LAURA MARIE ALTOM

LYNNETTE KENT

MARTA PERRY

CYNTHIA RUTLEDGE

The Christmas Treasury

HARLEQUIN®

TORONTO • NEW YORK • LONDON
AMSTERDAM • PARIS • SYDNEY • HAMBURG
STOCKHOLM • ATHENS • TOKYO • MILAN • MADRID
PRAGUE • WARSAW • BUDAPEST • AUCKLAND

ISBN: 0-373-15313-9

THE CHRISTMAS TREASURY

Copyright © 2005 by Harlequin Books S.A.

The publisher acknowledges the copyright holder
of the excerpts from the individual works as follows:

A HOME FOR CHRISTMAS
Copyright © 2005 by Harlequin Books S.A.

SEASON OF WONDER
Copyright © 2002 by Harlequin Books S.A.

SUGAR AND SPICE
Copyright © 2002 by Harlequin Books S.A.

A SEASON FOR MIRACLES
Copyright © 2001 by Harlequin Books S.A.

This edition published by arrangement with Harlequin Books S.A.

® and TM are trademarks of the publisher. Trademarks indicated with
® are registered in the United States Patent and Trademark Office, the
Canadian Trade Marks Office and in other countries.

www.eHarlequin.com

Printed in U.S.A.

CONTENTS

A HOME FOR CHRISTMAS

Laura Marie Altom

Chapter One

"Rachel!"

Ignoring Chance Mulgrave, her husband's best friend, Rachel Finch gripped her umbrella handle as if it were the only thing keeping her from throwing herself over the edge of the cliff, at the base of which thundered an angry Pacific. Even for Oregon Coast standards, the day was hellish. Brutal winds, driving cold rain…

The wailing gloom suited her. Only ten minutes earlier, she'd left the small chapel where her presumed dead husband's memorial service had just been held.

"Please, Rachel!" Chance shouted above the storm. Rachel didn't see Chance since her back was to him, but she could feel him thumping toward her on crutches. "Honey…"

He cupped his hand to her shoulder and she flinched, pulling herself free of his hold. "Don't."

"Sure," he said. "Whatever. I just—"

She turned to him, too exhausted to cry. "I'm pregnant."

"What?"

"Wes didn't know. I'd planned on telling him after he'd finished this case."

"God, Rache." Sharing the suffocating space beneath her umbrella, his demeanor softened. "I'm sorry. Or maybe happy. Hell, I'm not sure what to say."

"There's not much anyone can say at this point," she responded. "Wes is gone. I'm having his child…but how can I even think of being a mother when I'm so emotionally…"

"Don't worry about a thing," he said. "No matter what you need, I'm here for you. Wes and I made a pact. Should anything happen to either of us, we'd watch after each other's family."

"But you don't have a family," she pointed out.

"Yet. But it could've just as easily been me whose life we were celebrating here today." He bowed his head. "Seeing you like this…so sad…makes me almost wish it was."

Me, too.

There. Even if Rachel hadn't given voice to her resentment, it was at least out there, for the universe to hear. Ordinarily, Chance and her husband worked together like a well-oiled team, watching each other's backs. But then Chance had had to go and bust his ankle while helping one of their fellow Deputy U.S. Marshals move into a new apartment.

If Chance had really cared for Wes, he'd have been more careful. He wouldn't have allowed his friend to be murdered at the hands of a madman—a rogue marshal who'd also come uncomfortably close to taking out one of the most key witnesses the Marshal's Service had ever had.

Her handful of girlfriends had tried consoling her,

suggesting maybe Wes wasn't really dead…but Rachel knew. There had been an exhaustive six-week search for Wes's body. Combined with that, of the five marshals who'd been on that assignment, only two had come home alive. Another two bodies had been found, both shot. It didn't take rocket science to assume the same had happened to her dear husband.

"Let me take you home," Chance said. Despite his crutches, he tried to angle her away from the thrashing sea and back to the parking lot, to the sweet little chapel where less than a year earlier she and Wes had taken their wedding vows.

"You're soaked. Being out here in this weather can't be good for you or the baby."

"I'm all right," she said, again wrenching free of his hold. This time, it had been her elbow he'd grasped. She was trying to regain her dignity after having lost it in front of the church filled with Wes's co-workers and friends, and she just wanted to be left alone. "Please… leave. I can handle this on my own."

"Rachel, that's just it," he said, awkwardly chasing after her as she strode down the perilous trail edging the cliff.

His every step tore at her heart. Why was he alive and not her husband? The father of her child. What was she going to do? How was she ever going to cope with raising a baby on her own?

"Honey, you don't have to deal with Wes's passing on your own. If you'd just open up to me, I'm here for you—for as long as you need."

That was the breaking point. Rachel stopped abruptly. She tossed her umbrella out to sea, tipped her head up to the battering rain and screamed.

Tears returned with a hot, messy vengeance. Only, in

the rain it was impossible to tell where tears left off and rain began. Then, suddenly, Chance was there, drawing her against him, into his island of strength and warmth, his crutches braced on either side of her like walls blocking the worst of her pain.

"That's it," he crooned into her ear. "Let it out. I'm here. I'm here."

She did exactly as he urged, but then, because she'd always been an intensely private person and not one prone to histrionics, she stilled. Curiously, the rain and wind also slowed to a gentle patter and shush.

"Thank you," she eventually said. "You'll never know how much I appreciate you trying to help, but…"

"I'm not just trying," he said. "If you'd let me in, we can ride this out together. I'm hurting, too."

"I know," she said, looking to where she'd white-knuckle gripped the soaked lapels of his buff-colored trench. "But I—I can't explain. I have to do this on my own. I was alone before meeting Wes, and now I am again."

"But you don't have to be. Haven't you heard a word I've said? I'm here for you."

"No," she said, walking away from him again, this time in the direction of her car.

"Thanks, but definitely, no."

Chapter Two

Eighteen months later...

Through the rain-drizzled, holiday-themed windows of bustling Hohlmann's Department Store, Chance caught sight of a woman's long, buttery blond hair. Heart pounding, his first instinct was to run that way, seeking an answer to the perpetual question: Was it her? Was it Rachel?

No. It wasn't her. And this time, just as so many others, the disappointment landed like a crushing blow to his chest.

That day at the chapel had been the last time he'd seen her. Despite exhaustive efforts to track her, she'd vanished—destroying him inside and out.

When eventually he'd had to return to work and his so-called normal life, he'd put a private investigator on retainer, telling the man to contact him upon finding the slightest lead.

"You all right?" his little sister, nineteen-year-old Sarah, asked above an obnoxious Muzak rendition of "Jingle Bells." She was clutching the prewrapped perfume box she'd just purchased for their mother. "You look like you've seen a ghost."

"Might as well have," he said, taking the box from her to add to his already bulging bag. "Got everything you need?"

"Sure," she said, giving him *The Look*. The one that said she knew he was thinking about Rachel again, and that her wish for Christmas was that her usually wise big brother would once and for all put the woman—his dead best friend's wife—out of his heart and head.

Two hours later, Chance stuck his key in the lock of the Victorian relic his maternal grandmother had left him, shutting out hectic holiday traffic and torrential rain. Portland had been swamped under six inches in the past twenty-four hours. The last time they'd had such a deluge had been the last time he'd seen Rachel.

"Where are you?" he asked softly, as the wind bent gnarled branches, eerily scratching them against the back porch roof.

Setting his meager selection of family gifts on the wood bench parked alongside the door, he looked away from the gray afternoon and to the blinking light on his answering machine. Expecting the message to be from Sarah, telling him she'd left a gift or glove in his Jeep, he pressed Play.

"Chance," his P.I. said, voice like gravel from too many cigarettes and not enough broccoli. "I've got a lead for you on that missing Finch girl. It's a long shot, but you said you wanted everything, no matter how unlikely…"

Despite the fact that Rachel had run off without the decency of a proper—or even improper—goodbye, her tears still haunted him when he closed his eyes.

Chance listened to the message three times before committing the information to memory, then headed to his computer to book a flight to Denver.

"Wesley, sweetie, please stop crying," Rachel crooned to her ten-month-old baby boy, the only bright spot in what was becoming an increasingly frightening life. Having grown up in an orphanage, Rachel was no stranger to feeling alone in a crowd, or having to make it on her own. So why, after six months, was this still so hard?

Despite her hugging and cooing, the boy only wailed more.

"Want me to take him?"

She looked up to see one of Baker Street Homeless Shelter's newest residents wave grungy hands toward her child. She hadn't looked much better when she'd first arrived, and Rachel still couldn't get past the shock that she and her baby were now what most people would call "bums."

After reverting back to the name she'd gone by at the orphanage, Rachel Parkson, she'd traveled to Denver to room with her friend Jenny. But while Jenny had gotten lucky, landing a great job transfer to Des Moines, Rachel had descended into an abyss of bad luck.

A tough pregnancy had landed her in hospital. While she'd been blessed with a beautiful, healthy baby, at the rate she was going, the hefty medical bill wouldn't be gone till he was out of high school. Wes's life insurance company had repeatedly denied her claim, stating that without a body it wouldn't pay.

Making a long, sad story short, she'd lost everything, and here she was, now earning less than minimum wage doing bookkeeping for the shelter while trying to finish out her business degree one night course at a time through a downtown Denver community college.

She was raising her precious son in a shelter with barely enough money for diapers, let alone food and a place of their own. She used to cry herself to sleep every night, but now, she was just too exhausted. She used to pray, as well, but it seemed God, just like her husband, had deserted her.

Baby Wesley continued to wail.

"Sorry for all the noise," she said to the poor soul beside her, holding her son close as she wearily pushed to her feet with her free hand. She had to get out of here, but how? How could she ever escape this downward financial spiral?

"Rachel?"

That voice…

She paused before looking up. But when she did, tingles climbed her spine.

"Chance?"

Chapter Three

After all this time, was it really Rachel? Raising Wes's child in a homeless shelter? Why, why hadn't she just asked for help?

Chance pressed the heel of his hand to stinging eyes.

"Y-you look good," he said, lying through his teeth at the waiflike ghost of the woman he used to know. Dark shadows hollowed pale blue eyes. Wes used to brag about the silky feel of Rachel's long hair cascading against his chest when they'd made love—but it was now shorn into a short cap. "And the baby. He's wonderful, Rachel. You did good."

"Thanks," she said above her son's pitiful cry. "We're okay." She paused. "What are you doing here?"

"I'm here to see you…to help you…"

"I don't need help."

"Bull," he said, taking the now screaming baby from her, cradling him against his chest, nuzzling the infant's downy hair beneath his chin. "What's his name?"

"Wesley," she said, refusing to meet his gaze.

He nodded, fighting a sudden knot at the back of his throat. Such a beautiful child, growing up in such cruel surroundings. And why? All because of Rachel's foolish pride.

"Get your things," he growled between clenched teeth, edging her away from a rag-clothed derelict reeking of booze.

"W-what?"

"You heard me. You tried things your way, honey, and apparently it didn't work out. Now we're doing it *my* way. Your husband's way."

"I—I'm fine," she said, raising her chin, a partial spark back in her stunning eyes. "Just a little down on my luck. But things will change. They'll get better."

"Damn straight they will." Clutching the infant with one arm, he dragged her toward the shelter's door with the other. "You don't want charity from me, fine. But is this really what you want for your son? Wes's son?"

While Chance regretted the harshness of his words, he'd never retract them. Years ago he'd made a promise to her husband, and he sure as hell wasn't about to back out on it now.

He glanced away from Rachel to take in a nearly bald, fake Christmas tree that'd been decorated with homemade ornaments. Pipe cleaner reindeer and paper angels colored with crayons. Though the tree's intent was kind, he knew Rachel deserved better.

While killing time on endless stakeouts, Wes would ramble for hours about his perfect wife. About how much he loved her, how she was a great cook, how she always managed to perfectly balance the checkbook. Wes went so far as to offer private morsels he should've kept to himself—locker room details that should've been holy between a man and his wife. But because of Wes's ever-flapping mouth, whether he'd wanted to or not, Chance knew everything about Rachel from her favorite songs to what turned her on.

Another thing he knew were Wes's dreams for her. How because she'd grown up in an orphanage, he'd always wanted to have a half-dozen chubby babies with her and buy her a great house and put good, reliable tires on her crappy car.

Chance had made a promise to his best friend; one that put him in charge of picking up where Wes left off. It was a given he'd steer clear of the husband/wife physical intimacies—she was off limits. Totally. But when it came to making her comfortable, happy…by God, if it took every day for the rest of his life, that's what Chance had come to Denver prepared—and okay, he'd admit it, secretly hoping—to do.

Looking back to Rachel, he found her eyes pooled. Lips trembling, she met his stare.

"Come on," he said. "It's time to go home."

Baby Wesley had fallen asleep in Chance's arms. His cheeks were flushed, and he sucked pitifully at his thumb.

"I—I tried breastfeeding him," she said. "But my milk dried up."

"That happens," he said, not knowing if it did or didn't or why she'd even brought it up…just willing to say anything to get her to go with him.

Shaking her head, looking away to brush tears, she said, "Wait here. I'll get our things."

For Rachel, being at the airport and boarding the plane was surreal. As was driving through a fog-shrouded Portland in Chance's Jeep, stopping off at an all-night Wal-Mart for a car seat and over five hundred dollars worth of clothes, diapers, formula and other baby supplies. The Christmas decorations, hundreds and thousands of colorful lights lining each new street they traveled, struck her as foreign. As if from a world where she was no longer welcome.

"I'll repay you," she said from the passenger seat, swirling a pattern in the fogged window. Presumably, he was heading toward his lovely hilltop home she'd always secretly called the real estate version of a wedding cake. "For everything. The clothes. Plane ticket. I'll pay it all back. I—I just need a breather to get back on my feet."

"Sure," he said. Was it her imagination, or had he tightened his grip on the wheel?

"Really," she said, rambling on about how Wes's life insurance company refused to pay. "Just as soon as I get the check, I'll reimburse you."

"Know how you can pay me?" he asked, pressing the garage door remote on the underbelly of his sun visor.

She shook her head.

He pulled the Jeep into the single stall detached garage she'd helped Wes and him build, that same enchanted summer she and her future husband had become lovers.

It is said a woman's heart is a deep well of secrets and Rachel knew hers was no different. Squeezing her eyes shut, she saw Chance as she had that first night they'd met at Ziggy's Sports Bar—before she'd even met Wes. Despite his physical appearance—six-three, with wide, muscular shoulders and a chest as broad and strong as an oak's trunk—Chance's shy, kind spirit made him a gentle giant to whom she'd instinctively gravitated. Never the brazen type,

Rachel had subtly asked mutual friends about him, and every so often, when their eyes met from opposite ends of the bar during the commercial breaks of *Monday Night Football*, she'd thought she'd caught a glimmer of interest. And if only for an instant, hope that he might find her as attractive as she found him would soar. But then he'd look away and the moment would be gone.

Then she'd met Wes—who'd made it known in about ten exhilaratingly sexy seconds that he didn't just want to be her *friend*. Handsome, five-eleven with a lean build and quick smile, Wes hadn't had to work too hard to make her fall for him—or his knack of making any and all occasions magic.

Chance turned off the engine and sighed. The only light was that which spilled from the weak bulb attached to the automatic opener, the only sounds those of rain pattering the roof and the baby's sleepy gurgle…. Angling on his seat, Chance reached out to Rachel, whispering the tip of his index finger so softly around her lips…she might've imagined his being there at all.

"Know how you can repay me?" he repeated.

Heartbeat a sudden storm, she swallowed hard.

"By bringing back your smile."

Chapter Four

Rachel awoke the next morning to unfamiliar softness, and the breezy scent of freshly laundered sheets. Sunshine streamed through tall, paned windows. After a moment of initial panic, fearing she may have died and moved on to Heaven, she remembered herself not on some random cloud, but safely tucked in Chance's guest bed in the turret-shaped room she'd urged him to paint an ethereal sky blue.

The room was the highest point in his home, reached by winding stairs, and its view never failed to stir her. Mt. Hood was to the west, while to the east—long ago, while standing on a ladder, paint brush in hand, nose and cheeks smudged blue—she'd sworn she could see all the way to the shimmering Pacific. Wesley and Chance had laughed at her, but she'd ignored them.

To Rachel, the room represented freedom from all that had bound her in her early, depressing, pre-Wes life.

The panoramic views, just as her marriage, made her feel as if her soul was flying.

As she inched up in the sumptuous feather bed to greet a day as chilly as it was clear, the room still wielded its calming effect. She'd awakened enough to realize how late it must be…and yet Wesley hadn't stirred.

Tossing back covers, she winced at the wood floor's chilly bite against her bare feet. With one look at the portable crib that had been among their purchases the previous night, Rachel realized that Wesley's cries hadn't woken her because he wasn't there.

Bounding to the kitchen, she found her son sitting proud in his new high chair, beaming, covered ear to ear in peachy-smelling orange *goo*.

"Morning, sleepyhead." Baby spoon to Wesley's cooing lips, Chance caught her off guard with the size of his smile.

"You should've woken me," she said, hustling to where the two guys sat at a round oak table in a sunny patch of the country kitchen. "I'm sure you have better things to do."

"Nope," he said. "I took the day off."

"I'll pay you for your time."

He'd allowed her to take the spoon as she'd pulled out a chair and sat beside him, but now, his strong fingers clamped her wrist. "Stop."

"What?"

"The whole defensive routine. It doesn't become you."

"S-sorry. That's who I am."

"Bull."

"E-excuse me?" He released her, and the spoon now trembled in her still tingling wrist.

"I knew you as playful. Fun. Now, you seem like you're in attack mode."

"And why shouldn't I be?" she asked. "Aside from Wesley, name one thing that's gone right for me in the past year?"

"That's easy," he said, cracking a slow and easy grin that, Lord help her, had Rachel's pulse racing yet again. Had the man always been this attractive?

Judging by the massive crush she'd had on him all those years ago…yes.

Making things worse—or better, depending how you looked at it—he winked. "One thing that's gone very right is how you're finally back with me."

Sensing Rachel needed two gifts above all else that Christmas season—time and space—Chance returned to work Tuesday, and every day for the rest of the week. Come Saturday, though, despite her protests that they should stay at the house, he bustled her and the baby into his Jeep and started off for the traditional holiday ride he'd loved as a kid, but had given up as an adult.

"Well?" he asked a silent Rachel an hour later, pulling into a snow-covered winter wonderland. "See anything that'd fit in the living room bay window?"

She glanced at him, then at the sprawling Christmas tree farm that might as well have been Santa's North Pole as everywhere you looked, Christmas was in full swing. Kids laughing and sledding and playing tag while darting in and out amongst fragrant trees. Families hugging the fires built in river rock pits, sipping steaming mugs of cocoa. Upbeat carols played from a tiny speaker.

"It's—" she cautiously glanced at the idyllic scene before them, as if they didn't belong, then back to him "—amazing. But if you want a tree, wouldn't it be cheaper to—"

"Look—" he sighed "—I wasn't going to bring this

up until it's a done deal, but I told my boss about your situation—with Wes's flaky life insurance—and fury didn't begin to describe his reaction. Wheels are turning, and I'd say you'll have a check by the end of next week."

"Really?"

Just then, she was seriously gorgeous, eyes brimming with hope and a shimmering lake of tears. "Yeah," Chance said. "I'm serious. So what's with the waterworks? I thought you'd be thrilled to be rich?"

"I would be—I mean, I am. It's just that after all these months of barely scraping by, not sleeping because I've literally been afraid to close my eyes, it seems a bit surreal to have such a happy ending at all, let alone in such a happy place."

He laughed, unfastening his seat belt to grab the baby from his seat. "Don't you think after what you've been through you two deserve a little happiness?"

Turning away from him while she sniffled and dried her cheeks, he couldn't tell if she was nodding or shaking her head. "Well?" he asked. "Was that a yes or no?"

"I don't know," she said with a laugh. "Maybe both. I'm just so confused. And grateful. Very, *very* grateful."

"Yeah, well, what you need to be," he said, Wesley snug in his arms, "is energized."

"Oh yeah?" she asked, again blasting him with a tremulous smile. "How come?"

"Because me and this kid of yours are about to *whomp* you in a snowball fight."

Chapter Five

"It's beautiful," Rachel said, stepping back to admire the nine-foot fir they'd finished decorating. Heirloom glass ornaments and twinkling white lights hung from each branch. "Perfect."

With Chance beside her, carols softly playing and a fire crackling in the hearth, Rachel couldn't have ordered a more enchanting holiday scene.

"I don't know," Chance said, finger to his lips as he stood beside her, surveying their afternoon's work. "Something's missing."

"You're right," Rachel said. "We forgot the angel."

"I didn't see it, did you?"

"Not in the boxes we've been through. Maybe—" She looked down to see Wesley sucking the top corner of the angel's box. "Aha! Found it."

"Thanks, bud." Chance took the box from the baby, replacing it with the teething ring he had been contentedly gumming. "How about you do the honors?" he suggested, handing the golden angel to her.

"I'd like that," Rachel said, embarrassed to admit just how much the small gesture meant.

At the orphanage, placing the angel on top of the tree was generally a task reserved for the child who was newest to the home. Since Rachel had gone to live there the summer just before her fourth birthday when her parents had been killed in a car accident, she'd never had the chance. By the time Christmas rolled around, she had only been the third-newest kid.

Knowing this, Wes had made their first Christmas together as a married couple extra special by taking her to pick out an especially extravagant angel that they really couldn't afford. In Denver, at a desperation yard sale she'd held in a futile attempt to stay financially afloat, it had devastated her to have to sell that precious angel to a cranky old guy for the princely sum of three dollars.

Rachel swallowed hard at the bittersweet memory of how dearly she'd loved sharing Christmas with Wes. There was a part of her struggling with the guilt that she was once again immersed in holiday cheer…but Wes was gone. It somehow felt disloyal for her to be so happy.

Trying to focus on the task at hand, Rachel climbed onto the small step ladder she'd used to hang the ornaments from the highest branches, but she still wasn't tall enough to reach the tree's top.

"Let me help," Chance said, inching up behind her, settling his hands around her waist, then lifting her the extra inches needed to get the job done.

His nearness was overwhelming, flooding her senses to the point she nearly failed her mission. Had his hands lingered on her waist longer than necessary after he'd set her back to her feet? Was that the reason for her erratically beating heart? What kind of woman was she to one minute reminisce about her deceased husband, and the next wonder at the feel of another man's strong hands?

"Thank you," she said, licking her lips, by habit going to push at her long hair that was no longer there.

"You're welcome." As if he'd sensed the awareness between them, too, they both fell into awkward step, bustling to clean the wreckage of tissue paper and boxes.

Once they'd finished hauling the mess to a spare bedroom Chance used for storage, they were in the dark upstairs hall when Chance asked, "Why'd you cut your hair?"

The question caught her off guard, made her feel even more uncomfortable than she already did. "It was too much trouble," she said.

"It was beautiful. Not that it's any of my business, but you should grow it back."

She looked down to hands she'd clenched at her waist.

"Not that you aren't still attractive," he said. "It's just that Wes always had a thing for your hair. I think he'd be sad to see it gone."

What about you, Chance? Did you like my hair?

Rachel was thankful for the hall's lack of light—the question, even if asked only in her head, made her uncomfortable. Why would she even care what Chance thought of the way she used to style her hair? Worse yet, why did his question leave her feeling lacking?

Suddenly, she was wishing she at least had a little more length to work into an attractive style instead of the boyish cut that'd been easy to keep clean and neat at the homeless shelter. This cut hardly made her feel feminine or desirable. But then until her reunion with Chance, she'd had no use for vanity.

"Chance?" she asked, her voice a croaked whisper.

"Yes?"

"When we first met, you know, back when you, me and Wes used to just be friends, hanging out at Ziggy's, did you find me pretty?"

He cleared his throat. "What kind of question is that?"

"I don't know." She shook her head. "Sorry I asked."

Because she truly didn't know, Rachel returned to the living room, where holiday cheer and the sight of her contented child banished doubts and fears. The question had been silly. As was her growing awareness of her husband's best friend. For a moment she felt better, but then Chance returned, his essence filling the room.

"For the record," he said, perching alongside her on the toasty fireplace hearth, "yes. I thought you were pretty back then, but you're even prettier now."

Chance had a tough time finding sleep. Why had Rachel asked him such a loaded question? Why did he feel his final, almost flirty answer had been a betrayal of his friend's trust? Yeah, Chance thought she was pretty—gorgeous, in fact. But for Wes's sake, couldn't he have just skirted the issue?

Sunday morning, he woke to a breakfast spread fit for a five-star hotel. "Wow," he said. "What's all this for?"

Looking more gorgeous than any woman had a right to first thing in the morning, she shrugged. "Guess I just wanted to say thanks for the great day we had yesterday. Never having had a family growing up, I always wished for that kind of traditional family fun."

"Is that what we are?" he asked, forking a bite of pancake. "A family?"

"You know what I mean," she said, avoiding his glance by drinking orange juice.

He broke off a piece of bacon and handed it to Wesley.

"Yeah," he said. "I know what you mean. But *is* that what we are, Rache?"

Sitting with her and Wesley, from out of nowhere Chance was struck with the realization that no matter how she answered his question, he very much *wanted* them to be a family. They'd already fallen into husband and wife roles. The only things missing were emotional and physical closeness.

And as reluctant as he was to admit it, from the day he'd set eyes on her all those years ago, kissing Rachel was something he'd always longed to do. And therein lay the rub. Somehow, he had to find it within himself to squelch that want.

"We're sort of a family," she said. "But I suppose, once I get Wes's life insurance you'll probably be glad to get the house back to yourself."

Boldly reaching across the table for her hand, stroking her palm, lying to himself by labeling it a casual, friendly touch, he said, "Actually, it's nice having you two here. Waking up to you in the morning, coming home to you at night."

She laughed off his admission. "You're just being polite. No bachelor actually enjoys being strapped with another man's wife and child."

"That's just it," he said. "Crazy as it may seem, I like you being here—a lot."

Chapter Six

Another week passed, during which Rachel had too much time to ponder Chance's curious statement. He liked having her and Wesley sharing his house? If only he truly felt that way because truth be told, she liked being there, and judging by Wesley's easy grins, he did, too.

Being with Chance made her feel safe—an emotion that'd been sorely lacking from the past eighteen months of her life. Being with him now told her what a fool she'd been for ever denying his offer of help and companionship. He was a wonderful man.

The only reason she was now standing at the front window on a sunny Friday afternoon, watching for his Jeep to head up the winding lane leading to his home was because she was thankful to him…right? No way could it be something more.

Trouble was, try as she might to pass off the growing feelings she had for him as simply affection between friends, she *did* feel something more. Twinges of attraction. Flickering flames.

Whatever the label, it had wrongfully been there Sunday morning when he'd held her hand across the breakfast table. And Monday night when their hands brushed while Chance helped with Wesley's bath. Again still Tuesday and Wednesday when they'd shared the usually dull duty of cleaning up after dinner.

Instead of being ho-hum, washing dishes with Chance towering beside her, making her feel small and cherished and protected, had been—in a word—intoxicating.

But why? Why couldn't she keep at the forefront of her mind the fact that Chance had been Wes's best friend? To follow through on any attraction for him would be wrong.

Finally, she saw him pulling into the drive. Though she wanted to run to the back door to greet him like a giddy school girl, she somehow managed to rein her emotions. Instead, with Wesley in her arms, she checked on the latest fragrant batch of sugar cookies still in the oven.

"Smells wonderful in here," Chance said with a gorgeous grin on his way through the back door. "You must be psychic."

"Why's that?" she asked, telling herself the heat from the oven had her cheeks flushed—not the pleasure of being the recipient of his smile.

"My parents invited us for dinner. Sugar cookies are Dad's favorite—not that he'll need a reason to fall for you or my buddy Wesley." After slipping off his coat, then setting his keys and wallet on the blue tile counter, he took the baby from her, swooping him high into the air, then snug against his chest for a cuddle and kiss. "Mmm...I missed you," he said, nuzzling the infant's head.

Rachel fought irrational jealousy strumming through

her as she realized she wanted Chance to have missed her, too. Almost as much as she wanted a welcome home kiss…

Relaxing over almond bundt cake and coffee with Chance's mother, Helen, while the men washed up after dinner, Rachel would've been hard pressed to name a time she'd ever felt more content.

Helen had decorated her home from top to bottom in holiday décor ranging from elegant to goofy fun. The crackling fire and Elvis CD of holiday love songs playing softly in the background only made the night that much more special.

"Please don't think me forward for bringing this up," Helen said after they'd had a few moments to finish their cake, "but my son's a different person around you and Wesley. Better, in every conceivable way."

Rachel was so caught off guard by the woman's random statement that she darned near choked on her last bite of dessert. "Oh?"

"He loves you, you know. Has loved you ever since you first met all those years ago. Bless his heart…" She paused for a sip of coffee. "He was always the strong, silent type. His father and I urged him to tell you how he felt before you and Wes grew close, but he missed his window of opportunity and seeing how he and Wes were always such good friends, he did the gentlemanly thing and bowed out."

Not knowing what to say, her head and heart reeling, Rachel was hard pressed to say much else but another, "Oh."

"He'd kill me if he knew I was telling you all of this, it's just that—" she peeked over her shoulder to make sure they were alone "—I'm not getting any younger and the thought of having an instant grandson, as well as a daughter-in-law whose company I'm very much enjoying, fills me with indescribable joy."

Chance loves me.

Lying in bed that night, listening to Wesley softly snore from the beautiful crib Chance had bought for him on a wondrously hectic shopping trip Tuesday afternoon, Rachel wasn't sure what to do with this knowledge.

Part of her wished Chance's mother had kept her nose out of her son's affairs. Another part, the part of Rachel increasingly craving Chance's touch, was secretly thrilled. But if she was falling for Chance, what did that say about her love for her poor husband? What kind of wife was she to so soon be falling head over heels for Wes's best friend?

Finding sleep impossible, she tossed back the covers and padded barefoot downstairs. Cookies and milk. That's all she needed to get this ridiculous notion from her head.

She *wasn't* falling for Chance. He was like her brother.

She was grateful to him.

"Hey, gorgeous," he said from in front of the open fridge, the dim light washing over the muscles of his bare chest. "Fancy meeting you here." He winked.

Her mouth went dry. That gratitude she was supposedly feeling for him? One sight of his rock-hard pecs and abs and there was no denying it. She wanted the guy— bad. Not in a friendly way, but in a way she had no business even thinking about, let alone aching to act upon.

"Um, hi," she mumbled, biting her lower lip.

"Want milk?" he asked, wagging the gallon jug.

"Yes, please."

While he poured, she grabbed the foil-wrapped plate of cookies from the kitchen's center island.

They reunited at the kitchen table.

"Why can't you sleep?" he asked.

For a long time, she stayed silent, toying with her cookie. "Truth? You."

Gracing her with a slow, sexy grin that turned her resolve to think of him as a brother to mush, he said, "I'm flattered. At least, I hope I have reason to be."

Swallowing hard, she nodded. Everything about him was good. So why, then, did the realization that she was falling for him hurt so bad?

"Rachel?" Setting his milk glass on the table, he asked, "You okay?"

In a last ditch effort to prove to herself—to both of them—that the two of them as a couple would never work, she blurted, "Kiss me."

Chapter Seven

Per Rachel's request, Chance did kiss her. At first, softly, reverently. But then, the closer she melded to him, the more he increased his pressure, dizzying her with fervent strokes of his tongue.

And then, just as abruptly as their kiss had begun, it ended with Chance pulling away.

Fingers sliding into the hair at his temples, breathing ragged, he said, "Sorry."

"For what?" she asked, eyes welling with emotion. "That was beautiful. It's been so long since I've felt anything but pain. Your kiss…it was as if somewhere deep inside me, the wall of grief I've been hiding behind has been shattered."

"That's all well and good," he said with a sharp laugh. "But what about Wes? Don't you feel guilty? As if our being attracted to each other is a betrayal of his trust?"

Eyes closed, she took a deep breath. "Honestly," she

said, eyes open, facing Chance straight on, "I know how awful it must sound, but from the moment your lips touched mine, all I could think about was you."

Two days later, with Wes's life insurance check safely in the bank and her bills paid, Rachel should've been on top of the world. But as she finished wrapping the last of the presents she'd purchased for Chance and his family, all she really felt was sad. He'd invited her to stay with him through New Year's—longer if she liked—but after their kiss, she was more convinced than ever that maybe what would be best for them both was for her and Wesley to move on.

She'd already caused Chance so much trouble. Why stick around if their attraction would only bring him— not to mention, her—pain?

"You look pretty," he said from the living room door, hands behind his back.

"When's the last time you had your eyes checked? I'm a mess." From the oriental rug where she'd parked herself in front of the fire with a mess of bows, boxes and ribbons, she grinned up at him. Dressed in comfy, but hardly flattering sweats, her short hair sticking out at crazy angles and no makeup, she was sure she'd never looked worse.

"My eyes are fine," he said, wading his way through the mess. "Seeing you like this, so at ease in my home… it's my heart I'm worried about."

"Have you always been such a charmer?" she asked, batting her eyelashes exaggeratedly.

"I don't know, you tell me…" From behind his back, he withdrew a perfect cluster of mistletoe.

With him kneeling beside her, holding the sprig over her head, it would've been rude not to follow through with tradition. Seeing how she'd long since put Wesley to bed, Rachel had no qualms about reaching Chance halfway for a mesmerizing kiss.

"You know," Chance said the next afternoon, Wesley gurgling high on his shoulders as they crunched their way through freshly fallen snow in the neighborhood's park, "at work this afternoon, I had some downtime while the jury was deliberating. I did some thinking."

"'Bout time," Rachel quipped.

Her sassy comment earned her a snowball fight. And like the day at the tree farm, the guys once again got the better of her. Laughing so hard her lungs burned from the cold, she cried, "Stop! I give up!"

"Oh no," Chance said, setting a bundled Wesley beside him so he could tackle her with both hands. "You don't get to surrender until you apologize."

"Sorry, sorry," she laughingly cried, her foggy breath mingling with his.

He kissed her, and despite the fact they were lying in the snow, she felt warmed inside. Which was wrong. She shouldn't be on fire for this man who was her husband's best friend.

"You're forgiven," he said a few minutes later, when her every defense had been shattered. "Now, back to what I was saying before you so rudely interrupted…I've been thinking about how you said you felt like you should find a place of your own. And then I got to thinking how much I enjoy having you both here. And how big this rambling old house of mine is for just me. And how Wesley made me promise to look after you if anything should ever happen to him…"

Heart galloping like a herd of runaway reindeer, Rachel alternately dreaded, yet prayed for what she knew Chance would say next.

"And so, anyway, what would you think of the two of us getting hitched? You could still keep your own room, if that's what you wanted, but at least then it'd be official. Me watching out for you and Wesley, I mean."

Tears of joy and sadness stung her eyes.

"Well?" he asked while she blinked.

"Oh, Chance…" Holding her mittened fingers to her mouth, she bit off the fuzzy wool, then cupped her hand to his cold, whiskered cheek. "I would love nothing more than to marry you. If only there wasn't so much history between us…"

"Say no more," he said, pushing himself off of her. "I understand." Snatching up Wesley, he trudged toward the house, telling her without a single word that he didn't truly understand—at all.

After turning down Chance's proposal, to say there was tension between them would've been a major understatement—which was why Rachel sat alone in the kitchen that quiet Christmas Eve morning, scanning apartment ads while Chance had gone off to work.

Sipping cocoa while Wesley crumbled a cookie in his high chair, she was startled when the doorbell rang.

"Chance?" she said, running for the front door, hoping now that he'd had time to think about it, he was okay with her suggestion that they remain just friends.

"Sorry," a well-dressed older man said, clearing his throat. "Are you Rachel Finch?"

"Y-yes." She fingered the pearls Helen had given her at her throat.

After introducing himself as Wes's old boss, he said, "Forgive me for dropping by, especially today of all days, but…there's no easy way to say this…a fisherman netted your husband's body. I thought you'd like to have his few personal effects."

Chapter Eight

Within fifteen minutes of Rachel's call, Chance roared his Jeep up his normally quiet street. Yes, he'd been mortally wounded by her turning down his proposal, but that didn't mean he was now going to let her down.

He heard the news through the office grapevine—and he also found out Franks had dropped by to pass the news along to Rachel. Chance fully planned to be by her side as she dealt with it all.

"You okay?" he asked, finding her alone at the kitchen table. She had opened the watertight pouch Wes had been using as a wallet the day he'd been shot. His gold watch, wedding band and the navy wallet all lay in front of her.

Wes had been the consummate Boy Scout, and he'd also hated boats. Back when they were kids, Chance kept a rowboat on his paternal grandparents' farm pond. One sunny afternoon when they'd been about ten, he and Wes had been out rowing when the boat tipped.

Wes didn't get upset often, but when his prized base-ball cards fell in the water, he'd freaked—kind of like when he'd learned he was the only guy from the Port-land marshal's office assigned to that unconventional-as-hell mission, trying to protect a witness who'd refused to leave his private island.

Had Wes known there was a chance he wouldn't be coming home?

"Rachel?" She still hadn't answered his question.

Looking shell-shocked, she nodded. "Yeah. I'm all right."

"Where's Wesley?"

"Down for his nap."

Pulling out the chair beside her, he asked, "You sure you don't want to be alone for this?"

She shook her head, and off they went on a journey down memory lane. Wes's driver's license and credit cards, photos and fast-food coupons—all of it was in pristine condition.

In the last pocket was a folded slip of yellow legal paper.

Hands trembling, Rachel opened it. "Oh, God," she said. "It's a note."

"*If you're reading this*," she read aloud, "*then I'm so sorry, sweetie, but…*" She broke down. "I c-can't do this," she said. "Please, Chance. You read it."

He cleared his throat, continuing where she'd left off. "*…but I've apparently croaked. I know, I know, right about now you're probably wanting to smack me for try-ing to find humor in this, but I suppose everybody's gotta go eventually, and unfortunately, it seems my time's up.*

"*That said, you're not allowed to be sad—well, maybe you could mope a little for the first week, or two, but after that, I want to be staring down from Heaven at your beautiful smile. I want you having babies and good times and toasting me whenever the top's popped on a beer."*

"You do this next part," Chance said, closing stinging eyes. "It's too personal."

She took the letter and read on. *"By now, Chance has no doubt told you about the promise he made me to always watch over you. But what he probably didn't tell you is how he's always had a secret thing for you. Back when we first started dating, he was too much of a gentleman and friend to stand in the way of me marrying you. If I have died, Rachel, he'd be a good man for you. The best—second only to me. Wink, wink. Be sure and give him a shot at…"* She paused to catch her breath. *"…winning your heart."*

Sobbing, Rachel clung to Chance, drinking in his goodness and kindness and strength.

"Shh…" Chance crooned, stroking her short hair.

"Even in death, he put my needs before his own," she said softly, gently setting the letter on the table. "And the timing…of all times for me to have finally gotten his letter, on Christmas Eve. What a gift. Makes you wonder if he's up there, watching over us."

"You doubted it?" Chance teased, sliding Rachel off her chair and onto his lap.

"After the rocky months I've had, I doubted not only Wes, but God."

"Gotta admit," he said, thumb brushing her lower lip. "Having you disappear on me like that—I've had my doubts, too."

"Yet look at us now," she said, resting her head on his shoulder. "Maybe Wes knew that without time and space between us, we'd have both been too loyal to his memory to give each other a try?"

"Whatever the reason," Chance said, "we don't have to feel guilty or pained anymore." He smiled at her, gently. "Now, with Wes's blessing, will you marry me, so that you, me and Wesley can start a family all our own?"

"What do you mean, *start*? I thought we already were a family?"

"Right," he said before a spellbinding kiss. "How could I forget?"

Christmas morning, Wesley snug between them on the living room sofa, a fire crackling in the hearth and the scent of fresh-baked cinnamon rolls flavoring the air, Rachel opened gift after gift that Chance had secretly stashed in nooks and crannies all over the house.

Later, they'd go to his parents' for Christmas dinner with his sisters and extended family, but for now, it was just the three of them, opening sweaters and perfume and books and china figurines and fishing lures and hats and for Wesley, toys, toys and more toys—most of which Rachel guessed he wouldn't be able to play with until he was three!

Once they'd finished their gift extravaganza and all the wrappings had been cleared, Chance stood beside the Christmas tree and said, "Look, honey, here's another package in this bird's nest, and it's tagged for you."

"Chance," Rachel complained, heading his direction. "You've already given me too much."

"Look here, the label says it's from Santa," he said, holding out a tiny, robin's egg blue box that screamed Tiffany's.

Heart racing, hands trembling, Rachel lifted the lid to peek inside. "Chance…" Tearing at the sight of the glowing, pear-shaped diamond solitaire, she crushed him in a hug. "It's gorgeous. Yes, I'll marry you!"

"Whoa," he said with a sexy grin, pushing her back and shaking his head. "I don't recall asking anything. This was all Santa's doing."

"Well, then, *Santa*," she said, tilting her head back to talk to the high ceiling, "I accept your proposal."

"Now, wait a minute…" Chance pulled her back into his arms. "Not so fast. I thought the two of us had reached an understanding. Those kisses you gave me last night implied a certain level of intimacy and trust. You can't just make out with me, then leave me for a big, jolly guy in a red suit."

"Then what do you suggest?" she asked, standing on her tiptoes to press a kiss to his delicious, cinnamon-flavored lips.

"Just to be safe, you'd better marry me right away."

"Yeah, but do I get to keep the ring?"

He winked. "Why not? With any luck, Mr. Ho Ho Ho will go back to his wife…leaving me plenty of time under the mistletoe with mine."

SEASON OF WONDER
Marta Perry

Chapter One

It was his angel-girl. David Caldwell stopped dead, letting the waves wash over his feet. He hadn't seen Allison March in fifteen years, but he knew her instantly, with the kind of bone-deep knowledge that didn't require explanation. Once again, Christmas had brought Allison back to Caldwell Island, South Carolina.

He waded out of the surf, his footsteps marring the smooth wet sand as he walked toward the two figures on a blanket near the weather-worn cottage in the dunes. He didn't have to think twice about the identity of the child. The little girl must be about six, the age Allison had been that first Christmas, and she looked the way Ally had then—hair the pale platinum of the sea oats, a delicate heart-shaped face, and huge blue eyes. Just like the angel on their Christmas tree.

"Allison." He stopped short of the blanket. "Merry Christmas." It was what he'd said then.

She shaded her eyes against the December sunshine with her hand. "Hello, David."

He grinned. "You're supposed to say, 'Hello, boy.'"

Her answering smile was as cool and brittle as a shell washed up in the tide. "You're not a boy any longer."

She'd changed. Fine lines spelled worry on her face, and her lips were stiff. Even her hands, thin and elegant, seemed clenched for battle.

David squatted, careful not to track sand on the blanket. "What happened to you, Allison?" That was blunt, but he and Allison had always been able to speak their thoughts, as if they'd known each other forever and always would.

She didn't answer. Instead, she turned to the child. "Kristie, this is David Caldwell. He lives here on the island. David, my daughter, Kristie."

"Hi." He held out his hand. The child hesitated, then nodded and put her small hand in his. It was like holding a sand dollar, soft and quivering on his palm.

He didn't let his gaze stray toward the heavy brace on her leg, nor the child-size wheelchair at the edge of the blanket. But maybe he understood what had wiped the sense of wonder from Allison's blue eyes.

"So you've come to spend Christmas at the beach, just like your momma used to do when she was your age."

Her eyes lit. "Did you know my mommy when she was little?"

"I sure did. I taught her everything she knows about the ocean." He glanced at Allison. No wedding band on her left hand, only the faintest pale line. "Didn't I?"

"I'm afraid I've forgotten most of it." Her smile

brushed him off as coolly as a sweep of her hand would a sand fly. "It's too long ago."

He lifted an eyebrow. "Is it?"

"Yes." Her mouth clamped shut on the word, dismissing their friendship as if it had never been.

Well. He sat back on his heels. Allison clearly didn't want to go back to the way things had been.

But as for him—

He hadn't changed. He wanted to see his angel-girl again.

Chapter Two

David didn't look as if her rebuff had had much effect on him, Allison decided. He sat barefoot in the sand, much as he had at ten or twelve.

He was sun-browned, as he'd been years ago; his hair streaked to a sand color, and his eyes the changeable blue-green of the ocean. And he still had that easy lopsided smile that had once lodged itself in her heart.

But he wasn't that boy any longer. The height and breadth of him startled her, as if some trick of photography had taken the boy she knew and turned him into a man.

David sifted sand through his fingers, apparently content to laze on the beach all day. A spurt of irritation hit her. Was that what he'd turned into—a beachcomber?

"What brings you back after all this time?" he asked.

It had been a lifetime, but he didn't need to know that.

"I promised to show Kristie the island. What are you doing these days?" Besides walking on the beach. She didn't add that, but he probably caught the implication in her tone.

His eyes crinkled, as if he laughed at her on the inside. He'd always done that when she'd betrayed her ignorance of this natural space between mainland and ocean that he called home.

"A little of this, a little of that. I help at the inn, run dolphin tours for the tourists."

Exasperation filled her. "You're a bright person, David. You could have done anything with your life."

The moment the words were out, she regretted them. Her own track record wasn't exactly stellar.

"This is what I want to do." His voice was gentle. "Maybe you and Kristie would like to go with me one day to see the dolphins."

"I'm afraid we won't have time for that." She glanced at the cottage, her only tangible asset she'd held on to since the divorce. It was a wonder Richard hadn't tried to take that, too. "I'll be too busy getting the cottage fixed up."

She'd have to work quickly if she wanted to get the place on the market soon. At least she had her priorities straight now: sell the cottage so she'd have a nest egg; get Kristie through her next surgery; start the new job in Atlanta that would make her and her daughter independent. That left no time in her schedule for something as frivolous as a dolphin tour.

"I guess you'll want the cottage in shape for a real sea-island Christmas. Maybe I can give you a hand."

"I can take care of it myself." She stood, brushing sand from her slacks. "Time to go now, Kristie."

David picked up the wheelchair. "Let me."

She snatched it from him. "I don't need any help, thanks."

No help, no one to depend on. She'd learned that the hard way. From now on she would be tough and practical, and she'd depend only on herself.

"If that's the way you want it." A hint of sadness showed in David's eyes.

"It is."

He shrugged. "See you around, then."

No, she wouldn't see him. She'd been rude enough that David wouldn't come back again, and that was for the best.

So why did she feel as if she'd just lost something important?

Chapter Three

"Are you sure she won't come over to supper?" David's mother turned from the stove to give him a perplexed frown. "There's plenty, and we'd love to have them."

He couldn't help but smile. There was always plenty to eat at the Dolphin Inn, even when there were no guests checked in. His mother and his gran were used to cooking for a horde of Caldwells.

"Not today, Momma. Maybe later." Maybe not at all, judging by the way his angel-girl had brushed him off.

Gran, her blue eyes wise behind her wire-rimmed glasses, handed him a cookie tin. "You take these cookies for the little girl, then. She won't turn down something for her child."

He kissed her firm cheek. "What makes you so smart?"

"A lot of livin'." She swatted him gently on the arm. "You remember, boy. Whatever's wrong there, Christmas works wonders on the heart."

Gran's words lingered in his mind as he drove down the lane to Allison's cottage. Christmas works wonders. Would even Christmas be enough to bring back the friendship he'd cherished?

He pulled into the drive, turned off the engine, and hesitated, recognizing the tightness in his belly for what it was. When had he ever been nervous about seeing Allison?

Something's hurt her bad, Father, he prayed silently. Something even worse than the child's problems. Show me what I can do.

He went to the back door.

"David." Allison clearly hadn't expected to see him. "I'm rather busy."

"This won't take a minute." He edged past her into the kitchen. The child sat at the round oak table, looking at him warily. "I brought something." He held up the tin.

Allison stiffened. "I don't need—"

"It's not for you." He handed the tin to Kristie. "My gran was baking Christmas cookies. Thought you might like some."

"For me?" Her cheeks grew pink when she lifted the lid and saw the iced bells and reindeer. "May I, Mommy? Please?"

Allison's shell seemed to melt when she looked at her daughter. "Just one now. I'm making supper." She glanced at the elderly gas range. "If I can get that monster lit, anyway."

He'd learned his lesson when he'd picked up that wheelchair without permission. "May I?" he asked.

She studied his face before she nodded. "Okay."

She watched him as he got the burners going, her attitude that of someone looking at a museum piece. "Are you sure it's safe?" Her glance toward Kristie was fiercely protective.

"Seems okay. But you'd best not use the oven until I can check it out."

Her face tightened. "I can hire someone to do that."

"Sure you can. But why should you?" He leaned against the stove. "Way I see it, you've got a lot to do to get this place ready for Christmas. I'm not busy just now. I'd like to give you a hand."

There. He'd said it. He held his breath, waiting for the rejection he was sure would come.

Chapter Four

David's offer of help hung in the air between them. Instinct told Allison to reject both his help and his friendship.

He reminded her too much of the girl she used to be— the dreamer who'd expected promises would last forever.

But she already felt overwhelmed by the amount of work that had to be done on the cottage, and despite her quick words, she really couldn't afford to hire someone.

"Maybe you'd better see how bad the cottage is before you make an offer like that."

She didn't miss the relief on his face, and it gave her a twinge of shame. David couldn't help it that he reminded her she'd once seen the world with a foolish sense of wonder.

She led the way into the living room. Showing him around didn't commit her to anything, after all.

"This doesn't look bad." He tugged at a piece of dangling wallpaper. "The paper will come off, and a coat of paint will do wonders."

A wave of relief swept over her at his assessment.

He nodded toward the steps. "How's the upstairs?"

"Not as bad as this." She hesitated, caught between what she wanted and what she needed. "Are you sure you have time to help?"

His smile was like sunlight on the water. "Absolutely. It'll be pure pleasure getting this place ready for you and Kristie to enjoy. It's been empty too long."

She almost told him she wasn't getting it ready to enjoy. She was getting it ready to sell.

Some instinctive caution stilled the words. David might not be so eager to help if he knew she had no intention of staying. Thoughts of her dwindling bank account and Kristie's upcoming surgery hung heavy. Perhaps it would be best if David didn't know her plans.

She wasn't lying to him. She just wasn't telling him everything.

"Well, that's great." She managed to produce a smile. "Since you're here, maybe you'd give me a hand with these windows." Anyone buying the place would want to enjoy the ocean breezes. "They're stuck."

"Sure thing." He gave the nearest window an experimental tug. "Do you have a knife I can use to loosen this paint?"

She should not be noticing the way his muscles flexed, nor the glint of sunlight on his tanned arms. "I'll get one."

She scurried to the kitchen and back. She gave him the knife, then started to step away. David took her hand.

"Just hold this for a minute—" he pressed her palm against the frame "—until I can wedge the blade in place."

Inches separated them. He was so close she could count the sun wrinkles around his eyes, smell his fresh masculine scent, hear the quick intake of his breath.

She was not attracted to David Caldwell, she told herself sternly, trying to control her own breathing. He was nothing but an old childhood friend.

So why couldn't she get her pulse under control?

Chapter Five

"Please, Kristie." Allison's voice floated down the stairs of the cottage the next day. "You have to exercise to get well."

The child's answer was muted, stubborn, and unco-operative.

Clearly Allison had a basketful of troubles. Talking with an old friend might help, if David could get her to open up.

He resumed scraping as she came down. "Hey, Ally."

"I see you still say 'hey' instead of 'hi.'" Her smile flickered. "I guess things don't change on the island."

"Not much. Folks get married, have babies, have troubles, but life keeps on going."

She picked up a scraper and started working next to

him. If she'd seen his words as a conversation opener, she ignored the invitation.

Maybe he'd best be a bit more direct. "Sounds like that little girl of yours is as stubborn as her momma."

Allison ripped a strip of paper loose. "She won't exercise. The doctors say she has to build up strength for her next surgery."

"Next surgery?" Poor child. Poor mother, too.

She was silent for a moment, as if deciding whether or not to confide in him. "Kristie was born with a malformed hip. She's had a series of operations. The one next month should be the last."

His heart hurt for them. "So you feel like you have to push her."

"It's not just the exercises. She doesn't want the surgery." She shoved the scraper so hard it dug into the plaster. "I understand that, but we can't give up now."

He leaned against the wall, studying her determined expression, trying to understand. "So you brought her here."

She turned, her arm brushing his as she looked out at the beach. "I remembered how peaceful the island is."

He had a brief, fleeting memory of the angel-girl who'd loved the island so much on her vacation visits. She wanted Kristie to have that, too.

"I thought this place would be good for her—that the change in scene would encourage her to try again."

She was talking to him as easily as she always had. Maybe that meant he could ask the question that was haunting his thoughts.

"What about Kristie's father? Doesn't he help with her?"

Her face tightened. "No."

He waited, sure there was more.

"Everything always had to be perfect for Richard.

His wife, his car, his apartment. When his daughter wasn't…he walked away." She looked at him, blue eyes direct. "Was that what you wanted to know?"

Chapter Six

Maybe she'd been wrong to come back to the island. Allison unloaded groceries from the car, frowning. She'd thought this would be good for Kristie, but Kristie hadn't responded.

She longed to see her daughter running along the beach the way she used to, arms spread wide as if to take flight with the gulls. No classes, no dance or music lessons, no approved play dates with children from her mother's social set. Just freedom.

And David. She seemed to see two figures on the shining sand left by the ebb tide. Always the tanned gangly boy had encouraged, taught, shared the wonders of his world. How much credit was David's for the happiness she'd found here?

That was past. This was now. She hauled the remaining bag from the trunk and slammed the lid. David had his life, such as it was. Peaceful, probably, but certainly lacking in ambition.

And she had hers. She had to keep her eyes pinned on her goals. Sell the cottage. Get Kristie through her final surgery. Start the job that would make them independent.

Repeating the words in her mind, she went into the cottage.

She set groceries on the table, registering the sounds from the living room. David seemed to be using her absence to play a game with Kristie instead of getting on with the painting.

She couldn't complain, she supposed, since she wasn't paying him. But still—

She stopped in the doorway, her annoyance draining away.

"Simon says, 'Put your hand on your head,'" Kristie said importantly, doing the motion. "Sit on the floor."

David, smiling, sat down.

"I caught you!" Kristie crowed. "I didn't say 'Simon says.' You have to be it."

"Maybe your momma should," he suggested.

For a moment Allison's throat was too tight to respond. Kristie, moving as if the heavy brace on her leg weighed nothing. Laughing as she hadn't laughed in what seemed like months.

"I'll be it," she managed finally. "Just let me put the cold things in the fridge first." She turned away before either of them could see the tears in her eyes.

"I'll give you a hand." David followed her to the kitchen. "Hope you don't mind," he said softly. "I didn't let her do anything too lively."

"Mind?" She reached to him impulsively. "I'm grateful."

He caught her hand in a strong grasp that warmed her to her heart. "No need. She's a great kid. Just like her momma."

She tried to ignore the way her heart thumped. Perhaps David's low-key approach would be as good for Kristie as it had once been for her.

"Mommy, guess what?" Kristie stood in the doorway, bracing herself with her hands. "David's going to take us out on his boat tomorrow to look for dolphins. Isn't that great?"

Allison pulled her hand away from his, her gaze chilling. Maybe David was good for Kristie. But he had no right to make plans for her—for them—without talking to her first.

Chapter Seven

David steered the Spyhop slowly into the channel. Kristie, life jacket bright over her navy jacket, bounced with excitement. Allison clasped her daughter, every tense line of her body saying she didn't want to be here.

"I've never run you aground before. I won't today."

She turned a startled face to him. "I don't think that."

"You grip that rail any tighter, you're going to bend it."

"Not unless I've been eating my collard greens."

The unexpected response took him back to evenings when Allison had joined the Caldwells for supper. Gran had teased her to try things her own mother wouldn't have served on her table.

"Come to supper and you can have some." He liked seeing her face relax at his teasing. Allison shouldn't have to go through life tensed up as if waiting for a blow to fall.

"When will we see the dolphins?" Kristie edged forward.

"We're headed for the sound on the other side of the island. The pod is usually there about now."

"And if not?" Allison smiled as she got in a little teasing of her own. "How will the dolphin expert explain that?"

He shook his head in mock sorrow. "I don't know. They might make me give back my degree."

"Degree?"

He enjoyed her surprise. "Oceanography. Sorry, sugar. I know you had me pegged as a beach bum."

"I did not." But the flush in her cheeks said differently. "I remember you talked about college that last Christmas."

He nodded, making the wide turn around the end of the island. They skimmed over the waves toward the sound.

He remembered that last Christmas, too—especially the look on her mother's face when she'd seen them walking along the beach, hand in hand. "You never came back. I was sorry."

"My mother always had other plans for Christmas." She smoothed her hand along Kristie's hair, ruffled by the wind. "And then—well, college, marriage…"

"Life intervened," he suggested.

"I guess." Her face tightened again. "I haven't had much time for vacations. I've had to be practical."

Practical. It seemed a sad word in connection with the girl who'd danced along the beach, hair flowing in the wind.

"Look." He throttled back, letting the Spyhop idle on the waves. "There they are." He pointed as first one, then another dolphin made a silver arc through the waves.

"Oh." Eyes shining, Kristie clasped her hands in awe.

She should look that way more often. The child needed a sense of wonder to sustain her through the difficult times ahead. Didn't Allison see that?

He looked at Ally, and his heart seemed to stop at her expression. Ally needed to regain that sense of wonder, too, just as much as her daughter did.

And if he thought all he wanted from Allison was friendship, he'd been kidding himself.

Chapter Eight

Allison held her breath as the dolphins cartwheeled through the waves. How could she have forgotten that incredible sight?

"They seem so—" she sought for words "—free."

David leaned on the rail next to her, letting the boat rock gently. "They are that. I remember you always loved them."

His voice was soft, recalling the past they'd shared. Somehow in the busy stressful years she'd forgotten that, but now it seemed to be here, waiting for her.

"Look at that one, David." Her daughter's face was lit with wonder. "Do they live here always?"

"They travel, but they always come back to us."

He bent close to Kristie as he began telling her some fanciful story about dolphins saving a shipwrecked sailor. Their faces wore identical looks of childlike innocence. Allison had felt that way, too, when she was Kristie's age. A longing swept over her, powerful as a riptide, to feel that way again.

No. Her rejection was almost panic-stricken. She couldn't go back. She had to be practical. She had to take care of herself and Kristie, because no one else would.

"Do you remember counting dolphins with me, Ally?" David's smile invited her back into that world she'd left.

"No." That was a lie. She remembered. But she shouldn't. "Is this what you're doing with your oceanography degree?" She wielded the question like a weapon to push him away.

He shrugged, refusing to take offense. "Maybe the degree helps me appreciate it more."

"You can't build a career on appreciation. Or dreams."

"You can't build a life without both."

He didn't seem to expect a response to that. He just leaned on the railing next to Kristie, watching the dolphins, apparently content to let the day slip away with the tide.

She should be telling him how improvident he was. Instead all she could think was how secure he seemed. "You're happy, aren't you?"

The fine lines crinkled around his eyes. "Why not? I live in a place I love. A place my family has loved for generations. Gran says that Caldwells always come back to Caldwell Island, because this is where we belong."

Suddenly, Allison realized he wasn't searching for anything, because he already had it all.

"You're a lucky man, David. You have everything you want."

Some emotion she couldn't identify touched his eyes. "Nobody has that. Maybe someday." He stretched, muscles flexing under his denim shirt. "Today, I'll settle for this." His gesture took in the sea, the dolphins, even her and Kristie.

That sense of freedom she'd felt when she caught her first glimpse of the dolphins seized her again. Maybe today she could push away all the things she should do in favor of what she wanted—to be here, right now, with David and Kristie.

Just for today.

Chapter Nine

David eased the boat toward the dock, watching Allison's relaxed expression harden. Her cares were a visible weight, making his Ally into the brittle, determined woman she'd become.

"Thank you." Her voice surprised him with its softness. "I guess you were right. We both needed this."

"A little relaxation never hurt anyone." He had to keep it light, or he'd give in to the longing to try and take her cares away permanently, and that was beyond him.

He nodded toward the dock. "You'd better get ready. Looks like they've sent out the big guns."

"What are you talking about?"

"Gran's waiting for us. My loving interfering family thinks you should stay for supper. Nobody ever refuses Gran."

"I can't. I have to go home and get some work done."

He shrugged. "Don't tell me. Tell Gran."

He busied himself tying the boat while Ally and his grandmother skirmished. The result was predictable.

"Have another piece of key lime pie," his mother urged.

Allison shook her head. "I couldn't possibly."

They'd had dessert and coffee in the living room, watching as his sister Miranda and her boy, Sammy, lured Kristie into making Christmas tree ornaments out of shells. Kristie, shy at first, had thawed under the flow of warmth from his family.

Ally had, too, but she was fighting it. "I really have to go home and get some work done," she said for the third time.

"No need to hurry off." His father stretched long legs out toward the fire. "If David's not giving you enough help, you say the word and I'll bring Daniel and Theo over to work."

Allison looked a little overwhelmed at the thought of all those Caldwell men in her small cottage. "Thanks, but we're doing fine. I do need to get Kristie home before she falls asleep."

"I'm awake." Kristie's words were interrupted by a yawn.

David grinned and got up. "I'll drive you."

Daniel and Theo embarked on a mock battle over who got to carry Kristie to the car that had the child giggling. David's mother shoved a plate of pie into Allison's hands.

"Come again tomorrow," she urged. "Or if you can't do that, at least promise you'll spend Christmas Eve with us."

Ally evaded the invitation politely, and they finally

escaped the clutch of family. David paused for a moment on the porch, waiting while Theo put Kristie in the backseat.

"Do you remember telling me once you wanted a family like mine?" He looked at Allison, laughter in his voice.

"I remember." For an instant, unguarded longing shone in her eyes.

David's heart clenched. Was that what she'd tried to have with Richard?

And after a failure like that, would she ever be willing to try again?

Chapter Ten

What on earth had gotten into her? Allison stared at live oaks draped with Spanish moss as David drove them back to the cottage. She'd practically agreed to spend Christmas with the Caldwells.

She was as drawn to their warmth now as she had been years ago, when she'd seen the contrast with her cold, barren home life. But now she had Kristie and her own independence to hold on to.

The car pulled up to the cottage. She'd left lights on, and they showed yellow and welcoming through the new curtains.

"It looks like home," he said lightly.

"Yes." She shook off the tempting thought. "I'm afraid our apartment in Atlanta isn't quite so cozy."

"How soon will you go?" He sounded as if it mattered.

"I promised Kristie we'd stay until her surgery. Mid-January." She glanced toward the backseat. "She's asleep."

"I'll get her."

He was lifting Kristie before Allison could get out. Having David around didn't do her drive for independence a lot of good. She opened the front door and nodded toward the couch.

"Just put her there. I'll take her up in a bit."

David settled Kristie on the couch, tucking the afghan around her gently. He smoothed her tousled hair. "What a sweetheart she is."

There was a lump in her throat the size of a baseball. He saw the beauty in Kristie that her own father had never discerned.

"Yes. I wish— " She wished so much for her child.

"She's going to be fine."

"Yes." She had to believe that. She cleared her throat. "Thank you, David. For everything." She held the door open.

He started through, then paused on the threshold and touched her arm, nodding toward the ocean. "Look."

She stepped out onto the porch with him. A nearly full moon cast a shimmering silver pathway across the dark water, mesmerizing in its beauty.

"Your grandmother used to tell us a story," she said softly. "Something about sailing off on a stream of moonbeams to wonderful adventures. I dreamed about that for years."

"Good dreams, I hope." He was very close, his voice a low baritone rumble.

"The best." An odd, somehow familiar longing touched her. She wanted— What? She didn't know.

That sent a tinge of panic through her. She knew

what she wanted—sell the cottage; get through Kristie's surgery; start her new job. Why did she feel so uncertain? She shivered.

"You're cold. You should go in." David touched her, his palms warm on her arms.

She should. But somehow her gaze tangled with David's; somehow his hands were drawing her close, his lips finding hers, and the world went spinning away along the path of moonbeams.

She pulled away, her lips cold where his had been. This was crazy. She turned and bolted into the cottage before she could do something even crazier, like kiss him again.

Chapter Eleven

David whistled as he drove down the lane. Ally was going back to Atlanta in three weeks, but she and Kristie would come for weekends, maybe longer while Kristie recuperated.

Even Allison's rapid retreat after their kiss didn't discourage him. They had plenty of time for their relationship to grow, and they had years of friendship to build it on.

He parked and took the box he'd brought into the cottage, finding Kristie at the kitchen table.

"Hey, sugar. I have something for you from Sammy."

Kristie slid from the chair, grabbed her crutches, and went into the living room without even acknowledging his presence.

So much for all his good cheer.

"I'm sorry." Ally kept her voice low. "Kristie woke up when we were on the porch last night. She saw us."

"Saw us kissing, you mean."

Her gaze evaded his. "I tried to explain that we're just friends. That it didn't mean anything."

He put the sand dollar he'd brought on the table, then arranged the glue and glitter in a neat row. "Didn't it?"

"No." That sounded firm, but she didn't meet his eyes.

"Maybe I should talk to her."

"I think it's better to forget it." She did meet his gaze then, and he saw that she didn't just mean Kristie.

She might be able to forget, but he didn't think he would.

"Well, guess I'd better get to work, then." He carried a paint can into the living room. Kristie was curled on the couch with a book. "Sammy sent you a sand dollar shell and some glitter and glue. So you can make a Christmas ornament if you want."

Kristie put the book down, still not speaking.

He bent to open the paint can. "If you need any help, just tell me." He started painting.

By the time Allison got her brush and joined him, Kristie had made her way to the table and was bending over the shell.

"Thank you." Allison concentrated on the paint she was applying. "And tell Sammy thanks, too."

He suppressed a smile. Ally and her daughter were alike in more than just looks.

By the time they'd finished the woodwork along one wall, Allison was talking normally again, as if determined to show him that she had forgotten that kiss.

"David?" Kristie's voice was small. "Could you help me?"

"Sure thing." He found her ready to attach the hanging string. "Hey, great job. Do you know why we use the sand dollar for Christmas?" He felt Ally move, standing behind him.

Kristie shook her head. "Tell me."

"See, on this side is the shape of an Easter lily, and inside it is a star." He turned it over. "On the other side is a poinsettia. So the sand dollar is perfect for Christmas."

Kristie dangled the ornament from one finger. "Thank you for helping me. I'm sorry I acted mean."

He touched her cheek lightly. "Friends help each other."

Kristie's smile flashed. Apparently their crisis was over.

But Ally—he could feel the tension that went through her at his words. And he didn't have the slightest idea why.

Chapter Twelve

Allison had felt guilty all afternoon, and nothing she had said to herself seemed to help. She scrubbed paint off her hands at the kitchen sink, trying to ignore the feeling. She couldn't.

David had gone home after painting all day, whistling as happily as if she'd given him a gift by letting him work. She didn't feel that carefree, unfortunately.

His innocent comment to Kristie about friends helping each other had stung her. David helped because he had a good heart, and because he lived in a place where such simple acts of kindness were routine.

And all the while she was deceiving him—carefully avoiding the truth about why she was fixing up the cottage. If he knew she intended to sell it…

Well, what? Did she imagine he'd stop helping her

if he knew that? That was silly. David wasn't that kind of person.

Maybe she was just afraid of the disappointment in his eyes if he knew she'd kept it from him. David's honesty had always made her want to measure up. Somehow that hadn't changed.

A car pulling into the drive brought her to the window with a ridiculous leap of her heart. It wasn't David. His grandmother came toward the door, carrying a basket.

She opened the door. "Mrs. Caldwell, how nice to see you."

"Just dropping by with a little something for your supper. I know you and David have been painting all day." She bustled in, put the basket on the table, and started unloading it.

"You didn't need to do that." She felt helpless in the face of all this goodwill. She couldn't very well close the door to keep out kindness, but it only increased her guilt.

"This is chicken pot pie, and that one's pickled beets. And I brought another tin of my Christmas cookies, 'cause David said your little girl really enjoyed them."

"You're all being too kind."

"I don't reckon there's such a thing as too kind." Her faded blue eyes, sharp behind her glasses, inspected Allison.

"David's here every day helping, and now you come with food." There was a ridiculous stinging behind her eyes.

"David comes because he wants to. After all, the two of you were always special to each other. Now that you're back, it's only natural he wants to help."

Special to each other. "I'm not here to stay for good, you know. I'll be starting a job in Atlanta in a few months."

Gran Caldwell just smiled and shook her head. "You still belong here, even if you spend some of the time away."

"I don't—"

But David's grandmother was already picking up her basket. "I'd best get home. Don't you worry about David. Land, that boy was over here fixing the roof when we didn't know if you'd ever come back. He's not going to mind a bit of painting."

She whisked out the door before Allison could say anything, even supposing the huge ball of guilt in her throat would have allowed her to speak. David had fixed the roof, and he'd never even mentioned it. How much more did she owe him?

Chapter Thirteen

Allison waited, nervous but determined, for David to arrive. She had to find out how much the materials had cost to fix the roof, even if he wouldn't take money for labor. And she also had to tell him the truth about why she was fixing the place.

This was no big deal, she assured herself. But that didn't seem to erase the sensation of dread in her stomach.

It was just as well that she had to be out for the rest of the day. Tomorrow was Christmas Eve, and they'd skip working. By the time the holiday was over, they'd both be back to normal.

The sound of his footstep on the porch sent her pulse accelerating. Yes, indeed, normal was certainly a good idea.

"Hey." He stopped, taking in her business suit. "What's happening? You don't look ready for painting."

"I have to go to Beaufort today. The firm I'm going to be working for asked me to take care of something for them."

"The day before Christmas Eve? Can't they wait until after the holiday?"

She'd asked herself that, but it annoyed her coming from him. "This job could take me right to the top. I can't refuse the first thing they've asked me to do."

His gaze assessed her. "Fine. Kristie can stay with me."

"No, I'll take Kristie along." She swallowed. Just say it. "But I wanted to ask you something. Your grandmother said you fixed the roof on the cottage. I'm sure that must have cost something for materials, and I want to pay you."

He looked just as offended by that as she'd thought he would. "You don't owe me a thing," he said flatly.

"But the roofing materials—"

"We always have stuff like that around the inn for repairs. We don't want money for doing a neighbor a good turn."

Her frustration probably didn't make sense, but she felt it anyway. "But I wasn't even here then. And after the way my parents let the place deteriorate, I'd think you'd be glad to see it fall down."

"I knew you'd want the cottage someday."

"How?" She wanted to shout at him. "How did you know?"

He shrugged. "I knew. People don't change all that much. You always loved this place, even though your folks didn't. I knew you could never sell it."

Now was clearly the moment to tell him that she was

doing just that. Unfortunately the words seemed lodged in her throat, unwilling to come out.

As little as she wanted to acknowledge it, she knew why.

She didn't want to lose what they had. It could never be anything but friendship, but she didn't want to risk it.

Kristie appeared in the doorway, still in her pajamas.

"Kristie, what are you doing? I said to get dressed."

"I don't want to go. I want to stay with David."

"You can't." She glanced at her watch. This had taken more time than it should, and she was already late.

"She can stay with me." David smiled. "No problem."

No problem for him. For her, it was just one more reason to feel grateful to him. And one more reason to feel guilty.

Chapter Fourteen

"The wise man built his house upon the rock," Kristie sang as she patted sand onto her sandcastle.

David grinned. "We just have sand to build on here."

Kristie glanced toward the cottage. "Do the houses fall down, then?" Her small face was serious.

"Not your house," he assured her. He patted the sandcastle. "The tide will take this away, but your house is structurally sound. That means it's strong inside, even if we did need to do a little painting to make it look nice."

His thoughts slipped to Ally, as they had a tendency to do too often. When he'd seen her dressed in her power suit instead of her jeans and sweatshirt, every hair in place, she'd been a different person—smart, ambitious, determined.

But that brittle sophistication was on the surface, wasn't it? Underneath, where it counted, Ally was sound.

Kristie scraped at the sand with a shell. "I wish we didn't ever have to go away from here."

I wish that, too, sugar, David thought. But he couldn't say it.

"Your momma told me you don't want to have your operation," he said carefully. "But it sure would be nice if next time you come, we could play sandpiper tag."

Kristie looked up, intrigued. "What's sandpiper tag?"

"Your momma and I used to play that." He saw Ally running, laughing, happy. He pointed to a row of sandpipers strutting along the wet sand. "It's like tag, but you can't tap someone without running between the sandpipers first."

"I can't do that." She frowned at her brace.

"After you have your operation, you will." Please, God.

"But if I'm well—" She paused, digging her fingers into the sand. "If I'm better, Mommy will go to work all the time."

He hesitated, aware that Ally probably wouldn't appreciate his interference. But the child deserved someone to listen.

"I guess maybe she'll have to, so she can earn money to take care of you. She'll still spend a lot of time with you."

Kristie shook her head, her silky blond hair obscuring her expression. "She'll work all the time, like Daddy. I heard her one time. She told him he was doing it to stay away from me."

"Oh, honey." His heart hurt for them. "That's not true for your momma. She loves you more than anything."

Her lower lip came out. "Maybe that's why Mommy wants me to have the operation. So she can go to work every day instead of staying with me."

He took her sandy hand in a firm grip. "Now, that's just plain silly. Your momma wants you to have that operation so you can be better. So you can run and play and have fun. I know that as well as I know that the tide's gonna come in."

Kristie looked up at him, fear and hope battling in her blue eyes. "You sure?"

"Positive." He made it just as strong as he could, relieved when hope won out in her expression.

He'd talk to Ally. He'd help her understand Kristie's fears. They'd find a solution to make both of them happy.

To make all three of them happy.

Chapter Fifteen

If Allison's mind whirled any faster, she wouldn't be able to drive. She crossed the bridge onto the island, trying to think this through rationally. The firm actually wanted her to start her new job two days after Christmas.

Her initial reaction had been that it was impossible, but that wasn't an option. Needing someone in the office immediately, her future boss had made it clear: She started, or the job went to someone else.

So she had no choice. She'd have to put the cottage on the market tomorrow, if she could find a Realtor open. Get a nanny for Kristie—

Kristie would not be happy. She'd remind Allison of her promise to stay on the island until the time of the surgery. Somehow, Allison would have to make her daughter understand. This job would secure their future.

She had to tell someone else, too. David would be—what? Sad? Disappointed? Angry?

She didn't know. But as she pulled in next to his car, she knew she was about to find out.

They were sitting at the table in the kitchen, playing a board game. She paused for a moment. They made a nice picture.

"Mommy!" Kristie's face lit up. "I beat David two times!"

"That's great, honey." She put her bag down and took a deep breath. The moment was here, and she didn't know how to say it.

"Has something happened?" David read her too easily.

"I have some news." She took another breath. It didn't help. "I talked to my new boss today. He wants me to start my job right away. Right after Christmas."

Kristie went from smiling to tearful in a second. "Mommy, no! You promised we'd stay here until my operation. I don't want to go back."

"I know I promised, Kristie, but I have to do this. It'll be okay. I'll find someone really nice to stay with you."

"I don't want someone nice. I want to stay here!" Kristie slid off her chair and lurched toward the other room. "I hate you!"

"Kristie—" Allison started after her, her eyes swimming with tears. But David caught her hand.

"Wait."

She tried to shake him off. "I have to go to her."

"There's something you have to hear first." His eyes were very serious. "Something Kristie told me today."

She stopped, held by his expression. "What?"

Now David looked reluctant to speak. "She talked about why she doesn't want to have the operation."

She seemed to feel his heart beating through his

hand. He was going to say something she didn't want to hear—she knew it.

"Kristie said she doesn't want to have the operation because if she's well, you'll leave her to go to work. She said that's what her father did. He worked a lot, so he didn't have to be around her."

The words stabbed straight to her heart.

Chapter Sixteen

David didn't want to cause her pain, but however it hurt, Ally had to know why Kristie was so opposed to the surgery.

"I'm sorry." His words were inadequate.

"Why did she tell you? What did you say to her?"

"I tried to reassure her that you love her, that's all. We were talking about all the things she could do when you come back to the island after her operation."

"We won't be back."

Now it was his turn to stare, stunned. "What?"

Her face had lost all the softness it had acquired since she'd returned. "I'm selling the cottage. I can't afford a vacation house, and our future is in Atlanta, not here."

He shook his head slowly, trying to take it in. "Why didn't you tell me?"

"Because I thought you wouldn't help if you knew."

"Ally—" He didn't know what to say to that. "You know that's not true. We're friends."

She rubbed her forehead, and for an instant he thought her eyes shimmered with tears. "I'm sorry. I didn't mean that. I just couldn't figure out how to tell you."

He tried to push away his own feelings long enough to figure out what she needed. "Look, are you sure this is what you really want? A job so demanding it will consume your life?"

"It's a good job," she said, looking as stubborn as Kristie sometimes did.

"Good for you and Kristie? Or good because it will bring in a high salary?"

Her temper flared. "That's not fair. I have a child to support. I can't afford to work only when I want to. I need a real job."

This was probably not the moment to say that his job was real, even though it wasn't as prestigious as the position that waited for her in Atlanta.

"You don't have to go back to the city for that. You could work in Beaufort and live right here in the cottage. Kristie could have friends around her and the kind of life you always said you wanted."

"I was twelve when I said that. I didn't know anything." Her mouth firmed. "I've learned, believe me. I can't count on anyone else. I've made my plans, and I'll follow them."

"Gran would say we're not in charge of planning our own lives."

"Your grandmother is a lovely person, but I have to do what I think is best for my child."

With her face hard and determined and her voice brittle, she didn't look anything like the girl he remembered.

"All right, Ally." He felt a flicker of anger. "But while you're doing what you've planned, just be careful you don't turn into the same kind of person your husband was."

Chapter Seventeen

"Come on, Kristie. Help me put some ornaments on the tree." Allison had run out on Christmas Eve to get a small tree, in spite of the fact that they'd be leaving soon, hoping that might make her daughter happy. It wasn't working.

"I want to go to David's house." Kristie shoved her lower lip out. "They invited us, remember?"

"I know, but—" But what? She could hardly tell her daughter that she wasn't sure of her welcome there. Or that she didn't want to be confronted by David, challenging her decisions.

I'm right. I know. I have to take care of my daughter.

But David's words kept coming back to her every moment that she wasn't actively pushing them away. *Are you sure you're doing what's right for Kristie?* That was what his argument amounted to. *Are you sure you aren't turning into the same kind of person your husband was?*

Of course she wasn't. Was she arguing with David or with God?

You gave me this special child. Surely You expect me to take care of her as best I can.

Turning into the same kind of person your husband was? Had she really begun measuring herself by Richard's standards?

She rejected that, a little panic-stricken. If she didn't have the plans she'd been relying on, what did she have?

Help me. Please, she prayed. Show me that the decisions I've made are right for us.

The knock at the door came on the heels of her prayer, almost like an Amen.

She opened it to find David standing on the porch. For a moment she could only stare at him. "David."

He lifted an eyebrow. "It's Christmas Eve. You promised to spend it with us, remember?"

"I don't remember promising anything."

"Mommy, you did. You promised." Kristie's pout had vanished as she hobbled to the door. "We have to go to David's. I want to put my sand dollar on his tree."

David smiled at her. "You go get it, okay?"

"Okay." She hurried toward the kitchen, eyes shining.

David looked at Allison, and she felt a ridiculous longing to step forward into his arms and rest her head on his shoulder.

"Well?"

"I wasn't sure you'd want us to come now."

He reached out, taking her hands in both of his. "Sugar, if that isn't the silliest thing I ever heard, I don't know what is."

His warmth flowed along her skin.

"Come on," he teased. "You know we're friends, no matter where we are."

She did know that, didn't she? "Okay. Christmas Eve with the Caldwells it is."

Chapter Eighteen

The whole downstairs of the inn overflowed with Caldwells—sisters, brothers, cousins. And kids, running
around, dodging between adults, filled with all the excitement of Christmas. His mother, Gran, and Miranda
had filled countless trays with more food than anyone
could possibly eat, but everyone who came through the
door brought more. The air was filled with the mingled
scents of pine, cookies, baked ham, roast turkey.

David spotted Kristie in the living room near the
tree. She wasn't running, of course, but she seemed to
be having a good time. Sammy, bless his good heart,
was sitting on the rug playing a game with her.

When David had lifted her up to hang her sand dollar on the tree, she'd put her arms around his neck and
squeezed. He'd felt as if she was squeezing his heart.

He'd managed to put himself in a position so he could see Ally wherever she moved. Right now she was helping his sister arrange cookies on a platter. Their heads were together, and they were laughing.

In a few days she'd be gone. She and Kristie would go back out of his life as suddenly as they'd appeared, and he might never see them again.

There's nothing you can do, he told himself. Ally's changed. She's not the girl you remember.

Had she changed? Maybe. Or maybe he was being a coward.

He'd given her every reason she should stay on the island. Except the real one.

Don't go. Stay with me. I love you.

He couldn't say that to her. She hadn't given him any indication that she would welcome it.

Except for the kiss. That had been real.

It wasn't very practical of him, falling in love on the basis of one kiss.

But it hadn't just been one kiss—it had been a lifetime of knowing her.

And she already thought he wasn't very practical.

His gaze found her again. Now she stood in the archway, chatting with his grandmother. As if she felt his gaze, she looked up at him. Her eyes, wide and startled, were the eyes of the girl he'd known.

Ally was actually the one person who might understand if he came right out with what was in his heart. They'd always been able to speak to each other heart to heart, without worrying about what they should say or how it would sound.

He'd tell her. He owed it to both of them to say it at least once before she left.

He shoved away from the mantel he'd been leaning

against. It shouldn't be hard to detach her from Gran. Gran always had a sixth sense about things like that.

He'd taken one step toward her when he heard a clatter, a crash, and a cry. He spun around, searching automatically for Kristie.

One of the running children had bumped into the Christmas tree. Kristie stood, hands pressed against her lips, eyes desolate. Her sand dollar lay shattered on the floor.

Chapter Nineteen

Allison would have recognized that cry anywhere. Kristie. She turned toward the living room, gaze searching for her daughter.

She was all right. At least, she didn't seem to be hurt. Allison hurried across the room toward the tree, weaving through the running children.

David had reached Kristie first. He knelt next to her, drawing her into the circle of his arms. Allison was caught by the tender expression on his face and by the way her daughter leaned against him.

She vaguely heard Miranda shepherding the other children into the dining room. The room grew quiet around them, and she moved closer to David and Kristie.

"I know," David's soft drawl was even softer than

usual. "I know how disappointed you are, sugar. It was a beautiful ornament, and you made it yourself."

Kristie sniffled. "You gave me the shell. I wanted it to be on your tree forever and ever, so you wouldn't forget me."

Allison tried to swallow, but her throat wouldn't work. David had been more of a father to Kristie in one week than Richard had in her whole life.

"Honey, I couldn't forget you." David sounded as if he had trouble with his throat, too. "No matter how far away you go, I could never, ever, forget you. We're friends for always. And I'll find you another sand dollar. Promise."

Kristie wiped tears with the back of her hand. "It won't be the same." She looked down at the shattered shell.

David held her closer. "You remember the story I told you about why we use the sand dollar for Christmas?"

"Because it has the poinsettia on it."

"That's right. But there's something else I didn't tell you." He leaned over the broken shell, pointing. "See those five white things that came out of the shell?"

Kristie nodded. "They look like little birds."

"That's what they are. There are five tiny doves inside each sand dollar, and when it's broken, they go free."

Allison knelt next to them carefully, as if the moment might shatter like the shell. "That's a beautiful story, isn't it, Kristie?"

Her daughter nodded slowly, as if unwilling to give up her sorrow. "I guess so." She leaned closer. "They really are like little doves."

Free. The thought confused Allison. They're free.

Kristie's smile flickered, lighting her face. "Can I get Sammy and show him?"

David tousled her hair. "Sure thing."

Kristie hurried toward the other room, her brace thumping.

Allison's vision blurred with the tears she hadn't wanted her daughter to see. Oddly enough, she could still make out the doves, flying free. They gave her an odd sensation, the way she'd felt when she'd watched the dolphins arcing through the waves.

She'd asked for a sign, hadn't she?

Chapter Twenty

David saw the tears on Allison's cheeks. He caught her hands, drawing her to her feet, wanting to wipe away the tears and not quite daring to.

"She's going to be all right."

"Thanks to you."

It looked as if he had the chance he'd wanted. "Can we talk?"

She nodded. "There's something I need to tell you."

Kristie was coming back into the living room, accompanied by a flood of kids who slowed their steps to hers.

"Looks like privacy's going to be in short supply in here." David nodded toward the door. "Let's step out onto the porch."

The wraparound porch was dim and cool. Out in the darkness, the Christmas lights strung on the boats reflected the stars. This was Christmas for him—not sleigh bells and snow, but lights shimmering on the water.

He turned to Ally. "You said you wanted to tell me something." Whatever it was, he couldn't let it deter him from telling her how he felt.

"I couldn't get away from what you said yesterday." She looked at him, her eyes troubled. "I kept thinking about it all day. That I was turning myself into someone like Richard."

"I shouldn't have said that."

"Yes, you should." She hesitated, and he heard the whisper of her breath. "I'd begun to see that the life I had with Richard wasn't right, even before Kristie. But I intended to hold our marriage together. I was devastated when it broke apart."

The Ally he remembered didn't give up once she'd started something. "It wasn't your fault."

"No. But I didn't realize…until you said what you did. I've been trying to rebuild that same world for Kristie, even though it was never what I wanted. I didn't realize I could be free. I could create a different life for us."

Like the doves. Freed by breaking.

She drew a shuddering breath. "I'm not taking the job. It wouldn't be fair to Kristie. I need to get her through the surgery before I do anything. Then…we'll see."

That was his cue, wasn't it? He took her hands.

"Don't go away, Allison. You belong here. Stay." He breathed a silent prayer. "I love you. No pressure. I know you're not going to rush into anything. You have Kristie to consider. But I love you. Both of you. And I'll wait as long as I have to."

She tilted her head back, her hair flowing over her shoulders. The starlight seemed to be reflected in her eyes.

She looked at him for a long moment. Then she smiled. "You don't have to wait." She lifted her face for his kiss.

He had his angel-girl back...to stay.

SUGAR AND SPICE
Lynnette Kent

Chapter One

Ian Baker heaved a sigh of relief as the garage door closed behind him. He'd written today's date a hundred times during the past fifteen hours, yet hadn't realized the significance until he drove home from work to find the streets of his neighborhood crowded with Hobbits, Star Wars storm troopers, and Powerpuff girls, firefighters and Special Forces soldiers. Halloween, of course. His newly adopted community—New Skye, North Carolina—appeared to celebrate the holiday with great enthusiasm.

The front doorbell rang as he came into the kitchen, then rang again. Ian jogged to the entry hall, fished his keys out of his pocket, and turned the big brass lock.

On the porch, upward of ten little goblins stared

hopefully at him. "Trick or treat!" A contingent of adults stood on his front lawn, just outside the circle of light.

Ian wiped his hand over his face. "Uh…I…" He didn't have any candy in the house. No apples or oranges. Handfuls of cereal wouldn't cut it. What the heck could he give these kids?

He held up a hand. "Wait just a second." Back in the kitchen, he surveyed his pantry. A box of Grape Nuts, a loaf of bread, a jar of peanut butter. There was jam in the fridge, but he doubted PBJs would go over well.

The light shining in the laundry room caught his eye. He'd left it on this morning when he was searching for matching socks in the dryer. And on top of the dryer… *That's it!*

At the front door again, he crouched to kid level and held out the gallon pickle jar in which he saved the change from his pockets.

"One fistful apiece, okay?"

"All right!" They lined up efficiently to take their turns at the jar. "Thanks, mister."

"This is cool!"

"Awesome!"

His impromptu treat appeared to do the trick.

Wincing at his own stupid pun, Ian straightened to watch the kids flee across the grass to his neighbor's porch, followed by their adult bodyguards. Then he turned to go inside to prepare his nightly gourmet dinner—a couple of PBJs and a glass of milk. What the menu lacked in variety, it made up in predictability.

"Dr. Baker?"

Hearing a woman's voice, he swung back around, automatically offering the jar. "Did I miss somebody?"

She stepped out of the darkness and onto the porch. "Not at all. And I'm betting the handout at Dr. Baker's house will be the talk of New Skye Elementary School to-

morrow morning. But you and I have an appointment."
Her smile was wide and bright as she offered a handshake. "Cass Stuart. Sugar and Spice, Incorporated."

Ian stared at her, his mind a total blank. "I'm sorry,
it's been a really long day." Belatedly, he closed his
palm against her warm one. "Come on in, please."

He led her through the dark family room to the adjoining kitchen, where there was light, a table, and
chairs. "Have a seat." Setting the pickle jar on the table,
he crossed his arms and leaned his hips back against the
counter to take some of the weight off his tired feet.
"Now, Ms. Stuart, I hate to admit it, but I don't have a
clue as to why you're here. What are we meeting
about?"

"Food."

"Food." Ian scoured his brain. "Dinner?" Yes, he
worked hard. Some nights he got home so tired he could
hardly spell his own name correctly. But surely he
would remember having asked this very attractive
woman for a date.

She nodded, her big brown eyes sparkling with
laughter. "Thanksgiving dinner."

"Thanksgiv—" He snapped his fingers as the pieces
clicked into place. "Right. I remember—I asked my office manager to find somebody to make dinner for my
family."

"And she called me. Sugar and Spice is a catering
firm." She definitely fit the description, with her shiny,
cinnamon brown hair, cinnamon sugar freckles sprinkled
over her creamy skin, and those deep chocolate brown
eyes. "I'm here to discuss the menu with you." She'd
pulled her hair back from her face with an orange velvet
band and wore black cats dangling from her earlobes.

The touch of whimsy made him realize he hadn't
thought about how much fun Halloween could be

for…fifteen years? Twenty? "That's great." He heard his stomach growl and, from the quirk of Cass Stuart's full lips, knew she'd heard, too. "Would you mind if I made a sandwich? I haven't eaten since…" The memory escaped him and he shrugged. "Whenever."

She opened her hands in a generous gesture. "Be my guest. But since I'm in the business of feeding people, I'd be glad to make a sandwich for you, if you'd like."

He turned from the pantry with bread and peanut butter in his arms. "No, that's…" Then again, the idea of someone else making him a simple meal seemed close to heaven. "Will you join me? If you get the sandwiches, I could change clothes."

"Sounds like a plan." She came to the counter as he set down the supplies. "I'll find what I need. Come back in ten minutes."

"Right."

Cass watched the gorgeous Dr. Baker disappear into the shadows beyond the kitchen. Rita, his new office manager and Cass's best friend since high school, had warned her. Now, she believed—believed in the broad, rangy shoulders, the athletic build, the curly blond hair cut close to his beautifully shaped head. And the deep-set blue eyes, looking warily out on the world as if he hoped for friendship but didn't expect it.

The house was nearly as magnificent as the man. As a kitchen aficionado, Cass definitely approved of the granite countertops and professional-grade appliances, although she wasn't sure the room had ever been used for meaningful cooking. A peek inside the spotless double ovens pretty much confirmed that guess.

She put together four neat peanut butter and strawberry jam sandwiches, moved the pickle jar to the counter and set the glass-topped table with plates and two glasses of milk. Then, since Dr. Baker hadn't yet reappeared, she turned on the one lamp in the family room. Twice as large as the huge kitchen, this space offered a fireplace framed in black marble surrounded by exquisite paneling and built-in bookcases. Two long brown leather couches faced each other across the hearth, complemented by two tapestry armchairs and the lamp table between them.

Otherwise, the room was empty. No curtains or drapes, no pictures on the walls, no rugs on the floor. Not a single accessory, not even a poker with which to stir a fire, should one ever be lit in that pristine space. Altogether, Dr. Baker's house looked like a cold, heartless place.

Cass was still standing in the center of the room when Dr. Baker returned. He stopped short by the fireplace wall. "Something wrong?"

"Not at all. Let's eat." They sat at the table and spent a couple of silent moments inhaling their food. Finally, Cass sighed. "This is good. I haven't had a bite since dawn."

He raised a straight blond eyebrow. "A caterer doesn't get to eat?"

"Too busy cooking." She reached into her purse for her notebook. "Now, do you have an idea of what kind of food you'd like for Thanksgiving dinner?"

"Just the usual—turkey and dressing, mashed potatoes, sweet potatoes, rolls, vegetables, pies. Cranberry sauce. My mother likes cranberry sauce."

Making notes, she shook her head. "You don't really need a caterer for this. Every grocery store will have all these dishes prepared and available the day before."

"Yeah, I know." He put a hand on the back of his neck and rolled his head, obviously trying to loosen kinks. "But, see, this is a big deal. I just moved to New Skye to start my CT surgery practice."

"CT?"

"Cardiothoracic—heart surgery. Coronary artery by-passes, that kind of work. Anyway, my whole family wants to drive over from Atlanta and celebrate the holiday. They weren't happy about my coming here, so my plan is to demonstrate that I'm doing fine and they don't need to worry anymore. I'd like everything to be really special, including the food. That's where you come in."

"I understand." Cass added a couple of notes to her list. "But I have to tell you, Dr. Baker—"

"Ian." He finished the last of his milk and looked at her with an endearing white mustache above his firm—and very kissable—mouth. "Call me Ian."

Cass repressed her smile. "I have to tell you, Ian, that your grand plan doesn't stand a snowball's chance in hell of working out."

Chapter Two   .

"'A snowball's chance in hell'? What are you talking about?" Frowning, Ian wiped away his milk mustache with the paper towel Cass had provided as a napkin. "What's wrong with my plan?"

She braced her elbows on the table and shrugged, trying to keep her attention on the subject at hand, rather than on that well-shaped mouth. "You can hire me or any other caterer in town to prepare a terrific Thanksgiving dinner. But you don't have a place for your family to stay."

"Of course, I do—five thousand square feet of house, including four bedrooms, besides mine, and six extra baths. What more do I need?" He'd changed out of his surgical scrubs into a dark blue, long-sleeved T-shirt over soft, comfortable jeans, and socks, but no shoes. Something about the white socks, and those strong shoulders under blue cotton, made thinking a challenge.

Cass pushed back from the table and walked into the family room. With a safe distance between them, she turned to face him, holding out her arms. "Does this look like a home to you? Does this resemble the house where you grew up?"

Ian glanced around, his brows drawn together in concentration. "Well, my mother has more furniture. And lots of...of stuff."

"Don't you think she'll expect something like that here?"

He shook his head. "Nope. No way. I had to do the dusting when I was a kid. Spent my Saturday mornings wiping off little china dogs and monkeys and fancy boxes and painted plates on tiny stands when I wanted to be out playing ball. I'm not having that clutter in my house."

Given such a pitiful portrait, Cass held up her hands in surrender. "But there's middle ground between bare and unbearable. Your family—which means who, by the way?"

"Mother, Dad, sister and husband, brother and wife and two kids."

She widened her eyes. "That's a boatload of family, all right. And they won't be comfortable if you don't offer more than just the essentials in furniture. You need chairs, tables, lamps, a television for the kids...."

"You sound as if I've got time to do that kind of shopping." He rolled his shoulders, then rubbed the back of his neck again. "I was in surgery at six this morning. Even if I knew what to look for, I can't possibly make time for wandering around town to find it."

"How long have you lived in this house?" Cass clenched her fists against the urge to massage his neck and shoulders, get out those kinks that were driving him crazy.

"Six months."

"And all you've done is work?"

"That's why I'm here. CT surgeons are plentiful in Atlanta. There was only one overworked guy in New Skye. I came where the patients needed me."

"So now there are two overworked guys." Cass smiled and stepped close enough to put her hand on his arm. "I'll be glad to prepare a dinner your family can enjoy together. But I really do think you need to soften the house if they're going to be comfortable. And, more important, if they're going to believe you are."

After a silent minute, he nodded decisively. "Okay. You do it."

To Ian's immense regret, Cass stepped back again, dropping her hand from his arm. "I beg your pardon?"

He persevered. "I'll pay you whatever you ask to make the place look like it should."

Those deep brown eyes had gone round with surprise. "I'm not a decorator."

"I don't want a decorator." *This* was the right plan. And the right woman to carry it out. He wasn't sure how he knew that. But he did. "I want somebody who understands my aversion to clutter and somebody who understands what needs to be here so my family will stop bugging me about coming back to Atlanta."

Her gaze focused, intensified. "You don't want to go back?"

"I went to college at Georgia Tech and med school at Emory, in Atlanta. Did my training there, as well, but I never knew how tied down I was until I finally came up for air and realized I'd never left home." He shook his head. "I was thirty-three and still a little kid. I decided it was time to grow up."

Cass gazed up at him, and he didn't look away, didn't try to avoid the frank interest in her face. He'd never said any of that to a woman. Somehow, though, he knew he could trust Cass Stuart with his confession.

She took a deep breath. "Well, then, I'll see what I can do about the house. Is there a color you especially hate?"

He thought for a second. "Pink. In any form."

"Your mother likes pink?"

"Loves it."

She laughed, and he loved the sound of it in his house. "No pink. Do you want to show me what I'm up against?"

"Right this way." He led her upstairs and turned on the lights in the guest bedrooms. Each room had a bed, an armchair, and a chest of drawers or a dresser and mirror. The armchairs were identical, upholstered in a green damask he'd seen on a sample at the furniture store, and the four beige bedspreads were all the same, because he'd liked the heavy cotton fabric. Off-white blinds hung at the windows, matching the off-white paint on the walls. The off-white baths were supplied with green towels.

Cass stood in the last room and shook her head. "Dr. Baker, you are seriously color-challenged."

He considered that he'd done pretty well. "I had one free day before I started work. This was all I could manage."

"Now we've got four weeks. Place yourself in my capable hands and I guarantee the results will be breathtaking."

Ian couldn't help the interpretation his mind chose to put on those words. "Sounds good. I'm game."

The woman across the room looked puzzled, and then horrified. "That's not what I meant!"

"Unfortunately, I know that." He grinned and turned the light off to give her time to recover. Starting down the stairs, he glanced up as she came to the top step. "Do you want to have your way in my bedroom, too?"

After a second's pause, Cass chuckled. "Of course," she said, in a voice suddenly gone deep and sexy. "What woman wouldn't?"

A kitten was waiting on her doorstep when she got home from Ian's house—tiny, shivering, all big green eyes and orange stripes. Cass picked the little thing up and warmed it in her arms.

"What are you doing here? Where did you come from?" The baby mewed pitifully. "Is somebody missing you?" Inside her apartment, she wrapped a towel around her houseguest and went to the kitchen for a bowl of milk.

"Pretty stripes." Cass sat on the floor nearby as the cat lapped up the last of her half-and-half. "Like ginger and cream. But I know naming you means you're staying…." She resisted the urge for all of a minute. "I think I'll call you Ginger. I'll be good, though, I promise. I'll put up signs, in case they're looking for you."

Ginger crawled into her lap, made herself comfortable in the folds of Cass's sweater, and began to clean her paws.

"I don't think they were taking very good care of you." When she stroked a finger along those stripes, the ribs underneath were all too obvious. "I'll have to check them out before I let you go back.

"Meantime," she said, settling her shoulders against the oven with Ginger dozing in her arms, "we have to get your shots. The right food. And a litter box. You need to be well trained, as soon as possible.

"Because, Ginger, my dear, there's this doctor I know—a really great guy—who needs just the kind of care you and I have to give."

Chapter Three

On Monday, Cass got her early morning cooking done, then went to Ian's house and let herself in with the key he had given her. She walked through the rooms alone and tried to imagine coming home every night to such emptiness. How could the man survive like this?

That was the problem, she decided. He survived, and that was all. He had no ties outside the hospital, nothing and no one to draw him away from his work. Ian had isolated himself with his studies and his training until his life withered around him. Even his reason for moving to New Skye had to do with the patients who needed him.

But Cass believed that, somewhere deep inside, he'd known he had to find a place to do more than just exist. A place to *live*.

And her job—her calling—was to show him how.

Why she should believe that, after only one meeting, she couldn't say. Love at first sight had never been part of her agenda. Destiny was not a concept with which she felt comfortable. Life was work in progress, and she intended to make her work worthwhile.

And to share it with Dr. Ian Baker, for as long as they both should live.

In the following days, every moment she could squeeze from her cooking schedule she spent prowling fabric shops and furniture stores, searching for the right touches that would make Ian's house a *home*. She read *Consumer Reports* in bed at night to choose the best television and sound system. She renewed her close acquaintance with the man at the paint-and-wallpaper outlet.

Her own small apartment accumulated the fruits of her searches—pillows and candlesticks and pottery, fabric samples and paint chips and wallpaper books. Kate Bowdrey, a longtime friend and expert on décor, spent several evenings sitting on Cass's living room floor, helping her choose patterns and colors and playing with Ginger.

"I can't go too bold," Cass warned. "He wants a very quiet, soothing house. After a day at the hospital, I expect he needs peace."

"I'm sure." Kate compared two shades of gold at the same time she dangled a feather toy in front of the kitten. "When do I get to meet this paragon?"

"Did I say he was a paragon?" She hadn't realized she'd revealed quite so much.

Kate smiled. "You said he was gorgeous, dedicated, intelligent, and…oh, yes, gorgeous. Sounds like a paragon to me."

"No, that's the way you talk about Dixon." Kate was waiting for her divorce to become final so she and Dixon

Bell, another high school classmate, could become engaged. She had already asked Cass to cater the wedding,
but the arrangement was a secret between the two of
them.

"Oh, all right. You're just passionately involved in
creating a comfortable home for this man in whom you
have no personal interest. Who wouldn't understand
something so…illogical?"

But, of course, Cass did have a personal interest.
And every time she ran into him, that interest deepened. Just last night, she'd come over late, after work,
to measure the upstairs windows. And Ian had come up
to see why his guest room lights had been left on.

"The Decorating Fairy, I presume." He stood at the
foot of her ladder. "I'm reminded of the Shoemaker and
the Elves. They finished his work for him every night
and made him rich."

Cass grinned. "That's right, and at the end his wife
sewed them clothes and he cobbled them each a cute little pair of boots."

"So, should I write you a coupon for a free bypass?
That's my only skill, I'm afraid."

She turned sideways, leaned an elbow on the top of
the ladder and propped her chin in her hand. "Somehow,
I doubt that."

He stepped onto the bottom rung, aligning their bodies and bringing their faces very close together. "You
doubt what?"

"That surgery is your only skill." Maybe it was
their seductive position—or, more likely, the fantasies
she'd been having about him as she lay alone in her
bed at night—but Cass was feeling bold. "You'd have
to be good with your hands to be a successful surgeon.
So I'm sure…" At the glint in his eyes, her courage
failed her.

"You're sure…?"

"I'm sure you'd be quite dexterous with…with knots and c-carpentry…all sorts of— of manual tasks."

Ian stared at her for a long moment, his gaze intent, wondering. And then he dropped lightly back to the floor. "That's what you mean, hmm?"

She tried to recover her breath. "What else?"

"I'm wondering," he said, then winked at her and left the room.

The second week of November was one of the hardest Ian had yet experienced in his new practice. Emergency bypass surgeries popped up every time he turned around, and the regular surgery schedule was booked solid. Follow-up visits and consultations with other doctors took time. Several nights he simply walked straight through the house from the garage to his bedroom and fell facedown on the bed, asleep before he hit the pillow.

On Saturday, he got home early—about seven p.m.—and stepped into a strange new world.

The house smelled faintly of…cider, he decided. He tracked the scent to the dozen or more gold candles in brass holders of various heights now grouped on the mantel. A low, square table sat between the two leather sofas, with a bowl of green apples—real apples, he discovered with approval—on top. A soft, tapestry-patterned blanket had been draped over the back of one couch, while velvet pillows in gold and green lay against the arm of the other. The space provided in the bookcase now housed a new, state-of-the-art television, and the remote control waited next to the bowl of apples. Firewood had been stacked neatly on the grate, ready for lighting.

Ian found himself tempted to lie down, put his feet up and look for a ballgame on TV. But he was hungry.

More important, he wanted to see what other changes Cass had brought to his house.

A tour upstairs yielded…nothing. That seemed strange, when she'd been so appalled by the lack of color. His bedroom hadn't been touched, either.

Or had it? He couldn't remember making the bed this morning—he'd been called in at five a.m. for a trauma case. But now the sheets were smooth, the pillows plump. And did he imagine that hint of spiced peaches in the air?

His stomach did the proverbial growling routine, and he decided he had to get sustenance or he would keel over. The refrigerator was his usual destination, so he went there first, wishing for something besides strawberry jelly. Grape would be a nice change. Maybe tomorrow he'd get to the grocery store.

But the fridge yielded those surprises he hadn't found upstairs—a foil container with a paper top marked "chicken and rice, heat in microwave four minutes on high." A big bowl of green salad. A whole apple pie and a pitcher of iced tea. Plus orange juice, fresh milk, bagels, butter, and cream cheese.

Ian stood and stared for a long time. The pillows and blankets and candles—part of their agreement, and he expected to see a bill. Food, though…what did food mean?

Maybe Cass Stuart, caterer, couldn't stand to see *anyone* go hungry.

Or maybe—just maybe—Cass Stuart, an attractive and generous woman, cared enough about Ian Baker to be sure he got fed on Saturday night. And if that was the case…

What should be *his* next move?

Chapter Four

His next move turned out to be far easier than Ian had imagined. Maybe even predestined. He woke up Sunday morning to find chilly November rain pouring down outside the windows. For some reason, the idea of going to a worship service occurred to him.

And the first person he saw, as he shut the church door on a wet gust of wind, was Cass Stuart.

"Ian!" Her lovely face shone with pleasure as she came toward him. "Welcome to St. Peter's. Is this your first visit?"

He shook the hand she extended, then discovered he was reluctant to release her. So he didn't. "I thought I should get back in the habit of showing up on Sundays." Impulsively, he added, "That was even before I knew you were here."

She made no attempt to take her hand back. At his words, her gaze warmed like a goblet of fine liqueur held over a flame. "I'm glad you chose our church this morning. Let me find you a seat." Even as she turned away, her fingers clung to his for a few seconds. Ian missed her touch as soon as it was gone.

Their progress to a suitable pew was delayed by introductions. Cass, it would seem, knew everyone in the congregation, from the grandparents to the youngest of babies. Ian suspected he would have met them all, if the service hadn't started.

"I'm ushering today," she whispered, as she seated him. "But I'll find you later."

Her introductions continued after the service, in addition to several encounters with doctors and nurses Ian knew from work. He was feeling quite comfortable as they reached the front door and the minister who stood there to greet each member of the departing flock.

But then Cass stepped up ahead of him and hugged the robed man around the neck. "Daddy, I want you to meet somebody." Before Ian could assimilate what he'd just heard, she caught his hand and drew him forward. "This is Dr. Ian Baker, the client I've been telling you and Mom about. Ian, this is my dad, Andrew Stuart."

Ian put his arm out for a handshake, though he wasn't sure a word could get past the lump in his throat. "—I'm glad t-to m-meet you, sir. I enjoyed your sermon very much." There didn't seem to be much more he could offer, especially since his brain had frozen solid. And the idea he'd come up with about asking Cass to lunch—which was why he hadn't paid attention to who was preaching—seemed completely hopeless.

The reverend turned to his daughter. "Honey, maybe Dr. Baker would like to join us at home for dinner. Your mother always has an extra place set."

Paralyzed now, as well as speechless, Ian felt Cass squeeze his hand. "Thanks, Daddy, but we've already made lunch plans. We'll take a rain check, okay?" Still holding on, Cass led Ian out onto the front porch of the church. She looked up at him with a blush on her cheeks and a shy smile in her brown eyes. "You don't actually have to go to lunch with me. But I knew you weren't prepared for lunch with them."

When her hand started to slip away, Ian held tight. "But I do want to go to lunch with you. I was thinking about that instead of the sermon." He hung his head in mock shame. "If I'd known I was going to meet your dad, I would have listened better."

Cass stared at him for a second, her soft, wide lips parted in surprise. "That's…" She shook her head, laughing. "That's perfect."

They went down the church steps and Ian turned her toward his car. "So where should we eat?"

"Don't worry," she said, with another of those smiles he'd become addicted to. "I know just the place."

At the Carolina Diner, Cass introduced Ian to the owner, Charlie Brannon, and his daughter, Abby, both of whom stared in shock when he ordered fried chicken.

"It's bad for you, son." Charlie shook his head. "You, being a heart surgeon and all, should know that."

Ian nodded. "Oh, I do. I see enough clogged arteries in a week to make you plan your meals around celery, carrots, and lettuce." Then he shrugged and grinned. "But what's the point of living a long life if you don't enjoy it? A little fried chicken now and then won't hurt."

Charlie went back to the kitchen, nodding to himself, obviously pleased. But Abby frowned. "Now see what you've done? He's gonna feed me that line every time I remind him the doctor wants him to lose weight.

Thanks a lot, Ian. Thanks a whole lot." She stomped off, pretending to be mad until she got behind the counter, then gave them both a smile and a wave.

Chuckling, Cass turned to face Ian across the table. "If they only knew how you eat most of the time, they'd probably come hog-tie you and drag you down here every night for a decent dinner."

"Speaking of which," he said, fixing her with that deep blue gaze, "I really appreciate the food you left yesterday. I got home early enough to enjoy the chicken and two pieces of pie and a ballgame on TV. I don't know when I've had such a normal Saturday night."

She could feel a blush climbing to her face. "I'm glad. As long as I was there, I thought…" Taking a deep breath, she looked up from the napkin she'd been pleating. "What did you think of the candles and the table? Are the pillows too much?"

Ian reached over and covered her right hand with his left. "Everything looked really good. I knew I could trust you." He tightened his hold for a second, then sat back and drew his hand away as Abby approached. "With everything."

His voice was so low, Cass wasn't sure she hadn't imagined that last part. Could he possibly mean…?

But then she got busy making more introductions, as friends she'd known since childhood arrived for Sunday dinner. Rob Warren and his daughter Ginny came over to say hello, and then Adam DeVries, who needed no introduction at all since he'd built Ian's house to begin with.

"Rob, Adam, Abby, and I graduated from high school the same year," Cass explained as they drove back to the church, where she'd left her car. "Kate Bowdrey, who's helping me on your house, was our valedictorian and her brother-in-law, Pete Mitchell, was in the same class. And Charlie's been running the diner ever since we were in elementary school. It's a pretty small world, I guess. But I like being able to count on seeing friends wherever I go in town."

They reached the church parking lot, where her SUV sat alone in the rain. Ian turned to face her. "Do you have plans for the rest of the afternoon?"

Cass wished fiercely that she could say no. "I have to go to work," she said, instead. "We're serving lunch to the Women's Club tomorrow. Sixty plates of chicken Florentine with wild rice pilaf, cranberry-pecan salad, and pumpkin mousse for dessert. I'm making the mousse today."

"Alone?" There was no mistaking the hope in his mellow voice.

A hope she had to destroy. "Two other people will be at the shop at three o'clock." She glanced at her watch. "Which gives me a whole five minutes. Good thing it's a small town."

Before Ian could stir, she opened her door and stepped out into the rain. But when she got to the driver's side of her own car, he was there beside her.

"Okay, I give up." He heaved a mock sigh. "But it'll only take you three minutes to drive to your shop. So you've got two minutes to spare."

She stared at him, confused. "For what?"

He cupped her face in his warm hands, took the one step that separated their bodies. Then he bent his head until their lips were a mere whisper apart.

"For this."

Chapter Five

Kissing Cass was like coming home...only better, because his empty house didn't welcome him the way she did, with an instant melting against him, the warmth of her palms holding his wrists, the spicy sweet taste of her lips moving, giving under his. He could have stood in the rain with her forever.

Except that she was pulling away. He lifted his head to look at her and found her eyes closed, her smile dreamy. "Ian." He'd never heard his name sighed that way before, wanted to hear it over and over again. Then she opened her eyes. "I have to go. It's not heart surgery." She smiled, wistfully. "But people do count on me."

A sudden clutch in his gut protested. But commitment was a characteristic he respected. And this was a woman he'd come to care about too much to dishonor.

"I know." He stepped back, set her free. "Can I see you sometime this week? I don't know my schedule, but…" Like he ever had free time during the week for something as ordinary, as sociable, as a date.

Cass smiled at him over her shoulder as she unlocked her car. "Oh, I imagine we'll run into each other. After all, this is a really small town."

They next ran into each other on his staircase, as Ian was using his last ounce of energy climbing up and Cass was skipping down. He gazed up at her, sniffing the air. "Is that paint I smell?"

She stopped, blocking his way. "Paint, it is. Top quality latex."

Ian had liked the white walls. After a day of chaos at the hospital—a day like this one where it seemed everything had gone wrong—white was quiet. Soothing. He came to the step just below the one on which Cass stood, but when he edged to the right, so did she. "You didn't tell me you were going to paint."

"You didn't ask." When Ian stepped to her left, she followed.

Hands on his hips, he frowned. "What color?"

"Which room?"

"You're painting all the rooms different colors?" He swallowed hard. "And the bathrooms?"

"Paper."

Worse and worse. Visions of his mother's flower-covered walls assailed him. Again, he tried to move past her. Again, Cass blocked. "Please, let me by," he said through clenched jaws, barely remembering his manners. "I want to see what you're doing."

"Why don't you wait until it's done and get the whole effect?"

"Because it doesn't make sense to have you do something, pay for everything, and then have to do it over when I hate it. I'd rather stop this process as early as possible."

"Whoa." The woman above him backed up a step. "What happened to trusting me?"

He had said that. And meant it. But tonight, he just couldn't take the chance.

"What happened to making things comfortable without any major changes?" he retorted.

There was no doubt he'd roused her temper. She had her chin up in the air and her eyes were hard. "Your family will appreciate these changes."

"My family will be here three nights. I live here all the time. If I'd wanted the walls all sorts of wild colors, I would have had them painted that way."

Cass jammed her hands in the pockets of her overalls. "Excuse me, but that's not quite the impression you gave me of the way you finished this house." When Ian opened his mouth, she shook her head. "Never mind. Feel free to go up and make your judgment. If you hate it, tell the guys to paint over the color and charge the paint to me. I wouldn't stick you with a room you didn't like any more than I would a meal you couldn't eat. Good night." Brushing past him, she hurried down the stairs. The slam of the front door rattled the windows in every room.

Ian ran his hands over his face and through his hair. Then, wearily, he climbed the rest of the way to the second floor to see what disaster awaited him there.

The room at the top had two walls painted a soft green, lighter than the chair fabric he'd chosen, but in the same shade. With the woodwork left white, he had to admit the effect was cool, crisp. Pleasant. There were no flowers in the bathroom, just a pale green, marble-patterned paper with rolls of a Greek key border waiting to be installed.

So it went. As he viewed each bedroom, Ian found a variation of paint against which his green chair looked...well, great. Soft gold, a light brown. The most unusual color was orange—not a harsh or bright tone, just a moment pulled from a cozy blaze in the fireplace and expanded to glow on the walls. He felt warm and comfortable, standing there in the half-painted room.

At the same time, he felt like an absolute jerk. A heel. An ungrateful, stupid, ill-natured boor.

And there was nobody in the house to tell him he was wrong.

Cass turned her answering machine off and refused to answer the first six calls that rang after she got home. She didn't want to talk to anyone on the entire planet, not even Russell Crowe. Didn't need any more work. Didn't want any more friends. Just expected to sit on the couch next to Ginger with a pint of Häagen Dazs and eat until her teeth froze and her brain exploded.

"When?" she asked the kitten. "When will I learn?" All her life, she'd been smart, fast, organized. And bossy. How many times had she heard that from teachers, from other girls? From *boys*? And when would she stop expecting to find a man who actually appreciated her talent for getting things done?

Today might just be the day. Ian Baker had accomplished what no man had done before. He'd shut Cass Stuart up.

A pint of Häagen Dazs didn't last long enough for this kind of pain, and Cass realized she would have to go out for more. She set the carton on the floor for Ginger to clean and was dragging on her jacket, debating between French Vanilla and Bailey's Irish Cream, when the phone rang again.

"'Lo?" Then she remembered, and swore.

"Cass, it's Ian. Don't hang up." The words reached her even as she aimed the receiver at its hook. "Please, let me apologize."

She brought the phone back to her ear long enough to say, "Don't bother." Then, for some reason, she didn't hang up, but stood there like a fool, one arm in her coat and one out. Waiting.

"Listen, Cass, I was wrong. Totally, miserably wrong." He sounded breathless, frantic. "I looked at the rooms upstairs and the colors are great. Perfect. I wouldn't change one, and the bathroom papers are fantastic, too. I'm really sorry I acted like such a...a..."

"Would you like me to supply the word?"

"I'm sure you could. Let's just take it as already said." She heard the smile in his voice. "My only excuse is that I had a really bad day. A patient died during bypass surgery. Not my case but, still, it throws everybody."

Immediately, she felt horrible. "Oh, Ian, I'm so sorry. Why didn't you say something?"

"I didn't give myself a chance, did I? Instead, I jumped down your throat and made everything worse. But if you'll forgive me, that'll help."

How could she refuse? "Of course. Do you want me to keep going? It's up to you."

"Definitely." No doubt at all. "And I want to make up to you for being a jerk."

Cass smiled, the ice cream forgotten. "How do you propose to do that?"

"You'd like to know, wouldn't you?" Ian now sounded his usual, in-control self. "Just meet me here at eight Friday night. I guarantee an evening you won't forget!"

Chapter Six

Wearing a velvet dress and sexy heels, Cass arrived at eight p.m. on Friday to find Ian's house dark and apparently empty. She waited in her car for a few minutes, thinking he might be running late. Then she wondered if he expected her to let herself in with her key. He might even be planning to spring some kind of surprise when she did.

No surprise. No Ian. Just the chill and the dark and the smell of fresh paint met her at the front door.

She turned on the lights in the family room—she'd placed two floor lamps and another table, with the right lamp to set on it, by the sofas. She sat in an armchair for a while, staring at the blank television. The apples smelled good, and Cass finally acknowledged how hungry she was.

In the refrigerator, she found hints of Ian's plans, including chicken breasts, a bottle of white wine, fresh broccoli, and fresh pasta. The thought of what she could do with those ingredients made her mouth water and her stomach growl.

But tonight she would not take charge. She would let Ian keep control.

By nine-thirty, she was ready to weep with hunger. He hadn't called and she didn't know how to contact him, except through the answering service, which wouldn't give her any information except to say he wasn't on call tonight. Great. So where was he?

At ten, she consigned his male ego and his desire for control to hell. First, she turned on the gas igniter in the fireplace and set the logs to blazing. Then, she pounded the chicken breasts thin, dredged them in flour, and set about making chicken Piccata with the lemons and capers she found in the fridge. Great minds think alike.

Just as she was stirring the sauce, lights flashed outside and the garage door lifted. In another moment, Ian came into the house. He closed the door behind him and leaned back against it, staring at Cass with an expression very close to despair.

"Smells good," he said quietly. And then, "I am so sorry. I'd have called, but I was in surgery the whole time."

Cass looked at him a moment, and her irritation bled away. "It's okay. Why don't you get out of your scrubs while I dish this up, and we can eat in front of the fireplace?"

Ian squeezed his eyes shut. "Sounds great. I—" But then he opened his eyes, shook his head, and went to his room without finishing the thought.

When he came out again, the plates were set on the coffee table, with glasses of wine waiting and a CD

Cass liked playing softly. "I have no idea what kind of music you enjoy," she said as they sat on the floor opposite each other. "Is this okay?"

"I haven't had much time for music. But this is good." He took a bite of chicken. "Mmm. So's this." He toasted her with his wine. "How is it you always end up taking care of me? I really meant to do the honors tonight."

"You take care of people all day long."

"You feed people all day long."

"Not the same level of pressure as heart surgery."

"Sometimes being fed is more important."

"Give it up, Dr. Baker. I'm not going to let you take the blame. Just eat your dinner."

"Yes, ma'am."

She wouldn't let him clean up afterward, either. With the dishes in the dishwasher, she brought the wine bottle out, refilled their glasses, then turned off the lamps and curled up on the couch where she could watch Ian, still on the floor, and the fire. "Thank you for a lovely dinner. Consider yourself cleared of all obligation."
"You cooked, cleaned up, and waited two hours to begin with."

Cass shrugged. "I'm a take-charge kind of person. Being waited on really doesn't suit me."

Ian pushed himself up off the floor and onto the opposite sofa, bracing his elbows on his thighs as he held his wineglass in both hands. "What does suit you?"

The answer slipped out before she could stop it. "Being needed."

"Yeah?" He moved to her couch, setting his glass on the table. "What else?" The fire flickered over his face, striking blue sparks deep in his eyes.

"Um...being comfortable."

Reaching out, he slipped off her shoes. "Better?"

Cass smiled and wiggled her toes. "Much."

"Anything else?"

Staring into her wine, she debated asking *That I want you to take off?* but decided she wasn't brave enough to be quite that blunt. She risked a quick glance at the man next to her. "That suits me?"

"Well?"

His hand still rested on her ankle, his fingers circling lightly on her skin. The tremor caused by his touch streaked straight up her leg and set off an earthquake deep inside of her.

"To be wanted," Cass said, barely above a whisper.

He took the wine goblet from her shaky fingers and set it beside his on the table. "So, there are a few things I can do for you, after all." His fingers tilted her face up. His mouth touched the point of her chin, grazed the line of her cheek, placed a kiss on each eyelid. "I've wanted you from that first night," he said softly, skimming his fingers, then his lips, over her ear. "You were like a candle coming into my darkness, leaving warmth and light behind even when you weren't here."

His kisses, light as they were, pressed her back into the soft leather sofa. She raised her hands to grip his shoulders, bring him closer, but Ian held back. "Are you warm enough? Too warm?" He set his mouth to her throat, nibbled lightly.

"Ian…" She was losing the ability to think.

"You're the first thing that comes to my mind in the morning when I wake up." He ran his fingers along the edge of her dress, over the sensitive skin of her shoulders, the tops of her breasts. "Seems like you're the sunshine that starts my day." He followed the trail of his fingers with his lips. "I need that thought of you to get me going."

Crazy with her own need, Cass pulled his face to

hers, seized his mouth for a breathless eternity of kisses. She let her hands roam freely, as his were, and soon they lay together with no barriers at all, except a desire to prolong the pleasure as long as possible. Finally, Ian settled over her, joining their bodies with a deliberation that drove her even wilder.

Then he lifted his head to look into her eyes, his own glinting with a smile. "Are you okay? Comfortable enough?"

"I'm going to kill you." Cass adjusted her hips with a move that made him groan.

"You know, lady," he said breathlessly, "I think you might be right."

Chapter Seven

Thanksgiving drew near and the pace of Cass's life accelerated from busy to frantic. She'd always been an early riser, but when she stayed over at Ian's—which happened more often than not—she got up an hour earlier than her regular six a.m. That meant she got more cooking done before the stores opened at ten.

But the house was almost finished. And she knew Ian was pleased with what she'd done. Pleased to see that his guest rooms provided a quiet elegance with which he felt comfortable. Pleased that his family room offered welcome and comfort—to him and anyone else who came in—with accents of color, contrasts of texture, and simple luxuries.

Most of all, maybe, pleased that his kitchen had become a functional place, with food in the pantry and the refrigerator and, most nights, dinner on the table when he finally got home. She managed to be there at some point in the afternoon or evening and, even if she couldn't stay, to leave him something to eat. The extra cooking put more strain on her hectic schedule, but taking care of Ian was a pleasure well worth the effort.

The weekend before the big day, she decided to introduce him to Ginger. He had two days off from the hospital, plenty of time for them to get to know each other. Late Friday afternoon, she packed up Ginger's household and went to Ian's, prepared to offer homemade lasagna and her little feline surprise when he walked in the door.

Predictably, he still wasn't there by nine, so she cut herself a piece of lasagna, then curled up on the sofa with Ginger under the tapestry throw to watch the fire and wait.

Warm, cozy, she dreamed that Ian was bending over her, his smile wide and sexy as he leaned in for a kiss.

"Hey, beautiful. Where've you been all my life?"

She smiled and kissed him back, and then realized with pleasure that it was real. He'd come home.

Stretching, she reached up to put her arms around him. "Mmmm. What time is it?" Ginger stirred and peeked out from underneath the throw.

"Midni—" His gaze dropped. He straightened up out of her hold. "What is *that*?"

The cat scrambled away from his harsh tone, clawing at Cass's shoulder. "A kitten, of course. Ginger."

"Did you find it outside the house? Are there more?"

"No. I've had her since Halloween." Getting control of the trembling creature, she turned the sweet face toward him. "I brought her for you."

Ian sneezed, and sneezed again. "N-no, thanks."

"Are you getting a cold? And what do you mean, 'No, thanks'?"

"I don't want a cat. I'm allergic." He backed around the coffee table to the other sofa. "You'll have to take her away."

Allergic. How awful. "Are you sure?"

Another series of sneezes. "Oh, I'm sure."

She grappled frantically for a solution. "There are allergy shots you can take. Medicines. And you need a cat. Someone to be here when you come home." *Until you ask me to be.* "A reason to do something besides work. Ginger's perfect." Although as she kept trying to get away, she was pulling threads from Cass's brand-new velour sweater.

Ian ran a hand over his face. "Look, I appreciate the thought—though it would have been better if you'd asked me first, and saved us both the hassle. I just can't have a cat." He dropped down on the couch and put his head back. "Man, what a day."

Hassle. That meant she'd done it *again.* Evidently, she never would learn not to be bossy. "What am I supposed to do with Ginger?"

He opened one eye. "You can keep a cat at your place, right?"

Her heart stopped for a long moment. "Of course." Now feeling very, very cold, she got to her feet and moved toward the door.

"Cass?" Ian was on his feet again, staring at her across the vast expanse of his family room and kitchen.

The space was friendly now, and inviting, with the fire crackling cheerfully, the lamplight glinting on gold and red and green accents, the scent of cider spicing the air. His family would know how good his life could be here in New Skye. And they'd never know that she had expected to be part of it.

"I have to go." She opened the door and hurried outside, trying to keep hold of the cat and hold back her tears at the same time.

What he'd just said, essentially, was that she had no more of a role in his life than the cat did. He hadn't used the *L* word yet. And Cass had been waiting on him, trying, for once, not to control the situation. Trying to let Ian take the lead.

Good thing. This would hurt much worse if she'd told him she loved him.

On the other hand, she wasn't sure it could hurt any worse.

The only thing Ian knew for sure was that he had no clue. Cass had brought a cat to his house and when he didn't want it, she'd cut off all communication. He had some experience with women, though he didn't think of himself as Don Juan. Still, this was the strangest situation he'd ever encountered.

To make matters worse, he didn't have time to do anything about it. The guy who was on call on Sunday came down with the flu Saturday afternoon and begged Ian to take over. So he spent Sunday in the hospital before beginning the regular workweek. People didn't much like seeing doctors in the days before Thanksgiving, so he made it home most nights by eight.

But Cass wouldn't answer the phone, at work or at home. The finishing touches for the house magically appeared during the day, but she wasn't waiting for him anymore, with her warm smile and her hot kisses and her generous soul. How was he supposed to get through a week without waking up with Cass in his arms?

Wednesday night, he came in to discover a mouthwatering aroma in the air, compliments of the pies on the counter—pumpkin, pecan, and mincemeat, just as he'd ordered.

Thursday morning, he went in for rounds at seven a.m., knowing no surgeries had been scheduled for the holiday. His family would be arriving about two. He should be home in plenty of time to talk with Cass and get this whole mess straightened out before they arrived. He really wanted his family to meet her.

The news about a ten-car pileup on the interstate just outside of town only reached him after he got to work.

Chapter Eight

When Cass arrived at ten on Thanksgiving morning to find Ian's house empty, she drew a huge sigh of relief. As long as they weren't alone together, she could function as simply the hired help. She'd make dinner, be polite to his family, and then she'd never have to see him again. Him or his beautiful home.

The turkey went into the oven at noon, and Ian hadn't shown up. She started on her special green bean casserole, peeled the potatoes, and put them in the pot, and he still hadn't arrived. Two o'clock drew ever closer. Ian didn't come home.

Just as she set the yeast dough to rise for the first time, the front doorbell rang. With no other choice, she smoothed her hair, took off her apron, and prepared to face the Baker family. Alone.

She opened the door. Standing on the porch was an assortment of adults, while a couple of little boys raced around the front lawn.

Cass swallowed hard and called up some kind of smile. "Hi. You must be Mr. and Mrs. Baker." She searched for the oldest faces. "I'm Cassandra Stuart. Please, come in."

As Mrs. Baker stepped inside, Cass realized that Ian looked like his mother. The same bone structure, the same deep-set blue eyes, which were surveying her now with outright suspicion. "Where is Ian?"

"Where do you think he is, Dorothy?" Mr. Baker came in behind his wife, an approachable man with dark hair and twinkling eyes. "Where he always is—at work." He held out a hand. "I'm Jeff Baker, Ms. Stuart. Good to meet you." His grin was like Ian's, definitely sexy even in his rounder face. "This is my son Jeff, Junior, and his wife, Honey, and that's our daughter, Melissa, with her husband, Todd. Those hooligans outside are Jason and Joshua."

"I'm pleased to meet all of you." Cass held on to her poise by a thread. "Ian is still at the hospital—there was an accident on the interstate this morning and I imagine he's been called in to operate. But I'll make you as comfortable as I can. Would you like to go to your rooms for a bit? And then I'll serve some appetizers while we wait for Ian to get here."

With Mrs. Baker's assent, they went upstairs. Cass showed them to the rooms she'd thought they would like, and was gratified to hear murmurs of appreciation up and down the hall. Okay, she'd gotten that part right. Now, all she had to do was survive the rest of the afternoon.

Ian drove home at six-thirty in a state of exhaustion coupled with dread. No woman would forgive a man who put her in the position he'd left Cass facing today—welcoming strangers to a house where she had no real place or authority.

That wasn't true, of course. Cass was the heart of his home, the soul of his life. If he hadn't realized that truth before, these past days without her would have done it. Today had brought him, once again, up against life or death choices and the realization of how precious time can be. There might never be enough.

As he came in from the garage, he was surprised to hear his father's roar of laughter in the dining room. Baffled by sounds of celebration where he'd expected chilly silence, Ian stopped in the doorway to survey the scene.

His family was clearly enjoying its collective self. His brother and sister and their spouses looked comfortable. He didn't see the nephews at first, but a quick glance into the family room found them playing some kind of video game on his new TV.

Cass had joined them at the dining room table, her face flushed with effort and pleasure and, maybe, a glass of wine. She seemed perfectly at ease with his dad and his siblings. No one was ever at ease with Dorothy Baker, but as far as he could tell, Cass appeared to have made a truce.

Of course she had. She was too gracious, too generous, not to have charmed even his mother.

Ian cleared his throat. "Hi, everybody. Sorry I'm late."

Chairs scraped the floor as they all surged around him for hugs. The chaos finally subsided when his mother filled his plate with her own hands and set it before him, along with a full glass of wine. Since he hadn't eaten since dawn, Ian was glad to dig in. As he looked around before that first bite, however, he found one face missing.

"Where's Cass?" They all looked puzzled—no one

had seen her leave. Ian got to his feet again. "Excuse me a minute." His mother protested, but he waved her back. He would not let the woman he loved get away this time.

He found her standing on the driveway staring at her car, blocked at the rear by his dad's SUV and on the side by his Saab. She would have to drive on the grass to get out. And Cass wasn't the kind to drive on the grass.

"Where are you going?" he asked quietly, coming up behind her in the chilly darkness.

"I left the kitchen clean," she said, without facing him. "You'll just need to put the dishes in to wash and store the leftovers."

Ian smiled. "But isn't that part of what I hired you to do?"

"Well, I'm sorry." She faced him, then, and he could see her temper had flared. "I wasn't supposed to have to entertain people all afternoon as well as cook. I thought the least you could do was clean up, but if that's too much…" Marching past him, she headed toward the house.

"Cass." He caught her arm, pulled her up against him and heard her gasp. "I'm apologizing again. I'm not sure exactly what for, though. I mean…why did you get so upset over a cat?"

With surprising strength, she tried to pull away. "Because it's more than the cat, idiot! If you don't want her, you don't want me. Is that too hard to understand?"

But Ian didn't let her go. And, after a minute of concentrated thought, he began to see. He'd told her to keep the cat he didn't want. Which meant… "Boy, did I blow it." Chuckling, he put his arms around her stiff shoulders. "I'm sorry. I didn't mean to send you away. I was too tired to think straight."

"Are you allergic to me, too?" Though she didn't look up, she'd softened in his arms.

"Not in the least. You, I can't live without." He lifted her chin so he could see her beautiful brown eyes. "And there are allergy shots. If you'll only come to me with the cat, then that's the way it'll have to be."

"Ian…" Cass stopped, and dropped her gaze. He simply held her, waiting.

Drawing a deep breath, she met his eyes. "I love you."

"Yeah? What took you so long?"

Finally, that wonderful smile warmed her face. "I was waiting for you, of course."

"That's something you'll be doing a lot of, I guess. I can't seem to show up on time." Then he lowered his head, kissed her softly once, and again. "But never again for this. I love you, Cass Stuart. Today and always." They shared a real kiss, then, the kind he'd ached for in the long, lonely nights just past. When he raised his head, they were both breathing hard. "Let's go in and introduce my mother to the future Mrs. Baker."

Halfway up the steps, Cass stopped and tugged on his hand. "That's really neat, you know."

"What?"

"I'll be Cassandra Baker."

He bent down for another kiss. "I like the idea, myself."

She gave him the kiss, but then shook her head. "No, I mean I'll be Cassandra Baker…of Sugar and Spice, Inc. Perfect, isn't it?"

Ian grinned. "Whatever you think, love. You're the boss."

A SEASON FOR MIRACLES
Cynthia Rutledge

Chapter One

"I won't do it." Shannon O'Connor painted the last toenail and lifted her head to gaze at her twin. "I'm surprised you'd even ask."

Erin took a sip of her diet soda and met her sister's gaze. Her green eyes narrowed.

"Well, that makes us even. I'm surprised you're saying no."

"I'm not going to go away with your boyfriend for the weekend and pretend to be you. You're the one who promised to go to that wedding with him, not me." Shannon twisted the cap on the pale pink polish with unnecessary force. "We're 26, not 16. Impersonating each other is kids' stuff. Besides, Jake doesn't deserve that kind of treatment."

"You like the guy." Erin's lips curved up in a satisfied smile.

"Of course I do," Shannon said, the image of the tall, broad-shouldered man with an easy smile flashing before her. "Who wouldn't?"

Her sister had started dating Jake Kinkaid three months ago. Though Shannon hadn't seen a lot of Erin's new boyfriend, she knew he was intelligent, considerate, and treated Erin like a princess. The handsome architect had been a refreshing change from the superficial men Erin usually favored. Which made it hard to understand why her sister was willing to take a chance on throwing it all away. Especially for the likes of Dillon Clark.

"If Jake finds out I'm going to Aspen with Dillon, it'll be over."

"So don't go." Shannon couldn't keep the exasperation from her voice. "You and Dillon haven't been together since last summer and now, all of a sudden, you *have* to go away with him? I don't understand."

"He says he's missed me." Erin lowered her gaze and picked a piece of lint from the sleeve of her cashmere sweater. "And I've missed him."

"Last I heard he was an overbearing jerk who you never wanted to see again."

"You know me. Sometimes I exaggerate a little," Erin said with a wry grin.

"A little?" Shannon couldn't help but laugh. Though she loved her sister dearly, she wasn't blind to her sister's faults. Erin *could* be difficult. If growing up in the same household hadn't instilled that in her, the four years they'd shared an apartment since college had more than made that clear.

"And I'm not stupid," Erin said. "I know that getting back together with Dillon is a long shot. But Jake's a great guy. I'd like to still have him around in case things don't work out with Dillon."

"But that's not fair to Jake."

"Oh Shannon, can't you see?" Erin leaned forward, her voice pleading. "What isn't fair is for me to date Jake, not knowing how I feel about Dillon. Can't you help me out? Just this once?"

Shannon pushed the thin wire-rimmed glasses up on her nose and shook her head.

"You promised Jake over a month ago you'd go with him to this wedding. You're just going to have to reschedule with Dillon. Tell him something came up and you're not free this weekend, after all."

"I can't," Erin said.

"Can't?" Shannon raised an eyebrow.

"All right, I could but I don't want to." Erin flopped back in the overstuffed leather chair. "I'm just going to tell Jake the truth. If he wants to break it off, that's his choice."

Shannon thought quickly. She hated to see her sister throw away a great guy for one she'd probably hate before the weekend was over. Shannon abhorred deceit. On the other hand, she couldn't bear the thought of her sister losing Jake over a foolish whim.

"I don't like it. But if it's just for the weekend, I guess…"

Erin squealed, jumped up, and crossed the room to give Shannon a quick hug. "I knew I could count on you."

The doorbell rang and Erin headed toward the door. "That'll be Jake now. You won't regret saying yes."

Shannon smiled weakly. She already regretted it.

In only moments, Erin was back, her arm wrapped around the sleeve of the man at her side.

"Hello, Shannon." With his wavy dark hair cut conservatively short and his brilliant blue eyes, Jake Kin-

kaid could have been a GQ model instead of a successful St. Louis architect.

An easy smile played at the corners of his mouth.

Shannon's heart picked up speed.

Dear God, what had she gotten herself into?

Chapter Two

Shannon desperately wished she'd had time to change out of her sweatpants and do something with her hair before Jake had shown up. After all, she hated to look like a frump in front of such a good-looking guy.

About six feet tall with broad shoulders and a lean muscular build, Jake was the perfect size. The first time Erin had brought him home, Shannon had told her sister that he had to be one of the handsomest men she'd ever seen.

Erin had only laughed and said he wasn't really her type, but she guessed he'd do. Erin usually preferred big guys with thick necks and broad chests. Guys like Dillon Clark who'd played football in college and who still bragged about how much they could bench-press.

"It's been a while." Jake's gaze shifted from Shannon back to Erin. "I swear you two look less alike every time I see you together."

Shannon felt the heat rise up her neck. Though she could tell by his expression he didn't mean anything derogatory, the words still stung.

Erin laughed. "It's just those silly glasses Shannon insists on wearing that make us look different."

But Shannon knew it was more than the glasses. She'd let her hair grow long while Erin's short bob barely made it past her ears. And the honey-colored highlights her sister had added had changed her back to the blond of their youth, while Shannon's color hovered somewhere between a light to medium brown.

Shannon's gaze shifted to her sister. The physical differences were manageable. But what had ever made her think she could pretend to be her sister for a whole weekend? Erin could wrap a man around her finger without even trying. She was confident, witty and *fun*.

The more Shannon thought about it, the more she realized that for this masquerade to succeed, they were going to need a miracle.

Twenty-four hours later, Shannon stared in the mirror and the image of her sister stared back. Except Erin wasn't here. She was hundreds of miles away in Aspen, partying with Dillon and his friends.

Her fingers reached up and touched the wisps of blond hair. Though it had taken her a long time to grow her hair out, she didn't really miss it now that it was gone. She smiled at her reflection. Erin had been right: A haircut, some highlights, and contacts were all it took to make them identical again.

A car door slammed outside and Shannon's heart clenched. This would be the real test. She crossed the room, reaching the door just as the bell rang. Counting to 20, she took a deep breath and pulled it open.

"Jake, hello."

"You look fabulous." His gaze slid to her rust-colored leather miniskirt. "Have I seen that before?"

Shannon shook her head. The skirt was from her sister. Erin had called it a gift. Shannon had called it a bribe. "It's new."

"I like it." His admiring gaze lingered on her legs.

"Thank you."

"These are for you." He thrust a bouquet of roses into Shannon's hands. "I realize it doesn't make sense to bring flowers when we'll be out of town all weekend, but I wanted you to know how much I appreciated you coming with me."

Shannon smiled and lowered her face to the roses, inhaling their sweet fragrance. It had been eons since she'd been on a date. Eons since she'd received flowers from a man. But she reminded herself she hadn't received these, Erin had. "They're lovely."

He smiled and waited expectantly. It only took Shannon an instant to realize what he was waiting for. Erin had always been effusive in her affections and at the very least would have rewarded such thoughtfulness with a kiss.

But he was her sister's boyfriend and therefore strictly off-limits.

But she was supposed to be her sister.

How was she ever supposed to pull this off?

Chapter Three

Shannon laid the bouquet on the side table and took a step closer to Jake, her hand rising to rest on his shoulder. She leaned forward and lightly brushed his cheek with her lips. "Thank you so much."

She started to step back when his arms tightened around her. He pulled her close and he molded her tightly against his lean muscular body.

Her heart picked up speed. The delicious fragrance of his cologne enveloped her and Shannon drank it in, drowning in unfamiliar sensations.

But when his lips lowered, Shannon slipped from his arms and forced a bright smile. She headed toward the stairs, her heart racing, her brain pure mush.

"Hey, where are you going?" Jake called out.

"Upstairs," Shannon said. "Come with me."

Jake stared. *Was she asking what he thought she was?*

He hoped not. It wasn't that he didn't like Erin. He wouldn't have asked her to his cousin's wedding in Kansas City if he didn't. But they'd only been dating casually for a few months and he wasn't sure if he was ready to take her up on this invitation. Not yet anyway.

"Jake?"

His gaze shifted to the stairs. Still, she was so beautiful....

"Aren't you going to help me with my bag?"

"Your bag?"

"My overnight bag. In my bedroom." She shifted from one foot to the other. "I know we're only going for the weekend, but it's kind of heavy."

"That's why you wanted me to come to your bedroom?" he asked. "To carry your bag?"

"Why else?" Her green eyes widened.

He didn't know whether to feel insulted or relieved. But her innocent expression didn't fool him. She was playing with him. Though he didn't know what she was up to, Jake decided to play, too.

He chuckled. "I thought maybe you wanted to get an early start. You know this will be our first weekend trip together."

Shannon's breath caught in her throat. She'd never once considered what expectations Jake might have for the next two days. Could he have really thought by agreeing to come, she'd agreed to sleep with him?

Erin had never gone into detail about her physical relationship with Jake, other than to say he was a pretty good kisser. Surely her sister would have told her if they had been more intimate.

But it didn't matter what Erin had agreed to or what she had done in the past; Shannon wasn't taking one step out the door until the misunderstanding was cleared up. "I agreed to go to a wedding with you, nothing more."

"You invited me upstairs."

"To-get-my-bag." Shannon spoke clearly and emphasized every word. "Nothing more."

"So, you don't want to sleep with me?"

"No, I don't."

"Not even a little bit?" His boyish smile caught her off guard and she had to smile.

He reached over and took her hand, planting a kiss in her palm. "Okay, we'll play it your way this weekend. No sex. Just lots of kissing."

Chapter Four

The drive to Kansas City was a long one. But Shannon didn't mind. She and Jake talked the entire way and by the time they reached KC, she felt as if she'd known him forever. He had a sense of humor in sync with her own and, as they talked, she realized they shared common attitudes on everything from religion to politics.

The prenuptial dinner and wedding were a blur. The perfect host, Jake stayed close to her side the entire time. Shannon only wished her sister had warned her that Jake was an affectionate guy. If he wasn't taking her hand to pull her over to meet someone, he was leaning over to whisper something in her ear.

By the wedding reception, she'd grown comfortable with his attentiveness. She liked having him take her arm or put his hand against the small of her back when they made their way through the crowded hall.

And it seemed so natural to reciprocate; to lean into him when they stood talking to his cousins or to grab his hand and pull him onto the dance floor.

They danced until Shannon's head spun. She wasn't sure if it was from the champagne or Jake's closeness.

"Are you ready to take a break?" Jake had removed his suit jacket and loosened his tie earlier, but the room was hot and little beads of sweat still dotted his brow. Though he'd shaved that morning his cheeks wore a faint shadow.

He looked, Shannon thought, simply magnificent.

"Sounds good to me." She smiled and pushed back a strand of hair that fell across her forehead.

"Since we'll be sitting anyway, how about we go talk to my grandfather for a few minutes? He had hip surgery last month, and he's still not very steady on his feet."

"Have I met him?" Shannon had met so many people, it was hard to keep them all straight.

"I don't think so," Jake said. "He wasn't at the dinner last night."

"I've really enjoyed meeting your relatives."

"I wasn't sure you would. I know you don't normally like these kinds of things." Jake squeezed her shoulder. "But you've been such a good sport about all this and I really appreciate it. I promise, when we get back to St. Louis I'll make it up to you."

"Don't worry about it." Shannon waved a hand. "I'm having fun just being with you."

It was the polite thing to say, but Shannon really meant it. The wedding had been beautiful and even though he'd talked about "lots of kissing" when they'd left St. Louis, he'd been a perfect gentleman. This weekend just confirmed her belief that he was a great guy and her sister was lucky to have him.

They strolled across the hall hand in hand, stopping finally in front of an older gentleman sitting in a wheelchair. The white-haired man had a glass of champagne in one hand, an unlit cigar in the other.

"Grandpa Al, I'd like you to meet a friend of mine. This is—"

"Introductions can wait." The old man waved a dismissive hand.

Shannon slanted a look at Jake.

"Grandpa—"

"The mistletoe, boy." Grandpa Al pointed with the hand holding the cigar to a sprig hanging above Shannon. "Don't tell me young people nowadays don't know what that means."

Jake shifted his gaze to Shannon and she could see in his eyes that he planned on kissing her.

Her insides twisted into knots. How could she refuse? In the eyes of his grandfather she was Erin, Jake's girlfriend. And in Jake's eyes, too.

Did a mistletoe kiss really count anyway? Wouldn't it be like a kiss between friends on New Year's Eve? It didn't mean you liked the guy, or wanted him for your own.

Did it?

Chapter Five

Shannon smiled and Jake took a step forward. Using his left hand, he pushed Shannon's hair gently back from her face and lowered his lips to hers.

With one soft touch all the feelings Shannon had held inside surged to the surface. She closed her eyes and kissed him back, losing herself in the lightning bolt of emotion that ripped through her.

Jake wrapped his arms around her and pulled her close, molding his body to hers. He kissed her hard, crushing his mouth to hers, catching her by surprise.

For a moment in his arms, Shannon forgot he belonged to her sister.

It was Jake that finally pulled back. He studied her with a puzzled expression.

For a moment Shannon just stood there, trying to get her bearings, her chest heaving.

"Now that's what I call a kiss." His grandfather cackled. "Come on over here and let me meet this friend of yours."

Jake took a deep breath and Shannon realized that though he might outwardly appear composed, he was as shaken as she was by the electricity between them.

But he took her hand and smiled confidently at his grandfather. "Grandfather, this is Erin O'Connor. Erin, this is my grandfather, Alfred Kinkaid."

"Pleased to meet you, Miss."

"It's nice to meet you too, Mr. Kinkaid." The polite words flowed from Shannon's mouth automatically even as her mind whirled and skidded. What had gotten into her, kissing Jake like that?

"Have you enjoyed your weekend with my grandson?" Though he had to be close to 80, Alfred Kinkaid's eyes were bright and Shannon had the feeling he missed very little.

"Very much," Shannon said, glad she could answer honestly. "Everyone has been so nice."

"From what I've heard, you've made quite a hit with the Kinkaid clan. And we're a difficult bunch to please." Grandpa Al shifted his gaze to Jake. "I hope you're planning to come to our big Christmas get-together. It'll be in St. Louis. I live there, you know."

Shannon nodded. Jake had already explained that his family was pretty evenly split between St. Louis and Kansas City, so the fact that his grandfather lived in St. Louis wasn't a surprise. And she'd already heard all about the plans for Christmas Day from one of Jake's aunts. Apparently everyone would attend church in the morning together, then head over to Grandpa Al's for his famous Christmas brunch. In the evening it would be eggnog and spice cake in front of the fireplace. Though

Shannon thought it sounded lovely, she knew her sister would probably turn up her nose at the invitation.

"So will you come?" Grandpa Al met her gaze.

"I don't know...."

"We'll have lots of mistletoe. I promise." The old man wiggled one eyebrow.

Shannon smiled even as her face warmed.

"It's very kind of you to invite me," she said. "But that sounds like a family celebration and I wouldn't want to intrude."

"I'd love to have you come with me," Jake said.

"We'll see." Shannon gave a noncommittal smile. Of course, if it were up to her she'd say yes in a heartbeat.

But it wasn't up to her.

It was up to Erin.

Chapter Six

Shannon glanced out the parlor window of the Park-side Bed-and-Breakfast Sunday morning. The snow that had started out as flurries the night before now blanketed the ground. The latest weather reports warned areas west of Kansas City to expect heavy snow, up to a foot or more in some places. The storm was then supposed to veer north, leaving areas east of KC with only minimal precipitation.

She sighed. That meant that she and Jake should be able to make the drive home to St. Louis with only a light dusting of snow on the road. She should be happy. Her weekend masquerade was almost over. Tonight her life would return to normal. Erin would have Jake and she would have her memories.

"I wondered where you were."

Shannon hurriedly brushed a tear from her eye and pasted on a smile. "I was so tired last night, I thought I'd sleep forever. Unfortunately my internal alarm didn't get the message. It went off right on time."

"You should have knocked on my door."

"Why would I do that?" Shannon said lightly. "You were sleeping."

She shifted her gaze back to the window. "It's snowing outside."

"I see that."

He came up behind her and his arms slid around her waist. How had the smell of his cologne and the feel of his arms become so familiar? Shannon leaned back against him, wishing this moment could last forever.

Jake's arms tightened around her. "Penny for your thoughts."

"I can't believe this weekend is almost over." She stared at the bleak landscape and her heart filled with despair.

"I know." He sighed. "It's gone so fast."

"Too fast."

Something in her tone must have alerted him because he turned her in his arms and tipped her face up with his hand. Concern filled his gaze. "You've been crying. Tell me what's wrong."

"Nothing." Shannon blinked back her tears.

"Something has to be wrong. You never cry. Is it something I said?" His brow furrowed. "Or something I did? Tell me—"

"It's not you." She shook her head. "It's me. I don't want to go back to the real world."

I don't want to go back to a life without you.

"But the real world isn't all that bad." His arms closed around her in a comforting embrace and he laid his head against hers. "We live in the same town. I know we haven't seen each other much lately, but that's going to change. I wasn't being polite last night. I really want you to spend Christmas with my family. If your sister doesn't have plans, maybe she can join us. I'd like to get to know her better...."

"Jake—" She pulled away but he pressed her head back against his chest.

"Shh, just hear me out. There's no reason to be sad. Don't you see? This weekend isn't the end, it's just the beginning."

Shannon swallowed a sob. She'd always believed things happened for a reason. And usually she could see why something happened the way it did. But not this time.

After all, falling in love with your sister's boyfriend made no sense.

No sense at all.

Chapter Seven

"*Miss O'Connor?*"

Shannon raised her head from the comforting warmth of Jake's shoulder.

"Yes?"

Mrs. Graham, Parkside's proprietor, held out a cordless telephone. "I'm sorry to interrupt, but you have a call."

Shannon took the phone, her palms suddenly clammy. Only Erin knew where she was staying. But why would she be calling?

Unless something was wrong?

Shannon offered Mrs. Graham a tiny smile and pressed the receiver to her ear.

"This is…Erin."

Though she tried to act calm and nonchalant, Jake

must have sensed her trepidation because he moved to her side, his eyes filled with concern.

"Hey Shanny, how's KC?"

Shannon could tell by her sister's tone that everything was okay. Releasing the breath she didn't realize she'd been holding, Shannon covered the receiver with her hand and turned to Jake. "It's just my sister checking up on us."

To her horror, Jake reached for the phone. "Let me talk to her."

She fought an instinctive urge to step back and hug the receiver tightly to her chest. Instead, she lifted it to her lips. "Shannon, Jake wants to say hello."

She handed him the phone.

"Hello, Shannon…."

Shannon heard him ask her sister about her weekend. He laughed and they talked for a few moments longer. Between the roaring in her ears and the pounding of her heart, Shannon heard little of the conversation.

"Here, she wants to talk to you." Jake shoved the phone into her hand. His lips brushed Shannon's cheek. "I'm going to check the weather."

She waited until he'd left the room before lifting the receiver to her ear. "It's me."

"He certainly seems in a good mood." Erin's voice was light and teasing. "You must be doing a good job impersonating me."

Shannon wanted to tell her sister that she'd done nothing more than be herself this weekend, but instead she gave a weak laugh. "Just doing what you asked, dear sister."

"And I appreciate it. I know you didn't want to do this." Erin's voice turned serious. "And I feel terrible about wasting your time."

"Wasting my time?" Shannon said slowly. "I don't understand."

"I mean it may have all been for nothing." Erin's voice lowered. "Oh, Shannon. I'm having the most fabulous time. Dillon is so wonderful. I like him so much, I can't imagine dating anyone else."

"What are you saying? You don't want Jake, after all?" Shannon couldn't stop a surge of excitement from racing through her body. Last night she'd been so sure he could never be hers. Could she have been wrong?

"Dillon loves me," Erin said. "He told me so last night."

"The question is, do you love him?" Though Shannon wanted Jake, she couldn't, in good conscience, push Erin toward a man that in the past had only caused her sister heartache.

"Yes." Erin spoke so softly that even with the receiver pressed tight against her ear, Shannon could barely hear. "I think I do."

"So, where does that leave Jake?"

"Available," Erin said with a laugh. "He'll find someone else. Even though he and I never clicked, he's a great guy."

"I agree," Shannon said. "I think there are any number of women who would love to have a guy like Jake."

"Well, as far as I'm concerned, they're welcome to him."

"You really mean that?" Shannon's heart picked up speed.

"Absolutely."

But did she really mean anyone?

Chapter Eight

Shannon clicked off the phone, her thoughts whirling. As the weekend had progressed Shannon had found herself wishing Jake were free, though she'd never thought it would really happen.

But then again she'd never believed her sister would fall in love with Dillon Clark. But Erin was in love. Shannon could hear it in her voice. She could only hope and pray that this time around, her sister and Dillon were mature enough to make the relationship work.

Now, all that was left was for Shannon to square things with Jake. But how? And what was he going to say when she told him the truth? Would he tell her he couldn't abide liars and that he never wanted to see her again?

Shannon's gaze drifted out the window. Two or three inches of snow now covered Jake's Jeep and the snow continued to fall. Shannon wrapped her arms around herself and shivered.

"Is everything okay with your sister?"

Shannon jumped. She'd been so focused on imagining the worst she hadn't heard Jake return.

"Of course." Shannon pasted a smile on her face. "Why do you ask?"

"You looked so solemn. Not like your usual perky self." His hand lightly touched her arm. "Come here. Let me give you a hug."

He opened his arms and she stepped forward, burying her head against his chest, slipping her hands around his waist. The scent of soap mixed with the tantalizing fragrance of his cologne.

His hand reached up and stroked her hair. He could have said a thousand words but none would have been as comforting as his touch.

Shannon didn't know how long they stood there. All she knew was that the icy coldness that filled her after the troubling phone call was replaced by growing warmth.

Sometime, she wasn't quite sure when, she became conscious of his breath against her neck, of the beating of his heart against her breast, of the hardness of his body pressed against hers.

A strange aching started deep inside and she couldn't help but remember the feel of his lips against hers and wish that there were mistletoe hanging above them so she would have an excuse to kiss him.

As if Jake could read her thoughts, he took a step back and his hand moved upward to cup her face. His eyes searched hers. Though she knew she should look away and not let him see her naked longing, she met his gaze.

"You are so beautiful." His gaze slid over her, lingering at the hollow of her neck, her breasts, passing down to her hips, then returning to her eyes.

Her palms grew damp and she moistened her lips with the tip of her tongue. It was all the invitation he needed.

His head dipped and his lips brushed hers. They were soft and warm, slightly parted, barely touching. He continued to tease her with his mouth, planting little kisses along her jaw line and down her neck.

It was torture, sweet delicious torture.

Her senses swirled. She wanted more and she went up on tiptoe, slanting her mouth across his and deepening the kiss.

She caught a flash of surprise in his eyes before his tongue met hers, and the world exploded in a wave of heat and passion.

Footsteps sounded in the distance, but Shannon paid no attention. She reached up, raking her fingers through his thick dark hair, pulling him closer still. Now that she had him, she wasn't ever going to let him go.

Chapter Nine

"I'm sorry to interrupt."

Like two guilty teenagers, Jake and Shannon jerked apart.

Running her fingers through her disheveled curls, Shannon turned and lifted her chin.

Mrs. Graham stood in the doorway to the parlor. Though the proprietor's smile was apologetic, amusement filled her gaze. "They've revised the weather forecast and I thought you'd be interested to know we're now in a winter storm warning. The police are saying the roads both in the metro area and outside the city are extremely hazardous and are urging everyone to stay put. The report also said I-70 west just closed."

Shannon widened her gaze. "But the radio said there was only going to be a dusting west of here."

Mrs. Graham laughed. "You know what they say about weather forecasters. They're only right about 50 percent of the time."

Jake chuckled.

"But what are we going to do?" Shannon's voice rose and her gaze shifted to Jake.

"I know we were supposed to check out today," Jake said, flashing the innkeeper that devastating smile that always made Shannon go weak in the knees. "But would it be possible to extend our stay a day or two?"

Mrs. Graham paused. "Normally in bad weather we have some cancellations and letting you keep your rooms wouldn't be a problem. But several of the guests who had reservations for tonight have already arrived."

"Are you saying there are no rooms available?" Shannon asked.

"Not at all," Mrs. Graham said. "But I can only give you one room. So, if you're willing to share, you're in luck."

Shannon cast a sideways glance at Jake.

Jake met her gaze. "It's up to you."

Shannon didn't have to think long. The curious excitement that surged at the thought of spending the night with him was enough to send up a warning flag. Shannon had long ago resolved that the only man she would make love with would be her husband. So she'd made it a practice to steer clear of situations that could get her into trouble. Spending the night in the same room with Jake would be the height of foolishness.

"This can't be our only option." Shannon said. "There have to be some motels nearby that would have two rooms available."

"I can give you a list and some numbers." Mrs. Graham's gaze shifted from Jake to Shannon. "But I think you'll find they're in the same boat we are."

"We'd still like to check," Shannon said.

"I can hold the room for a half hour. But I'll have to know by then if you want it or not," Mrs. Graham said apologetically. "I have others calling."

"I understand," Shannon said. She knew the room situation would be tight, but she couldn't believe there weren't two rooms available in the whole area.

Twenty-five minutes and a dozen phone calls later, Shannon conceded defeat.

Lead me not into temptation....

Shoving the thought aside, Shannon clicked off the phone and turned to Jake. "I guess you and I are going to have to be roomies, after all."

Chapter Ten

"Do you *want* to share a room?" Jake's gaze searched hers. "I mean, is that okay with you?"

Shannon looked into his handsome face and her heart fluttered. No, it wasn't okay with her. The thought of spending the night in the same room with Jake was way too appealing to be okay.

"I don't think we have a choice." Shannon sighed. "Between the two of us, we've called every place in a 20 mile radius and they're all full."

"There is one other option," Jake said quietly. "You could take the room and I could see if Mrs. Graham would let me sleep in the parlor."

Some guys might have made the offer just for the show, but the look in Jake's eyes told her he was dead serious.

"No way." Shannon shook her head. If the parlor had a foldout couch it would have been one thing, but the delicate antique Victorian furniture made crashing on the sofa impossible. "We're two responsible adults. Just because we sleep in the same room together doesn't mean we have to let things get out of control."

"You're right. That's a choice, not a given." Jake's gaze lingered on her face and her heart flip-flopped. "I'll go tell Mrs. Graham we'll take the room."

Shannon's gaze followed him out into the hall. He looked so cute in his jeans and navy sweater. His dark hair glimmered in the light and the color of the sweater made his eyes look even bluer. Several female guests standing in the foyer cast interested glances his way, but he passed by with only a smile.

All weekend he'd scarcely glanced at another woman. She'd had his full attention. It was still hard for her to believe that this handsome, kind, wonderful man was really hers.

Until he found out who she was.

And how she had lied.

Jake looked up from the black-and-red checkerboard and flashed Erin a triumphant smile. "King me."

She groaned. "This game is rigged."

"You've still got a chance."

"I don't think so. You have five kings and I have none." She pushed back from the table in the parlor and walked to the window. With one hand she slipped open the lace curtains.

With her lean lithe body, Erin made a beautiful silhouette in the firelight. Jake let his gaze linger. He couldn't believe she was his.

Though they'd been dating for almost three months, he hadn't really known her. Oh, they'd had fun, but they'd never really connected. For a time he'd even wondered if there was another guy in the picture. But ever since he'd picked her up on Friday, she'd been different, more open, nicer.

Her blond hair shimmered in the firelight. If someone would have told him, he'd fall in love this weekend, he would have said they were crazy. Now he was the crazy one, crazy in love with Erin.

Jake moved to her side. The blowing snow coupled with the ice on the window made it difficult to see much past the front porch.

"It's still coming down," she said almost to herself. "We may be here awhile."

"I thought you wanted to delay your return to the real world," Jake teased.

"I do," she said. "But this same-room thing still bothers me."

"I don't snore," Jake wrapped his arms around her and pulled her close, "or leave the toilet seat up, or scatter my shaving stuff all over the bathroom. So you have absolutely nothing to worry about."

Jake felt himself grow warm at the contact between them. Nothing to worry about? Erin wouldn't, but as for him—he wasn't so sure.

Chapter Eleven

"How long has it been since you built a snowman?" Jake asked as if sensing Shannon's reluctance to go upstairs.

"It's dark outside." Shannon took another sip of her cappuccino and shifted her gaze out the window.

"There's a streetlight at the end of the driveway." Jake pushed his chair back and stood, holding out a hand. "More than enough light for what we'll be doing."

The old Victorian home was cozy and warm and Shannon knew that though the wind had quit blowing, it would be cold outside. She knew Erin wouldn't have considered it for a moment. The only time Erin was willing to brave the snow was on a pair of skis. But Erin wasn't here this weekend, Shannon was, and Jake's expression was so hopeful, Shannon didn't have the heart to say no.

"Okay, but I'll have to go upstairs and change first."

He gazed admiringly at her formfitting black pants and sweater. "Need any help?"

Shannon laughed at his silly leer. "I think I can manage just fine."

"Remember your stuff is in my room now."

She paused. The thought of sharing a room with Jake was still unsettling. Putting her lotion next to his razor had been way too intimate.

But they had no choice. At least they had a place to stay. And they were warm and dry, at least for the moment. Shannon glanced longingly at the fire.

"Sure you want to go outside?"

"If you don't want to…" Though his smile never dimmed, the light in his eyes faded. "We can skip it."

Tempted though she was, Shannon thought of all the nice things he'd done for her this weekend.

"No. Let's do it," she said with as much enthusiasm as she could muster. "It'll be fun."

Forty-five minutes later, Shannon plopped back in the snow, chilled to the bone, but determined to not go inside until she'd made her snow angel. She flapped her arms and legs outward, moving the snow aside.

"You look beautiful lying there." Jake gazed down at her, his cheeks red from the cold.

"I'm sure," Shannon scoffed. "My nose is as bright as Rudolph's and if I don't get out of the snow right this minute, I'm going to be as frozen solid as Frosty."

"We can't have that." Jake smiled and reached down, pulling her up and dusting her off. "No more snow."

Shannon glanced down at the angel. "She's beautiful, isn't she?"

His gaze never left Shannon's face. "Yes, she is."

Shannon licked her dry lips, heat spreading throughout her body at the look in his eyes.

"I had a great time tonight." He lowered his head and brushed her lips. "Thank you."

"You're very welcome." Her gloved finger traced a line down his cheek and his eyes darkened. But before he could kiss her again, Shannon stepped back from his arms and headed for the house.

She welcomed the arctic blast of air that hit her face. It had gotten entirely too warm for her outside.

Chapter Twelve

"Honey, I'm home."

Shannon laughed and opened the door. "You look like you've had a hard day at the office."

Jake had hung his coat up downstairs but their time in the snow had taken its toll. His jeans were wet and his hair stuck up in dark tufts. He looked, Shannon thought, magnificent.

"It was rough," he said with a grin. "But now that I'm home I'm sure you can make it all better."

Even when he didn't try he was charming. But when he did...

Shannon steeled her resolve. "Jake, let's sit and talk for a minute."

"Before or after I get undressed?"

Her head jerked up, but when she saw his teasing

smile she had to grin. "Before would probably be best. I wouldn't want to be distracted."

His eyes lit up and he rose and crossed the room. "Distractions can be fun."

She placed her hand flat against his chest and pushed him back. "Rule number one. While we're in the bedroom, we keep our hands to ourselves."

"That doesn't sound like much fun."

"You're right. It doesn't." Shannon sat on the edge of the bed and twisted the edge of her sweatshirt. "I mean we've dated for three months...."

"And most people have slept together by then," he added. "But you and I both wanted to wait until we knew each other better."

Shannon exhaled the breath she didn't realize she'd been holding. Though she hadn't thought Erin had slept with him, until this moment she hadn't been positive. She smiled in relief. "That's right."

"But I'd say we know each other quite well now." He sat beside her on the bed and his gaze met hers. "And I love you, Erin O'Connor. With all my heart."

Shannon could only stare. Jake loved Erin.

Of course he did. After all, her sister was the one he'd dated for the past three months. Shannon was just the fill-in for the weekend. She'd been foolish to think there had been anything special between her and Jake. The whole time he'd held her, kissed her, teased her, he'd been seeing Erin.

Shame mixed with despair. What should she do now? Tell him who she really was? Or play this out as Erin and no one would ever be the wiser?

"Erin," Jake took her hand. "I just wanted you to know how I felt. If you don't feel the same, I understand."

This was her opportunity to let him down gently and tell him she was getting back with her old boyfriend. If she didn't do it now, then Erin would have to do it when they got back to St. Louis. And Erin might not be as kind.

Still, Shannon couldn't bring herself to say the words. "I'm so confused."

The look of pain in his eyes broke her heart.

"I don't know what I feel—"

"Shh." His fingers closed her lips. "There's no need to talk about that now. We have more important things to decide."

"We do?" she asked. "Such as?"

"Such as—" his lips quirked upward "—do you want the right side of the bed? Or the left?"

Which side of the bed?

Shannon groaned. Her gaze shifted to the floor. She eyed the oval rug in front of the fireplace. Though she knew hardwood floors could be cold, maybe he'd be warm enough if she gave him the comforter off the bed.

A knock sounded at the door. "Could someone open the door, please?"

Recognizing Mrs. Graham's voice, Shannon opened the door.

The woman held out a stack of blankets. "These are for you."

"Thank you." Shannon took the bundle and set them on the bed.

"I thought you could use some extra blankets and I found an old air mattress." The landlady's gaze shifted from Jake to Shannon. "Of course, if you don't want it…"

"Actually—" Jake began.

"Actually we were just about to discuss who would get the floor," Shannon said. "So you couldn't have come at a better time."

"Sleep tight," Mrs. Graham whispered as she shut the door.

"Sleep tight? On the floor?" Jake muttered.

"Not on the floor." Shannon smiled. "On the air mattress."

Chapter Thirteen

Shannon jerked upright in bed, her body drenched in sweat, her heart pounding.

Something was wrong. Dreadfully wrong.

Her chest hurt and she could barely catch her breath. She hadn't felt this bad since she'd been 10 and Erin had fallen from the parallel bars and had gotten the air knocked out of her.

Something is wrong with Erin.

Shannon tried to reassure herself that Erin was perfectly safe with Dillon in Colorado. But once the thought hit her, it wouldn't let go. After a half hour of trying to convince herself she was being silly, Shannon eased herself out of the bed and padded silently across the cold hardwood floor in her bare feet.

Her sweatpants and sweatshirt were warm but Shannon found herself shivering as she dialed the number of Dillon's condo in Aspen. On the 10th ring she hung up and dialed her parents.

"Hello." Even though it was three in the morning her mother sounded wide-awake, almost as if she'd been expecting a call.

"Mom, this is Shannon." Shannon spoke in a low tone and cast a quick glance at the floor, reassured that Jake hadn't moved at all. "I didn't mean to wake you. But I have the most awful feeling—"

"I'm so glad you called." Her mother's voice sounded odd, as if she was coming down with a cold. "I knew you were in Kansas City, but I'd lost your number—"

"Mom," Shannon interrupted. "I'm worried about Erin. I just need to know if you've talked to her? I had the most awful feeling and I need to know she's okay."

"The doctors think she'll be fine. Of course, they can't say for sure...." Her mother's voice broke.

"Think she'll be fine? What's wrong with her?" Though a fire burned in the fireplace and Shannon was dressed warmly in a sweatshirt and sweatpants, she shivered.

"Shannon, this is Dad."

Shannon forced herself to stay calm. Her mother often overreacted. Her father had always been the calm, logical one. "Dad. Tell me what's going on with Erin. Is she okay?"

"Honey, Erin was in a skiing accident yesterday. She broke a bone in her leg and hit her head pretty hard."

"But she's okay? I mean people break their legs every day."

Her father hesitated. "At first she was doing fine. But then she...she took a turn for the worse. She started having trouble breathing...."

Shannon's hand dropped to her side, the phone dangling loosely in her grasp. The sweatshirt and sweat-pants couldn't assuage the icy chill that raced through her body. For a second Shannon thought she would faint. She sat down, her knees too weak to hold her. Tears spilled from her lids and a sob rose from the depths of her soul.

Suddenly Jake was at her side, taking the phone from her hand. "This is Jake Kinkaid. Who am I speaking with?"

His troubled gaze lingered on Erin. When he'd awakened to find her on the phone, he'd thought he was dreaming. Until he'd heard her cry out.

"This is Mike O'Connor. Is my daughter okay?"

"She's very upset," Jake said. "Can you tell me what's going on?"

"I was just telling her that Erin broke her leg in a skiing accident in Colorado. When Dillon first called with the news, we didn't think much of it. After all, people break their legs all the time. But she had a concussion and they kept her for observation. Then—" the older man paused and took a breath "—she developed trouble breathing. They think a blood clot went to her lung."

"Is she okay?"

"They've got her on blood thinners. The first 24 hours are most critical. Helen and I have a six a.m. flight to Denver."

Jake took down all the pertinent information and hung up the phone. Though Mike O'Connor seemed fairly together, Jake knew he must be more distraught than he seemed. In the course of their brief conversation he'd gotten Erin's and Shannon's names mixed up several times.

"Is my sister dead?"

Jake looked up to find Erin's tear-filled gaze staring at him.

"Oh, honey, no. She's not dead." He sat beside her on

the bed and took her in his arms. "She's in the hospital and they're taking good care of her. She'll be just fine."

"She couldn't breathe." Her hand rose to her throat.

"A blood clot went to her lung." Jake tried to keep his voice matter-of-fact, as if a pulmonary embolism were just a minor inconvenience and not a life-threatening event. "But your father said they're treating her with some kind of blood thinners and they expect her to make a full recovery."

"My mother was crying."

"She was upset," he acknowledged. "But your father said he thought she'd be fine once she saw your sister was okay."

"My dad will take good care of her."

"That's right, he will." Jake brushed the hair back from her face with one hand. "And I'll take good care of you. Because that's what you do when you love someone."

Chapter Fourteen

Though Shannon wanted nothing more than to remain cosseted in Jake's loving arms, her sister came first. "I can't stay here. I have to go to Erin. She needs me."

"Erin?" Jake's brows drew together.

Shannon stared at him, realizing what she'd just said.

The confusion in his gaze cleared. His jaw tensed. "You're not Erin. You're Shannon."

The hurt and anger in his eyes tore at her heart. Last night she'd had several opportunities to tell the truth, to explain what had happened. Why hadn't she told him when she'd had the chance? She'd never wanted him to find out this way. Shannon swallowed past the sudden lump in her throat. "I never meant to hurt you."

"Don't give me that." He stood abruptly and strode to the window. He leaned forward, his hands on the windowsill for a long moment before shifting his gaze back to Shannon.

"Jake—"

"So, there couldn't have been a conflict. The only reason I can think of is that she got a better offer. Is that it, Shannon? Did Erin get a better offer?"

Shannon lowered her gaze.

"Dillon." Jake snapped his fingers. "Your father said something about Dillon calling with the news. That was Erin's old boyfriend's name, wasn't it?"

Shannon's heart clenched at the pain in his voice.

"I'll take your silence as a yes." Jake raked his fingers through his hair. "I've been such a fool. I even thought I was in love with you. But I don't even know who you are."

He shook his head and turned back to the window.

Shannon knew there was nothing she could say that would ease his pain. She didn't want to leave him like this, but she didn't have a choice. She had to go to Erin. She grabbed her bag and in a matter of minutes she was fully packed.

Jake still stood with his back to her. "It's quit snowing."

"I'm going to the airport," Shannon said.

"I'll take you."

"I can call a cab."

Jake turned. "It'll be faster if I take you."

Shannon hesitated. She knew he was right. Still, she was exhausted and the last thing she wanted was to argue all the way to the airport.

"Don't worry. It'll be fine. We don't need to talk." His voice was matter-of-fact instead of angry and it was almost as if he could read her mind. "After all, there's really nothing more to say."

They'd barely spoken since they'd left the bed-and-breakfast. Jake preferred it that way. After all, he certainly wasn't in the mood for small talk and as he'd said, what was there left to say?

She'd lied and played him for a fool.

He'd found out.

He didn't want anything more to do with her.

Still, on the way to the airport, his gaze kept drifting sideways.

Her blond hair stuck out in little spikes and her green eyes were rimmed with red, but she still was the most beautiful woman he'd ever seen. She'd kept her gaze focused straight ahead for most of the drive, but now her hands were folded in her lap and her eyes were closed.

He wondered for a moment if she had fallen asleep, but then he saw her lips move and realized she wasn't sleeping, she was praying.

For a moment his heart softened. Until he reminded himself she had a lot to pray about.

And she'd better hope God would forgive her, because he sure wasn't going to.

Chapter Fifteen

A week later, Shannon sat across from her sister in their apartment living room and breathed a prayer of thanks. Erin had recovered quickly from her blood clot and the cast on her leg barely slowed her down at all. From the time she'd left the hospital and returned to St. Louis, Erin and Dillon had been inseparable. Tonight at dinner, they'd made the big announcement.

"I can't believe you're engaged." Shannon stared at the huge diamond on her sister's finger.

"Being with Dillon again made me realize that he was the man for me." A little smile hovered at the corners of Erin's lips. "I'm so glad I went to Aspen."

"I'm happy for you, Erin. I really am."

"So what about you and Jake?" Erin took a sip of iced

tea and peered at Shannon over the top of the glass. "You've barely said 10 words about the guy since we got home."

"There's not much to say." Shannon kept her tone light and gave her sister a brief summary of her and Jake's time together, starting with the drive and ending with Jake discovering the truth. "He knows you chose Dillon. And he was okay with that decision."

"That was nice of him to send the flowers to the hospital."

"He's a thoughtful guy," Shannon said past the sudden lump in her throat.

"And the most handsome man you've ever seen." Erin's lips twitched. "I still remember when you told me that. I knew right then that you should have been the one with him, not me."

"But you were the one he chose," Shannon pointed out. "Not me."

"That's because he didn't know any better." Erin laughed. "I mean, he's a great guy but he never was my type. And I'm really not his." Erin's gaze narrowed. "But you, you were just his type. And you liked him. Don't try to tell me you didn't."

"I didn't want to like him," Shannon said. "But I did. And I feel guilty about that. I mean, he was your guy."

"We can't help what we feel," Erin said, her voice uncharacteristically soft and gentle. "We can only help what we do about it. I might want a necklace in Tiffany's window, but there's no crime unless I snatch it out of the case and run out of the store."

"I kissed him, Erin." Shannon's heart twisted. "He was your boyfriend and I kissed him."

"Big deal. You and I both know if I had wanted Jake, regardless of how much you loved him, you would have let me have him. So there's no crime and absolutely nothing to forgive." Erin's tone was so confident Shannon couldn't help but believe her.

"You're sure?"

"Positive." Erin put her ring under the light. "Hey, did I tell you Kellie called today to ask how I was doing and she mentioned that Jake's grandfather was in the hospital?"

"What's the matter with him?"

"I didn't ask." Erin held out her hand, the diamond glittering in the bright light. "Isn't this the most beautiful ring you've ever seen?"

"Did they say what hospital he was in?"

"Who?"

"Jake's grandfather."

"I don't know." Erin set her glass on the table. "I didn't really pay much attention. I've never been much for old people. Plus, I don't even know the guy."

But I do, Shannon thought. Alfred Kinkaid was a sweet old man who'd gone out of his way to make her feel comfortable.

Would it be wrong to stop by and say hello?

"I think I might call around," Shannon said in an offhand tone. "Find out where he's at."

"Why would you want to do that?" Erin couldn't have looked more shocked if Shannon had told her she'd decided to dye her hair green.

"Because I like the guy. Because it's the week before Christmas and he might be lonely," Shannon said. "Because it's the right thing to do."

"Good for you," Erin said, glancing down at her ring again. "Tell Gramps hello for me. And, if you see Jake, give him a kiss from me, will you?"

Shannon paused. She'd forgotten that Jake might be there. She almost reconsidered her decision to go, until she remembered he'd told her that he played handball on Thursday nights. She grabbed her keys and headed out the door.

Chapter Sixteen

"Erin, my dear." Alfred Kinkaid stretched out his bony arms in welcome. "How good of you to come by. And on such a snowy night, too."

Despite the IV tubing taped to one arm, Jake's grandfather looked remarkably healthy.

"Hello, Mr. Kinkaid." Shannon crossed the room and gave him a quick hug being careful to avoid the tubing. "And before we go any further, I'm Shannon. Somehow the names got mixed up when we were introduced before. Erin is my twin sister's name."

Shannon didn't want to cause Jake any embarrassment, so she didn't go into detail, but she was through pretending to be anyone but herself.

"Shannon." Jake's grandfather rolled the name around on his tongue. "I like it. Shannon it is. And you can call me Grandpa Al."

The request tore at her heartstrings. If things had turned out differently, he might one day have been her grandfather.

"I'm glad you stopped." His pale blue eyes gleamed. "I've been asking Jake to bring you by."

Shannon kept her expression impassive, but she couldn't help but wonder why the old man had made the request. He had to know the odds of his grandson bringing his ex-girlfriend along weren't good. Unless, Shannon thought, Grandpa Al still thought she and Jake were together.

"It's been a long week." Grandpa Al sighed. "I've been poked and prodded so much I feel like a pincushion."

Suddenly Shannon understood why Jake hadn't told him. The older gentleman had enough on his mind without worrying about his grandson's love life.

"Are you going to have to be here much longer?" Shannon asked.

"Tomorrow is D day," the old man said holding up one hand with his fingers crossed.

"D day?" Shannon widened her eyes. She'd worked in a nursing home in high school and thought she knew most medical acronyms but this was one she hadn't heard before.

"Dismissal Day." A broad smile split Grandpa Al's face, making him look 10 years younger.

Shannon impulsively gave him another hug. "I'm so glad."

"You're a sweet girl, Shannon." Grandpa Al's gaze lingered on her face. "By the way, just so you know, there's been a change in plans. Christmas brunch won't be at my house this year."

"Why not?" Though she wasn't planning on going, had never planned on going, from what Jake had told her, Christmas was always held at his grandfather's home. Concern welled up inside her. She hoped this change in plans didn't mean that Grandpa Al's condition was more tenuous than it appeared.

"Because I'm under strict orders to take it easy. I'll be staying with Jake until I'm back on my feet. The doctors didn't want me going home alone and I certainly wasn't going to any nursing home."

Though the nursing home she'd once worked at had been very nice, Shannon knew many elderly people had fears about such facilities. Unfortunately, most didn't have another option. Not many had family able to step in and help.

Or willing. Shannon's heart clenched. Jake was such a good guy.

"Sounds like it all worked out for you." Shannon smiled. "I'm so glad."

"He's got a nice house, don't you think?" Grandpa Al's gaze lingered speculatively on Shannon.

Shannon took a seat in the turquoise vinyl chair next to the bed and forced a nonchalant air. "Actually, I've never seen it."

"Really?" Grandpa Al raised an eyebrow. "It's nice. Large two story in Wildwood. All the place needs is a woman's touch and a couple of kids."

The older man's penetrating gaze met hers.

"My church is in Wildwood. Over on Clayton." Flustered, Shannon rattled on about the congregation, hoping his grandfather would take the hint and change the subject. But the minute she paused to take a breath, Grandpa Al jumped into the conversation.

"I know you and my grandson had some kind of falling out. But I know he loves you." Alfred smiled. "You just stop by the house, real casual-like. I'll bring the mistletoe. This season is the perfect time for kissing and making up."

As much as Shannon wished it could be that simple, she knew it would never work. And anyway, it would be wrong.

And Shannon was through doing the wrong thing. Even for the right reason.

Chapter Seventeen

Jake decided to stop by the hospital on the way home from the gym. Though he'd dropped by for a short time after work, he knew his grandfather got lonely. Jake knew how that felt. He'd had the same feeling since returning from Kansas City.

Jake shoved the maudlin thoughts aside. Shannon was in the past. Out of his life. Thank goodness he didn't have to see or think about her ever again.

Pushing open the hospital door, he forced a cheery smile. "How's it going this evening?"

"You just missed Shannon," Grandpa Al said. "Looking prettier than ever, I might add."

"Really?" Jake smiled and kept his tone nonchalant. "What was she doing here?"

"She came to visit me," Grandpa Al said. "Said she'd

heard I was in the hospital and wanted to make sure I was okay. She's a wonderful girl."

Jake ignored the comment. "How's she doing?"

"Why don't you ask her yourself?"

"We don't talk much anymore."

"I gathered as much." His grandfather's eyes narrowed. "You two had a spat, didn't you?"

Jake shifted his gaze out the window.

"Don't tell me this is about the name thing?" Al chuckled. "So she gave you the wrong name. Your grandma told me she was born in '26. I didn't find out until years later, she was born in '24."

"It's not that simple." Jake knew his grandfather wouldn't give up until he knew the whole story. "I'd been dating Erin O'Connor casually for a couple of months. She'd promised to attend the wedding with me but instead, she sent her twin sister, Shannon, in her place."

"And you couldn't tell?" Grandpa Al's tone was clearly disbelieving.

Jake shifted in his chair. He knew it made no sense. How *could* he have dated a woman for three months and not been able to tell the difference between her and her sister? Though they might be identical on the outside, inside they weren't the same. Not at all.

Their discussion in the car on the way to KC had been his first clue. They'd talked about things that really mattered, instead of what new concerts were coming to the area or what the hottest new vacation spots were. But he'd told himself she must have finally decided to open up, to let him get to know her.

And then there was the reception. He'd expected her to be bored stiff. After all, there had been a lot of elderly relatives present and Erin had told him more than once she wasn't into old people. But instead of begging to cut out early, she'd been charming and gracious and had actually seemed to enjoy his relatives and the evening.

But the biggest clue had been the way she kissed. She kissed him as if she really cared. As if she...loved him. Jake's chest tightened.

"I told her I loved her." Jake shook his head and gave a humorless laugh. "I was going to ask her to marry me."

"Sounds serious."

"But it was all a joke," Jake said. "Don't you understand? She was just filling in for her sister. I didn't mean anything to her."

"Son, I've been on this earth for 80 years and I saw the way she looked at you." Grandpa Al paused. "If you can't see that she loves you, then all I can say is your eyesight must be worse than mine."

Jake stared at his grandfather, the first faint stirrings of hope coursing through his veins. Could the older man be right? Could it be that Shannon really did love him?

As mad as he'd been at first, now he understood. And he'd had a wonderful weekend. If he was in love with her, maybe it was time he did something about it and not let his pride stand in the way.

Chapter Eighteen

"C'mon, Shannon. Don't be a poop. Come with us to church." Erin lined her lips with a cinnamon-colored stick before lifting her gaze from the dressing table mirror. "It's Christmas Eve. You don't want to go alone."

Of course she didn't want to go alone. But Shannon didn't want to be a fifth wheel, either. Normally she could have gone with her parents, but her brother's newest baby had arrived earlier than expected and her parents had left for Texas two days ago. So she was on her own this year.

"I don't mind." Shannon forced a casual shrug. "And I like to go to my own church on Christmas Eve."

"Let me talk to Dillon." Erin rose with a fluid grace her sister had always envied. "We can go with his family another time."

Shannon grabbed her arm as she reached for the phone. "Erin, no. Go with Dillon. There will be plenty of people I know at church. Aunt Janice even asked if I'd save her a seat."

Of course, that was before her elderly aunt had come down with a migraine this afternoon.

"Are you sure?" Relief warred with the suspicion in Erin's gaze.

"Positive." Shannon hugged her sister. "I'll be just fine."

The last thing Jake wanted to do was put up mistletoe.

"A little to the right." Grandpa Al leaned forward in the wheelchair, his gaze narrowing. "It's not centered in the doorway."

Jake bit back a sharp retort. It wasn't his grandfather's fault that the mistletoe made him think of a certain green-eyed blonde. The mere touch of the tiny sprig brought back the memory of that night at the reception hall, the softness of her hair, the sweetness of her kiss. Though it was crazy, after his talk with his grandfather, he'd kept thinking about Shannon, wondering if he should give her a call.

"Are you going to hang it or stand there looking at it all day?"

The abrupt tone jerked Jake back to reality. He moved the mistletoe a half-inch to the right. "How's this?"

"Perfect." Grandpa Al nodded approvingly.

Breathing a sigh of relief, Jake secured the sprig.

"What time will we be leaving for church?"

"I thought we might skip services tonight." With this whole thing about Shannon still up in the air, Jake couldn't muster up much of the Christmas spirit. He knew it was wrong, but he shoved aside his guilt. "You've had a long day. We'll be going with the family tomorrow, anyway."

"But it's Christmas Eve. I haven't missed a Christmas Eve service in 50 years." The older man's jaw jutted out, but it was the distress in his voice that tugged at Jake's heart.

"The roads are icy."

"We don't have to go far. Someone told me about a little church not too far from here. Over on Clayton. We can go there."

An hour later, Jake sat with his grandfather in the back pew of a church he'd only driven past before. The roads had been as icy as he'd feared, but he'd snagged a close parking space and the parking lot had been well salted.

The church was packed. Jack scanned the crowd, his gaze lingering on all the families. The little boys in their shirts and ties, the little girls in their velvet dresses. It was hard to believe that only a few short weeks ago, such a life had seemed within his reach.

"I was such a fool," Jake muttered.

"What did you say?" Grandpa Al's eyes were bright with curiosity.

"Nothing." Jake shifted his gaze to the front of the church. "Look at all those poinsettias."

"So beautiful," his grandfather murmured, but the old man's gaze wasn't on the plants. It was on a blonde who'd just walked through the door.

Jake froze in his seat.

What was *she* doing here?

Chapter Nineteen

"Shannon. Over here."

Shannon turned in the direction of the voice and stopped dead in her tracks. For a moment she was tempted to pretend she hadn't seen Alfred Kinkaid. But she'd been taught to respect her elders and she couldn't ignore him. Or the dark-haired man sitting at his side.

God give me strength.

Shannon made her way through the crowd, and by the time she reached the end of the long pew, her heart had slowed back to a normal rhythm. "Mr. Kinkaid, what a surprise. I never expected to see you this evening."

"God works in mysterious ways." The old man's grin was so infectious Shannon couldn't help but smile. "Jake's church is way across town and with the roads being bad, we decided to go somewhere close."

"I'm glad you did," Shannon said. "I can't imagine not being in church on Christmas Eve."

"That's exactly what I told Jake." Grandpa Al's eyes twinkled. "You remember my grandson, don't you?"

"Of course." Shannon forced a smile. She'd spent the day telling herself that everything worked out for the best. After all, Erin had Dillon and seemed blissfully happy. But it wasn't as easy now, seeing Jake and realizing she'd never have the man she loved. "Merry Christmas, Jake."

"Merry Christmas." Jake's gaze lingered. "Where's your family this evening?"

"My brother just had a new baby and my parents went to Texas to be with him," Shannon said. "My sister and her fiancé are attending services this evening with his family."

Jake looked up at the word "fiancé" and she realized he didn't know Erin was engaged. But, of course, how could he? They hadn't talked since Kansas City.

"So you're alone this evening?" Grandpa Al said in a conversational tone.

"Yes, but—"

"Miss, we're about to start," the usher whispered. "Could you take your seat?"

"We've got a spot for you." Grandpa Al patted the space next to him on the end. "Right here."

Shannon glanced around the church. During the time she'd spent talking, the sanctuary had filled up and she couldn't see one empty seat except for the one in front of her. Shannon gave a resigned sigh. At least Jake was on the other side of his grandfather.

But when Shannon started to sit, the old man slid to the end of the pew, opening a space between him and Jake.

"I like to sit on the outside." Grandpa Al shot her an apologetic smile. "You don't mind sitting in the middle, do you?"

The old man's innocent expression didn't fool Shannon in the least. She sat down and smoothed the skirt of her dress, telling herself that they were all adults and if she just focused on the service she'd be fine.

But with Jake's leg pressed against hers and the familiar scent of his cologne wafting about her, Shannon found it difficult enough just to breathe, much less concentrate.

Halfway through the service she realized she was staring at him and he was staring back. She licked her dry lips.

His own lips parted as if he were about to say something but then forgot what it was.

She reached for the hymnal and his fingers closed around it, brushing hers. She felt the blood surge from her fingertips all the way to her toes.

His gaze slowly swept down her body, studying her, inch by inch.

Though the church was well heated, her skin turned to gooseflesh. It was crazy. She felt languid and tense at the same time.

He held her gaze and his eyes seemed to glitter, suddenly looking more green and brown than blue.

Her heart hammered against her ribs, drowning out the sound of the familiar Christmas hymn.

Her eyes locked with his and their breathing came in unison.

"We need to talk," he said, his lips barely moving.

Chapter Twenty

"Come to my house after church," Jake said softly. "We can talk there."

"But it's Christmas Eve," she said in a low tone.

"We need to talk," he repeated, meeting her gaze. "I don't want to wait any longer, do you?"

Shannon shook her head.

The rest of the service passed in a blur. It seemed only a matter of minutes before Shannon found herself walking through the front door of Jake's home. The minute they got inside, Grandpa Al started complaining about his hip. But when he headed to his room, Shannon noticed he wasn't limping at all and he barely used his four-pronged cane.

"I'm going to go to my room and lie down." Grandpa Al smiled at Shannon and gave his grandson a wink. "You two kids have fun."

"He seems to be walking okay," Shannon said, after she'd heard a door shut down the hall. "Do you think his hip is really bothering him?"

"With him, who really knows," Jake said with a smile. "If I had to bet, I'd say no. I think he wanted to give us some time alone together."

"He's really a sweet man."

"Yes, he is," Jake said. "But we're not here to talk about him. We're here to talk about us."

"Before you say anything, I just want to say again that I'm sorry." Shannon met his gaze. "I never meant to hurt you. I'm not the kind of person that normally lies. Erin wanted to see if there was still something there with Dillon. I didn't want her to lose you. That's why I agreed to do it. But it was wrong."

"You know I believe," he said, taking her hand in his, "that things happen for a reason."

"You do?" Shannon drew a shaky breath.

"I never really knew Erin," he said. "If you wouldn't have come with me that weekend we might never have gotten to know each other."

Hope grew inside her. Could this be what God had planned all along? Erin had gotten the man she loved. Could it happen to her, too?

"You know how in church the minister talked about this being a time of beginnings?"

Shannon pushed a strand of hair back with her hand. "Actually, I was so preoccupied I didn't catch much of the sermon."

Jake smiled. "I didn't get it all, either. But I liked the part about beginnings. I found myself thinking we could start over. Pretend we just met and go from there. What do you think?"

"I think it could work." Shannon's smile widened. "When do you want to start?"

"No time like the present." Jake extended his hand. "I don't believe we've met. I'm Jake Kinkaid."

Shannon took his hand. A shiver traveled up her spine at his touch. "Shannon O'Connor."

"Shannon." He kept hold of her hand and his gaze flickered for a moment, down to her mouth. "Do you believe in kissing on the first date?"

"Not usually." Her gaze shifted pointedly to the mistletoe overhead. "But in this case I might be willing to make an excep—"

Jake tugged her toward him and stopped her words by covering her mouth with his own. She quivered at the sweet tenderness of his kiss.

"Marry me," Jake whispered in her hair.

Shannon's heart fluttered wildly in her breast. "We just met."

Jake stepped back and held her at arm's length.

"I feel like I've known you forever." His gaze traveled over her face and searched her eyes. "I love you, Shannon."

Shannon stared into Jake's eyes for a long second as his words seemed to echo in the room. *I love you, Shannon.*

He loved her. Jake loved her. Not her sister, but *her*.

"And I love you." Tears of happiness stung her eyes and as she brushed them aside, her gaze drifted to the mistletoe. *Grandpa Al, the matchmaker.* Now that he'd succeeded in bringing them together, she knew they'd never hear the end of it. Her lips curved upward. "You know what this means, don't you?"

"I know exactly what it means." Jake's gaze never left her face. "It means I've got the right twin. And I'm never going to let her go."

HARLEQUIN®
Live the emotion™

Upbeat,
All-American Romances

 flip**side**
Romantic Comedy

Harlequin Historicals®
Historical,
Romantic Adventure

INTRIGUE
Romantic Suspense

HARLEQUIN ROMANCE®
The essence of
modern romance

HARLEQUIN®
Presents
Seduction and passion
guaranteed

Super ROMANCE®
Emotional,
Exciting, Unexpected

Temptation
Sassy, Sexy, Seductive!

A LAODICEAN

THOMAS HARDY was born in Higher Bockhampton, Dorset, on 2 June 1840; his father was a builder in a small way of business, and he was educated locally and in Dorchester before being articled to an architect. After sixteen years in that profession and the publication of his earliest novel *Desperate Remedies* (1871), he determined to make his career in literature; not, however, before his work as an architect had led to his meeting, at St Juliot in Cornwall, Emma Gifford, who became his first wife in 1874.

In the 1860s Hardy had written a substantial amount of unpublished verse, but during the next twenty years almost all his creative effort went into novels and short stories. *Jude the Obscure*, the last written of his novels, came out in 1895, closing a sequence of fiction that includes *Far from the Madding Crowd* (1874), *The Return of the Native* (1878), *Two on a Tower* (1882), *The Mayor of Casterbridge* (1886), and *Tess of the d'Urbervilles* (1891).

Hardy maintained in later life that only in poetry could he truly express his ideas; and the more than nine hundred poems in his collected verse (almost all published after 1898) possess great individuality and power.

In 1910 Hardy was awarded the Order of Merit; in 1912 Emma died and two years later he married Florence Dugdale. Thomas Hardy died in January 1928; the work he left behind—the novels, the poetry, and the epic drama *The Dynasts*—forms one of the supreme achievements in English imaginative literature.

JANE GATEWOOD teaches English and directs the Writing Center at Mary Washington College, Fredericksburg, Virginia.

THE WORLD'S CLASSICS

THOMAS HARDY

A Laodicean

Edited with an Introduction by
JANE GATEWOOD

Oxford   New York

OXFORD UNIVERSITY PRESS

Oxford University Press, Great Clarendon Street, Oxford OX2 6DP

Oxford New York
Athens Auckland Bangkok Bogota Bombay
Buenos Aires Calcutta Cape Town Dar es Salaam
Delhi Florence Hong Kong Istanbul Karachi
Kuala Lumpur Madras Madrid Melbourne
Mexico City Nairobi Paris Singapore
Taipei Tokyo Toronto Warsaw

and associated companies in
Berlin Ibadan

Oxford is a trademark of Oxford University Press

Introduction, Note on the Text, Select Bibliography, Explanatory Notes,
Notes of Revisions, Text © Jane Gatewood 1991
Chronology © Simon Gatrell 1985

First published as a World's Classics paperback 1991

British Library Cataloguing in Publication Data
Data available

Library of Congress Cataloging in Publication Data
Hardy, Thomas, 1840–1928.
A Laodicean : Thomas Hardy: edited with an introduction by Jane Gatewood.
p. cm. – (The World's classics)
I. Gatewood, Jane. II. Title. III. Series.
PR4750.L26 1991 823'.8–dc20 91-8262
ISBN 0-19-282783-9

7 9 10 8 6

Printed in Great Britain by
Caledonian International Book Manufacturing Ltd, Glasgow

CONTENTS

GENERAL EDITOR'S PREFACE

THE first concern in The World's Classics editions of Hardy's works has been with the texts. Individual editors have compared every version of the novel or stories that Hardy might have revised, and have noted variant readings in words, punctuation, and styling in each of these substantive texts; they have thus been able to exclude much that their experience suggests that Hardy did not intend. In some cases this is the first time that the novel has appeared in a critical edition purged of errors and oversights; where possible Hardy's manuscript punctuation is used, rather than what his compositors thought he should have written.

Some account of the editor's discoveries will be found in the Note on the Text in each volume, while the most interesting revisions their work has revealed are included as an element of the Explanatory Notes. In some cases a Clarendon Press edition of the novel provides a wealth of further material for the reader interested in the way Hardy's writing developed from manuscript to final collected edition.

SIMON GATRELL

INTRODUCTION

DURING the eight-year interval between *The Return of the Native* in 1878 and *The Mayor of Casterbridge* in 1886, Hardy experimented with both form and subject-matter, apparently trying to satisfy the demand for romantic fiction by adding distinctive motifs to the love stories he knew were acceptable to his audience. He made notes at the British Museum before writing *The Trumpet-Major* (1880), a romance that plays against the background of the Napoleonic wars. In *A Laodicean* (1881) and *Two on a Tower* (1882), he turned to contemporary settings, creating in the latter a romance laced with astronomical technicalities verified by a visit to Greenwich Observatory. But *A Laodicean or The Castle of the De Stancys*, subtitled "A Story of To-day", required no research to give its architectural motif authenticity, for Hardy drew from memories of sixteen years in his first profession.

On 14 December 1881, soon after the publication of the three-volume first edition of *A Laodicean*, Hardy responded to a letter from Alexandra Sutherland Orr, who had written on 12 December to praise the serial version of the story just completing its run in *Harper's New Monthly Magazine* and to express her regret that she had "missed the proper time" for reviewing the book. Wishing that all of his critics "were as appreciative" as Mrs Orr and "so well able to express their appreciation", Hardy commented on the connection between himself and the story's architect hero: "The architectural portion of the novel embodies, as you will have guessed, much of my own experience, which enabled me to write the story with, I think, less effort than others have cost me."[1] According to William Lyon Phelps, Hardy told him in 1900 that "*A Laodicean* contained more of the facts of his own life than anything else he had ever written".[2]

Certainly George Somerset strongly resembles Thomas Hardy. A would-be poet, he has made a "contrite return to

---

[1] *The Collected Letters of Thomas Hardy*, vii (Oxford: Clarendon Press, 1988), 93-4.

[2] *Autobiography With Letters* (London: Oxford University Press, 1939), 391.

architecture" after publishers failed to appreciate his verse written in "every conceivable metre except an original one, and on every conceivable subject, from Wordsworthian sonnets on the singing of his tea-kettle to epic fragments on the Fall of Empires" (p. 10). The opening chapter introduces us to this "summer traveller from London" on an excursion in the country to study and sketch Gothic churches, as Hardy had often done while working for John Hicks in Dorchester and as the "Gothic draughtsman" for Arthur Blomfield in London.[3] Like *The Return of the Native*'s Clym Yeobright, Somerset is an introspective modern, having the look of the "future human type", with lines in his forehead revealing a "too dominant speculative activity" (p. 8). His bewilderment on the question of styles mirrors Hardy's restless doubts about his career in architecture and suggests that Somerset may be the Laodicean of the title:

His mind flew back to his past life, and deplored the waste of time that had resulted from his not having been able to make up his mind which of the many fashions of art that were coming and going in kaleidoscopic change was the true point of departure for himself. He had suffered from the modern malady of unlimited appreciativeness as much as any living man of his own age. (p. 12)

The reflective, almost poignant, mood of the first chapter establishes Somerset's uncertainty about architectural styles and his hesitancy to commit himself to his profession as he wishes for "inexorable blinkers" so that he cannot see alternatives (p. 12). Packing up his tools at sunset and beginning a leisurely stroll to a roadside inn, he comes upon a "recently-erected chapel of red brick", different from the six-hundred-year-old church he has been sketching not only because it has "neither beauty, quaintness, nor congeniality to recommend it", but also because light shines from its windows and there is an "intense and busy energy" inside—a "living human interest" (pp. 13–14). The contrast between the "bold and quaint" Gothic church and the ugly Nonconformist chapel implies that the novel will explore a choice between the traditional order,

---

[3] *The Early Life of Thomas Hardy* (London: Macmillan, 1928), 40–8.

or medievalism, and the new order, modernism, an opposition
that becomes more explicit as Somerset continues his walk,
following a telegraph wire until it ends in a "fossil of feudalism", a half-ruined castle:

There was a certain unexpectedness in the fact that the hoary memorial
of a stolid antagonism to the interchange of ideas, the monument of
hard distinctions in blood and race, of deadly mistrust of one's
neighbour in spite of the Church's teaching, and of a sublime
unconsciousness of any other force than a brute one, should be the
goal of a machine which beyond everything may be said to symbolise
cosmopolitan views and the intellectual and moral kinship of all
mankind. (pp. 22–3)

In his "moonlight meditations", Somerset also thinks of the
"fairer side of feudalism—leisure, light-hearted generosity,
intense friendships, hawks, hounds, revels, healthy complexions, freedom from care, and such a living power in
architectural art as the world may never again see" and finds
the "modern mental fever and fret which consumes people
before they can grow old" (p. 23) a poor alternative. At this
point we expect to explore, in the company of a sensitive,
intelligent individual, a novel organized by vividly contrasting
images—the sun sets on a beautiful Gothic church but light
shines from an ugly Baptist chapel, telegraph wires bring the
modern world into a ruined castle. Its focus will be the
conflicting demands of intellect and emotions as Somerset's
mind reasons that the old order no longer serves its purpose,
while his heart argues that the new does not appeal to his
imagination or satisfy him aesthetically. The model for Somerset appears to be Hardy; as Michael Millgate points out, they
share "a reluctance to adopt absolute or even firm positions, a
willingness to see virtue in all sides of a question, an insistence
upon the provisionality of [their] opinions, and the need to
register them rather as a series of tentative impressions than as
the systematic formulations of a philosopher".[4]

While at the chapel, Somerset spies on Paula Power as she
refuses to be baptized by a flustered minister who then subjects
her to a blistering sermon about her uncertainty, using as his

⁴ *Thomas Hardy: A Biography* (Oxford: Clarendon Press, 1982), 220.

text the third chapter of Revelation's condemnation of the lukewarm Christians in Laodicea. Like Somerset, Paula is a modern who can't make up her mind. She is, of course, the heroine of a romance, and as such must make another decision: she must choose a husband. Here the trouble begins, as Hardy tried to integrate his exploration of the ambiguities of modernism with the love story his audience expected. After meeting Paula, Somerset assumes his role as the hero in a romance, and the story's focal point is the contrary impulses of its heroine, not its hero. Of all the autobiographical elements in *A Laodicean*, the most interesting is that once the love story comes into play, Somerset shares Hardy's background, but Paula shares his temperament. As the romantic hero, Somerset must be knowledgeable, assertive, and confident so that he can guide the impressionable and indecisive heroine.

Paula Power is a wealthy young woman who has moved into an ancient and dilapidated castle inherited from her father, a famous railway contractor. "Emphatically a modern type of maidenhood" (p. 17), she immediately adds a telegraph system and a gymnasium modelled on those in the new colleges for women, and subscribes to the leading periodicals to keep abreast of current affairs. Nevertheless, the castle casts its spell and she soon longs to be "romantic and historical" (p. 111), like the De Stancys whose portraits line the walls of their ancestral home. After slaying dragons unlike any slain before or since in defence of a fair maiden, debating with the Baptist minister on paedobaptism,[5] and trouncing the rival architect Havill in a discussion about the castle's history, Somerset is hired to restore Stancy Castle. He must compete for the attention of Paula, a "modern flower in a mediæval flower-pot" (p. 38–9), with Captain De Stancy, an army officer with the aristocratic background she yearns for. If Paula were a De Stancy, she would love her castle and "adore every stone, and think feudalism the only true romance of life" (p. 92). Somerset fears that her *prédilection d'artiste* for aristocratic

---

[5] Hardy drew from memories of arguments participated in twenty years earlier with Bastow, another architectural pupil in the office of John Hicks in Dorchester, and the sons of Perkins, the Baptist minister who was the model for Woodwell. See *Early Life*, 37–40.

families (p. 113) will draw her closer to a man who resembles the De Stancys in the portraits.

His original assumption, that she was a personification of the modern spirit, who had been dropped, like a seed from the bill of a bird, into a chink of mediævalism, required some qualification. . . . But romanticism, which will exist in every human breast as long as human nature itself exists, had asserted itself in her. Veneration for things old, not because of any merit in them, but because of their long continuance, had developed in her; and her modern spirit was taking to itself wings and flying away. (p. 273)

Hardy incorporated into this passage a note he had made late in 1880: "Romanticism will exist in human nature as long as human nature itself exists. The point is (in imaginative literature) to adopt that form of romanticism which is the mood of the age."[6] The note indicates the experimental nature of the novel, its self-conscious modernity, and the extent to which Hardy saw the heroine's dilemma as the centre of the story.

Paula's infatuation with medievalism evidently suggests the persistent tendency in human nature to romanticize traditional beliefs and institutions even though, like the dingy portraits of the De Stancys and the De Stancys themselves, they have fallen into decay. No elegy for a lost past, *A Laodicean* presumably was meant to be a comic investigation of the "incongruities that were daily shaping themselves in the world under the great modern fluctuations of classes and creeds" (p. 39). Far from being elegiac and nostalgic, the tone of the book now insists on the energy of the new order and mocks the De Stancys, who show up by contrast the vitality of the moderns, Paula and Somerset. The ambiguities promised in the early chapters give way to a less than subtle comedy of manners. As the impressionable Paula moves among the fools in her world—the De Stancys, who are portrayed almost farcically at times—she must be tutored by Somerset, whose good sense will temper her romantic notions.

In part because Captain De Stancy is not a credible alternative to the man Paula obviously loves, the choice-of-suitors

[6] *Early Life*, 189.

pattern is too frail to support the complexities of the intellectual, religious, moral, aesthetic, and social uncertainty that
Hardy attempted to embody in her. Paula's longing for "real
logical dogmatism" (p. 62) seems unrelated to her predicament
of choosing a husband. In his letter of 14 December 1881 to
Mrs Orr, Hardy said: "I am much pleased to find that you feel
De Stancy *might* have proved a very satisfactory husband for
Paula, & that poetic justice did not demand Somerset's success
too exclusively. That much may be said on both sides is my
continual feeling, on real situations as well as on ideal ones in
life." It is, however, difficult to believe that Paula really has to
make a choice between the two men; her behaviour seems
more related to the demands of the plot than to her doubt.
Because there is no analysis of her motives and no revelation
of her inner life, the attempt to read *A Laodicean* as a realistic
novel and to discuss it in terms of what Paula learns as she
chooses between men representing opposing attitudes and ways
of life can only lead to frustration. The narrator adores Paula,
spies on her, tells us how she walks and talks and the colour of
her hair and of her dresses, but doesn't say what is going on
inside her mind—or her heart, for in this novel Somerset tends
to think and Paula to feel.

Paul Ward distinguishes between what he sees as essential
in the "organic structure" of *A Laodicean*, Paula's dilemma as
she chooses between her suitors, and what is "ornamental",
the mystery plot involving William Dare and the tour of
Europe, and concludes that Hardy did not do what he needed
to do to make the book successful: "engage in a sensitive
exploration of Paula's inner psychology" so that she is "accessible to the reader".[7] Ward's comment that there is a "funda-
mental antagonism" between the novel's subject-matter and
Hardy's technique of characterization indicates that he thinks
A Laodicean is essentially a realistic story.

In *An Essay on Hardy* John Bayley explores the premiss that
the nature of the heroine in a Hardy novel determines its form.
He proposes a new category for Hardy's fiction, "heroines as
fictional forms", a category that excludes only *The Hand of*

[7] "A Laodicean", *Thomas Hardy Year Book*, 11 (1984), 28–30.

Ethelberta and *A Laodicean*, for these "hybrid" novels "evade such a determination". Unlike Tess or Bathsheba, for example, Ethelberta and Paula "fail . . . to be realized as heroines", while Fancy Day of the pastoral novel *Under the Greenwood Tree* and Anne Garland of the historical novel *The Trumpet-Major* are "bogus heroines" tailored to fit a predetermined form.[8] Bayley doesn't mention the possibility that Paula may not be entirely convincing because she narrowly escapes being a bogus heroine of a novel built on a conventional form.

Because there is so much going on in *A Laodicean*, it does not fall easily into any category. Bayley's description of the novel as a "hybrid" echoes what its first critics noted: its disparate elements. The *World* saw *A Laodicean* as a "curious . . . mixture of sensationalism, philosophy, religion, spiritual affection, and carnal suggestiveness" (11 January 1882, p. 18), while the *Observer* found it "original in its mixture of pedantry and simplicity, melodrama and philosophy" (2 April 1882, p. 1). The most astute observation of all may have been that of Arthur Barker, who tentatively said that the novel "seems to be a conventional love-tale" (*Academy*, 7 January 1882, p. 5).

The framework of *A Laodicean* is the sentimental love story as it was told in popular fiction and drama. George Somerset is a virtuous, sensible, high-minded, "nice young man" (p. 8) who sees and straightway loves Paula Power, an attractive, virtuous, and high-minded young woman. If these sweethearts in their tender and devoted love—so different from the destructive passion associated with Hardy's fiction—are unlikely to provide the obstacles needed to block the course of true love for thirteen instalments, external circumstances will, so that the story can be continued to its "predetermined cheerful ending", as Hardy wryly noted in the 1896 preface. If Paula is a melodramatic heroine rather than a realistic one, no subtle analysis of her feelings is needed. If she doesn't control the circumstances that separate her from Somerset, there is no reason to examine her motives. Villains Hardy borrowed from a familiar gallery of stock characters keep the lovers apart. Uncle Abner is the mysterious figure from the past in the role

---

[8] *An Essay on Hardy* (Cambridge: Cambridge University Press, 1978), 142–3.

of the parental tyrant. William Dare, the illegitimate son of Captain De Stancy, would be recognized as the villain on any stage, even without Hardy's references to Satan, as he swaggers about flashing his cheap jewellery and smoking cigarettes. His accomplice, the rival architect Havill, is the cowardly villain who deserts to the side of goodness. Other characters are as unoriginal as the villains. Captain De Stancy is the Byronic hero, a melancholy officer imprisoned by his past, almost redeemed by his love for the virtuous Paula, while his sister Charlotte is the delicate, timid, loyal companion who sacrifices her own happiness by telling the truth at just the right moment. Her illnesses brought on by emotional distress further the plot and add the required measure of pathos. The landlord of the inn at Sleeping-Green provides comic relief both by his commentary on how Sir William De Stancy squandered his family's fortune and lost their home and by his opinions on the religious issues that concern Paula and Somerset.

Hardy borrowed from melodrama not only his characters but also much of his plot, most notably the convention of the misunderstanding based on false information. A fake telegram and a fake photograph sabotage the innocent Somerset's chances with Paula, but in spite of the obstacles that separate the lovers, they are destined to be together and all will be well in the end.

That a Hardy novel is melodramatic should come as no surprise since most of his fiction wavers between realism and melodrama. As critics began to discuss A Laodicean in light of their knowledge of the unusual circumstances of its composition, they saw the book as breaking into two distinct sections: the opening one-third, representing the success, Hardy's attempt to write a comedy of ideas, and the last two-thirds, representing the failure, his surrender to melodrama when illness forced him to abandon his original plan. In October 1880, with what roughly corresponds to Book I completed, Hardy became seriously ill and had to dictate much of the remainder of the novel to his wife Emma to meet his obligation to Harper's, which began serialization of the thirteen-part story in December 1880. A rather extreme example of the tendency to overrate the first book and to ridicule the rest of the novel is the discussion by Guerard, who understood the opening to be a "study of Jamesian nuances, told in the manner of Edith Wharton", in which Hardy established the "materials for a minute psychological comedy of temperamental differences" before the story collapsed into implausibility.[9] J. I. M. Stewart recognized a similar pattern in other novels, a reliance on melodrama when inspiration failed, and refused to explain the book's unevenness in terms of Hardy's illness or the pressures of serialization. In *A Laodicean* as well as in *Two on a Tower*, Stewart noted "a failure of nerve or stamina, an inability to hold on to a new and exploratory form of ironic comedy".[10]

Although they are not as likely to make a melodrama of the composition of *A Laodicean*, more recent critics also speak of the novel as though social comedy at some point gives way to melodrama, with their operational definition of melodrama being a story with improbable characters, implausible events, and sensational elements. The novel does abruptly shift its point of view at Book II—where Hardy is believed to have begun dictation—as the focus moves from Somerset to other characters, but the organization of the novel into books concentrating on specific characters must have been in place all along and suggests a problem with point of view that might have little to do with Hardy's illness. Whenever attention returns to Somerset, the book recovers to a certain extent the tone of the earlier chapters, although he is for the most part playing his role in the love story rather than musing over the ambiguities of the old and the new. The design of the book as well as its execution may be at fault, and a better way to describe *A Laodicean* is to say that it wavers between disparate modes and tones from the beginning. A complex theme demanding a realistic treatment of character struggles to emerge from a melodrama that rather than dramatizing convincingly the central character's dilemma seems to put her at the mercy of a plot. Most disconcerting about the story is that Hardy tried to dramatize difficult choices in a mixture of two

[9] Albert Guerard, *Thomas Hardy: The Novels and Stories* (Cambridge, Mass.: Harvard University Press, 1949), 53–4.
[10] *Thomas Hardy: A Critical Biography* (London: Longman, 1971), 157.

genres that depend on certainty: the satirical comedy of manners with its insistence that we accept as worthy a norm or standard that the heroine eventually embraces and the sentimental melodrama in which virtuous characters triumph over adversities so that the story can come to its happy ending.

If read as a comedy of manners, *A Laodicean* would show that contrasting groups of characters representing opposing values and ways of life work out a pattern of ideas. The ending will be a happy one, for the new order must oust the old. If read as melodrama, *A Laodicean* would evoke tears for Charlotte, boos for William Dare, and above all cheers for Paula as she marches in and announces to Somerset that if he still wants to marry her, she is "here to be asked". Either scenario relies on certainty, but *A Laodicean* has no certainty, in part because its hero and heroine threaten at times to be realistic and break out of the form, and in part because its unresolved issues and shifting tones are not convincing. Perhaps we prefer our Victorians to be "wandering between two worlds" as in Arnold's "Stanzas from the Grande Chartreuse"—"children reared in shade | Beneath some old world abbey wall"—rather than the comic figure of Sir William de Stancy living in the "mushroom modernism" of Myrtle Villa in the shadows of Stancy Castle or Somerset cheerfully contemplating building a "new house, eclectic in style" near the ruins of that castle after it is destroyed by fire.

It would be perverse to call *A Laodicean* a successful novel. The story was an experiment that failed, perhaps because its author was writing under unusual stress and in an uncongenial mode. But that it is Hardy's experiment will always make it significant to those who value his fiction. J. B. Bullen notes that this "curious exercise in literary form" in "its very rawness and the presence in the text of unresolved and unassimilated ideas" provides "unusual evidence of Hardy's literary practices".[11] As Bullen's comment indicates, the fictional world of *A Laodicean* may be less interesting than what the novel reveals about the way Hardy looked at the world and

---

[11] *The Expressive Eye: Fiction and Perception in the Work of Thomas Hardy* (Oxford: Clarendon Press, 1986), 118.

the way he struggled to realize his vision in fiction. Although unable to integrate successfully his ambivalent feelings about modernism with the sentimental love story he supposed his audience wanted, constrained by conventions acceptable to his readers and by his imagination, Hardy must have enjoyed undercutting the convention of the happy ending, letting emotion mock intellect after all of Somerset's bravado about "the march of mind—the steamship, and the railway, and the thoughts that shake mankind" (p. 92) and his conviction that Paula will soon be herself again, free from the "warp" given to her mind by the medievalism of Stancy Castle:

"Very well, I'll keep straight on; and we'll build a new house beside the ruin, and show the modern spirit for evermore. . . . But, George, I wish—" And Paula repressed a sigh.

"Well?"

"I wish my castle wasn't burnt; and I wish you were a De Stancy!"

NOTE ON THE TEXT

A Laodicean has generally been available only in editions that follow the 1912 text because scholars have worked on the assumption that Hardy had a single goal that remained constant through thirty-two years until the novel reached its intended form in the Wessex Edition. Analysis of the five authorial versions leads to a different understanding of the 1912 *A Laodicean*: not an organic whole with parts that necessarily relate to all other parts but a whole made up of diverse parts reflecting Hardy's shifting intentions during the book's long history.

This text of *A Laodicean* is based on the three-volume edition published by Sampson Low in 1881. By presenting the novel as Hardy originally wrote it, the first finished version, and by providing information about other versions, this edition and a full scholarly edition now under way challenge readers to reconstruct *A Laodicean* by tracing the stages through which Hardy expressed his intentions, thereby gaining an understanding of what the novel is as a whole—a series of versions published in 1880–1, 1881, 1882, 1896, and 1912.

This edition cannot adequately present the extensive stylistic changes made in 1881 as Hardy refined what had essentially been a work in progress, the serialization in the European edition of *Harper's New Monthly Magazine* from December 1880 to December 1881. Variant readings listed in the appendix illustrate Hardy's attempt in the autumn of 1881 to refocus the novel's heroine, Paula Power. The notes also include the few changes made in response to criticism of the first edition, particularly concerning the portrayal of Paula, as Hardy prepared copy for the New Edition, the cheaper one-volume book published by Sampson Low in 1882.

Hardy made two further revisions of *A Laodicean*: in 1896 for the first collected edition published by Osgood, McIlvaine and in 1912 for Macmillan's Wessex Edition. The notes cannot cover the several hundred stylistic changes made in 1896, but thoroughly trace revisions relating to Wessex because they especially mark the later texts as products of 1896 and 1912.

By 1896, Hardy and his public had become fascinated with the correspondence between the half-imaginary world of Wessex and actual locations in Dorset and the surrounding counties. A contemporary story with much of its action set on the continent as the characters wander around Europe, *A Laodicean* clearly does not fit into the pattern established by the books depicting rural life and customs. The novel takes place in Wessex, when Paula and her entourage are at home, but has few rustic characters, little local colour, and might be set anywhere in England. Hardy removed the few references to Dorset (South Wessex) and substituted names to hint that the adjoining county of Somerset was the locale he had had in mind. With only two dozen changes, he accomplished the task, a far easier one than incorporating *A Laodicean* into the heart of Wessex. Hardy's main concern in 1912 was to adjust distances and place-names to make more specific the relationship between the landscape of the novel and actual locations in the county of Somerset. Dismissing his efforts in the novel's preface by saying that its "sites, mileages, and architectural details" could "hardly seem satisfactory to the investigating topographist", he nevertheless yielded to those who wanted a more reliable guidebook to Outer Wessex. After months spent revising the other novels and checking proofs, Hardy may not have had the time or the energy to give the last of the novels to be prepared his careful attention. The notes fully present the attempt to bring *A Laodicean* into Wessex so that readers may compare the novel of 1881 to 1912's adaptation for a new audience.

The 1912 text, undoubtedly representing Hardy's last intentions, has undeniable historical significance. Rather than replacing an edition more or less representing that text, this edition supplements it so that its readers may better understand what they are reading. This edition also provides an alternative—a pre-Wessex novel embodying Hardy's original concept of the story, a different novel.

This edition bases its punctuation and styling on the first edition, emending only where compositorial error can be inferred. While the words here are almost certainly authorial, the punctuation and styling may not be. William Clowes and

Sons, the printing house responsible for both the *Harper's* text and the first edition, imposed its own style on the manuscript. Because the manuscript does not survive, it is impossible to distinguish between authorial intentions and those of editors and compositors. Following the styling of the first edition is most appropriate for an edition essentially historical in its orientation, but I did not make the decision without consideration of the dominant editorial practice of the last four decades and recent challenges to it. The full scholarly edition will treat in detail the choice of copy-text.

SELECT BIBLIOGRAPHY

READERS interested in Hardy's life should consult *Thomas Hardy: A Biography* by Michael Millgate (Oxford: Clarendon Press, 1982) and *The Early Life of Thomas Hardy* and *The Later Years of Thomas Hardy* (London: Macmillan, 1928 and 1930), published under the name of Hardy's wife Florence but mostly written by Hardy. The two works were combined in one volume in *The Life of Thomas Hardy* (London: Macmillan, 1962) and the typescripts were edited by Michael Millgate as *The Life and Work of Thomas Hardy* (London: Macmillan, 1985).

Also of interest are the seven-volume work *The Collected Letters of Thomas Hardy* (Oxford: Clarendon Press, 1978–88), edited by R. L. Purdy and Michael Millgate; Hardy's personal notebooks, edited by Richard Taylor (London: Macmillan, 1978); the literary notebooks, edited in 2 volumes by Lennart Björk (London: Macmillan, 1985); and the architectural notebook edited by C. J. P. Beatty (Dorchester: Dorset Natural History and Archeological Society, 1966). The standard bibliographical work is R. L. Purdy's *Thomas Hardy: A Bibliographical Study* (Oxford: Clarendon Press, 1954, repr. 1978). For an overview of Hardy's career as a fiction writer, see Simon Gatrell's *Hardy the Creator: a Textual Biography* (Oxford: Clarendon Press, 1988).

Few essays centre on *A Laodicean*. Richard Taylor's *The Neglected Hardy: Thomas Hardy's Lesser Novels* (London: Macmillan, 1982) and Michael Millgate's *Thomas Hardy: His Career as a Novelist* (London: Bodley Head, 1971) provide good introductions that integrate biographical and bibliographical information with critical commentary. David J. De Laura's essay "'The Ache of Modernism' in Hardy's Later Novels" (*Journal of English Literary History*, 34 (1967), 380–99) does not discuss *A Laodicean* but its remarks on Hardy's response to modernism touch on the issues explored in the novel. J. B. Bullen focuses on *A Laodicean* in an interesting chapter entitled "Architecture as Symbol" in *The Expressive Eye: Fiction and Perception in the Work of Thomas Hardy* (Oxford: Clarendon Press, 1986).

A CHRONOLOGY OF
THOMAS HARDY

1840   2 June: Thomas Hardy born, first child of Thomas and
        Jemima (Hand) Hardy, five and a half months after their
        marriage. His father was a builder in a small but slowly
        developing way of business, thus setting the family apart
        socially from the "work-folk" whom they clearly resembled
        in financial circumstances.

1848   Entered the newly opened Stinsford National School.

1849   Sent to Dorchester British School kept by Isaac Last.

1853   Last established an independent "commercial academy", and
        Hardy became a pupil there. His education was practical
        and effective, including Latin, some French, theoretical and
        applied mathematics, and commercial studies.

1856   11 July: articled to Dorchester architect John Hicks. Soon
        after this he became friendly with Horace Moule, an import-
        ant influence on his life.

1860   Summer: Hardy's articles, having been extended for a year,
        completed. Employed by Hicks as an assistant.

1862   17 April: Without a position; travelled to London, but soon
        employed by Arthur Blomfield as a "Gothic draughtsman".
        November: Elected to the Architectural Association; began
        to find his feet in London.

1863   Won architectural prizes; began to consider some form of
        writing as a means of support.

1863-7 Possibly became engaged to Eliza Nicholls.

1865   March: "How I Built myself a House" published in *Cham-
        bers' Journal*. Began to write poetry.

1866   Hardy's commitment to the Church and his religious belief
        seem to have declined though he probably experienced no
        dramatic loss of faith.

1867   Returned to Dorset. Began his first unpublished novel.

1868   Sent MS of *The Poor Man and the Lady* to four publishers,
        where it was read by Morley and Meredith, amongst others,
        but finally rejected.

1869   Worked in Weymouth for the architect Crickmay; began
        writing *Desperate Remedies*.

1870   In order to take "a plan and particulars" of the church,
        Hardy journeyed to St Juliot, near Boscastle in North
        Cornwall; there he met Emma Lavinia Gifford, who became
        his wife four years later.

1871   *Desperate Remedies* published after Hardy had advanced £75.

1872   *Under the Greenwood Tree* published; the copyright sold to
        Tinsley for £30. Hardy moved temporarily to London to
        work in the offices of T. Roger Smith. Contracted to provide
        serial for *Tinsleys' Magazine* for £200 (to include first edition
        rights). *A Pair of Blue Eyes* began to appear in September.
        Hardy decided to relinquish architecture and concentrate on
        writing. Leslie Stephen requested a serial for the *Cornhill
        Magazine*.

1873   *A Pair of Blue Eyes* published in three volumes; Horace
        Moule, his close adviser and friend, committed suicide in
        Cambridge.

1874   *Far From the Madding Crowd* begun as a serial in *Cornhill*
        under Leslie Stephen's editorship and published later in the
        year in two volumes. Hardy married Emma Gifford on 17
        September; they honeymooned in Paris and returned to live
        in London.

1875   *Cornhill* serialized *The Hand of Ethelberta*. The Hardys
        moved from London to Swanage in Dorset.

1876   Further moves to Yeovil and Sturminster Newton, where
        Hardy began writing *The Return of the Native*.

1878   Return to London (Tooting). *The Return of the Native*
        serialized in *Belgravia* and published in three volumes, to
        which Hardy affixed a map of the novel's environment.
        Made researches in the British Museum for the background
        of *The Trumpet-Major*.

1879   With "The Distracted Young Preacher", began regularly to
        publish short stories.

1880   *Good Words* serialized *The Trumpet-Major*, which was also
        published in three volumes with covers designed by Hardy.
        In October he became seriously ill and believed himself close
        to death; the cause of his illness uncertain, but led to five
        months' total inactivity.

1881   *A Laodicean*, mostly written from his bed, published as a serial in *Harper's New Monthly Magazine* (the first in the new European edition), and in three volumes. The Hardys returned to Dorset, living at Wimborne Minster.

1882   Controversy with Pinero over Hardy's adaptation of *Far From the Madding Crowd* and Pinero's use of the same material. Hardy's third novel in three years, *Two on a Tower*, serialized in the *Atlantic Monthly* and issued in three volumes.

1883   The final move of his life—from Wimborne to Dorchester, though into temporary accommodation while his own house was being built.

1884   Made a Justice of the Peace and began to receive invitations from aristocracy. Began writing *The Mayor of Casterbridge*.

1885   Max Gate, designed by Hardy and built by his brother Henry, completed; on the outskirts of Dorchester, it remained his home for the rest of his life.

1886   *The Mayor of Casterbridge* serialized in the *Graphic* and brought out in two volumes; in the same year *The Woodlanders* began its run in *Macmillan's Magazine*. William Barnes, the Dorset poet and friend of Hardy, died.

1887   *The Woodlanders* issued in three volumes. The Hardys visited France and Italy. Began work on *Tess of the d'Urbervilles*.

1888   Hardy's first collection of short stories, *Wessex Tales*, published in two volumes. Also published the first of three significant essays on the theory of fiction, *The Profitable Reading of Fiction*.

1889   The novel that was to become *Tess* rejected by Tillotson's Fiction Bureau, which had commissioned it; subsequent further rejections fuelled the bitterness behind a second essay, *Candour in English Fiction*, published in January of the following year.

1890   *A Group of Noble Dames* appeared in the *Graphic*.

1891   *Tess of the d'Urbervilles* serialized in the *Graphic* and published in three volumes; *A Group of Noble Dames* brought out in one volume. The third important essay, *The Science of Fiction*, appeared. A Copyright Bill passed through the United States Congress in time for *Tess* to benefit from its provisions, a factor of considerable financial significance in Hardy's career.

1892   Father died 20 July. *The Pursuit of the Well-Beloved* serialized in the *Illustrated London News*.

1893   Met Florence Henniker, subject of the intensest of his romantic attachments to artistic ladies. Wrote *The Spectre of the Real* in collaboration with her. Began writing *Jude the Obscure*.

1894   Third volume of short stories, *Life's Little Ironies*, published in one volume.

1895   First collected edition of Hardy's work begun; published by Osgood, McIlvaine, it included the first edition of *Jude the Obscure*, previously serialized in *Harper's New Monthly Magazine*. Some reviews of *Jude* quite savage, a contributory factor to Hardy's writing no further novels. Hardy dramatized *Tess*.

1896   The first group of major poems with identifiable dates written since the 1860s; they included the three *In Tenebris* poems and *Wessex Heights*.

1897   *The Well-Beloved*, substantially revised from the 1892 serialization, published as part of the Osgood, McIlvaine edition. Visited Switzerland.

1898   Hardy's first collection of verse published, *Wessex Poems*; comprising mainly poems written in the 1860s and 1890s, and illustrated by himself.

1899   Boer War began, to which Hardy responded in verse. The gradual physical separation between Hardy and Emma intensified, following the mental separation that set in after the publication of *Jude the Obscure*.

1901   *Poems of the Past and the Present* published.

1902   Changed publishers for the last time, to Macmillan.

1904   First part of *The Dynasts* appeared. 3 April: Hardy's mother died, leaving a tremendous gap in his life.

1905   Met Florence Dugdale. Received LL.D. from Aberdeen University.

1906   Part Two of *The Dynasts* published.

1908   *The Dynasts* completed with the publication of the third part; it embodied Hardy's most complete statement of his philosophical outlook. Also published his *Select Poems of William Barnes*, undertaken as a memorial to his great predecessor. The first Dorchester dramatization of a Hardy novel, *The*

Trumpet-Major. Meredith and Swinburne died, leaving Hardy as the greatest living English writer.

1909 Relationship with Florence Dugdale deepened. *Time's Laughingstocks*, Hardy's third volume of poems, published.

1910 Awarded the Order of Merit, having previously refused a knighthood. Received the freedom of Dorchester.

1912 Second collected edition of Hardy's works begun, the Wessex Edition. Received the gold medal of the Royal Society of Literature. 27 November: Emma Hardy died; as a direct result Hardy began writing the poems of 1912–13.

1913 Visited Cornwall in search of his and Emma's youth. Awarded Litt.D. at Cambridge and became an Honorary Fellow of Magdalene College—a partial fulfilment of an early aspiration. His final collection of short stories published, *A Changed Man*.

1914 10 February: married Florence Dugdale. *Satires of Circumstance* published. First World War began; Hardy's attitude to the future of humanity coloured by it in a profound way.

1915 At the age of 75 Hardy began to become reclusive. Frank George, his chosen heir, killed at Gallipoli. Hardy's sister Mary died 24 November.

1916 *Selected Poems of Thomas Hardy* published.

1917 Hardy's fifth collection of verse published, *Moments of Vision*. He and Florence began work on what was eventually to become *The Life of Thomas Hardy*.

1919–20 The de luxe edition of Hardy's work issued, the Mellstock Edition.

1922 *Late Lyrics and Earlier*, with its important Preface, published.

1923 Florence Henniker died. The Prince of Wales visited Max Gate. Friendship with T. E. Lawrence developed. *The Queen of Cornwall* published.

1924 Hardy's adaptation of *Tess* acted in Dorchester with the last of his romantic attachments, Gertrude Bugler, in the title role.

1925 *Tess* acted in London, but not by Miss Bugler. *Human Shows Far Phantasies Songs and Trifles*, Hardy's seventh volume of verse, published.

1928 11 January: Hardy died. His final book of poems, *Winter Words*, published posthumously.

A LAODICEAN;

OR,

THE CASTLE OF THE DE STANCYS.

A STORY OF TO-DAY.

BY

THOMAS HARDY

CONTENTS

CONTENTS

BOOK THE FIRST

GEORGE SOMERSET

CHAPTER I

THE sun blazed down and down, till it was within half an hour of its setting; but the sketcher still lingered at his occupation of measuring and copying the chevroned doorway—a bold and quaint example of a transitional style of architecture, which formed the tower entrance to an English village church. The graveyard being quite open on its western side, the tweed-clad figure of the young man, and the tall mass of antique masonry which rose above him to a battlemented parapet, were fired to a great brightness by the uninterrupted solar rays, that crossed the neighbouring mead like a warp of gold threads, in whose mazes groups of equally lustrous gnats danced and wailed incessantly.

He was so absorbed in his pursuit that he did not mark the brilliant chromatic effect of which he composed the central feature, till it was brought home to his intelligence by the warmth of the moulded stonework under his touch when measuring; which led him at length to turn his head and gaze on its cause.

There are few in whom the sight of a sunset does not beget as much meditative melancholy as contemplative pleasure, the human decline and death that it illustrates being too obvious to escape the notice of the simplest observer. The sketcher, as if he had been brought to this reflection many hundreds of times before by the same spectacle, showed that he did not wish to pursue it just now by turning away his face after a few moments, to resume his architectural studies.

He took his measurements carefully, and as if he reverenced the old workers whose trick he was endeavouring to acquire six hundred years after the original performance had ceased and the performers passed into the unseen. By means of a strip of lead called a leaden tape, which he pressed around and into the fillets and hollows with his finger and thumb, he transferred the exact contour of each moulding to his drawing, that lay on a sketching-stool a few feet distant; where were also a sketching-block, a small T-square, a bow-pencil, and other mathematical instruments. When he had marked down the line thus fixed, he returned to the doorway to copy another as before.

It being the month of August, when the pale face of the townsman and stranger is to be seen among the brown skins of remotest uplanders, not only in England, but throughout the temperate zone, few of the homeward-bound labourers paused to notice him further than by a momentary turn of the head. They had beheld such gentlemen before, not exactly measuring the church so accurately as this one seemed to be doing, but painting it from a distance, or at least walking round the mouldy pile. At the same time the present visitor, even exteriorly, was not altogether commonplace. His features were good, his eyes of the dark deep sort called eloquent by the sex that ought to know, and with that ray of light in them which announces a heart susceptible to beauty of all kinds,—in woman, in art, and in inanimate nature. Though he would have been broadly characterised as a young man, his face bore contradictory testimonies to his precise age. This was conceivably owing to a too dominant speculative activity in him, which, while it had preserved the emotional side of his constitution, and with it the significant flexuousness of mouth and chin, had played upon his forehead and temples till, at weary moments, they exhibited some trace of being over-exercised. A youthfulness about the mobile features, a mature forehead—though not exactly what the world has been familiar with in past ages—is now growing common; and with the advance of juvenile introspection it probably must grow commoner still. Briefly, he had more of the beauty—if beauty it ought to be called—of the future human type than of the past; but not so much as to make him other than a nice young man.

His build was somewhat slender and tall; his complexion, though a little browned by recent exposure, was that of a man who spent much of his time indoors. Of beard he had but small show, though he was as innocent as a Nazarite of the use of the razor; but he possessed a moustache all-sufficient to hide the subtleties of his mouth, which could thus be tremulous at tender moments without provoking inconvenient criticism.

Owing to his situation on high ground, open to the west, he remained enveloped in the lingering aureate haze till a time when the eastern part of the churchyard was in obscurity, and damp with rising dew. When it was too dark to sketch further he packed up his drawing, and, beckoning to a lad who had been idling by the gate, directed him to carry the stool and implements to a roadside inn which he named, lying a mile or two ahead. The draughtsman leisurely followed the lad out of the churchyard, and along a lane in the direction signified.

The spectacle of a summer traveller from London sketching mediæval details in these neo-Pagan days, when a lull has come over the study of English Gothic architecture, through a re-awakening to the art-forms of times that more nearly neighbour our own, is accounted for by the fact that George Somerset, son of the Academician of that name, was a man of independent tastes and excursive instincts, who unconsciously, and perhaps unhappily, took greater pleasure in floating in lonely currents of thought than with the general tide of opinion. When quite a lad, in the days of the French Gothic mania which immediately succeeded to the great English-pointed revival under Britton, Pugin, Rickman, Scott, and other mediævalists, he had crept away from the fashion to admire what was good in Palladian and Renaissance. As soon as Jacobean, Queen-Anne, and kindred accretions of decayed styles began to be popular, he purchased such old-school works as Revett and Stuart, Chambers, and the rest, and worked diligently at the Five Orders; till quite bewildered on the question of style, he concluded that all styles were extinct, and with them all architecture as a living art. Somerset was not old enough at that time to know that, in practice, art had at all times been as full of shifts and compromises as every other mundane thing; that ideal perfection was never achieved by Greek, Goth, or Hebrew Jew, and never would be; and thus he was thrown into a mood of disgust with his profession, from which mood he was only delivered by recklessly abandoning these studies and indulging in an old enthusiasm for poetical literature. For two whole years he did nothing but avoid his barber and write verse in every conceivable metre except an original one, and on every conceivable subject, from Wordsworthian sonnets on the singing of his tea-kettle to epic fragments on the Fall of Empires. His discovery at the age of five-and-twenty that these inspired works were not jumped at by the publishers with all the eagerness they deserved, coincided in point of time with a severe hint from his father that unless he went on with his legitimate profession he might have to look elsewhere than at home for an allowance. Mr. Somerset junior then awoke to realities, became intently practical, rushed back to his dusty drawing-boards, and worked up the styles anew, with a view of regularly starting in practice on the first day of the following January.

It is an old story, and perhaps only deserves the light tone in which the soaring of a young man into the empyrean, and his descent again, is always narrated. But as has often been said, the light and the truth may be on the side of the dreamer: a far wider view than the wise ones have may be his at that recalcitrant time, and his reduction to common measure be nothing less than a tragic event. The operation called lunging, in which a colt having a rope attached to its head is made to trot round and round a horsebreaker with the other end of the rope in his hand, till it makes the beholder dizzy to look at them, is a very unhappy one for the animal concerned. During its progress the colt springs upward, across the circle, stops still, flies over the turf with the velocity of a bird, and indulges in all sorts of graceful antics; but he always ends in one way— thanks to the knotted whipcord—in a level trot round the lunger with the regularity of a horizontal wheel, and in the loss for ever to his character of the bold contours which the fine hand of Nature gave it. Yet the process is considered to be the making of him.

Whether Somerset became permanently made under the action of the inevitable lunge, or whether he lapsed into mere dabbling with the artistic side of his profession only, it is premature to say; but at any rate it was the impetus of his contrite return to architecture as a calling that sent him on the sketching excursion under notice. Feeling that something still was wanting to round off his knowledge before he could take

his professional line with confidence, he was led to remember
that his own native Gothic was the one form of design that he
had totally neglected from the beginning, through its having
greeted him with wearisome iteration at the opening of his
career. Now it had again returned to silence; indeed—such is
the surprising instability of art "principles" as they are
facetiously called—it was just as likely as not to sink into the
neglect and oblivion which had been its lot in Georgian times.
This accident of being out of vogue lent English Gothic an
additional charm to one of his proclivities; and away he went
to make it the business of a summer circuit in the west.

The quiet time of evening, the secluded neighbourhood, the
unusually gorgous liveries of the clouds lying packed in a pile
over that quarter of the heavens in which the sun had
disappeared, were such as to make a traveller loiter on his
walk. Coming to a stile, Somerset mounted himself on the top
bar, to imbibe the spirit of the scene and hour. The evening
was so still that every trifling sound could be heard for miles.
There was the rattle of a returning waggon, mixed with the
smacks of the waggoner's whip: the team must have been at
least three miles off. From far over the hill came the faint
periodic yell of kennelled hounds; while from the nearest
village resounded the voices of boys at play in the twilight.
Then a powerful clock struck the hour; it was not from the
direction of the church, but rather from the wood behind him;
and he thought it must be the clock of some mansion that way.

But the mind of man cannot always be forced to take up
subjects by the pressure of their material presence, and Somerset's thoughts were often, to his great loss, apt to be even more
than common truants from the tones and images that met his
outer senses on walks and rides. He would sometimes go
quietly through the queerest, gayest, most extraordinary town
in Europe, and let it alone, provided it did not meddle with
him by its beggars, beauties, innkeepers, police, coachmen,
mongrels, bad smells, and such like obstructions. This feat of
questionable utility he began performing now. Sitting on the
three-inch ash rail that had been peeled and polished like glass
by the rubbings of all the small-clothes in the parish, he forgot
the time, the place, forgot that it was August—in short,

everything of the present altogether. His mind flew back to his past life, and deplored the waste of time that had resulted from his not having been able to make up his mind which of the many fashions of art that were coming and going in kaleidoscopic change was the true point of departure for himself. He had suffered from the modern malady of unlimited appreciativeness as much as any living man of his own age. Dozens of his fellows in years and experiences, who had never thought specially of the matter, but had blunderingly applied themselves to whatever form of art confronted them at the moment of their making a move, were by this time acquiring renown as new lights; while he was still unknown. He wished that some accident could have hemmed in his eyes between inexorable blinkers, and sped him on in a channel ever so worn.

Thus balanced between believing and not believing in his own future, till the poise became so delicate that a bubble of opinion turned either scale, he was recalled to the scene without by hearing the notes of a solemn familiar hymn, rising in subdued harmonies from an unexplored valley below. He listened more heedfully. It was his old friend the "New Sabbath," which he had never once heard since the lisping days of childhood, and whose existence, much as it had then been to him, he had till this moment quite forgotten. Where the "New Sabbath" had kept itself all these years—why that sound and hearty melody had disappeared from all the cathedrals, parish churches, minsters, and chapels-of-ease that he had been acquainted with during his apprenticeship to life, and until his ways had become irregular and uncongregational—he could not, at first, say. But then he recollected that the tune appertained to the old west-gallery period of church-music, anterior to the great choral reformation and the rule of Monk—that old time when the repetition of a word, or half-line of a verse, was not considered a disgrace to an episcopal choir.

Willing to be interested in anything which would keep him out-of-doors, Somerset dismounted from the stile and descended the hill before him, to learn whence the singing proceeded.

CHAPTER II

HE found that it had its origin in a building standing alone in a field; and though the evening was not yet dark without, lights shone from the windows. In a few moments Somerset stood before the edifice. Being just then *en rapport* with ecclesiasticism by reason of his recent occupation, he could not help murmuring, "Shade of Pugin, what a monstrosity!"

Perhaps this exclamation (being one rather out of date since the discovery that Pugin himself often nodded to an amazing extent) would not have been indulged in by Somerset but for his new architectural resolves, which caused professional opinions to officiously advance themselves to his lips whenever occasion offered. The building was, in short, a recently-erected chapel of red brick, with pseudo-classic ornamentation, and the white regular joints of mortar could be seen streaking its surface in geometrical oppressiveness from top to bottom. The roof was of blue slate, clean as a table, and unbroken from gable to gable; the windows were glazed with sheets of plate glass, a temporary iron stove-pipe passing out near one of these and running up to the height of the ridge, where it was finished by a covering like a parachute. Walking round to the end, he perceived an oblong white stone let into the wall just above the plinth, on which was inscribed in block letter:

ERECTED 187—, at the sole expense of JOHN
POWER, ESQ., M.P.

The "New Sabbath" still proceeded line by line, with all the emotional swells and cadences that had of old characterised the tune; and the body of vocal harmony that it evoked implied a large congregation within, to whom it was plainly as familiar as it had been to church-goers of a past generation. With a whimsical sense of regret at the secession of his once favourite air Somerset moved away, and would have quite withdrawn from the field had he not at that moment observed two young men with pitchers of water coming up from a stream hard by, and hastening with their burdens into the chapel vestry by a side door. Almost as soon as they had entered they emerged again with empty pitchers, and proceeded to the stream to fill them as before, an operation which they repeated several times. Somerset went forward to the stream, and waited till the young men came out again.

"You are carrying in a great deal of water," he said, as each dipped his pitcher.

One of the young men modestly replied, "Yes: we filled the cistern this morning; but it leaks, and requires a few pitcher-fuls more."

"Why do you do it?"

"There is to be a baptism, sir."

Somerset was not at the moment sufficiently interested to develop a further conversation, and observing them in silence till they had again vanished into the building, he went on his way. Reaching the brow of the hill he stopped and looked back. The chapel was still in view, and the shades of night having deepened, the lights shone from the windows yet more brightly than before. A few steps further would hide them, and the edifice, and all that belonged to it from his sight, possibly for ever. There was something in the thought which led him to linger in a way he had not at all expected. The chapel had neither beauty, quaintness, nor congeniality to recommend it: the dissimilitude between the new utilitarianism of the place and the scenes of venerable Gothic art which had occupied his daylight hours could not well be exceeded. But Somerset, as has been said, was an instrument of no narrow gamut: he had a key for other touches than the purely æsthetic, even on such an excursion as this. His mind was arrested by the intense and busy energy which must needs belong to an assembly that required such a glare of light to do its religion by; in the heaving of that tune there was an earnestness which made him thoughtful, and the shine of those windows he had characterised as ugly reminded him of the shining of the good deed in a naughty world. The chapel and its shabby plot of ground, from which the herbage was all trodden away by busy feet, had a living human interest that the numerous minsters and churches knee-deep in fresh green grass, visited by him during the foregoing week, had often lacked. Moreover there was going to be a baptism: that meant the immersion of a grown-up person; and he had been told that Baptists were earnest people and that the scene was most impressive. What manner of man would it be who on an ordinary plodding and bustling evening of the nineteenth century could single himself out as one different from the rest of inhabitants, banish all shyness, and come forward to undergo such a trying ceremony? Who was he that had pondered, gone into solitudes, wrestled with himself, worked up his courage and said, I will do this, though few else will, for I believe it to be my duty?

Whether on account of these thoughts, or from the circumstance that he had been alone amongst the tombs all day without communion with his kind, he could not tell in after years (when he had good reason to think of the subject); but so it was that Somerset went back, and again stood under the chapel-wall.

Instead of entering he passed round to where the stove-chimney came through the bricks, and holding on to the iron stay he rested on the plinth and looked in at the window. The building was quite full of people belonging to that vast majority of society who are denied the art of articulating their higher emotions, and crave dumbly for a fugleman—respectably dressed working people, whose faces and forms were worn and contorted by years of dreary toil. On a platform at the end of the chapel a haggard man of more than middle age, with grey whiskers ascetically cut back from the fore part of his face so far as to be almost banished from the countenance, stood reading a chapter. Between the minister and the congregation was an open space, and in the floor of this was sunk a tank full of water, which just made its surface visible above the blackness of its depths by reflecting the lights overhead.

After glancing miscellaneously at the assemblage for some moments Somerset endeavoured to discover which one among them was to be the subject of the ceremony. But nobody appeared there who was at all out of the region of commonplace. The people were all quiet and settled; yet he could discern on their faces something more than attention, though it was less than excitement: perhaps it was expectation. And as if to bear out his surmise he heard at that moment the noise of wheels behind him, which led him to turn his head.

His gaze into the lighted chapel made what had been an evening scene when he looked away from the landscape night itself on looking back; but he could see enough to discover that a brougham had driven up to the side-door used by the young water-bearers, and that a lady in white-and-black half-mourning was in the act of alighting, followed by what appeared to be a waiting-woman carrying wraps. They entered the vestry-room of the chapel, and the door was shut. The service went on as before till at a certain moment the door between vestry and chapel was opened, when a woman came out clothed in an ample robe of flowing white, which descended to her feet. Somerset was unfortunate in his position; he could not see her face, but her gait suggested at once that she was the lady who had arrived just before. She was rather tall than otherwise, and the contour of her head and shoulders denoted a girl in the heyday of youth and activity. His imagination, stimulated by this beginning, set about filling in the meagre outline with most attractive details.

She stood upon the brink of the pool, and the minister descended the steps at its edge till the soles of his shoes were moistened with the water. He turned to the young candidate, but she did not follow him: instead of doing so she remained rigid as a stone. He stretched out his hand, but she still showed reluctance, till, with some embarrassment, he went back, and spoke softly in her ear, afterwards saying in a voice audible to all who were near, "You will descend?"

She approached the edge, looked into the water, and gently turned away. Somerset could for the first time see her face. Though humanly imperfect, as is every face we see, it was one which made him think that the best in woman-kind no less than the best in psalm-tunes had gone over to the Dissenters. He had certainly seen nobody so interesting in his tour hitherto; she was about twenty or twenty-one—perhaps twenty-three, for years have a way of stealing marches even upon beauty's anointed. The total dissimilarity between the expression of her lineaments and that of the countenances around her was not a little surprising, and was productive of hypotheses without measure as to how she came there. She was, in fact, emphatically a modern type of maidenhood, and she looked ultra-modern by reason of her environment: a presumably sophisticated being among the simple ones—not wickedly so, but one who knew life fairly well for her age. Her hair, of good English brown, neither light nor dark, was abundant—too abundant for convenience in tying, as it seemed; and it threw off the lamp-light in a hazy lustre. As before observed, it could not be said of her features that this or that was flawless—quite the contrary, indeed; but the nameless charm of them altogether was only another instance of how beautiful a woman can be as a whole without attaining in any one detail to the lines marked out as absolutely correct. The spirit and the life were there; and material shapes could be disregarded.

This was all that could be gleaned of her: whatever moral characteristics it might be the surface of, enough was shown to assure Somerset that she had had some experience of things far removed from her present circumscribed horizon, and could live, and was even at that moment living, a clandestine, stealthy inner life which had very little to do with her present outward one. The repression of nearly every external sign of that distress under which Somerset knew, by a sudden intuitive sympathy, that she was labouring, added strength to these convictions.

"And you refuse?" said the astonished minister, as she still stood immoveable on the brink of the pool. He added to the force of his pleading by persuasively taking her sleeve between his finger and thumb as if to draw her; but she resented this by a quick movement of displeasure, and he released her, seeing that he had gone too far.

"But, my dear lady," he whispered, "you promised! Consider your profession, and that you stand in the eyes of the whole church as an exemplar of your faith."

"I cannot do it!"

"But your father's memory, miss; his last dying request!"

"I cannot help it," she said, turning to get away.

"You came here with the intention to fulfil the Word?"

"But I was mistaken."

"Then why did you come?"

She tacitly implied that to be a question she did not care to answer. "Please say no more to me," she murmured, and hastened to withdraw.

During this unexpected dialogue (which had distinctly reached Somerset's ears, the windows standing open for ventilation, and his perch being close behind the speakers) that young man's feelings had flown hither and thither between minister and lady in a most capricious manner: it had seemed at one moment a rather uncivil thing of her, charming as she was, to give the minister and the water-bearers so much trouble for nothing; the next, it seemed like reviving the ancient cruelties of the ducking-stool to try to force a girl into that dark water if she had not a mind for it. But the minister was not without insight, and he had seen that it would be useless to say more. The crestfallen old man had to turn round upon the congregation and declare officially that the baptism was postponed.

She passed through the door into the vestry. During the exciting moments of her recusancy there had been a perceptible flutter among the sensitive members of the congregation; nervous Dissenters seeming to be at one with nervous Episcopalians in this at least, that they heartily disliked a scene during service. Calm was restored to their minds by the minister starting a rather long hymn in minims and semibreves, amid the singing of which he ascended the pulpit. His face had a severe and even denunciatory look as he gave out his text, and Somerset began to understand that this meant mischief to the person who had caused the hitch.

"In the third chapter of Revelation and the fifteenth and following verses, you will find these words:

"'*I know thy works, that thou are neither cold nor hot: I would thou wert cold or hot. So then because thou art lukewarm, and neither cold nor hot, I will spue thee out of my mouth. . . . Thou sayest, I am rich, and increased with goods, and have need of nothing; and knowest not that thou art wretched, and miserable, and poor, and blind, and naked.*'"

The sermon straightway began, and went on, and it was

soon apparent that the commentary was to be no less forcible than the text. It was also apparent that the words were, virtually, not directed forward in the line in which they were uttered, but through the chink of the vestry-door, that had stood slightly ajar since the exit of the young lady. The listeners appeared to feel this no less than Somerset did, for their eyes, one and all, became fixed upon that vestry-door as if they would almost push it open by the force of their gazing. The preacher's heart was full and bitter; no book or note was wanted by him; never was spontaneity more absolute than here. His enthusiasm had been suddenly made to take a negative turn by pressure of unexpected circumstances. It was no timid reproof of the ornamental kind, but a direct denunciation, all the more vigorous perhaps from the limitation of mind and language under which the speaker laboured. Yet fool that he had been made by the candidate there was nothing acrid in his attack. Genuine flashes of rhetorical fire were occasionally struck by that plain and simple man, who knew what straightforward conduct was, and who did not know the illimitable caprice of a woman's mind.

At this moment there was not in the whole chapel a person whose imagination was not centred on what was invisibly taking place within the vestry-door. The thunder of the minister's eloquence echoed, of course, through the weak sister's cavern of retreat no less than round the public assembly. What she was doing inside there—whether listening contritely, or haughtily hastening to get away from the chapel and all it contained—was obviously the thought of each member. What changes were tracing themselves upon that lovely face: did it rise to phases of Raffaelesque resignation, or sink so low as to flush and frown? was Somerset's inquiry; and a half-explanation occurred when, during the discourse, the door which had been ajar was gently pushed to.

Looking on as a stranger it seemed to him more than probable that this young woman's power of persistence in her unexpected repugnance to the rite was strengthened by wealth and position of some sort, and was not the unassisted gift of nature. The manner of her arrival, and her dignified bearing before the assembly, strengthened the belief. A woman who did not feel something extraneous to her mental self to fall back upon would be so far overawed by the people and the crisis as not to retain sufficient resolution for a change of mind.

The sermon ended, the minister wiped his steaming face and turned down his cuffs, and nods and sagacious glances went round. Yet many, even of those who had presumably passed the same ordeal with credit, exhibited gentler judgment than the preacher's on a tergiversation of which they had probably recognised some germ in their own bosoms when in the lady's situation.

For Somerset there was but one scene: the imagined scene of the girl herself as she sat alone in the vestry. The fervent congregation rose to sing again, and then Somerset heard a slight noise on his left hand which caused him to turn his head. The brougham, which had retired into the field to wait, was back again at the door: the subject of his rumination came out from the chapel—not in her mystic robe of white, but dressed in ordinary fashionable costume—followed as before by the attendant with other articles of clothing on her arm, including the white gown. Somerset fancied that the younger woman was drying her eyes with her handkerchief, but there was not much time to see: they quickly entered the carriage, and it moved on. Then a cat suddenly mewed, and he saw a white Persian standing forlorn where the carriage had been. The door was opened, the cat taken in, and the carriage rolled away.

The young stranger's form stamped itself deeply on Somerset's soul. He strolled on his way quite oblivious to the fact that the moon had just risen, and that the landscape was one for him to linger over, especially if there were any Gothic architecture in the line of the lunar rays. The inference was that though this girl must be of a serious turn of mind, caprice was not foreign to her composition: and upon the whole it was probable that her daily doings evinced without much abatement the unbroken spirit and pride of life natural to her age.

The little village inn at which Somerset intended to pass the night lay two miles further on, and retracing his way up to the stile he rambled along the lane, now beginning to be streaked like a zebra with the shadows of some young trees that edged the road. But his attention was attracted to the other side of the way by a hum as of a night-bee, which arose from the play of the breezes over a single wire of telegraph running parallel with his track on tall poles that had appeared by the road, he hardly knew when, from a branch route, probably leading from some town in the neighbourhood to the village he was approaching. He did not know the population of Sleeping-Green, as the village of his search was called, but the presence of this mark of civilisation seemed to signify that its inhabitants were not quite so far in the rear of their age as might be imagined; a glance at the still ungrassed heap of earth round the foot of each post was, however, sufficient to show that it was at no very remote period that they had made their advance.

Aided by this friendly wire Somerset had no difficulty in keeping his course, till he reached a point in the ascent of a hill at which the telegraph branched off from the road, passing through an opening in the hedge, to strike across an undulating down, while the road wound round to the left. For a few moments Somerset doubted and stood still: the cut over the down had no mark of a path or drive, but on the other hand it might be a shorter though steeper way to the same place. The wire sang on overhead with dying falls and melodious rises that invited him to follow; while above the wire rode the stars in their courses, the low nocturn of the former seeming to be the voices of those stars,

Still quiring to the young-eyed cherubim.

Recalling himself from these reflections Somerset decided to follow the lead of the wire. It was not the first time during his present tour that he had found his way at night by the help of these musical threads which the post-office authorities had erected all over the country for quite another purpose than to guide belated travellers. Plunging with it across the down he soon came to a hedgeless road that entered a park or chase, which flourished in all its original wildness. Tufts of rushes and brakes of fern rose from the hollows, and the road was in places half overgrown with green, as if it had not been tended for many years; so much so that, where shaded by trees, he found some difficulty in keeping it. Though he had noticed the remains of a deer-fence further back no deer were visible, and it was scarcely possible that there should be any in the existing state of things; but rabbits were multitudinous, every hillock being dotted with their seated figures till Somerset approached and sent them limping into their burrows. The road next wound round a clump of underwood beside which lay heaps of faggots for burning, and then there appeared against the sky the walls and towers of a castle, half ruin, half residence, standing on an eminence hard by.

Somerset stopped to examine it. The castle was not exceptionally large, but it had all the characteristics of its most important fellows. Irregular, dilapidated, and muffled in creepers as a great portion of it was, some part—a comparatively modern wing as nearly as he could discover at a glance—was inhabited, for a light or two steadily gleamed from some upper windows; in others a reflection of the moon denoted that unbroken glass yet filled their casements. Over all rose the keep, a square solid tower apparently not much injured by wars or weather, and darkened with ivy on one side, wherein wings could be heard flapping uncertainly, as if they belonged to a bird unable to find a proper perch. Hissing noises supervened, and then a hoot, proclaiming that a brood of young owls were residing there in the company of older ones. In spite of the habitable and more modern wing, neglect and decay had set their mark upon the outworks of the pile, unfitting them for a more positive light than that of the present hour.

He walked up to a modern arch spanning the ditch—now dry and green—over which the drawbridge once had swung. The large door under the porter's archway was closed and locked. While standing here the singing of the wire, which for the last few minutes he had quite forgotten, again struck upon his ear, and retreating to a convenient place he observed its final course: from the poles amid the trees it leaped across the moat, over the girdling wall, and thence by a tremendous stretch towards the keep where, to judge by sound, it vanished through an arrow-slit into the interior. This fossil of feudalism, then, was the journey's end of the wire, and not the village of Sleeping-Green.

There was a certain unexpectedness in the fact that the hoary memorial of a stolid antagonism to the interchange of ideas, the monument of hard distinctions in blood and race, of deadly mistrust of one's neighbour in spite of the Church's teaching, and of a sublime unconsciousness of any other force than a brute one, should be the goal of a machine which beyond everything may be said to symbolise cosmopolitan views and the intellectual and moral kinship of all mankind. In that light the little buzzing wire had a far finer significance to the student Somerset than the vast walls which neighboured it. But, on the other hand, the modern mental fever and fret which consumes people before they can grow old was also signified by the wire; and this aspect of to-day did not contrast well (at least in his moonlight meditations) with the fairer side of feudalism—leisure, light-hearted generosity, intense friendships, hawks, hounds, revels, healthy complexions, freedom from care, and such a living power in architectural art as the world may never again see—civilisation having at present a stronger attachment to lath and plaster than to walls of a thickness sufficient for the perpetuation of grand ideas.

Somerset withdrew till neither the singing of the wire nor the hisses of the irritable owls could be heard any more. A clock in the castle struck ten, and he recognised the strokes as those he had heard when sitting on the stile. It was indispensable that he should retrace his steps and push on to Sleeping-Green if he wished that night to reach his lodgings, which had been secured by letter at a little inn in the straggling line of roadside houses called by the above name, where his luggage had by this time probably arrived. In a quarter of an hour he was again at the point where the wire left the road, and following the highway over a hill he saw the hamlet at his feet.

CHAPTER III

BY half-past ten the next morning Somerset was once more approaching the precincts of the building which had interested him the night before. Referring to his map he had learnt that it bore the name of Stancy Castle or Castle de Stancy; and he had been at once struck with its familiarity, though he had never understood its position in the county, believing it further to the west. If report spoke truly there was some excellent vaulting in the interior, and a change of study from ecclesiastical to secular Gothic was not unwelcome for a while.

The entrance-gate was open now, and under the archway the outer ward was visible, a great part of it being laid out as a flower-garden. This was in process of clearing from weeds and rubbish by a set of gardeners, and the soil was so encumbered that in rooting out the weeds such few hardy flowers as still remained in the beds were mostly brought up with them. The groove wherein the portcullis had run was as fresh as if only cut yesterday, the very tooling of the stone being visible. Close to this hung a bell-pull formed of a large wooden acorn attached to a vertical rod. Somerset's application brought a woman from the porter's door, who informed him that the day before having been the weekly show-day for visitors, it was doubtful if he could be admitted now.

"Who is at home?" said Somerset.

"Only Miss De Stancy," the porteress replied.

To him Miss De Stancy seemed a great deal, and his dread of being considered an intruder was such that he thought at first there was no help for it but to wait till the next week. But before retreating many steps he changed his mind: he had already through his want of effrontery lost a sight of many interiors, whose exhibition would have been rather a satisfaction to the inmates than a trouble. It was inconvenient to wait: he knew nobody in the neighbourhood from whom he could get an introductory letter: he turned and passed the woman, crossed the ward where the gardeners were at work, over a second and smaller bridge, and up a flight of stone stairs, open to the sky, along whose steps sunburnt Tudor soldiers and other renowned dead men had doubtless many times walked. It led to the principal door on this side. Thence he could observe the walls of the lower court in detail, and the old mosses with which they were padded—mosses that from time immemorial had been burnt brown every summer, and every winter had grown green again. The arrow-slit and the electric wire that entered it, like a worm uneasy at being unearthed, were distinctly visible now. So also was the clock, not, as he had supposed, a chronometer coeval with the fortress itself, but new and shining, and bearing the name of a recent maker.

The door was opened by a bland, intensely shaven man out of livery, who took Somerset's name and politely worded request to be allowed to inspect the architecture of the more public portions of the castle. He pronounced the word "architecture" in the tone of a man who knew and practised that art; "for," he said to himself, "if she thinks I am a mere idle tourist, it will not be so well."

No such uncomfortable consequences ensued. Miss De Stancy had great pleasure in giving Mr. Somerset full permission to walk through whatever parts of the building he chose.

It was as if he had come from winter to summer at this intelligence. He followed the butler into the inner buildings of the fortress, the ponderous thickness of whose walls made itself felt like a physical pressure. An internal stone staircase, ranged round four sides of a square, was next revealed, leading at the top of one flight into a spacious hall, which seemed to occupy the whole area of the keep. From this apartment a corridor floored with black oak led to the more modern wing, where light and air were treated in a less gingerly fashion.

Here the passages were broader than in the oldest portion, and upholstery enlisted in the service of the fine arts hid to a great extent the coldness of the walls.

Somerset was now left to himself, and roving freely from room to room he found time to inspect the different objects of interest that abounded there. Not all the chambers, even of the habitable division, were in use as dwelling-rooms, though these were still numerous enough for the wants of an ordinary country family. In a long gallery with a coved ceiling of arabesques which had once been gilded, hung a series of paintings representing the past personages of the De Stancy line. It was a remarkable array—even more so on account of the incredibly neglected condition of the canvases than for the artistic peculiarities they exhibited. Many of the frames were dropping apart at their angles, and some of the canvas was so dingy that the face of the person depicted was only distinguishable as the moon through mist. For the colour they had now they might have been painted during an eclipse; while, to judge by the webs tying them to the wall, the spiders that ran up and down their backs were such as to make the fair originals shudder in their graves.

He wondered how many of the lofty foreheads and smiling lips of this pictorial pedigree could be credited as true reflections of their prototypes. Some were wilfully false, no doubt; many more so by unavoidable accident and want of skill. Somerset felt that it required a profounder mind than his to disinter from the lumber of conventionality the lineaments that really sat in the painter's presence, and to discover their history behind the curtain of mere tradition. Perhaps a true account of the sweetest and softest among these who looked so demurely at him over their pearl necklaces was a story which, related in its bareness, would be hardly credible to the more self-repressing natures of the present day.

The painters of this long collection were those who usually appear in such places: Holbein, Jansen, and Vandyck; Sir Peter, Sir Geoffrey, Sir Joshua, and Sir Thomas. Their sitters, too, had mostly been sirs; Sir William, Sir John, or Sir George De Stancy—some undoubtedly having a nobility stamped upon them beyond that conferred by their robes and orders; and others not so fortunate. Their respective ladies hung by their sides—feeble and watery, or fat and comfortable, as the case might be; also their fathers and mothers-in-law, their brothers and remoter relatives; their contemporary reigning princes, and their intimate friends. Of the De Stancys pure there ran through the collection a mark by which they might surely have been recognised as members of one family; this feature being the upper part of the nose. Every one, even if lacking other points in common, had the special indent at this point in the face—sometimes moderate in degree, sometimes excessive.

While looking at the pictures—which, though not in his regular line of study, interested Somerset more than the architecture, because of their singular dilapidation, it occurred to his mind that he had in his youth been schoolfellow for a very short time with a pleasant boy bearing a surname attached to one of the paintings—the name of Ravensbury. The boy had vanished he knew not how—he thought he had been removed from school suddenly on account of ill health. But the recollection was vague, and Somerset moved on to the rooms above and below. In addition to the architectural details of which he had as yet obtained but glimpses, there was a great collection of old moveables and other domestic art-work—all more than a century old, and mostly lying as lumber. There were suites of tapestry hangings, common and fine; green and scarlet leather-work, on which the gilding was still but little injured; venerable damask curtains; quilted silk table-covers, ebony cabinets, worked satin window-cushions, carved bed-steads, and embroidered bed-furniture which had apparently screened no sleeper for these many years. Downstairs there was also an interesting collection of armour, together with several huge trunks and coffers. A great many of them had been recently taken out and cleaned, as if a long dormant interest in them were suddenly revived. Doubtless they were those which had been used by the living originals of the phantoms that looked down from the frames.

This excellent hoard of suggestive designs for woodwork, metalwork, and work of other sorts, induced Somerset to divert his studies from the ecclesiastical direction in which they had flowed too exclusively of late, to acquire some new ideas from the objects here for domestic application. Yet for the present he was inclined to keep his sketch-book closed and his ivory rule folded, and devote himself to a general survey. Emerging from the ground-floor by a small doorway, he found himself on a terrace to the north-east, and on the other side than that by which he had entered. It was bounded by a parapet breast high, over which a view of the distant country met the eye, stretching from the foot of the slope to a distance of many miles. Somerset went and leaned over, and looked down upon the tops of the bushes beneath. The prospect included the village he had passed through on the previous day: and amidst the green lights and shades of the meadows he could discern the red brick chapel whose recalcitrant inmate had so engrossed him.

Before his attention had long strayed over the incident which romanticised that utilitarian structure, he became aware that he was not the only person who was looking from the terrace towards that point of the compass. At the right-hand corner, in a niche of the curtain-wall, reclined a girlish shape; and asleep on the bench over which she leaned was a white cat—the identical Persian as it seemed—that had been taken into the carriage at the chapel-door.

By a natural train of thought Somerset began to muse on the probability or otherwise of the backsliding Baptist and this young lady resulting in one and the same person; and almost without knowing it he found himself deeply hoping for such a charming unity. It was hoping quite out of bounds; yet at the present moment it was impossible to say they were not the same. The object of his inspection was idly leaning, and this somewhat disguised her figure. It might have been tall or short, curvilinear or angular. She carried a light sunshade which she fitfully twirled until, thrusting it back over her shoulder, her head was revealed sufficiently to show that she wore no hat or bonnet. This token of her being an inmate of the castle, and not a visitor, as Somerset had conjectured, rather damped his expectations: but so unreasonable is hope, particularly when allied with a young man's fancy, that he persisted in believing her look towards the chapel must have a meaning in it, till she suddenly stood erect, and revealed herself as short in stature—almost dumpy—at the same time giving him a distinct view of her profile. She was not at all like the heroine of the chapel; he saw the dinted nose of the De Stancys distinctly outlined with Holbein shadowlessness against the blue-green of the distant wood. But it was not the De Stancy face with all its original specialities: it was, so to speak, a defective reprint of that face: for the nose tried hard to turn up and deal utter confusion to the family shape.

As for the rest of the countenance, Somerset was obliged to own that it was not beautiful: Nature had done there many things that she ought not to have done, and left undone much that she should have executed. It would have been decidedly plain but for a precious quality which no perfection of chiselling can give when the temperament denies it, and which no facial irregularity can take away—a tender affectionateness which might almost be called yearning; such as is often seen in all its intensity in the women of Correggio when they are painted in profile, and which a slight elevation of the lower part of her face helped to accentuate. Perhaps the plain features of Miss De Stancy—who she undoubtedly was—were rather severely handled by Somerset's judgment owing to his impression of the previous night. And, indeed, a beauty of a sort would have been lent by the flexuous contours of the mobile parts but for that unfortunate condition the poor girl was burdened with, of having to hand on a traditional feature with which she did not find herself otherwise in harmony.

She glanced at him for a moment in turning, and presently showed by an imperceptible movement that he had made his presence felt. Not to embarrass her, if it were true, as it seemed, that she was not much accustomed to strangers, Somerset instantly hastened to withdraw, at the same time that she passed round to the other part of the terrace, followed by the cat, in whom Somerset could imagine a certain denominational cast of countenance, notwithstanding her company. But as white cats are much like each other at a distance, it was reasonable to suppose this creature was not the same one as that possessed by the beauty.

CHAPTER IV

HE descended the stone stairs to a lower storey of the castle, in which was a crypt-like hall covered by vaulting of exceptional and massive ingenuity:

> Built ere the art was known,
> By pointed aisle and shafted stalk
> The arcades of an alleyed walk
> To emulate in stone.

It happened that the central pillar whereon the vaults rested, reputed to exhibit some of the most hideous grotesques in England upon its capital, had been enclosed with a modern partition, cutting off a portion of the large area for domestic purposes. A locked door barred Somerset's ingress, and he was tempted to ask a servant for permission to open it till he heard that the inner room was temporarily used for plate, the key being kept by Miss De Stancy, at which Somerset said no more. But afterwards he heard the active housemaid redescending the stone steps; she entered the crypt with a bunch of keys in one hand, and in the other a candle, followed by the young lady whom Somerset had seen on the terrace. The servant advanced with the key, but the young lady stood back; he saw that something hung upon her lips to say to him which she could not get off; he slightly bowed to encourage her.

"I shall be very glad to unlock anything you may want to see," she now found tongue to say. "So few people take any real interest in what is here that we do not leave it open."

Somerset expressed his thanks.

Miss De Stancy, a little to his surprise, had a touch of rusticity in her manner, and that forced absence of reserve which seclusion from society lends to young women more frequently than not. She seemed glad to have something to do; the arrival of Somerset was plainly an event sufficient to set some little mark upon her day. Deception had been written on the faces of those frowning walls in their implying the insignificance of Somerset, when he found them tenanted only by this little woman whose life was narrower than his own.

"We have not been here long," continued Miss De Stancy, "and that's why everything is in such a dilapidated and confused condition."

Somerset entered the dark store-closet, thinking less of the ancient pillar revealed by the light of the candle than what a singular remark the latter was to come from a member of the family which appeared to have been there five centuries. He held the candle above his head, and walked round, and presently Miss De Stancy came back.

"There is another vault below," she said, with the severe face of a young woman who speaks only because it is absolutely necessary. "Perhaps you are not aware of it? It was the dungeon: if you wish to go down there too, the servant will show you the way. It is not at all ornamental: rough, unhewn arches and clumsy piers."

Somerset thanked her, and would perhaps take advantage of her kind offer when he had examined the spot where he was, if it were not causing inconvenience.

"No; I am sure Paula will be glad to know that anybody thinks it interesting to go down there—which is more than she does herself."

Some obvious inquiries were suggested by this, but Somerset said, "I have seen the pictures, and have been much struck by them; partly," he added, with some hesitation, "because one or two of them reminded me of a schoolfellow—I think his name was John Ravensbury?"

"Yes," she said, almost eagerly. "He was my cousin!"

"So that we are not quite strangers?"

"But he is dead now. . . . He was unfortunate: he was mostly spoken of as 'that unlucky boy.' . . . You know, I suppose, Mr. Somerset, why the paintings are in such a decaying state?—it is owing to the peculiar treatment of the castle during Mr. Wilkins's time. He was blind; so one can imagine he did not appreciate such things as there are here."

"The castle has been shut up, you mean?"

"Oh, yes, for many years. But it will not be so again. We

are going to have the pictures cleaned, and the frames mended, and the old pieces of furniture put in their proper places. It will be very nice then. Did you see those in the east closet?"

"I have only seen those in the gallery."

"I will just show you the way to the others, if you would like to see them?"

They ascended to the room designated the east closet. The paintings here, mostly of smaller size, were in a better condition, owing partly to the fact that they were hung on an inner wall, and had hence been kept comparatively free from damp. Somerset inquired the names and histories of one or two.

"I really don't quite know," Miss De Stancy replied after some thought. "But Paula knows, I am sure. I don't study them much—I don't see the use of it." She swung her sunshade, so that it fell open, and turned it up till it fell shut. "I have never been able to give much attention to ancestors," she added, with her eyes on the parasol.

"These *are* your ancestors?" he asked, for her position and tone were matters which perplexed him. In spite of the family likeness and other details he could scarcely believe this frank and communicative country maiden to be the modern represent-ative of the De Stancys.

"Oh, yes, they certainly are," she said laughing. "People say I am like them: I don't know if I am—well, yes, I know I am: I can see that, of course, any day. But they have gone from my family, and perhaps it is just as well that they should have gone. . . . They are useless," she added, with serene conclusiveness.

"Ah! they have gone, have they?"

"Yes, castle and furniture went together: it was long ago—long before I was born. It doesn't seem to me as if the place ever belonged to a relative of mine."

Somerset corrected his smiling manner to one of solicitude.

"But you live here, Miss De Stancy?"

"Yes—a great deal now; though sometimes I go home to sleep."

"This is home to you, and not home?"

"I live here with Paula—my friend: I have not been here

long, neither has she. For the first six months after her father's death she did not come here at all."

They walked on, gazing at the walls, till the young man said, as if he were rather speaking of the portrait over which his eyes were playing than of her previous statement: "I fear I may be making some mistake: but I am sure you will pardon my inquisitiveness this once. *Who is* Paula?"

"Ah, you don't know! Of course you don't—local changes don't get talked of far away. She is the owner of this castle and estate. My father sold it when he was quite a young man, years before I was born, and not long after his father's death. It was purchased by a man named Wilkins, a rich man who became blind soon after he had bought it, and never lived here; so it was left uncared for."

She went out upon the terrace; and without exactly knowing why, Somerset followed.

"Your friend——"

"Has only come here quite recently. She is away from home to-day. . . . It was very sad," murmured the young girl thoughtfully. "No sooner had Mr. Power bought it of the representatives of Mr. Wilkins—almost immediately indeed— he died from a chill caught after a warm bath. On account of that she did not take possession for several months; and even now she has only had a few rooms prepared as a temporary residence till she can think what to do. Poor thing, it is sad to be left alone!"

Somerset heedfully remarked that he thought he recognised that name Power, as one he had seen lately, somewhere or other.

"Perhaps you have been hearing of her father. Do you know what he was?"

Somerset did not.

She looked across the distant country, where undulations of dark-green foliage formed a prospect extending for miles. And as she watched, and Somerset's eyes, led by hers, watched also, a white streak of steam, thin as a cotton thread, could be discerned ploughing that green expanse. "Her father made *that*," Miss De Stancy said, directing her finger towards the object.

"That what?"

"That railway. He was Mr. John Power, the great railway contractor. And it was through making the railway that he discovered this castle—the railway was diverted a little on its account."

"A clash between ancient and modern."

"Yes, but he took an interest in the locality long before he purchased the estate. And he built the people a chapel on a bit of freehold he bought for them. He was a staunch Baptist up to the day of his death—a much stauncher one," she said significantly, "than his daughter is."

"Ah, I begin to spot her!"

"You have heard about the baptism?"

"I know something of it."

"Her conduct has given mortal offence to the scattered people of the denomination that her father was at such pains to unite into a body, and build a chapel for."

Somerset could guess the remainder, and in thinking over the circumstances did not state what he had seen. She added, as if disappointed at his want of curiosity:

"She would not submit to the rite when it came to the point. The water looked so cold and dark and fearful, she said, that she could not do it to save her life."

"Surely she should have known her mind before she had gone so far?" Somerset's words had a condemnatory form, but perhaps his actual feeling was that if Miss Power had known her own mind, she would have not interested him half so much.

"Paula's own mind had nothing to do with it!" said Miss De Stancy, warming up to staunch partisanship in a moment. "It was all undertaken by her from a mistaken sense of duty. It was her father's dying wish that she should make public profession of her—what do you call it—of the denomination she belonged to, as soon as she felt herself fit to do it: so when he was dead she tried and tried, and didn't get any more fit; and at last she screwed herself up to the pitch, and thought she must undergo the ceremony out of pure reverence for his memory. It was very short-sighted of her father to put her in such a position; because she is now very sad as she feels she can never try again after such a sermon as was delivered against her."

Somerset presumed that Miss Power need not have heard this Knox or Bossuet of hers if she had chosen to go away?

"She did not hear it in the face of the congregation; but from the vestry. She told me some of it when she reached home. Would you believe it, the man who preached so bitterly is a tenant of hers? I said, 'Surely you will turn him out of his house?'—But she answered, in her calm, deep, nice way, that she supposed he had a perfect right to preach against her, that she could not in justice molest him at all. I wouldn't let him stay if the house were mine. But she has often before allowed him to scold her from the pulpit in a smaller way—once it was about an expensive dress she had worn—not mentioning her by name, you know; but all the people are quite aware that it is meant for her, because only one person of her wealth or position belongs to the Baptist body in this county."

Somerset was looking at the homely affectionate face of the little speaker. "You are her good friend, I am sure," he remarked.

She looked into the distant air with tacit admission of the impeachment. "So would you be if you knew her," she said; and a blush slowly rose to her cheek, as if the person spoken of had been a lover rather than a friend.

"But you are not a Baptist any more than I?" continued Somerset.

"Oh no. And I never knew one till I knew Paula. I think they are very nice; though I sometimes wish Paula was not one, but the religion of reasonable persons."

They walked on, and came opposite to where the telegraph emerged from the trees, leaped over the parapet, and up through the loophole into the interior.

"That looks strange in such a building," said her companion.

"Miss Power had it put up to know the latest news from town. It costs six pounds a year for each mile. She can work it herself, beautifully: and so can I, but not so well. It was a great delight to learn. Miss Power was so interested at first that she was sending messages from morning till night. And did you hear the new clock?"

"Oh! is it a new one?—Yes, I heard it."

"The old one was quite worn out; so Paula has put it in the cellar, and had this new one made, though it still strikes on the old bell. It tells the seconds, but the old one, which my very great grandfather erected in the eighteenth century, only told the hours. Paula says that time, being so much more valuable now, must of course be cut up into smaller pieces."

"She does not appear to be much impressed by the spirit of this ancient pile."

Miss De Stancy shook her head too slightly to express absolute negation.

"Do you wish to come through this door?" she asked. "There is a singular chimney-piece in the kitchen which is considered a unique example of its kind, though I myself don't know enough about it to have an opinion on the subject."

When they had looked at the corbelled chimney-piece they returned to the hall, where his eye was caught anew by a large map that he had conned for some time when alone, without being able to divine the locality represented. It was called "General Plan of the Town," and showed streets and open spaces corresponding with nothing he had seen in the county.

"Is that town here?" he asked.

"It is not anywhere but in Paula's brain; she has laid it out from her own design. The site is supposed to be near our railway-station, just across there, where the land belongs to her. She is going to grant cheap building leases, and develop the manufacture of pottery."

"Pottery—how very practical she must be!"

"Oh no! no!" replied Miss De Stancy in tones showing how supremely ignorant he must be of Miss Power's nature if he characterised her in those terms. "It is *Greek* pottery she means—Hellenic pottery she tells me to call it, only I forget. There is beautiful clay at the place, her father told her: he found it in making the railway tunnel. She has visited the British Museum, continental museums, and Greece, and Spain; and hopes to imitate the old fictile work in time, especially the Greek of the best period, four hundred years after Christ, or before Christ—I forget which it was Paula said. . . . Oh no, she is not practical in the sense you mean, at all."

"A mixed young lady, rather."

Miss De Stancy appeared unable to settle whether this new definition of her dear friend should be accepted as kindly, or disallowed as decidedly sarcastic. "You would like her if you knew her," she insisted, in half tones of pique; after which she walked on a few steps.

"I think very highly of her," said Somerset.

"And I! And yet at one time I could never have believed that I should have been her friend. One is prejudiced at first against people who are reported to have such differences in feeling, associations, and habit, as she seemed to have from mine. But it has not stood in the least in the way of our liking each other. I believe the difference makes us the more united."

"It says a great deal for the liberality of both," answered Somerset warmly. "Heaven send us more of the same sort of people! They are not too numerous at present."

As this remark called for no reply from Miss De Stancy, she took advantage of an opportunity to leave him alone, first repeating her permission to him to wander where he would. He walked about for some time, sketch-book in hand, but was conscious that his interest did not lie much in the architecture. In passing along the corridor of an upper floor he observed an open door, through which was visible a room containing one of the finest Renaissance cabinets he had ever seen. It was impossible, on close examination, to do justice to it in a hasty sketch; it would be necessary to measure every line, and get impressions of every surface, if he would bring away anything of practical utility to him as a designer. Deciding to reserve this gem for another opportunity he cast his eyes round the room, and blushed a little. Without knowing it he had intruded into the absent Miss Paula's own particular set of chambers, including a boudoir and sleeping apartment. On the tables of the sitting-room were most of the popular papers and periodicals that he knew, not only English, but from Paris, Italy, and America. Satirical prints, though they did not unduly preponderate, were not wanting. Besides these there were books from a London circulating library, paper-covered light literature in

French and choice Italian, and the latest monthly reviews; while between the two windows stood the telegraph apparatus whose wire had been the means of bringing him hither.

These things, ensconced amid so much of the old and hoary, were as if a stray hour from the nineteenth century had wandered like a butterfly into the thirteenth, and lost itself there.

The door between this ante-chamber and the sleeping-room stood open. Without venturing to cross the threshold, for he felt that he would be abusing hospitality to go so far, Somerset looked in for a moment. It was a pretty place, and seemed to have been hastily fitted up. In a corner, overhung by a blue and white canopy of silk, was a little cot, hardly large enough to impress the character of bedroom upon the old place. Upon a counterpane lay a parasol and a silk neckerchief. On the other side of the room was a tall mirror of startling newness, draped like the bedstead, in blue and white. Thrown at random upon the floor was a pair of satin slippers that would have fitted Cinderella. A dressing-gown lay across a settee; and opposite, upon a small easy-chair in the same blue and white livery, were a Bible, the *Baptist Magazine*, Wardlaw on Infant Baptism, Walford's County Families, and the *Court Journal*. On and over the mantelpiece were nicknacks of various descriptions, and photographic portraits of the artistic, scientific, and literary celebrities of the day.

A dressing-room lay beyond; but, becoming conscious that his study of ancient architecture would hardly bear stretching further in that direction without injury to his morals, Mr. Somerset retreated to the outside, passing by, without notice, the gem of Renaissance that had led him in.

"She affects blue," he was thinking. "Then she is fair."

On looking up, some time later, at the new clock that told the seconds, he found that the time at his disposal for work had flown without his having transferred a single feature of the building or furniture to his sketch-book. He remained but a little longer that day. Before leaving he sent in for permission to come again, and then walked across the fields to the inn at Sleeping-Green, reflecting less upon Miss De Stancy (so little force of presence had she possessed) than upon the modern flower in a mediæval flower-pot whom Miss De Stancy's information had so vividly brought before him, and upon the incongruities that were daily shaping themselves in the world under the great modern fluctuations of classes and creeds.

Somerset was still full of the subject when he arrived at the end of his walk, and he fancied that some loungers at the bar of the inn were discussing the heroine of the chapel-scene just at the moment of his entry. On this account, when the landlord came to clear away the dinner, Somerset was led to inquire of him, by way of opening a conversation, if there were many Baptists in the neighbourhood.

The landlord (who was a serious man on the surface, though he occasionally smiled beneath) replied that there were a great many—far more than the average in country parishes. "Even here, in my house, now," he added, "when folks get a drop of drink into 'em, and their feelings rise to a song, some man will strike up a hymn by preference. Though, I find no fault with that; for though 'tis hardly human nature to be so calculating in yer cups, a feller may as well sing to gain something as sing to waste."

"How do you account for there being so many?"

"Well you see, sir, some says one thing, and some another; I think they does it to save the expense of a Christian burial for their children. Now there's a poor family out in Long Lane—the husband used to smite for Jimmy More the blacksmith till 'a hurt his arm—they'd have no less than eleven children if they'd not been lucky t'other way, and buried five when they were three or four months old. Now every one of them children was given to the sexton in a little box that any journeyman could nail together in a quarter of an hour, and he buried 'em at night for a shilling a head; whereas 'twould have cost a couple of pounds each if they'd been christened at church. . . . Of course there's the new lady at the castle, she's a chapel member, and that may make a little difference; but she's not been here long enough to show whether 'twill be worth while to join 'em for the profit o't, or whether 'twill not. No doubt if it turns out that she's of a sort to relieve folks in trouble, more will join her set than belongs to it already. 'Any port in a storm,' of course, as the saying is."

"As for yourself, you are a Churchman at present, I presume?"

"Yes, sir, but I was a Methodist once—ay, for a length of time. 'Twas owing to my taking a house next door to a chapel; so that what with hearing the organ bizz like a bee through the wall, and what with finding it saved umbrellas on wet Sundays, I went over to that faith for two years—though I believe I dropped money by it—I wouldn't be the man to say so if I hadn't. Howsomever, when I moved into this house I turned back again to my old religion. Faith, I don't see much difference: be you one, or be you t'other, you've got to get your living."

"The De Stancys, of course, have not much influence here now, for that or any other thing?"

"Oh, no no; not any at all. They be very low upon ground, and always will be now, I suppose. It was thoughted worthy of being recorded in history—you've read it, sir, no doubt?"

"Not a word."

"Oh, then, you shall. I've got the history somewhere. 'Twas gay manners that did it. The only bit of luck they have had of late years is Miss Power's taking to little Miss De Stancy, and making her her company-keeper. I hope 'twill continue."

That the two daughters of these antipodean families should be such intimate friends was a situation which pleased Somerset as much as it did the landlord. It was an engaging instance of that human progress on which he had expended many charming dreams in the years when poetry, theology, and the reorganisation of society had seemed matters of more importance to him than a profession which should help him to a big house and income, a fair Deïopeia, and a lovely progeny. When he was alone he poured out a glass of wine, and silently drank the healths of the two generous-minded young women who, in this lonely country district, had found sweet communion a necessity of life, and by pure and instinctive good sense had broken down a barrier which men thrice their age and repute would probably have felt it imperative to maintain. But perhaps this was premature: the omnipotent Miss Power's character—practical or ideal, politic or impulsive—he as yet knew nothing of; and giving over reasoning from insufficient data he lapsed into mere conjecture.

CHAPTER V

THE next morning Somerset was again at the castle. He passed some considerable interval on the walls before encountering Miss De Stancy, whom at last he observed going towards a pony-carriage that waited near the door.

A smile gained strength upon her face at his approach, and she was the first to speak. "I am sorry Miss Power has not returned," she said to him, and proceeded to account for that lady's absence by her distress at the event of two evenings earlier.

"But I have driven over to my father's—Sir William De Stancy's—house this morning," she went on. "And on mentioning your name to him, I found he knew it quite well. You will, will you not, forgive my ignorance in having no better knowledge of the elder Mr. Somerset's works than a dim sense of his fame as a painter? But I was going to say that my father would much like to include you in his personal acquaintance, and wishes me to ask if you will give him the pleasure of lunching with him to-day. My cousin John, whom you once knew, was a great favourite of his, and used to speak of you sometimes. It will be so kind if you can come. My father is an old man, out of society, and he would be glad to hear the news of town."

Somerset said he was glad to find himself among friends where he had only expected strangers; and promised to come that day, if she would tell him the way.

That she could easily do. The short way was across that glade he saw there—then over the stile into the wood, following the path till it came out upon the turnpike-road. He would then be almost close to the house. The distance was about two miles and a half. But if he thought it too far for a walk, she would drive on to the town, where she had been going when he came, and instead of returning straight to her father's would come back and pick him up.

It was not at all necessary, he thought. He was a walker, and could find the path.

At this moment a servant came to tell Miss De Stancy that the telegraph was calling her.

"Ah—it is lucky that I was not gone again!" she exclaimed. "John seldom reads it right if I am away."

It now seemed quite in the ordinary course that, as a friend of her father's, he should accompany her to the instrument. So up they went together, and immediately on reaching it she applied her ear to the instrument, and began to gather the message. Somerset fancied himself like a person overlooking another's letter, and moved aside.

"It is no secret," she said, smiling.

"*'Paula to Charlotte,'* it begins."

"That's very pretty."

"Oh—and it is about—you," murmured Miss De Stancy.

"Me?" The architect blushed a little.

She made no answer, and the machine went on with its story. There was something curious in watching this utterance about himself, under his very nose, in language unintelligible to him. He conjectured whether it were inquiry, praise, or blame, with a sense that it might reasonably be the latter, as the result of his surreptitious look into that blue bedroom, possibly observed and reported by some servant of the house.

"*'Direct that every facility be given to Mr. Somerset to visit any part of the castle he may wish to see. On my return I shall be glad to welcome him as the acquaintance of your relatives. I have two of his father's pictures.'*"

"Dear me, the plot thickens," he said, with surprise, as Miss De Stancy announced the words. "How could she know about me?"

"I sent a message to her this morning when I saw you crossing the park on your way here—telling her that Mr. Somerset, son of the Academician, was making sketches of the castle, and that my father knew something of you. That's her answer."

"Where are the pictures by my father that she has purchased?"

"Oh, not here—at least, not unpacked."

Miss De Stancy then left him to proceed on her journey to Markton (so the nearest little town was called), informing him that she would be at her father's house to receive him at two o'clock.

Just about one he closed his sketch-book, and set out in the direction she had indicated. At the entrance to the wood a man was at work, pulling down a rotten gate that bore on its battered lock the initials "W. De S." and erecting a new one whose ironmongery exhibited the letters "P. P."

The warmth of the summer noon did not inconveniently penetrate the dense masses of foliage which now began to overhang the path, except in spots where a ruthless timber-felling had taken place in previous years for the purpose of sale. It was that particular half-hour of the day in which the birds of the forest prefer walking to flying; and there being no wind, the hopping of the smallest songster over the dead leaves reached his ear from behind the undergrowth. The tract had originally been a well-kept winding drive, but a deep carpet of moss and leaves overlaid it now, though the general outline still remained to show that its curves had been set out with as much care as those of a lawn walk, and the gradient made easy for carriages where the natural slopes were great. Felled trunks occasionally lay across it, and alongside were the hollow and fungous boles of trees sawn down in long-past years.

After a walk of three-quarters of an hour he came to another gate, where the letters "P. P." again supplanted the historical "W. De S." Climbing over this, he found himself on a highway which presently dipped down towards the town of Markton, a place he had never yet seen. It appeared in the distance as a quiet little borough of six or eight thousand inhabitants; and, without the town boundary on the side he was approaching, stood half a dozen genteel and modern houses, of the detached kind usually found in such suburbs. On inquiry, Sir William De Stancy's residence was indicated as one of these.

It was almost new, of streaked brick, having a central door, and a small bay window on each side to light the two front parlours. A little lawn spread its green surface in front, divided from the road by iron railings, the low line of shrubs immediately within them being coated with pallid dust from the highway. On the neat piers of the neat entrance gate were chiselled the words "Myrtle Villa." Genuine roadside respectability sat smiling on every brick of the eligible dwelling.

"How are the mighty fallen!" murmured Somerset, as he pulled the bell.

Perhaps that which impressed him more than the mushroom modernism of Sir William De Stancy's house was the air of healthful cheerfulness which pervaded it. Somerset was shown in by a neat maidservant in black gown and white apron, a canary singing a welcome from a cage in the shadow of the window, the voices of crowing cocks coming over the chimneys from somewhere behind, and sun and air riddling the house everywhere.

Being a dwelling of those well-known and popular dimensions which allow the proceedings in the kitchen to be distinctly heard in the parlours, it was so planned that a raking view might be obtained through it from the front door to the end of the back garden. The drawing-room furniture was comfortable, in the walnut-and-green-rep style of some years ago. Somerset had expected to find his friends living in an old house with remnants of their own antique furniture, and he hardly knew whether he ought to meet them with a smile or a gaze of condolence. His doubt was terminated, however, by the cheerful and tripping entry of Miss De Stancy, who had returned from her drive to Markton; and in a few more moments Sir William came in from the garden.

He was an old man of tall and spare build, with a considerable stoop, his glasses dangling against his waistcoat-buttons, and the front corners of his coat-tails hanging lower than the hinderparts, so that they swayed right and left as he walked. He nervously apologised to his visitor for having kept him waiting.

"I am so glad to see you," he said, with a mild benevolence of tone, as he retained Somerset's hand for a moment or two; "partly for your father's sake, whom I met more than once in my younger days, before he became so well-known; and also because I learn that you were a friend of my poor nephew John Ravensbury." He looked over his shoulder to see if his daughter were within hearing; finding she was not, he bent towards Somerset, and, with the impulse of the solitary to make a confidence at the first opportunity, continued in a low tone: "She, poor girl, was to have married John: his death was a sad blow to her and to all of us.—Pray take a seat, Mr. Somerset."

The reverses of fortune which had brought Sir William De Stancy to this comfortable cottage awakened in Somerset a warmer emotion than curiosity, and he sat down with a heart as responsive to each detail of speech uttered as if it had seriously concerned himself, while his host gave some words of information to his daughter on the trifling events that had marked the morning just passed; such as that the cow had got out of the paddock into Miss Power's field, that the smith who had promised to come and look at the kitchen range had not arrived, that two wasps' nests had been discovered in the garden bank, and that Nick Jones's baby had fallen downstairs. Sir William had large cavernous arches to his eye-sockets, reminding the beholder of the vaults in the castle he once had owned. His hands were long and almost fleshless, each knuckle showing like a bamboo-joint from beneath his coat-sleeves, which were small at the elbow and large at the wrist. All the colour had gone from his beard and locks, except in the case of a few isolated hairs of the former, which retained dashes of their original shade at sudden points in their length, revealing that all had once been raven black.

But to study a man to his face is a species of ill-nature which requires a colder temperament, or at least an older heart, than the architect's was at that time, to carry it on long. Incurious unobservance is the true attitude of cordiality, and Somerset blamed himself for having fallen into an act of inspection even for so short a time. He would wait for his host's conversation, which would doubtless be of the essence of historical romance.

"The favourable Bank-returns have made the money-market much easier to-day, as I learn?" said Sir William.

"Oh, have they?" said Somerset. "Yes, I suppose they have."

"And something is meant by this unusual quietness in Foreign stocks since the late remarkable fluctuations," insisted the old man, significantly. "Is the current of speculation quite arrested, or is it but a temporary lull?"

Somerset said he was afraid he could not give an opinion, and entered very lamely into the subject; but Sir William seemed to find sufficient interest in his own thoughts to do away with the necessity of acquiring fresh impressions from other people's replies; for often after putting a question he looked on the floor, as if the subject were at an end. Lunch was now ready, and when they were in the dining-room Miss De Stancy, to introduce a topic of more general interest, asked Somerset if he had noticed the myrtle on the lawn?

Somerset had noticed it, and thought he had never seen such a full-blown one in the open air before. His eyes were, however, resting at the moment on the only objects at all out of the common that the dining-room contained. One was a singular glass case over the fireplace, within which were some large mediæval door-keys, black with rust and age; and the others were two full-length oil portraits in the costume of the end of the last century—so out of all proportion to the size of the room they occupied that they almost reached to the floor.

"Those originally belonged to the castle yonder," said Miss De Stancy, or Charlotte, as her father called her, noticing Somerset's glance at the keys. "They used to unlock the principal entrance-doors, which were knocked to pieces in the civil wars. New doors were placed afterwards, but the old keys were never given up, and have been preserved by us ever since."

"They are quite useless—mere lumber—particularly to me," said Sir William.

"And those huge paintings were a present from Paula," she continued. "They are portraits of my great-grandfather and mother. Paula would give all the old family pictures back to me if we had room for them; but they would fill the house to the ceilings."

Sir William was impatient of the subject. "What is the utility of such accumulations?" he asked. "Their originals are but clay now—mere forgotten dust, not worthy a moment's inquiry or reflection at this distance of time. Nothing can retain the spirit, and why should we preserve the shadow of the form?—London has been very full this year, sir, I have been told?"

"It has," said Somerset, and he asked if they had been up that season. It was plain that the matter with which Sir William De Stancy least cared to occupy himself before visitors was the history of his own family, in which he was followed with more simplicity by his daughter Charlotte.

"No," said the baronet. "One might be led to think there is a fatality which prevents it. We make arrangements to go to town almost every year, to meet some old friend who combines the rare conditions of being in London with being mindful of me; but he has always died or gone elsewhere before the event has taken place. . . . But with a disposition to be happy, it is neither this place nor the other that can render us the reverse. In short, each man's happiness depends upon himself, and his ability for doing with little." He turned more particularly to Somerset, and added with an impressive smile: "I hope you cultivate the art of doing with little?"

Somerset said that he certainly did cultivate that art, partly because he was obliged to.

"Ah,—you don't mean to the extent that I mean. The world has not yet learned the riches of frugality, says, I think, Cicero somewhere; and nobody can testify to the truth of that remark better than I. If a man knows how to spend less than his income, however small that may be, why—he has the philosopher's stone." And Sir William looked in Somerset's face with frugality written in every pore of his own, as much as to say, "And here you see one who has been a living instance of those principles from his youth up."

Somerset soon found that whatever turn the conversation took, Sir William invariably reverted to this topic of frugality. When luncheon was over he asked his visitor to walk with him into the garden, and no sooner were they alone, than he continued: "Well, Mr. Somerset, you are down here sketching architecture for professional purposes. Nothing can be better: you are a young man, and your art is one in which there are innumerable chances."

"I had begun to think they were rather few," said Somerset.

"No, they are numerous enough: the difficulty is to find out where they lie. It is better to know where your luck lies than where your talent lies: that's an old man's opinion."

"I'll remember it," said Somerset.

"And now give me some account of your new clubs, new hotels, and new men. . . . What I was going to add, on the subject of finding out where your luck lies, is that nobody is so unfortunate as not to have a lucky star in some direction or other. Perhaps yours is at the antipodes; if so, go there. All I say is, discover your lucky star."

"I am looking for it."

"You may be able to do two things; one well, the other but indifferently, and yet you may have more luck in the latter. Then stick to that one, and never mind what you can do best. Your star lies there."

"There I am not quite at one with you, Sir William."

"You should be. Not that I mean to say that luck lies in any one place long, or at any one person's door. Fortune likes new faces, and your wisdom lies in bringing your acquisitions into safety while her favour lasts. To do that you must make friends in her time of smiles—make friends with people, wherever you find them. My daughter has unconsciously followed that maxim. She has struck up a warm friendship with our neighbour, Miss Power, at the castle. We are diametrically different from her in associations, traditions, ideas, religion—she comes of a violent dissenting family among other things—but I say to Charlotte what I say to you: win affection and regard wherever you can, and accommodate yourself to the times. I put nothing in the way of their intimacy, and wisely so, for by this so many pleasant hours are added to the sum total vouchsafed to humanity."

It was quite late in the afternoon when Somerset took his leave. Miss De Stancy did not return to the castle that night, and he walked through the wood as he had come, feeling that he had been talking with a man of simple nature, who flattered his own understanding by devising Machiavellian theories after the event, to account for any spontaneous action of himself, or his daughter, which might otherwise seem eccentric or irregular.

Before Somerset reached the inn he was overtaken by a

slight shower, and on entering the house he walked into the general room, where there was a fire, and stood with one foot on the fender. The landlord was talking to some guest who sat behind a screen; and, probably because Somerset had been seen passing the window, and was known to be sketching at the castle, the conversation turned on Sir William De Stancy.

"I have often noticed," observed the landlord, "that folks who have come to grief, and quite failed, have the rules how to succeed in life more at their fingers' ends than folks who have succeeded. I assure you that Sir William, so full as he is of wise maxims, never acted upon a wise maxim in his life, until he had lost everything, and it didn't matter whether he was wise or no. You know what he was in his young days, of course?"

"No, I don't," said the invisible stranger.

"Oh, I thought everybody knew poor Sir William's history. He was the star, as I may say, of fashion forty years ago. I remember him in the height of his splendour, as I used to see him when I was a very little boy, and think how great and wonderful he was. I can seem to see now the exact style of his clothes; it was always of a very light colour—a neat white hat, white trousers, white silk handkerchief; ay, and his handsome face, as white as his clothes with keeping late hours. There was nothing black about him but his hair and his eyes—he wore no beard at that time—and they were black indeed. The like of his style of coming on the race-course was never seen there before nor since. He drove his barouche himself; and it was always drawn by four beautiful white horses, and two outriders on matches to 'em, rode in harness bridles. In his rear was a saddle-horse groom leading a thoroughbred hack, and at the rubbing-post was another groom—all in splendid liveries— waiting with another hack. What a 'stablishment he kept up at that time! I can mind him, sir, with thirty race-horses in training at once, seventeen coach-horses, twelve hunters at his box t'other side of London, four chargers at Budmouth, and ever so many hacks."

"And he lost all by his racing speculations?" the stranger observed; and Somerset fancied that the voice had in it something more than the languid carelessness of a casual sojourner.

"Partly by that, partly in other ways. He spent a mint o' money in a visionary project of founding a watering-place; and sunk thousands in a useless silver mine; so 'twas no surprise that the castle that bears his name passed into other hands. . . . The way it was done was curious. Mr. Wilkins, who was the first owner after it went from Sir William, actually sat down as a guest at his table, and got up as the owner. He took off, at a round sum, everything saleable, furniture, plate, pictures, even the milk and butter in the dairy. That's how the pictures and furniture come to be in the castle still; worm-eaten rubbish some of it, and hardly worth moving."

"And off went the baronet to Myrtle Villa?"

"Oh no! he went away for many years. 'Tis quite recently, since his illness, that he came to that little place, within sight of the buildings that once were the pride of his ancestors and himself."

"From what I hear, he has not the manner of a broken-hearted man?"

"Not at all. Since that severe illness he has been happy, as you see him; no pride or regret, quite calm and mild; at new moon quite childish. 'Tis that makes him able to live there: before he was so ill he couldn't bear a sight of the place; but since then he is happy nowhere else, and never leaves the parish further than to drive once a week to Markton. His head won't stand society nowadays, and he lives quite lonely as you see, only seeing his daughter, or his son whenever he comes home, which is not often. They say that if his brain hadn't softened a little he would ha' died—'twas that saved his life."

"What's this I hear about his daughter? Is she really hired companion to the new owner?"

"Now that's a curious thing again, these two girls being so fond of one another; one of 'em a dissenter, and all that, and the other a De Stancy. Oh no, not hired exactly, but she mostly lives with Miss Power, and goes about with her, and I dare say Miss Power makes it worth her while. One can't move a step without the other following; though judging by ordinary folks you'd think 'twould be a cat and dog friendship rather."

"But 'tis not?"

"'Tis not; they are more like lovers than girl and girl. Miss

Power is looked up to by little De Stancy as if she were a god-a'mighty, and Miss Power lets her love her to her heart's content. But whether Miss Power loves back again I can't say, for she's as deep as the North Star."

The landlord here left the stranger to go to some other part of the house, and Somerset drew near to the glass partition to gain a glimpse of a man whose interest in the neighbourhood seemed to have arisen so simultaneously with his own. But the inner room was empty: the man had apparently departed by another door.

CHAPTER VI

THE telegraph had almost the attributes of a human being at Stancy Castle. When its bell rang people rushed to the old tapestried chamber allotted to it, and waited its pleasure with all the deference due to such a novel inhabitant of that ancestral pile. This happened on the following afternoon about four o'clock, while Somerset was sketching in the room adjoining that occupied by the instrument. Hearing its call, he looked in to learn if anybody were attending, and found Miss De Stancy bending over it.

She welcomed him without the least embarrassment. "Another message," she said.—"'*Paula to Charlotte.—Have returned to Markton. Am starting for home. Will be at the gate between four and five if possible.*'"

Miss De Stancy blushed with pleasure when she raised her eyes from the machine. "Is she not thoughtful to let me know beforehand?"

Somerset said she certainly appeared to be, feeling at the same time that he was not in possession of sufficient data to make the opinion of great value.

"Now I must get everything ready, and order what she will want, as Mrs. Goodman is away. What will she want? Dinner would be best—she has had no lunch, I know; or tea perhaps, and dinner at the usual time. Still, if she has had no lunch— Hark, what do I hear?"

She ran to an arrow-slit, and Somerset, who had also heard something, looked out of an adjoining one. They could see from their elevated position a great way along the white road, stretching like a tape amid the green expanses on each side. There had arisen a cloud of dust, accompanied by a noise of wheels.

"It is she," said Charlotte. "Oh yes—it is past four—the telegram has been delayed."

"How would she be likely to come?"

"She has doubtless hired a carriage at the King's Arms: she said it would be useless to send to meet her, as she couldn't name a time. . . . Where is she now?"

"Just where the boughs of those beeches overhang the road—there she is again!"

Miss De Stancy went away to give directions, and Somerset continued to watch. The vehicle, which was of no great pretension, soon crossed the bridge and stopped: there was a ring at the bell; and Miss De Stancy reappeared.

"Did you see her as she drove up—is she not interesting?"

"I could not see her."

"Ah, no—of course you could not from this window because of the tree. Mr. Somerset, will you come downstairs? You will have to meet her, you know."

Somerset felt an indescribable backwardness. "I will go on with my sketching," he said. "Perhaps she will not be——"

"Oh, but it would be quite natural, would it not? Our manners are easier here, you know, than they are in town, and Miss Power has adapted herself to them."

A compromise was effected by Somerset declaring that he would hold himself in readiness to be discovered on the landing at any convenient time.

A servant entered. "Miss Power?" said Miss De Stancy, before he could speak.

The man advanced with a card: Miss De Stancy took it up, and read thereon: "Mr. William Dare."

"It is not Miss Power who has come, then?" she asked, with a disappointed face.

"No, ma'am."

She looked again at the card. "This is some man of business, I suppose—does he want to see me?"

"Yes, miss. Leastwise, he would be glad to see you if Miss Power is not at home."

Miss De Stancy left the room, and soon returned, saying, "Mr. Somerset, can you give me your counsel in this matter? This Mr. Dare says he is a photographic amateur, and it seems that he wrote some time ago to Miss Power, who gave him permission to take views of the castle, and promised to show him the best points. But I have heard nothing of it, and scarcely know whether I ought to take his word in her absence. Mrs. Goodman, Miss Power's relative, who usually attends to these things, is away."

"I dare say it is all right," said Somerset.

"Would you mind seeing him? If you think it quite in order, perhaps you will instruct him where the best views are to be obtained?"

Thereupon Somerset at once went down to Mr. Dare. His coming as a sort of counterfeit of Miss Power disposed Somerset to judge him with as much severity as justice would allow, and his manner for the moment was not of a kind calculated to dissipate antagonistic instincts. Mr. Dare was standing before the fireplace with his feet wide apart, and his hands in the pockets of his coat-tails, looking at a carving over the mantelpiece. He turned quickly at the sound of Somerset's footsteps, and revealed himself as a person quite out of the common.

His age it was impossible to say. There was not a hair upon his face which could serve to hang a guess upon. In repose he appeared a boy; but his actions were so completely those of a man that the beholder's first estimate of sixteen as his age was hastily corrected to six-and-twenty, and afterwards shifted hither and thither along intervening years as the tenor of his sentences sent him up or down. He had a broad forehead, vertical as the face of a bastion, and his hair, which was parted in the middle, hung as a fringe or valance above, in the fashion sometimes affected by the other sex. He wore a heavy ring, of which the gold seemed good, the diamond questionable, and the taste indifferent. There were the remains of a swagger in his body and limbs as he came forward, regarding Somerset with a confident smile, as if the wonder were, not why Mr. Dare should be present, but why Somerset should be present likewise; and the first tone that came from Dare's lips wound up his listener's opinion that he did not like him.

A latent power in the man, or boy, was revealed by the circumstance that Somerset did not feel, as he would ordinarily have done, that it was a matter of profound indifference to him whether this gentleman-photographer were a likeable person or no.

"I have called by appointment; or rather, I left a card stating that to-day would suit me, and no objection was made?" Somerset recognised the voice; it was that of the invisible stranger who had talked with the landlord about the De Stancys. Mr. Dare then proceeded to explain his business.

Somerset found from his inquiries that the man had unquestionably been instructed by somebody to take the views he spoke of; and concluded that Dare's curiosity at the inn was, after all, naturally explained by his errand to this place. Blaming himself for a too hasty condemnation of the stranger, who though visually a little too assured was civil enough verbally, Somerset proceeded with the young photographer to sundry corners of the outer ward, and thence across the moat to the field, suggesting advantageous points of view. The office, being a shadow of his own pursuits, was not uncongenial to Somerset, and he forgot other things in attending to it.

"Now in our country we should stand further back than this, and so get a more comprehensive *coup d'œil*," said Dare, as Somerset selected a good situation.

"You are not an Englishman, then," said Somerset.

"I have lived mostly in India, Malta, Gibraltar, the Ionian Islands, and Canada. I there invented a new photographic process, which I am bent upon making famous. Yet I am but a dilettante, and do not follow this art at the base dictation of what men call necessity."

"Oh, indeed," Somerset replied.

As soon as this business was disposed of, and Mr. Dare had brought up his van and assistant to begin operations, Somerset returned to the castle entrance. While under the archway a man with a professional look drove up in a dog-cart and inquired if Miss Power were at home to-day.

"She has not yet returned, Mr. Havill," was the reply.

Somerset, who had hoped to hear an affirmative by this time, thought that Miss Power was bent on disappointing him in the flesh, notwithstanding the interest she expressed in him by telegraph; and as it was now drawing towards the end of the afternoon, he walked off in the direction of his inn.

There were two or three ways to that spot, but the pleasantest was by passing through a rambling shrubbery, between whose bushes trickled a broad shallow brook, occasionally intercepted in its course by a transverse chain of old stones, evidently from the castle walls, which formed a miniature waterfall. The walk lay along the river brink. Soon Somerset saw before him a circular summer-house formed of short sticks nailed to ornamental patterns. Outside the structure, and immediately in the path, stood a man with a book in his hand; and it was presently apparent that this gentleman was holding a conversation with some person inside the pavilion, but the back of the building being towards Somerset, the second individual could not be seen.

The speaker at one moment glanced into the interior, and at another at the advancing form of the architect, whom, though distinctly enough beheld, the other scarcely appeared to heed in the absorbing interest of his own discourse. Somerset became aware that it was the Baptist minister, whose rhetoric he had heard in the chapel yonder.

"Now," continued the Baptist minister, "will you express to me any reason or objection whatever which induces you to withdraw from our communion? It was that of your father, and of his father before him. Any difficulty you may have met with, I will honestly try to remove; for I need hardly say that in losing you we lose one of the most valued members of the Baptist church in this district. I speak with all the respect due to your position, when I ask you to realise how irreparable is the injury you inflict upon the cause here by this lukewarm backwardness."

"I don't withdraw," said a woman's low voice within.

"What do you do?"

"I decline to attend for the present."

"And you can give no reason for this?"

There was no reply.

"Or for your refusal to proceed with the baptism?"

"I have been christened."

"My dear young lady, it is well known that your christening was the work of your aunt, who did it unknown to your parents when she had you in her power, out of pure obstinacy to a church with which she was not in sympathy, taking you

surreptitiously, and indefensibly, to the font of the Establishment; so that the rite meant and could mean nothing at
all. . . . But I fear that your new position has brought you into
contact with the Pædobaptists, that they have disturbed your
old principles, and so induced you to believe in the validity of
that trumpery ceremony!"

"It seems sufficient."

"I will demolish the basis of that seeming in three minutes,
give me but that time as a listener."

"I have no objection."

"Very well. . . . First, then, I will assume that those who
have influenced you in the matter have not been able to make
any impression, upon one so well grounded as yourself in our
distinctive doctrine, by the stale old argument drawn from
Circumcision?"

"You may assume it."

"Good—that clears the ground. And we now come to the
New Testament."

The minister began to turn over the leaves of his little Bible,
which it impressed Somerset to observe was bound with a flap,
like a pocket-book, the black surface of the leather being worn
brown at the corners by long usage. He turned on till he came
to the beginning of the New Testament, and then commenced
his discourse. After explaining his position, the old man ran
very ably through the arguments, citing well-known writers on
the point in dispute when he required more finished sentences
than his own.

The minister's earnestness and interest in his own case led
him unconsciously to include Somerset in his audience as the
young man drew nearer; till, instead of fixing his eyes exclusively on the person within the summer-house, the preacher
began to direct a good proportion of his discourse upon his
new auditor, turning from one listener to the other attentively,
without seeming to feel Somerset's presence as superfluous.

"And now," he said in conclusion, "I put it to you, sir, as to
her: do you find any flaw in my argument? Is there, madam, a
single text which honestly interpreted, affords the least foot-
hold for the Pædobaptists; in other words, for your opinion on
the efficacy of the rite administered to you in your unconscious

infancy? I put it to you both as honest and responsible beings."
He turned again to the young man.

It happened that Somerset had been over this ground long
ago. Born, so to speak, a High-Church infant, in his youth he
had been of a thoughtful turn, till at one time an idea of his
entering the Church had been entertained by his parents. He
had formed acquaintances with men of almost every variety of
doctrinal practice in this country; and, as the pleadings of each
assailed him before he had arrived at an age of sufficient mental
stability to resist new impressions, however badly substanti-
ated, he inclined to each denomination as it presented itself,
was

> Everything by starts, and nothing long,

till he had travelled through a great many beliefs and doctrines
without feeling himself much better than when he set out.

Fully conscious of the inexpediency of contests on minor
ritual differences, he yet felt a sudden impulse towards a mild
intellectual tournament with the eager old man—to do now,
purely as an exercise of his wits in the defence of a fair girl,
what he had once done with all the earnestness of a lad fighting
for vital principles and not quite able to maintain them.

"Sir, I accept your challenge to us," said Somerset, advancing to the minister's side.

CHAPTER VII

AT the sound of a new voice the lady in the bower started, as he could see by her outline through the crevices of the woodwork and creepers. The minister looked surprised.

"You will lend me your Bible, sir, to assist my memory?" he continued.

The minister held out the Bible with some reluctance, but he allowed Somerset to take it from his hand. The latter, stepping upon a large moss-covered stone which stood near, and laying his hat on a flat beech bough that rose and fell behind him, pointed to the minister to seat himself on the grass. The minister looked at the grass, and looked up again at Somerset, but did not move.

Somerset for the moment was not observing him. His new position had turned out to be exactly opposite the open side of the bower, and now for the first time he beheld the interior. On the seat was the woman who had stood beneath his eyes in the chapel, the "Paula" of Miss De Stancy's enthusiastic eulogies. She wore a summer hat, beneath which her fair curly hair formed a thicket round her forehead. It would be impossible to describe her as she then appeared. Not sensuous enough for an Aphrodite, and too subdued for a Hebe, she would yet, with the adjunct of doves or nectar, have stood sufficiently well for either of those personages, if presented in a pink morning light, and with mythological scarcity of attire.

Half in surprise she glanced up at him; and lowering her eyes again, as if no surprise were ever let influence her actions for more than a moment, she sat on as before, looking past Somerset's position at the view down the river, visible for a long distance before her till it was lost under the bending trees. Somerset turned over the leaves of the minister's Bible, and began:

"The words of my text are taken from the First Epistle to the Corinthians, the seventh chapter and the fourteenth verse."

Here the young lady raised her eyes in spite of her reserve, but it being apparently, too much labour to keep them raised, allowed her glance to subside upon her jet necklace, extending it with the thumb of her left hand.

"Sir!" said the Baptist excitedly, "I know that passage well—it is the last refuge of the Pædobaptists—I foresee your argument. I have met it dozens of times, and it is not worth that snap of the fingers! It is worth no more than the argument from Circumcision, or the Suffer-little-children argument."

"Then turn to the sixteenth chapter of the Acts, and the thirty-third——"

"That, too," cried the minister, "is answered by what I said before! I perceive, sir, that you adopt the method of a special pleader, and not that of an honest inquirer. Is it, or is it not, an answer to my proofs from the eighth chapter of the Acts, the thirty-sixth and thirty-seventh verses; the sixteenth of Mark, sixteenth verse; second of Acts, forty-first verse; the tenth and the forty-seventh verse; or the eighteenth and eighth verse?"

"Very well, then: I will not stick to my text, since you are predetermined not to be convinced by my sermon. Let me prove the point by other reasoning—by the argument from Apostolic tradition." He threw the minister's book upon the grass, and proceeded with his contention at length, which comprised:

First: A lucid discourse on the earliest practice of the Church.

Secondly: Inferences from the same, to wit; that the inquiry being about a fact which could not but be publicly and perfectly known in the ages immediately succeeding that of the Apostles, the sense of those ages concerning this fact must needs be nearly conclusive.

(When he reached this point an interest in his ingenious argument was revealed in spite of herself by the mobile bosom of Miss Paula Power, though otherwise she still occupied herself by drawing out the necklace.)

Thirdly: Testimony from Justin Martyr as to persons who were proselyted or made disciples from their infancy.

Fourthly: Inference from Irenæus in the expression,

"Omnes enim venit per semetipsum salvare; omnes inquam, qui per eum renascuntur in Deum, *infantes* et parvulos et pueros et juvenes."

(At the sound of so much learning Paula turned her eyes upon the speaker with attention.)

Fifthly: Proof of the signification of "renascor" in the writings of the Fathers, as reasoned by Wall.

Sixthly: Argument from Tertullian's advice to defer the rite.

Seventhly: Citations from Cyprian, Clemens Alexandrinus, Nazianzen, Basil, Ambrose, Chrysostom, and Jerome.

Eighthly: A summing up of the whole matter.

Somerset looked around for the minister as he concluded the address, which had occupied about fifteen minutes in delivery. The old man had, after standing face to face with the speaker, gradually turned his back upon him, and during the latter portions of the discourse had moved slowly away. He now looked back; his countenance was full of commiserating reproach as he lifted his hand, twice shook his head, and said, "In the Epistle to the Philippians, first chapter and sixteenth verse, it is written that there are some who preach in contention, and not sincerely. And in the Second Epistle to Timothy, fourth chapter and fourth verse, attention is drawn to those whose ears refuse the truth, and are turned unto fables. I wish you good-afternoon, sir, and that priceless gift, *sincerity*."

The minister vanished behind the trees; Somerset and Miss Power being left confronting each other alone.

Somerset stepped down from the stone, hat in hand, at the same moment in which Miss Power rose from her seat. She hesitated for an instant, and said, with a pretty girlish dignity, sweeping back the skirt of her dress to free her toes in turning, "Although you are personally unknown to me, I cannot leave you without expressing my deep sense of your profound scholarship, and my admiration for the thoroughness of your studies in divinity."

"Your opinion gives me great pleasure," said Somerset, bowing, and fairly blushing. "But, believe me, I am no scholar, and no theologian. My knowledge of the subject arises simply from the accident that some few years ago I looked into the question on my own account, and some of the arguments I then learnt up still remain with me."

"If your sermons at the church only match your address to-day, I shall not wonder at hearing that the parishioners are at last willing to attend."

It flashed upon Somerset's mind that she supposed him to be the new curate, of whose arrival he had casually heard, during his sojourn at the inn. Before he could bring himself to correct an error to which, perhaps, more than to anything else, was owing the friendliness of her manner, she went on, as if to escape the embarrassment of silence:

"I need hardly say that I at least do not doubt the sincerity of your arguments."

"Nevertheless, I was not altogether sincere," he answered.

She was silent.

"Then why should you have delivered such a defence of me?" she asked with simple curiosity.

Somerset involuntarily looked in her face for his answer.

Paula again teased the necklace. "Would you have spoken so eloquently on the other side if I—if occasion had served?" she inquired shyly.

"Perhaps I would."

Another pause, till she said, "I, too, was insincere."

"You?"

"I was."

"In what way?"

"In letting him, and you, think I had been at all influenced by authority, scriptural or patristic."

"May I ask, why, then, did you decline the ceremony the other evening?"

"Ah, you, too, have heard of it?" she said quickly.

"No."

"What then?"

"I saw it."

She blushed and looked past him down the river. "I cannot give my reasons," she said.

"Of course not," said Somerset respectfully.

"I would give a great deal to possess real logical dogmatism."

"So would I."

There was a moment of embarrassment: she wanted to get away, but did not precisely know how. He would have withdrawn had she not said, as if rather oppressed by her conscience, and evidently, still thinking him the curate: "I cannot but feel that Mr. Woodwell's heart has been unnecessarily wounded."

"The minister's?"

"Yes. He is single-mindedness itself. He gives away nearly all he has to the poor. He works among the sick, carrying them necessaries with his own hands. He teaches the ignorant men and lads of the village when he ought to be resting at home, till he is absolutely prostrate from exhaustion, and then he sits up at night writing encouraging letters to those poor people who formerly belonged to his congregation in the village, and have now gone away. He always offends ladies, because he can't help speaking the truth as he believes it; but he hasn't offended me!"

Her feelings had risen towards the end, so that she finished quite warmly, and turned aside.

"I was not in the least aware that he was such a man," murmured Somerset, looking wistfully after the minister. . . . "Whatever you may have done, I fear that I have grievously wounded a worthy man's heart from an idle wish to engage in a useless, unbecoming, dull, last-century argument."

"Not dull," she murmured, "for it interested me."

Somerset accepted her correction willingly. "It was ill-considered of me, however," he said; "and in his distress he has forgotten his Bible." He went and picked up the worn volume from where it lay on the grass.

"You can easily win him to forgive you, by just following, and returning the book to him," she observed.

"I will," said the young man impulsively. And, bowing to her, he hastened along the river brink after the minister. He walked some distance, and at length saw his friend before him, leaning over the gate which led from the private path into a lane, his cheek resting on the palm of his hand with every outward sign of abstraction. He was not conscious of Somerset's presence till the latter touched him on the shoulder.

Never was a reconciliation effected more readily. When

Somerset said that, fearing his motives might be misconstrued, he had followed to assure the minister of his goodwill and esteem, Mr. Woodwell held out his hand, and proved his friendliness in return by preparing to have the controversy on their religious differences over again from the beginning, in an amicable spirit, and with exhaustive detail. Somerset evaded this with alacrity, and once having won his companion to other subjects, he found that the austere man had a smile as pleasant as an infant's on the rare moments when he indulged in it; moreover, that he was warmly attached to Miss Power.

"Though she gives me more trouble than all the rest of the Baptist church in this district," he said, "I love her as my own daughter. But I am sadly exercised to know what she is at heart. Heaven supply me with fortitude to contest her wild opinions, and intractability! But she has sweet virtues, and her conduct at times can be most endearing."

"I believe it!" said Somerset, with more fervour than mere politeness required.

"Sometimes I think those Stancy towers and lands will be a curse to her. The spirit of old papistical times still lingers in the nooks of those silent walls, like a bad odour in a still atmosphere, dulling the iconoclastic emotions of the true Puritan. It would be a pity indeed if she were to be tainted by the very situation that her father's indomitable energy created for her."

"Do not be concerned about her," said Somerset gently, for the minister was evidently in trouble. "She's not a Pædobaptist at heart, although she seems so."

Mr. Woodwell placed his finger on Somerset's arm, saying, "If she's not a Pædobaptist, or Episcopalian; if she is not vulnerable to the mediæval influences of her mansion, lands, and new acquaintance, it is because she's been vulnerable to what is worse: to doctrines beside which the errors of Pædobaptists, Episcopalians, Roman Catholics, are but as air."

"How? You astonish me."

"Have you heard in your metropolitan experience of a curious body of New lights, as they think themselves?" The minister whispered a name to his listener, as if he were fearful of being overheard.

"Oh no," said Somerset, shaking his head, and smiling at the minister's horror. "She's not that; at least, I think not. . . . She's a woman; nothing more. Don't fear for her; all will be well."

The poor old man sighed. "I love her as my own. I will say no more."

Somerset was now in haste to get back to the lady, to ease her apparent anxiety as to the result of his mission, and also because time seemed heavy in the loss of her discreet voice and soft, buoyant look. Every moment of delay began to be as two. But the minister was too earnest in his converse to see his companion's haste, and it was not till perception of the same was forced upon him by the actual retreat of Somerset that he remembered time to be a limited commodity. He then expressed his wish to see Somerset at his house to tea any afternoon he could spare, and receiving the other's promise to call as soon as he could, allowed the younger man to set out for the summer-house, which he did at a smart pace. When he reached it he looked around, and found she was gone.

Somerset was immediately struck by his own lack of social dexterity. Why did he act so readily on the whimsical suggestion of another person, and follow the minister, when he might have said that he would call on Mr. Woodwell to-morrow, and, making himself known to Miss Power as the visiting architect of whom she had heard from Miss De Stancy, have had the pleasure of attending her to the castle? "That's what any other man would have had wit enough to do!" he said.

There then arose the question whether her despatching him after the minister was such an admirable act of good-nature to a good man as it had at first seemed to be. Perhaps it was simply a manœuvre for getting rid of himself; and he remembered his doubt whether a certain light in her eyes when she inquired concerning his sincerity were innocent earnestness or the reverse. As the possibility of levity crossed his brain, his face warmed; it pained him to think that a woman so interesting could condescend to a trick of even so mild a complexion as that. He wanted to think her the soul of all that was tender, and noble, and kind. The pleasure of setting himself to win a minister's goodwill was a little tarnished now.

"Oh no," said Somerset, shaking his head, and smiling at
the minister's horror. "She's not that; at least, I think not.
She's a woman; nothing more. Don't fear for her; all will be
well."

The poor old man ... ... my own, I will say
no more."

... ...

expressed his wish to see Somerset at his ...
... ...

... ...

... ...

of whom she had heard from Miss De Stancy.

... ...

... ...

bered his doubt whether a certain habit in her ...
... ...

... ...

as that. He wanted to think her the soul of all that was ...

CHAPTER VIII

THAT evening Somerset was so preoccupied with these things
that he left all his sketching implements out-of-doors in the
castle grounds. He went somewhat earlier the next morning to
secure them from being stolen or spoiled. Meanwhile he was
hoping to have an opportunity of rectifying in the mind of
Paula the mistake about his personality, which having served a
very good purpose in introducing them to a mutual conversation, might possibly be made just as agreeable as a thing to be
explained away.

He fetched his drawing instruments, rods, sketching-blocks
and other articles from the field where they had lain, and was
passing under the walls with them in his hands, when there
emerged from the outer archway an open landau, drawn by a
pair of black horses of fine action and obviously strong
pedigree, in which Paula was seated, under the shade of a
white parasol with black and white ribbons fluttering on the
summit. The morning sun sparkled on the equipage, its
newness being made all the more noticeable by the ragged old
arch behind.

She bowed to Somerset in a way which might have been
meant to express that she had discovered her mistake; but
there was no embarrassment in her manner, and the carriage
bore her away without her making any sign for checking it. He
had not been walking towards the castle entrance, and she
could not be supposed to know that it was his intention to
enter that day.

She had looked such a bud of youth and promise that his
disappointment at her departure might have shown itself in his
face as he observed her. However, he went on his way, entered
a turret, ascended to the leads of the great tower, and stepped
out.

From this elevated position he could still see the carriage
and the white surface of Paula's parasol in the glowing sun.

While he watched these objects the landau stopped, and in a few moments the horses were turned, the wheels and the panels flashed, and the carriage came bowling along towards the castle again.

Somerset descended the stone stairs. Before he had quite got to the bottom he saw Miss De Stancy standing in the outer hall.

"When did you come, Mr. Somerset?" she gaily said, looking up surprised. "How industrious you are to be at work so regularly every day! We didn't think you would be here to-day: Paula has gone to a vegetable show at Markton, and I am going to join her there soon."

"Oh! gone to a vegetable show. But I think she has altered her——"

At this moment the noise of the carriage was heard in the ward, the door was thrown open, and after the lapse of a few seconds Miss Power came in—Somerset being invisible from the door where she stood.

"Oh, Paula, what has brought you back?" said Miss De Stancy.

"I have forgotten something."

"Mr. Somerset is here. Will you not speak to him?"

Somerset, being by this time in sight, came forward, and Miss De Stancy presented him to her friend. Mr. Somerset acknowledged the pleasure by a respectful inclination of his person, and said some words about the meeting yesterday.

"Yes," said Miss Power, with a serene deliberateness quite noteworthy in a girl of her age: "I have seen it all since. I was mistaken about you, was I not? Mr. Somerset, I am glad to welcome you here, both as a friend of Miss De Stancy's family, and as the son of your father—which is indeed quite a sufficient introduction anywhere."

"You have two pictures painted by Mr. Somerset's father, have you not? I have already told him about them," said Miss De Stancy. "Perhaps Mr. Somerset would like to see them, if they are unpacked?"

As Somerset had from his infancy suffered from a plethora of those productions, excellent as they were, he did not reply quite so eagerly as Miss De Stancy seemed to expect to her kind suggestion, and Paula remarked to him, "You will stay to lunch? Do order it at your own time, if our hour should not be convenient."

Her voice was a voice of low note, in quality that of a flute at the grave end of its gamut. If she sang, she was a pure contralto unmistakably.

"I am making use of the privilege you have been good enough to accord me—of sketching what is valuable within these walls."

"Yes, of course, I am willing for anybody to come. People hold these places in trust for the nation, in one sense. You lift your hands, Charlotte; I see I have not convinced you on that point yet."

Miss De Stancy laughed, and said something to no purpose.

Somehow Miss Power seemed not only more woman than Miss De Stancy, but more woman than Somerset was man; and yet in years she was inferior to both. Though becomingly girlish and modest, she appeared to possess a good deal of composure, which was well expressed by the shaded light of her eyes.

"You have then met Mr. Somerset before?" said Charlotte.

"He was kind enough to deliver an address in my defence yesterday. I suppose I seemed quite unable to defend myself."

"Oh no!" said he.

When a few more words had passed she turned to Miss De Stancy and spoke of some domestic matter, upon which Somerset withdrew, Paula accompanying his exit with a remark that she hoped to see him again a little later in the day.

Somerset retired to the chambers of antique lumber, keeping an eye upon the windows to see if she re-entered the carriage and resumed her journey to Markton. But when the horses had been standing a long time the carriage was driven round to the stables. Then she was not going to the vegetable show. That was rather curious, seeing that she had only come back for something forgotten.

These queries and thoughts occupied the mind of Somerset until the bell was rung for luncheon. Owing to the very dusty condition in which he found himself after his morning's labours among the old carvings he was rather late in getting down-stairs, and seeing that the rest had gone in he went straight to the dining-hall.

The population of the castle had increased in his absence. There were assembled Paula and her friend Charlotte; a bearded man some years older than himself, with a cold grey eye, who was cursorily introduced to him in sitting down as Mr. Havill, an architect of Markton; also an elderly lady of dignified aspect, in a black satin dress, of which she apparently had a very high opinion. This lady, who seemed to be a mere dummy in the establishment, was, as he now learnt, Mrs. Goodman by name, a widow of a recently deceased gentleman, and aunt to Paula—the identical aunt who had smuggled Paula into a church in her helpless infancy, and had her christened without her parents' knowledge. Having been left in narrow circumstances by her husband, she was at present living with Miss Power as chaperon and adviser on practical matters—in a word, as ballast to the management. Beyond her Somerset discerned his new acquaintance Mr. Woodwell, who on sight of Somerset was for hastening up to him and performing a laboured shaking of hands in earnest recognition.

Paula had just come in from the garden, and was carelessly laying down her large shady hat as he entered. Her dress, a figured material in black and white, was short, allowing her feet to appear. There was something in her look, and in the style of her corsage, which reminded him of several of the bygone beauties in the gallery. The thought for a moment crossed his mind that she might have been imitating one of them, but it was scarcely likely.

"Fine old screen, sir!" said Mr. Havill, in a long-drawn voice across the table when they were seated, pointing in the direction of the traceried oak divison between the dining-hall and a vestibule at the end. "As good a piece of fourteenth-century work as you shall see in this part of the county."

"You mean fifteenth century, of course?" said Somerset.

Havill was silent. "You are one of the profession, perhaps?" asked the latter, after a while.

"You mean that I am an architect?" said Somerset. "Yes."

"Ah—one of my own honoured vocation." Havill's face had been not unpleasant until this moment, when he smiled;

whereupon there instantly gleamed over him a phase of meanness, remaining until the smile died away. It might have been a physical accident; it might have been otherwise.

Havill continued, with slow watchfulness: "What enormous sacrileges are committed by the builders every day, I observe! I was driving yesterday to Helterton, where I am erecting a town-hall, and passing through a village on my way I saw the workmen pulling down a chancel-wall in which they found imbedded a unique specimen of Perpendicular work—a capital from some old arcade—the mouldings wonderfully undercut. They were smashing it up as filling-in for the new wall."

"It must have been unique," said Somerset, in the too-readily controversial tone of the educated young man who has yet to learn diplomacy. "I have never seen much undercutting in Perpendicular stone-work; nor anybody else, I think."

"Oh yes—lots of it!" said Mr. Havill, nettled. His glance at Somerset as he answered had a peculiar shade in it, suggesting that he was readily convertible into an enemy.

Paula looked from one to the other. "Which am I to take as guide?" she asked. 'Are Perpendicular capitals undercut, as you call it, Mr. Havill, or no?"

"It depends upon circumstances," said Mr. Havill.

But Somerset had answered at the same time: "There is seldom or never any marked undercutting in moulded work later than the middle of the fourteenth century."

Havill looked keenly at Somerset for a time: then he turned to Paula: "As regards that fine Saxon vaulting you did me the honour to consult me about the other day, I should advise taking out some of the old stones and reinstating new ones exactly like them."

"But the new ones won't be Saxon," said Paula. "And then in time to come, when I have passed away, and those stones have become stained like the rest, people will be deceived. I should prefer an honest patch to any such make-believe of Saxon relics."

As she concluded, she let her eyes rest on Somerset for a moment, as if to ask him to side with her. Much as he liked talking to Paula, he would have preferred not to enter into this discussion with another professional man, even though that man were a spurious article; but he was led on to enthusiasm by a sudden pang of regret at finding that the masterly workmanship in this fine castle was likely to be tinkered and spoilt by such a man as Havill.

"You will deceive nobody into believing that anything is Saxon here," he said, warmly. "There is not a square inch of Saxon work, as it is called, in the whole castle."

Paula, in doubt, looked to Mr. Havill.

"Oh yes, sir; you are quite mistaken," said that gentleman, slowly. "Every stone of those lower vaults was reared in Saxon times."

"I can assure you," said Somerset, deferentially, but firmly, "that there is not an arch or wall in this castle of a date anterior to the year 1100; no one whose attention has ever been given to the study of architectural details of that age can be of a different opinion."

"I have studied architecture, and I am of a different opinion. I have the best reason in the world for the difference, for I have history herself on my side. What will you say when I tell you that it is a recorded fact that King Edred, great uncle of Edward the Confessor, gave this castle to a certain abbess, and that, in addition, the castle is mentioned in Domesday as a building of long standing?"

"I shall say that has nothing to do with it," replied the young man. "I don't deny that there may have been a castle here in the time of Edward; what I say is, that none of the architecture we now see was standing at that date."

There was a silence of a minute, disturbed only by a murmured dialogue between Mrs. Goodman and the minister, during which Paula was looking thoughtfully on the table, as if framing a question.

"Can it be," she said to Somerset, "that such certainty has been reached in the study of architectural dates? Now, would you really risk anything on your belief? Would you agree to be shut up in the vaults and fed upon bread and water for a week if I could prove you wrong?"

"Willingly," said Somerset. "The date of those groins is matter of absolute certainty. The details are notorious, as being what are called Transition or semi-Norman; their growth can be traced out of earlier forms; everything is known about them from repeated observations made all over England and the Continent. More than that, I have found an arch-ornament here which is exactly copied from a similar one I sketched in the crypt of the Abbaye aux Dames at Caen last year. That it should have been built before the Conquest is as unlikely as, say, that the rustiest old gun with a percussion lock should be older than the date of Waterloo."

"How I wish I knew something precise of an art which makes one so independent of written history!"

Mr. Havill had lapsed into a mannerly silence that was only sullenness disguised. Paula turned her conversation to Miss De Stancy, who had simply looked from one to the other during the discussion, never venturing to put in a word, though she might have been supposed to have a prescriptive right to a few remarks on the matter. A commonplace talk ensued, till Havill, who had not joined in it, privately began at Somerset again with a mixed manner of cordiality, contempt, and misgiving.

"You have a practice, I suppose, sir?"

"I am not in practice just yet."

"Just beginning?"

"I am about to begin."

"In London, or near here?"

"In London probably."

"H'm. . . . I am practising in Markton."

"Indeed. Have you been at it long?"

"Not particularly. I designed the chapel built by this lady's late father; it was my first undertaking—I owe my start, in fact, to Mr. Power. Ever built a chapel?"

"Never. I have sketched a good many churches."

"Ah—there we differ. I didn't do much sketching in my youth, nor have I time for it now. Sketching and building are two different things, to my mind. I was not brought up to the profession—got into it through sheer love of it. I began as a landscape gardener, then I became a builder, then I was a road-contractor. Every architect might do worse than have some such experience. But nowadays 'tis the men who can draw pretty pictures who get recommended, not the practical men. Young prigs win Institute medals for a pretty design or two which, if anybody tried to build them, would fall down like a house of cards; then they get travelling studentships and what not, and then they start as architects of some new school or other, and think they are the masters of us experienced ones."

While Somerset was reflecting how far this statement was true, he heard the voice of Paula inquiring, "Who can he be?"

Her eyes were bent on the window. Looking out, Somerset saw, in the mead beyond the dry ditch, Dare, with his photographic apparatus.

"He is the young gentleman who called about taking views of the castle," said Charlotte.

"Oh yes—I remember; it is quite right. He met me in the village and asked me to suggest him some views. I thought him a respectable young fellow."

"I think he is a Canadian," said Somerset.

"No," said Paula, "he is an East Indian—at least he implied that he was so to me."

"There is Italian blood in him," said Charlotte, brightly. "For he spoke to me with an Italian accent. But I can't think whether he is a boy or a man."

"It is to be earnestly hoped that the gentleman does not prevaricate," said the minister, for the first time attracted by the subject. "I accidentally met him in the lane, and he said something to me about having lived in Malta. I think it was Malta, or Gibraltar—even if he did not say that he was born there."

"His manners are no credit to his nationality," observed Mrs. Goodman, also speaking publicly for the first time. "He asked me this morning to send him out a pail of water for his process, and before I had turned away he began whistling. I don't like whistlers."

"Then it appears," said Somerset, "that he is a being of no age, no nationality, and no behaviour."

"A complete negative," added Havill, brightening into a civil sneer. "That is, he would be, if he were not a maker of negatives well known in Markton."

"Not well known, Mr. Havill," answered Mrs. Goodman,

firmly. "For I lived in Markton for thirty years ending three months ago, and he was never heard of in my time."

"He is something like you, Charlotte," said Paula, smiling playfully on her companion.

All the men looked at Charlotte, on whose face a delicate nervous blush thereupon made its appearance.

"'Pon my word there is a likeness, now I think of it," said Havill.

Paula bent down to Charlotte and whispered: "Forgive my rudeness, dear. He is not a nice enough person to be like you. He is really more like one or other of the old pictures about the house. I forget which, and really it does not matter."

"People's features fall naturally into groups and classes," remarked Somerset. "To an observant person they often repeat themselves; though to a careless eye they seem infinite in their differences."

The conversation flagged, and they idly observed the figure of the cosmopolite Dare as he walked round his instrument in the mead, and busied himself with an arrangement of curtains and lenses, occasionally withdrawing a few steps and looking contemplatively at the towers and walls.

CHAPTER IX

SOMERSET returned to the top of the great tower with a vague consciousness that he was going to do something up there—perhaps sketch a general plan of the structure, with a view to measuring it in detail. But he began to discern that this Stancy-Castle episode in his studies of Gothic architecture might be less useful than ornamental to him as a professional man, though it was too agreeable to be abandoned. Finding after a while that his drawing progressed but slowly, by reason of infinite joyful thoughts more allied to his nature than to his art, he relinquished rule and compass, and entered one of the two turrets opening on the roof. It was not the staircase by which he had ascended, and he proceeded to explore its lower part. Entering from the blaze of light without, and imagining the stairs to descend as usual, he became aware after a few steps that there was suddenly nothing to tread on, and found himself precipitated downwards to a distance of several feet.

Arrived at the bottom, he was conscious of the happy fact that he had not seriously hurt himself, though his leg was twisted awkwardly. Next he perceived that the stone steps had been removed from the turret, so that he had dropped into it as into a dry well; that, owing to its being walled up below, there was no door of exit on either side of him; that he was, in short, a prisoner.

Placing himself in a more comfortable position he calmly considered the best means of getting out, or of making his condition known. For a moment he tried to drag himself up by his arms, but it was a hopeless attempt, the height to the first step being far too great.

He next looked around at a lower level. Not far from his left elbow, in the concave of the outer wall, was a slit for the admission of light, and he perceived at once that through this slit alone lay his chance of communicating with the outer world. At first it seemed as if it were to be done by shouting, but when he learnt what little effect was produced by his voice in the midst of such a mass of masonry, his heart failed him for a moment. Yet, as either Paula or Miss De Stancy would probably guess his visit to the top of the tower, there was no cause for terror, if some for alarm.

He put his handkerchief through the window-slit, so that its length fluttered outside, and, fixing it in its place by a large stone drawn from the loose ones around him, awaited succour as best he could. To begin this course of procedure was easy but to abide in patience till it should produce fruit was an irksome task. As nearly as he could guess—for his watch had been stopped by the fall—it was now about four o'clock, and it would be scarcely possible for evening to approach without some eye or other noticing the white signal. So Somerset waited, his eyes lingering on the little world of objects around him, till they all became quite familiar. Spiders'-webs in plenty were there, and one in particular just before him was in full use as a snare, stretching across the arch of the window, with radiating threads as its ribs. Somerset had plenty of time, and he counted their number—fifteen. He remained so silent that the owner of this elaborate structure soon forgot the disturbance which had resulted in the breaking of his diagonal ties, and crept out from the corner to mend them. In watching the process, Somerset noticed that on the stonework behind the web sundry names and initials had been cut by explorers in years gone by. Among these antique inscriptions he observed two bright and clean ones, consisting of the words "De Stancy" and "W. Dare," crossing each other at right angles. From the state of the stone they could not have been cut more than a month before this date, and, musing on the circumstance, Somerset passed the time until the sun reached the slit in that side of the tower, where, beginning by throwing in a streak of fire as narrow as a corn-stalk, it enlarged its width till the dusty nook was flooded with cheerful light. It disclosed something lying in the corner, which on examination proved to be a dry bone. Whether it was human, or had come from the castle larder in bygone times, he could not tell. One bone was not a whole skeleton; but it made him think of Ginevra of Modena, the heroine of the Mistletoe Bough, and other cribbed and confined wretches, who had fallen into such traps and been discovered after a cycle of years.

The sun's rays had travelled some way round the interior when Somerset's waiting ears were at last attracted by footsteps above, each tread being brought down by the hollow turret with great fidelity. He hoped that with these sounds would arise that of a soft voice he had begun to like well. Indeed, during the solitary hour or two of his waiting here he had pictured Paula straying alone on the terrace of the castle, looking up, noting his signal, and ascending to deliver him from his painful position by her own exertions. It seemed that at length his dream had been verified. The footsteps approached the opening of the turret; and, attracted by the call which Somerset now raised, began to descend towards him. In a moment, not Paula's face, but that of a dreary footman of her household, looked over the edge of the lowest stair.

Somerset mastered his disappointment, and the man speedily fetched a ladder, by which means the prisoner of two hours ascended to the roof in safety. During the process he ventured to ask for the ladies of the house, and learnt that they had gone out for a drive together.

Before he left the castle, however, they had returned, a circumstance unexpectedly made known to him by his receiving a message, through a servant, from Miss Power, to the effect that she would be glad to see him at his convenience. Wondering what it could possibly mean, he followed the messenger to her room—a small modern library in the Elizabethan wing of the house, adjoining that in which the telegraph stood, and arranged for her temporary use till things were more in order.

She was alone, sitting behind a table littered with letters and sketches, and looking fresh from her drive. Perhaps it was because he had been shut up in that dismal dungeon all the afternoon that he felt something in her presence which at the same time charmed and refreshed him.

She signified that he was to sit down; but finding that he was going to place himself on a straight-backed chair some distance off she said, "Will you sit nearer to me?" and then, as if rather oppressed by her dignity, she left her own chair of business and seated herself at ease on an ottoman which was among the diversified furniture of the apartment.

"I want to consult you professionally," she went on. "I have been much impressed by your great knowledge of castellated architecture. Will you sit in that leather chair at the table, as you may have to take notes?"

The young man assented, expressed his gratification, and went to the chair she designated.

"But, Mr. Somerset," she continued from the ottoman—the width of the table only dividing them—"I first should like to know, and I trust you will excuse my inquiry, if you are an architect in practice, or only as yet studying for the profession?"

"I am just going to practise. I open my office on the first of January next," he answered.

"You would not mind having me as a client—your first client?" She was reclining, and looked curiously from her sideway face across the table, as she said this.

"Can you ask it!" said Somerset, warmly. "What are you going to build?"

"I am going to restore the castle."

"What, all of it?" said Somerset, astonished at the audacity of such an undertaking.

"Not the parts that are absolutely ruinous: the walls battered by the Parliament artillery had better remain as they are, I suppose. But we have begun wrong; it is I who should ask you, not you me. . . . I fear," she went on, in that low note which was somewhat difficult to catch at a distance, but which he did not wish her to raise to a louder tone, "I fear what the antiquarians will say if I am not very careful. They come here a great deal in summer, and if I were to do the work wrong they would put my name in the papers as a dreadful person, wilfully destroying what is by rights the property of all. But I must live here, as I have no other house, except the one in London, and hence I must make the place habitable, which it hardly is at present. I do hope I can trust to your judgment?"

"I hope so," he said, with diffidence, for far from having much professional confidence, he often mistrusted himself. "I am a Fellow of the Society of Antiquaries, and a Member of the Institute of British Architects—not a Fellow of that body yet, though I soon shall be."

"Then I am sure you must be trustworthy," she said, with some enthusiasm. "Well, what am I to do?—How do we begin?"

Somerset began to feel more professional, what with the business chair, and the table, and the writing-paper, notwithstanding that these articles, and the room they were in, were hers instead of his; and an evenness of manner which he had momentarily lost returned to him. "The very first step," he said, "is to decide upon the outlay—what is it to cost?"

He faltered a little, for it seemed to disturb the softness of their relationship to talk thus of hard cash. But her sympathy with his feeling was apparently not great, and she said, "The expenditure shall be what you advise."

"What a heavenly client!" he thought. "But you must just give some idea," he said gently. "For the fact is, any sum almost may be spent on such a building: five thousand, ten thousand, twenty thousand, fifty thousand, a hundred thousand."

"I want it done well; so suppose we say a hundred thousand? My father's solicitor—my solicitor now—says I may go to a hundred thousand without extravagance, if the expenditure is scattered over two or three years."

Somerset looked round for a pen. With her habitual quickness of insight she knew what he wanted, and signified where one could be found. He wrote down in large figures—

£100,000.

It was more than he had expected; and for a young man just beginning practice, and wishing to make his name known, the opportunity of playing with another person's money to that extent would afford an exceptionally handsome opening, not so much from the commission it represented, as from the attention that would be bestowed by the art world on such an undertaking.

Paula had sunk into a reverie. "I was intending to entrust the work to Mr. Havill, a local architect," she said. "But I gathered from his conversation with you to-day that his ignorance of styles might compromise me very seriously. In short, though my father employed him in one or two little matters, it would not be right—even a morally culpable thing—to place such an historically valuable building in his hands."

"Has Mr. Havill ever been led to expect the commission?" he asked.

"He may have guessed that he would have it. I have spoken of my intention to him more than once."

Somerset thought over his conversation with Havill. Well, he did not like Havill personally; and he had strong reasons for suspecting that in the matter of architecture Havill was a quack. But was it quite generous to step in thus, and take away what would be a golden opportunity to such a man of making both ends meet comfortably for some years to come, without giving him at least one chance? He reflected a little longer, and then spoke out his feeling.

"I venture to propose a slightly modified arrangement," he said. "Instead of committing the whole undertaking to my hands without better proof of my ability to carry it out than you have at present, let there be a competition between Mr. Havill and myself—let our rival plans for the restoration and enlargement be submitted to a committee of the Royal Institute of British Architects—and let the choice rest with them, subject of course to your approval."

"It is indeed generous of you to suggest it." She looked thoughtfully at him; he appeared to strike her in a new light. "You really recommend it?" she asked, as if the fairness which had prompted his words inclined her still more than before to resign herself entirely to him in the matter.

"I do," said Somerset deliberately.

"I will think of it, since you wish it," she replied. "And now, what general idea have you of the plan to adopt? I do not positively agree to your suggestion as yet," she added; "so I may perhaps ask the question."

Somerset, being by this time familiar with the general plan of the castle, took out his pencil, and made a rough sketch. While he was doing it she rose, and coming slowly to the back of his chair, bent over him in silence.

"Ah, I begin to see your conception," she murmured; and the breath of her words fanned his ear. He finished the sketch, and held it up to her, saying—

"I would suggest that you walk over the building with Mr. Havill and myself, and detail your ideas to us on each portion."

"Is it necessary?"

"Clients mostly do it."

"I will, then. But it is too late for me this evening. Please meet me to-morrow at ten."

CHAPTER X

AT ten o'clock they met in the same room, Paula appearing in a straw hat having a bent-up brim lined with plaited silk, so that it surrounded her forehead like a nimbus; and Somerset armed with sketch-book, measuring-rod, ivory rule, and other apparatus of his craft.

"And Mr. Havill?" said the young man.

"I have not decided to employ him: if I do he shall go round with me independently of you," she replied rather brusquely.

Somerset was by no means sorry to hear this. His duty to Havill was done.

"And now," she said, as they walked on together through the passages, "I must tell you that I am not a mediævalist myself; and perhaps that's a pity."

"What are you?"

"I am Greek—that's why I don't wish to influence your design."

Somerset, as they proceeded, pointed out where roofs had been and should be again, where gables had been pulled down, and where floors had vanished, showing her how to reconstruct their details from marks in the walls, much as a comparative anatomist reconstructs an antediluvian from fragmentary bones and teeth. She appeared to be interested, listened attentively, but said little in reply. They were ultimately in a long narrow passage, indifferently lighted, when Somerset, treading on a loose stone, felt a twinge of weakness in one knee, and knew in a moment that it was the result of the twist given by his yesterday's fall. He paused, leaning against the wall.

"What is it?" said Paula, with a sudden timidity in her voice.

"I slipped down yesterday," he said. "It will be right in a moment."

"I—can I help you?" said Paula. But she did not come near him; indeed, she withdrew a little. She looked up the passage, and down the passage, and became conscious that it was long and gloomy, and that nobody was near. A curious coy uneasiness seemed to take possession of her. Whether she thought, for the first time, that she had made a mistake—that to wander about the castle alone with him was compromising, or whether it was the mere shy instinct of maidenhood, nobody knows; but she said suddenly, "I will get something for you, and return in a few minutes."

"Pray don't—it has quite passed!" he said, stepping out again.

But Paula had vanished. When she came back it was in the rear of Charlotte De Stancy. Miss De Stancy had a tumbler in one hand, half full of wine, which she offered him; Paula remaining in the background.

He took the glass, and, to satisfy his companions, drank a mouthful or two, though there was really nothing whatever the matter with him beyond the slight ache above mentioned. Charlotte was going to retire, but Paula said, quite anxiously, "You will stay with me, Charlotte, won't you? Surely you are interested in what I am doing?"

"What is it?" said Miss De Stancy.

"Planning how to mend and enlarge the castle. Tell Mr. Somerset what I want done in the quadrangle—you know quite well—and I will walk on."

She walked on; but instead of talking on the subject as directed, Charlotte and Somerset followed chatting on indifferent matters. They came to an inner court not unlike a cloister-garth, and found Paula standing there.

She met Miss De Stancy with a smile. "Did you explain?" she asked.

"I have not explained yet." Paula seated herself on a stone bench and Charlotte went on: "Miss Power thought of making a Greek court of this. But she will not tell you so herself, because it seems such dreadful anachronism."

"I said I would not tell any architect myself," interposed Paula, correctly. "I did not then know that he would be Mr. Somerset."

"It is rather startling," said Somerset.

"A Greek colonnade all round, you said, Paula," continued her less reticent companion. "A peristyle you called it—you

saw it in a book, don't you remember?—and then you were
going to have a fountain in the middle, and statues like those
in the British Museum."

"I did say so," remarked Paula, pulling the leaves from a
young sycamore-tree that had sprung up between the joints of
the paving.

From the spot where they sat they could see over the roofs
the upper part of the great tower wherein Somerset had met
with his misadventure. The tower stood boldly up in the sun,
and from one of the slits in the corner something white waved
in the breeze.

"What can that be?" said Charlotte. "Is it the fluff of owls,
or a handkerchief?"

"It is my handkerchief," Somerset answered, carelessly. "I
fixed it there with a stone to attract attention, and forgot to
take it away."

All three looked up at the handkerchief with interest. "Why
did you want to attract attention?" asked Paula, in a low voice.

"Oh, I fell into the turret: but I got out very easily."

"Oh, Paula," said Charlotte, turning to her friend. "That
must be the place where the man fell in, years ago, and was
starved to death!"

"Starved to death?" said Paula.

"They say so. Oh, Mr. Somerset, what an escape!" And
Charlotte De Stancy walked away to a point from which she
could get a better view of the treacherous turret.

"Whom did you think to attract?" asked Paula, after a
pause.

"I thought you might see it."

"Me personally?" And, blushing faintly, her eyes rested
upon him.

"I hoped for anybody. I thought of you," said Somerset.

She did not continue. In a moment she arose and went
across to Miss De Stancy. "Don't *you* go falling down and
becoming a skeleton," she said—Somerset overheard the
words, though Paula was unaware of it—after which she
clasped her fingers behind Charlotte's neck, and smiled tenderly in her face.

It seemed to be quite unconsciously done, and Somerset

thought it a very beautiful action. Presently Paula returned to him and said, "Mr. Somerset, I think we have had enough architecture for to-day."

The two women then wished him good morning and went away. Somerset, feeling that he had now every reason for prowling about the castle, remained near the spot endeavouring to evolve some plan of procedure for the project entertained by the beautiful owner of those weather-scathed walls. But for a long time the mental perspective of his new position so excited the emotional side of his nature that he could not concentrate on feet and inches. As Paula's architect (supposing Havill not to be admitted as a competitor), he must of necessity be in constant communication with her for a space of two or three years to come; and particularly during the next few months. She, doubtless, cherished far too ambitious views of her career to feel any personal interest in this enforced relationship with him; but he would be at liberty to feel what he chose: and to be the victim of an unrequited passion, while afforded such splendid opportunities of communion with the one beloved, deprived that passion of its most deplorable features. Accessibility is a great point in matters of love, and perhaps of the two there is less misery in loving without return a goddess who is to be seen and spoken to every day, than in having an affection tenderly reciprocated by one always hopelessly removed.

With this view of having to spend a considerable time in the neighbourhood, Somerset shifted his quarters that afternoon from the little inn at Sleeping-Green to the King's Arms Hotel at Markton. He required more rooms in which to carry out Paula's instructions than the former place afforded, and a more central position. Having reached and dined at the King's Arms he found the evening tedious, and again strolled out in the direction of the castle.

When he reached it the light was declining, and a solemn stillness overspread the pile. The great tower was in full view. That spot of white which looked like a pigeon fluttering from the loophole was his handkerchief, still hanging in the place where he had left it. His eyes yet lingered on the walls when he noticed, with surprise, that the handkerchief suddenly vanished.

Believing that the breezes, though weak below, might have been strong enough at that height to blow it into the turret, and in no hurry to get off the premises, he leisurely climbed up to find it, ascending by the second staircase, crossing the roof, and going to the top of the treacherous turret. The ladder by which he had escaped still stood within it, and beside the ladder he beheld the dim outline of a woman, in a meditative attitude, holding his handkerchief in her hand.

Somerset felt himself an intruder and softly withdrew. When he had reached the ground he looked up. A girlish form was standing at the top of the tower looking over the parapet upon him—possibly not seeing him, for it was dark on the lawn.

It was either Miss De Stancy or Paula; one of them had gone there alone for his handkerchief and had remained awhile, pondering on his escape. But which? "If I were not a faint-heart I should run all risk and wave my hat or kiss my hand to her, whoever she is," he thought. But he was faint-hearted in the circumstances, and did not do either, feeling that, if it were Miss Power, his acquaintance was too desirable a thing to be trifled with, even by an act which would easily have borne the interpretation of playful gallantry.

So he lingered about silently in the shades, and then thought of strolling to his rooms at Markton. Just at leaving, as he passed under the inhabited wing, whence one or two lights now blinked, he heard a piano, and a voice singing "The Mistletoe Bough." The song had probably been suggested to the romantic fancy of the singer by her visit to the scene of his captivity.

CHAPTER XI

THE identity of the lady whom he had seen on the tower and afterwards heard singing was established the next day.

"I have been thinking," said Miss Power, on meeting him, "that you may require a studio on the premises. If so, the one I showed you yesterday as suitable for such a purpose is at your service. If I employ Mr. Havill to compete with you I will offer him a similar one."

Somerset did not decline; and when they had discussed further arrangements she added, "In the same room you will find the handkerchief that was left on the tower."

"Ah, I saw that it was gone. Somebody brought it down?"

"I did," she quietly remarked, looking up for a second under her shady hat-brim.

"I am much obliged to you."

"Oh no—that's not necessary. I went up last night to see where the accident happened, and there I found it. When you came up were you in search of it, or did you want me?"

"Then she saw me," he thought. "I went for the handker-chief only; I was not aware that you were there," he answered simply. It could hardly be assumed that she was conscious of any sentimental meaning which might have been attached to her words. "Did you want me?" and he involuntarily sighed.

It was very soft, but she might have heard him, for there was interest in her voice as she continued, "Did you see me before you went back?"

"I did not know it was you; I saw that some lady was there, and I would not disturb her. I wondered all the evening if it were you."

Paula hastened to explain: "We understood that you would stay to dinner, and as you did not come in we wondered where you were. That made me think of your accident, and after dinner I went up to the place where it happened."

Somerset almost wished she had not explained so lucidly.

And now followed the piquant days to which his position as her architect, or, at worst, as one of her two architects, naturally led. His anticipations were for once surpassed by the reality. Perhaps Somerset's inherent unfitness for a professional life under ordinary circumstances was only proved by his great zest for it now. Had he been in regular practice, with numerous other clients, instead of having merely made a start with this one, he would have totally neglected their business in his exclusive attention to Paula's.

The idea of a competition between Somerset and Havill had been highly approved by Paula's solicitor, but she would not assent to it as yet, seeming quite vexed that Somerset should not have taken the good the gods provided without questioning her justice to Havill. The room she had offered him was prepared as a studio. Drawing-boards and Whatman's paper were sent for, and in a few days Somerset began serious labour. His first requirement was a clerk or two, to do the drudgery of measuring and figuring; but for the present he preferred to sketch alone. Sometimes, in measuring the outworks of the castle, he ran against Havill strolling about with no apparent object, who bestowed on him an envious nod, and passed by.

"I hope you will not roughly make your sketches," she said, looking in upon him one day, with serio-playfulness, as he sat in the room which had been lent him, "and then go away to your studio in London and think of your other buildings and forget mine. I am in haste to begin, and wish you not to neglect me."

"I have no other building to think of," said Somerset, rising and placing a chair for her. "I had not begun practice, as you may know. I have nothing else in hand but your castle."

"I suppose I ought not to say I am glad of it; but it is an advantage to have an architect all to one's self. The architect whom I at first thought of told me before I knew you that if I placed the castle in his hands he would undertake no other commission till its completion."

"I agree to the same," said Somerset.

"I don't wish to bind you," she returned. "But I hinder you now—do pray go on without reference to me. When will there be some drawing for me to see?"

"I will take care that it shall be soon."

He had a metallic tape in his hand, and went out of the room to take some dimension in the corridor. As the assistant for whom he had advertised had not arrived, he attempted to fix the end of the tape by sticking his penknife through the ring into the wall. Paula looked on at a distance.

"I will hold it," she said, after watching in silence for some time and seeing his difficulty.

She went to the required corner and held the end in its place. She had taken it the wrong way, and Somerset went over and placed it properly in her fingers, carefully avoiding to touch them. He did this without speaking; she obediently raised her hand to the corner again, and stood till he had finished, when she asked, "Is that all?"

"That is all," said Somerset. "Thank you." Without further speech she looked at his sketch-book, while he marked down the lines just acquired.

"You said the other day," she observed, "that early Gothic work might be known by the under-cutting, or something to that effect. I have looked in Rickman and the Oxford Glossary, but I cannot quite understand what you meant."

It was only too evident to her lover, from the way in which she turned to him, that she *had* looked in Rickman and the Glossary, and was thinking of nothing in the world but of the subject of her inquiry.

"I can show you, by actual example, if you will come to the chapel?" he returned, hesitatingly.

"Don't go on purpose to show me—when you are there on your own account I will come in."

"I shall be there in half an hour."

"Very well," said Paula. She looked out of a window, and, seeing Miss De Stancy on the terrace, left him.

Somerset stood thinking of what he had said. He had no occasion whatever to go into the chapel of the castle that day. He had been tempted by her words to say he would be there, and "half an hour" had come to his lips almost without his knowledge. This community of interest—if it were not any-thing more tender—was growing serious. What had passed between them amounted to an appointment; they were going to meet in the most solitary chamber of the whole solitary pile. Could it be that Paula had well considered this in replying with her passive "Very well"? Probably not. She might think of it between now and then, and might not come.

Somerset proceeded to the chapel and waited. With the progress of the seconds towards the half-hour he began to discover that a dangerous admiration for this girl had risen within him. Yet so imaginative was his passion that he hardly knew a single feature of her countenance well enough to remember it in her absence. The meditative judgment of things and men which had been his habit up to the moment of seeing her in the Baptist chapel seemed to have left him—nothing remained but a distracting wish to be always near her, and it was quite with dismay that he recognised what immense importance he was attaching to the question whether she would keep the trifling engagement or not.

The chapel of Stancy Castle was a silent place, heaped up in corners with a lumber of old panels, framework, and broken coloured glass. Here no clock could be heard beating out the hours of the day—here no voice of priest or deacon had for generations uttered the daily service denoting how the year rolls on. The stagnation of the spot was sufficient to draw Somerset's mind for a moment from the subject which absorbed it, and he thought, "So, too, will time triumph over all this fervour within me."

The sombre mood quite vanished when, lifting his eyes from the floor on which his foot had been tapping nervously, he saw Paula standing at the other end. It was not so pleasant when he also saw that Mrs. Goodman accompanied her. The latter lady however, obligingly remained where she was resting, while Paula came forward, and, as usual, paused on a half-smile without speaking.

"It is in this little arcade that the example occurs," said Somerset.

"Oh yes," she answered, turning to look at it.

"Early piers, capitals, and mouldings, generally alternate with deep hollows, so as to form strong shadows. Now look under the abacus of this capital; you will find the stone hollowed out wonderfully; and also in this arch-mould. It is often difficult to understand how it could be done without cracking off the stone. The difference between this and late work can be felt by the hand even better than it can be seen." He suited the action to the word and placed his hand in the hollow.

She listened attentively; then stretched up her own hand to test the cutting as he had done; she was not quite tall enough; she would step upon this piece of wood. Having done so she tried again, and succeeded in putting her finger on the spot. No; she could not understand it through her glove even now. She pulled off her glove, and, her hand resting in the stone channel, her eyes became abstracted in the effort of realisation, the ideas derived through her hand passing into her face.

"No, I am not sure now," she said.

Somerset placed his own hand in the cavity. Now their two hands were close together again. They had been close together half an hour earlier, and he had sedulously avoided touching here. He dared not let such an accident happen now. And yet—surely she saw the situation! Was the inscrutable serious-ness with which she applied herself to his lesson a mockery? There was such a bottomless depth in her eyes that it was impossible to guess truly. Let it be that destiny alone had ruled that their hands should be together a second time.

All rumination was cut short by an impulse. He seized her forefinger between his own finger and thumb, and drew it along the hollow, saying, "That is the curve I mean."

Somerset's hand was hot and trembling; Paula's, on the contrary, was cool and soft as an infant's.

"Now the arch-mould," continued he. "There—the depth of that cavity is tremendous, and it is not geometrical, as in later work." He drew her unresisting fingers from the capital to the arch, and laid them in the little trench as before.

She allowed them to rest quietly there till he relinquished them. "Thank you," she then said, withdrawing her hand, brushing the dust from her finger-tips, and putting on her glove.

Her imperception of his feeling was the very sublimity of maiden innocence if it were real; if not, well, the coquetry was no great sin. But he would not think of it as pretence or flirtation; the pleasure of this day would be marred by such commonplace suppositions.

"Mr. Somerset, will you allow me to have the Greek court I mentioned?" she asked tentatively, after a long break in their discourse, as she scanned the green stones along the base of the arcade, with a conjectural countenance as to his reply.

"Will your own feeling for the genius of the place allow you?"

"I am not a mediævalist: I am an eclectic."

"You don't dislike your own house on that account."

"I did at first—I don't so much now. . . . I should love it, and adore every stone, and think feudalism the only true romance of life, if——"

"What?"

"If I were a De Stancy, and the castle the long home of my forefathers."

Somerset was a little surprised at the avowal: the minister's words on the effects of her new environment recurred to his mind. "Miss De Stancy doesn't think so," he said. "She cares nothing about those things."

Paula now turned to him: hitherto her remarks had been sparingly spoken, her eyes being directed elsewhere: "Yes, that is very strange, is it not?" she said. "But it is owing to the joyous freshness of her nature, which precludes her from dwelling on the past—indeed, the past is no more to her than it is to a sparrow or robin. She is scarcely an instance of the wearing out of old families, for a younger mental constitution than hers I never knew."

"Unless that very simplicity represents the second childhood of her line, rather than her own exclusive character."

Paula shook her head. "In spite of the Greek court, she is more Greek than I."

"You represent science rather than art, perhaps."

"How?" she asked quickly, glancing from under her hat.

"I mean," he answered quietly, "that you represent the march of mind—the steamship, and the railway, and the thoughts that shake mankind."

She weighed his words, and said slowly: "Ah, yes: you allude to my father. My father was a great man; but I am more and more forgetting his greatness: that kind of greatness is what a woman can never truly enter into. I am less and less his daughter every day that goes by."

She walked away a few steps to rejoin the excellent Mrs. Goodman, who, as Somerset still perceived, was waiting for Paula at the discreetest of distances in the shadows at the further end of the building. Surely Paula's voice had faltered, and she had turned to hide a tear; were he sure of that, the ambiguous manner, which he could not unriddle, would have no cold-hearted meaning in it, but would be only an external peculiarity of her nature.

She came back again. "Did you know that my father made half the railways in Europe, including that one over there?" she said, waving her little gloved hand in the direction whence low rumbles were occasionally heard during the day.

"Yes."

"How did you know?"

"Miss De Stancy told me a little; and I then found his name and doings were quite familiar to me."

Curiously enough, or perhaps naturally, since it was a main line of railway, with his words there came through the broken windows the murmur of a train in the distance, sounding clearer and more clear. It was nothing to listen to, yet they both listened; till the increasing noise suddenly broke off into dead silence.

"It has gone into the tunnel," said Paula. "Have you seen the tunnel my father made? the curves are said to be a triumph of science. There is nothing else like it in this part of England."

"There is not: I have heard so. But I have not seen it."

"Do you think it a thing more to be proud of that one's father should have made a great tunnel and railway like that, than that one's remote ancestor should have built a great castle like this?"

What could Somerset say? It would have required a casuist to decide whether his answer should depend upon his conviction, or upon the family ties of such a questioner. His own family had been rather of the high old-fashioned sort, he himself was rather an artist than a man of science; and had his interrogator been a De Stancy, there is not much doubt about the answer that would have risen spontaneously to his lips. "From a modern point of view, railways are no doubt, things more to be proud of than castles," he said; "though perhaps I myself, from mere association, should decide in favour of the ancestor who built the castle." The serious anxiety that Somerset threw into his observation, as if nothing but honest truth were available, was more than the circumstance required. But she herself was in such a thoughtful mood that mere politeness without conviction would, after all, hardly have met the case. "To design great engineering works," he added musingly, and without the least eye to the disparagement of her parent, "requires no doubt a leading mind. But to execute them requires, of course, only a following mind."

His reply did not altogether please her; and there was a distinct reproach conveyed by her slight movement towards Mrs. Goodman. He saw it, and was grieved that he should have spoken so. "I am going to walk over and inspect that famous tunnel of your father's," he added gently. "It will be a pleasant study for this afternoon."

She went away. "I am no man of the world," he thought. "I ought to have praised that father of hers straight off. I shall not win her respect; much less her love!"

CHAPTER XII

SOMERSET did not forget what he had planned, and when lunch was over he walked away through the trees. The tunnel was more difficult of discovery than he had anticipated, and it was only after considerable winding among green lanes, whose deep ruts were like Cañons of Colorado in miniature, that he reached the slope in the distant upland where the tunnel began. A road stretched over its crest, and thence along one side of the railway-cutting.

He there unexpectedly saw standing Miss Power's carriage; and on drawing nearer he found it to contain Paula herself, Miss De Stancy, and Mrs. Goodman.

"How singular!" exclaimed Miss De Stancy gaily.

"It is most natural," said Paula, instantly. "In the morning two people discuss a feature in the landscape, and in the afternoon each has a desire to see it from what the other has said of it. Therefore they accidentally meet."

Now Paula had distinctly heard Somerset declare that he was going to walk there; how then could she say this so coolly? It was with a pang at his heart that he returned to his old thought of her being possibly a finished coquette and dissembler. Whatever she might be, she was not a creature starched very stiffly by Puritanism.

Somerset looked down on the mouth of the tunnel. The absurdity of the popular commonplace that science, steam, and travel must always be unromantic and hideous, was proved on the spot. On either slope of the deep cutting, green with long grass, grew drooping young trees of ash, beech, and other flexible varieties, their foliage almost concealing the actual railway which ran along the bottom, its thin steel rails gleaming like silver threads in the depths. The vertical front of the tunnel, faced with brick that had once been red, was now weather-stained, lichened, and mossed over in harmonious hues of rusty-browns, pearly greys, and neutral greens, at the

very base appearing a little blue-black spot like a mouse-hole—
the tunnel's mouth.

The carriage was drawn up quite close to the wood railing,
and Paula was looking down at the same time with him; but he
made no remark to her.

Mrs. Goodman broke the silence by saying, "If it were not a
railway we should call it a lovely dell."

Somerset agreed with her, adding that it was so charming
that he felt inclined to go down.

"If you do, perhaps Miss Power will order you up again, as
a trespasser," said Charlotte De Stancy. "You are one of the
largest shareholders in the railway, are you not, Paula?"

Miss Power did not reply.

"I suppose as the road is partly yours you might walk all the
way to London along the rails, if you wished, might you not,
dear?" Charlotte continued.

Paula smiled, and said, "No, of course not."

Somerset, feeling himself superfluous, raised his hat to his
companions as if he meant not to see them again for a while,
and began to descend by some steps cut in the earth, when
Miss De Stancy asked Mrs. Goodman to accompany her to a
barrow over the top of the tunnel; and they left the carriage,
Paula remaining alone.

Down Somerset plunged through the long grass, bushes,
late summer flowers, moths, and caterpillars, vexed with
himself that he had come there, since Paula was so inscrutable,
and humming the notes of some song he did not know. The
tunnel that had seemed so small from the surface was a vast
archway when he reached its mouth, which emitted, as a
contrast to the sultry heat on the slopes of the cutting, a cool
breeze, that had travelled a mile underground from the other
end. Far away in the darkness of this silent subterranean
corridor he could see that other end as a mere speck of light.

When he had conscientiously admired the construction of
the massive archivault, and the majesty of its nude ungarnished
walls, he looked up the slope at the carriage; it was so small to
the eye that it might have been made for a performance by
canaries; Paula's face being still smaller, as she leaned back in
her seat, idly looking down at him. There seemed something

roguish in her attitude of criticism, and to be no longer the subject of her contemplation he entered the tunnel out of her sight.

In the middle of the speck of light before him appeared a speck of black; and then a shrill whistle, dulled by millions of tons of earth, reached his ears from thence. It was what he had been on his guard against all the time,—a passing train; and instead of taking the trouble to come out of the tunnel he stepped into a recess, till the train had rattled past, and vanished onward round a curve.

Somerset still remained where he had placed himself, mentally balancing science against art, the grandeur of this fine piece of construction against that of the castle, and thinking whether Paula's father had not, after all, the best of it, when all at once he saw Paula's form confronting him at the entrance of the tunnel. He instantly went forward into the light where she was; to his surprise she was as pale as a lily.

"Oh, Mr. Somerset!" she exclaimed, impulsively. "You ought not to frighten me so—indeed you ought not! The train came out almost as soon as you had gone in, and as you did not return—an accident was possible!"

Somerset at once perceived that he had been to blame in not thinking of this.

"Please do forgive my thoughtlessness in not reflecting how it would strike you!" he pleaded. "I—I see I have alarmed you."

Her alarm was, indeed, much greater than he had at first thought: she trembled so much that she was obliged to sit down, at which he went up to her full of solicitousness.

"You ought not to have done it!" she said. "I naturally thought—any person would——"

Somerset, perhaps wisely, said nothing at this outburst; the cause of her vexation was, plainly enough, his perception of her discomposure. He stood looking in another direction, till in a few moments she had risen to her feet again, quite calm.

"It would have been dreadful," she said with faint gaiety, as the colour returned to her face; "if I had lost my architect, and been obliged to engage Mr. Havill without an alternative."

"I was really in no danger; but of course I ought to have considered," he said.

"I forgive you," she returned good-naturedly. "I knew there was no *great* danger to a person exercising ordinary discretion; but artists and thinkers like you are indiscreet for a moment sometimes. I am now going up again. What do you think of the tunnel?"

They were crossing the railway to ascend by the opposite path, Somerset keeping his eye on the interior of the tunnel for safety, when suddenly there arose a noise and shriek from the contrary direction behind the trees. Both knew in a moment what it meant, and each seized the other as they rushed off the permanent way. The ideas of both had been so centred on the tunnel as the source of danger, that the probability of a train from the opposite quarter had been forgotten. It rushed past them, causing Paula's dress, hair, and ribbons to flutter violently, and blowing up the fallen leaves in a shower over their shoulders.

Neither spoke, and they went up several steps, holding each other by the hand, till, becoming conscious of the fact, she withdrew hers; whereupon Somerset stopped and looked earnestly at her; but her eyes were averted towards the tunnel wall.

"What an escape!" he said.

"We were not so very near, I think, were we?" she asked quickly. "If we were I think you were—very good to take my hand."

They reached the top at last, and the new level and open air seemed to give her a new mind. "I don't see the carriage anywhere," she said, in the common tones of civilisation.

He thought it had gone over the crest of the hill; he would accompany her till they reached it.

"No—please—I would rather not—I can find it very well." Before he could say more she had inclined her head and smiled and was on her way alone.

The tunnel-cutting appeared a dreary gulf enough now to the young man, as he stood leaning over the rails above it, beating the herbage with his stick. For some minutes he could not criticise or weigh her conduct; the warmth of her presence still encircled him. He recalled her face as it had looked out at him from under the white silk puffing of her black hat, and the speaking power of her eyes at the moment of danger. The breadth of that clear-complexioned forehead—almost concealed by the masses of brown hair bundled up around it—signified that if her disposition were oblique and insincere enough for trifling, coquetting, or in any way making a fool of him, she had the intellect to do it cruelly well.

But it was ungenerous to ruminate so suspiciously. A girl not an actress by profession could hardly turn pale artificially as she had done, though perhaps mere fright meant nothing, and would have arisen in her just as readily had he been one of the labourers on her estate. Upon the whole it was a perplexity.

The reflection that such feeling as she had exhibited could have no tender meaning returned upon him with masterful force when he thought of her wealth and the social position into which she had drifted. Somerset, being of a solitary and studious nature, was not quite competent to estimate precisely the disqualifying effect, if any, of her non-conformity, her newness of blood, and other things, among the old county families established round her; but the toughest prejudices, he thought, were not likely to be long invulnerable to such cheerful beauty and brightness of intellect as Paula's. When she emerged, as she was plainly about to do, from the comparative seclusion in which she had been living since her father's death, she would inevitably win her way among her neighbours. She would become the local topic. Fortune-hunters would learn of her existence and draw near in shoals. What chance would there then be for him?

The points in his favour were indeed few, but they were just enough to keep a tantalising hope alive. Modestly leaving out of count his personal and intellectual qualifications, he thought of his family. It was an old stock enough, though not a rich one. His great-uncle had been the well-known Vice-admiral Sir Armstrong Somerset, who served his country well in the Baltic, the Indies, China, and the Caribbean Sea. His grandfather had been a notable metaphysician. His father, the Royal Academician, was popular. But perhaps this was not the sort of reasoning likely to occupy the mind of a young woman; the personal aspect of the situation was in such circumstances of far more import. He had come as a wandering stranger—that possibly lent some interest to him in her eyes. He was installed in an office which would necessitate free communion with her for some time to come; that was another advantage, and would be a still greater one if she showed, as Paula seemed disposed to do, such artistic sympathy with his work as to follow up with interest the details of its progress.

The carriage did not reappear, and he went on towards Markton, disinclined to return again that day to the studio which had been prepared for him at the castle. He heard feet brushing the grass behind him, and, looking round, saw the Baptist minister.

"I have just come from the village," said Mr. Woodwell, who looked worn and weary, his boots being covered with dust, "and I have learnt that which confirms my fears for her."

"For Miss Power?"

"Most assuredly."

"What danger is there?" said Somerset.

"The temptations of her position have become too much for her! She is going out of mourning next week, and will give a large dinner-party on the occasion; for though the invitations are partly in the name of her relative Mrs. Goodman, they must come from her. The guests are to include people of old cavalier families who would have treated her grandfather, sir, and even her father, with scorn for their religion and connections; also the parson and curate—yes, actually people who believe in the Apostolic Succession; and, what's more, they're coming. My opinion is, that it has all arisen from her friendship with Miss De Stancy."

"Well," cried Somerset, warmly, "this only shows liberality of feeling on both sides! I suppose she has invited you as well?"

"She has not invited me! . . . Mr. Somerset, not withstanding your erroneous opinions on important matters, I speak to you as a friend, and I tell you that she has never in her secret heart forgiven that sermon of mine, in which I likened her to the church at Laodicea. I admit the words were harsh, but I was doing my duty, and if the case arose to-morrow I would do it again. Her displeasure is a deep grief to me; but I serve

One greater than she. . . . You, of course, are invited to this dinner?"

"I have heard nothing of it," murmured the young man.

Their paths diverged; and when Somerset reached the King's Arms Hotel he was informed that somebody was waiting to see him.

"Man or woman?" he asked.

The landlady, who always like to reply in person to Somerset's inquiries, apparently thinking him, by virtue of his drawing implements and liberality of payment, a possible lord of Burleigh, came forward and said it was certainly not a woman, but whether man or boy she could not say. "His name is Mr. Dare," she added.

"Oh—that youth," he said.

Somerset went upstairs, along the passage, down two steps, round the angle, and so on to the room reserved for him in this rambling edifice of stage-coach memories, where he found Dare waiting. Dare came forward, pulling out the cutting of an advertisement.

"Mr. Somerset, this is yours, I believe, from the *Architectural World*?"

Somerset said that he had inserted it.

"I think I should suit your purpose as assistant very well."

"Are you an architect's draughtsman?"

"Not specially. I have some knowledge of the same, and want to increase it."

"I thought you were a photographer."

"Also of photography," said Dare, with a bow. "Though but an amateur in that art, I can challenge comparison with Regent Street or Broadway."

Somerset looked upon his table. Two letters only, addressed in initials, were lying there as answers to his advertisement. He asked Dare to wait, and looked them over. Neither was satisfactory. On this account he overcame his slight feeling against Mr. Dare, and put a question to test that gentleman's capacities. "How would you measure the front of a building, including windows, doors, mouldings, and every other feature, for a ground plan, so as to combine the greatest accuracy with the greatest despatch?"

"In running dimensions," said Dare.

As this was the particular kind of work he wanted done, Somerset thought the answer promising. Coming to terms with Dare, he requested the would-be student of architecture to wait at the castle the next day, and dismissed him.

A quarter of an hour later, when Dare was taking a walk in the country, he drew from his pocket eight other letters addressed to Somerset in initials, which, to judge by their style and stationery, were from men far superior to those two whose communications alone Somerset had seen. Dare looked them over for a few seconds as he strolled on, then tore them into minute fragments, and, burying them under the leaves in the ditch, went on his way again.

CHAPTER XIII

THOUGH exhibiting indifference, Somerset had felt a pang of
disappointment when he heard the news of Paula's approaching dinner-party. It seemed a little unkind of her to pass him
over, seeing how much they were thrown together just now.
That dinner meant more than it sounded. Notwithstanding the
roominess of her castle, she was at present living somewhat
incommodiously, owing partly to the stagnation caused by her
recent bereavement, and partly to the necessity for overhauling
the De Stancy lumber piled in those vast and gloomy chambers
before they could be made tolerable to nineteenth-century
fastidiousness.

To give dinners on any large scale before Somerset had at
least set a few of these rooms in order for her, showed, to his
thinking, an overpowering desire for society.

During the week he saw less of her than usual, her time
being to all appearance much taken up with driving out to
make calls on her neighbours and receiving return visits. All
this he observed from the windows of his studio overlooking
the castle ward, in which room he now spent a great deal of his
time, bending over drawing-boards and instructing Dare, who
worked as well as could be expected of a youth of such varied
attainments.

Nearer came the Wednesday of the party, and no hint of
that event reached Somerset, but such as had been communicated by the Baptist minister. At last, on the very afternoon,
an invitation was handed into his studio—not a kind note in
Paula's handwriting, but a formal printed card in the joint
names of Mrs. Goodman and Miss Power. It reached him just
four hours before the dinner-time. He was plainly to be used
as a stop-gap at the last moment because somebody could not
come.

Having previously arranged to pass a quiet evening in his
rooms at the King's Arms, in reading up chronicles of the

castle from the county history, with the view of gathering some
ideas as to the distribution of rooms therein before the
demolition of a portion of the structure, he decided off-hand
that Paula's dinner was not of sufficient importance to him as
a professional man and student of art to justify a waste of the
evening by going. He accordingly declined Mrs. Goodman's
and Miss Power's invitation; and at five o'clock left the castle
and walked across the fields to the little town.

He dined early, and, clearing away heaviness with a cup of
coffee, applied himself to that volume of the county history
which contained the record of Stancy Castle.

Here he read that "when this picturesque and ancient
structure was founded, or by whom, is extremely uncertain.
But that a castle stood on the site in very early times appears
from many old books of charters. In its prime it was such a
masterpiece of fortification as to be the wonder of the world,
and it was thought, before the invention of gunpowder, that it
never could be taken by any force less than divine."

He read on to the times when it first passed into the hands
of "De Stancy, Chivaler," and received the family name, and
so on from De Stancy to De Stancy till he was lost in the
reflection whether Paula would or would not have thought
more highly of him if he had accepted the invitation to dinner.
Applying himself again to the tome, he learnt that in the year
1504 Stephen the carpenter was 'paid eleven pence for neces-
sarye repayrs," and William the mastermason eight shillings
"for whyt lyming of the kitchen, and the lyme to do it with,"
including "a new rope for the fyer bell;" also the sundry
changes for "vij crockes, xiij lytyll pans, a pare of pot hookes,
a fyer pane, a lanterne, a chafynge dyshe, and xij candyll
stychs."

Bang went eight strokes of the clock: it was the dinner-hour.

"There, now I can't go, anyhow!" he said bitterly, jumping
up, and picturing her receiving her company. How would she
look; what would she wear? Profoundly indifferent to the early
history of the noble fabric, he felt a violent reaction towards
modernism, eclecticism, new aristocracies, everything, in
short, that Paula represented. He even gave himself up to
consider the Greek court that she had wished for and passed

the remainder of the evening in making a perspective view of the same.

The next morning he awoke early, and, resolving to be at work betimes, started promptly. It was a fine calm hour of day; the grass slopes were silvery with excess of dew; and the blue mists hung in the depths of each tree for want of wind to blow them out. Somerset entered the drive on foot, and when near the castle he observed in the gravel the wheel-marks of the carriages that had conveyed the guests thither the night before. There seemed to have been a large number, for the road where newly repaired was quite cut up. Before going indoors he was tempted to walk round to the wing in which Paula slept.

Rooks were cawing, sparrows were chattering there; but the blind of her window was as closely drawn as if it were midnight. Probably she was sound asleep, dreaming of the compliments which had been paid her by her guests, and of the future triumphant pleasures that would follow in their train. Reaching the outer stone stairs leading to the great hall, he found them shadowed by an awning brilliantly striped with red and blue, within which rows of flowering plants in pots bordered the pathway. She could not have made more preparation had the gathering been a ball. He passed along the gallery in which his studio was situated, entered the room, and seized a drawing-board to put into correct drawing the sketch for the Greek court that he had struck out the night before, thereby abandoning his art principles to please the whim of a girl. Dare had not yet arrived, and after a time Somerset threw down his pencil and leant back.

His eye fell upon something that moved. It was white, and lay in the folding-chair on the opposite side of the room. On near approach he found it to be a fragment of swan's-down, fanned into motion by his own movements, and partially squeezed into the chink of the chair as though by some person sitting on it.

None but a woman would have worn or brought that swan's-down into his studio, and it made him reflect on the possible one. Nothing interrupted his conjectures till ten o'clock, when Dare came. Then one of the servants tapped at the door to know if Mr. Somerset had arrived. Somerset asked if Miss Power wished to see him, and was informed that she had only wished to know if he had come. Somerset sent a return message that he had a design on the board which he should soon be glad to submit to her, and the messenger departed.

"Fine doings here last night, sir," said Dare, as he dusted his T-square.

"Oh, indeed!"

"A dinner-party, I hear; eighteen guests."

"Oh," said Somerset.

"The young lady was magnificent—sapphires and opals— she carried as much as a thousand pounds upon her head and shoulders during that three or four hours. Of course they call her charming; *Compuesta no hay muger fea*, as they say at Madrid."

"I don't doubt it for a moment," said Somerset with reserve.

Dare said no more, and presently the door opened, and there stood Paula.

Somerset nodded to Dare to withdraw into an adjoining room, and offered her a chair.

"You wish to show me the design you have prepared?" she asked, without taking the seat.

"Yes; I have come round to your opinion. I have made a plan for the Greek court you were anxious to build." And he elevated the drawing-board against the wall.

She regarded it attentively for some moments, her finger resting lightly against her chin, and said, "I have given up the idea of a Greek court."

He showed his astonishment, and was almost disappointed. He had been grinding up Greek architecture entirely on her account; had wrenched his mind round to this strange arrangement, all for nothing.

"Yes," she continued; "on reconsideration I perceive the want of harmony that would result from inserting such a piece of marble-work in a mediæval fortress; so in future we will limit ourselves strictly to synchronism of style—that is to say, make good the Norman work by Norman, the Perpendicular by Perpendicular, and so on. I have informed Mr. Havill of the same thing."

Somerset pulled the Greek drawing off the board, and tore it in two pieces.

She involuntarily turned to look in his face, but stopped before she had quite lifted her eyes high enough. "Why did you do that?" she asked with suave sauciness.

"It is of no further use," said Somerset, tearing the drawing in the other direction, and throwing the pieces into the fireplace. "You have been reading up orders and styles to some purpose, I perceive." He regarded her with a faint smile.

"I have had a few books down from town. It is desirable to know a little about the architecture of one's own house."

She remained looking at the torn drawing, when Somerset, observing on the table the particle of swan's-down he had found in the chair, gently blew it so that it skimmed across the table under her eyes.

"It looks as if it came off a lady's dress," he said idly.

"Off a lady's fan," she replied.

"Oh, off a fan?"

"Yes; off mine."

At her reply Somerset stretched out his hand for the swan's-down, and put it carefully in his pocket-book; whereupon Paula, moulding her cherry-red lower lip beneath her upper one in arch self-consciousness at his act, turned away to the window, and after a pause said softly as she looked out, "Why did you not accept our invitation to dinner?"

It was impossible to explain why. He impulsively drew near and confronted her, and said, "I hope you pardon me?"

"I don't know that I can quite do that," answered she with ever so little reproach. "I know why you did not come—you were mortified at not being asked sooner! But it was purely by an accident that you received your invitation so late. My aunt sent the others by post, but as yours was to be delivered by hand it was left on her table, and was overlooked."

Surely he could not doubt her words; those nice friendly accents were the embodiment of truth itself.

"I don't mean to make a serious complaint," she added, in injured tones, showing that she did. "Only we had asked nearly all of them to meet you, as the son of your illustrious father, whom many of my friends know personally; and—they were disappointed."

It was now time for Somerset to be genuinely grieved at what he had done. Paula seemed so good and honourable at that moment that he could have laid down his life for her.

"When I was dressed I came in here to ask you to reconsider your decision," she continued; "or to meet us in the drawing-room if you could not possibly be ready for dinner. But you were gone."

"And you sat down in that chair, didn't you, darling, and remained there a long time musing!" he thought. But that he did not say.

"I am very sorry," he murmured.

"Will you make amends by coming to our garden-party? I ask you the very first."

"I will," replied Somerset. To add that it would give him great pleasure, etc., seemed an absurdly weak way of expressing his feelings, and he said no more.

"It is on the nineteenth. Don't forget the day."

He met her eyes in such a way that, if she were woman, she must have seen the meaning as plainly as words: "Do I look as if I could forget anything you say!"

She must, indeed, have understood much more by this time—the whole of his open secret. But he did not understand her. History has revealed that a supernumerary lover or two is rarely considered a disadvantage by a woman, from queen to cottage girl: and the thought made him pause.

CHAPTER XIV

WHEN she was gone he went on with the drawing, not calling in Dare, who remained in the room adjoining. Presently a servant came and laid a paper on his table, which Miss Power had sent. It was one of the morning newspapers, and was folded so that his eye fell immediately on a letter headed "Restoration or Demolition."

The letter was professedly written by a dispassionate person solely in the interests of art. It drew attention to the circumstance that the ancient and interesting castle of the De Stancys had unhappily passed into the hands of an iconoclast by blood, who, without respect for the tradition of the county, or any feeling whatever for history in stone, was about to demolish much, if not all, that was interesting in that ancient pile, and insert in its midst a monstrous travesty of some Greek temple. In the name of all lovers of mediæval art, conjured the simple-minded writer, let something be done to save a building which, injured and battered in the Civil Wars, was now to be made a complete ruin by the freaks of an irresponsible owner.

Her sending him the paper seemed to imply that she required his opinion on the case, and in the afternoon, leaving Dare to measure up a wing according to directions, he went out in the hope of meeting her, having learnt that she had gone to the village. On reaching the church he saw her crossing the churchyard path with her aunt and Miss De Stancy. Somerset entered the enclosure, and as soon as she saw him she came across.

"What is to be done?" she asked.

"You need not be concerned about such a letter as that."

"I am concerned."

"I think it dreadful impertinence," spoke up Charlotte, who had joined them. "Can you think who wrote it, Mr. Somerset?"

Somerset could not.

"Well, what am I do?" repeated Paula.

"Just as you would have done before."

"That's what *I* say," observed Mrs. Goodman emphatically.

"But I have already altered—I have given up the Greek court."

"Oh—you had seen the paper this morning before you looked at my drawing."

"I had," she answered.

Somerset thought it a forcible illustration of her natural reticence that she should have abandoned the design without telling him the reason; but he was glad she had not done it from mere caprice.

She turned to him and said quietly, "I wish *you* would answer that letter."

"It would be ill-advised," said Somerset. "Still if, after consideration, you wish it much, I will. Meanwhile let me impress upon you again the expediency of calling in Mr. Havill—to whom, as your father's architect, expecting this commission, something perhaps is owed—and getting him to furnish an alternative plan to mine, and submitting the choice of designs to some members of the Royal Institute of British Architects. This letter makes it still more advisable than before."

"Very well," said Paula reluctantly.

"Let him have all the particulars you have been good enough to explain to me—so that we start fair in the competition."

She looked negligently on the grass. "I will tell the building-steward to write them out for him," she said.

The party separated and entered the church by different doors. Somerset went to a nook of the building that he had often intended to visit. It was called the Stancy aisle; and in it stood the tombs of that family. Somerset examined them: they were unusually rich and numerous, beginning with cross-legged knights in hauberks of chain-mail, their ladies beside them in wimple and cover-chief, all more or less coated with the green mould and dirt of ages: and continuing with others of later date, in fine alabaster, gilded and coloured, some of them wearing round their necks the Yorkist collar of suns and roses, the livery of Edward the Fourth. In scrutinising the tallest canopy over these he beheld Paula behind it, as if in contemplation of the same objects.

"You came to the church to sketch these monuments, I suppose, Mr. Somerset?" she asked as soon as she saw him.

"No. I came to speak to you about the letter."

She sighed. "Yes: that letter," she said. "I am persecuted! If I had been one of these it would never have been written." She tapped the alabaster effigy of a recumbent lady with her parasol.

"They are interesting, are they not?" he said. "She is beautifully preserved. The gilding is nearly gone, but beyond that she is perfect."

'She is like Charlotte," said Paula. And what was much like another sigh escaped her lips.

Somerset admitted that there was a resemblance, while Paula drew her forefingers across the marble face of the effigy, and at length took out her handkerchief, and began wiping the dust from the hollows of the features. He looked on, wondering what her sigh had meant, but guessing that it had been somehow caused by the sight of these sculptures in connection with the newspaper writer's denunciation of her as an irresponsible outsider.

The secret was out when in answer to his question, idly put, if she wished she were like of these, she said, with exceptional vehemence for one of her demeanour:

"I don't wish I was like one of them: I wish I *was* one of them."

"What—you wish you were a De Stancy?"

"Yes. It is very dreadful to be denounced as a barbarian. I want to be romantic and historical."

"Miss De Stancy seems not to value the privilege," he said, looking round at another part of the church where Charlotte was innocently prattling to Mrs. Goodman, quite heedless of the tombs of her forefathers.

"If I were one," she continued, "I should come here when I feel alone in the world as I do to-day; and I would defy people and say, 'You cannot spoil what has been!'"

They walked on till they reached the old black pew attached

to the castle—a vast square enclosure of oak panelling occupying half the aisle, and surmounted with a little balustrade above the framework. Within, the baize lining that had once been green, now faded to the colour of a common in August, was torn, kicked and scraped to rags by the feet and hands of the ploughboys who had appropriated the pew as their own special place of worship since it had ceased to be used by any resident at the castle, because its height afforded convenient shelter for playing at marbles and pricking with pins.

Charlotte and Mrs. Goodman had by this time left the building, and could be seen looking at the headstones outside.

"If you were a De Stancy," said Somerset, who had pondered more deeply upon that new wish of hers than he had seemed to do, "you would be a churchwoman, and sit here."

"And I should have the pew done up," she said readily, as she rested her pretty chin on the top rail and looked at the interior, her cheeks pressed into deep dimples. Her quick reply told him that the idea was no new one with her, and he thought of poor Mr. Woodwell's shrewd prophecy as he perceived that her days as a separatist were numbered.

"Well, why can't you have it done up, and sit here?" he said warily.

Paula shook her head.

"You are not at enmity with Anglicanism, I am sure?"

"I want not to be. I want to be—what——"

"What the De Stancys were, and are," he said insidiously; and her silenced bearing told him that he had hit the nail.

It was a strange idea to get possession of such a nature as hers, and for a minute he felt himself on the side of the minister. So strong was Somerset's feeling of wishing her to show the quality of fidelity to paternal dogma and party that he could not help adding:

"But have you forgotten that other nobility—the nobility of talent and enterprise?"

"No. But I wish I had a well-known line of ancestors."

"You have. Archimedes, Newcomen, Watt, Telford, Stephenson, those are your father's direct ancestors. Have you forgotten them? Have you forgotten your father, and the railways he made over half Europe, and his great energy and skill, and all connected with him, as if he had never lived?"

She did not answer for some time. "No, I have not forgotten it," she said, still looking into the pew. "But I have a *prédilection d'artiste* for ancestors of the other sort, like the De Stancys."

Her hand was resting on the low pew next the high one of the De Stancys. Somerset looked at the hand, or rather at the glove which covered it, then at her averted cheek, then beyond it into the pew, then at her hand again, until by an indescribable consciousness that he was not going too far he laid his own upon it.

"No, no," said Paula quickly, withdrawing her hand. But there were nothing resentful or haughty in her tone—nothing, in short, which makes a man in such circumstances feel that he has done a particularly foolish action.

The flower on her bosom rose and fell somewhat more than usual as she added, "I am going away now—I will leave you here." Without waiting for a reply she adroitly swept back her skirts to free her feet and went out of the church blushing.

Somerset took her hint and did not follow; and when he knew that she had rejoined her friends, and heard the carriage roll away, he made towards the opposite door. Pausing to glance once more at the alabaster effigies before leaving them to their silence and neglect, he beheld Dare bending over them, to all appearance intently occupied.

He must have been in the church some time—certainly during the tender episode between Somerset and Paula, and could not have failed to perceive it. Somerset blushed: it was unpleasant that Dare should have seen the interior of his heart so plainly. He went across and said, "I think I left you to finish the drawing of the north wing, Mr. Dare?"

"Three hours ago, sir," said Dare. "Having finished that, I came to look at the church—fine building—fine monuments—two interesting people looking at them."

"What?"

"I stand corrected. *Pensa molto, parla poco*, as the Italians have it."

"Well, now, Mr. Dare, suppose you get back to the castle?"

"Which history dubs Castle Stancy. . . . Certainly."

"How do you get on with the measuring?"

Dare sighed whimsically. "Badly in the morning, when I have been tempted to indulge overnight, and worse in the afternoon when I have been tempted in the morning!"

Somerset looked at the youth, and said, "I fear I shall have to dispense with your services, Dare, for I think you have been tempted to-day."

"On my honour no. My manner is a little against me, Mr. Somerset. But you need not fear for my ability to do your work. I am a young man wasted, and am thought of slight account; it is the true men who get snubbed, while traitors are allowed to thrive!"

"Hang sentiment, Dare, and off with you!" A little ruffled, Somerset had turned his back upon the interesting speaker, so that he did not observe the sly twist Dare threw into his right eye as he spoke. The latter went off in one direction and Somerset in the other, pursuing his pensive way towards Markton with thoughts not difficult to divine.

From one point in her nature he went to another, till he again recurred to her romantic interest in the De Stancy family. To wish she was one of them: how very inconsistent of her. That she really did wish it was unquestionable; for the feeling had been so strong as to break through her natural silentness.

CHAPTER XV

IT was the day of the garden-party. The weather was too cloudy to be called perfect, but was as sultry as the most thinly clad young lady could desire. Great trouble had been taken by Paula to bring the lawn to a fit condition after the neglect of recent years, and Somerset had suggested the design for the tents. As he approached the precincts of the castle he discerned a flag of newest fabric floating over the keep, and soon his phaeton fell in with the stream of carriages that were passing over the bridge into the outer ward.

Mrs. Goodman and Paula were receiving the people in the drawing-room. Somerset came forward in his turn; but as he was immediately followed by others there was not much opportunity, even had she felt the wish, for any special mark of feeling in the younger lady's greeting of him.

He went on through a canvas passage, lined on each side with flowering plants, till he reached the tents; thence, after nodding to one or two guests slightly known to him, he proceeded to the grounds with a sense of being rather lonely. Few visitors had as yet got so far in, and as he walked up and down a shady alley his mind dwelt upon the new aspect under which Paula had greeted his eyes that afternoon. Her black-and-white costume had finally disappeared, and in its place she had adopted a picturesque dress of ivory white, with satin enrichments of the same hue; while upon her bosom she wore a blue flower. Her days of infestivity were plainly ended, and her days of gladness were to begin.

His reverie was interrupted by the sound of his name, and looking round he beheld Havill, who appeared to be as much alone as himself.

Somerset already knew that Havill had been appointed to compete with him, according to his recommendation. In measuring a dark corner a day or two before, he had stumbled upon Havill engaged in the same pursuit with a view to the rival design. Afterwards he had seen him receiving Paula's instructions precisely as he had done himself. It was as he had wished, for fairness' sake; and yet he felt a regret for he was less Paula's own architect now.

"Well, Mr. Somerset," said Havill, "since we first met an unexpected rivalry has arisen between us! But I dare say we shall survive the contest, as it is not one arising out of love. Ha-ha-ha!" He spoke in a level voice of fierce pleasantry, and uncovered his regular white teeth.

Somerset supposed him to allude to the castle competition?

"Yes," said Havill. "Her proposed undertaking brought out some adverse criticism till it was known that she intended to have more than one architectural opinion. An excellent stroke of hers to disarm criticism. You saw the second letter in the morning papers?"

"No," said the other.

"The writer states that he has discovered that the competent advice of two architects is to be taken, and withdraws his accusations."

Somerset said nothing for a minute. "Have you been supplied with the necessary data for your drawings?" he asked, showing by the question the track his thoughts had taken.

Havill said that he had. "But possibly not so completely as you have," he added, again smiling fiercely. Somerset did not quite like the insinuation, and the two speakers parted, the younger going towards the musicians, who had now begun to fill the air with their strains from the embowered enclosure of a drooping ash. When he got back to the marquees they were quite crowded, and the guests began to pour out upon the grass, the toilets of the ladies presenting a brilliant spectacle—here being coloured dressed with white devices, there, white dresses with coloured devices, and yonder transparent dresses with no device at all. A lavender haze hung in the air, the trees were as still as those of a submarine forest; while the sun, in colour like a brass plaque, had a hairy outline in the livid sky.

After watching a while some young people who were so madly devoted to lawn-tennis that they had set about it like day-labourers at the moment of their arrival, he turned and saw approaching a graceful figure in cream-coloured hues, whose gloves lost themselves beneath her lace ruffles, even when she lifted her hands to make firm the blue flower at her breast, and whose hair hung under her hat in great knots so well compacted that the sun gilded the convexity of each knot like a ball.

"You seem to be alone," said Paula, who had at last escaped from the duty of receiving guests.

"I don't know many people."

"Yes: I thought of that while I was in the drawing-room. But I could not get out before. I am now no longer a responsible being: Mrs. Goodman is mistress for the remainder of the day. Will you be introduced to anybody? Whom would you like to know?"

"I am not particuarly unhappy in my solitude."

"But you must be made to know a few."

"Very well—I submit readily."

She looked away from him, and while he was observing upon her cheek the moving shadow of leaves cast by the declining sun, she said, "Oh, there is my aunt," and beckoned with her parasol to that lady, who approached in the comparatively youthful guise of a grey silk dress that whistled at every touch.

Paula left them together, and Mrs. Goodman then made him acquainted with a few of the best people, describing what they were in a whisper before they came up, among them being the Radical member for Markton who had succeeded to the seat rendered vacant by the death of Paula's father. While talking to this gentleman on the proposed enlargement of the castle, Somerset raised his eyes and hand towards the walls, the better to point out his meaning; in so doing he saw a face in the square of darkness formed by one of the open windows, the effect being that of a high-light portrait by Vandyck or Rembrandt.

It was his assistant Dare, leaning on the window-sill of the studio, as he smoked his cigarette and surveyed the gay groups promenading beneath.

After holding a chattering conversation with some ladies from a neighbouring country seat who had known his father in bygone years, and handing them ices and strawberries till they were satisfied, he found an opportunity of leaving the grounds, wishing to learn what progress Dare had made in the survey of the castle.

Dare was still in the studio when he entered. Somerset informed the youth that there was no necessity for his working later that day, unless to please himself, and proceeded to inspect Dare's achievements thus far. To his vexation Dare had not plotted three dimensions during the previous two days. This was not the first time that Dare, either from incompetence or indolence, had shown his inutility as a house-surveyor and draughtsman.

"Mr. Dare," said Somerset, "I fear you don't suit me well enough to make it necessary that you should stay after this week."

Dare removed the cigarette from his lips and bowed. "If I don't suit, the sooner I go the better; why wait the week?" he said.

"Well, that's as you like."

Somerset drew the inkstand towards him, wrote out a cheque for Dare's services, and handed it across the table.

"I'll not trouble you to-morrow," said Dare, seeing that the payment included the week in advance.

"Very well," replied Somerset. "Please lock the door when you leave." Shaking hands with Dare and wishing him well, he left the room and descended to the lawn below.

There he contrived to get near Miss Power again, and inquired of her for Miss De Stancy.

"Oh! did you not know?" said Paula; "her father is unwell, and she preferred staying with him this afternoon."

"I hoped he might have been here."

"Oh no; he never comes out of his house to any party of this sort; it excites him, and he must not be excited."

"Poor Sir William!" murmured Somerset.

"No," said Paula. "he is grand and historical."

"That is hardly an orthodox notion for a Puritan," said Somerset mischievously.

"I am not a Puritan," insisted Paula.

The day turned to dusk, and the guests began going in relays to the dining-hall. When Somerset had taken in two or three ladies to whom he had been presented, and attended to their wants, which occupied him three quarters of an hour, he returned again to the large tent, with a view to finding Paula and taking his leave. It was now brilliantly lighted up, and the musicians, who during daylight had been invisible behind the ash-tree, were ensconced at one end with their harps and violins. It reminded him that there was to be dancing. The tent had in the mean time half filled with a new set of young people who had come expressly for that pastime. Behind the girls gathered numbers of newly arrived young men with low shoulders and diminutive moustaches, who were evidently prepared for once to sacrifice themselves as partners.

Somerset felt something of a thrill at the sight. He was an infrequent dancer, and particularly unprepared for dancing at present; but to dance once with Paula Power he would give a year of his life. He looked round; but she was nowhere to be seen. The first set began; old and middle-aged people gathered from the different rooms to look on at the gyrations of their children, but Paula did not appear. When another dance or two had progressed, and an increase in the average age of the dancers was making itself perceptible, especially on the masculine side, Somerset was aroused by a whisper at his elbow:

"You dance, I think? Miss Deverell is disengaged. She has not been asked once this evening." The speaker was Paula.

Somerset looked at Miss Deverell—a sallow lady with black twinkling eyes, yellow costume and gay laugh, who had been there all the afternoon—and said something about having thought of going home.

"Is that because I asked you to dance?" she murmured. "There—she is appropriated." A young gentleman had at that moment approached the uninviting Miss Deverell, claimed her hand and led her off.

"That's right," said Somerset. "I ought to leave room for younger men."

"You need not say so. That bald-headed gentleman is forty-five. He does not think of younger men."

"Have *you* a dance to spare for me?"

Her face grew stealthily redder in the candle-light. "Oh—I have no engagement at all—I have refused. I hardly feel at liberty to dance; it would be as well to leave that to my visitors."

"Why?"

"My father, though he allowed me to be taught, never liked the idea of my dancing."

"Did he make you promise anything on the point?"

"He said he was not in favour of such amusements—no more."

"I think you are not bound by that, on an informal occasion like the present."

She was silent.

"You will just once?" said he.

Another silence. "If you like," she venturesomely answered at last.

Somerset closed the hand which was hanging by his side, and somehow hers was in it. The dance was nearly formed, and he led her forward. Several persons looked at them significantly, but he did not notice it then, and plunged into the maze.

Never had Mr. Somerset passed through such an experience before. Had he not felt her actual weight and warmth, he might have fancied the whole episode a figment of the imagination. It seemed as if those musicians had thrown a double sweetness into their notes on seeing the mistress of the castle in the dance, that a perfumed southern atmosphere had begun to pervade the marquee, and that human beings were shaking themselves free of all inconvenient gravitation.

Somerset's feelings burst from his lips. "This is the happiest moment I have ever known," he said. "Do you know why?"

"I think I saw a flash of lightning through the opening of the tent," said Paula, with roguish abruptness.

He did not press for an answer. Within a few minutes a long growl of thunder was heard. It was as if Jove could not refrain from testifying his jealousy of Somerset for taking this covetable woman so presumptuously in his arms.

The dance was over, and he had retired with Paula to the back of the tent, when another faint flash of lightning was visible through an opening. She lifted the canvas, and looked out, Somerset looking out behind her. Another dance was begun, and, being on this account left out of notice, Somerset did not hasten to leave Paula's side.

"I think they begin to feel the heat," she said.

"A little ventilation would do no harm." He flung back the tent door where he stood, and the light shone out upon the grass.

"I must go to the drawing-room soon," she added. "They will begin to leave shortly."

"It is not late. The thunder-cloud has made it seem dark—see there; a line of pale yellow stretches along the horizon from west to north. That's evening—not gone yet. Shall we go into the fresh air for a minute?"

She seemed to signify assent, and he stepped off the tent-floor upon the ground. She stepped off also.

The air out-of-doors had not cooled, and without definitely choosing a direction they found themselves approaching a little wooden tea-house that stood on the lawn a few yards off. Arrived here, they turned, and regarded the tent they had just left, and listened to the strains that came from within it.

"I feel more at ease now," said Paula.

"So do I," said Somerset.

"I mean," she added in an undeceiving tone, "because I saw Mrs. Goodman enter the tent again just as we came out here; so I have no further responsibility."

"I meant something quite different. Try to guess what."

She teasingly demurred, finally breaking the silence by saying, "The rain is come at last," as great drops began to fall upon the ground with a smack, like pellets of clay.

In a moment the storm poured down with sudden violence, and they drew further back into the summer-house. The side of the tent from which they had emerged still remained open, the rain streaming down between their eyes and the lighted interior of the marquee like a tissue of glass threads, the brilliant forms of the dancers passing and repassing behind the watery screen, as if they were people in an enchanted submarine palace.

"How happy they are!" said Paula. "They don't even know that it is raining. I am so glad that my aunt had the tent lined;

otherwise such a downpour would have gone clean through it."

The thunder-storm showed no symptoms of abatement, and the music and dancing went on more merrily than ever.

"We cannot go in," said Somerset. "And we cannot shout for umbrellas. We will stay here till it is over, will we not?"

"Yes," she said, "if you care to. Ah!"

"What is it?"

"Only a big drop came upon my head."

"Let us stand further in."

Her hand was hanging by her side, and Somerset's was close by. He took it, and she did not draw it away. Thus they stood a long while, the rain hissing down upon the grass-plot, and not a soul being visible outside the dancing-tent save themselves.

"May I call you Paula?" asked her.

"Yes, occasionally," she murmured.

"Dear Paula!—may I call you that?"

"Oh no—not yet."

"But you know I love you?" he insisted.

"I can give a shrewd guess," she said slily.

"And shall I love you always?"

"If you wish to."

"And will you love me?"

Paula did not reply.

"Will you, Paula?" he repeated.

"You may love me."

"But don't you love me in return?"

"I love you to love me."

"Won't you say anything more explicit?"

"Not a single word!"

Somerset emitted half a sigh: he wished she had been more demonstrative, yet felt that this passive way of assenting was as much as he could hope for. Had there been anything cold in her passivity he might have felt repressed; but her stillness suggested the stillness of motion imperceptible from its intensity.

"We must go in," said she. "The rain is almost over, and there is no longer any excuse for this."

Somerset bent his lips toward hers.

"No," said the fair Puritan decisively.

"Why not?" he asked.

"Nobody ever has."

"But!——" expostulated Somerset.

"To everything there is a season, and the season for this is not just now," she answered, walking away.

They crossed the wet and glistening lawn, stepped under the tent and parted. She vanished, he did not know whither; and, standing with his gaze fixed on the dancers, the young man waited, till, being in no mood to join them, he went slowly through the artificial passage lined with flowers, and entered the drawing-rooms. Mrs. Goodman was there, bidding good-night to the early goers, and Paula was just behind her, apparently in her usual mood. His parting with her was quite formal, but that he did not mind, for her colour rose decidedly higher as he approached, and the light in her eyes was like the ray of a diamond.

When he reached the door he found that his brougham from the King's Arms, which had been waiting more than an hour, could not be heard of. That vagrancy of spirit which love induces would not permit him to wait; and, leaving word that the man was to follow him when he returned, he went past the glare of carriage-lamps ranked in the ward, and under the outer arch. The night was now clear and beautiful, and he strolled along his way full of mysterious elation till the vehicle overtook him, and he got in.

Up to this point Somerset's progress in his suit had been, though incomplete, so uninterrupted, that he almost feared the good chance he enjoyed. How should it be in a mortal of his calibre to command success with such a sweet woman for long? He might, indeed, turn out to be one of the singular exceptions which are said to prove rules; but when Fortune means to men most good, observes the bard, she looks upon them with a threatening eye. Somerset would even have been content that a little disapproval of his course should have occurred in some quarter, so as to make his wooing more like ordinary life. But Paula was not clearly won, and that was drawback sufficient. In these phenomenal agonies and questionable delights he passed the journey to Markton.

BOOK THE SECOND

DARE AND HAVILL

CHAPTER I

YOUNG Dare sat thoughtfully at the window of the studio in which Somerset had left him, till the gay scene beneath became embrowned by the twilight, and the brilliant red stripes of the marquees, the bright sunshades, the many-tinted costumes of the ladies, were indistinguishable from the blacks and greys of the masculine contingent moving among them. He had occasionally glanced away from the outward prospect to study a small old volume that lay before him on the drawing-board. Near scrutiny revealed the book to bear the title "Moivre's Doctrine of Chances."

The evening had been so still that Dare had heard conversations from below with a clearness unsuspected by the speakers themselves; and among the dialogues which thus reached his ears was that between Somerset and Havill on their professional rivalry. When they parted, and Somerset had mingled with the throng, Havill went to a seat at a distance. Afterwards he rose, and walked away; but on the bench he had quitted there remained a small object resembling a book or leather case.

Dare put away the drawing-board and plotting-scales which he had kept before him during the evening as a reason for his prsence at that post of espial, locked up the door, and went downstairs. Notwithstanding his dismissal by Somerset, he was so serene in countenance and easy in gait as to make it a fair conjecture that professional servitude, however profitable, was no necessity with him. The gloom now rendered it practicable for any unbidden guest to join Paula's assemblage without criticism, and Dare walked boldly out upon the lawn. The crowd on the grass was rapidly diminishing; the tennis-players had relinquished sport; many people had gone in to dinner or supper; and many others, attracted by the cheerful radiance of the candles, were gathering in the large tent that had been lighted up for dancing.

Dare went to the garden-chair on which Havill had been seated, and found the article left behind to be a pocket-book. Whether because it was unclasped and fell open in his hand, or whether for any other reason, he did not hesitate to examine the contents. Among a mass of architects' customary memoranda occurred a draft of the letter abusing Paula as an iconoclast or Vandal by blood, which had appeared in the newspaper: the draft was so interlined and altered as to bear evidence of being the original conception of that ungentlemanly attack.

The lad read the letter, smiled, and strolled about the grounds, only met by an occasional pair of individuals of opposite sex in deep conversation, the state of whose emotions led them to prefer the evening shade to the publicity and glare of the tents and rooms. At last he observed the white waistcoat of the man he sought.

"Mr. Havill, the architect, I believe?" said Dare. "The author of most of the noteworthy buildings in this neighbourhood?"

Havill assented blandly.

"I have long wished for the pleasure of your acquaintance, and now an accident helps me to make it. This pocket-book, I think, is yours?"

Havill clapped his hand to his pocket, examined the book Dare held out to him, and took it with thanks. "I see I am speaking to the artist, archæologist, Gothic photographer—Mr. Dare."

"Professor Dare."

"Professor? Pardon me, I should not have guessed it—so young as you are."

"Well, it is merely ornamental; and in truth, I drop the title in England, particularly under present circumstances."

"Ah—they are peculiar, perhaps? Ah, I remember. I have heard that you are assisting a gentleman in preparing a design in opposition to mine—a design——"

"'That he is not competent to prepare himself,' you were perhaps going to add?"

"Not precisely that."

"You could hardly be blamed for such words. However, you are mistaken. I did assist him, to gain a little further insight into the working of architectural plans; but our views on art are antagonistic, and I assist him no more. Mr. Havill, it must be very provoking to a well-established professional man to have a rival sprung at him in a grand undertaking which he had a right to expect as his own."

Professional sympathy is often accepted from those whose condolence on any domestic matter would be considered intrusive. Havill walked up and down beside Dare for a few moments in silence, and at last showed that the words had told, by saying: "Every one may have his opinion. Had I been a stranger to the Power family, the case would have been different; but having been specially elected by the lady's father as a competent adviser in such matters, and then to be degraded to the position of a mere competitor, it wounds me to the quick——"

"Both in purse and in person, like the ill-used hostess of the Garter."

"A lady to whom I have been a staunch friend," continued Havill, not heeding the interruption.

At that moment sounds seemed to come from Dare which bore a remarkable resemblance to the words, "Ho, ho, Havill!" It was hardly credible, and yet, could he be mistaken? Havill turned. Dare's eye was twisted comically upward.

"What does that mean?" said Havill coldly, and with some amazement.

"Ho, ho, Havill! 'Staunch friend' is good—especially after 'an iconoclast and Vandal by blood'—'monstrosity in the form of a Greek temple,' and so on, eh!"

"Sir, you have the advantage of me. Perhaps you allude to that anonymous letter?"

"O—ho, Havill!" repeated the boy-man, turning his eyes yet further towards the zenith. "To an outsider such conduct would be natural; but to a friend who finds your pocket-book, and looks into it before returning it, and kindly removes a leaf bearing the draft of a letter which might injure you if dis- covered there, and carefully conceals it in his own pocket—

why, such conduct is unkind!" Dare held up the abstracted leaf.

Havill trembled. "I can explain," he began.

"It is not necessary: we are friends," said Dare assuringly.

Havill looked as if he would like to snatch the leaf away, but altering his mind, he said, grimly: "Well, I take you at your word: we are friends. That letter was concocted before I knew of the competition: it was during my first disgust, when I believe myself entirely supplanted."

"I am not in the least surprised. But if she knew *you* to be the writer!"

"I should be ruined as far as this competition is concerned," said Havill carelessly. "Had I known I was to be invited to compete, I should not have written it, of course. To be supplanted is hard; and thereby hangs a tale."

"Another tale? you astonish me."

"Then you have not heard the scandal, though everybody is talking about it."

"A scandal implies indecorum."

"Well, 'tis indecorous. Her infatuated partiality for him is patent to the eyes of a child; a man she has only known a few weeks, and one who obtained admission to her house in the most irregular manner! Had she a watchful friend beside her, instead of that moonstruck Mrs. Goodman, she would be cautioned against bestowing her favours on the first adventurer who appears at her door. It is a pity, a great pity!"

"Oh, there is love-making in the wind?" said Dare slowly. "That alters the case for me. But it is not proved?"

"It can easily be proved."

"I wish it were, or disproved."

"You have only to come this way to clear up all doubts."

Havill took the lad towards the tent, from which the strains of a waltz now proceeded, and on whose sides flitting shadows told of the progress of the dance. The companions looked in. The rosy silk lining of the marquee, and the numerous coronas of wax lights, formed a canopy to a radiant scene which, to two at least of those who composed it, was an intoxicating one. Paula and Somerset were dancing together.

"That proves nothing," said Dare.

"Look at their rapt faces, and say if it does not," sneered Havill.

Dare objected to a judgement based on looks alone.

"Very well—time will show," said the architect, dropping the tent-curtain. . . "Good God! a girl worth fifty thousand and more a year to throw herself away upon a fellow like that—she ought to be whipped."

"Time must *not* show!" said Dare.

"You speak with emphasis."

"I have reason. I would give something to be sure on this point, one way or the other. Let us wait till the dance is over, and observe them more carefully. *Hörensagen ist halb gelogen*! Hearsay is half lies."

Sheet-lightnings increased in the northern sky, followed by thunder like the indistinct noise of a battle. Havill and Dare retired to the trees. When the dance ended Somerset and his partner emerged from the tent, and slowly moved towards the tea-house. Divining their goal Dare seized Havill's arm; and the two worthies entered the building unseen, by first passing round behind it. They seated themselves in the back part of the interior, where darkness prevailed.

As before related, Paula and Somerset came and stood within the door. When the rain increased they drew themselves further inward, their forms being distinctly outlined to the gaze of those lurking behind by the light from the tent beyond. But the hiss of the falling rain and the lowness of their tones prevented their words from being heard.

"I wish myself out of this!" breathed Havill to Dare as he buttoned his coat over his white waistcoat. "I told you it was true, but you wouldn't believe. I wouldn't she should catch me here eavesdropping for the world!"

"Courage, Man Friday," said his cooler comrade.

Paula and her lover backed yet further, till the hem of her skirt touched Havill's feet. Their attitudes were sufficient to prove their relations to the most obstinate Didymus who should have witnessed them. Tender emotions seemed to pervade the summer-house like an aroma. The calm ecstasy of the condition of at least one of them was not without a coercive effect upon the two invidious spectators, so that they must need have remained passive had they come there to disturb or annoy. The serenity of Paula was even more impressive than the hushed ardour of Somerset: she did not satisfy curiosity as Somerset satisfied it; she piqued it. Poor Somerset had reached a perfectly intelligible depth—one which had a single blissful way out of it, and nine calamitous ones; but Paula remained an enigma all through the scene.

The rain ceased, and the pair moved away. The enchantment worked by their presence vanished, the details of the meeting settled down in the watchers' minds, and their tongues were loosened. Dare, turning to Havill, said, "Thank you; you have done me a timely turn today."

"What! had you hopes that way?" asked Havill, satirically.

"I! The woman that interests my heart has yet to be born," said Dare, with a steely coldness strange in such a juvenile, and yet almost convincing. "But though I have not personal hopes, I have an objection to this courtship. Now I think we may as well fraternise, the situation being what it is?"

"What is the situation?"

"He is in your way as her architect; he is in my way as her lover: we don't want to hurt him, but we wish him clean out of the neighbourhood."

"I'll go as far as that," said Havill.

"I have come here at some trouble to myself, merely to observe: I find I ought to stay to act."

"If you were myself, a married man with people dependent on him, who has had a professional certainty turned to a miserably remote contingency by these events, you might say you ought to act; but what conceivable difference it can make to you who it is the young lady takes to her heart and home, I fail to understand."

"Well, I'll tell you—thus much at least. I want to keep the place vacant for another man."

"The place?"

"The place of husband to Miss Power, and proprietor of that castle and domain."

"That's a scheme with a vengeance. Who is the man?"

"It is my secret at present."

"Certainly." Havill drew a deep breath, and dropped into a tone of depression. "Well, scheme as you will, there will be small advantage to me," he murmured. "The castle commission is as good as gone, and a bill for two hundred pounds falls due next week."

"Cheer up, heart! My position, if you only knew it, has ten times the difficulties of yours, since this disagreeable discovery. Let us consider if we can assist each other. The competition drawings are to be sent in—when?"

"In something over six weeks—a fortnight before she returns from Brighton, for which place she leaves here in a few days."

"Oh, she goes away—that's better. Our lover will be working here at his drawings, and she not present."

"Exactly. Perhaps she is a little ashamed of the intimacy."

"And if your design is considered best by the committee, he will have no further reason for staying, assuming that they are not definitely engaged to marry by that time?"

"I suppose so," murmured Havill discontentedly. "The conditions, as sent to me, state that the designs are to be adjudicated on by three members of the Institute called in for the purpose; so that she may return, and have seemed to show no favour."

"Then it amounts to this: your design *must* be best. It must combine the excellences of your invention with the excellences of his. Meanwhile a coolness should be made to arise between her and him: and as there would be no artistic reason for his presence here after the verdict is pronounced, he would perforce hie back to town. Do you see?"

"I see the ingenuity of the plan, but I also see two insurmountable obstacles to it. The first is, I cannot add the excellences of his design to mine without knowing what those excellences are, which he will of course keep a secret. Second, it will not be easy to promote a coolness between such hot ones as they."

"You make a mistake. It is only he who is so ardent. She is only lukewarm. If we had any spirit, a bargain would be struck between us: you would appropriate his design; I should cause the coolness."

"How could I appropriate his design?"

"By copying it, I suppose."

"Copying it?"

"By going into his studio and looking it over."

Havill turned to Dare, and stared. "By George, you don't stick at trifles, young man! You don't suppose I would go into a man's rooms and steal his inventions like that?"

"I scarcely suppose you would," said Dare indifferently, as he rose.

"And if I were to," said Havill curiously, "how is the coolness to be caused?"

"By the second man."

"Who is to produce him?"

"Her Majesty's Government."

Havill looked meditatively at his companion, and shook his head. "In these idle suppositions we have been assuming conduct which would be quite against my principles as an honest man."

other was the unfortunate creditor with his hat on. Though
Dare's entry surprised them, both parties seemed relieved.
"I have called in passing to congratulate you, Mr. Havill,"
said Dare gaily. "Such a commission as has been entrusted to
you will make you famous."
"How do you do?—I wish it would make me rich," said

CHAPTER II

A FEW days after the party at Stancy Castle Dare was walking
down the High Street of Markton, a cigarette between his lips
and a silver-topped cane in his hand. His eye fell upon a brass
plate on an opposite door, bearing the name of Mr. Havill,
Architect. He crossed over, and rang the office bell.

The clerk who admitted him stated that Mr. Havill was in
his private room, and would be disengaged in a short time.
While Dare waited the clerk affixed to the door a piece of
paper bearing the words "Back at 2," and went away to his
dinner, leaving Dare in the room alone.

Dare looked at the different drawings on the boards about
the room. They all represented one subject, which, though
unfinished as yet, and bearing no inscription, was recognized
by the visitor as the design for the enlargement and restoration
of Stancy Castle. When he had glanced it over Dare sat down.

The doors between the office and private room were double;
but the one towards the office being only ajar Dare could hear
a conversation in progress within. It presently arose to an
altercation, the tenour of which was obvious. Somebody had
come for money.

"Really I can stand it no longer, Mr. Havill—really I will
not!" said the creditor excitedly. "Now this bill overdue
again—what can you expect? Why, I might have negotiated it;
and where would you have been then? Instead of that, I have
locked it up out of consideration for you; and what do I get for
my considerateness? I shall let the law take its course!"

"You'll do me inexpressible harm, and get nothing whatever," said Havill. "If you would renew for another three
months there would be no difficulty in the matter."

"You have said so before: I will do no such thing."

There was a silence; whereupon Dare arose without hesitation, and walked boldly into the private office. Havill was
standing at one end, as gloomy as a thundercloud, and at the

other was the unfortunate creditor with his hat on. Though Dare's entry surprised them, both parties seemed relieved.

"I have called in passing to congratulate you, Mr. Havill," said Dare gaily. "Such a commission as has been entrusted to you will make you famous!"

"How do you do?—I wish it would make me rich," said Havill drily.

"It will be a lift in that direction, from what I know of the profession. What is she going to spend?"

"A hundred thousand."

"Your commission as architect, five thousand. Not bad, for making a few sketches. Consider what other great commissions such a work will lead to."

"What great work is this?" asked the creditor, pricking up his ears.

"Stancy Castle," said Dare, since Havill seemed too agape to answer. "You have not heard of it, then? Those are the drawings, I presume, in the next room?"

Havill replied in the affirmative, beginning to perceive the manœuvre. "Perhaps you would like to see them?" he said to the creditor.

The latter offered no objection, and all three went into the drawing-office.

"It will certainly be a magnificent structure," said the creditor, after regarding the elevations through his spectacles. "Stancy Castle: I had no idea of it! and when do you begin to build, Mr. Havill?" he inquired in mollified tones.

"In three months, I think?" said Dare, looking to Havill.

Havill assented.

"Five thousand pounds commission," murmured the creditor. "Paid down, I suppose?"

Havill nodded.

"And the works will not linger for lack of money to carry them out, I imagine," said Dare. "Two hundred thousand will probably be spent before the work is finished."

"There is not much doubt of it," said Havill.

"You said nothing to me about this?" whispered the creditor to Havill, taking him aside, with a look of regret.

"You would not listen!"

"It alters the case greatly." The creditor retired with Havill to the door, and after a subdued colloquy in the passage he went away, Havill returning to the office.

"What the devil do you mean by hoaxing him like this, when the job is no more mine than Inigo Jones's?"

"Don't be too curious," said Dare, laughing. "Rather thank me for getting rid of him."

"But it is all a vision!" said Havill, ruefully regarding the pencilled towers of Stancy Castle. "If the competition were really the commission that you have represented it to be there might be something to laugh at."

"It must be made a commission, somehow," returned Dare carelessly. "I am come to lend you a little assistance. I must stay in the neighbourhood, and I have nothing else to do."

A carriage slowly passed the window, and Havill recognized the Power liveries. "Hullo—she's coming here!" he said under his breath as the carriage stopped by the kerb. "What does she want, I wonder? Dare, does she know you?"

"I would just as soon be out of the way."

"Then go into the garden."

Dare went out through the back office as Paula was shown in at the front. She wore a grey travelling costume, and seemed to be in some haste.

"I am on my way to the railway-station," she said to Havill. "I shall be absent from home for several weeks, and since you requested it, I have called to inquire how you are getting on with the design."

"Please look it over," said Havill, placing a seat for her.

"No," said Paula. "I think it would be unfair. I have not looked at Mr.—— the other architect's plans since he has begun to design seriously, and I will not look at yours. Are you getting on quite well, and do you want to know anything more? If so, go to the castle, and get anybody to assist you. Why would you not make use of the room at your disposal in the castle, as the other architect has done?"

In asking the question her face was towards the window, and suddenly her cheeks became a rosy red. She instantly looked another way.

"Having my own office so near, it was not necessary, thank

you," replied Havill, as, noting her countenance, he allowed his glance to stray into the street. Somerset was walking past on the opposite side.

"The time is—the time fixed for sending in the drawings is the first of November, I believe," she said confusedly; "and the decision will be come to by three gentlemen who are prominent members of the Institute of Architects."

Havill then accompanied her to the carriage and she drove away.

Havill went to the back window to tell Dare that he need not stay in the garden; but the garden was empty. The architect remained alone in his office for some time; at the end of a quarter of an hour, when the scream of a railway whistle had echoed down the still street, he beheld Somerset repassing the window in a direction from the railway, with somewhat of a sad gait. In another minute Dare entered, humming the latest air from Offenbach.

"'Tis a mere piece of duplicity!" said Havill.

"What is?"

"Her pretending indifference as to which of us comes out successful in the competition, when she colours carmine the moment Somerset passes by." He described Paula's visit, and the incident.

"It may not mean Cupid's Entire XXX after all," said Dare judicially. "The mere suspicion that a certain man loves her would make a girl blush at his unexpected appearance. Well, she's gone from him for a time; the better for you."

"He has been privileged to see her off at any rate."

"Not privileged."

"How do you know that?"

"I went out of your garden by the back-gate, and followed her carriage to the railway. He simply went to the first bridge outside the station, and waited. When she was in the train, it moved forward; he was all expectation, and drew out his handkerchief ready to wave, while she looked out of the window towards the bridge. The train backed before it reached the bridge, to attach the box containing her horses, and the carriage-truck. Then it started for good, and when it reached the bridge she looked out again, he waving his handkerchief to her."

"And she waving hers back?"

"No, she didn't."

"Ah!"

"She looked at him—nothing more. I wouldn't give much for his chance." After a while Dare added musingly: "You are a mathematician: did you ever investigate the doctrine of expectations?"

"Never."

Dare drew from his pocket his "Book of Chances," a volume as well thumbed as the minister's Bible. "This is a treatise on the subject," he said. "I will teach it to you some day."

The same evening Havill asked Dare to dine with him. He was just at this time living *en garçon*, his wife and children being away on a visit. After dinner they sat on till their faces were rather flushed. The talk turned, as before, on the castle-competition.

"To know his design is to win," said Dare. "And to win is to send him back to London where he came from."

Havill inquired if Dare had seen any sketch of the design while with Somerset?

"Not a line. I was concerned only with the old building."

"Not to know it is to lose, undoubtedly," murmured Havill. "Suppose we go for a walk that way, instead of consulting here?"

They went down the town, and along the highway. When they reached the entrance to the park a man driving a basket-carriage came out from the gate and passed them by in the gloom.

"That was he," said Dare. "He sometimes drives over from the hotel, and sometimes walks. He has been working late this evening."

Strolling on under the trees they met three masculine figures, laughing and talking loudly.

"Those are the three first-class London draughtsmen, Bowles, Knowles, and Cockton, whom he has engaged to assist him, regardless of expense," continued Dare.

"O Lord!" groaned Havill. "There's no chance for me."

The castle now arose before them, endowed by the rayless shade with a more massive majesty than either sunlight or moonlight could impart; and Havill sighed again as he thought of what he was losing by Somerset's rivalry. "Well, what was the use of coming here?" he asked.

"I thought it might suggest something—some way of seeing the design. The servants would let us into his room, I dare say."

"I don't care to ask. Let us walk through the wards, and then homeward."

They sauntered on smoking, Dare leading the way through the gate-house into a corridor which was not inclosed, a lamp hanging at the further end.

"We are getting into the inhabited part, I think," said Havill.

Dare, however, had gone on, and knowing the tortuous passages from his few days' experience in measuring them with Somerset, he came to the butler's pantry. Dare knocked, and nobody answering he entered, took down a key which hung behind the door, and rejoined Havill. "It is all right," he said. "The cat's away; and the mice are at play in consequence."

Proceeding up a stone staircase he unlocked the door of a room in the dark, struck a light inside, and returning to the door called in a whisper to Havill, who had remained behind. "This is Mr. Somerset's studio," he said.

"How did you get permission?" inquired Havill, not knowing that Dare had seen no one.

"Anyhow," said Dare, carelessly. "We can examine the plans at leisure; for if the placid Mrs. Goodman, who is the only one at home, sees the light, she will only think it is Somerset still at work."

Dare uncovered the drawings, and young Somerset's brain-work for the last six weeks lay under their eyes. To Dare, who was too cursory to trouble himself by entering into such details, it had very little meaning; but the design shone into Havill's head like a light into a dark place. It was original; and it was fascinating. Its originality lay partly in the circumstance that Somerset had not attempted to adapt an old building to the wants of the new civilisation. He had placed his new erection beside it as a slightly attached structure, harmonising with the old; heightening and beautifying, rather than subduing it. His work formed a palace, with a ruinous castle annexed as a curiosity. To Havill the conception had more charm than it could have to the most appreciative outsider; for when a mediocre and jealous mind that has been cudgelling itself over a problem capable of many solutions, lights on the solution of a rival, all possibilities in that kind seem to merge in the one beheld.

Dare was struck by the arrested expression of the architect's face. "Is it rather good?" he asked.

"Yes, rather," said Havill, subduing himself.

"More than rather?"

"Yes, the clever devil!" exclaimed Havill, unable to depreciate longer.

"How?"

"The enigma that has worried me three weeks he has solved in a way which is simplicity itself. He has got it, and I am undone!"

"Nonsense, don't give way. Let's make a tracing."

"The ground-plan will be sufficient," said Havill, his courage reviving. "The idea is so simple, that if once seen it is not easily forgotten."

A rough tracing of Somerset's design was quickly made, and blowing out the candle with a wave of his hand the younger gentleman locked the door, and they went downstairs again.

"I should never have thought of it," said Havill, as they walked homeward.

"One man has need of another every ten years: *Ogni dieci anni un uomo ha bisogno dell' altro*, as they say in Italy. You'll help me for this turn if I have need of you?"

"I shall never have the power."

"Oh yes you will. A man who can contrive to get admitted to a competition by writing a letter abusing another man has any amount of power. The stroke was a good one."

Havill was silent till he said, "I think these gusts mean that we are to have a storm of rain."

Dare looked up. The sky was overcast, the trees shivered,

and a drop or two began to strike into the walkers' coats from
the east. They were not far from the inn at Sleeping-Green,
where Dare had lodgings, occupying the rooms which had
been used by Somerset till he gave them up for more commodi-
ous chambers at Markton; and they decided to turn in there
till the rain should be over.

Having possessed himself of Somerset's brains Havill was
inclined to be jovial, and ordered the best in wines that the
house afforded. Before starting from home they had drunk as
much as was good for them; so that their potations here soon
began to have a marked effect upon their tongues. The rain
beat upon the windows with a dull dogged pertinacity which
seemed to signify boundless reserves of the same and long
continuance. The wind rose, the sign creaked, and the candles
waved. The weather had, in truth, broken up for the season,
and this was the first night of the change.

"Well, here we are," said Havill, as he poured out another
glass of the brandied liquor called old port at Sleeping-Green;
"and it seems that here we are to remain for the present."

"I am at home anywhere!" cried the lad, whose brow was
hot and eye wild.

Havill who had not drunk enough to affect his reasoning,
held up his glass to the light and said, "I never can quite make
out what you are, or what your age is. Are you sixteen, one-
and-twenty, or twenty-seven? And are you an Englishman,
Frenchman, Indian, American, or what? You seem not to have
taken your degrees in these parts."

"That's a secret, my friend," said Dare. "I am a citizen of
the world. I owe no country patriotism, and no king or queen
obedience. A man whose country has no boundary is your only
true gentleman."

"Well, where were you born—somewhere, I suppose?"

"It would be a fact worth the telling. The secret of my birth
lies here." And Dare slapped his breast with his right hand.

"Literally, just under your shirt-front; or figuratively, in
your heart?" asked Havill.

"Literally there. It is necessary that it should be recorded,
for one's own memory is a treacherous book of reference,

should verification be required at a time of delirium, disease, or death."

Havill asked no further what he meant, and went to the door. Finding that the rain still continued he returned to Dare who was by this time sinking down in a one-sided attitude, as if hung up by the shoulder. Informing his companion that he was but little inclined to move far in such a tempestuous night, he decided to remain in the inn till next morning.

On calling in the landlord, however, they learnt that the house was full of farmers on their way home from a large sheep-fair in the neighbourhood, and that several of these, having decided to stay on account of the same tempestuous weather, had already engaged the spare beds. If Mr. Dare would give up his room, and share a double-bedded room with Mr. Havill, the thing could be done, but not otherwise.

To this the two companions agreed, and presently went upstairs with as gentlemanly a walk and vertical a candle as they could exhibit under the circumstances.

The other inmates of the inn soon retired to rest, and the storm raged on unheeded by all local humanity.

CHAPTER III

AT two o'clock the rain lessened its fury. At half-past two the obscured moon shone forth; and at three Havill awoke. The blind had not been pulled down overnight, and the moonlight streamed into the room, across the bed whereon Dare was sleeping. He lay on his back, his arms thrown out; and his well-curved youthful form looked like an unpedestaled Dionysus in the colourless lunar rays.

Sleep had cleared Havill's mind from the drowsing effects of the last night's sitting, and he thought of Dare's mysterious manner in speaking of himself. This lad resembled the Etruscan youth Tages, in one respect, that of being a boy with, seemingly, the wisdom of a sage; and the effect of his presence was now heightened by all those sinister and mystic attributes which are lent by nocturnal environment. He who in broad daylight might be but a young *chevalier d'industrie* was now an unlimited possibility in social phenomena. Havill remembered how the lad had pointed to his breast, and said that his secret was literally kept there. The architect was too much of a provincial to have quenched the common curiosity that was part of his nature by the acquired metropolitan indifference to other people's lives which, in essence more unworthy even than the former, causes less practical inconvenience in its exercise.

Dare was breathing profoundly. Instigated as above mentioned, Havill got out of bed and stood beside the sleeper. After a moment's pause he gently pulled back the unfastened collar of Dare's nightshirt and saw a word tattooed in distinct characters on his breast. Before there was time for Havill to decipher it Dare moved slightly, as if conscious of disturbance, and Havill hastened back to bed. Dare bestirred himself yet more, whereupon Havill breathed heavily, though keeping an intent glance on the lad through his half-closed eyes to learn if he had been aware of the investigation.

Dare was certainly conscious of something, for he sat up, rubbed his eyes, and gazed around the room; then after a few moments of reflection he drew some article from beneath his pillow. A blue gleam shone from the object as Dare held it in the moonlight, and Havill perceived that it was a small revolver.

A clammy dew broke out upon the face and body of the architect when, stepping out of bed with the weapon in his hand, Dare looked under the bed, behind the curtains, out of the window, and into a closet, as if convinced that something had occurred, but in doubt as to what it was. He then came across to where Havill was lying and still keeping up the appearance of sleep. Watching him awhile and mistrusting the reality of this semblance, Dare brought it to the test by holding the revolver within a few inches of Havill's forehead.

Havill could stand no more. Crystallised with terror he said, without however moving more than his lips, in dread of hasty action on the part of Dare: "Oh, good Lord, Dare, Dare, I have done nothing!"

The youth smiled and lowered the pistol. "I was only finding out whether it was you or some burglar who had been playing tricks upon me. I find it was you."

"Do put away that thing! It is too ghastly to produce in a respectable bedroom. Why do you carry it!"

"Cosmopolites always do. Now answer my questions. What were you up to?" and Dare as he spoke played with the pistol again.

Havill had recovered some coolness. "You could not use it upon me," he said sardonically, watching Dare. "It would be risking your neck for too little an object."

"I did not think you were shrewd enough to see that," replied Dare carelessly, as he returned the revolver to its place. "Well, whether you have outwitted me or no, you will keep the secret as long as I choose."

"Why?" said Havill.

"Because I keep your secret of the letter abusing Miss P., and of the pilfered tracing you carry in your pocket."

"It is quite true," said Havill.

They went to bed again. Dare was soon asleep; but Havill

did not attempt to disturb him again. The elder man slept but fitfully. He was aroused in the morning by a heavy rumbling and jingling along the highway overlooked by the window, the front wall of the house being shaken by the reverberation.

"There is no rest for me here," he said, rising and going to the window, carefully avoiding the neighbourhood of Mr. Dare. When Havill had glanced out he returned to dress himself.

"What's that noise?" said Dare, awakened by the same rumble.

"It is the Artillery going away."

"From where?"

"Markton barracks."

"Hurrah!" said Dare, jumping up in bed. "I have been waiting for that these six weeks."

Havill did not ask questions as to the meaning of his unexpected remark.

When they were downstairs Dare's first act was to ring the bell and ask if his *Army and Navy Gazette* had arrived.

While the servant was gone Havill cleared his throat and said, "I am an architect, and I take in the *Architect*; you are an architect, and you take in the *Army and Navy Gazette*."

"I am not an architect any more than I am a soldier; but I have taken in the *Army and Navy Gazette* these many weeks."

When they were at breakfast the paper came in. Dare hastily tore it open and glanced at the pages.

"I am going to Markton after breakfast!" he said suddenly, before looking up; "we will walk together, if you like?"

They walked together as planned, and entered Markton about ten o'clock.

"I have just to make a call here," said Dare, when they were opposite the barrack-entrance on the outskirts of the town, where wheel-tracks and a regular chain of hoofmarks left by the departed batteries were imprinted in the gravel between the open gates. "I shall not be a moment." Havill stood still while his companion entered and asked the commissary in charge, or somebody representing him, when the new batteries would arrive to take the place of those which had gone away. He was informed that it would be about noon.

"Now I am at your service," said Dare, "and will help you to rearrange your design by the new intellectual light we have acquired."

They entered Havill's office and set to work. When contrasted with the tracing from Somerset's plan, Havill's design, which was not far advanced, revealed all its weaknesses to him. After seeing Somerset's scheme the bands of Havill's imagination were loosened: he laid his own previous efforts aside, got fresh sheets of drawing-paper and drew with vigour.

"I may as well stay and help you," said Dare. "I have nothing to do till twelve o'clock; and not much then."

So there he remained. At a quarter to twelve children and idlers began to gather against the railings of Havill's house. A few minutes past twelve the noise of an arriving host was heard at the entrance to the town. Thereupon Dare and Havill went to the window.

The X and Y Batteries of the Z Brigade, Royal Horse Artillery, were entering Markton, each headed by the major with his bugler behind him. In a moment they came abreast and passed, every man in his place:

Six shining horses, in pairs, harnessed by rope-traces white as milk, with a driver on each near horse:

Two gunners on the lead-coloured stout-wheeled limber, their carcases jolted to a jelly for lack of springs:

Two gunners on the lead-coloured stout-wheeled gun-carriage, in the same personal condition:

The nine-pounder gun, dipping its heavy head to earth, as if ashamed of its office in these enlightened times:

The complement of jingling and prancing troopers, riding at the wheels and elsewhere:

Six shining horses with their drivers, and traces white as milk, as before:

Two more gallant jolted men, on another jolting limber, and more stout wheels and lead-coloured paint:

Two more jolted men on another drooping gun:

More jingling troopers on horseback:

Again six shining draught-horses, traces, drivers, gun, gunners, lead paint, stout wheels and troopers as before.

So each detachment lumbered slowly by, all eyes martially forward, except when wandering in quest of female beauty.

"He's a fine fellow, is he not?" said Dare, denoting by a nod a mounted officer, with a sallow, yet handsome face, and black moustache, who came up on a bay gelding with the men of his battery.

"What is he?" said Havill.

"A captain who lacks advancement."

"Do you know him?"

"I know him?"

"Yes; do you?"

Dare made no reply; and they watched the captain as he rode past with his drawn sword in his hand, the sun making little suns upon its blade, and upon his brilliantly polished long-boots and bright spurs; also warming his gold cross-belt and braidings, white gloves, busby with its red bag, and tall white plume.

Havill seemed too indifferent to press his questioning; and when all the soldiers had passed by, Dare observed to his companion that he should leave him for a short time; but would return in the afternoon or next day.

After this he walked up the street in the rear of the artillery, following them to the barracks. On reaching the gates he found a crowd of people gathered outside, looking with admiration at the guns and gunners drawn up within the enclosure. When the soldiers were dismissed to their quarters the sightseers dispersed, and Dare went through the gates to the barrack-yard.

The guns were standing on the green; the soldiers and horses were scattered about, and the handsome captain whom Dare had pointed out to Havill was inspecting the buildings in the company of the quartermaster. Dare made a mental note of these things, and apparently changing a previous intention, went out from the barracks and returned to the town.

CHAPTER IV

TO return for a while to George Somerset. The sun of his later existence having vanished from that young man's horizon, he confined himself closely to the studio, superintending the exertions of his draughtsmen Bowles, Knowles, and Cockton, who were now in the full swing of working out Somerset's creations from the sketches he had previously prepared.

He had so far got the start of Havill in the competition that, by the help of these three gentlemen, his design was soon finished. But he gained no unfair advantage on this account, an additional month being allowed to Havill to compensate for his later information.

Before sealing up his drawings Somerset wished to spend a short time in London, and dismissing his assistants till further notice, he locked up the rooms which had been appropriated as office and studio, and prepared for the journey.

It was afternoon. Somerset walked from the castle in the direction of the wood to reach Markton by a detour. He had not proceeded far when there approached his path a man riding a bay horse with a square-cut tail. The equestrian wore a grizzled beard, and looked at Somerset with a piercing eye as he noiselessly ambled nearer over the soft sod of the park. He proved to be Mr. Cunningham Haze, chief constable of the district, who had become slightly known to Somerset during his sojourn here.

"One word, Mr. Somerset," said the constable, after they had exchanged nods of recognition, reining his horse as he spoke.

Somerset stopped.

"You have a studio at the castle in which you are preparing drawings?"

"I have."

"Have you a clerk?"

"I had three till yesterday, when I paid them off."

"Would they have any right to enter the studio late at night?"

"There would have been nothing wrong in their doing so. Either of them might have gone back at any time for something forgotten. They lived quite near the castle."

"Ah, then all is explained. I was riding past over the grass on the night of last Thursday and I saw two persons in your studio with a light. It must have been about half-past nine o'clock. One of them came forward and pulled down the blind, so that the light fell upon his face. But I only saw it for a short time."

"If it were Knowles or Cockton he would have had a beard."

"He had no beard."

"Then it must have been Bowles. A young man?"

"Quite young. His companion in the background seemed older."

"They are all about the same age really. By the way—it couldn't have been Dare—and Havill, surely! Would you recognize them again?"

"The young one possibly. The other not at all, for he remained in the shade."

Somerset endeavoured to discern in a description by the chief constable the features of Mr. Bowles; but it seemed to approximate more closely to Dare in spite of himself. "I'll make a sketch of the only one who had no business there, and show it to you," he presently said. "I should like this cleared up."

Mr. Cunningham Haze said he was going to Casterbridge that afternoon, but would return in the evening before Somerset's departure. With this they parted. A possible motive for Dare's presence in the rooms had instantly presented itself to Somerset's mind, for he had seen Dare enter Havill's office more than once, as if he were at work there.

He accordingly sat on the next stile, and taking out his pocket-book began a pencil sketch of Dare's head, to show to Mr. Haze in the evening; for if Dare had indeed found admission with Havill, or as his agent, the design was lost.

But he could not make a drawing that was a satisfactory likeness. Then he luckily remembered that Dare, in the intense warmth of admiration he had affected for Somerset on the first day or two of their acquaintance, had begged for his photograph, and in return for it had left one of himself on the mantelpiece, taken as he said by his own process. Somerset resolved to show this production to Mr. Haze, as being more to the purpose than a sketch, and instead of finishing the latter proceeded on his way.

He entered the old overgrown drive which wound indirectly through the wood to Markton. The road, having been laid out for idling rather than for progress, bent sharply hither and thither among the fissured trunks and layers of horny leaves which lay there all the year round, interspersed with cushions of vivid green moss that formed oases in the rust-red expanse.

Reaching a point where the road made one of its bends between two large beeches, a man and woman revealed themselves at a few yards' distance, walking slowly towards him. In the short and quaint lady he recognized Charlotte De Stancy, whom he remembered not to have seen for several days.

She slightly blushed and said, "Oh, this is pleasant, Mr. Somerset! Let me present my brother to you, Captain De Stancy, of the Royal Horse Artillery."

Her brother came forward and shook hands heartily with Somerset; and they all three rambled on together, talking of the season, the place, the fishing, the shooting, and whatever else came uppermost in their minds.

Captain De Stancy was a personage who would have been called interesting by women well out of their teens. He was ripe, without having declined a digit towards fogeyism. He was sufficiently old and experienced to suggest a goodly accumulation of touching amourettes in the chambers of his memory, and not too old for the possibility of increasing the store. He was apparently about eight-and-thirty, less tall than his father had been, but admirably made; and his every movement exhibited a fine combination of strength and flexibility of limb. His face was somewhat thin and thoughtful, its complexion being naturally pale, though darkened by exposure to a warmer sun than ours. His features were somewhat striking; his moustache and hair raven black; and his eyes, denied the attributes of military keenness by reason of the largeness and darkness of their aspect, acquired thereby a softness of expression that was in part womanly. His mouth as far as it could be seen reproduced this characteristic, which might have been called weakness, or goodness, according to the mental attitude of the observer. It was large but well formed, and showed an unimpaired line of teeth within. His dress at present was a heather-coloured rural suit, cut close to his figure.

"You knew my cousin, Jack Ravensbury?" he said to Somerset, as they went on. "Poor Jack: he was a good fellow."

"He was a very good fellow."

"He would have been made a parson if he had lived—it was his great wish. I, as his senior, and a man of the world as I thought myself, used to chaff him about it when he was a boy, and tell him not to be a milksop, but to enter the army. But I think Jack was right—the parsons have the best of it, I see now."

"They would hardly admit that," said Somerset, laughing. "Nor can I."

"Nor I," said the captain's sister. "See how lovely you all looked with your big guns and uniform when you entered Markton; and then see how stupid the parsons look by comparison, when they flock into Markton at a Visitation."

"Ah, yes," said De Stancy, a little pensively:

> "Doubtless it is a brilliant masquerade;
> But when of the first sight you have had your fill,
> It palls—at least it does so upon me,
> This paradise of pleasure and ennui.

When one is getting on for forty;

> When we have made our love, and gamed our gaming,
> Dressed, voted, shone, and maybe, something more;
> With dandies dined, heard senators declaiming;
> Seen beauties brought to market by the score,

and so on, there arises a strong desire for a quiet old-fashioned country life, in which incessant movement is not a necessary part of the programme."

"But you are not forty, Will?" said Charlotte.

"My dear, I was thirty-nine last January."

"Well, men about here are youths at that age. It was India used you up so, when you served in the line, was it not? I wish you had never gone there!"

"So do I," said De Stancy, drily. "But I ought to grow a youth again, like the rest, now I am in my native air."

They came to a narrow brook, not wider than a man's stride, and Miss De Stancy halted on the edge.

"Why, Lottie, you used to jump it easily enough," said her brother. "But we won't make her do it now." He took her in his arms, and lifted her over, giving her a gratuitous ride for some additonal yards, and saying, "You are not a pound heavier, Lott, than you were at ten years old. . . . What do you think of the country here, Mr. Somerset? Are you going to stay long?"

"I think very well of it," said Somerset. "But I leave to-morrow morning, which makes it necessary that I turn back in a minute or two from walking with you."

"That's a disappointment. I had hoped you were going to finish out the autumn with shooting. There's some, very fair, to be got here on reasonable terms, I've just heard."

"But you need not hire any!" spoke up Charlotte. "Paula would let you shoot anything, I am sure. She has not been here long enough to preserve much game, and the poachers had it all in Mr. Wilkins' time. But what there is you might kill with pleasure to her."

"No, thank you," said De Stancy, grimly. "I prefer to remain a stranger to Miss Power—Miss Steam-Power, she ought to be called—and all her possessions."

Charlotte was subdued, and did not insist further; while Somerset, before he could feel himself able to decide on the mood in which the gallant captain's joke at Paula's expense should be taken, wondered whether it were a married man or a bachelor who uttered it.

He had not been able to keep the question of De Stancy's domestic state out of his head from the first moment of seeing him. Assuming De Stancy to be a husband, he felt there might be some excuse for his remark; if unmarried, Somerset liked the satire still better; in such circumstances there was a relief in the thought that Captain De Stancy's prejudices might be infinitely stronger than those of his sister or father.

"Going to-morrow, did you say, Mr. Somerset?" asked Miss De Stancy. "Then will you dine with us to-day? My father is anxious that you should do so before you go. I am sorry there will be only our own family present to meet you; but you can leave as early as you wish."

Her brother seconded the invitation, and Somerset promised, though his leisure for that evening was short. He was in truth somewhat inclined to like De Stancy; for though the captain had said nothing of any value either on war, commerce, science, or art, he had seemed attractive to the younger man. Beyond the natural interest a soldier has for imaginative minds in the civil walks of life, De Stancy's occasional manifestations of *tædium-vitæ* were too poetically shaped to be repellent. Gallantry combined in him with a sort of ascetic self-repression, in a way that was curious. He was a dozen years older than Somerset: his life had been passed in grooves remote from those of Somerset's own life; and the latter decided that he would like to meet the artillery officer again.

Bidding them a temporary farewell, he went away to Markton by a shorter path than that pursued by the De Stancys, and after spending the remainder of the afternoon preparing for departure, he sallied forth just before the dinner-hour towards the suburban villa.

He had become yet more curious whether a Mrs. De Stancy existed; if there were one he would probably see her to-night. He had an irrepressible hope that there might be such a lady. On entering the drawing-room only the father, son, and daughter were assembled. Somerset fell into talk with Charlotte during the few minutes before dinner, and his thought found its way out.

"There is no Mrs. De Stancy?" he said in an undertone.

"None," she said; "my brother is a bachelor."

The dinner having been fixed at any early hour to suit Somerset, they had returned to the drawing-room at eight o'clock. About nine he was aiming to get away.

"You are not off yet?" said the captain.

"There would have been no hurry," said Somerset, "had I

not just remembered that I have left one thing undone which I want to attend to before my departure. I want to see the chief constable to-night."

"Cunningham Haze?—he is the very man I too want to see. But he went out of town this afternoon, and I hardly think you will see him to-night. His return has been delayed."

"Then the matter must wait."

"I have left word at his house asking him to call here if he gets home before half-past ten; but at any rate I shall see him tomorrow morning. Can I do anything for you, since you are leaving early?"

Somerset replied that the business was of no great importance, and briefly explained the suspected intrusion into his studio; that he had with him a photograph of the suspected young man. "If it is a mistake," added Somerset, "I should regret putting my draughtsman's portrait into the hands of the police, since it might injure his character; indeed, it would be unfair to him. So I wish to keep the likeness in my own hands, and merely to show it to Mr. Haze: that's why I prefer not to send it."

"My matter with Haze is that the barrack furniture does not correspond with the inventories. If you like, I'll ask your question at the same time with pleasure."

Thereupon Somerset gave Captain De Stancy an unfastened envelope containing the portrait, asking him to destroy it if the constable should declare it not to correspond with the face that met his eye at the window. Soon after, Somerset took his leave of the household.

He had not been absent ten minutes when other wheels were heard on the gravel without, and the servant announced Mr. Cunningham Haze, who had returned earlier than he had expected and had called as requested.

They went into the dining-room to discuss their business. When the barrack matter had been arranged De Stancy said, "I have a little commission to execute for my friend Mr. Somerset. I am to ask you if this portrait of the person he suspects of unlawfully entering his room is like the man you saw there?"

The speaker was seated on one side of the dining-table and

Mr. Haze on the other. As he spoke De Stancy pulled the envelope from his pocket, and half drew out the photograph, which he had not as yet looked at, to hand it over to the constable. In the act his eye fell upon the portrait, with its uncertain expression of age, assured look, and hair worn in a fringe like a girl's.

Captain De Stancy grew sickly pale, and fell back gasping in his chair, having previously had sufficient power over himself to close the envelope and return it to his pocket.

"Good heavens, you are ill, Captain De Stancy?" said the chief constable.

"It was only momentary," said De Stancy faintly; "better in a minute—a glass of water will put me right."

Mr. Haze got him a glass of water from the sideboard.

"These spasms occasionally overtake me," said De Stancy when he had drunk. "I am already better. What were we saying? Oh, this affair of Mr. Somerset's. I find that this envelope is not the right one." He ostensibly searched his pocket again. "I must have mislaid it," he continued, rising. "I'll be with you again in a moment."

De Stancy went into the room adjoining, opened an album of portraits that lay on the table, and selected one of a young man quite unknown to him, whose age was somewhat akin to Dare's, but who in no other attribute resembled him.

De Stancy placed this picture in the original envelope, and returned with it to the chief constable, saying he had found it at last.

"Thank you, thank you," said Cunningham Haze, looking it over. "Ah—I perceive it is not what I expected to see. Mr. Somerset was mistaken."

When the chief constable had left the house, Captain De Stancy shut the door and drew out the original photograph. As he looked at the transcript of Dare's features he was moved by a painful agitation till, recalling himself to the present, he carefully put the portrait into the fire.

During the following days Captain De Stancy's manner on the roads, in the streets, and at barracks, was that of Crusoe after seeing the print of a man's foot on the sand.

CHAPTER V

ANYBODY who had closely considered Dare at this time would have discovered that, shortly after the arrival of the Royal Horse Artillery at Markton Barracks, he gave up his room at the inn at Sleeping-Green and took permanent lodgings over a broker's shop at the upper end of the town above-mentioned. The peculiarity of the rooms was that they commanded a view lengthwise of the barrack road along which any soldier, in the natural course of things, would pass either to enter the town, to call at Myrtle Villa, or to go to Stancy Castle.

Dare seemed to act as if there were plenty of time for his business. Some few days had slipped by when, perceiving Captain De Stancy walk past his window and down the town, Dare took his hat and cane, and followed in the same direction. When he was about fifty yards short of Myrtle Villa on the other side of the town he saw De Stancy enter its gate.

Dare mounted a stile beside the highway and patiently waited. In about twenty minutes De Stancy came out again and turned back in the direction of the town, till Dare was revealed to him on his left hand. When De Stancy recognized the youth he was visibly agitated, though apparently not surprised. Standing still a moment he dropped his glance upon the ground, and then came forward to Dare, who having alighted from the stile stood before the captain with a smile.

"My dear lad!" said De Stancy, much moved by recollections. He held Dare's hand for a moment in both his own, and turned askance.

"You are not astonished," said Dare, still retaining his smile, as if to his mind there were something comic in the situation.

"I knew you were somewhere near. Where do you come from?"

"From going to and fro in the earth, and walking up and

down in it, as Satan said to his Maker.—Southampton last, in common speech."

"Have you come here to see me?"

"Entirely. I divined that your next quarters would be Markton, the previous batteries that were at your station having come on here. I have wanted to see you badly."

"You have?"

"I am rather out of cash. I have been knocking about a good deal since you last heard from me."

"I will do what I can again."

"Thanks, captain."

"But Willy, I am afraid it will not be much at present. You know I am as poor as a mouse."

"But such as it is, could you write a cheque for it now?"

"I will send it to you from the barracks."

"I have a better plan. By getting over this stile we could go round at the back of the villas to Sleeping-Green Church. There is always a pen-and-ink in the vestry, and we can have a nice talk on the way. It would be unwise for me to appear at the barracks just now."

"That's true."

De Stancy sighed, and they were about to walk across the fields together. "No," said Dare, suddenly stopping. "My plans make it imperative that we should not run the risk of being seen in each other's company for long. Walk on, and I will follow. You can stroll into the churchyard, and move about as if you were ruminating on the epitaphs. There are some with excellent morals. I'll enter by the other gate, and we can meet easily in the vestry-room."

De Stancy looked gloomy, and was on the point of acquiescing when he turned back and said, "Why should your photograph be shown to the chief constable?"

"By whom?"

"Somerset the architect. He suspects your having broken into his office or something of the sort." De Stancy briefly related what Somerset had explained to him at the dinner-table.

"It was merely diamond cut diamond between us, on an

architectural matter," murmured Dare. "Ho! and he suspects, and that's his remedy! I must be on my guard."

"I hope this is nothing serious?" asked De Stancy gravely.

"I peeped at his drawing—that's all. But since he chooses to make that use of my photograph, which I gave him in friendship, I'll make use of his, in a way he little dreams of. Well now, let's on."

A quarter of an hour later they met in the vestry of the church at Sleeping-Green.

"I have only just transferred my account to the bank here," said De Stancy, as he took out his cheque book, "and it will be more convenient to me at present to draw but a small sum. I will make up the balance afterwards."

When he had written it Dare glanced over the paper and said ruefully, "It is small, dad. Well, there is all the more reason why I should broach my scheme, with a view to making such documents larger in the future."

"I shall be glad to hear of any such scheme," answered De Stancy, with a languid attempt at jocularity.

"Then here it is. The plan I have arranged for you is of the nature of a marriage."

"You are very kind!" said De Stancy, agape.

"The lady's name is Miss Paula Power, who, as you may have heard since your arrival, is in absolute possession of her father's property and estates, including Stancy Castle. As soon as I heard of her I saw what a marvellous match it would be for you, and your family; it would make a man of you, in short, and I have set my mind upon your putting no objection in the way of its accomplishment."

"But Willy, it seems to me that, of us two, it is you who exercise paternal authority?"

"True, it is for your good. Let me do it."

"Well, one must be indulgent under the circumstances, I suppose. . . . But," added De Stancy, simply, "Willy, I— don't want to marry, you know. I have lately thought that some day we may be able to live together, you and I: go off to America or New Zealand, where we are not known, and there lead a quiet, pastoral life, defying social rules and troublesome observances."

"I can't hear of it, captain," replied Dare, reprovingly. "I am what events have made me, and having fixed my mind upon getting you settled in life by this marriage, I have put things in train for it at an immense trouble to myself. If you had thought over it o' nights as much as I have, you would not say nay."

"But I ought to have married your mother if anybody. And as I have not married her, the least I can do in respect to her is to marry no other woman."

"You have some sort of duty to me, have you not, Captain De Stancy?"

"Yes, Willy, I admit that I have," the elder replied reflectively. "And I don't think I have failed in it thus far?"

"This will be the crowning proof. Paternal affection, family pride, the noble instinct to reinstate yourself in the castle of your ancestors, all demand the step. And when you have seen the lady! She has the figure and motions of a sylph, the face of an angel, the eye of love itself. What a sight she is crossing the lawn on a sunny afternoon, or gliding airily along the corridors of the old palace the De Stancys knew so well! Her lips are the softest, reddest, most distracting things you ever saw. Her hair is as soft as silk, and of the rarest, tenderest brown."

The captain moved uneasily. "Don't take the trouble to say more, Willy," he observed. "You know how I am. My cursed susceptibility to these matters has already wasted years of my life, and I don't want to make myself a fool about her too."

"You must see her."

"No, don't let me see her," De Stancy expostulated. "If she is only half so good-looking as you say, she will drag me at her heels like a blind Samson. You are a mere youth as yet, but I may tell you that the misfortune of never having been my own master where a beautiful face was concerned obliges me to be cautious if I would preserve my peace of mind."

"Well, to my mind, Captain De Stancy, your objections seem trivial. Are those all?"

"They are all I care to mention just now to you."

"Captain! can there be secrets between us?"

De Stancy paused and looked at the lad as if his heart wished to confess what his judgment feared to tell. "There should not be—on this point," he murmured.

"Then tell me—why do you so much object to her?"

"I once vowed a vow."

"A vow!" said Dare, rather disconcerted.

"A vow of infinite solemnity. I must tell you from the beginning; perhaps you are old enough to hear it now, though you have been too young before. Your mother's life ended in much sorrow, and it was occasioned entirely by me. In my regret for the wrong done her I swore to her that though she had not been my wife, no other woman should stand in that relationship to me; and this to her was a sort of comfort. When she was dead my knowledge of my own plaguy impressibility, which seemed to be ineradicable—as it seems still—led me to think what safeguards I could set over myself with a view to keeping my promise to live a life of celibacy; and among other things I determined to forswear the society, and if possible the sight, of women young and attractive, as far as I had the power to do."

"It is not so easy to avoid the sight of a beautiful woman if she crosses your path, I should think?"

"It is not easy; but it is possible."

"How?"

"By directing your attention another way."

"But do you mean to say, captain, that you can be in a room with a pretty woman who speaks to you, and not look at her?"

"I do: though mere looking has less to do with it than mental attentiveness—allowing your thoughts to flow out in her direction—to comprehend her image."

"But it would be considered very impolite not to look at the woman or comprehend her image?"

"It would be, and is. I am considered the most impolite officer in the service. I have been nicknamed the man with the averted eyes—the man with the detestable habit—the man who greets you with his shoulder, and so on. Ninety-and-nine fair women at the present moment hate me like poison and death for having persistently refused to plumb the depths of their offered eyes."

"How can you do it, who are by nature courteous?"

"I cannot always—I break down sometimes. But upon the whole recollection holds me to it: dread of a lapse. Nothing is so potent as fear well maintained."

De Stancy narrated these details in a grave meditative tone with his eyes on the wall, as if he were scarcely conscious of a listener.

"But haven't you reckless moments, captain?—when you have taken a little more wine than usual, for instance?"

"I don't take wine."

"Oh, you are a teetotaller?"

"Not a pledged one—but I don't touch alcohol unless I get wet, or anything of that sort."

"Don't you sometimes forget this vow of yours to my mother?"

"No, I wear a reminder."

"What is that like?"

De Stancy held up his left hand, on the third finger of which appeared an iron ring.

Dare surveyed it, saying, "Yes, I have seen that before, though I never knew why you wore it. Well, I wear a reminder also, but of a different sort."

He threw open his shirt-front, and revealed tattooed on his breast the letters DE STANCY; the same marks which Havill had seen in the bedroom by the light of the moon.

The captain rather winced at the sight. "Well, well," he said hastily, "that's enough. . . . Now, at any rate, you understand my objection to know Miss Power."

"But, captain," said the lad coaxingly, as he fastened his shirt; "you forget me and the good you may do me by marrying? Surely that's a sufficient reason for a change of sentiment. This inexperienced sweet creature owns the castle and estate which bears your name, even to the furniture and pictures. She is the possessor of at least forty thousand a year—how much more I cannot say—while she lives at the rate of twelve hundred in her simplicity."

"It is very good of you to set this before me. But I prefer to go on as I am going."

"Well, I won't bore you any more with her to-day. A monk in regimentals!—'tis strange." Dare arose and was about to open the door, when, looking through the window, Captain De Stancy said, "Stop." He had perceived his father Sir William De Stancy walking among the tombstones without.

"Yes, indeed," said Dare, turning the key in the door. "It would look strange if he were to find us here."

As the old man seemed indisposed to leave the churchyard just yet they sat down again.

"What a capital card-table this green cloth would make," said Dare, as they waited. "You play, captain, I suppose?"

"Very seldom."

"The same with me. But as I enjoy a hand of cards with a friend, I don't go unprovided." Saying which, Dare drew a pack from the tail of his coat. "Shall we while away this leisure with the witching things?"

"Really, I'd rather not."

"But," coaxed the young man, "I am in the humour for it; so don't be unkind!"

"But, Willy, why do you care for these things? Cards are harmless enough in their way; but I don't like to see you carrying them in your pocket. It isn't good for you."

"It was by the merest chance I had them. Now come, just one hand, since we are prisoners. I want to show you how nicely I can play. I won't corrupt you!"

"Of course not," said De Stancy, as if ashamed of what his objection had implied. "You are not corrupt enough yourself to do that, I should hope."

The cards were dealt and they began to play, Captain De Stancy abstractedly, and with his eyes mostly straying out of the window upon the large yew, whose boughs as they moved were distorted by the old green window-panes.

"It is better than doing nothing," said Dare, cheerfully, as the game went on. "I hope you don't dislike it?"

"Not if it pleases you," said De Stancy, listlessly.

"And the consecration of this place does not extend further than the aisle wall."

"Doesn't it?" said De Stancy, as he mechanically played out his cards. "What became of that box of books I sent you with my last cheque?"

"Well, as I hadn't time to read them, and as I knew you

would not like them to be wasted, I sold them to a bloke who peruses them from morning till night. Ah, now you have lost a pony altogether—how queer! We'll double the stakes. So, as I was saying, just at the time the books came I got an inkling of this important business, and literature went to the wall."

"Important business—what?"

"The capture of this lady, to be sure."

De Stancy sighed impatiently. "I wish you were less calculating, and had more of the impulse natural to your years!"

"Game—by Jove! You have lost again, captain. That makes—let me see—nine pounds fifteen to square us."

"I owe you that?" said De Stancy, startled. "It is more than I have in cash. I must write another cheque."

"Never mind. Make it payable to yourself, and our connection will be quite unsuspected."

Captain De Stancy did as requested, and rose from his seat. Sir William, though further off, was still in the churchyard.

"How can you hesitate for a moment about this girl?" said Dare, pointing to the bent figure of the old man. "Think of the satisfaction it would be to him to see his son within the family walls again. It should be a religion with you to compass such a legitimate end as this."

"Well, well, I'll think of it," said the captain, with an impatient laugh. "You are quite a Mephistopheles, Will—I say it to my sorrow!"

"Would that I were in your place."

"Would that you were! Fifteen years ago I might have called the chance a magnificent one."

"But you are a young man still, and you look younger than you are. Nobody knows our relationship, and I am not such a fool as to divulge it. Of course, if through me you reclaim this splendid possession, I should leave it to your feelings what you would do for me."

Sir William had by this time cleared out of the churchyard, and the pair emerged from the vestry and departed. Proceeding towards Markton by the same by-path, they presently came to an eminence covered with bushes of blackthorn, and tufts of yellowing fern. From this point a good view of the woods and glades about Stancy Castle could be obtained. Dare stood still on the top and stretched out his finger; the captain's eye followed the direction, and he saw above the many-hued foliage in the middle distance the towering keep of Paula's castle.

"That's the goal of your ambition, captain—ambition do I say?—most righteous and dutiful endeavour! How the hoary shape catches the sunlight—it is the *raison d'être* of the landscape, and its possession is coveted by a thousand hearts. Surely it is an hereditary desire of yours? You must make a point of returning to it, and appearing in the map of the future as in that of the past. I delight in this work of encouraging you, and pushing you forward towards your own. You are really very clever, you know, but—I say it with respect—how comes it that you want so much waking up?"

"Because I know the day is not so bright as it seems, my boy. However, you make a little mistake. If I care for anything on earth, I do care for that old fortress of my forefathers. I respect so little among the living that all my reverence is for my own dead. But manœuvring even for my own, as you call it, is not in my line. It is distasteful—it is positively hateful to me."

"Well, well, let it stand thus for the present. But will you refuse me one little request—merely to see her? I'll contrive it so that she may not see you. Don't refuse me, it is the one thing I ask, and I shall think it hard if you deny me."

"Oh Will!" said the captain wearily. "Why will you plead so? No—even though your mind is particularly set upon it, I cannot see her, or bestow a thought upon her, much as I should like to gratify you."

CHAPTER VI

WHEN they had parted Dare walked along towards Markton, with resolve on his mouth and an unscrupulous light in his prominent black eye. Could any person who had heard the previous conversation have seen him now, he would have found little difficulty in divining that, notwithstanding De Stancy's obduracy, the reinstation of Captain De Stancy in the castle, and the possible legitimation and enrichment of himself, was still the dream of his brain. Even should any legal settlement or offspring intervene to nip the extreme development of his projects, there was abundant opportunity for his glorification. Two conditions were imperative. De Stancy must see Paula before Somerset's return. And it was necessary to have help from Havill, even if it involved letting him know all.

Whether Havill already knew all was a nice question for Mr. Dare's luminous mind. Havill had had opportunities of reading his secret, particularly on the night they occupied the same room. If so, by revealing it to Paula, Havill might utterly blast his project for the marriage. Havill, then, was at all risks to be retained as an ally.

Yet Dare would have preferred a stronger check upon his confederate than was afforded by his own knowledge of that anonymous letter and the competition trick. For were the competition lost to him, Havill would have no further interest in conciliating Miss Power; would as soon as not let her know the secret of De Stancy's relation to him, Dare, in retaliation for the snubbing and fright he had received by the production of the revolver.

Fortune as usual helped him in his dilemma. Entering Havill's office, Dare found him sitting there; but the drawings had all disappeared from the boards. The architect held an open letter in his hand.

"Well, what news?" said Dare.

"Miss Power has returned to the castle, Somerset is detained in London, and the competition is decided," said Havill, with a glance of quiet dubiousness.

"And you have won it?"

"No. We are bracketed—it's a tie. The judges say there is no choice between the designs—that they are singularly equal and singularly good. That she would do well to adopt either. Signed So-and-So, Fellows of the Royal Institute of British Architects. The result is that she will employ which she personally likes best. It is as if I had spun a guinea in the air and it had alighted on its edge. The least false movement will make it tails; the least wise movement heads."

"Singularly equal. Well we owe that to our nocturnal visit, which must not be known."

"Oh Lord no!" said Havill apprehensively.

Dare felt secure of him at those words. Havill had much at stake; the slightest rumour of his trick in bringing about the competition would be fatal to Havill's reputation; his own position was consequently safe.

"The permanent absence of Somerset is then desirable architecturally on your account, matrimonially on mine."

"Matrimonially? By the way—who was that captain you pointed out to me when the artillery entered the town?"

"Captain De Stancy—son of Sir William De Stancy. He's the husband. Oh you needn't look incredulous: it is practicable; but we won't argue that. In the first place I want him to see her, and to see her in the most love-kindling, passion-begetting circumstances that can be thought of. And he must see her surreptitiously, for he refuses to meet her."

"Let him see her going to church or chapel?"

Dare shook his head.

"Driving out?"

"Common-place."

"Walking in the gardens?"

"Ditto."

"At her toilet?"

"Ah—if it were possible!"

"Which it hardly is. Well, you had better think it over and make inquiries about her habits, and as to when she is in a favourable aspect for observation, as the almanacs say."

Shortly afterwards Dare took his leave. In the evening he made it his business to sit smoking on the bole of a tree which commanded a view of the upper ward of the castle, and also of the old postern-gate, now enlarged and used as a tradesmen's entrance. It was half-past six o'clock; the dressing-bell rang, and Dare saw a light-footed young woman hasten at the sound across the ward from the servant's quarter. A light appeared in a chamber which he knew to be Paula's dressing-room; and there it remained half an hour, a shadow passing and repassing on the blind in the style of head-dress worn by the girl he had previously seen. The dinner-bell sounded and the light went out.

As yet it was scarcely dark out of doors, and in a few minutes Dare had the satisfaction of seeing the same young woman cross the ward and emerge upon the slope without. This time she was bonneted, and carried a little basket in her hand. A nearer view showed her to be, as he had expected, Milly Birch, Paula's maid, who had friends living in Markton, whom she was in the habit of visiting almost every evening during the three hours of leisure which intervened between Paula's retirement from the dressing-room and return thither at ten o'clock. When the young woman had descended the road and passed into the large drive Dare rose and followed her.

"Oh, it is you, Miss Birch," said Dare, on overtaking her. "I am glad to have the pleasure of walking by your side."

"Yes, sir. Oh, it's Mr. Dare. We don't see you at the castle now, sir."

"No. And do you get a walk like this every evening when the others are at their busiest?"

"Almost every evening; that's the one return to the poor lady's-maid for losing her leisure when the others get it—in the absence of the family from home."

"Is Miss Power a hard mistress?"

"No."

"Rather fanciful than hard, I presume?"

"Just so, sir."

"And she likes to appear to advantage, no doubt."

"I suppose so," said Milly laughing. "We all do."

"When does she appear to the best advantage? When riding, or driving, or reading her book?"

"Not altogether then, if you mean the very best."

"Perhaps it is when she sits looking in the glass at herself, and you let down her hair."

"Not particularly, to my mind."

"When does she to your mind? When dressed for a dinner-party or ball?"

"She's middling, then. But there is a time when she looks more bewitching than at any. It is when she is in the gymnasium."

"Oh—gymnasium?"

"Because when she is there she wears such a pretty boy's costume, and is so charming in her movements, that you think she is a lovely youth and not a girl at all."

"When does she go to this gymnasium?"

"Not so much as she used to. Only on wet mornings now, when she can't get out for walks or drives. But she used to do it every day."

"I should like to see her there."

"Why, sir?"

"I am a poor artist, and can't afford models. To see her attitudes would be of great assistance to me in the art I love so well."

Milly shook her head. "She's very strict about the door being locked. If I were to leave it open she would dismiss me, as I should deserve."

"But consider, dear Miss Birch, the advantage to a poor artist the sight of her would be: if you could hold the door ajar it would be worth five pounds to me, and a good deal to you."

"No," said the incorruptible Milly, shaking her head. "Beside, I don't always go there with her. Oh no, I couldn't!"

Milly remained so firm at this point that Dare said no more. When he had left her he returned to the castle grounds, and though there was not much light he had no difficulty in discovering the gymnasium, the outside of which he had observed before, without thinking to inquire its purpose. Like the erections in other parts of the shrubberies it was constructed of wood, the interstices between the framing being filled up with short billets of fir nailed diagonally. Dare, even when without a settled plan in his head, could arrange for probabilities; and wrenching out one of the billets he looked inside. It seemed to be a simple oblong apartment, fitted up with ropes, with a little dressing-closet at one end, and lighted by a skylight or lantern in the roof. Dare replaced the wood and went on his way.

Havill was smoking on his doorstep when Dare passed up the street. He held up his hand.

"Since you have been gone," said the architect, "I've hit upon something that may help you in exhibiting your lady to your gentleman. In the summer I had orders to design a gymnasium for her, which I did; and they say she is very clever on the ropes and bars. Now——"

"I've discovered it. I shall contrive for him to see her there on the first wet morning, which is when she practices. What made her think of it?"

"As you may have heard, she holds advanced views on social and other matters; and in those on the higher education of women she is very strong, talking a good deal about the physical training of the Greeks, whom she adores, or did. Every philosopher and man of science who ventilates his theories in the monthly reviews has a devout listener in her; and this subject of the physical development of her sex has had its turn with other things in her mind. So she had the place built on her very first arrival, according to the latest lights on athletics, and in imitation of those at the new colleges for women."

"How deuced clever of the girl! She means to live to be a hundred."

health, you say. Have a pull for safety's sake." He presented a
flask to De Stancy.

The military officer looked down at his nether garments.

"I don't break my rule without good reason," he observed.

"I am afraid that——"

"I am afraid it does. What have you got?"

CHAPTER VII

THE wet day arrived with all the promptness that might have
been expected of it in this land of rains and mists. The alder
bushes behind the gymnasium dripped monotonously leaf
upon leaf, added to this being the purl of the shallow stream a
little way off, producing a sense of satiety in watery sound.
Though there was drizzle in the open meads, the rain here in
the thicket was comparatively slight, and two men with fishing
tackle who stood beneath one of the large bushes found its
boughs a sufficent shelter.

"We may as well walk home again as study nature here,
Willy," said the taller and elder of the twain. "I feared it would
continue when we started. The magnificent sport you speak of
must rest for to-day."

The other looked at his watch, but made no particular reply.

"Come, let us move on. I don't like intruding into other
people's grounds like this," De Stancy continued.

"We are not intruding. Anybody walks outside this fence."
He indicated an iron railing newly tarred, dividing the wilder
underwood amid which they stood from the inner and well-
kept parts of the shrubbery, and against which the back of the
gymnasium was built.

Light footsteps upon a gravel walk could be heard on the
other side of the fence, and a trio of cloaked and umbrella-
screened figures were for a moment discernible. They vanished
behind the gymnasium; and again nothing resounded but the
river murmurs and the clock-like drippings of the leafage.

"Hush!" said Dare.

"No pranks, my boy," said De Stancy, suspiciously. "You
should be above them."

"And you should trust to my good sense, captain," Dare
remonstrated. "I have not indulged in a prank since the sixth
year of my pilgrimage: I have found them too damaging to my
interests. Well, it is not too dry here, and damp injures your

health, you say. Have a pull for safety's sake." He presented a flask to De Stancy.

The artillery officer looked down at his nether garments.

"I don't break my rule without good reason," he observed.

"I am afraid that reason exists at present."

"I am afraid it does. What have you got?"

"Only a little wine."

"What wine?"

"Do try it. I call it 'the blushful Hippocrene,' that the poet describes as

'Tasting of Flora and the country green;
Dance, and Provençal song, and sun-burnt mirth.'"

De Stancy took the flask, and drank a little.

"It warms, does it not?" said Dare.

"Too much," said De Stancy with misgiving. "I have been taken unawares. Why, it is three parts brandy, to my taste, you scamp!"

Dare put away the wine. "Now you are to see something," he said.

"Something—what is it?" Captain De Stancy regarded him with a puzzled look.

"It is quite a curiosity, and really worth seeing. Now just look in here."

The speaker advanced to the back of the building, and withdrew the wood billet from the wall.

"Will, I believe you are up to some trick," said De Stancy, not, however, suspecting the actual truth in these unsuggestive circumstances, and with a comfortable resignation, produced by the potent liquor, which would have been comical to an outsider; but which, to one who had known the history and relationship of the two speakers, would have worn a sadder significance. "I am too big a fool about you to keep you down as I ought; that's the fault of me, worse luck."

He pressed the youth's hand with a smile, went forward, and looked through the hole into the interior of the gymnasium. Dare withdrew to some little distance, and watched Captain De Stancy's face, which presently began to change.

What was the captain seeing? A sort of optical poem.

Paula, in a pink flannel costume, was bending, wheeling, and undulating in the air like a gold-fish in its globe, sometimes ascending by her arms nearly to the lantern, then lowering herself till she swung level with the floor. Her aunt Mrs. Goodman, and Charlotte De Stancy, were sitting on camp-stools at one end, watching her gyrations, Paula occasionally addressing them with such an expression as—"Now, Aunt, look at me—and you, Charlotte—is not that shocking to your weak nerves!" when some adroit feat would be repeated, which, however, seemed to give much more pleasure to Paula herself in performing it than to Mrs. Goodman in looking on, the latter sometimes saying, "Oh, it is terrific—do not run such a risk again!"

It would have demanded the poetic passion of some joyous Elizabethan lyrist like Lodge, Nash, or Constable, to fitly phrase Paula's presentation of herself at this moment of absolute abandonment to every muscular whim that could take possession of such a supple form. The white manilla ropes clung about the performer like snakes as she took her exercise, and the colour in her face deepened as she went on. Captain De Stancy felt that, much as he had seen in early life of beauty in woman, he had never seen beauty of such a real and living sort as this. A bitter recollection of his vow, together with a sense that to gaze on the festival of this Bona Dea was, though so pretty a sight, hardly fair or gentlemanly, would have compelled him to withdraw his eyes, had not the sportive fascination of her appearance glued them there in spite of all. And as if to complete the picture of Grace personified and add the one thing wanting to the charm which bound him, the clouds, till that time thick in the sky, broke away from the upper heaven, and allowed the noonday sun to pour down through the lantern upon her, irradiating her with a warm light that was incarnadined by her pink doublet and hose, and reflected in upon her face. She only required a cloud to rest on instead of the green silk net which actually supported her reclining figure for the moment, to be quite Olympian; save indeed that in place of haughty effrontery there sat on her countenance only the healthful sprightliness of an English girl.

Dare had withdrawn to a point at which another path crossed

the path occupied by De Stancy. Looking in a side direction, he saw Havill idling slowly up to him over the silent grass. Havill's knowledge of the appointment had brought him out to see what would come of it. When he neared Dare, but was still partially hidden by the boughs from the third of the party, the former simply pointed to De Stancy, upon which Havill still stood and peeped at him. "Is she within there?" he inquired.

Dare nodded, and whispered, "You need not have asked, if you had examined his face."

"That's true."

"A fermentation is beginning in him," said Dare, half-pitifully; "a purely chemical process; and when it is complete he will probably be clear, and fiery, and sparkling, and quite another man than the good, weak, easy fellow that he was."

To precisely describe Captain De Stancy's look was impossible. A sun rising in his face, such was somewhat the effect. By watching him they could almost see the aspect of her within the wall, so accurately were her changing phases reflected in him. He seemed to forget that he was not alone.

"And is this," he murmured, in the manner of one only half apprehending himself, "and is this the end of my vow?"

Paula was saying at this moment, "Ariel sleeps in this posture, does he not, Auntie?" Suiting the action to the word, she flung out her arms behind her head as she lay in the green silk hammock, idly closed her pink eyelids, and swung herself to and fro.

BOOK THE THIRD

DE STANCY

CHAPTER I

CAPTAIN DE STANCY was a changed man. A hitherto well-repressed energy was giving him motion towards long-shunned consequences. His features were, indeed, to cursory observation, much the same as before; though had a physiognomist chosen to study them with the closeness of an astronomer scanning the universe, he would doubtless have discerned abundant novelty.

In recent years De Stancy had been an easy, melancholy, unaspiring officer, enervated and depressed by a parental affection quite beyond his control for the graceless lad Dare—the obtrusive memento of a shadowy period in De Stancy's youth, who threatened to be the curse of his old age. Throughout a long space he had persevered in his system of rigidly incarcerating within himself all instincts towards the opposite sex, with a resolution that would not have disgraced a much stronger man. By this habit, maintained with fair success, a chamber of his nature had been preserved intact during many later years, like the one solitary sealed-up cell occasionally retained by bees in a lobe of drained honey-comb. And thus, though he had irretrievably exhausted the relish of society, of ambition, of action, and of his profession, the love-force that he had kept immured alive was still a reproducible thing.

The sight of Paula in the gymnasium, which the judicious Dare had so carefully planned, led up to and heightened by subtle accessories, operated on De Stancy's surprised soul with a promptness almost magical.

On the evening of the self-same day, having dined as usual, he retired to his rooms, where he found a hamper of wine awaiting him. It had been anonymously sent, and the account was paid. He smiled grimly, but no longer with heaviness. In this he instantly recognised the handiwork of Dare, who, having at last broken down the barrier which De Stancy had erected round his heart for so many years, acted like a skilled strategist, and took swift measures to follow up the advantage so tardily gained.

Captain De Stancy knew himself conquered; he knew he should yield to Paula—had indeed yielded; but there was now, in his solitude, an hour or two of reaction. He did not drink from the bottles sent. He went early to bed, and lay tossing thereon till far into the night, thinking over the collapse. His teetotalism had, with the lapse of years, unconsciously become the outward and visible sign to himself of his secret vows; and a return to its opposite, however mildly done, signified with ceremonious distinctness the formal acceptance of delectations long forsworn.

But the exceeding freshness of his feeling for Paula, which by reason of its long arrest was that of a man far under thirty, and was a wonder to himself every instant, would not long brook weighing in balances. He wished suddenly to commit himself; to remove the question of retreat out of the region of debate. The clock struck two: and the wish became determination. He arose, and wrapping himself in his dressing-gown went to the next room, where he took from a shelf in the pantry several large bottles, which he carried to the window, till they stood on the sill a goodly row. There had been sufficient light in the room for him to do this without a candle. Now he softly opened the sash, and the radiance of a gibbous moon riding in the opposite sky flooded the apartment. It fell on the labels of the captain's bottles, revealing their contents to be simple aërated waters for drinking.

De Stancy looked out and listened. The guns that stood drawn up within the yard glistened in the moonlight reaching them from over the barrack-wall: there was an occasional stamp of horses in the stables; also a measured tread of sentinels—one or more at the gates, one at the hospital, one between the wings, two at the magazine, and others further off. Recurring to his intention he drew the corks of the mineral waters, and inverting each bottle one by one over the window-sill, heard its contents dribble in a small stream on to the gravel below.

He then opened the hamper which Dare had sent. Uncorking one of the bottles he murmured, "To Paula!" and drank a glass of the ruby liquor.

"A man again after eighteen years," he said, shutting the sash and returning to his bedroom.

The first overt result of his kindled interest in Miss Power was his saying to his sister the day after the surreptitious sight of Paula: "I am sorry, Charlotte, for a word or two I said the other day."

"Well!"

"I was rather disrespectful to your friend Miss Power."

"I don't think so—were you?"

"Yes. When we were walking in the wood, I made a stupid joke about her. . . . What does she know about me—do you ever speak of me to her?"

"Only in general terms."

"What general terms?"

"You know well enough, William; of your idiosyncrasies and so on—that you are a bit of a woman-hater, or at least a confirmed bachelor, and have but little respect for your own family."

"I wish you had not told her that," said De Stancy with dissatisfaction.

"But I thought you always liked women to know your principles!" said Charlotte, in injured tones; "and would particularly like her to know them, living so near."

"Yes, yes," replied her brother hastily. "Well, I ought to see her, just to show her that I am not quite a brute."

"That would be very nice!" she answered, putting her hands together in agreeable astonishment. "It is just what I have wished, though I did not dream of suggesting it after what I have heard you say. I am going to stay with her again to-morrow, and I will let her know about this."

"Don't tell her anything plainly, for heaven's sake. I really want to see the interior of the castle: I have never entered its walls since my babyhood." He raised his eyes as he spoke to where the walls in question showed their ashlar faces over the trees.

"You might have gone over it at any time."

"Oh yes. It is only recently that I have thought much of the place: I feel now that I should like to examine the old building thoroughly, since it was for so many generations associated with our fortunes, especially as most of the old furniture is still there. My sedulous avoidance hitherto of all relating to our family vicissitudes has been, I own, stupid conduct for an intelligent being; but impossible grapes are always sour, and I have unconsciously adopted Radical notions to obliterate disappointed hereditary instincts. But these have a trick of re-establishing themselves as one gets older, and the castle and what it contains have a keen interest for me now."

"It contains Paula."

De Stancy's pulse, which had been beating languidly for many years, beat double at the sound of that name.

"I meant furniture and pictures for the moment," he said; "but I don't mind extending the meaning to her, if you wish it."

"She is the rarest thing there."

"So you have said before." He might have added, "but never with the present effect upon me."

"The castle and our family history have as much romantic interest for her as they have for you," Charlotte went on. "She delights in visiting our tombs and effigies, and ponders over them for hours."

"Indeed!" said De Stancy, allowing his surprise to hide the satisfaction which accompanied it. "That should make us friendly. . . . Does she see many people?"

"Not many as yet. And she cannot have many staying there during the alterations."

"Ah! yes—the alterations. Didn't you say that she has had a London architect stopping there on that account? What was he—old or young?"

"He is a young man: he has been to our house. Don't you remember you met him there?"

"What was his name?"

"Mr. Somerset."

"Oh, that man! Yes, yes, I remember. . . . Hullo, Lottie!"

"What?"

"Your face is as red as a peony. Now I know a secret!" Charlotte vainly endeavoured to hide her confusion. "Very well,—not a word! I won't say more," continued De Stancy, good-humouredly, "except that he seems to be a very nice fellow."

De Stancy had turned the dialogue on to this little well-preserved secret of his sister's with sufficient outward lightness; but it had been done in instinctive concealment of the disquieting start with which he had recognised that Somerset, Dare's enemy, whom he had intercepted in placing Dare's portrait into the hands of the chief constable, was a man beloved by his sister Charlotte. This novel circumstance might lead to a curious complication. But he was to hear more.

"He may be very nice," replied Charlotte, with an effort, after this silence. "But he is nothing to me, more than a very good friend."

"There's no engagement, or thought of one between you?"

"Certainly there's not!" said Charlotte, with brave emphasis. "It is more likely to be between Paula and him than me and him."

De Stancy's bare military ears and closely cropped poll flushed hot. "Miss Power and him?"

"I don't mean to say there is, because Paula denies it; but I mean that he loves Paula. That I do know."

De Stancy was dumb. This item of news which Dare had kept from him, not knowing how far De Stancy's sense of honour might extend, was decidedly grave. Indeed, he was so greatly impressed with the fact, that he could not help saying as much aloud: "This is very serious!"

"Why?" she murmured tremblingly, for the first leaking out of her tender and sworn secret had disabled her quite.

"Because I love Paula too."

"What do you say, William, you?—a woman you have never seen?"

"I have seen her—by accident. And now, my dear little sis, you will be my close ally, won't you? as I will be yours, as brother and sister should be." He placed his arm coaxingly round Charlotte's shoulder.

"Oh, William, how can I?" at last she stammered.

"Why, how can't you? I should say. We are both in the same ship. I love Paula, you love Mr. Somerset; it behoves both of us to see that this flirtation of theirs ends in nothing."

"I don't like you to put it like that—that I love him—it frightens me," murmured the girl, visibly agitated. "I don't want to divide him from Paula; I couldn't, I wouldn't do anything to separate them. Believe me, Will, I could not! I am sorry you love there also, though I should be glad if it happened in the natural order of events that she should come round to you. But I cannot do anything to part them and make Mr. Somerset suffer. It would be *too* wrong and blamable."

"Now, you silly Charlotte, that's just how you women fly off at a tangent. I mean nothing dishonourable in the least. Have I ever prompted you to do anything dishonourable. Fair fighting allies was all I thought of."

Miss De Stancy breathed more freely. "Yes, we will be that, of course; we are always that, William. But I hope I can be your ally, and be quite neutral; I would so much rather."

"Well, I suppose it will not be a breach of your precious neutrality if you get me invited to see the castle?"

"Oh no!" she said brightly; "I don't mind doing such a thing as that. Why not come with me to-morrow? I will say I am going to bring you. There will be no trouble at all."

De Stancy readily agreed. The instant effect upon him of the information now acquired was to intensify his ardour tenfold.

The stimulus was no doubt partly due to a perception that Somerset, with a little more knowledge, would have in his hands a card which could be played with disastrous effect against himself. Were his relationship to Dare once discovered by Somerset, in the latter's already manifested doubt of Dare's personal character, he would, without question, be stimulated by the heat of rivalry to disclose that relationship instantly. Nay—and it added yet more excitement to this game to know it, though the pang was so much the greater—Dare's character was of a kind to justify such an exposure by any man of common probity, without the stimulus of rivalry. And to a lady of such Puritan antecedents as Paula's this would probably mean her immediate severance from himself as an unclean thing.

"Is Miss Power a severe pietist, or precisian; or is she a compromising lady?" he asked abruptly.

"She is severe and uncompromising—if you mean in her judgements on morals," said Charlotte, not quite hearing. The remark was peculiarly apposite, and De Stancy was silent.

He spent some following hours in a close study of the castle history, which till now had unutterably bored him. More particularly did he dwell over documents and notes which referred to the pedigree of his own family. He wrote out the names of all—and they were many—who had been born within those domineering walls since their first erection; of those among them who had been brought thither by marriage with the owner, and of stranger knights and gentlemen, fewer, yet more interesting in present circumstances, who had entered the castle by marriage with its mistress. He refreshed his memory on the strange loves and hates that had arisen in the course of the family history; on memorable attacks, and the dates of the same, the most memorable among them being the occasion on which the party represented by Paula battered down the castle walls that she was now about to mend, and, as he hoped, return in their original intact shape to the family dispossessed, by marriage with himself, its living representative.

In Sir William's villa were small engravings after many of the portraits in the castle galleries, some of them hanging in the dining-room in plain maple frames, and others preserved in portfolios. De Stancy spent much of his time over these, and in getting up the romances of their originals' lives from memoirs and other records, all which stories were as great novelties to him as they could possibly be to any stranger. Most interesting to him was the life of an Edward De Stancy, who had lived just before the Civil Wars, and to whom Captain De Stancy bore a very traceable likeness. This ancestor had a mole on his cheek, black and distinct as a fly in cream; and as in the case of the first Lord Amherst's wart, and Bennet, Earl of Arlington's nose-scar, the painter had faithfully reproduced the defect on canvas. It so happened that the captain had a mole, though not exactly on the same spot of his face; and this made the resemblance still greater.

He took infinite trouble with his dress that day, showing an amount of anxiety on the matter which for him was quite abnormal. At last, when fully equipped, he set out with his sister to make the call proposed. Charlotte was rather unhappy at sight of her brother's earnest attempt to make an impression on Paula; but she could say nothing against it, and they proceeded on their way.

It was the darkest of November weather, when the days are so short that morning seems to join with evening without the intervention of noon. The sky was lined with low cloud, within whose dense substance tempests were slowly fermenting for the coming days. Even now a windy turbulence troubled the half-naked boughs, and a lonely leaf would occasionally spin downwards to rejoin on the grass the scathed multitude of its comrades which had preceded it in its fall. The river by the pavilion, in the summer so clear and purling, now slid onwards brown and thick and silent, and enlarged to double size.

CHAPTER II

MEANWHILE Paula was alone. Of any one else it would have been said that she was finding the afternoon rather dreary in the vast halls not of her forefathers; but of Miss Power it was unsafe to predicate so surely. She walked from room to room in a black velvet dress which gave decision to her outline without depriving it of softness. She occasionally clasped her hands behind her head and looked out of a window; but she more particularly bent her footsteps up and down the Long Gallery, where she had caused a large fire of logs to be kindled, in her endeavour to extend cheerfulness somewhat beyond the precincts of the sitting-rooms.

The fire glanced up on Paula, and Paula glanced down at the fire, and at the gnarled beech fuel, and at the wood-lice which ran out from beneath the bark to the extremity of the logs, as the heat approached them. The low-down ruddy light spread over the dark floor like the setting sun over a moor, fluttering on the grotesque countenances of the bright andirons, and touching all the furniture on the underside.

She now and then crossed to one of the deep embrasures of the windows, to decipher some sentence from a letter she held in her hand. The daylight would have been more than sufficient for any bystander to discern that the capitals in that letter were of the peculiar semi-gothic type affected at the time by Somerset and other young architects of his school in their epistolary correspondence. She was very possibly thinking of him, even when not reading his letter, for the expression of softness with which she perused the page was more or less with her when she appeared to examine other things.

She walked about for a little time longer, then put away the letter, looked at the clock, and thence returned to the windows, straining her eyes over the landscape without, as she murmured, "I wish Charlotte was not so long coming!"

As Charlotte continued to keep away, Paula became less

reasonable in her desires, and proceeded to wish that Somerset would arrive; then that anybody would come; then, walking towards the portraits on the wall, she flippantly asked one of those cavaliers to oblige her fancy for company by stepping down from his frame. The temerity of the request led her to prudently withdraw it almost as soon as conceived: old paintings had been said to play queer tricks in extreme cases, and the shadows this afternoon were funereal enough for anything in the shape of revenge on an intruder who embodied the antagonistic modern spirit to such an extent as she. However, Paula still stood before the picture which had attracted her; and this, by a coincidence common enough in fact, though scarcely credited in chronicles, happened to be that one of the seventeenth-century portraits of which De Stancy had studied the engraved copy at Myrtle Villa the same morning.

Whilst she remained before the picture, wondering her favourite wonder, how would she feel if this and its accompanying canvases were pictures of her own ancestors, she was surprised by a light footstep upon the carpet which covered part of the room, and turning quickly she beheld the smiling little figure of Charlotte De Stancy.

"What has made you so late?" said Paula. "You are come to stay, of course?"

Charlotte said she had come to stay. "But I have brought somebody with me!"

"Ah—whom?"

"My brother happened to be at home, and I have brought him."

Miss De Stancy's brother had been so continuously absent from home in India, or elsewhere, so little spoken of, and, when spoken of, so truly though unconsciously represented as one whose interests lay wholly outside this antiquated neighbourhood, that to Paula he had been a mere nebulosity whom she had never distinctly outlined. To have him thus cohere into substance at a moment's notice lent him the novelty of a new creation.

"Is he in the drawing-room?" said Paula in a low voice.

"No, he is here. He would follow me. I hope you will forgive him."

And then Paula saw emerge into the red beams of the dancing fire, from behind a half-drawn hanging which screened the door, the military gentleman whose acquaintance the reader has already made.

"You know the house, doubtless, Captain De Stancy?" said Paula, somewhat shyly, when he had been presented to her.

"I have never seen the inside since I was three weeks old," replied the artillery officer gracefully; "and hence my recollections of it are not remarkably distinct. A year or two before I was born the entail was cut off by my father and grandfather; so that I saw the venerable place only to lose it; at least, I believe that's the truth of the case. But my knowledge of the transaction is not profound, and it is a delicate point on which to question one's father."

Paula assented, and looked at the interesting and noble figure of the man whose parents had seemingly righted themselves at the expense of wronging him.

"The pictures and furniture were sold about the same time, I think?" said Charlotte.

"Yes," murmured De Stancy. "They went in a mad bargain of my father with his visitor, as they sat over their wine. My father sat down as host on that occasion, and arose as guest."

He seemed to speak with such a courteous absence of regret for the alienation, that Paula, who was always fearing that the recollection would rise as a painful shadow between herself and the De Stancys, felt reassured by his magnanimity.

De Stancy looked with interest round the gallery; seeing which Paula said she would have lights brought in a moment.

"No, please not," said De Stancy. "The room and ourselves are of so much more interesting a colour by this light!"

As they moved hither and thither, the various expressions of De Stancy's face made themselves picturesquely visible in the unsteady shine of the blaze. In a short time he had drawn near to the painting of the ancestor whom he so greatly resembled. When her quick eye noted the speck on the face, indicative of inherited traits strongly pronounced, a new and romantic feeling that the De Stancys had stretched out a tentacle from their genealogical tree to seize her by the hand and draw her in to their mass took possession of Paula. As has been said, the

De Stancys were a family on whom the hallmark of membership was deeply stamped, and by the present light the representative under the portrait and the representative in the portrait seemed beings not far removed. Paula was continually starting from a reverie and speaking irrelevantly, as if such reflections as those seized hold of her in spite of her natural unconcern.

When candles were brought in Captain De Stancy ardently contrived to make the pictures the theme of conversation. From the nearest they went to the next, whereupon Paula as hostess took up one of the candlesticks and held it aloft to light up the painting. The candlestick being tall and heavy, De Stancy relieved her of it, and taking another candle in the other hand, he imperceptibly slid into the position of exhibitor rather than spectator. Thus he walked in advance, holding the two candles on high, his shadow forming a gigantic figure on the neighbouring wall, while he recited the particulars of family history pertaining to each portrait, that he had learnt up with such eager persistence during the previous four-and-twenty hours.

"I have often wondered what could have been the history of this lady, but nobody has ever been able to tell me," Paula observed, pointing to a Vandyck which represented a beautiful woman wearing curls across her forehead, a square-cut bodice, and a heavy pearl necklace upon the smooth expanse of her neck.

"I don't think anybody knows," Charlotte said.

"Oh yes," replied her brother promptly, seeing with enthusiasm that it was yet another opportunity for making capital of his acquired knowledge, with which he felt himself as inconveniently crammed as a candidate for a government examination. "That lady has been largely celebrated under a fancy name, though she is comparatively little known by her own. Her parents were the chief ornaments of the almost irreproachable court of Charles the First, and were not more distinguished by their politeness and honour than by the affections and virtues which constitute the great charm of private life."

The stock verbiage of the family memoir was somewhat apparent in this effusion; but it much impressed his listeners;

and he went on to point out that from the lady's necklace was suspended a heart-shaped portrait—that of the man who broke his heart by her persistent refusal to encourage his suit. De Stancy then led them a little further, where hung a portrait of the lover, one of his own family, who appeared in full panoply of plate mail, the pommel of his sword standing up under his elbow. The gallant captain then related how this personage of his line wooed the lady fruitlessly; how, after her marriage with another, she and her husband visited the parents of the disappointed lover, the then occupiers of the castle; how, in a fit of desperation at the sight of her, he retired to his room, where he composed some passionate verses, which he wrote with his blood, and after directing them to her ran himself through the body with his sword. Too late the lady's heart was touched by his devotion; she was ever after a melancholy woman, and wore his portrait despite her husband's prohibition. "This," continued De Stancy, leading them through the doorway into the hall where the coats of mail were arranged along the wall, and stopping opposite a suit which bore some resemblance to that of the portrait, "this is his armour, as you will perceive by comparing it with the picture, and this is the sword with which he did the rash deed."

"What unreasonable devotion!" said Paula practically. "It was too romantic of him. She was not worthy of such a sacrifice."

"He also is one whom they say you resemble a little in feature, I think," said Charlotte.

"Do they?" replied De Stancy. "I wonder if it's true." He set down the candles, and asking the girls to withdraw for a moment, was inside the upper part of the suit of armour in incredibly quick time. Going then and placing himself in front of a low-hanging painting near the original, so as to be enclosed by the frame while covering the figure, arranging the sword as in the one above, and setting the light that it might fall in the right direction, he recalled them; when he put the question, "Is the resemblance strong?"

He looked so much like a man of bygone times that neither of them replied, but remained curiously gazing at him. His modern and comparatively sallow complexion, as seen through the open visor, lent an ethereal ideality to his appearance which the time-stained countenance of the original warrior totally lacked.

At last Paula spoke, so stilly that she seemed a statue enunciating: "Are the verses known that he wrote with his blood?"

"Oh yes, they have been carefully preserved." Captain De Stancy, with true wooer's instinct, had committed some of them to memory that morning from the printed copy. "I fear I don't remember them all," he said, "but they begin in this way:

'From one that dyeth in his discontent,
Dear Faire, receive this greeting to thee sent;
And still as oft as it is read by thee,
Then with some deep sad sigh remember mee!

O 'twas my fortune's error to vow dutie,
To one that bears defiance in her beautie!
Sweete poyson, precious wooe, infectious jewell—
Such is a Ladie that is faire and cruell.

How well could I with ayre, camelion-like,
Live happie, and still gazeing on thy cheeke,
In which, forsaken man, meethink I see
How goodlie Love doth threaten cares to mee.

Why dost thou frowne thus on a kneelinge soule,
Whose faultes in love thou may'st as well controule?—
In love—but O, that word; that word I feare
Is hatefull still both to thy hart and eare!

Ladie, in breefe, my fate doth now intend
The period of my daies to have an end:
Waste not on mee thy pittie, precious Faire:
Rest you in much content; I, in despaire!'"

A solemn silence followed the close of the recital, which De Stancy improved by turning the point of the sword to his breast, resting the pommel upon the floor, and saying:

"After writing that we may picture him turning this same sword in this same way, and falling on it thus." He inclined his body forward as he spoke.

"Don't, Captain De Stancy, please don't!" cried Paula, involuntarily.

"No, don't show us any further, William!" said his sister. "It is too tragic."

De Stancy put away the sword, himself rather excited—not, however, by his own recital, but by the direct gaze of Paula at him.

This Protean quality of De Stancy's, by means of which he could assume the shape and situation of almost any ancestor at will, had impressed her, and he perceived it with a throb of fervour. But it had done no more than impress her; for though in delivering the lines he had so fixed his look upon her as to suggest, to any maiden practised in the game of the eyes, a present significance in the words, the idea of any such double-entendre had by no means commended itself to her soul.

At this time a messenger from Markton barracks arrived at the castle and wished to speak to Captain De Stancy in the hall. Begging the two ladies to excuse him for a moment the captain went out.

While De Stancy was talking in the twilight to the messenger at one end of the apartment, some other arrival was shown in by the side door, and in making his way after the conference across the hall to the room he had previously quitted, De Stancy encountered the new-comer. There was just enough light to reveal the countenance to be Dare's; he bore a portfolio under his arm, and had begun to wear a moustache, in case the chief constable should meet him anywhere in his rambles, and be struck by his resemblance to the man in the studio.

"What the devil are you doing here?" said Captain De Stancy, in tones he had never used before to the young man.

Dare started back in surprise, and naturally so. De Stancy, having adopted a new system of living, and relinquished the meagre diet and enervating waters of his past years, was rapidly recovering tone. His voice was firmer, his cheeks were less pallid; and above all, he was authoritative towards his present companion, whose ingenuity in vamping up a Frankenstein for his ambitious experiments seemed likely to be rewarded by his discomfiture at the hands of his own creature.

"What the devil are you doing here, I say?" repeated De Stancy.

"You can talk to me like that, after my working so hard to get you on in life, and make a rising man of you!" expostulated Dare, like one who felt himself no longer the protagonist in this enterprise.

"But," said the captain less harshly, "if you let them discover any relations between us here, you will ruin the fairest prospects man ever had!"

"Oh, I like that, captain—when you owe all of it to me!"

"That's too cool, Will."

"No; what I say is true. However, let that go. So now you are here on a call; but how are you going to get here often enough to win her before the other man comes back? If you don't see her every day—twice, three times a day—you will not capture her in the time."

"I must think of that," said De Stancy.

"There is only one way of being constantly here: you must come to copy the pictures or furniture, something in the way he did."

"I'll think of it," muttered De Stancy, hastily, as he heard the voices of the ladies, whom he hastened to join as they were appearing at the other end of the room. His countenance was gloomy as he recrossed the hall, for Dare's words on the shortness of his opportunities had impressed him. Almost at once he uttered a hope to Paula that he might have further chance of studying, and if possible of copying, some of the ancestral faces with which the building abounded.

Meanwhile Dare had come forward with his portfolio, which proved to be full of photographs. While Paula and Charlotte were examining them he said to De Stancy, as a stranger: "Excuse my interruption, sir, but if you should think of copying any of the portraits, as you were stating just now to the ladies, my patent photographic process is at your service, and is, I believe, the only one which would be effectual in the dim indoor lights."

"It is just what I was thinking of," said De Stancy, now so far cooled down from his irritation as to be quite ready to accept Dare's adroitly suggested scheme for frequenting Paula's halls.

On application to Paula she immediately gave De Stancy permission to photograph to any extent, and told Dare he might bring his instruments as soon as Captain De Stancy required them.

"Don't stare at her in such a brazen way!" whispered that officer to the young man, when Paula had withdrawn a few steps. "Say, 'I shall value the privilege highly of assisting Captain De Stancy in such a work.'"

Dare obeyed, and before leaving De Stancy arranged to begin performing on his venerated forefathers the next morning, the youth so accidentally engaged agreeing to be there at the same time to assist in the technical operations.

The weather was frequently wet during these operations, and Paula, Miss De Stancy, and her brother, were often in the house whole mornings together. By constant urging and coaxing, the latter would induce his gentle sister, much against her conscience, to leave him opportunities for speaking to Paula alone. It was mostly before some print or painting that these conversations occurred, while De Stancy was ostensibly occupied with its merits, or in giving directions to his photographer how to proceed. As soon as the dialogue began, the latter would withdraw out of earshot, leaving Paula to imagine him the most deferential young artist in the world.

"You will soon possess duplicates of the whole gallery," she said on one of these occasions, examining some curled sheets which Dare had printed off from the negatives.

"No," said the soldier, "I shall not have patience to go on. I get ill-humoured, and indifferent, and then leave off."

"Why ill-humoured?"

"I scarcely know—more than that I acquire a general sense of my own family's want of merit through seeing how meritorious the people are around me. I see them happy and thriving without any necessity for me at all; and then I regard these canvas grandfathers and grandmothers, and ask.. Why was a line so antiquated and out of date prolonged till now?"

She chid him good-naturedly for such views. "They will do

DE STANCY 103

accept Dare's adroitly suggested scheme for frequenting
Paula's halls.

On application to Paula she immediately gave De Stancy
permission to photograph to any extent, and told Dare he
might bring his instrument whenever Captain De Stancy
required them.

CHAPTER III

As he had promised, De Stancy made use the next day of
the coveted permission that had been brought about by the
ingenious Dare. Dare's second timely suggestion of tendering
assistance himself had the practical result of relieving the other
of all necessity for occupying his time with the proceeding,
further than to bestow a perfunctory superintendence now and
then, to give a colour to his regular presence in the fortress,
the actual work of taking copies being carried on by the
younger man.

The weather was frequently wet during these operations,
and Paula, Miss De Stancy, and her brother, were often in the
house whole mornings together. By constant urging and coaxing the latter would induce his gentle sister, much against her
conscience, to leave him opportunities for speaking to Paula
alone. It was mostly before some print or painting that these
conversations occurred, while De Stancy was ostensibly occupied with its merits, or in giving directions to his photographer
how to proceed. As soon as the dialogue began, the latter
would withdraw out of earshot, leaving Paula to imagine him
the most deferential young artist in the world.

"You will soon possess duplicates of the whole gallery," she
said on one of these occasions, examining some curled sheets
which Dare had printed off from the negatives.

"No," said the soldier. "I shall not have patience to go on. I
get ill-humoured, and indifferent, and then leave off."

"Why ill-humoured?"

"I scarcely know—more than that I acquire a general sense
of my own family's want of merit through seeing how meritorious the people are around me. I see them happy and thriving
without any necessity for me at all; and then I regard these
canvas grandfathers and grandmothers, and ask, 'Why was a
line so antiquated and out of date prolonged till now?'"

She chid him good-naturedly for such views. "They will do

you an injury," she declared. "Do spare yourself, Captain De Stancy!"

De Stancy shook his head as he turned the painting before him a little further to the light.

"But, do you know," said Paula, "that notion of yours of being a family out of date is delightful to some people. I talk to Charlotte about it often. I am never weary of examining those canopied effigies in the church, and almost wish they were those of my relations."

"I will try to see things in the same light for your sake," said De Stancy, fervently.

"Not for my sake; for your own was what I meant, of course," she replied, with a repressive air.

Captain De Stancy bowed.

"What are you going to do with your photographs when you have them?" she asked, as if still anxious to obliterate the previous sentimental lapse.

"I shall put them into a large album, and carry them with me in my campaigns; and may I ask, now I have an opportunity, that you would extend your permission to copy a little further, and let me photograph one other painting that hangs in the castle, to fittingly complete my set?"

"Which?"

"That half-length of a lady which hangs in the morning-room. I remember seeing it in the Academy last year."

Paula involuntarily closed herself up. The picture was her own portrait. "It does not belong to your series," she said somewhat coldly.

De Stancy's secret thought was, I hope from my soul it will belong some day! He answered with mildness: "There is a sort of connection—you are my sister's friend."

Paula assented.

"And hence, might not your friend's brother photograph your picture?"

Paula demurred.

A gentle sigh rose from the bosom of De Stancy. "What is to become of me?" he said, with a light distressed laugh. "I am always inconsiderate and inclined to ask too much. Forgive me! What was in my mind when I asked I dare not say."

"I quite understand your interest in your family pictures—and all of it," she remarked more gently, willing not to hurt the sensitive feelings of a man so full of romance.

"And in that *one*!" he said, looking devotedly at her. "If I had only been fortunate enough to include it with the rest, my album would indeed have been a treasure to pore over by the bivouac fire!"

"Oh, Captain De Stancy, this is provoking perseverance!" cried Paula, laughing half-crossly. "I expected that after expressing my decision so plainly the first time I should not have been further urged upon the subject." Saying which she turned and moved decisively away.

It had not been a productive meeting, thus far. "One word!" said De Stancy, following and almost dropping on one knee. "I have given offence, I know; but do let it all fall on my own head—don't tell my sister of my misbehaviour! She loves you deeply and it would wound her to the heart."

"You deserve to be told upon," said Paula as she withdrew, with just enough playfulness to show that her anger was not too serious.

Charlotte looked at Paula uneasily when the latter joined her in the drawing-room. She wanted to say, "What is the matter?" but guessing that her brother had something to do with it, forbore to speak at first. But she could not contain her anxiety long. "Were you talking with my brother?" she said.

"Yes," returned Paula, with reservation. However she soon added, "he not only wants to photograph his ancestors, but *my* portrait too. They are a dreadfully encroaching sex, and perhaps being in the army makes them worse!"

"I'll give him a hint, and tell him to be careful."

"Don't say I have definitely complained of him; it is not worth while to do that; the matter is too trifling for repetition. Upon the whole, Charlotte, I would rather you said nothing at all."

De Stancy's hobby of photographing his ancestors seemed to become a perfect mania with him. Almost every morning discovered him in the larger apartments of the castle, taking down and rehanging the dilapidated pictures, with the assistance of the indispensable Dare; his fingers stained black with dust, and his face expressing a busy attention to the work in hand, though always reserving a look askance for the presence of Paula.

Thus much must be said for Captain De Stancy; that though there was something of subterfuge, there was no double subterfuge in all this. It is true that he took no particular interest in his ancestral portraits; but he was enamoured of Paula to weakness. Perhaps the composition of his love would hardly bear looking into, but it was passionately frank and not quite mercenary. His photographic scheme was nothing worse than a lover's not too scrupulous contrivance. After the refusal of his request to copy her picture he fumed and fretted at the prospect of Somerset's return before any impression had been made on her heart by himself; he swore at Dare, and asked him hotly why he had dragged him into such a hopeless dilemma as this.

"Hopeless? Somerset must still be kept away, so that it is not hopeless. I will consider how to prolong his stay."

Thereupon Dare considered.

The time was coming—had indeed come—when it was necessary for Paula to make up her mind about her architect, if she meant to begin building in the spring. The two sets of plans, Somerset's and Havill's, were hanging on the walls of the room that had been used by Somerset as his studio, and were accessible by anybody. Dare took occasion to go and study both sets, with a view to finding a flaw in Somerset's which might have been passed over unnoticed by the committee of architects, owing to their absence from the actual site. But not a blunder could he find.

He next went to Havill; and here he was met by an amazing state of affairs. Havill's creditors, at last suspecting something mythical in Havill's assurance that the grand commission was his, had lost all patience; his house was turned upside-down, and a poster gleamed on the front wall, stating that the excellent modern household furniture was to be sold by auction on Friday next. As an illustration of the truism that troubles come in battalions, Dare was informed by a bystander that Havill's wife was seriously ill also.

Without staying for a moment to enter his friend's house, back went Mr. Dare to the castle, and told Captain De Stancy of the architect's desperate circumstances, begging him to convey the news in some way to Miss Power. Though Dare's object in making this request was purely to bring about that which actually resulted from it, De Stancy, being a simpler character, promised to make representations in the proper quarter without perceiving that he was doing the best possible deed for himself thereby.

De Stancy told Paula of Havill's misfortunes in the presence of his sister, who turned pale. With a woman's quickness she had discerned how this misfortune would bear upon the undecided competition.

"Poor man," murmured Paula. "He was my father's architect, and somehow expected, though I did not promise it, the work of rebuilding the castle."

Then De Stancy saw Dare's aim, and, seeing it, concurred: Somerset was his rival, and all was fair. "And is he not to have the work of the castle after expecting it?" he asked with simplicity of tone.

Paula was lost in reflection. "The other architect's design and Mr. Havill's are exactly equal in merit, and we cannot decide how to give it to either," explained Charlotte.

"That is our difficulty," Paula murmured. "A bankrupt, and his wife ill—dear me! I wonder what's the cause."

"He has borrowed on the expectation of having to execute the castle works, and now he is unable to meet his liabilities."

"It is very sad," said Paula.

"Let me suggest a remedy for this deadlock," said De Stancy.

"Do," said Paula.

"Do the work of building in two halves or sections. Give Havill the first half, since he is in need; when that is finished, the second half can be given to your London architect. If, as I understand, the plans are identical except in ornamental details, there will be no difficulty about it at all."

Paula sighed—just a little one; and yet the suggestion seemed to satisfy her by its reasonableness. She turned sad, wayward, and yet was impressed by De Stancy's manner and words. She appeared indeed to have a smouldering desire to please him. In the afternoon she said to Charlotte, "I mean to do as your brother says."

A note was despatched to Havill that very day, and in an hour the crestfallen architect presented himself at the castle. Paula instantly gave him audience, commiserated him, and commissioned him to carry out a first section of the buildings, comprising work to the extent of about twenty thousand pounds expenditure; and then, with a prematureness quite phenomenal among architects' clients, she handed him over a cheque for five hundred pounds on account.

When he had gone, Paula's bearing showed some sign of her being disquieted at what she had done; but she covered her mood under a cloak of saucy serenity. Perhaps a tender remembrance of a certain thunderstorm in the foregoing August, when she stood with Somerset in the arbour, and did not own that she loved him, was pressing on her memory, and bewildering her. She had not seen quite clearly, in adopting De Stancy's suggestion, that Somerset would now have no professional reason for being at the castle for the next twelve months.

But the captain had, and when Havill entered the castle he rejoiced with great joy. Dare, too, rejoiced in his cold way, and went on with his photography, saying, "The game progresses, captain."

"Game? Call it Divine Comedy, rather!" said the captain, exultingly.

"He is practically banished for a year or more. What can't you do in a year, captain!"

Havill, in the mean time, having respectfully withdrawn from the presence of Paula, passed by Dare and De Stancy in the gallery as he had done in entering. He spoke a few words to Dare, who congratulated him. While they were talking somebody was heard in the hall, inquiring hastily for Mr. Havill.

"What shall I tell him?" demanded the porter.

"His wife is dead," said the messenger.

Havill overheard the words, and hastened away.

"An unlucky man!" said Dare.

"That, happily for us, will not affect his installation here," said De Stancy. "Now hold your tongue and keep at a distance. She may come this way."

Surely enough in a few minutes she came. De Stancy, to make conversation, told her of the new misfortune which had just befallen Mr. Havill.

Paula was very sorry to hear it, and remarked that it gave her great satisfaction to have appointed him as architect of the first wing before he learnt the bad news. "I owe you best thanks, Captain De Stancy, for showing me such an expedient."

"Do I really deserve thanks?" asked De Stancy with a meditative smile upon her. "I wish I deserved a reward; but I must bear in mind the fable of the priest and the jester."

"I never heard it."

"The jester implored the priest for alms, but the smallest sum was refused, though the holy man readily agreed to give him his blessing. Query, its value?"

"How does it apply?"

"You give me unlimited thanks, but deny me the tiniest substantial trifle I desire."

"What persistence!" exclaimed Paula, colouring. "Very well, if you *will* photograph my picture you must. It is really not worthy further pleading. Take it when you like."

When Paula was alone she seemed vexed with herself for having given way; and rising from her seat she went quietly to the door of the room containing the picture, intending to lock it up till further consideration, whatever he might think of her. But on casting her eyes round the apartment the painting was gone. The captain, wisely taking the current when it served, already had it in the gallery, where he was to be seen bending attentively over it, arranging the lights and directing Dare with the instruments. On leaving he thanked her, and said that he had obtained a splendid copy. Would she look at it?

Paula was severe and icy. "Thank you—I don't wish to see it," she said.

De Stancy bowed with civil reserve, and departed in a glow of triumph; satisfied, notwithstanding her frigidity, that he had compassed his immediate aim, which was that she might not be able to dismiss from her thoughts him and his persevering desire for the shadow of her face during the next four-and-twenty hours. And his confidence was well founded: she could not.

"I fear this Divine Comedy will be a slow business for us, captain," said Dare, who had heard her cold words.

"Oh no!" said De Stancy, flushing a little: he had not been perceiving that the lad had the measure of his mind so entirely as to gauge his position at any moment. But he would show no shamefacedness. "Even if it is, my boy," he answered, "there's plenty of time before the other can come."

At that hour and minute of De Stancy's remark "the other," to look at him, seemed indeed securely shelved. He was sitting lonely in his chambers far away, wondering why she did not write, and yet hoping to hear—wondering if it had all been but a short-lived strain of tenderness. He knew as well as if it had been stated in words that her serious acceptance of him as a suitor would be her acceptance of him as an architect—that her schemes in love would be expressed in terms of art; and conversely that her refusal of him as a lover would be neatly effected by her choosing Havill's plans for the castle, conveying to him, Somerset, the news that his design was deemed less suitable than the other, and returned with thanks. The position was so clear: he was so well walled in by the shape of circumstances that he was absolutely helpless.

To wait for the line that would not come—the letter saying that, as she had desired, his was the design that pleased her— was still the only thing to do. The (to Somerset) surprising accident that the committee of architects should have pronounced the designs absolutely equal in point of merit, and thus have caused the final choice to revert after all to Paula, had been a joyous thing to him when he first heard of it, full of confidence in her favour. But the fact of her having again become the arbitrator, though it had made acceptance of his plans all the more probable, made refusal of them, should it happen, all the more crushing. He could have conceived himself favoured by Paula as her lover, even had the committee decided in favour of Havill as her architect. But not to be chosen as architect now was to be rejected in both kinds.

"I fear this Divine Comedy will be a slow business for us, captain," said Dare, who had heard her cold words.

"Oh no!" said De Stancy, sighing a little: he had not been perceiving that she had had the measure of his mind so entirely as to gauge his position. . . . . would show no chamfacedness. "Even if it is, my boy," he answered, "there is a suitor . . . . .

CHAPTER IV

IT was the Sunday following the funeral of Mrs Havill, news of whose death had been so unexpectedly brought to her husband at the moment of his exit from Stancy Castle. The minister, as was his custom, improved the occasion by a couple of sermons on the uncertainty of life. One was preached in the morning in the old chapel of Markton; the second at evening service in the little rural chapel near Stancy Castle, built by Paula's father, which bore to the first somewhat the relation of an episcopal chapel-of-ease to the mother church.

The unscreened lights blazed through the plate-glass windows of the smaller building and outshone the steely stars of the early night, just as they had done when Somerset was attracted by their glare four months before. The fervid minister's rhetoric equalled its force on that more romantic occasion: but Paula was not there. She was not a frequent attendant now at her father's votive building. The mysterious tank, with its dark waters that had so repelled her at the last moment, was boarded over: a table stood on its centre, with an open quarto Bible upon it; behind which Havill, in a new suit of black, sat in a large chair. Havill held the office of deacon: and he had mechanically taken the deacon's seat as usual to-night, in the face of the congregation, and under the nose of Mr. Woodwell.

Mr. Woodwell was always glad of an opportunity. He was gifted with a burning natural eloquence, which though perhaps a little too freely employed in exciting the "Wertherism of the uncultivated" had in it genuine power. He was a master of that oratory which no limitation of knowledge can repress, and which no training can impart. The neighbouring rector could eclipse Woodwell's scholarship, and the freethinker at the corner shop in Markton could demolish his logic; but the Baptist could do in five minutes what neither of these had done in a lifetime; he could move some of the hardest men to tears.

Thus it happened that, when the sermon was fairly under

way, Havill began to feel himself in a trying position. It was not that he had bestowed much affection upon his deceased wife, irreproachable woman as she had been; but the suddenness of her death had shaken his nerves, and Mr. Woodwell's address on the uncertainty of life involved considerations of conduct on earth that bore with singular directness upon Havill's unprincipled manœuvre for victory in the castle competition. He wished he had not been so inadvertent as to take his customary chair in the chapel. People who saw Havill's agitation did not know that it was most largely owing to his sense of the fraud which had been practised on the unoffending Somerset: and when, unable longer to endure the torture of Woodwell's words, he rose from his place and went into the chapel vestry, the preacher little thought that remorse for a contemptibly unfair act, rather than grief for a dead wife, was the cause of the architect's withdrawal.

When Havill got into the open air his morbid excitement calmed down, but a sickening self-abhorrence for the proceeding instigated by Dare did not abate. To appropriate another man's design was no more nor less than to embezzle his money or steal his goods. The intense reaction from his conduct of the past two or three months did not leave him when he reached his own house and observed where the handbills of the countermanded sale had been torn down, as the result of the payment made in advance by Paula of money which should really have been Somerset's.

The mood went on intensifying when he was in bed. He lay awake till the clock reached those still, small, ghastly hours when the vital fires burn at their lowest in the human frame, and death seizes more of his victims than in any other of the twenty-four. Havill could bear it no longer; he got a light, went down into his office and wrote the note subjoined.

"MADAM,

"The recent death of my wife necessitates a considerable change in my professional arrangements and plans with regard to the future. One of the chief results of the change is, I regret to state, that I no longer find myself in a position to carry out the enlargement of the castle which you had so generously entrusted to my hands.

"I beg leave therefore to resign all further connection with the same, and to express, if you will allow me, a hope that the commission may be placed in the hands of the other competitor. Herewith is returned a cheque for one-half of the sum so kindly advanced in anticipation of the commission I should receive; the other half, with which I had cleared off my immediate embarrassments before perceiving the necessity for this course, shall be returned to you as soon as some payments from other clients drop in. I beg to remain, Madam, your obedient servant,

"JAMES HAVILL."

Havill would not trust himself till the morning to post this letter. He sealed it up, went out with it into the street, and walked through the sleeping town to the post-office. At the mouth of the box he held the letter long. By dropping it, he was dropping at least two thousand five hundred pounds which, however obtained, were now securely his. It was a great deal to let go; and there he stood till another wave of conscience bore in upon his soul the absolute nature of the theft, and made him shudder. The footsteps of a solitary policeman could be heard nearing him along the deserted street; hesitation ended, and he let the letter go.

When he awoke in the morning he thought over the circumstances by the cheerful light of a low eastern sun. The horrors of the situation seemed much less formidable; yet it cannot be said that he actually regretted his act. Later on he walked out, with the strange sense of being a man who, from one having a large professional undertaking in hand, had, by his own act, suddenly reduced himself to an unoccupied nondescript. From the upper end of the town he saw in the distance the grand grey towers of Stancy Castle looking over the leafless trees; he felt stupefied at what he had done, and said to himself with bitter discontent: "Well, well, what is more contemptible than a half-hearted rogue!"

That morning the post-bag had been brought to Paula and Mrs. Goodman in the usual way, and Miss Power read the letter. His resignation was a surprise: the question whether he would or would not repay the money was passed over; the necessity of installing Somerset after all as sole architect was an agitation, or emotion, the precise nature of which it is impossible to accurately define.

However, she went about the house after breakfast with very much the manner of one who had had weight removed either from her heart or from her conscience; moreover, her face was a little flushed when, in passing by Somerset's late studio, she saw the plans bearing his motto, and knew that his and not Havill's would be the presiding presence in the coming architectural turmoil. She went on further, and called to Charlotte, who was now regularly sleeping in the castle, to accompany her, and together they ascended to the telegraph-room in the donjon tower.

"Whom are you going to telegraph to?" said Miss De Stancy when they stood by the instrument.

"My architect."

"Oh—Mr. Havill."

"Mr. Somerset."

Miss De Stancy had schooled her emotions on that side cruelly well, and she asked calmly, "What, have you chosen him after all?"

"There is no choice in it—read that," said Paula, handing Havill's letter, as if she felt that Providence had stepped in to shape ends that she was too undecided or unpractised to shape for herself.

"It is very strange," murmured Charlotte; while Paula applied herself to the machine and despatched the words:

Miss Power, Stancy Castle, to G. Somerset, Esq., F.S.A., F.R.I.B.A., Queen Anne's Chambers, St. James's:—

Your design is accepted in its entirety. It will be necessary to begin soon. I shall wish to see and consult you on the matter about the 10*th instant.*

When the message was fairly gone out of the window Paula seemed still further to expand. The strange spell cast over her by something or other—probably the presence of De Stancy, and the weird romanticism of his manner towards her, which was as if the historic past had touched her with a yet living hand—in a great measure became dissipated, leaving her the arch and serene maiden that she was before.

About this time Captain De Stancy and his Achates were approaching the castle, and had arrived about fifty paces from the spot at which it was Dare's custom to drop behind his companion, in order that their appearance at the lodge should be that of master and man.

Dare was saying, as he had said before: "I can't help fancying, captain, that your approach to this castle and its mistress is by a very tedious system. Your trenches, zigzags, counterscarps, and ravelins may be all very well, and a very sure system of attack in the long run; but upon my soul they are almost as slow in maturing as those of Uncle Toby himself. For my part I should be inclined to try an assault."

"Don't pretend to give advice, Willy, on matters beyond your years."

"I only meant it for your good, and your proper advancement in the world," said Dare in wounded tones.

"Different characters, different systems," returned the captain. "This lady is of a reticent, independent, complicated disposition, and any sudden proceeding would put her on her mettle. You don't dream what my impatience is, my boy. It is a thing transcending your utmost conceptions! But I proceed slowly; I know better than to do otherwise. Thank God there is plenty of time. As long as there is no risk of Somerset's return my situation is sure."

"And professional etiquette will prevent him coming yet. Havill and he will be like the men in the weather-house; when Havill walks out, he'll walk in, and not a moment before."

"That will not be till eighteen months have passed. And, as the Jesuit said, 'Time and I against any two.' . . . Now drop to the rear," added Captain De Stancy authoritatively. And they passed under the walls of the castle.

The grave fronts and bastions were wrapped in silence; so much so that, standing a while in the inner ward, they could hear through an open window a faintly clicking sound from within.

"She's at the telegraph," said Dare, throwing forward his voice softly to the captain. "What can that be for so early?

That wire is a nuisance, to my mind; such constant intercourse with the outer world is bad for our romance."

The speaker entered to arrange his photographic apparatus, of which, in truth, he was getting weary; and De Stancy smoked on the terrace till Dare should be ready. While he waited his sister looked out upon him from an upper casement, having caught sight of him as she came from Paula in the telegraph-room.

"Well, Lotty, what news this morning?" he said gaily.

"Nothing of importance. We are quite well." . . . She added with hesitation, "There is one piece of news; Mr. Havill—but perhaps you have heard it in Markton?"

"Nothing."

"Mr. Havill has resigned his appointment as architect to the castle."

"What?—who has it, then?"

"Mr. Somerset," she faltered.

"Appointed?"

"Yes—by telegraph."

"When is he coming?" said De Stancy in consternation.

"About the tenth, we think."

Charlotte was concerned to see her brother's face, and withdrew from the window that he might not question her further. De Stancy went into the hall, and on to the gallery, where Dare was standing as still as a caryatid.

"I have heard every word," said Dare.

"Well, what does it mean? Has that fool Havill done it on purpose to annoy me? What conceivable reason can the man have for throwing up an appointment he has worked so hard for, at the moment he has got it, and in the time of his greatest need?"

Dare guessed, for he had seen a little way into Havill's soul during the brief period of their confederacy. But he was very far from saying what he guessed. Yet he unconsciously revealed by other words the nocturnal shades in his character which had made that confederacy possible.

"Somerset coming after all!" he replied. "By God: that little six-barrelled friend of mine, and a good resolution, and he would never arrive!"

"What!" said Captain De Stancy, paling with horror as he looked at the other and gathered his sinister meaning.

Dare instantly recollected himself. "One is tempted to say anything at such a moment," he replied hastily.

"Since he is to come, let him come, for me," continued De Stancy, with reactionary distinctness, and still gazing gravely into the young man's face. "The battle shall be fairly fought out. Fair play, even to a rival—remember that, my boy. . . . Why are you here?—unnaturally concerning yourself with the passions of a man of my age, as if you were the parent, and I the son? Would to Heaven, Willy, you had done as I wished you to do, and led the life of a steady, thoughtful young man! Instead of meddling here, you should now have been in some studio, college, or professional man's chambers, engaged in a useful pursuit which might have made one proud to own you. But you were so precocious and headstrong; and this is what you have come to: you promise to be worthless!"

"I think I shall go to my lodgings to-day instead of staying here over these pictures," said Dare, after a silence, during which Captain De Stancy endeavoured to calm himself. "I was going to tell you that my dinner today will unfortunately be one of herbs, for want of the needful. I have come to my last stiver.—You dine at the mess, I suppose, captain?"

De Stancy had walked away; but Dare knew that he played a pretty sure card in that speech. De Stancy's heart could not withstand the suggested contrast between a lonely meal of bread-and-cheese and a well-ordered dinner amid cheerful companions.— "Here," he said, emptying his pocket and returning to the lad's side. "Take this, and order yourself a good meal. You keep me as poor as a crow. There shall be more to-morrow."

The peculiarly bifold nature of Captain De Stancy, as shown in his conduct at different times, was something rare in life, and perhaps happily so. That mechanical admixture of black and white qualities without coalescence, on which the theory of men's characters was based by moral analysts before the rise of modern ethical schools, fictitious as it was in general application, would have almost hit off the truth as regards Captain De Stancy. Removed to some half-known century, his deeds would have won a picturesqueness of light and shade that might have made him a fascinating subject for some gallery of illustrious historical personages. It was this tendency to moral chequer-work which accounted for his varied bearings towards Dare.

Dare withdrew to take his departure. When he had gone a few steps, despondent, he suddenly turned, and ran back with some excitement.

"Captain—he's coming on the tenth, don't they say? Well, four days before the tenth comes the sixth. Have you forgotten what's fixed for the sixth?"

"I had quite forgotten!"

"That day will be worth three months of quiet attentions: with luck, skill, and a bold heart, what mayn't you do?"

Captain De Stancy's face softened with satisfaction.

"There is something in that; the game is not up after all. The sixth—it had gone clean out of my head, by gad!"

CHAPTER V

THE cheering message from Paula to Somerset sped through the loophole of Stancy Castle keep, over the trees, along the railway, under bridges, across three counties—from extreme antiquity of environment to sheer modernism—and finally landed itself on a table in Somerset's chambers in the midst of a cloud of fog. He read it and, in the moment of reaction from the depression of his past days, clapped his hands like a child.

Then he considered the date at which she wanted to see him. Had she so worded her despatch he would have gone that very day; but there was nothing to complain of in her giving him a week's notice. Pure maiden modesty might have checked her indulging in a too ardent recall.

Time, however, dragged somewhat heavily along in the interim, and on the second day he thought he would call on his father and tell him of his success in obtaining the appointment.

The elder Mr. Somerset lived in a detached house in the north-west part of fashionable London; and ascending the chief staircase the young man branched off from the first landing and entered his father's painting-room. It was an hour when he was pretty sure of finding the well-known painter at work, and on lifting the tapestry he was not disappointed, Mr. Somerset being busily engaged with his back towards the door.

Art and vitiated nature were struggling like wrestlers in that apartment, and art was getting the worst of it. The overpowering gloom pervading the clammy air, rendered still more intense by the height of the window from the floor, reduced all the pictures that were standing around to the wizened feebleness of corpses on end. The shadowy parts of the room behind the different easels were veiled in a brown vapour, precluding all estimate of the extent of the studio, and only subdued in the foreground by the ruddy glare from an open stove of Dutch tiles. Somerset's footsteps had been so noiseless over the carpeting of the stairs and landing that his father was unaware of his presence; he continued at his work as before, which he performed by the help of a complicated apparatus of lamps, candles, and reflectors, so arranged as to eke out the miserable daylight to a power apparently sufficient for the neutral touches on which he was at that moment engaged.

The first thought of an unsophisticated stranger on entering that room could only be the amazed inquiry why a professor of the art of colour, which beyond all other arts requires pure daylight for its exercise, should fix himself on the single square league in habitable Europe to which light is denied at noonday for weeks in succession.

"Oh! it's you, George, is it?" said the Academician, turning from the lamps, which shone over his bald crown at such a slant as to reveal every cranial irregularity. "How are you this morning? Still a dead silence about your grand castle competition?"

Somerset told the news. His father duly congratulated him, and added genially, "It is well to be you, George. One large commission to attend to, and nothing to distract you from it. I am bothered by having a dozen irons in the fire at once. And people are so unreasonable.—Only this morning, among other things, when you got your order to go on with your single study, I received a letter from a woman, an old friend whom I can scarcely refuse, begging me as a great favour to design her a set of theatrical costumes, in which she and her friends can perform for some charity. It would occupy me a good week to go into the subject and do the thing properly. Such are the sort of letters I get. I wish, George, you could knock out something for her before you leave town. It is positively impossible for me to do it with all this work in hand, and these eternal fogs to contend against."

"I fear costumes are rather out of my line," said the son. "However, I'll do what I can. What period and country are they to represent?"

His father didn't know. He had never looked at the play of late years. It was "Love's Labour's Lost." "You had better read it for yourself," he said, "and do the best you can."

During the morning Somerset junior found time to refresh

his memory of the play, and afterwards went and hunted up materials for designs to suit the same, which occupied his spare hours for the next three days. As these occupations made no great demands upon his reasoning faculties he mostly found his mind wandering off to imaginary scenes at Stancy Castle: particularly did he dwell at this time upon Paula's lively interest in the history, relics, tombs, architecture,—nay, the very Christian names, of the De Stancy line, and her "artistic" preference for Charlotte's ancestors instead of her own. Yet what more natural than that a clever meditative girl, encased in the feudal lumber of that family, should imbibe at least an antiquarian interest in it? Human nature at bottom is romantic rather than ascetic, and the local habitation which accident had provided for Paula was perhaps acting as a solvent of the hard, morbidly introspective views thrust upon her in early life.

Somerset wondered if his own possession of a substantial genealogy like Captain De Stancy's would have had any appreciable effect upon her regard for him. His suggestion to Paula of her belonging to a worthy strain of engineers had been based on his content with his own intellectual line of descent through Phidias, Ictinus and Callicrates, Chersiphron, Vitruvius, Wilars of Cambray, William of Wykeham, and the rest of that long and illustrious roll; but Miss Power's marked preference for an animal pedigree led him to muse on what he could show for himself in that kind.

These thoughts so far occupied him that when he took the sketches to his father, on the morning of the fifth, he was led to ask: "Has any one ever sifted out our family pedigree?"

"Family pedigree?"

"Yes. Have we any pedigree worthy to be compared with that of professedly old families? I never remember hearing of any ancestor further back than my great-grandfather."

Somerset the elder reflected and said that he believed there was a genealogical tree about the house somewhere, reaching back to a very respectable distance. "Not that I ever took much interest in it," he continued, without looking up from his canvas; "but your great-uncle John was a man with a taste for those subjects, and he drew up such a sheet: he made several copies on parchment, and gave one to each of his brothers and sisters. The one he gave to my father is still in my possession, I think."

Somerset said that he should like to see it; but half an hour's search about the house failed to discover the document; and the Academician then remembered that it was in an iron box at his banker's. He had used it as a wrapper for some bonds and other valuable papers which were deposited there for safety. "Why do you want it?" he inquired.

The young man confessd his wish to know if his own antiquity would bear comparison with that of another person, whose name he did not mention; whereupon his father gave him a key that would fit the said chest, if he meant to pursue the subject further. Somerset, however, did nothing in the matter that day, but the next morning, having to call at the bank on other business, he remembered his intention.

It was about eleven o'clock. The fog, though not so brown as it had been on previous days, was still dense enough to necessitate lights in the shops and offices. When Somerset had finished his business in the outer office of the bank he went to the manager's room. The hour being somewhat early the only persons present in that sanctuary of balances, besides the manager who welcomed him, were two gentlemen, apparently lawyers, who sat talking earnestly over a box of papers. The manager, on learning what Somerset wanted, unlocked a door from which a flight of stone steps led to the vaults, and sent down a clerk and a porter for the safe.

Before, however, they had descended far a gentle tap came to the door, and in response to an invitation to enter a lady appeared, wrapped up in furs to her very nose.

The manager seemed to recognise her, for he went across the room in a moment, and set her a chair at the middle table, replying to some observation of hers with the words, "Oh yes, certainly," in a deferential tone.

"I should like it brought up at once," said the lady.

Somerset, who had seated himself at a table in a somewhat obscure corner, screened by the lawyers, started at the words. The voice was Miss Power's, and so plainly enough was the figure as soon as he examined it. Her back was towards him, and either because the room was only lighted in two places, or because she was absorbed in her own concerns, she seemed to be unconscious of any one's presence on the scene except the banker and herself. The former called back the clerk, and two other porters having been summoned they disappeared to get whatever she required.

Somerset, somewhat excited, sat wondering what could have brought Paula to London at this juncture, and was in some doubt if the occasion were a suitable one for revealing himself, her errand to her banker being possibly of a very private nature. Nothing helped him to a decision. Paula never once turned her head, and the progress of time was marked only by the murmurs of the two lawyers, and the ceaseless clash of gold and rattle of scales from the outer room, where the busy heads of cashiers could be seen through the partition moving about under the globes of the gas-lamps.

Footsteps were heard upon the cellar-steps, and the three men previously sent below staggered from the doorway, bearing a huge safe which nearly broke them down. Somerset knew that his father's box, or boxes, could boast of no such dimensions, and he was not surprised to see the chest deposited in front of Miss Power. When the immense accumulation of dust had been cleared off the lid, and the chest conveniently placed for her, Somerset was attended to, his modest box being brought up by one man unassisted and without much expenditure of breath.

His interest in Paula was of so emotional a cast that his attention to his own errand was of the most perfunctory kind. She was close to a gas-standard, and the lawyers, whose seats had intervened, having finished their business and gone away, all her actions were visible to him. While he was opening his father's box the manager assisted Paula to unseal and unlock hers, and he now saw her lift from it a morocco case, which she placed on the table before her, and unfastened. Out of it she took a dazzling object that fell like a cascade over her fingers. It was a necklace of diamonds and pearls, apparently of large size and many strands, though he was not near enough to see distinctly. When satisfied by her examination that she had got the right article she shut it into its case.

The manager closed the chest for her; and when it was again

secured Paula arose, tossed the necklace into her handbag, bowed to the manager, and was about to bid him good morning. Thereupon he said with some hesitation, "Pardon one question, Miss Power. Do you intend to take those jewels far?"

"Yes," she said simply, "to Stancy Castle."

"You are going straight there?"

"I have one or two places to call at first."

"I would suggest that you carry them in some other way— by fastening them into the pocket of your dress, for instance."

"But I am going to hold the bag in my hand and never once let it go."

The banker slightly shook his head. "Suppose your carriage gets overturned: you would let it go then."

"Perhaps so."

"Or if you saw a child under the wheels just as you were stepping in; or if you accidentally stumbled in getting out; or if there was a collision on the railway—you might let it go."

"Yes; I see I was too careless. I thank you."

Paula removed the necklace from the bag, turned her back to the manager, and spent several minutes in placing her treasure in her bosom, pinning it and otherwise making it absolutely secure.

"That's it," said the grey-haired man of caution, with evident satisfaction. "There is not much danger now: you are not travelling alone?"

Paula replied that she was not alone, and went to the door. There was one moment during which Somerset might have conveniently made his presence known; but the juxtaposition of the bank-manager, and his own disarranged box of securities, embarrassed him: the moment slipped by, and she was gone.

In the mean time he had mechanically unearthed the pedigree, and, locking up his father's chest, Somerset also took his departure at the heels of Paula. He walked along the misty street, so deeply musing as to be quite unconscious of the direction of his walk. What, he inquired of himself, could she want that necklace for so suddenly? He recollected a remark of Dare's to the effect that her appearance on a particular occasion at Stancy Castle had been magnificent by reason of the jewels she wore; which proved that she had retained a sufficient quantity of those valuables at the castle for ordinary requirements. What exceptional occasion, then, was impending on which she wished to glorify herself beyond all previous experience? He could not guess. He was interrupted in these conjectures by a carriage nearly passing over his toes at a crossing in Bond Street: looking up he saw between the two windows of the vehicle the profile of a thickly mantled bosom, on which a camellia rose and fell. All the remainder part of the lady's person was hidden; but he remembered that flower of convenient season as one which had figured in the bank parlour half an hour earlier to-day.

Somerset hastened after the carriage, and in a minute saw it stop opposite a jeweller's shop. Out came Paula, and then another woman, in whom he recognised Mrs. Birch, one of the lady's-maids at Stancy Castle. The young man was at Paula's side before she had crossed the pavement.

CHAPTER VI

A QUICK arrested expression in her two sapphirine eyes, accompanied by a little, a very little, blush which loitered long, was all the outward disturbance that the sight of her lover caused. The habit of self-repression at any new emotional impact was instinctive with her always. Somerset could not say more than a word; he looked his intense solicitude, and Paula spoke.

She declared that this was an unexpected pleasure. Had he arranged to come on the tenth as she wished? How strange that they should meet thus!—and yet not strange—the world was so small.

Somerset said that he was coming on the very day she mentioned—that the appointment gave him infinite gratification, which was quite within the truth.

"Come into this shop with me," said Paula, with good-humoured authoritativeness.

They entered the shop and talked on while she made a small purchase. But not a word did Paula say of her sudden errand to town.

"I am having an exciting morning," she said. "I am going from here to catch the one-o'clock train to Markton."

"It is important that you get there this afternoon, I suppose?"

"Yes. You know why?"

"Not at all."

"The Hunt Ball. It was fixed for the sixth, and this is the sixth. I thought they might have asked you."

"No," said Somerset, a trifle gloomily. "No, I am not asked. But it is a great task for you—a long journey and a ball all in one day."

"Yes: Charlotte said that. But I don't mind it."

"You are glad you are going. Are you glad?" he said softly.

Her air confessed more than her words. "I am not so very

glad that I am going to the Hunt Ball," she replied confidentially.

"Thanks for that," said he.

She lifted her eyes to his for a moment. Her manner had suddenly become so nearly the counterpart of that in the tea-house that to suspect any deterioration of affection in her was no longer generous. It was only as if a thin layer of recent events had overlaid her memories of him, until his presence swept them away.

Somerset looked up, and finding the shopman to be still some way off, he added, "When will you assure me of something in return for what I assured you that evening in the rain?"

"Not before you have built the castle. My aunt does not know about it yet, nor anybody."

"I ought to tell her."

"No, not yet. I don't wish it."

"Then everything stands as usual?"

She lightly nodded.

"That is, I may love you: but you still will not say you love me."

She nodded again, and directing his attention to the advancing shopman, said, "Please not a word more."

Soon after this, they left the jeweller's, and parted, Paula driving straight off to the station and Somerset going on his way uncertainly happy. His re-impression after a few minutes was that a special journey to town to fetch that magnificent necklace which she had not once mentioned to him, but which was plainly to be the medium of some proud purpose with her this evening, was hardly in harmony with her assertions of indifference to the attractions of the Hunt Ball.

He got into a cab and drove to his club, where he lunched, and mopingly spent a great part of the afternoon in making calculations for the foundations of the castle works. Late in the afternoon he returned to his chambers, wishing that he could annihilate the three days remaining before the tenth, particularly this coming evening. On his table was a letter in a strange writing, and indifferently turning it over he found from the superscription that it had been addressed to him days before at the King's Arms Hotel, Markton, where it had lain ever since, the landlord probably expecting him to return. Opening the missive he found to his surprise that it was, after all, an invitation to the Hunt Ball.

"Too late!" said Somerset. "To think I should be served this trick a second time!"

After a moment's pause, however, he looked to see the time of day. It was five minutes past five—just about the hour when Paula would be driving from Markton Station to Stancy Castle to rest and prepare herself for her evening triumph. There was a train at six o'clock, timed to reach Markton between eleven and twelve, which by great exertion he might save even now, if it were worth while to undertake such a scramble for the pleasure of dropping in to the ball at a late hour. A moment's vision of Paula moving to swift tunes on the arm of a person or persons unknown was enough to impart the impetus required. He jumped up, flung his dress suit into a portmanteau, sent down to call a cab, and in a few minutes was rattling off to the railway which had borne Paula away from London just five hours earlier.

Once in the train, he began to consider where and how he could most conveniently dress for the dance. The train would certainly be half an hour late; half an hour would be spent in getting to the town-hall, and that was the utmost delay tolerable if he would secure the hand of Paula for one spin, or be more than a mere dummy behind the earlier arrivals. He looked for an empty compartment at the next stoppage, and finding the one next his own unoccupied, he entered it and changed his raiment for that in his portmanteau during the ensuing run of twenty miles.

Thus prepared he awaited the Markton platform, which was reached as the clock struck twelve. Somerset called a fly and drove at once to the town-hall.

The borough natives had ascended to their upper floors, and were putting out their candles one by one as he passed along the street; but the lively strains that proceeded from the central edifice revealed distinctly enough what was going on among the temporary visitors from the neighbouring manors. The doors were opened for him, and entering the vestibule lined with flags, flowers, evergreens, and escutcheons, he stood looking into the furnace of gaiety beyond.

It was some time before he could gather his impressions of the scene, so perplexing were the lights, the motions, the toilets, the full-dress uniforms of officers and the harmonies of sound. Yet light, sound, and movement were not so much the essence of that giddy scene as an intense aim at obliviousness in the beings composing it. For two or three hours at least those whirling young people meant not to know that they were mortal. The room was beating like a heart, and the pulse was regulated by the trembling strings of the most popular quadrille band in Wessex. But at last his eyes grew settled enough to look critically around.

The room was crowded—too crowded. Every variety of fair one, beauties primary, secondary, and tertiary, appeared among the personages composing the throng. There were suns and moons; also pale planets of little account. Broadly speaking, these daughters of the county fell into two classes: one the pink-faced unsophisticated girls from neighbouring rectories and small country-houses, who knew not town except for an occasional fortnight, and who spent their time from Easter to Lammas Day much as they spent it during the remaining nine months of the year: the other class were the children of the wealthy landowners, who migrated each season to the town-house; these were pale and collected, showed less enjoyment in their countenances, and wore in general an approximation to the languid manners of the capital.

A quadrille was in progress, and Somerset scanned each set. His mind had run so long upon the necklace, that his glance involuntarily sought out that gleaming object rather than the personality of its wearer. At the top of the room there he beheld it; but it was on the neck of Charlotte De Stancy.

The whole lucid explanation broke across his understanding in a second. His dear Paula had fetched the necklace that Charlotte should not appear to disadvantage among the county people by reason of her poverty. It was generously done—a disinterested act of sisterly kindness; theirs was the friendship of Hermia and Helena. Before he had got further than to realise this, there wheeled round amongst the dancers a lady

whose *tournure* he recognised well. She was Paula; and to the
young man's vision a superlative something distinguished her
from all the rest. This was not dress or ornament, for she had
hardly a gem upon her, her attire being a model of effective
simplicity. Her partner was Captain De Stancy.

The discovery of this latter fact slightly obscured his appreciation of what he had discovered just before. It was with
rather a lowering brow that he asked himself whether Paula's
prédilection d'artiste, as she called it, for the De Stancy line
might not lead to a *prédilection* of a different sort for its last
representative which would be not at all satisfactory.

The architect remained in the background till the dance
drew to a conclusion, and then he went forward. The circumstance of having met him by accident once already that day
seemd to quench any surprise in Miss Power's bosom at seeing
him now. There was nothing in her parting from Captain De
Stancy, when he led her to a seat, calculated to make Somerset
uneasy after his long absence. Though, for that matter, this
proved nothing; for, like all wise maidens, Paula never ventured on the game of the eyes with a lover in public; well
knowing that every moment of such indulgence overnight
might mean an hour's sneer at her expense by the indulged
gentleman next day, when weighing womankind by the aid of
a cold morning light and a bad headache.

Whilst Somerset was explaining to Paula and her aunt the
reason of his sudden appearance, their attention was drawn to
a seat a short way off by a fluttering of ladies round the spot.
In a moment it was whispered that somebody had fallen ill,
and in another that the sufferer was Miss De Stancy. Paula,
Mrs. Goodman, and Somerset at once joined the group of
friends who were assisting her. Neither of them imagined for
an instant that the unexpected advent of Somerset on the scene
had anything to do with the poor girl's indisposition.

She was assisted out of the room, and her brother who now
came up prepared to take her home, Somerset exchanging a
few civil words with him, which the hurry of the moment
prevented them from continuing; though on taking his leave
with Charlotte, who was now better, De Stancy informed

Somerset in answer to a cursory inquiry that he hoped to be back again at the ball in half an hour.

When they were gone Somerset, feeling that now another dog might have his day, sounded Paula on the delightful question of a dance.

Paula replied in the negative.

"How is that?" asked Somerset with reproachful disappointment.

"I cannot dance again," she said in a somewhat depressed tone; "I must be released from every engagement to do so, on account of Charlotte's illness. I should have gone home with her if I had not been particularly requested to stay a little longer, since it is as yet so early, and Charlotte's illness is not very serious."

If Charlotte's illness was not very serious, Somerset thought, Paula might have stretched a point; but not wishing to hinder her in showing respect to a friend so well liked by himself, he did not ask it. De Stancy had promised to be back again in half an hour, and Paula had heard the promise. But at the end of twenty minutes, still seeming indifferent to what was going on around her, she said she would stay no longer, and reminding Somerset that they were soon to meet and talk over rebuilding, drove off with her aunt to Stancy Castle.

Somerset stood looking at the retreating carriage till it was enveloped in shades that the lamps could not disperse. The ballroom was now virtually empty for him, and feeling no great anxiety to return thither he stood on the steps for some minutes longer, looking into the calm mild night, and at the dark houses behind whose blinds lay the burghers with their eyes sealed up in sleep. He could not but think that it was rather too bad of Paula to spoil his evening for a sentimental devotion to Charlotte which could do the latter no appreciable good; and he would have felt seriously hurt at her move if it had not been equally severe upon Captain De Stancy, who was doubtless hastening back, full of a belief that she would still be found there.

The star of gas-jets over the entrance threw its light upon the walls on the opposite side of the street, where there were notice-boards of forthcoming events. In glancing over these for the fifth time, his eye was attracted by the first words of a placard in blue letters, of a size larger than the rest, and moving onward a few steps he read:—

STANCY CASTLE.

By the kind permission of MISS POWER,

A PLAY

Will shortly be performed at the above CASTLE,

IN AID OF THE FUNDS OF THE

COUNTY HOSPITAL,

By the Officers of the

ROYAL HORSE ARTILLERY,

MARKTON BARRACKS,

ASSISTED BY SEVERAL

LADIES OF THE NEIGHBOURHOOD.

The cast and other particulars will be duly announced in small bills. Places will be reserved on application to Mr. Clangham, High Street, Markton, where a plan of the room may be seen.

N.B.—The Castle is about fifteen minutes' drive from Markton Station, to which there are numerous convenient trains from all parts of the county.

In a profound study Somerset turned and re-entered the ball-room, where he remained gloomily standing here and there for about five minutes, at the end of which he observed Captain De Stancy, who had returned punctually to his word, crossing the hall in his direction.

The gallant officer darted glances of lively search over every group of dancers and sitters; and then with rather a blank look in his face he came on to Somerset. Replying to the latter's inquiry for his sister that she had nearly recovered, he said, "I don't see my father's neighbours anywhere."

"They have gone home," replied Somerset, a trifle dryly. "They asked me to make their apologies to you for leading you to expect they would remain. Miss Power was too anxious about Miss De Stancy to care to stay longer."

The eyes of De Stancy and the speaker met for an instant. That curious guarded understanding, or inimical confederacy, which arises at moments between two men in love with the same woman, was present here; and in their mutual glances each said as plainly as by words that her departure had ruined his evening's hope.

They were now about as much in one mood as it was possible for two such differing natures to be. Neither cared further for elaborating giddy curves on that town-hall floor. They stood talking languidly about this and that local topic, till De Stancy turned aside for a short time to speak to a dapper little lady who had beckoned to him. In a few minutes he came back to Somerset.

"Mrs. Camperton, the wife of Major Camperton of my battery, would very much like me to introduce you to her. She is an old friend of your father's, and has wanted to know you for a long time."

De Stancy and Somerset crossed over to the lady, and in a few minutes, thanks to her flow of spirits, she and Somerset were chatting with remarkable freedom.

"It is a happy coincidence," continued Mrs. Camperton, "that I should have met you here, immediately after receiving a letter from your father: indeed it reached me only this morning. He has been so kind! We are getting up some theatricals, as you know, I suppose, to help the funds of the County Hospital, which is in debt."

"I have just seen the announcement—nothing more."

"Yes, such an estimable purpose; and as we wished to do it thoroughly well, I asked Mr. Somerset to design us the costumes, and he has now sent me the sketches. It is quite a secret at present, but we are going to play Shakespeare's romantic drama, 'Love's Labour's Lost,' and we hope to get Miss Power to take the leading part. You see, being such a handsome girl, and so wealthy, and rather an undiscovered novelty in the county as yet, she would draw a crowded room, and greatly benefit the funds."

"Miss Power going to play herself?—I am rather surprised," said Somerset. "Whose idea is all this?"

"Oh, Captain De Stancy's—he's the originator entirely. You see he is so interested in the neighbourhood, his family having been connected with it for so many centuries, that naturally a charitable object of this local nature appeals to his feelings."

"Naturally!" her listener laconically repeated. "And have you settled who is to play the junior gentleman's part, leading lover, hero, or whatever he is called?"

"Not absolutely: though I think Captain De Stancy will not refuse it; and he is a very good figure. At present it lies between him and Mr. Mild, one of our young lieutenants. My husband, of course, takes the heavy line; and I am to be the second-lady, though I am rather too old for the part really. If we can only secure Miss Power for heroine the cast will be excellent."

"Excellent!" said Somerset, with a spectral smile.

romantic drama, 'Love's Labour's Lost,' and we hope to get
Miss Power to take the leading part. You see, being such a
handsome girl, and so wealthy, and rather an undiscovered
novelty in the country as yet, she would draw a crowded room,
and greatly benefit the—

"Miss Power going to play herself?—I am rather surprised,"
said Somerset, with an effort to conceal this

CHAPTER VII

WHEN he awoke the next morning at the King's Arms Hotel,
Somerset felt quite morbid on recalling the intelligence he had
received from Mrs. Camperton. But as the day for serious
practical consultation about the castle works, to which Paula
had playfully alluded, was now close at hand, he determined
to banish sentimental reflections on the frailties that were
besieging her nature, by active preparation for his professional
undertaking. To be her high-priest in art, to elaborate a
structure whose cunning workmanship would be meeting her
eye every day till the end of her natural life, and saying to her,
"He invented it," with all the eloquence of an inanimate thing
long regarded—this was no mean satisfaction, come what else
would.

He returned to town the next day to set matters there in
such trim that no inconvenience should result from his prolonged absences at the castle; for having no other commission
he determined (with an eye rather to heart-interests than to
increasing his professional practice) to make, as before, the
castle itself his office, studio, and chief abiding place till the
works were fairly in progress.

On the tenth he reappeared at Markton. Passing through
the town, on the road to Stancy Castle, his eyes were again
arrested by the notice-board which had conveyed such startling
information to him on the night of the ball. The small bills
now appeared thereon; but when he anxiously looked them
over to learn how the parts were to be allotted, he found that
intelligence still withheld. Yet they told enough; the list of
lady-players was given, and Miss Power's name was one.

That a young lady who, six months ago, would scarcely join
for conscientious reasons in a simple dance on her own lawn,
should now be willing to exhibit herself on a public stage,
simulating love-passages with a stranger, argued a rate of

development which under any circumstances would have surprised him, but which, with the particular addition, as leading colleague, of Captain De Stancy, inflamed him almost to anger. What clandestine arrangements had been going on in his absence to produce such a full-blown intention it were futile to guess, Paula's course was a race rather than a march, and each successive heat was startling in its eclipse of that which went before.

Somerset was, however, introspective enough to know that his morals would have taken no such virtuous alarm had he been the chief male player instead of Captain De Stancy.

He passed under the castle-arch and entered. There seemed a little turn in the tide of affairs when it was announced to him that Miss Power expected him, and was alone.

The well-known ante-chambers through which he walked, filled with twilight, draughts, and thin echoes that seemed to reverberate from two hundred years ago, did not delay his eye as they had done when he had been ignorant that his destiny lay beyond; and he followed on through all this ancientness to where the modern Paula sat to receive him.

He forgot everything in the pleasure of being alone in a room with her. She met his eye with that in her own which cheered him. It was a light expressing that something was understood between them. She said quietly in two or three words that she had expected him in the forenoon.

Somerset explained that he had come only that morning from London.

After a little more talk, in which she said that her aunt would join them in a few minutes, and that Miss De Stancy was still indisposed at her father's house, she rang for tea and sat down beside a little table. "Shall we proceed to business at once?" she asked him.

"I suppose so."

"First then, when will the working drawings be ready, which I think you said must be made out before the work could begin?"

While Somerset informed her on this and other matters, Mrs. Goodman entered and joined in the discussion, after which they found it would be necessary to adjourn to the

studio where the plans were hanging. On their walk thither
Paula asked if he stayed late at the ball.

"I left soon after you."

"That was very early, seeing how late you arrived."

"Yes. . . . I did not dance."

"What did you do, then?"

"I moped, and walked to the door; and saw an
announcement."

"I know—the play that is to be performed."

"In which you are to be the Princess."

"That's not settled.—I have not agreed yet. I shall not play
the Princess of France unless Mr. Mild plays the King of
Navarre."

This sounded rather well. The Princess was the lady beloved
by the King; and Mr. Mild the young lieutenant of the artillery
was a diffident, inexperienced, rather plain-looking fellow,
whose sole interest in theatricals lay in the consideration of his
costume and the sound of his own voice in the ears of the
audience. With such an unobjectionable person to enact the
part of lover, the prominent character of leading young lady or
heroine, which Paula was to personate, was really the most
satisfactory in the whole list for her. For although she was to
be wooed hard, there was just as much love-making among the
remaining personages; while, as Somerset had understood the
play, there could occur no flingings of her person upon her
lover's neck, or agonised downfalls upon the stage, in her
whole performance, as there were in the parts chosen by Mrs.
Camperton, the major's wife and some of the other ladies.

"Why do you play at all!" he murmured.

"What a question! How could I refuse for such an excellent
purpose? They say that my taking a part will be worth a
hundred pounds to the charity. My father always supported
the hospital, which is quite undenominational; and he said I
was to do the same."

"Do you think the peculiar means you have adopted for
supporting it entered into his view?" inquired Somerset,
regarding her with critical dryness. "For my part I don't."

"It is an interesting way," she returned persuasively, though
apparently in a state of mental equipoise on the point raised by

his question. "And I shall not play the Princess, as I said, to any other than that quiet young man. Now I assure you of this, so don't be angry and absurd! Besides, the King doesn't marry me at the end of the play, as in Shakespeare's other comedies. And if Miss De Stancy continues seriously unwell I shall not play at all."

The young man pressed her hand, but she gently slipped it away.

"Are we not engaged, Paula?" he asked.

She evasively shook her head.

"Come—yes we are! Shall we tell your aunt?" he continued. Unluckily at that moment Mrs. Goodman, who had followed them to the studio at a slower pace, appeared round the doorway.

"No,—to the last," replied Paula hastily. Then her aunt entered, and the conversation was no longer personal.

Somerset took his departure in a serener mood, though not completely assured.

CHAPTER VIII

His serenity continued during two or three following days, when, continuing at the castle, he got pleasant glimpses of Paula now and then. Her strong desire that his love for her should be kept secret, perplexed him; but his affection was generous, and he acquiesced in that desire.

Meanwhile news of the forthcoming dramatic performance radiated in every direction. And in the next number of the county paper it was announced, to Somerset's comparative satisfaction, that the cast was definitively settled, Mr. Mild having agreed to be the King and Miss Power the French Princess. Captain De Stancy, with becoming modesty for one who was the leading spirit, figured quite low down, in the secondary character of Sir Nathaniel.

Somerset remembered that, by a happy chance, the costume he had designed for Sir Nathaniel was not at all picturesque; moreover Sir Nathaniel scarcely came near the Princess through the whole play.

Every day after this there was coming and going to and from the castle of railway vans laden with canvas columns, paste-board trees, limp house-fronts, woollen lawns, and lath balus-trades. There were also frequent arrivals of young ladies from neighbouring country houses, and warriors from the X and Y batteries of artillery, distinguishable by their regulation shaving.

But it was upon Captain De Stancy and Mrs. Camperton that the weight of preparation fell. Somerset, through being much occupied in the drawing office, was seldom present during the consultations and rehearsals; until one day, tea being served in the drawing-room at the usual hour, he dropped in with the rest to receive a cup from Paula's table. The chatter was tremendous, and Somerset was at once consulted about some necessary carpentry which was to be specially made at Markton. After that he was looked on as one of the band, which resulted in a large addition to the number of his acquaintance in this part of England.

But his own feeling was that of being an outsider still. This vagary had been originated, the play chosen, the parts allotted, all in his absence, and calling him in at the last moment might, if flirtation were possible in Paula, be but a sop to pacify him. What would he have given to impersonate her lover in the piece! But neither Paula nor any one else had asked him.

The eventful evening came. Somerset had been engaged during the day with the different people by whom the works were to be carried out; and in the evening went to his rooms at the King's Arms, Markton, where he dined. He did not return to the castle till the hour fixed for the performance, and having been received by Mrs. Goodman entered the large apartment, now transfigured into a theatre, like any other spectator.

Rumours of the projected representation had spread far and wide. Six times the number of tickets issued might have been readily sold. Friends and acquaintances of the actors came from curiosity to see how they would acquit themselves; while other classes of people came because they were eager to see well-known notabilities in unwonted situations. When ladies, hitherto only beheld in frigid, impenetrable positions behind their coachmen in Markton High Street, were about to reveal their hidden traits, home attitudes, intimate smiles, nods, and perhaps kisses, to the public eye, it was a throwing open of fascinating social secrets not to be missed for money.

The performance opened with no further delay than was occasioned by the customary refusal of the curtain at these times to rise more than two feet six inches; but this hitch was remedied, and the play began. It was with no enviable emotion that Somerset, who was watching intently, saw, not Mr. Mild, but Captain De Stancy, enter as the King of Navarre.

Somerset as a friend of the family had had a seat reserved for him next to that of Mrs. Goodman, and turning to her he said with some excitement, "I understood that Mr. Mild had agreed to take that part?"

"Yes," she said in a whisper, "so he had; but he broke down. He did very well at the first rehearsal; then he got more and more nervous, and at last this very morning said he could not possibly enact the part. Luckily, Captain De Stancy was familiar with it, through having coached the others so persistently, and he undertook it off-hand. Being about the same figure as Lieutenant Mild the same dress fits him, with a little alteration by the tailor."

It did fit him indeed; and of the male costumes it was that on which Somerset had bestowed most pains when designing them. It shrewdly burst upon his mind that there might have been collusion between Mild and De Stancy, the former agreeing to take the captain's place and act as blind till the last moment. A greater question was, could Paula have possibly been aware of this, and would she perform as the Princess of France now De Stancy was to be her lover, or throw up the part and stop the play?

"Does Miss Power know of this change?" he inquired.

"She did not till quite a short time ago."

He asked no further question from very pride, and controlled his impatience till the beginning of the second act. The Princess entered; it was Paula. But whether the slight embarrassment with which she pronounced her opening words,

> Good Lord Boyet, my beauty, though but mean,
> Needs not the painted flourish of your praise,

was due to the newness of her situation, or to her knowledge that De Stancy had usurped Mild's part of her lover, he could not guess. De Stancy appeared, and Somerset felt grim as he listened to the gallant Captain's salutation of the Princess, and her response.

De S.—Fair Princess, welcome to the court of Navarre.
Paula.—Fair, I give you back again: and welcome, I have not yet.

Somerset listened to this and to all that which followed of the same sort, with the reflection that, after all, the Princess never throughout the piece compromised her dignity by showing her love for the King; and that the latter, on this account, never addressed her in words in which passion got the better of courtesy. Moreover, as Paula had herself observed, they did not marry at the end of the piece, as in Shakespeare's other comedies. Somewhat calm in this assurance, he waited on while the other couples respectively indulged in their love-making and banter, including Mrs. Camperton as the sprightly Rosaline. But he was doomed to be surprised out of this humour when the end of the act came on. In abridging the play for convenience of representation, the favours or gifts from the gentlemen to the ladies were personally presented; and now Somerset saw De Stancy advance with the necklace fetched by Paula from London, and clasp it on her neck.

This seemed to throw a less pleasant light on her hasty journey. To fetch a valuable ornament in order to lend it to a poorer friend was estimable; but to fetch it that the friend's brother should have something magnificent and attractive to use as a lover's offering to herself in public, that wore a different complexion. Moreover, if the article were recognised by the spectators as the same that Charlotte had worn at the ball, which it probably was, the presentation by De Stancy of what must seem to be an heirloom of his house assumed the colour of symbolising a union of the families.

De Stancy's mode of presenting the necklace, though unauthorised by Shakespeare, had the full approval of the company, and set them in good humour to receive Major Camperton as Armado the braggart. Nothing calculated to stimulate jealousy occurred again till the fifth act; and then there arose full cause for it.

The scene was the outside of the Princess's pavilion. De Stancy, as the King of Navarre, stood with his group of attendants awaiting the Princess, who presently entered from her door. The two began to converse as the play appointed, De Stancy turning to her with this reply:

> Rebuke me not for that which you provoke;
> The virtue of your eye must break my oath.

So far all was well; and Paula opened her lips for the set rejoinder. But before she had spoken De Stancy continued:

> If I profane with my unworthy hand
> (*Taking her hand*)
> This holy shrine, the gentle fine is this—
> My lips, two blushing pilgrims, ready stand
> To smooth that rough touch with a tender kiss.

Somerset stared. Surely in this comedy the King never addressed the Princess in such warm words; and yet they were Shakespeare's, for they were quite familiar to him. A dim suspicion crossed his mind. Mrs. Goodman had brought a copy of Shakespeare with her, which she kept in her lap and never looked at: borrowing it, Somerset turned to "Romeo and Juliet," and there he saw the words which De Stancy had introduced as gag, to intensify the mild love-making of the other play. Meanwhile De Stancy continued:

> Oh then, dear Saint, let lips do what hands do;
> They pray, grant thou, lest faith turn to despair.
> Then move not, while my prayer's effect I take.
> Thus from my lips, by yours, my sin is purg'd!

Could it be that De Stancy was going to do what came next in the stage direction—kiss her? Before there was time for conjecture on that point the sound of a very sweet and long-drawn osculation spread through the room, followed by loud applause from the people in the cheap seats. De Stancy withdrew from bending over Paula, and she was very red in the face. Nothing seemed clearer than that he had actually done the deed. The applause continuing, Somerset turned his head. Five hundred faces had regarded the act; and four hundred and fifty mouths in those faces were smiling. About one half of them were tender smiles; these came from the women. The other half were at best humorous, and mainly satirical; these came from the men. It was a profanation without parallel, and his face blazed like a coal.

The play was now nearly at an end, and Somerset sat on, feeling what he did not and could not express. More than ever was he assured that there had been collusion between the two artillery officers to bring about this end. That he should have been the unhappy man to design those picturesque dresses in which his rival so audaciously played the lover to his, Somerset's, mistress, was an added point to the satire. He could hardly go so far as to assume that Paula was a consenting party to this startling interlude; but her otherwise unaccountable wish that his own love should be clandestinely shown lent immense force to a doubt of her sincerity. The ghastly thought that she had merely been keeping him on, like a pet spaniel, to amuse her leisure moments till she should have found appropriate opportunity for an open engagement with some one else, trusting to his sense of chivalry to keep secret their little episode, filled him with a grim heat.

that she had merely been keeping him on, like a pet spaniel, to
amuse her leisure moments till she should have found appropriate opportunity for an open engagement with some one else,
trusting to his sense of chivalry to keep secret their little
episode, filled him w

CHAPTER IX

AT the back of the room the applause had been loud at the
moment of the kiss, real or counterfeit. The cause was partly
owing to an exceptional circumstance which had occurred in
that quarter early in the play.

The people had all seated themselves, and the first act had
begun, when the tapestry that screened the door was lifted
gently and a figure appeared in the opening. The general
attention was at this moment absorbed by the newly disclosed
stage, and scarcely a soul noticed the stranger. Had any one of
the audience turned his head, there would have been sufficient
in the countenance to detain his gaze, notwithstanding the
counter-attraction forward.

He was obviously a man who had come from afar. There
was not a square inch about him that had anything to do with
modern English life. His visage, which was of the colour of
light porphyry, had little of its original surface left; it was a
face which had been the plaything of strange fires or pestil-
ences, that had moulded to whatever shape they chose his
orginally supple skin, and left it pitted, puckered, and seamed
like a dried water-course. But though dire catastrophes or the
treacherous airs of remote climates had done their worst upon
his exterior, they seemed to have affected him but little within,
to judge from a certain robustness which showed itself in his
manner of standing.

The face-marks had a meaning, for any one who could read
them, beyond the mere suggestion of their origin: they signified that this man had either been the victim of some terrible
necessity as regarded the occupation to which he had devoted
himself, or that he was a man of dogged obstinacy, from sheer
sang froid holding his ground amid malign forces when others
would have fled affrighted away.

As nobody noticed him, he dropped the door-hangings after
a while, walked silently along the matted alley, and sat down

in one of the back chairs. His manner of entry was enough to show that the strength of character which he seemed to possess had phlegm for its base and not ardour. One might have said that perhaps the shocks he had passed through had taken all his original warmth out of him. His beaver hat, which he had retained on his head till this moment, he now placed under the seat, where he sat absolutely motionless till the end of the first act as if he were indulging in a monologue which did not quite reach his lips.

When Paula entered at the beginning of the second act he showed as much excitement as was expressed by a slight movement of the eyes. When she spoke he turned to his next neighbour, and asked him in cold level words which had once been English, but which seemed to have lost the accent of nationality: "Is that the young woman who is the possessor of this castle—Power by name?"

His neighbour happened to be the landlord at Sleeping-Green, and he informed the stranger that she was what he supposed.

"And who is that gentleman whose line of business seems to be to make love to Power?"

"He's Captain De Stancy, Sir William De Stancy's son, who used to own this property."

"Baronet or knight?"

"Baronet—a very old-established family about here."

The stranger nodded, and the play went on, no further word being spoken till the fourth act was reached, when the stranger again said, without taking his narrow black eyes from the stage: "There's something in that love-making between Stancy and Power that's not all sham!"

"Well," said the landlord, "I have heard different stories about that, and wouldn't be the man to say what I couldn't swear to. The story is that Captain De Stancy, who is as poor as a gallicrow, is in full cry after her, and that his only chance lies in his being heir to a title and the old name. But she has not shown a genuine hanker for anybody yet."

"If she finds the money, and this Stancy finds the name and blood, 'twould be a very neat match between 'em,—hey?"

"That's the argument."

Nothing more was said again for a long time, but the stranger's eyes showed more interest in the passes between Paula and De Stancy than they had shown before. At length the crisis came, as described in the last chapter, De Stancy saluting her with that semblance of a kiss which gave such umbrage to Somerset. The stranger's thin lips lengthened a couple of inches with satisfaction; he put his hand into his pocket, drew out two half-crowns which he handed to the landlord, saying, "Just applaud that, will you, and get your comrades to do the same."

The landlord, though a little surprised, took the money, and began to clap his hands as desired. The example was contagious, and spread all over the room; for the audience, gentle and simple, though they might not have followed the blank verse in all its bearings, could at least appreciate a kiss. It was the unusual acclamation raised by this means which had led Somerset to turn his head.

When the play had ended the stranger was the first to rise, and going downstairs at the head of the crowd he passed out of the door, and was lost to view. Some questions were asked by the landlord as to the stranger's individuality; but few had seen him; fewer had noticed him, singular as he was; and none knew his name.

While these things were going on the quarter allotted to the commonalty, Somerset in front had waited the fall of the curtain with those sick and sorry feelings which should be combated by the aid of philosophy and a good conscience, but which really are only subdued by time and the abrading rush of affairs. He was, however, stoical enough, on the fall of the curtain, to accept Mrs. Goodman's invitation to accompany her to the drawing-room, fully expecting to find there a large company, including Captain De Stancy.

But none of the acting ladies and gentlemen had emerged from their dressing-rooms as yet. Feeling that he did not care to meet any of them that night, he bade farewell to Mrs. Goodman after a few minutes of conversation, and left her. While he was passing along the corridor, at the side of the gallery which had been used as the theatre, Paula crossed it from the latter apartment towards an opposite door. She was still in the dress of the Princess, and the diamond and pearl necklace still hung over her bosom as placed there by Captain De Stancy.

Her eye caught Somerset's, and she stopped. Probably there was something in his face which told his mind, for she invited him by a smile into the room she was entering.

"I congratulate you on your performance," he said mechanically, when she pushed-to the door.

"Do you really think it was well done?" she asked, drawing near him with a sociable air.

"It was startlingly done—the part from 'Romeo and Juliet' pre-eminently so."

"Do you think I knew he was going to introduce it, or do you think I didn't know?" she said, with that gentle sauciness which shows itself in the loved one's manner when she has had a triumphant evening without the lover's assistance.

"I think you may have known."

"No," she averred, decisively shaking her head. "It took me as much by surprise as it probably did you. But why should I have told!"

Without answering that question Somerset went on. "Then what he did at the end of his gag was of course a surprise also."

"He didn't really do what he seemed to do," she serenely answered.

"Well, I have no right to make observations—your actions are not subject to my surveillance; you float above my plane," said the young man with some bitterness. "But to speak plainly, surely he—kissed you?"

"No," she said. "He only kissed the air in front of me—ever so far off."

"Was it six inches off?"

"No, not six inches."

"Nor three."

"It was quite one," she said, with an ingenuous air.

"I don't call that very far."

"A miss is as good as a mile, says the time-honoured proverb; and it is not for us modern mortals to question its truth."

"How can you be so off-hand!" broke out Somerset. "I love you wildly and desperately, Paula, and you know it well!"

"I have never denied knowing it," she said softly.

"Then why do you, with such knowledge, adopt an air of levity at such a moment as this! You keep me at arm's-length, and won't say whether you care for me one bit, or no. I have owned all to you; yet never once have you owned anything to me!"

"I have owned much. And you do me wrong if you consider that I show levity. But even if I have not owned everything, and you all, it is not altogether such a grievous thing."

"You mean to say that it is not grievous, even if a man does love a woman, and suffers all the pain of feeling he loves in vain? Well, I say it is quite the reverse, and I have grounds for knowing."

"Now, don't fume so, George Somerset, but hear me. My not owning all may not have the dreadful meaning you think, and therefore it may not be really such a grievous thing. There are genuine reasons for women's conduct in these matters as well as for men's, though it is sometimes supposed to be regulated entirely by caprice. And if I do not give way to every feeling—I mean demonstration—it is because I don't want to. There, now, don't expect me to say more."

"Very well," said Somerset, with repressed sadness, "I will not expect you to say more. But you do like me a little, Paula?"

"Now!" she said, shaking her head with symptoms of tenderness and looking into his eyes. "What have you just promised? Perhaps I like you a little more than a little, which is much too much! Yes—Shakespeare says so, and he is always right. Do you still doubt me? Ah, I see you do!"

"Because somebody has stood nearer to you to-night than I."

"An elderly man like him!—half as old again as either of us! How can you mind him? What shall I do to show you that I do not for a moment let him come between me and you?"

"It is not for me to suggest what you should do. Though what you should permit *me* to do is obvious enough."

She dropped her voice: "You mean, permit you to do really and in earnest what he only seemed to do in the play."

Somerset signified by a look that such had been his thought.

Paula was silent. "No," she murmured at last. "That cannot be. He did not, nor must you."

It was said none the less decidedly for being spoken low.

"You quite resent such a suggestion: you have a right to. I beg your pardon, not for speaking of it, but for thinking it."

"I don't resent it at all, and I am not offended one bit. But I am not the less of opinion that it is possible to be premature in some things; and to do this just now would be premature. I know what you would say—that you would not have asked it, but for that unfortunate improvisation of it in the play. But that I was not responsible for, and therefore owe no reparation to you now . . . Listen!"

"Paula—Paula! Where in the world are you?" was heard resounding along the corridor in the voice of her aunt. "Our friends are all ready to leave, and you will surely bid them good-night!"

"I must be gone—I won't ring for you to be shown out—come this way."

"But how will you get on in repeating the play to-morrow evening if that interpolation is against your wish?" he asked, looking her hard in the face.

"I'll think it over during the night. Come to-morrow morning to help me settle. But," she added, with coy yet genial independence, "listen to me. Not a word more about a—what you asked for, mind. I don't want to go so far, and I will not—not yet at least—I mean not at all. You must promise that, or I cannot see you again alone."

"It shall be as you request."

"Very well. And not a word of this to a soul. My aunt suspects: but she is a good aunt and will say nothing. Now that is clearly understood, I should be glad to consult with you to-morrow early. I will come to you in the studio or Pleasance as soon as I am disengaged."

She took him to a little chamfered doorway in the corner, which opened into a descending turret; and Somerset went down. When he had unfastened the door at the bottom, and stepped into the lower corridor she asked, "Are you down?" And on receiving an affirmative reply she closed the top door.

Somerset signified by a look that such had been his thought.
Paula was silent. "No," she murmured at last. "That cannot
be. He did not, nor must you."

It was said none the less decidedly for being spoken low.

"You quite resent . . . . . you have a right to.
I beg your pardon, not for speaking of it, but for thinking it."

CHAPTER X

SOMERSET was in the studio the next morning about ten
o'clock, superintending the labours of Knowles, Bowles, and
Cockton, whom he had again engaged to assist him with the
drawings on his appointment to carry out the works. When he
had set them going he ascended the staircase of the great tower
for some purpose that bore upon the forthcoming repairs of
this part. Passing the door of the telegraph-room he heard little
sounds within which led him to pause. They came from the
instrument, that somebody was working. Only two people in
the castle, to the best of his knowledge, knew the trick of this;
Miss Power, and a page in her service, called John. Miss De
Stancy could also despatch messages, but she was at Myrtle
Villa.

The door was closed, and much as he would have liked to
enter, the possibility that Paula was not the performer led him
to withold his steps, since he had no legitimate reason for
intruding. He went on to where the uppermost masonry had
resisted the mighty hostility of the elements for five hundred
years without receiving worse dilapidation than half a century
produces upon the face of man. But he still wondered who was
telegraphing, and whether the message bore on the subject of
housekeeping, architecture, theatricals, or love.

Could Somerset have seen through the panels of the door in
passing, he would have beheld the room occupied by Paula
alone.

It was she who sat at the instrument, and the message she
was despatching ran as under:—

"*Can you send down a competent actress, who will undertake
the part of Princess of France in 'Love's Labour's Lost' this
evening in a temporary theatre here? Dresses already provided
suitable to a lady about the middle height. State price.*"

The telegram was addressed to a well-known theatrical agent
in London.

Off went the message, and Paula retired into the next room, which was her boudoir, leaving the door open between that and the one she had just quitted. Here she busied herself with writing some letters, till in less than an hour the telegraph instrument showed signs of life, and she hastened back to its side. The reply received from the agent was as follows:—

"Miss Barbara Bell of the Regent's Theatre could come. Quite competent. Her terms would be about twenty-five guineas."

Without a moment's pause Paula returned for answer:—

"The terms are quite satisfactory."

Presently she heard the instrument again, and emerging from the next room in which she had passed the intervening time as before, she read:—

"Miss Barbara Bell's terms were accidentally understated. They would be forty guineas, in consequence of the distance. Am waiting at the office for a reply."

Paula set to work as before and replied:—

"Quite satisfactory; only let her come at once."

She did not leave the room this time, but went to an arrow-slit hard by and gazed out at the trees till the instrument began to speak again. Returning to it with a leisurely manner, implying a full persuasion that the matter was settled, she was somewhat surprised to learn that

"Miss Bell, in stating her terms, understands that she will not be required to leave London till the middle of the afternoon. If it is necessary for her to leave at once, ten guineas extra would be indispensable, on account of the great inconvenience of such a short notice."

Paula seemed a little vexed, but not much concerned she sent back with a readiness scarcely politic in the circumstances:—

"She must start at once. Price agreed to."

Her impatience for the answer was mixed with curiosity as to whether it was due to the agent or to Miss Barbara Bell that the prices had grown like Jack's Bean-stalk in the negotiation. Another telegram duly came:—

"Travelling expenses are expected to be paid."

With decided impatience she dashed off:—

"Of course; but nothing more will be agreed to."

Then, and only then, came the desired reply:—

"*Miss Bell starts by the twelve o'clock train.*"

This business being finished, Paula left the chamber and descended into the inclosure called the Pleasance, a spot grassed down like a lawn. Here stood Somerset, who, having come down from the tower, was looking on while a man searched for old foundations under the sod with a crowbar. He was glad to see her at last, and noticed that she looked serene and relieved; but could not for the moment divine the cause. Paula came nearer, returned his salutation, and regarded the man's operations in silence awhile till his work led him to a distance from them.

"Do you still wish to consult me?" asked Somerset.

"About the building perhaps," said she. "Not about the play."

"But you said so?"

"Yes; but it will be unnecessary."

Somerset thought this meant skittishness, and merely bowed.

"You mistake me as usual," she said, in a low tone. "I am not going to consult you on that matter, because I have done all you could have asked for without consulting you. I take no part in the play to-night."

"Forgive my momentary doubt!"

"Somebody else will play for me—an actress from London. But on no account must the substitution be known beforehand, or the performance to-night will never come off; and that I should much regret."

"Captain De Stancy will not play his part if he knows you will not play yours—that's what you mean?"

"You may assume as much," she said smiling. "And to guard against this you must help me to keep the secret by being my confederate."

To be Paula's confederate; to-day, indeed, time had brought him something worth waiting for. "In anything!" cried Somerset.

"Only in this!" said she, with soft severity. "And you know what you have promised, George; and you remember there is to be no—what we talked about! Now will you go in the one-horse brougham to Markton Station this afternoon, and meet the four o'clock train? Inquire for a lady for Stancy Castle—a Miss Bell; see her safely into the carriage, and send her straight on here. I am particularly anxious that she should not enter the town, for I think she once came to Markton in a starring company, and she might be recognised, and my plan be thus defeated."

Thus she instructed her lover and devoted friend; and when he could stay no longer he left her in the garden to return to his studio. As Somerset went in by the garden door he met a strange-looking personage coming out by the same passage—a stranger, with the manner of a Dutchman, the face of a smelter, and the clothes of an inhabitant of Guiana. The stranger, whom we have already seen sitting at the back of the theatre the night before, looked hard from Somerset to Paula, and from Paula again to Somerset, as he stepped out. Somerset had an unpleasant conviction that this queer gentleman had been standing for some time in the doorway unnoticed, quizzing him and his mistress as they talked together. If so he might have learnt a secret.

When he arrived upstairs, Somerset went to a window commanding a view of the garden. Paula still stood in her place, and the stranger was earnestly conversing with her. Soon they passed round the corner and disappeared.

It was now time for him to see about starting for Markton, an intelligible zest for circumventing the ardent and coercive captain of artillery saving him from any unnecessary delay in the journey. He was at the station ten minutes before the train was due; and when it drew up to the platform the first person to jump out was Captain De Stancy in sportsman's attire and with a gun in his hand. Somerset nodded, and De Stancy spoke, informing the architect that he had been ten miles down the line shooting water-fowl. "That's Miss Power's carriage, I think," he added.

"Yes," said Somerset, carelessly. "She expects a friend, I believe. We shall see you at the castle again to-night?"

De Stancy assured him that they would, and the two men parted, Captain De Stancy, when he had glanced to see that the carriage was empty, going on to where a porter stood with a couple of dogs.

Somerset now looked again to the train. While his back had been momentarily turned to converse with the captain, a lady of five-and-thirty had alighted from the identical compartment occupied by De Stancy. She made an inquiry about getting to Stancy Castle, upon which Somerset, who had not till now observed her, went forward, and introducing himself assisted her to the carriage and saw her safely off.

De Stancy had by this time disappeared, and Somerset walked on to his rooms at the King's Arms, where he remained till he had dined, picturing the discomfiture of his alert rival when there should enter to him as Princess, not Paula Power, but Miss Bell of the Regent's Theatre, London. Thus the hour passed, till he found that if he meant to see the issue of the plot it was time to be off.

On arriving at the castle, Somerset entered by the public door from the hall as before, a natural delicacy leading him to feel that though he might be welcomed as an ally at the stage-door—in other words, the door from the corridor—it was advisable not to take too ready an advantage of a privilege which, in the existing secrecy of his understanding with Paula, might lead to an overthrow of her plans on that point.

Not intending to sit out the whole performance, Somerset contented himself with standing in a window recess near the proscenium, whence he could observe both the stage and the front rows of spectators. He was quite uncertain whether Paula would appear among the audience to-night, and resolved to wait events. Just before the rise of the curtain the young lady in question entered and sat down. When the scenery was disclosed and the King of Navarre appeared, what was Somerset's surprise to find that, though the part was the part taken by De Stancy on the previous night, the voice was that of Mr. Mild; to him, at the appointed season, entered the Princess, namely, Miss Barbara Bell.

Before Somerset had recovered from his crestfallen sensation at De Stancy's elusiveness, that officer himself emerged in evening dress from behind a curtain forming a wing to the proscenium, and Somerset remarked that the minor part originally allotted to him was filled by the subaltern who had enacted it the night before. De Stancy glanced across, whether by accident or otherwise Somerset could not determine, and his glance seemed to say he quite recognised there had been a trial of wits between them, and that, thanks to his chance meeting with Miss Bell in the train, his had proved the stronger.

The house being less crowded to-night there were one or two vacant chairs in the best part. De Stancy, advancing from where he had stood for a few moments, seated himself comfortably beside Miss Power.

On the other side of her he now perceived the same queer elderly foreigner (as he appeared) who had come to her in the garden that morning. Somerset was surprised to perceive also that Paula with very little hesitation introduced him and De Stancy to each other. A conversation ensued between the three, none the less animated for being carried on in a whisper, in which Paula seemed on strangely intimate terms with the stranger, and the stranger to show feelings of great friendship for De Stancy, considering that they must be new acquaintances.

The play proceeded, and Somerset still lingered in his corner. He could not help fancying that De Stancy's ingenious relinquishment of his part, and its obvious reason, was winning Paula's admiration. His conduct was homage carried to unscrupulous and inconvenient lengths, a sort of thing which a woman may chide, but which she can never resent. Who could do otherwise than talk kindly to a man, incline a little to him, and condone his fault, when the sole motive of so audacious an exercise of his wits was to escape acting with any other heroine than herself?

His conjectures were brought to a pause by the ending of the comedy, and the opportunity afforded him of joining the group in front. The mass of people were soon gone, and the knot of friends assembled around Paula were discussing the merits and faults of the two days' performance.

"My uncle, Mr Abner Power," said Paula suddenly to Somerset, as he came near, presenting the stranger to the astonished young man. "I could not see you before the performance, as I should have liked to do. The return of my uncle is so extraordinary, that it ought to be told in a less hurried way than this. He has been supposed dead by all of us for nearly ten years—ever since the time we last heard from him."

"For which I am to blame," said Mr. Power, nodding to Paula's architect. "Yet not I, but accident and a sluggish temperament. There are times, Mr. Somerset, when the human creature feels no interest in his kind, and assumes that his kind feel no interest in him. The feeling is not active enough to make him fly from their presence; but sufficient to keep him silent if he happens to be away. I may not have described it precisely; but this I know, that after my long illness, and the fancied neglect of my letters——"

"For which my father was not to blame, since he did not receive them," said Paula.

"For which nobody was to blame—after that, I say, I wrote no more."

"You have much pleasure in returning at last, no doubt," said Somerset.

"Sir, as I remained away without particular pain, so I return without particular joy. I speak the truth, and no compliments. I may add that there is one exception to this absence of feeling from my heart, namely, that I do derive great satisfaction from seeing how mightily this young woman has grown and prevailed."

This address, though delivered nominally to Somerset, was listened to by Paula, Mrs. Goodman, and De Stancy also. After uttering it, the speaker turned away, and continued his previous conversation with Captain De Stancy. From this time till the group parted he never again spoke directly to Somerset, paying him barely so much attention as he might have expected as Paula's architect, and certainly less than he might have supposed his due as her accepted lover.

The result of the appearance, as from the tomb, of this wintry man was that the evening ended in a frigid and formal way which gave little satisfaction to the sensitive Somerset, who was abstracted and constrained by reason of thoughts on how this resuscitation of the uncle would affect his relation with Paula. It was possibly also the thought of two at least of the others. There had, in truth, scarcely yet been time enough to adumbrate the possibilities opened up by this gentleman's return.

The only private word exchanged by Somerset with any one that night was with Mrs. Goodman, in whom he always recognised a friend to his cause, though the fluidity of her character rendered her but a feeble one at the best of times. She informed him that Mr. Power had no sort of legal control over Paula, or direction in her estates; but Somerset could not doubt that a near and only blood relation, even had he possessed but half the static force of character that made itself apparent in Mr. Power, might exercise considerable moral influence over the girl if he chose. And in view of Mr. Power's marked preference for De Stancy, Somerset had many misgivings as to its operating in a direction favourable to himself.

CHAPTER XI

SOMERSET was deeply engaged with his draughtsmen and builders during the three following days, and scarcely entered the occupied wing of the castle.

At his suggestion Paula had agreed to have the works executed as such operations were carried out in old times, before the advent of contractors. Each trade required in the building was to be represented by a master-tradesman of that denomination, who should stand responsible for his own section of labour, and for no other, Somerset himself as chief technicist working out his designs on the spot. By this means the thoroughness of the workmanship would be greatly increased in comparison with the modern arrangement, whereby a nominal builder, seldom present, who can certainly know no more than one trade intimately and well, and who often does not know that, undertakes the whole.

But notwithstanding its manifest advantages to the proprietor, the plan added largely to the responsibilities of the architect, who, with his master-mason, master-carpenter, master-plumber, and what not, had scarcely a moment to call his own. Still, the method being upon the face of it the true one, Somerset liked it, and supervised with a will.

But though so deeply occupied as to be removed from immediate contact with the household, there seemed to float across the court to him from the inhabited wing an intimation that things were not as they had been before; that an influence adverse to himself was at work behind the ashlared face of inner wall which confronted him hard by. Perhaps this was because he never saw Paula at the windows, or heard her footfall in that half of the building given over to himself and his myrmidons. There was really no reason other than a sentimental one why he should see her. The uninhabited part of the castle was almost an independent structure, and it was quite natural to exist for weeks in this wing without coming in contact with residents in the other.

But a more pronounced cause than vague surmise was destined to perturb him, and this in an unexpected manner. It happened one morning that, before leaving his chambers at the King's Arms, he glanced through a local paper while waiting for the pony-carriage to be brought round in which he often drove to the castle. The paper was two days old but to his unutterable amazement he read therein a paragraph which ran as follows:—

"We are informed that a marriage is likely to be arranged between Captain De Stancy, of the Royal Horse Artillery, only surviving son of Sir William De Stancy, Baronet, and Paula, only daughter of the late John Power, Esq., M.P., of Stancy Castle."

Somerset dropped the paper, and stared out of the window. Fortunately for his emotions, the horse and carriage were at this moment brought to the door, so that nothing hindered Somerset in driving off to the spot at which he would be soonest likely to learn what truth or otherwise there was in the newspaper report. From the first he doubted it: and yet how should it have got there? Such strange rumours, like paradoxical maxims, generally include a portion of the truth, and what this portion was he found it impossible to guess. Five days had elapsed since he last spoke to Paula; could anything have happened in that interval to lead the tantalising girl to smile encouragingly on De Stancy?

Reaching the castle he entered his own quarters as usual, and after setting the draughtsmen to work walked up and down, pondering how he might best see her without making the disturbing paragraph the ground of his request for an interview; for if it were absolutely a fabrication, such a reason would wound her pride in her own honour towards him, and if it were partly true, he would certainly do better in leaving her alone than in reproaching her. It would simply amount to a proof that Paula was an arrant coquette, the explanation of whose guarded conduct towards himself lay in the fact that she wished not to commit herself in playing her game with him.

But all this, or any of it, was too ungenerous a thought to

entertain for an instant. It reopened the whole problem of her bearing from the beginning, and was painful even when rejected as absurd.

In his meditation he stood still, closely scanning one of the jamb-stones of a doorless entrance, as if to discover where the old hinge-hook had entered the stonework. He heard a footstep behind him, and looking round saw Paula standing by. She held a newspaper in her hand. The spot was one quite hemmed in from observation, a fact of which she seemed to be quite aware.

"I have something to tell you," she said; "something important. But you are so occupied with that old stone that I am obliged to wait."

"It is not true, surely!" he said, looking at the paper.

"No, look here," she said, holding up the sheet. It was not what he had supposed, but a new one—the local rival to that which had contained the announcement, and was still damp from the press. She pointed and he read:

"We are authorised to state that there is no foundation whatever for the assertion of our contemporary that a marriage is likely to be arranged between Captain De Stancy and Miss Power of Stancy Castle."

Somerset pressed her hand, and spoke his feelings not by language, but by the more pathetic vehicle of eyes. "It disturbed me," he said, "though I did not believe it."

"It astonished me, as much as it disturbed you; and I sent this contradiction at once."

"How could it have got there?"

She shook her head.

"You have not the least knowledge?"

"Not the least. I wish I had."

"It was not from any friends of De Stancy's? or himself?"

"It was not. His sister has ascertained beyond doubt that he knew nothing of it. Well, now, don't say any more to me about the matter."

"I'll find out how it got into the paper."

"Not now—any future time will do. I have something else to tell you."

"I hope the news is as good as the last," he said, looking

into her face with anxiety; for though the face was blooming, it seemed full of doubt as to how her next information would be taken.

"Oh yes; it is good, because everybody says so. We are going to take a delightful journey. My new-created uncle, as he seems, and I, and my aunt, and perhaps Charlotte, if she is well enough, are going to Nice, and other places about there."

"To Nice!" said Somerset, rather blankly. "And I must stay here!"

"Why, of course you must, considering what you have undertaken," she said, looking with saucy composure into his eyes. "My uncle's reason for proposing the journey just now is, that he thinks the alterations will make residence here dusty and disagreeable during this spring. The opportunity of going with him is too good a one for us to lose, as I have never been there."

"I wish I was going to be one of the party! . . . What do *you* wish about it?"

She shook her head impenetrably. "Who knows? Time will tell."

"Are you really glad you are going, dearest?—as I *must* call you just once," said the young man, gazing earnestly into her face, which struck him as looking far too rosy and radiant to be consistent with ever so little regret at leaving him behind.

"I take great interest in foreign trips, especially to the shores of the Mediterranean; and everybody makes a point of getting away when their house is turned out of the window."

"But you do feel a little sadness, such as I should feel if our positions were reversed?"

"I think you ought not to have asked that so incredulously,' she murmured. "We can be near each other in spirit, when our bodies are far apart, can we not?" Her tone grew softer, and she drew a little closer to his side with a slightly nestling motion, as she went on, "May I be sure that you will not think unkindly of me when I am absent from your sight, and not begrudge me any little pleasure because you are not there to share it with me?"

"May you! Can you ask it? . . . As for me, I shall have no pleasure to be begrudged or otherwise. The only pleasure I have is, as you well know, in you. When you are with me, I am happy: when you are away, I take no pleasure in anything."

"I don't deserve it. I have no right to disturb you so," she said, very gently. "But I have given you some pleasure, have I not? A little more pleasure than pain, perhaps."

"You have, and yet. . . . But I don't accuse you, dearest. Yes, you have given me pleasure. One truly pleasant time was when we stood together in the summer-house on the evening of the garden-party, and you said you liked me to love you."

"Yes, it was a pleasant time," she returned, thoughtfully. "How the rain came down, and formed a gauze between us and the dancers, did it not; and how afraid we were—at least I was—lest anybody should discover us there, and how quickly I ran in after the rain was over!"

"Yes," said Somerset, "I remember it. But no harm came of it to you. . . . And perhaps no good will come of it to me."

"Do not be premature in your conclusions, sir," she said, archly. "If you really do feel for me only half what you say, we shall—you will make good come of it—I mean in some way or other."

"Dear Paula—now I believe you, and can bear anything."

"Then we will say no more; because, as you recollect, we agreed not to go too far. No expostulations, for we are going to be practical young people; besides, I won't listen if you utter them. I simply echo your words, and say I, too, believe you. Now I must go. Rely on me, and don't magnify trifles light as air."

"I *think* I understand you. And if I do, it will make a great difference in my conduct. You will have no cause to complain."

"Then you must not understand me so much as to make much difference; for your conduct as my architect is perfect. But I must not linger longer, though I wished you to know this news from my very own lips."

"Bless you for it! When do you leave?"

"The day after to-morrow."

"So early! Does your uncle guess anything? Do you wish him to be told just yet?"

"Yes, to the first; no, to the second."

"I may write to you?"

"On business, yes. It will be necessary."

"How can you speak so at a time of parting!"

"Now, George—you see I say George, and not Mr. Somerset, and you may draw your own inference—don't be so morbid in your reproaches! I have informed you that you may write, or still better, telegraph, since the wire is so handy—on business. Well, of course, it is for you to judge whether you will add postscripts of another sort. There, you make me say more than a woman ought, because you are so obtuse and literal. Good afternoon—good-bye! This will be my address."

She handed him a slip of paper, and was gone.

Though he saw her again after this, it was during the bustle of preparation, when there was always a third person present, usually in the shape of that breathing refrigerator, her uncle. Hence the few words that passed between them were of the most formal description, and chiefly concerned the restoration of the castle, and a church at Nice designed by him, which he wanted her to inspect.

They were to leave by an early afternoon train, and Somerset was invited to lunch that day. The morning was occupied by a long business consultation in the studio with Mr. Power and Mrs. Goodman on what rooms were to be left locked up, what left in charge of the servants, and what thrown open to the builders and workmen under the surveillance of Somerset. At present the work consisted mostly of repairs to existing rooms, so as to render those habitable which had long been used only as stores for lumber. Paula did not appear during this discussion; but when they were all seated in the dining-hall she came in dressed for the journey, and, to outward appearance, with blithe anticipation at its prospect blooming from every feature. Next to her came Charlotte De Stancy, still with some of the pallor of an invalid, but wonderfully brightened up, as Somerset thought, by the prospect of a visit to a delightful shore. It might have been this; and it might have been that Somerset's presence had a share in the change.

It was in the hall, when they were in the bustle of leave-taking, that there occurred the only opportunity for the two or three private words with Paula to which his star treated him on that last day. His took the hasty form of, "You will write soon?"

"Telegraphing will be quicker," she answered in the same low tone; and whispering, "Be true to me!" turned away.

How unreasonable he was! In addition to those words, warm as they were, he would have preferred a little paleness of cheek, or trembling of lip, instead of the bloom and the beauty which sat upon her undisturbed maidenhood, to tell him that in some slight way she suffered at his loss.

Immediately after this they went to the carriages waiting at the door. Somerset, who had in a measure taken charge of the castle, accompanied them and saw them off, much as if they were visitors. She stepped in, a general adieu was spoken, and she was gone.

While the carriages rolled away, he ascended to the top of the tower, where he saw them lessen to spots on the road, and turn the corner out of sight. The chances of a rival seemed to grow in proportion as Paula receded from his side; but he could not have answered why. He had bidden her and her relatives adieu on her own doorstep, like a privileged friend of the family, while De Stancy had scarcely seen her since the play-night. That the silence into which the captain appeared to have sunk was the placidity of conscious power, derived from sources that Somerset knew not of, was scarcely probable; yet that adventitious aids existed for De Stancy he could not deny. The link formed by Charlotte between De Stancy and Paula, much as he liked the ingenuous girl, was one that he could have wished away. It constituted a bridge of access to Paula's inner life and feelings which nothing could rival; except that one fact which, as he firmly believed, did actually rival it, giving him faith and hope; his own primary occupation of Paula's heart. Moreover, Mrs. Goodman would be an influence favourable to himself and his cause during the journey; though, to be sure, to set against her there was the phelgmatic and obstinate Abner Power, in whom, apprized by those subtle media of intelligence which lovers possess, he fancied he saw no friend.

Somerset remained but a short time at the castle that day. The light of its chambers had fled, the gross grandeur of the

dictatorial towers oppressed him, and the studio was hateful.
He remembered a promise made long ago to Mr. Woodwell of
calling upon him some afternoon; and a visit which had not
much attractiveness in it at other times recommended itself
now, through being the one possible way open to him of
hearing Paula named and her doings talked of, this being a
turn the discussion would inevitably take. Hence in walking
back to Markton, instead of going up the High Street, he
turned aside into the unfrequented footway that led to the
minister's cottage.

Mr. Woodwell was not indoors at the moment of his call,
and Somerset lingered at the doorway, and cast his eyes
around. It was a house which typified the drearier tenets of its
occupier with great exactness. It stood upon its spot of earth
without any natural union with it: no mosses disguised the stiff
straight line where wall met earth; not a creeper softened the
aspect of the bare front. The garden-walk was strewn with
loose clinkers from the neighbouring foundry, which rolled
under the pedestrian's foot and jolted his soul out of him
before he reached the porchless door. But all was clean, and
clear, and dry.

Whether Mr. Woodwell was personally responsible for this
condition of things, or whether it resulted from a landlord's
taste, unchallenged by a preoccupied tenant, there was not
time to closely consider, for at this minute Somerset perceived
the minister coming up the walk towards him. Mr. Woodwell
welcomed him heartily; and yet with the mien of a man whose
mind has scarcely dismissed some scene which has preceded
the one that confronts him. What that scene was soon
transpired.

"I have had a very busy afternoon," said the minister, as
they walked indoors; "or rather an exciting afternoon. Your
client at Stancy Castle, whose relative, as I imagine you know,
has so unexpectedly returned, has left with him to-day for the
south of France; and I wished to ask her before her departure
some questions as to how a charity organised by her father was
to be administered in her absence. But I have been very
unfortunate. She could not find time to see me at her own
house, and I awaited her at the station, all to no purpose,

owing to the presence of her friends. Well, well, I must see if a letter will find her."

Somerset asked if anybody of the neighbourhood was there to see them off.

"Yes, that was the trouble of it. Captain De Stancy was there, and quite monopolised her. I don't know what 'tis coming to, and perhaps I have no business to inquire, since she is scarcely a member of our church now. Who could have anticipated the daughter of my old friend John Power developing into the ordinary gay woman of the world as she has done? Who could have expected her to associate with people who show contempt for their Maker's intentions by flippantly assuming other characters than those in which He created them?"

"You mistake her," murmured Somerset, in a voice which he vainly endeavoured to attune to philosophy. "Miss Power has some very rare and beautiful qualities in her nature, though I confess I tremble—fear lest the De Stancy influence should be too strong."

"Sir, it is already! Do you remember my telling you that I thought the force of her surroundings would obscure the pure daylight of her spirit, as a monkish window of coloured images attentuates the rays of God's sun? I do not wish to indulge in rash surmises, but her oscillation from her family creed of Calvinistic truth towards the traditions of the De Stancys has been so decided, though so gradual, that—well, I may be wrong."

"That what?" said the young man sharply.

"I sometimes think she will take to her as husband the present representative of that impoverished line—Captain De Stancy—which she may easily do, if she chooses, as his behaviour to-day showed."

"He was probably there on account of his sister," said Somerset, trying to escape the mental picture of farewell gallantries bestowed on Paula.

"It was hinted at in the papers the other day."

"And it was flatly contradicted."

"Yes. Well, we shall know in the Lord's good time: I can do

no more for her. And now, Mr. Somerset, pray take a cup of tea."

The discovery that De Stancy had enjoyed the coveted privilege of seeing the last of her, coupled with the other words of the minister, depressed Somerset a little, and he did not stay long. As he went to the door Woodwell said, "There is a worthy man—the deacon of our chapel, Mr. Havill—who would like to be friendly with you. Poor man, since the death of his wife he seems to have something on his mind—some trouble which my words will not reach. If ever you are passing his door, please give him a look in. He fears that calling on you might be an intrusion."

Somerset did not clearly promise, and went his way. The minister's allusion to the mysterious announcement of the marriage reminded Somerset that she had expressed a wish to know how the paragraph came to be inserted. The wish had been but carelessly spoken; but so telling was the vacancy caused by her absence that any deed relating to her was attended with a sad satisfaction and he went to the newspaper office to make inquiries on the point.

The reply was unexpected. The reporter informed his questioner that in returning from the theatricals, at which he was present, he shared a fly homeward with a gentleman who assured him that such an alliance was certain, so obviously did it recommend itself to all concerned, as a means of strengthening both families. The gentleman's knowledge of the Powers was so precise that the reporter did not hesitate to accept his assertion. He was a man who had seen a great deal of the world, and his face was noticeable for the seams and scars on it.

Somerset recognised Paula's uncle in the portrait.

Hostilities, then, were beginning. The paragraph had been meant as the first slap. Taking her abroad was the second.

BOOK THE FOURTH

SOMERSET, DARE AND DE STANCY

CHAPTER I

THERE was no part of Paula's journey in which Somerset did
not think of her. He imagined her in the hotel at Havre, in her
brief rest at Paris; her drive past the Place de la Bastille to the
Boulevart Mazas to take the train for Lyons; her tedious
progress through the dark of a winter night till she crossed the
isothermal line which told of the beginning of a southern
atmosphere, and onwards to the ancient blue sea.

Thus, between the hours devoted to architecture, he passed
the next three days. One morning he set himself, by the help
of John, to practise on the telegraph instrument, expecting a
message. But though he watched the machine at every opportunity, or kept some other person on the alert in its neighbourhood, no message arrived to gratify him till after the lapse of
nearly a fortnight. Then she spoke from her new habitation
nine hundred miles away, in these meagre words:

"*Are settled at the address given. Can now attend to any inquiry
about the building.*"

The pointed implication that she could attend to inquiries
about nothing else, breathed of the veritable Paula so distinctly
that he could forgive its sauciness. His reply was soon
despatched:

"*Will write particulars of our progress. Always the same.*" The
last three words formed the sentimental appendage which she
had assured him she could tolerate, and which he hoped
she might desire.

He spent the remainder of the day in making a little sketch
to show what had been done in the castle since her departure.
This he despatched with a letter of explanation ending in a
paragraph of a different tenor:

"I have demonstrated our progress as well as I could; but
another subject has been in my mind, even whilst writing the
former. Ask yourself if you use me well in keeping me a

fortnight before you so much as say that you arrived? The one thing that reconciled me to your departure was the thought that I should hear early from you: my idea of being able to submit to your absence was based entirely upon that.

"But I have resolved not to be out of humour, and to believe that your scheme of reserve is not unreasonable; neither do I quarrel with your injunction to keep silence to all relatives. I do not know anything I can say to show you more plainly my acquiescence in your wish 'not to go too far' (in short, to keep yourself dear—by dear I mean not cheap—you have been dear in the other sense a long time, as you know), than by not urging you to go a single degree further in warmth than you please."

When this was posted he again turned his attention to her walls and towers, which indeed were a dumb consolation in many ways for the lack of herself. There was no nook in the castle to which he had not access or could not easily obtain access by applying for the keys, and this propinquity of things belonging to her served to keep her image before him even more constantly than his memories would have done.

Three days and a half after the despatch of his subdued effusion the telegraph called to tell him the good news that

"*Your letter and drawing are just received. Thanks for the latter. Will reply to the former by post this afternoon.*"

It was with cheerful patience that he attended to his three draughtsmen in the studio, or walked about the environs of the fortress during the fifty hours spent by her presumably tender missive on the road. A light fleece of snow fell during the second night of waiting, inverting the position of long-established lights and shades, and lowering to a dingy grey the approximately white walls of other weathers: he could trace the postman's footmarks as he entered over the bridge, knowing them by the dot of his walking-stick: on entering the expected letter was waiting upon his table. He looked at its direction with glad curiosity; it was the first letter he had ever received from her.

"Hôtel—, Nice, Feb. 14.

"MY DEAR MR. SOMERSET," (the "George," then, to which

SOMERSET, DARE, AND DE STANCY   265

she had so kindly treated him in her last conversation, was not
to be continued in black and white:)

"Your letter explaining the progress of the work, aided by
the sketch enclosed, gave me as clear an idea of the advance
made since my departure as I could have gained by being
present. I feel every confidence in you, and am quite sure the
restoration is in good hands. In this opinion both my aunt and
my uncle coincide. Please act entirely on your own judgement
in everything, and as soon as you give a certificate to the
builders for the first instalment of their money it will be
promptly sent by my solicitors.

"You bid me ask myself if I have used you well in not
sending intelligence of myself till a fortnight after I had left
you. Now, George, don't be unreasonable! Let me remind you
that there are a thousand things not bad in themselves, which,
nevertheless, custom and circumstances render inexpedient to
be done. I say this, not from pride in my own conduct, but to
offer you a very fair explanation of it. Your resolve not to be
out of humour with me suggests that you have been sorely
tempted that way, else why should such a resolve have been
necessary?

"If you only knew what passes in my mind sometimes you
would perhaps not be so ready to blame. Shall I tell you? No.
For if it is a great emotion it may afford you a cruel satisfaction
at finding I suffer through separation; and if it be a growing
indifference to you, it will be inflicting gratuitous unhappiness
upon you, if you care for me, as I *sometimes* think you may do
a little."

("Oh, Paula!" said Somerset.)

"Please which way would you have it? But it is better that
you should guess at what I feel than that you should distinctly
know it. Notwithstanding this assertion you will, I know,
adhere to your first prejudice in favour of prompt confessions.
In spite of that, I fear that upon trial such promptness would
not produce that happiness which your fancy leads you to
expect. Your heart would revolt in time, and when once that
happens, farewell to the emotion you have told me of. Analyse
your feelings strictly, and you will find this true. At the same

time I admit that a woman who is *only* a compound of evasions, disguises, and caprices, is very disagreeable.

"Do not write *very* frequently, and never write at all unless you have some real information about the castle works to communicate. I will explain to you on another occasion why I make this request. You will possibly set it down as additional evidence of my cold-heartedness. If so you must. Would you also mind writing the business letter on an independent sheet, with a proper beginning and ending? Whether you inclose another sheet is of course optional.

> "Sincerely yours,
> "PAULA POWER."

Somerset had a suspicion that her order to him not to neglect the business letter was to escape any invidious remarks from her uncle. He wished she would be more explicit, so that he might know exactly how matters stood with them, and whether Abner Power had ever ventured to express disapproval of him as her lover.

But not knowing, he waited anxiously for a new architectural event on which he might legitimately send her another line. This occurred about a week later, when the men engaged in digging foundations discovered remains of old ones which warranted a modification of the original plan. He accordingly sent off his professional advice on the point, requesting her assent or otherwise to the amendment, winding up the inquiry with "Yours faithfully." On another sheet he wrote:

"Do you suffer from any unpleasantness in the manner of others on account of me? If so, inform me, Paula. I cannot otherwise interpret your request for the separate sheets. While on this point I will tell you what I have learnt relative to the authorship of that false paragraph about your engagement. It was communicated to the paper by your uncle. Was the wish father to the thought, or could he have been misled, as many were, by appearances at the theatricals?

"If I am not to write to you without a professional reason, surely you can write to me without such an excuse? When you write, tell me of yourself. There is nothing I so much wish to hear of. Write a great deal about your daily doings, that she, whose words are the sweetest to me in the world, may express them upon the sweetest subject.

"You say nothing of having been to look at the chapel-of-ease I told you of, the plans of which I made when an architect's pupil, working in mètres instead of feet and inches, to my immense perplexity, that the drawings might be understood by the foreign workmen. Go there and tell me what you think of its design. I can assure you that every curve thereof is my own.

"How I wish you would invite me to run over and see you, if only for a day or two, for my heart runs after you in a most distracted manner. Dearest, you entirely fill my life! But I forget; we have resolved not to go *very far*. But the fact is I am half afraid lest, with such reticence, you should not remember how very much I am yours, and with what a dogged constancy I shall always remember you. Paula, sometimes I have horrible misgivings that something will divide us, especially if we do not make a more distinct show of our true relationship. True do I say? I mean the relationship which I think exists between us, but which you do not affirm too clearly.—Yours always."

Away southward like the swallow went the tender lines. He wondered if she would notice his hint of being ready to pay her a flying visit, if permitted to do so. His fancy dwelt on that further side of France, the very contours of whose shore were now lines of beauty for him. He prowled in the library, and found interest in the mustiest facts relating to that place, learning with æsthetic pleasure that the number of its population was fifty thousand, that the mean temperature of its atmosphere was 60° Fahrenheit, and that the peculiarities of a mistral were far from agreeable.

He waited over long for her reply; but it ultimately came. After the usual business preliminary, she said:—

"As requested, I have visited the little church you designed. It gave me great pleasure to stand before a building whose outline and details had come from the brain of such a valued friend and adviser."

("Valued friend and adviser," repeated Somerset critically.)

"I like the style much, especially that of the windows—
Early English are they not? I am going to attend service there
next Sunday, *because you were the architect, and for no godly
reason at all.* Does that content you? Fie your despondency!
Remember M. Aurelius: 'This is the chief thing: Be not
perturbed; for all things are of the nature of the Universal.'
Indeed I am a little surprised at your having forebodings after
my assurance to you before I left. I have none. My opinion is
that, to be happy, it is necessary not to think any place more
agreeable than the one where we happen to be. . . . You are
too faint-hearted, and that's the truth of it. I advise you not to
abandon yourself to idolatry too readily; you know what I
mean. It fills me with remorse when I think how very far
below such a position my actual worth removes me.

"I should like to receive another letter from you as soon as
you have got over the misgiving you speak of, but don't write
too soon. I wish I could write anything to raise your spirits,
but you may be so perverse that if, in order to do this, I tell
you of the races, routs, scenery, gaieties, and gambling going
on in this place and neighbourhood (into which of course I
cannot help being a little drawn), you may declare that my
words make you worse than ever. Don't pass the line I have
set down in the way you were tempted to do in your last; and
not too many Dearests—at least as yet. This is not a time for
effusion. You have my very warm affection, and that's enough
for the present."

As a love-letter this missive was tantalising enough, but
since its form was simply a continuation of what she had
practised before she left, and not a change from that practice,
it produced no undue misgiving in him. Far more was he impressed by her omitting to answer the two important questions
he had put to her. First, concerning her uncle's attitude
towards them, and his conduct in giving such strange information to the reporter. Second, on his, Somerset's, paying her a
flying visit some time during the spring. But he was not the
man to force opinion on these points, or on any others; and
since she had requested it, he made no haste in his reply.
When penned, it ran in the words subjoined, which, in

common with every line of their correspondence, acquired from the strangeness of subsequent circumstances an interest and a force that perhaps they did not intrinsically possess.

"People cannot" (he wrote) "be for ever in good spirits on this gloomy side of the Channel, even though you seem to be so on yours. However, that I can abstain from letting you know whether my spirits are good or otherwise, I will prove in our future correspondence. I admire you more and more, both for the warm feeling towards me which I firmly believe you have, and for your ability to maintain side by side with it so much dignity and resolution with regard to foolish sentiment. Sometimes I think I could have put up with a little more weakness if it had brought with it a little more romantic tenderness, but I dismiss all that when I mentally survey your other qualities. I have thought of fifty things to say to you of the *too far* sort, not one of any other; how unfortunate then is your prohibition, by which I am doomed to say things that do not rise spontaneously to my lips, but have to be made, shaped, and fashioned! You say that our shut-up feelings are not to be mentioned yet. How long is the yet to last?

"But, to speak more solemnly, matters grow very serious with us, Paula—at least with me; and there are times when this restraint is really unbearable. It is possible to put up with reserve and circumspection when the reserved and circumspect being is by one's side, for the eyes may reveal what the lips do not. But when absence is superadded, what was piquancy becomes harshness, tender railleries become cruel sarcasm, and tacit understandings misunderstandings. However that may be, you shall never be able to reproach me for touchiness. I still esteem you as a friend; I admire you and love you as a woman. This I shall always continue to do, however undemon-strative and unconfiding you prove."

common with every line of their correspondence, acquired
from the knowledge of subsequent circumstances an interest
and a force that perhaps they did not intrinsically possess.

"People cannot," she wrote, "always be in good spirits on
this gloomy side of the channel, and though you seem to be
so on yours. However, that I can banish from finding

CHAPTER II

WITHOUT knowing it, Somerset was drawing near to a crisis
in this soft correspondence which would speedily put his
assertions to the test; but the knowledge came upon him soon
enough for his peace.

Her next letter, dated March 9th, was the shortest of all he
had received, and beyond the portion devoted to the building-
works it contained only the following sentences:—

"I am almost angry with you, George, for being vexed
because I will not make you a formal confession. Why should
the verbal *I love you* be such a precious phrase? During the
seven or eight months that you have been endeavouring to
ascertain my sentiments you must have fairly well discovered
them. You have discovered my regard for you, what more can
you desire? Would a reiterated confession of passion really do
any good? Instead of pressing a lady upon this point, you
should endeavour to conceal from her the progress of her
interest in you. You should contrive to deeply involve her
heart before she perceives your designs; hiding her, as it were,
from her own observation. Then, on your side, can one
imagine a situation more charming than that of perceiving a
woman interested, without herself being exactly conscious of
the depth of her interest! What a triumph, to rejoice in secret
over what she will not recognise! This is what I should style
pleasure indeed. Women labour under great difficulties:
believe me that a declaration of love is always a mortifying
circumstance to us, and it is a natural instinct to retain the
power of obliging a man to hope, fear, pray, and beseech as
long as we think fit, before we confess to a reciprocal affection.

"I am now going to own to a weakness about which I had
intended to keep silent. It will not perhaps add to your respect
for me. My uncle, whom in many ways I like, is displeased
with me for keeping up this correspondence so regularly. I am

quite perverse enough to venture to disregard his feelings; but considering the relationship, and his kindness in other respects, I should prefer not to do so at present. Honestly speaking, I want the courage to resist him in some things. He said to me the other day that he was very much surprised that I did not depend upon his judgement for my future happiness. Whether that meant much or little, I have resolved to communicate with you only by telegrams for the remainder of the time we are here. Please reply by the same means only. There, now, don't flush and call me names! It is for the best, and we want no nonsense, you and I. I feel more than I say, and if I do not speak more plainly, you will understand what is behind after all I have hinted. I can promise you that you will not like me less upon knowing me better. Hope ever. I would give up a good deal for you. Good-bye!"

This brought Somerset some cheerfulness and a good deal of gloom. He silently reproached her, who was apparently so independent, for lacking independence in such a vital matter. Perhaps it was mere sex, perhaps it was peculiar to a few, that her independence and courage, like Cleopatra's, failed her occasionally at the last moment.

One curious impression which had often haunted him now returned with redoubled force. He could not see himself as the husband of Paula Power in any likely future. He could not imagine her his wife. People were apt to run into mistakes in their presentiments; but though he could picture her as queening it over him, as avowing her love for him unreservedly, even as compromising herself for him, he could not see her in a state of domesticity with him.

Telegrams being commanded, to the telegraph he repaired, when, after two days, an immediate wish to communicate with her led him to dismiss vague conjecture on the future situation. His first telegram took the following form:—

"*I give up the letter-writing. I will part with anything to please you but yourself. Your comfort with your relative is the first thing to be considered: not for the world do I wish you to make divisions within doors.—Yours.*"

Tuesday, Wednesday, Thursday passed, and on Saturday a telegram came in reply:—

"I can fear, grieve at, and complain of nothing, having your nice promise to consider my comfort always."

This was very pretty; but it admitted little. Such short messages were in themselves poor substitutes for letters, but their speed and easy frequency were good qualities which the letters did not possess. Three days later he replied:—

"You do not once say to me 'Come.' Would such a strange accident as my arrival disturb you much?"

She replied rather quickly:—

"I am indisposed to answer you too clearly. Keep your heart strong: 'tis a censorious world."

The vagueness there shown made Somerset peremptory, and he could not help replying somewhat more impetuously than usual:—

"Why do you give me so much cause for anxiety? Why treat me to so much mystification? Say once, distinctly, that what I have asked is given."

He waited for the answer, one day, two days, a week; but none came. It was now the end of March, and when Somerset walked of an afternoon by the river and pool in the lower part of the grounds, his ear newly greeted by the small voices of frogs and toads and other creatures who had been torpid through the winter, he became doubtful and uneasy that she alone should be silent in the awakening year.

He waited through a second week, and there was still no reply. It was possible that the urgency of his request had tempted her to punish him, and he continued his walks, to, fro, and around, with as close an ear to the undertones of nature, and as attentive an eye to the charms of his own art, as the grand passion would allow. Now came the days of battle between winter and spring. On these excursions, though spring was to the forward during the daylight, winter would reassert itself at night, and not unfrequently at other moments. Tepid airs and nipping breezes met on the confines of sunshine and shade; trembling raindrops that were still akin to frost crystals dashed themselves from the bushes as he pursued his way from town to castle; the birds were like an orchestra waiting for the signal to strike up, and colour began to enter into the country round.

But he gave only a modicum of thought to these proceedings. He rather thought such things as, "She can afford to be saucy, and to find a source of blitheness in my attachment, considering the power that wealth gives her to pick and choose almost where she will." He was bound to own, however, that one of the charms of her conversation was the complete absence of the note of the heiress from its accents. That, other things equal, her interest would naturally incline to a person bearing the name of De Stancy, was evident from her avowed predilections. His original assumption, that she was a personification of the modern spirit, who had been dropped, like a seed from the bill of a bird, into a chink of mediævalism, required some qualification. It had been based on her bold flights of thought, and her original innovations. But romanticism, which will exist in every human breast as long as human nature itself exists, had asserted itself in her. Veneration for things old, not because of any merit in them, but because of their long continuance, had developed in her; and her modern spirit was taking to itself wings and flying away. Whether his image was flying with the other was a question which moved him all the more deeply now that her silence gave him dread of an affirmative answer.

But he refused to give credit for more than brief spaces to those signs which at other moments convinced him that her passing fancy for him was declining like a summer day. Like other emotional natures, he was much more disposed to abandon himself blindly to his own passion than to reason out the grounds of a waning in hers.

For another seven days he stoically left in suspension all forecasts of his possibly grim fate in being the employed and not the beloved. The week passed: he telegraphed: there was no reply: he had sudden fears for her personal safety and resolved to break her command by writing.

"Stancy Castle, April 13.

"DEAR PAULA,

"Are you ill or in trouble? It is impossible in the very unquiet state you have put me into by your silence that I should abstain from writing. Without affectation, you sorely distress me, and I think you would hardly have done it could you know what a degree of anxiety you cost me. All the misgivings I had at your parting are nothing to those I feel since you have ceased to communicate. Why, Paula, do you not write or send to me? What have I done that you should treat me thus? Do write, if it is only to reproach me. I would rather have sharp words from your pen than none. I am compelled to pass the greater part of the day in a place which breathes constantly of you, but where you can no longer be found. To be honest in my supervision of what I have undertaken for you I must stay here, and the possibility of softening my disquietude by change of scene is thus denied me. I am unfortunate indeed that you have not been able to find half an hour during the last month to tell me at least that you are alive. I cannot help saying that your injustice and cruelty are extreme. How much misery would you not have saved me had you, when I first knew you, but shown as little tenderness as, according to appearances, you have latterly felt for me. You have always been ambiguous, it is true; but I thought I read encouragement in your eyes; encouragement certainly was in your eyes, and who would not have been deluded by them and have believed them sincere? It is difficult to learn to suspect the sincerity of one we admire. You charmed me by the sweetness of your manners, and my violent inclination led me on. The consequences of a love which, at the beginning was so pleasant and blissful, are now a ruinous disgust with everything I used to take an interest in, and I cannot say where it will end.

"You may say that in loving you, and being encouraged by you for a time, I have enjoyed transcendent pleasures, which are a fair return without further expectations. But consider what a price I pay for them now! Ask yourself if I may not pay too dearly. Had I resisted you; had I exerted my reason in opposition to the predilection I felt for you, then you might have had a right to punish me. But I did no such thing. There may, of course, be some deliberate scheming on the part of your relatives to intercept our communications; but I cannot think it. I know that the housekeeper has received a letter from your aunt this very week, in which she incidentally mentions that all are well, and in the same place as before. How then can I excuse you?

"Then write, Paula, or at least telegraph, as you proposed. Otherwise I am resolved to take your silence as a signal for discontinuing our avowals, to treat your fair words as wind, and to write to you no more."

CHAPTER III

HE despatched the letter, and half an hour afterwards felt sure that it would mortally offend her. But he had now reached a state of temporary indifference, and could contemplate the loss of such a tantalising property with reasonable calm.

In the interim of waiting for a reply he was one day walking to Markton, when, passing Myrtle Villa, he saw Sir William De Stancy ambling about his garden-path and examining the crocuses that palisaded its edge. Sir William saw him and asked him to come in. Somerset was in the mood for any diversion from his own affairs, and they seated themselves by the drawing-room fire.

"I am much alone now," said Sir William, "and if the weather were not very mild, so that I can get out into the garden every day, I should feel it a great deal."

"You allude to your daughter's absence?"

"And my son's. Strange to say, I do not miss her so much as I miss him. She offers to return at any moment; but I do not wish to deprive her of the advantages of a little foreign travel with her friend. Always, Mr. Somerset, give your spare time to foreign countries, especially those which contrast with your own in topography, language, and art. That's my advice to all young people of your age. Don't waste your money on expensive amusements at home. Practise the strictest economy at home, to have a margin for going abroad."

Economy, which Sir William had never practised, but to which, after exhausting all other practices, he now raised an altar, as the Athenians did to the unknown God, was a topic likely to prolong itself on the baronet's lips, and Somerset contrived to interrupt him by asking:

"Captain De Stancy, too, has gone? Has the artillery, then, left the barracks?"

"No," said Sir William. "But my son has made use of his leave in running over to see his sister at Nice."

The current of quiet meditation in Somerset changed to a busy whirl at this unexpected reply. Here was the key to her silence. That Paula should become indifferent to his existence from a sense of superiority, physical, spiritual, or social, was a sufficiently ironical thing; but that she should have relinquished him because of the presence of a rival fired him with indignation.

Sir William, noting nothing, continued in the tone of clever childishness which characterised him: "It is very singular how the present situation has been led up to by me. Policy, and policy alone, has been the rule of my conduct for many years past; and when I say that I have saved my family by it, I believe time will show that I am within the truth. I hope you don't let your passions outrun your policy, as so many young men are apt to do. Better be poor and politic, than rich and headstrong: that's the opinion of an old man. However, I was going to say that it was purely from policy that I allowed a friendship to develop between my daughter and Miss Power, and now events are proving the wisdom of my course. Straws show how the wind blows, and there are little signs that my son Captain De Stancy will return to Stancy Castle by the fortunate step of marrying its owner. I say nothing to either of them, and they say nothing to me; but my wisdom lies in doing nothing to hinder such a consummation, despite inherited prejudices."

Somerset had quite time enough to rein himself in during the old gentleman's locution, and the voice in which he answered was so cold and reckless that it did not seem his own: "But how will they live happily together when she is a dissenter, and a radical, and a New-light, and a Neo-Greek, and a person of red blood; while Captain De Stancy is the reverse of them all!"

"I anticipate no difficulty on that score," said the baronet. "My son's star lies in that direction, and, like the Magi, he is following it without trifling with his opportunity. You have skill in architecture, therefore you follow it. My son has skill in gallantry, and now he is about to profitably exercise it."

"May nobody wish him more harm in that exercise than I do!" said Somerset fervently.

★

A stagnant moodiness of several hours which followed his visit
to Myrtle Villa, and the intelligence there acquired, resulted in
a temper to which he had been warming for some time. It was
to journey over to Paula the very next day, and unravel the
whole mystery face to face with her. He now felt perfectly
convinced that the inviting of Captain De Stancy to visit them
at Nice was a second stage in the scheme of Paula's uncle, the
premature announcement of her marriage having been the
first. Somerset was not so blinded by his heart but that he
could see what an attraction the union would have for a frigid
calculator whose thoughts were like geometrical diagrams. The
roundness and neatness of the whole plan could not fail to
recommend it to the mind which delighted in putting involved
things straight, and such a mind Abner Power's seemed to be.
In fact, the felicity, in a politic sense, of pairing the captain
with the heiress furnished no little excuse for manœuvring to
bring it about, so long as that manœuvring fell short of
unfairness, which Mr. Power's could scarcely be said to do.

The next day was spent in furnishing the builders with such
instructions as they might require for a coming week or ten
days, and in dropping a short note to Paula; ending as
follows:—

"I am coming to see you. Possibly you will refuse me an
interview. Never mind, I am coming.—Yours,
                                        "G. SOMERSET."

The morning after that he was up and away. Between him
and Paula stretched nine hundred miles by the line of journey
that he found it necessary to adopt, namely, by way of London,
in order to inform his father of his movements and to make
one or two business calls. The afternoon was passed in
attending to these matters, the night in speeding onward, and
by the time that nine o'clock sounded next morning through
the sunless and leaden air of the English Channel coasts, he
had reduced the number of miles on his list by two hundred,
and cut off the sea from the impediments between him and
Paula.

Although his haste had involved an unpleasant night-passage
he did not wait for rest, pressing onward at once to Paris,

which he reached about noon. At present it was not the blithe and beautiful city that it had formerly been to him, but a stage marking three hundred and fifty miles as the number cleared off his score. He dined at an hotel without waiting for the regular *table d'hôte*, and about seven o'clock the same evening moved out of Paris on his southerly course, up the valley of the Seine and through the vine slopes of Burgundy. On awakening from a fitful sleep in the grey dawn of the next morning he looked out upon the great city whose name associates silk, in the fantastic imagination, with some of the ghastliest atrocities, Protestant, Catholic, and Revolutionary, that the civilised world has beheld. But all in Lyons was quiet enough now, the citizens being unaroused as yet even to the daily round of bread-winning, and enveloped in a haze of fog.

Six hundred and fifty miles of his journey had now been got over; there still intervened two hundred and fifty between him and the end of suspense. When he thought of that he was disinclined to pause; and pressed on by the same train, which set him down at Marseilles at mid-day.

Here he considered. By going on to Nice that afternoon he would arrive at too late an hour to call upon her at the hotel the same evening: it would therefore be advisable to sleep in Marseilles and proceed the next morning to his journey's end, so as to meet her in a brighter and more refreshed condition than he could boast of to-day. This he accordingly did, and leaving Marseilles the next morning about eight, found himself at Nice early in the afternoon.

Now that he was actually at the centre of his gravitation he seemed even further away from a feasible meeting with her than in England. While afar off, his presence at Nice had appeared to be the one thing needful for the solution of his trouble, but the very house fronts seemed now to ask him what right he had there. Unluckily, in writing from England, he had not allowed her time to reply before his departure, so that he did now know what difficulties might lie in the way of her seeing him privately. Before deciding what to do, he walked down the Avenue de la Gare to the Promenade between the shore and the Jardin Public, and sat down to think.

The hotel which she had given him as her address looked

right out upon him and the sea beyond, and he rested there
with the pleasing hope that her eyes might glance from a
window and discover his form. Everything in the scene was
sunny and gay. Behind him in the gardens a band was playing;
before him was the sea, the Great Sea, the historical and
original Mediterranean; the sea of innumerable characters in
history and legend that arranged themselves before him in a
long frieze of memories so diverse as to include both Æneas
and St. Paul.

Northern eyes are not prepared on a sudden for the impact
of such images of warmth and colour as meet them southward,
or for the vigorous light that falls from the sky of this favoured
shore. In any other circumstances the transparency and serenity of the air, the perfume of the sea, the radiant houses, the
palms and flowers, would have acted upon Somerset as an
enchantment, and wrapped him in a reverie; but at present he
only saw and felt these things as through a thick glass which
kept out half their atmosphere.

At last he made up his mind. He would take up his quarters
at her hotel, and catch echoes of her and her people, to learn
somehow if their attitude towards him as a lover were actually
hostile, before formally encountering them. Under this crystal-
line light, full of gaieties, sentiment, languor, seductiveness,
and ready-made romance, the memory of a solitary unimport-
ant man in the lugubrious North might have faded from her
mind. He was only her hired designer. He was an artist; but
he had been engaged by her, and was not a volunteer; and she
did not as yet know that he meant to accept no return for his
labours but the pleasure of presenting them to her as a love-
offering.

So off he went at once towards the imposing building
whither his letters had preceded him. Owing to a press of
visitors there was a moment's delay before he could be attended
to at the bureau, and he turned to the large staircase that
confronted him, momentarily hoping that her figure might
descend. Her dress must indeed have brushed the carpeting of
those steps scores of times. She must have gone in and out of
this portico daily. He now went to the hostess at the desk,

engaged his room, ordered his luggage to be sent for, and finally inquired for the party he sought.

"They left Nice yesterday, monsieur," replied madame.

Was she quite sure, Somerset asked her?

Yes, she was quite sure. Two of the hotel carriages had driven them to the station.

Did she know where they had gone to?

This and other inquiries resulted in the information that they had gone to the hotel at Monte Carlo; that how long they were going to stay there, and whether they were coming back again, was not known. His final question whether Miss Power had received a letter from England which must have arrived the day previous was answered in the affirmative.

Somerset's first and sudden resolve was to cancel his engagement to stay here for the night, and to follow on after them to the hotel named; but he finally decided to make his immediate visit to Monte Carlo only a cautious reconnoitre, returning to Nice to sleep.

Accordingly, after an early dinner, he again set forth through the broad Avenue de la Gare, and an hour on the coast railway brought him to the beautiful and sinister little spot to which the Power and De Stancy party had strayed in common with the rest of the frivolous throng.

He assumed that their visit thither would be chiefly one of curiosity, and therefore not prolonged. This proved to be the case in even greater measure than he had anticipated. On inquiry at the hotel he learnt that they had stayed only one night, leaving a short time before his arrival, though it was believed that some of the party were still in the town.

Somerset could not discover in which direction they had gone, and in a state of indecision he strolled into the gardens of the Casino, and looked out upon the sea. There it still lay, calm yet lively; of an unmixed blue, yet variegated; hushed, but articulate even to melodiousness. Everything about and around this coast appeared indeed jaunty, tuneful, and at ease, reciprocating with heartiness the rays of the splendid sun; everything, except himself. The palms and the flowers on the terraces before him were undisturbed by a single cold breath. The marble-work of parapets and steps was unsplintered by frosts. The whole was like a conservatory with the sky for its dome.

For want of other occupation he presently strolled round towards the public entrance to the Casino, and ascended the great staircase into the pillared hall. It was possible, after all, that after leaving the hotel and sending on their luggage they had taken another turn through the rooms, to follow by a later train. With more than curiosity, then, he scanned first the reading-rooms, only however to see not a face that he knew. He then crossed the vestibule to the gaming-tables.

CHAPTER IV

HERE he was confronted by a heated phantasmagoria of tainted splendour and a high pressure of suspense that seemed to make the air quiver. A low whisper of conversation prevailed, which might probably have been not wrongly defined as the lowest note of social harmony.

The people gathered at this negative pole of industry had come from all civilised countries; their tongues were familiar with many forms of utterance, that of each racial group or type being unintelligible in its subtler variations, if not entirely, to the rest. But the language of *meum* and *tuum* they collectively comprehended without translation. In a half-charmed spellbound state they had congregated in knots, standing, or sitting in hollow circles round the notorious oval tables marked with figures and lines. The eyes of all these sets of people were watching the Roulette. Somerset went from table to table, looking among the loungers rather than among the regular players, for faces, or at least for one face, which did not meet his gaze, there passing into his ears the while a confusion of sentences: "Messieurs, faites le jeu!" "Le jeu est-il fait?" "Rien ne va plus!" "Vingt-quatre." "Noir." "Pair et Passe," from the lips of the croupiers.

The suggestive charm which the centuries-old impersonality Gaming, rather than games and gamesters, had for Somerset, led him to loiter on even when his hope of meeting any of the Power and De Stancy party had vanished. As a non-participant in its profit and losses, fevers and frenzies, it had that stage effect upon his imagination which is usually exercised over those who behold Chance presented to them with spectacular piquancy without advancing far enough in its acquaintance to suffer from its ghastly reprisals and impish tricks, that strip it of all romance.

He beheld a hundred diametrically opposed wishes issuing from the murky intelligences around a table, and spreading down across each other upon the figured diagram in their midst, each to its own number. It was a network of hopes; which at the announcement, "Sept, Rouge, Impair, et Manque," disappeared like magic gossamer, to be replaced in a moment by new. That all the people there, including himself, could be interested in what to the eye of perfect reason was a somewhat monotonous thing—the property of numbers to recur at certain longer or shorter intervals in a machine containing them—in other words, the blind groping after fractions of a result the whole of which was well known—was one testimony among many of the powerlessness of logic when confronted with imagination. In some of the gamblers there was an intentness that reached the point of ferocity; in others a feline patience that was even less admirable. But these symptoms were after all secondary. The broad aspect of nearly every one was that of well-mannered calm, and a cursory view of the faces alone would have discovered nothing strongly contrasting with those of a mixed congregation listening to a church sermon. If they were all worshippers of Belial, they seemed to find that word quite as sustaining as the blessed Mesopotamia and its kin.

At this juncture our lounger discerned at one of the tables about the last person in the world he could have wished to encounter there. It was Dare, whom he had supposed to be a thousand miles off, hanging about the purlieus of Markton.

Dare was seated beside a table in an attitude of application, which seemed to imply that he had come early and engaged in this pursuit in a systematic manner. Somerset had never witnessed Dare and De Stancy together, neither had he heard of any engagement of Dare by the travelling party as artist, courier, or otherwise; and yet it crossed his mind that Dare might have had something to do with them, or at least have seen them. This possibility was enough to overmaster Somerset's reluctance to speak to the young man, and he did so as soon as an opportunity occurred.

Dare's face was as rigid and dry as if it had been encrusted with plaster, and he was like one turned into a computing machine which no longer had the power of feeling. He recognised Somerset as indifferently as if he had met him in the ward of Stancy Castle, and replying to his remarks by a word or two, concentrated on the game anew.

"Are you here alone?" said Somerset presently.

"Quite alone." There was a silence, till Dare added, "But I have seen some friends of yours." He again became absorbed in the events of the table. Somerset retreated a few steps, and pondered the question whether Dare could know where they had gone. He disliked to be beholden to Dare for information, but he would give a great deal to know. While pausing he watched Dare's play. He staked only five-franc pieces, but it was done with an assiduity worthy of larger coin. At every half-minute or so he placed his money on a certain spot, and as regularly had the mortification of seeing it swept away by the croupier's rake. After a while he varied his procedure. He risked his money, which from the look of his face seemed rather to have dwindled than increased, less recklessly against long odds than before. Leaving off backing numbers *en plein*, he laid his venture upon two columns *à cheval*; then tried it upon the dozens; then upon two numbers; then upon a square; and, apparently getting nearer and nearer defeat, at last upon the simple chances of even or odd, over or under, red or black. Yet with a few fluctuations in his favour fortune bore steadily against him, till he could breast her blows no longer. He rose from the table and came towards Somerset, and they both moved on together into the entrance-hall.

Dare was at that moment the victim of an intolerably overpowering mania for more money. His presence in the South of Europe had its origin, as may be guessed, in Captain De Stancy's journey in the same direction, whom he had followed, and occasionally troubled with persistent requests for more funds, though carefully keeping out of sight of Paula and the rest. His dream of involving Paula in the De Stancy pedigree knew no abatement. But Somerset had by accident lighted upon him at an instant when his chronic idea, though not displaced, was overwhelmed by a temporary rage for continuing play. He was so possessed with this desire that, in a hope of being able to gratify it by Somerset's aid, he was prepared to do almost anything to please the architect.

"You asked me," said Dare, stroking his impassive brow,

"if I had seen anything of the Powers. I have seen them; and if I can be of any use to you in giving information about them I shall only be too glad."

"What information can you give?"

"I can tell you where they are gone to."

"Where?"

"To the Grand Hotel, Genoa. They went on there this afternoon."

"Whom do you refer to by they?"

"Mrs. Goodman, Mr. Power, Miss Power, Miss De Stancy, and the worthy captain. He leaves them to-morrow: he comes back here for a day on his way to England."

Somerset was silent. Dare continued: "Now I have done you a favour, will you do me one in return?"

Somerset looked toward the gaming-rooms, and said dubiously, "Well?"

"Lend me two hundred francs."

"Yes," said Somerset; "but on one condition: that I don't give them to you till you are inside the hotel you are staying at."

"That can't be; it's at Nice."

"Well, I am going back to Nice, and I'll lend you the money the instant we get there."

"But I want it here, now, instantly!" cried Dare; and for the first time there was a wiry unreasonableness in his voice that fortified his companion more firmly than ever in his determination to lend the young man no money whilst he remained inside that building.

"You want it to throw it away. I don't approve of it; so come with me."

"But," said Dare, "I arrived here with a hundred napoleons and more, expressly to work out my theory of chances and recurrences, which is sound; I have studied it hundreds of times by the help of this." He partially drew from his pocket the little volume that we have before seen in his hands. "If I only persevere in my system, the certainty that I must win is almost mathematical. I have staked and lost two hundred and thirty-three times. Allowing out of that one chance in every thirty-six (which is the average of zero being marked), and two hundred and four times for the backers of the other numbers, I have the mathematical expectation of six times at least, which would nearly recoup me. And shall I, then, sacrifice that vast foundation of waste chances that I have laid down, and paid for, merely for want of a little ready money?"

"You might persevere for a twelvemonth, and still not get the better of your reverses. Time tells in favour of the bank. Just imagine for the sake of argument that all the people who have ever placed a stake upon a certain number to be one person playing continuously. Has that imaginary person won? The existence of the bank is a sufficient answer."

"But a particular player has the option of leaving off at any point favourable to himself, which the bank has not; and there's my opportunity."

"Which from your mood you will be sure not to take advantage of."

"I shall go on playing," said Dare, doggedly.

"Not with my money."

"Very well; we won't part as enemies," replied Dare, with the flawless politeness of a man whose speech has no longer any kinship with his feelings. "Shall we share a bottle of wine? You will not? Well, I hope your luck with your lady will be more magnificent than mine has been here; but—mind Captain De Stancy! he's a fearful wild fowl for you."

"He's a harmless, inoffensive officer, as far as I know. If he is not—let him be what he may for me."

"And do his worst to cut you out, I suppose?"

"Ay—if you will." Somerset, much against his judgement, was being stimulated by these pricks into words of irritation. "Captain De Stancy might, I think, be better employed than in dangling at the heels of a lady who can well dispense with his company. And you might be better employed than in wasting your wages here."

"Wages—a fit word for my money. May I ask you at what stage in the appearance of a man whose way of existence is unknown his money ceases to be called wages and begins to be called means?"

Somerset turned and left him without replying, Dare following his receding figure with a look of ripe resentment, not less likely to vent itself in mischief from the want of moral ballast in him who emitted it. He then fixed a nettled and unsatisfied gaze upon the gaming-rooms, and in another minute or two left the Casino also.

Dare and Somerset met no more that day. The latter returned to Nice by the evening train and went straight to the hotel. He now thanked his fortune that he had not precipitately given up his room there, for a telegram from Paula awaited him. His hand almost trembled as he opened it, to read the following few short words, dated from the Grand Hotel, Genoa.

"*Letter received. Am glad to hear of your journey. We are not returning to Nice, but stay here a week. I direct this at a venture.*"

This tantalising message—the first breaking of her recent silence—was saucy, almost cruel, in its dry frigidity. It led him to give up his idea of following at once to Genoa. That was what she obviously expected him to do, and it was possible that his non-arrival might draw a letter or message from her of a sweeter composition than this. That would at least be the effect of his tardiness if she cared in the least for him; if she did not he could bear the worst. The argument was good enough as far as it went, but, like many more, failed from the narrowness of its premises, the contingent intervention of Dare being entirely undreamt of. It was altogether a fatal miscalculation, which cost him dear.

Passing by the telegraph-office in the Rue Pont-Neuf at an early hour the next morning he saw Dare coming out from the door. It was Somerset's momentary impulse to thank Dare for the information given as to Paula's whereabouts, information which had now proved true. But Dare did not seem to appreciate his friendliness, and after a few words of studied civility the young man moved on.

And well he might. Five minutes before that time he had thrown open a gulf of treachery between himself and the architect which nothing in life would ever close. Before leaving the telegraph-office Dare had despatched the following message to Paula direct, as a set-off against what he called Somerset's ingratitude for valuable information, though it was really the fruit of many passions, motives, and desires:

"*G. Somerset, Nice, to Miss Power, Grand Hotel, Genoa.*

"*Have lost all at Monte Carlo. Have learnt that Capt. D. S. returns here to-morrow. Please send me one hundred pounds by him, and save me from disgrace. Will await him at eleven o'clock and four, on the Pont-Neuf.*"

FIVE hours after the despatch of that telegram Captain De Stancy was ratling along the coast railway of the Riviera from Genoa to Nice. He was returning to England by way of Marseilles; but before turning northwards he had engaged to perform on Miss Power's account a peculiar and somewhat disagreeable duty. This was to place in Somerset's hands a hundred and twenty-five napoleons which had been demanded from her by a message in Somerset's name. The money was in his pocket—all in gold, in a canvas bag, tied up by Paula's own hands, which he had observed to tremble as she tied it.

As he leaned in the corner of the carriage he was thinking over the events of the morning which had culminated in that literal response. At ten o'clock, before he had gone out from the hotel where he had taken up his quarters, which was not the same as the one patronised by Paula and her friends, he had been summoned to her presence in a manner so unexpected as to imply that something serious was in question. On entering her room he had been struck by the absence of that saucy independence usually apparent in her bearing towards him, notwithstanding the persistency with which he had hovered near her for the previous month, and gradually, by the position of his sister, and the favour of Paula's uncle in intercepting one of Somerset's letters and several of his telegrams, established himself as an intimate member of the travelling party. His entry, however, this time as always, had had the effect of a tonic, and it was quite with her customary self-possession that she had told him of the object of her message.

'You think of returning to Nice this afternoon?' she inquired.

De Stancy informed her that such was his intention, and asked if he could do anything for her there.

Then, he remembered, she had hesitated. 'I have received a

X). *Somerset, Nice, to Miss Power, Grand Hotel, Genoa. "Have lost all in Monte Carlo. Hope dearest that Capt. D. St. reaches here to-morrow. Please send me one hundred pounds by him, and save me from disgrace. Will meet him at eleven o'clock and join you on the Ponte"*

CHAPTER V

FIVE hours after the despatch of that telegram Captain De Stancy was rattling along the coast railway of the Riviera from Genoa to Nice. He was returning to England by way of Marseilles; but before turning northwards he had engaged to perform on Miss Power's account a peculiar and somewhat disagreeable duty. This was to place in Somerset's hands a hundred and twenty-five napoleons which had been demanded from her by a message in Somerset's name. The money was in his pocket—all in gold, in a canvas bag, tied up by Paula's own hands, which he had observed to tremble as she tied it.

As he leaned in the corner of the carriage he was thinking over the events of the morning which had culminated in that liberal response. At ten o'clock, before he had gone out from the hotel where he had taken up his quarters, which was not the same as the one patronised by Paula and her friends, he had been summoned to her presence in a manner so unexpected as to imply that something serious was in question. On entering her room he had been struck by the absence of that saucy independence usually apparent in her bearing towards him, notwithstanding the persistency with which he had hovered near her for the previous month, and gradually, by the position of his sister, and the favour of Paula's uncle in intercepting one of Somerset's letters and several of his telegrams, established himself as an intimate member of the travelling party. His entry, however, this time as always, had had the effect of a tonic, and it was quite with her customary self-possession that she had told him of the object of her message.

"You think of returning to Nice this afternoon?" she inquired.

De Stancy informed her that such was his intention, and asked if he could do anything for her there.

Then, he remembered, she had hesitated. "I have received a

telegram," she said at length; and so she allowed to escape her bit by bit the information that her architect, whose name she seemed reluctant to utter, had travelled from England to Nice that week, partly to consult her, partly for a holiday trip; that he had gone on to Monte Carlo, had there lost his money and got into difficulties, and had appealed to her to help him out of them by the immediate advance of some ready cash. It was a sad case, an unexpected case, she murmured, with her eyes fixed on the window. Indeed she could not comprehend it.

To De Stancy there appeared nothing so very extraordinary in Somerset's apparent fiasco, except in so far as that he should have applied to Paula for relief from his distresses instead of elsewhere. It was a self-humiliation which a lover would have avoided at all costs, he thought. Yet after a momentary reflection on his theory of Somerset's character, it seemed sufficiently natural that he should lean persistently on Paula, if only with a view of keeping himself linked to her memory, without thinking too profoundly of his own dignity. That the esteem in which she had held Somerset up to that hour suffered a tremendous blow by his apparent scrape was clearly visible in her, reticent as she was; and De Stancy, while pitying Somerset, thanked him in his mind for having gratuitously given a rival an advantage which that rival's attentions had never been able to gain of themselves.

After a little further conversation she had said: "Since you are to be my messenger, I must tell you that I have decided to send the hundred pounds asked for, and you will please to deliver them into no hands but his own." A curious little blush crept over her sobered face—perhaps it was a blush of shame at the conduct of the young man in whom she had of late been suspiciously interested—as she added, "He will be on the Pont-Neuf at four this afternoon and again at eleven to-morrow. Can you meet him there?"

"Certainly," De Stancy replied.

She then asked him, rather anxiously, how he could account for Mr. Somerset knowing that he, Captain De Stancy, was about to return to Nice?

De Stancy informed her that he left word at the hotel of his intention to return, which was quite true; moreover, there did not lurk in his mind at the moment of speaking the faintest suspicion that Somerset had seen Dare.

She then tied the bag and handed it to him, leaving him with a serene and impenetrable bearing, which he hoped for his own sake meant an acquired indifference to Somerset and his fortunes. Her sending the architect a sum of money which she could easily spare might be set down to natural generosity towards a man with whom she was artistically co-operating for the improvement of her home.

She came back to him again for a moment. "Could you possibly get there before four this afternoon?" she asked, and he informed her that he could just do so by leaving almost at once, which he was very willing to do, though by so forestalling his time he would lose the projected morning with her and the rest at the Palazzo Doria.

"I may tell you that I shall not go to the Palazzo Doria either, if it is any consolation to you to know it," was her reply. "I shall sit indoors and think of you on your journey."

The answer had admitted of two translations, but her manner had inclined him to the inference that her reason for abstaining from a visit to the palace was his enforced abandonment of it, and not her mental absorption in the result of his meeting with Somerset. These retrospections and conjectures filled the gallant officer's mind during the greater part of the journey. He arrived at the hotel they had all stayed at in succession about six hours after Somerset had left it for a little excursion to San Remo and its neighbourhood, as a means of passing a few days till Paula should write again to inquire why he had not come on. Had De Stancy and Somerset met at Nice a curious explanation would have resulted; but so it was that De Stancy saw no one he knew, and in obedience to Paula's commands he promptly set off on foot for the Pont-Neuf.

Though opposed to the architect as a lover, De Stancy felt for him as a poor devil in need of money, having had experiences of that sort himself, and he was really anxious that the needful supply entrusted to him should reach Somerset's hands. He was on the bridge five minutes before the hour, and when the clock struck a hand was laid on his shoulder: turning he beheld Dare.

Knowing that the youth was loitering somewhere along the coast, for they had frequently met together on De Stancy's previous visit, the latter merely said, "Don't bother me for the present, Willy, I have an engagement. You can see me at the hotel this evening."

"When you have given me the hundred pounds I will fly like a rocket, captain," said the young gentleman. "I keep the appointment instead of the other man."

De Stancy looked hard at him. "How—do you know about this?" he asked breathlessly.

"I have seen him."

De Stancy took the young man by the two shoulders and gazed into his eyes. The scrutiny seemed not altogether to remove the suspicion which had suddenly started up in his mind. "My soul," he said, dropping his arms, "can this be true?"

"What?"

"You know."

Dare shrugged his shoulders; "Are you going to hand over the money or no?" he said.

"I am going to make inquiries," said De Stancy, walking away with a vehement tread.

"Captain, you are without natural affection," said Dare, walking by his side, in a tone which showed his fear that he had over-estimated that emotion. "See what I have done for you. You have been my constant care and anxiety for I can't tell how long. I have stayed awake at night thinking how I might best give you a good start in the world by arranging this judicious marriage, when you have been sleeping as sound as a top with no cares upon your mind at all, and now I have got into a scrape—as the most thoughtful of us may sometimes—you go to make inquiries."

"I have promised the lady to whom this money belongs—whose generosity has been shamefully abused in some way—that I will deliver it into no hands but those of one man, and he has not yet appeared. I therefore go to find him."

Dare laid his hand upon De Stancy's arm. "Captain, we are both warm, and punctilious on points of honour; this will come to a split between us if we don't mind. So, not to bring matters to a crisis, lend me ten pounds here to enable me to get home, and I'll disappear."

In a state bordering on distraction, eager to get the young man out of his sight before worse revelations should rise up between them, De Stancy without pausing in his walk gave him the sum demanded. He soon reached the post-office, where he inquired if a Mr. Somerset had left any directions for forwarding letters.

It was just what Somerset had done. De Stancy was told that Mr. Somerset had commanded that any letters should be sent on to him at the Hôtel Victoria, San Remo.

It was now evident that the scheme of getting money from Paula was either of Dare's invention, or that Somerset, ashamed of his first impulse, had abandoned it as speedily as it had been formed. De Stancy turned and went out. Dare, in keeping with his promise, had vanished. Captain De Stancy resolved to do nothing in the case till further events should enlighten him, beyond sending a line to Miss Power to inform her that Somerset had not appeared, and that he therefore retained the money till further instructions.

BOOK THE FIFTH

DE STANCY AND PAULA

CHAPTER I

MISS POWER was reclining on a red velvet couch in the bedroom of an old-fashioned red hotel at Strasburg, and her friend Miss De Stancy was sitting by a window of the same apartment. They were both rather wearied by a long journey of the previous day. The hotel overlooked the large open Kleber Platz, erect in the midst of which the bronze statue of General Kleber received the rays of a warm sun that was powerless to brighten him. The whole square, with its people and vehicles going to and fro as if they had plenty of time, was visible to Charlotte in her chair; but Paula from her horizontal position could see nothing below the level of the many-dormered housetops on the opposite side of the Platz. After watching this upper story of the city for some time in silence, she asked Charlotte to hand her a binocular lying on the table, through which instrument she quietly regarded the distant roofs.

"What strange and philosophical creatures storks are," she said. "They give a taciturn, ghostly character to the whole town."

The birds were crossing and recrossing the field of the glass in their flight hither and thither between the Strasburg chimneys, their sad grey forms sharply outlined against the sky, and their skinny legs showing beneath like the limbs of dead martyrs in Crivelli's emaciated imaginings. The indifference of these birds to all that was going on beneath them impressed her: to harmonize with their solemn and silent movements the houses beneath should have been deserted, and grass growing in the streets.

Behind the long roofs thus visible to Paula over the window-sill, with their tiers of dormer-windows, rose the cathedral spire in airy openwork, forming the highest object in the scene; it suggested something which for a long time she appeared unwilling to utter; but natural instinct had its way.

"A place like this," she said, "where he can study Gothic architecture, would, I should have thought, be a spot more congenial to him than Monaco."

The person referred to was the misrepresented Somerset, whom the two had been gingerly discussing from time to time, allowing any casual subject, such as that of the storks, to interrupt the personal one at every two or three sentences.

"It would be more like him to be here," replied Miss De Stancy, trusting her tongue with only the barest generalities on this matter.

Somerset was again dismissed for the stork topic, but Paula could not let him alone; and she presently resumed, as if an irresistible fascination compelled what judgment had forbidden: "The strongest-minded persons are sometimes caught unawares at that place, if they once think they will retrieve their first losses; and I am not aware that he is particularly strong-minded."

For a moment Charlotte looked at her with a mixed expression, in which there was deprecation that a woman with any feeling should criticise Somerset so frigidly, and relief that it was Paula who did so. For, notwithstanding her assumption that Somerset could never be anything more to her than he was already, Charlotte's heart would occasionally step down and trouble her views so expressed.

Whether looking through a glass at distant objects enabled Paula to bottle up her affection for the absent one, or whether her friend Charlotte had so little personality in Paula's regard that she could commune with her as with a lay figure, it was certain that she evinced remarkable ease in speaking of Somerset, resuming her words about him in the tone of one to whom he was at most an ordinary professional adviser. "It would be very awkward for the works at the castle if he has got into a scrape. I suppose the builders were well posted up with instructions before he left: but he ought certainly to return soon. Why did he leave England at all just now?"

"Perhaps it was to see you."

"He should have waited; it would not have been so dreadfully long to May or June. Charlotte, how can a man who does such a hare-brained thing as this be deemed trustworthy in an important work like that of rebuilding Stancy Castle?"

There was such stress in the inquiry that, whatever factitiousness had gone before, Charlotte perceived Paula to be at last speaking her mind; and it seemed as if Somerset must have considerably lost ground in her opinion, or she would not have criticised him thus.

"My brother will tell us full particulars when he comes: perhaps it is not at all as we suppose," said Charlotte. She strained her eyes across the Platz and added, "He ought to have been here before this time."

While they waited and talked, Paula still observing the storks, the hotel omnibus came round the corner from the station. "I believe he has arrived," resumed Miss De Stancy; "I see something that looks like his portmanteau on the top of the omnibus. . . . Yes; it is his baggage. I'll run down to him."

De Stancy had obtained six weeks' additional leave on account of his health, which had somewhat suffered in India. The first use he made of his extra time was in hastening back to meet the travelling ladies here at Strasburg. Mr. Power and Mrs. Goodman were also in the hotel, and when Charlotte got downstairs, the former was welcoming De Stancy at the door.

Paula had not seen him since he set out from Genoa for Nice, commissioned by her to deliver the hundred pounds to Somerset. His note, stating that he had failed to meet Somerset, contained no details, and she guessed that he would soon appear before her now to answer any question about that peculiar errand.

Her anticipations were justified by the event: she had no sooner gone into the next sitting-room than Charlotte De Stancy appeared and asked if her brother might come up. The closest observer would have been in doubt whether Paula's ready reply in the affirmative was prompted by personal consideration for De Stancy, or by a hope to hear more of his mission to Nice. As soon as she had welcomed him she reverted at once to the subject.

"Yes, as I told you, he was not at the place of meeting," De Stancy replied. And taking from his pocket the bag of ready money he placed it intact upon the table.

De Stancy did this with a hand that shook somewhat more than a long railway journey was adequate to account for; and in truth it was the vision of Dare's position which agitated the unhappy officer: for had that young man, as De Stancy feared, been tampering with Somerset's name, his fate now trembled in the balance; Paula would unquestionably and naturally invoke the aid of the law against him if she discovered such an imposition.

"Were you punctual to the time mentioned?" she asked curiously.

De Stancy replied in the affirmative.

"Did you wait long?" she continued.

"Not very long," he answered, his instinct to screen the possibly guilty one confining him to guarded statements, while still adhering to the literal truth.

"Why was that?"

"Somebody came and told me that he would not appear."

"Who?"

"A young man who has been acting as his clerk. His name is Dare. He informed me that Mr. Somerset could not keep the appointment."

"Why?"

"He had gone on to San Remo."

"Has he been travelling with Mr. Somerset?"

"He had been with him. They know each other very well. But as you commissioned me to deliver the money into no hands but Mr. Somerset's, I adhered strictly to your instructions."

"But perhaps my instructions were not wise. Should it in your opinion have been sent by this young man? Was he commissioned to ask you for it?"

De Stancy murmured that Dare was not commissioned to ask for it; that upon the whole he deemed her instructions wise; and was still of opinion that the best thing had been done.

Although De Stancy was distracted between his desire to preserve Dare from the consequences of folly, and a gentlemanly wish to keep as close to the truth as was compatible with that condition, his answers had not appeared to Paula to be particularly evasive, the conjuncture being one in which a handsome heiress's shrewdness was prone to overleap itself by setting down embarrassment on the part of the man she questioned to a mere lover's difficulty in steering between honour and rivalry.

She put but one other question. "Did it appear as if he, Mr. Somerset, after telegraphing, had——had——regretted doing so, and evaded the result by not keeping the appointment?"

"That's just how it appears." The words, which saved Dare from ignominy, cost De Stancy a good deal. He was sorry for Somerset, sorry for himself, and very sorry for Paula. But Dare was to De Stancy what Somerset could never be: and "for his kin that is near unto him shall a man be defiled."

After that interview Charlotte saw with warring impulses that Somerset slowly diminished in Paula's estimate; slowly as the moon wanes, but as certainly. Charlotte's own love was of a clinging, uncritical sort, and though the shadowy intelligence of Somerset's doings weighed down her soul with regret, it seemed to make not the least difference in her affection for him.

In the afternoon the whole party, including De Stancy, drove about the streets. Here they looked at the house in which Goethe had lived, and afterwards entered the cathedral. Observing in the south transept a crowd of people waiting patiently, they were reminded that they unwittingly stood in the presence of the popular clock-work of Schwilgué.

Mr. Power and Mrs. Goodman decided that they would wait with the rest of the idlers and see the puppets perform at the striking. Charlotte also waited with them; but as it wanted eight minutes to the hour, and as Paula had seen the show before, she moved on into the nave.

Presently she found that De Stancy had followed. He did not come close till she, seeing him stand silent, said, "If it were not for this cathedral, I should not like the city at all; and I have even seen cathedrals I like better. Luckily we are going on to Baden to-morrow."

"Your uncle has just told me. He has asked me to keep you company."

"Are you intending to?" said Paula, probing the base-moulding of a pier with her parasol.

"I have nothing better to do, nor indeed half so good," said De Stancy. "I am abroad for my health, you know, and what's like the Rhine and its neighbourhood in early summer, before the crowd comes? It is delightful to wander about there, or anywhere, like a child, influenced by no fixed motive more than that of keeping near some friend, or friends, including the one we most admire in the world."

"That sounds perilously like love-making."

"'Tis love indeed."

"Well, love is natural to men, I suppose," rejoined the young lady. "But you must love within bounds; or you will be enervated, and cease to be useful as a heavy arm of the service."

"My dear Miss Power, your didactic and respectable rules won't do for me. If you expect straws to stop currents, you are sadly mistaken! But no—let matters be: I am a happy, contented mortal at present, say what you will. . . . You don't ask why? Perhaps you know. It is because all I care for in the world is near me, and that I shall never be more than a hundred yards from her as long as the present arrangement continues."

"We are in a cathedral, remember, Captain De Stancy, and should not keep up a secular conversation."

"If I had never said worse in a cathedral than what I have said here, I should be content to meet my eternal Judge without absolution. Your uncle has asked me this morning how I liked you."

"Well, there was no harm in that."

"How I like you! Harm, no; but you should have seen how silly I looked. Fancy the inadequacy of the expression when my whole sense is absorbed by you."

"Men allow themselves to be made ridiculous by their own feelings in an inconceivable way."

"True, I am a fool; but forgive me," he rejoined, observing her gaze, which wandered critically from roof to clerestory, and then to the pillars, without once lighting on him. "Don't mind saying yes.— You look at this thing and that thing, but you never look at me, though I stand here and see nothing but you."

"There, the clock is striking—and the cock crows. Please go across to the transept and tell them to come out this way."

De Stancy went. When he had gone a few steps he turned his head. She had at last ceased to study the architecture, and was looking at him. Perhaps his words had struck her, for it seemed at that moment as if he read in her bright eyes a genuine interest in him and his fortunes.

CHAPTER II

NEXT day they went on to Baden. De Stancy was beginning to cultivate the passion of love even more as an escape from the gloomy relations of his life than as matrimonial strategy. Paula's juxtaposition had the attribute of making him forget everything in his own history. She was a magic alterative; and the most foolish boyish shape into which he could throw his feelings for her was in this respect to be aimed at as the act of highest wisdom.

Hence he supplemented the natural warmth of feeling that she had wrought in him by every artifical means in his power, to make the distraction the more complete. He had not known anything like this self-obscuration for a dozen years, and when he conjectured that she might really learn to love him he felt exalted in his own eyes and purified from the dross of his former life. Such uneasiness of conscience as arose when he suddenly remembered Dare, and the possibility that Somerset was getting ousted unfairly, had its weight in depressing him; but he was inclined to accept his fortune without much question.

The journey to Baden, though short, was not without incidents on which he could work out this curious hobby of cultivating to superlative power an already positive passion. Handing her in and out of the carriage, accidentally getting brushed by her dress; of all such as this he made available fuel. Paula, though she might have guessed the general nature of what was going on, seemed unconscious of the refinements he was trying to throw into it, and sometimes, when in stepping into or from a railway carriage she unavoidably put her hand upon his arm, the obvious insignificance she attached to the action struck him with misgiving.

One of the first things they did at Baden was to stroll into the Trink-halle, where Paula sipped the water. She was about to put down the glass, when De Stancy quickly took it from her hands as though to make use of it himself.

"Oh, if that is what you mean," she said mischievously, "you should have noticed the exact spot. It was there." She put her finger on a particular portion of its edge.

"You ought not to act like that, unless you mean something, Miss Power," he replied gravely.

"Tell me more plainly."

"I mean, you should not do things which excite my heart to the hope that you care something for me, unless you really do."

"I put my finger on the edge and said it was there."

"Meaning, 'It was there my lips touched; let yours do the same.'"

"The latter part I wholly deny," she answered, with disregard, after which she went away, and kept between Charlotte and her aunt for the rest of the afternoon.

Since the receipt of the telegraphic message Paula had been frequently silent; she frequently stayed in alone, and sometimes she became quite gloomy—an altogether unprecedented phase for her. This was the case on the morning after the incident in the Trink-halle. Not to intrude on her, Charlotte walked about the landings of the sunny white hotel in which they had taken up their quarters, went down into the court, and petted the tortoises that were creeping about there among the flowers and plants; till at last, on going to her friend, she caught her reading some old letters of Somerset's.

Paula made no secret of them, and Miss De Stancy could see that more than half were written on blue paper, with diagrams amid the writing: they were, in fact, simply those sheets of his letters which related to the rebuilding. Nevertheless, Charlotte fancied she had caught Paula in a sentimental mood; and doubtless could Somerset have walked in at this moment instead of Charlotte it might have fared well with him, so insidiously do tender memories reassert themselves in the face of outward mishaps.

They took a short drive down the Lichtenthal road and into the forest, De Stancy and Abner Power riding on horseback alongside. The sun streamed yellow behind their backs as they wound up the long inclines, lighting the red trunks, and even the blue-black foliage itself. The summer had already made impression upon that mass of uniform colour by tipping every twig with a tiny sprout of virescent yellow; while the minute sounds which issued from the forest revealed that the apparently still place was becoming a perfect reservoir of insect life.

Abner Power was quite sentimental that day. "In such places as these," he said, as he rode alongside Mrs. Goodman, "nature's powers in the multiplication of one type strike me as much as the grandeur of the mass."

Mrs. Goodman agreed with him, and Paula said, "The foliage forms the roof of an interminable green crypt, the pillars being the trunks, and the vault the interlacing boughs."

"It is a fine place in a thunderstorm," said De Stancy. "I am not an enthusiast, but to see the lightning spring hither and thither, like lazy-tongs, bristling, and striking, and vanishing, is rather impressive."

"It must be indeed," said Paula.

"And in the winter winds these pines sigh like ten thousand spirits in trouble."

"Indeed they must," said Paula.

"At the same time I know a little fir-plantation, about a mile square, not far from Markton," said De Stancy, "which is precisely like this in miniature,—stems, colours, slopes, winds, and all. If we were to go there any time with a highly magnifying pair of spectacles it would look as fine as this—and save a deal of travelling."

"I know the place, and I agree with you," said Paula.

"You agree with me on all subjects but one," he presently observed, in a voice not intended to reach the others.

Paula looked at him, but was silent.

Onward and upward they went, the same pattern and colour of tree repeating themselves endlessly, till in a couple of hours they reached the castled hill which was to be the end of their journey, and beheld stretched beneath them the valley of the Murg. They alighted and entered the fortress.

"What did you mean by that look of kindness you bestowed upon me just now, when I said you agreed with me on all subjects but one?" asked De Stancy half humorously, as he held open a little door for her, the others having gone ahead.

"I meant, I suppose, that I was much obliged to you for not requiring agreement on that one subject," she said, passing on.

"Not more than that?" said De Stancy, as he followed her. "But whenever I involuntarily express towards you sentiments that there can be no mistaking, you seem truly compassionate."

"If I seem so, I feel so."

"If you mean no more than mere compassion, I wish you would show nothing at all, for your mistaken kindness is only preparing more misery for me than I should have if let alone to suffer without mercy."

"I implore you to be quiet, Captain De Stancy! Leave me, and look out of the window at the view here, or at the pictures, or at the armour, or whatever it is we are come to see."

"Very well. But pray don't extract amusement from my harmless remarks. Such as they are I mean them."

She stopped him by changing the subject, for they had entered an octagonal chamber on the first floor, presumably full of pictures and curiosities; but the shutters were closed, and only stray beams of light gleamed in to suggest what was there.

"Can't somebody open the windows?" said Paula.

"The attendant is about to do it," said her uncle; and as he spoke the shutters to the east were flung back, and one of the loveliest views in the forest disclosed itself outside.

Some of them stepped out upon the balcony. The river lay along the bottom of the valley, irradiated with a silver shine. Little rafts of pinewood floated on its surface like tiny splinters, the men who steered them not appearing larger than ants.

Paula stood on the balcony, looking for a few minutes upon the sight, and then came again into the shadowy room, where De Stancy had remained. While the rest were still outside she resumed: "You must not suppose that I shrink from the subject you so persistently bring before me. I respect deep affection—you know I do; but for me to say that I have any such for you, of the particular sort you only will be satisfied with, would be absurd. I don't feel it, and therefore there can be nothing between us. One would think it would be better to feel kindly towards you than to feel nothing at all. But if you object to that I'll try to feel nothing."

"I don't really object to your sympathy," said De Stancy, rather struck by her seriousness. "But it is very saddening to think you can feel nothing more."

"It must be so, since I *can* feel no more," she decisively replied, adding, as she dropped her seriousness: "You must pray for strength to get over it."

"One thing I shall never pray for; to see you give yourself to another man. But I suppose I shall witness that some day."

"You may," she gravely returned.

"You have no doubt chosen him already," cried the captain bitterly.

"No, Captain De Stancy," she said shortly, a faint involuntary blush coming into her face as she guessed his allusion.

This, and a few glances round at the pictures and curiosities, completed their survey of the castle. De Stancy knew better than to trouble her further that day with special remarks. During the return journey he rode ahead with Mr. Power and she saw no more of him.

She would have been astonished had she heard the conversation of the two gentlemen as they wound gently downwards through the trees.

"As far as I am concerned," Captain De Stancy's companion was saying, "nothing would give me more unfeigned delight than that you should persevere and win her. But you must understand that I have no authority over her—nothing more than the natural influence that arises from my being her father's brother."

"And for exercising that much, whatever it may be, in my favour, I thank you heartily," said De Stancy. "But I am coming to the conclusion tha. it is useless to press her further. She is right: I am not the man for her. I am too old, and too poor; and I must put up as well as I can with her loss—drown her image in old Falernian till I embark in Charon's boat for good!—Really, if I had the industry I could write some good Horatian verses on my unauspicious situation! . . . Ah, well;— in this way I affect levity over my troubles; but in plain truth my life will not be the brightest without her."

"Don't be down-hearted! You are too—too gentlemanly, De Stancy, in this matter—you are too soon put off—you should have a touch of the canvasser about you in approaching her; and not stick at things. You have my hearty invitation to travel with us all the way till we cross to England, and there will be heaps of opportunities as we wander on. I'll keep a slow pace to give you time."

"You are very good, my friend! Well, I will try again. I am full of doubt and indecision, mind, but at present I feel that I will try again. There is, I suppose, a slight possibility of something or other turning up in my favour, if it is true that the unexpected always happens—for I foresee no chance whatever. . . . Which way do we go when we leave here to-morrow?"

"To Carlsruhe, she says, if the rest of us have no objection."

"Carlsruhe, then, let it be, with all my heart; or anywhere."

To Carlsruhe they went next day, after a night of soft rain which brought up a warm steam from the Schwarzwald valleys, and caused the young tufts and grasses to swell visibly in a few hours. After the Baden slopes the flat thoroughfares of "Charles's Rest" seemed somewhat uninteresting, though a busy fair which was proceeding in the streets created a quaint and unexpected liveliness. On reaching the old-fashioned inn in the Lange-Strasse that they had fixed on, the women of the party betook themselves to their rooms, and showed little inclination to see more of the world that day than could be gleaned from the hotel windows.

"Don't be down-hearted. You are too—too gentlemanly, De
Stancy, in this matter:—you are too soon put off— you should
have a touch of the canvasser about you in approaching her,
and not stick at things. You lost her flattery invitation to travel
with us all the way. We shall reach England, and there will be
heaps of opportunities as we wander on. I'll keep a slow pace

CHAPTER III

WHILE the malignant tongues had been playing havoc with
Somerset's fame in the ears of Paula and her companion, the
young man himself was proceeding partly by rail, partly on
foot, below and amid the olive-clad hills, vineyards, carob
groves, and lemon gardens of the Mediterranean shores.
Arrived at San Remo he wrote to Nice to inquire for letters,
and such as had come were duly forwarded; but not one of
them was from Paula. This broke down his resolution to hold
off, and he hastened directly to Genoa, regretting that he had
not taken this step when he first heard that she was there.

Something in the very aspect of the marble halls of that city,
which at any other time he would have liked to linger over,
whispered to him that the bird had flown; and inquiry confirmed the fancy. Nevertheless, the architectural beauties of
the vast palace-bordered street, looking as if mountains of
marble must have been levelled to supply the materials for
constructing it, detained him there two days: or rather a feat
of resolution, by which he set himself to withstand the drag-
chain of Paula's influence, was operative for that space of time.

At the end of it he moved onward. There was no difficulty
in discovering their track northwards; and feeling that he
might as well return to England by the Rhine route as by any
other, he followed in the course they had chosen, getting scent
of them in Strasburg, missing them at Baden by a day, and
finally overtaking them at Carlsruhe, which town he reached
on the morning after the Power and De Stancy party had taken
up their quarters at the ancient inn above mentioned.

When Somerset was about to get out of the train at this
place, little dreaming what a meaning the word Carlsruhe
would have for him in subsequent years, he was disagreeably
surprised to see no other than Dare stepping out of the
adjoining carriage. A new brown leather valise in one of his
hands, a new umbrella in the other, and a new suit of

fashionable clothes on his back, seemed to denote considerable improvement in the young man's fortunes. Somerset was so struck by the phenomenal circumstance of his being on this spot that he almost missed his opportunity for alighting.

Dare meanwhile had moved on without seeing his former employer, and Somerset resolved to take the chance that offered, and let him go. There was something so mysterious in their common presence simultaneously at one place, five hundred miles from where they had last met, that he exhausted conjecture on whether Dare's errand this way could have anything to do with his own, or whether their juxtaposition a second time was the result of pure accident. Greatly as he would have liked to get this answered by a direct question to Dare himself, he did not counteract his first instinct, and remained unseen.

They went out in different directions, when Somerset for the first time remembered that, in learning at Baden that the party had flitted towards Carlsruhe, he had taken no care to ascertain the name of the hotel they were bound for. Carlsruhe was not a large place and the point was immaterial, but the omission would necessitate a little inquiry. To follow Dare on the chance of his having fixed upon the same quarters was a course which did not commend itself. He resolved to get some lunch before proceeding with his business—or fatuity—of discovering the elusive lady, and drove off to a neighbouring tavern, which did not happen to be, as he hoped it might, the one chosen by those who had preceded him.

Meanwhile Dare, previously master of their plans, went straight to the house which sheltered them, and on entering under the archway from the Lange-Strasse was saved the trouble of inquiring for Captain De Stancy by seeing him drinking bitters at a little table in the court. Had Somerset chosen this inn for his quarters instead of the one in the Market-Place which he actually did choose, the three must inevitably have met here at this moment, with some possibly striking dramatic results; though what they would have been remains for ever hidden in the darkness of the unfulfilled.

De Stancy jumped up from his chair, and went forward to the new-comer. "You are not long behind us, then," he said, with laconic disquietude. "I thought you were going straight home?"

"I was," said Dare, "but I have been blessed with what I may call a small competency since I saw you last. Of the two hundred francs you gave me I risked fifty at the tables, and I have multiplied them, how many times do you think? More than four hundred times"

De Stancy immediately looked grave. "I wish you had lost them," he said, with as much feeling as could be shown in a place where strangers were hovering near.

"Nonsense, captain! I have proceeded purely on a calculation of chances; and my calculations proved as true as I expected, notwithstanding a little in-and-out luck at first. Witness this as the result." He smacked his bag with his umbrella, and the chink of money resounded from within. "Just feel the weight of it!"

"It is not necessary. I'll take your word."

"Shall I lend you five pounds?"

"God forbid! As if that would repay me for what you have cost me! But come, let's get out of this place to where we can talk more freely." He put his hand through the young man's arm, and led him round the corner of the hotel towards the Schloss-Platz.

"These runs of luck will be your ruin, as I have told you before," continued Captain De Stancy. "You will be for repeating and repeating your experiments, and will end by blowing your brains out, as wiser heads than yours have done. I am glad you have come away, at any rate. Why did you travel this way?"

"Simply because I could afford it, of course.—But come, captain, something has ruffled you to-day. I thought you did not look in the best temper the moment I saw you. Every sip you took of your pick-up as you sat there showed me something was wrong. Tell your worry!"

"Pooh—I can tell you in two words," said the captain, satirically. "Your arrangement for my wealth and happiness—for I suppose you still claim it to be yours—has fallen through. The lady has announced to-day that she means to send for Somerset instantly. She is coming to a personal explanation with him. So woe to me—and in another sense, woe to you, as I have reason to fear, though I have hoped otherwise."

"Send for him!" said Dare, with the stillness of complete abstraction. "Then he'll come."

"Well," said De Stancy, looking him in the face. "And does it make you feel you had better be off? How about that telegram? Did he ask you to send it, or did he not?"

"One minute, or I shall be up such a tree as nobody ever saw the like of."

"Then what did you come here for?" burst out De Stancy. "'Tis my belief you are no more than a——. But I won't call you names; I'll tell you quite plainly that if there is anything wrong in that message to her—which I believe there is—no, I can't believe, though I fear it—you have the chance of appearing in drab clothes at the expense of the Government before the year is out, and I of being eternally disgraced!"

"No, captain, you won't be disgraced. I am bad to beat, I can tell you. And come the worst luck, I don't say a word."

"But those letters pricked in your skin would say a good deal, it strikes me."

"What! would they strip me?—but it is not coming to that. Look here, now, I'll tell you the truth for once; though you don't believe me capable of it. I *did* concoct that telegram—and sent it; just as a practical joke; and many a worse one has been only laughed at by honest men and officers. I could show you a bigger joke still—a joke of jokes—on the same individual."

Dare as he spoke put his hand into his breast-pocket, as if the said joke lay there; but after a moment he withdrew his hand empty, as he continued:

"Having invented it I have done enough; I was going to explain it to you, that you might carry it out. But you are so serious, that I will leave it alone. My second joke shall die with me."

"So much the better," said De Stancy. "I don't like your jokes, even though they are not directed against myself. They express a kind of humour which does not suit me."

"You may have reason to alter your mind," said Dare carelessly. "Your success with your lady may depend on it.

The truth is, captain, we aristocrats must not take too high a tone. Our days as an independent divison of society, which holds aloof from other sections, are past. This has been my argument (in spite of my strong Norman feelings) ever since I broached the subject of your marrying this girl, who represents both intellect and wealth—all, in fact, except the historical prestige that you represent. And we mustn't flinch at things. The case is even more pressing than ordinary cases—owing to the odd fact that the representative of the new blood who has come in our way actually lives in your own old house, and owns your own old lands. The ordinary reason for such alliances is quintupled in our case. Do then just think and be reasonable, before you talk tall about not liking my jokes, and all that. Beggars mustn't be choosers."

"There's really much reason in your argument," said De Stancy, with a bitter laugh; "and my own heart argues much the same way. But, leaving me to take care of my aristocratic self, I advise your aristocratic self to slip off at once to England like any hang-gallows dog; and if Somerset is here, and you have been doing wrong in his name, and it all comes out, I'll try to save you, as far as an honest man can. If you have done no wrong, of course there is no fear; though I should be obliged by your going homeward as quickly as possible, as being better both for you and for me. . . . Hullo—Damnation!"

They had reached one side of the Schloss-Platz, nobody apparently being near them save a sentinel who was on duty before the Palace; but turning as he spoke, De Stancy beheld a group consisting of his sister, Paula, and Mr. Power, strolling across the square towards them.

It was impossible to escape their observation, and putting a bold front upon it, De Stancy advanced with Dare at his side, till in a few moments the two parties met, Paula and Charlotte recognising Dare at once as the young man who assisted at the castle.

"I have met my young photographer," said De Stancy, cheerily. "What a small world it is, as every busybody truly observes! I am wishing he could take some views for us as we go on; but you have no apparatus with you, I suppose, Mr. Dare?"

"I have not, sir, I am sorry to say," replied Dare respectfully.

"You could get one, I suppose?" asked Paula of the interesting young photographer.

Dare declared that it would not be impossible: whereupon De Stancy said that it was only a passing thought of his; and in a few minutes the two parties again separated, going their several ways.

"That was awkward," said De Stancy, trembling with excitement. "I would advise you to keep further off in future."

Dare said thoughtfully that he would be careful, adding, "She is a prize for any man, indeed, leaving alone the substantial possessions behind her! Now was I too enthusiastic? Was I a fool for urging you on?"

"Wait till success justifies the undertaking. In case of failure it will have been anything but wise. It is no light matter to have a carefully preserved repose broken in upon for nothing—a repose that could never be restored!"

They walked down the Carl-Friedrichs-Strasse to the Margrave's Pyramid, and back to the hotel, where Dare also decided to take up his stay. De Stancy left him with the bookkeeper at the desk, and went upstairs to see if the ladies had returned.

go on; but you have no apparatus with you, I suppose, Mr. Dare.'

'I have not, sir; I am sorry to say,' replied Dare respectfully.

'You could get one at ——'. Paula of the interrupting young photographer.

'That was awkward,' said D——

—— astice Wa——

it will have been anything but wise. It is no——

—— returned.

CHAPTER IV

HE found them in their sitting-room with their bonnets on, as if they had just come in. Mr. Power was also present, reading a newspaper, but Mrs. Goodman had gone out to a neighbouring shop, in the windows of which she had seen something which attracted her fancy.

When De Stancy entered, Paula's thoughts seemed to revert to Dare, for almost at once she asked him in what direction the youth was travelling. With some hesitation De Stancy replied that he believed Mr. Dare was returning to England after a spring trip for the improvement of his mind.

"A very praiseworthy thing to do," said Paula. "What places has he visited?"

"Those which afford opportunities for the study of the old masters, I believe," said De Stancy, blandly. "He has also been to Turin, Genoa, Marseilles, and so on." The captain spoke the more readily to her questioning in that he divined her words to be dictated, not by any suspicions of his relations with Dare, but by her knowledge of Dare as the draughtsman employed by Somerset.

"Has he been to Nice?" she next demanded. "Did he go there in the company of my architect?"

"I think not."

"Has he seen anything of him? My architect Somerset once employed him. They know each other."

"I think he saw Somerset for a short time."

Paula was silent. "Do you know where this young man Dare is at the present moment?" she asked quickly.

De Stancy said that Dare was staying at the same hotel with themselves, and that he believed he was downstairs.

"I think I can do no better than send for him," said she. "He may be able to throw some light upon the matter of that telegram."

She rang and despatched the waiter for the young man in

question, De Stancy almost visibly trembling for the result. But he opened the town directory which was lying on a table, and affected to be engrossed in the names.

Before Dare was shown in she said to her uncle, "Perhaps you will speak to him for me?"

Mr. Power, looking up from the paper he was reading, assented to her proposition. Dare appeared in the doorway, and the waiter retired. Dare seemed a trifle startled out of his usual coolness, the message having evidently been unexpected, and he came forward somewhat uneasily.

"Mr. Dare, we are anxious to know something of Miss Power's architect; and Captain De Stancy tells us you have seen him lately," said Mr. Power sonorously over the edge of his newspaper.

Not knowing whether danger menaced or no, or, if it menaced, from what quarter it was to be expected, Dare felt that honesty was as good as anything else for him, and replied boldly that he had seen Mr. Somerset, De Stancy continuing to cream and mantle almost visibly, in anxiety at the situation of the speaker.

"And where did you see him?" continued Mr. Power.

"In the Casino at Monte Carlo."

"How long did you see him?"

"Only for half an hour. I left him there."

Paula's interest got the better of her reserve, and she cut in upon her uncle: "Did he seem in any unusual state, or in trouble?"

"He was rather excited," said Dare.

"And can you remember when that was?"

Dare considered, looked at his pocket-book, and said that it was on the evening of April the twenty-second.

The answer had a significance for Paula, De Stancy, and Charlotte, to which Abner Power was a stranger. The telegraphic request for money, which had been kept a secret from him by his niece, because of his already unfriendly tone towards Somerset, arrived on the morning of the twenty-third—a date which neighboured with painfully suggestive nicety that now given by Dare.

She seemed to be silenced, and asked no more questions.

Dare having furbished himself up to a gentlemanly appearance
with some of his recent winnings, was invited to stay on awhile
by Paula's uncle, who, as became a travelled man, was not
fastidious as to company. Being a youth of the world, Dare
made himself agreeable to that gentleman, and afterwards tried
to do the same with Miss De Stancy. At this the captain, to
whom the situation for some time had been amazingly uncomfortable, pleaded some excuse for going out, and left the room.

Dare continued his endeavours to say a few polite nothings
to Charlotte De Stancy, in the course of which he drew from
his pocket his new silk handkerchief. By some chance a card
came out with the handkerchief, and fluttered downwards. His
momentary instinct was to make a grasp at the card and
conceal it: but it had already tumbled to the floor, where it lay
face upward beside Charlotte De Stancy's chair.

It was neither a visiting nor a playing card, but one bearing
a photographic portrait of a peculiar nature. It was what Dare
had characterised as his best joke of all in speaking on the
subject to Captain De Stancy; he had in the morning put it
ready in his pocket to give to the captain, and had in fact held
it in waiting between his finger and thumb while talking to
him in the Platz, meaning that he should make use of it against
his rival whenever convenient. But his sharp conversation with
that officer had dulled his zest for this final joke at Somerset's
expense, had at least shown him that De Stancy would not
adopt the joke by accepting the photograph and using it
himself, and determined him to lay it aside till a more
convenient season. So fully had he made up his mind on this
course, that when the photograph slipped out he did not
perceive the appositeness of the circumstance, in putting into
his own hands the *rôle* he had intended for De Stancy, till after
a moment's reflection; though in an after-controversy on the
incident it was asserted that the whole scene was deliberately
planned. However, once having seen the accident, he seemed
resolved to take the current as it served, and, smiling
imperceptibly, waited events with cheerful inanition.

The card having fallen beside her, Miss De Stancy glanced
over it, which indeed she could not help doing. The smile that
had previously hung upon her lips was arrested as if by frost:

and she involuntarily uttered a little distressed cry of "Oh!" like one in bodily pain.

Paula, who had been talking to her uncle during this interlude, started round, and wondering what had happened, inquiringly crossed the room to poor Charlotte's side, asking her what was the matter. Charlotte had regained self-possession, though not enough to enable her to reply, and Paula asked her a second time what had made her exclaim like that. Miss De Stancy still seemed confused, whereupon Paula noticed that her eyes were continually drawn as by fascination towards the photograph on the floor, which, contrary to his first impulse, Dare, as has been said, now seemed in no hurry to regain. Surmising at last that the card, whatever it was, had something to do with the exclamation, Paula picked it up.

It was a portrait of Somerset; but by a device known in photography the operator, though contriving to produce what seemed to be a perfect likeness, had given it the distorted features and wild attitude of a man advanced in intoxication. No woman, unless specially cognisant of such possibilities, could have looked upon it and doubted that the photograph was a genuine illustration of a customary phase in the young man's private life.

Paula observed it, thoroughly took it in; but the effect upon her was by no means clear. Charlotte's eyes at once forsook the portrait to dwell on Paula's face. It paled a little, and this was followed by a hot blush—perceptibly a blush of shame. That was all. She flung the picture down on the table, and moved away.

It was now Mr. Power's turn. Anticipating Dare, who was advancing with a deprecatory look to seize the photograph, he also grasped it. When he saw whom it represented he seemed both amused and startled, and after scanning it a while handed it to the young man with a queer smile.

"I am very sorry," began Dare, in a low voice to Mr. Power. "I fear I was to blame for thoughtlessness in not destroying it. But I thought it was rather funny that a man should permit such a thing to be done, and that the humour would redeem the offence."

"In you, for purchasing it," said Paula, with haughty

quickness from the other side of the room. "Though probably his friends, if he has any, would say not in him."

There was silence in the room after this, and Dare, finding himself rather in the way, took his leave as unostentatiously as a cat that has upset the family china, though he continued to say among his apologies that he was not aware Mr. Somerset was a personal friend of the ladies.

Of all the thoughts which filled the minds of Paula and Charlotte De Stancy, the thought that the photograph might have been a fabrication was probably the last. To them that picture of Somerset had all the cogency of direct vision. Paula's experience, much less Charlotte's, had never lain in the fields of heliographic science, and they would as soon have thought that the sun could again stand still upon Gibeon, as that it could be made to falsify men's characters in delineating their features. What Abner Power thought he himself best knew. He might have seen such pictures before; or he might never have heard of them.

While pretending to resume his reading he closely observed Paula, as did also Charlotte De Stancy; but thanks to the self-management which was Miss Power's as much by nature as by art, she dissembled whatever emotion was in her.

"It is a pity a professional man should make himself so ludicrous," she said with such careless intonation that it was almost impossible, even for Charlotte, who knew her so well, to believe her indifference feigned.

"Yes," said Mr. Power, since Charlotte did not speak: "it is what I scarcely should have expected."

"Oh, I am not surprised!" said Paula quickly. "You don't know all." The inference was, indeed, inevitable that if her uncle were made aware of the telegram he would see nothing unlikely in the picture. "Well, you are very silent!" continued Paula, petulantly, when she found that nobody went on talking. "What made you cry out 'Oh,' Charlotte, when Mr. Dare dropped that horrid photograph?"

"I don't know; I suppose it frightened me," stammered the girl.

"It was a stupid fuss to make before such a person. One would think you were in love with Mr. Somerset."

"What did you say, Paula?" inquired her uncle, looking up from the newspaper which he had again resumed.

"Nothing, Uncle Abner." She walked to the window, and, as if to tide over what was plainly passing in their minds about her, she began to make remarks on objects in the street. "What a quaint being—look, Charlotte!" It was an old woman sitting by a stall on the opposite side of the way, which seemed suddenly to hit Paula's sense of the humorous, though beyond the fact that the dame was old and poor, and wore a white handkerchief over her head, there was really nothing note-worthy about her.

Paula seemed to be more hurt by what the silence of her companions implied—a suspicion that the discovery of Somer-set's depravity was wounding her heart—than by the wound itself. The ostensible ease with which she drew them into a bye conversation had perhaps the defect of proving too much: though her tacit contention that no love was in question was not incredible on the supposition that affronted pride alone caused her embarrassment. The chief symptom of her heart being really tender towards Somerset consisted in her apparent blindness to Charlotte's secret, so obviously suggested by her momentary agitation.

CHAPTER V

AND where was the subject of their condemnatory opinions all this while? Having secured a room at his inn, he came forth to complete the discovery of his dear mistress's halting-place without delay. After one or two inquiries he ascertained where such a party of English were staying; and arriving at the hotel, knew at once that he had tracked them to earth by seeing the heavier portion of the Power luggage confronting him in the hall. He sent up intelligence of his presence, and awaited her reply with a beating heart.

In the meanwhile Dare, descending from his pernicious interview with Paula and the rest, had descried Captain De Stancy in the public drawing-room, and entered to him forthwith. It was while they were here together that Somerset passed the door and sent up his name to Paula.

The incident at the railway station was now reversed, Somerset being the observed of Dare, as Dare had then been the observed of Somerset. Immediately on sight of him Dare showed real alarm. He had imagined that Somerset would eventually impinge on Paula's route, but he had scarcely expected it yet; and the architect's sudden appearance led Dare to ask himself the ominous question whether Somerset had discovered his telegraphic trick, and was in the mood for prompt measures.

"There is no more for me to do here," said the boy-man hastily to De Stancy. "Miss Power does not wish to ask me any more questions. I may as well proceed on my way, as you advised."

De Stancy, who had also gazed with dismay at Somerset's passing figure, though with dismay of another sort, was recalled from his vexation by Dare's remarks, and turning upon him he said sharply, "Well may you be in such a hurry all of a sudden!"

"True, I am superfluous now."

"You have been doing a foolish thing, and you must suffer its inconveniences.—Will, I am sorry for one thing; I am sorry I ever owned you; for you are not a lad to my mind. You have disappointed me—disappointed me almost beyond endurance."

"I have acted according to my illumination. What can you expect of a man born to dishonour?"

"That's mere speciousness. Before you knew anything of me, and while you thought you were the child of poverty on both sides, you were well enough; but ever since you thought you were more than that, you have led a life which is intolerable. What has become of your plan of alliance between the De Stancys and the Powers now? The man is gone upstairs who can overthrow it all."

"If the man had not gone upstairs, you wouldn't have complained of my nature or my plans," said Dare, dryly. "If I mistake not, he will come down again with the flea in his ear. However, I have done; my play is played out. All the rest remains with you. But, captain, grant me this! If when I am gone this difficulty should vanish, and things should go well with you, and your suit should prosper, will you think of him, bad as he is, who first put you on the track of such happiness, and let him know it was not done in vain?"

"I will," said De Stancy. "Promise me that you will be a better boy?"

"Very well—as soon as ever I can afford it. Now I am up and away, when I have explained to them that I shall not require my room."

Dare fetched his bag, touched his hat with his umbrella to the captain, and went out of the hotel archway. De Stancy sat down in the stuffy drawing-room, and wondered what other ironies time had in store for him.

A waiter in the interim had announced Somerset to the group upstairs. Paula started as much as Charlotte at hearing the name, and Abner Power stared at them both.

"If Mr. Somerset wishes to see me *on business*, show him in," said Paula.

In a few seconds the door was thrown open for Somerset. On receipt of the pointed message he guessed that a change had come. Time, absence, ambition, her uncle's influence, and a new wooer, seemed to account sufficiently well for that change, and he accepted his fate. But from a stoical instinct to show that he could regard her vicissitudes with the equanimity that became a man; a desire to ease her mind of any fear she might entertain that his connection with her past would render him troublesome in future, induced him to accept her permission, and see the act to the end.

"How do you do, Mr. Somerset?" said Abner Power, with sardonic geniality: he had been far enough about the world not to be greatly concerned at Somerset's apparent failing, particularly when it helped to reduce him from the rank of lover to his niece to that of professional adviser.

Miss De Stancy faltered a welcome as weak as that of the Maid of Neidpath, and Paula said coldly, "We are rather surprised to see you. Perhaps there is something urgent at the castle which makes it necessary for you to call?"

"There is something a little urgent," said Somerset slowly, as he approached her; "and you have judged rightly that it is the cause of my call." He sat down near her chair as he spoke, put down his hat, and drew a note-book from his pocket with a despairing sang-froid that was far more perfect than had been Paula's demeanour just before.

"Perhaps you would like to talk over the business with Mr. Somerset alone?" murmured Charlotte to Miss Power, hardly knowing what she said.

"Oh no," said Paula, "I think not. Is it necessary?" she said, turning to him.

"Not in the least," replied he, bestowing a penetrating glance upon his questioner's face, which seemed however to produce no effect; and turning towards Charlotte, he added, "You will have the goodness, I am sure, Miss De Stancy, to excuse the jargon of professional details."

He spread some tracings on the table, and pointed out certain modified features to Paula, commenting as he went on, and exchanging occasionally a few words on the subject with Mr. Abner Power by the distant window.

In this architectural dialogue over his sketches, Somerset's head and Paula's became unavoidably very close. The temptation was too much for the young man. Under cover of the rustle of the tracings, he murmured, "Paula, I could not get here before!" in a low voice inaudible to the other two.

She did not reply, only busying herself the more with the notes and sketches; and he said again, "I stayed a couple of days at Genoa, and some days at San Remo, and Mentone."

"But it is not the least concern of mine where you stayed, is it?" she said, with a cold yet disquieted look.

"Do you speak seriously?" Somerset brokenly whispered.

Paula concluded her examination of the drawings and turned from him with inexpressible disregard. He tried no further, but, when she had signified her pleasure on the points submitted, packed up his papers, and rose with the bearing of a man altogether superior to such a class of misfortune as this. Before going he turned to speak a few words of a general kind to Mr. Power and Charlotte.

"You will stay and dine with us?" said the former, rather with the air of being unhappily able to do no less than ask the question. "My charges here won't go down to the *table d'hôte*, I fear, but De Stancy and myself will be there."

Somerset excused himself, and in a few minutes withdrew. At the door he looked round for an instant, and his eyes met Paula's. There was the same miles-off expression in hers that they had worn when he entered; but there was also a look of distressful inquiry, as if she were earnestly expecting him to say something more. This of course Somerset did not comprehend. Possibly she was clinging to a hope of some excuse for the message he was supposed to have sent, or for the other and more degrading matter. Anyhow, Somerset only bowed and went away.

A moment after he had gone, Paula, impelled by something or other, crossed the room to the window. In a short time she saw his form in the broad street below, which he traversed obliquely to an opposite corner, his head somewhat bent, and his eyes on the ground. Before vanishing into the Ritterstrasse he turned his head and glanced at the hotel windows, as if he knew that she was watching him. Then he disappeared; and the only real sign of emotion betrayed by Paula during the whole episode escaped her at this moment. It was a slight trembling of the lip and a sigh so slowly breathed that scarce anybody could hear—scarcely even Charlotte, who was reclining on a couch, her face on her hand and her eyes downcast.

Not more than two minutes had elapsed when Mrs. Goodman came in with a manner of haste.

"You have returned," said Mr. Power. "Have you made your purchases?"

Without answering, she asked, "Whom, of all people on earth, do you think I have met? Mr. Somerset! Has he been here?—he passed me almost without speaking!"

"Yes, he has been here," said Paula. "He is on the way from Genoa home, and called on business."

"You will have him here to dinner, of course?"

"I asked him," said Mr. Power, "but he declined."

"Oh, that's unfortunate! Surely we could get him to come. You would like to have him here, would you not, Paula?"

"No, indeed. I don't want him here," said she.

"You don't?"

"No!" she said sharply.

"You used to like him well enough, anyhow," bluntly rejoined Mrs. Goodman.

Paula sedately: "It is a mistake to suppose that I have ever particularly liked the gentleman mentioned."

"Then you are wrong, Mrs. Goodman, it seems," said Mr. Power.

Mrs. Goodman, who had been growing quietly indignant, notwithstanding a vigorous use of her fan, at this said: "Fie, fie, Paula! you did like him. You said to me only a week or two ago that you should not at all object to marry him."

"It is a mistake," repeated Paula calmly. "I meant the other one of the two we were talking about."

"What, Captain De Stancy?"

"Yes."

Knowing this to be a fiction, Mrs. Goodman made no remark, and hearing a slight noise behind, turned her head. Seeing her aunt's action, Paula also looked round. The door had been left ajar, and De Stancy was standing in the room.

The last words of Mrs. Goodman and Paula's reply, must have been quite audible to him.

They looked at each other much as if they had unexpectedly met at the altar; but after a momentary start Paula did not flinch from the position into which hurt pride had betrayed her. De Stancy bowed gracefully, and she merely walked to the furthest window, whither he followed her.

"I am eternally grateful to you for avowing that I have won favour in your sight at last," he whispered.

She acknowledged the remark with a somewhat reserved bearing. "Really I don't deserve your gratitude," she said. "I did not know you were there."

"I know you did not—that's why the avowal is so sweet to me. Can I take you at your word?"

"Yes, I suppose."

"Then your preference is the greatest honour that has ever fallen to my lot. It is enough: you accept me?"

"As a lover on probation—no more."

The conversation being carried on in low tones, Paula's uncle and aunt took it as a hint that their presence could be spared, and severally left the room—the former gladly, the latter with some vexation. Charlotte De Stancy followed.

"And to what am I indebted for this happy change?" inquired De Stancy, as soon as they were alone.

"You shouldn't look a gift-horse in the mouth," she replied brusquely.

"You mistake my motive. I am like a reprieved criminal, and can scarcely believe the news."

"You shouldn't say that to me, or I shall begin to think I have been too kind," she answered, some of the archness of her manner returning. "Now, I know what you mean to say in answer; but I don't want to hear any more at present; and whatever you do, don't fall into the mistake of supposing I have accepted you in any other sense than the way I say. If you don't like such a limitation you can go away. I dare say I shall get over it."

"Go away! Could I go away?—But you are beginning to tease, and will soon punish me severely; so I will make my escape while all is well. It would be presumptuous to expect more in one day."

"It would indeed," said Paula, with her eyes on a bunch of flowers.

CHAPTER VI

ON leaving the hotel, Somerset's first impulse was to get out
of sight of its windows, and his glance upward had perhaps not
the tender significance that Paula imagined, the last look
impelled by any such whiff of emotion having been the
lingering one he bestowed upon her in passing out of the room.
Unluckily for the prospects of this attachment, Paula's conduct
towards him now, as a result of misrepresentations, had
enough in common with her previous silence at Nice to make
it not unreasonable as a further development of that silence.
Moreover, her social position as a woman of wealth, always felt
by Somerset as a perceptible bar to that full and free eagerness
with which he would fain have approached her, rendered it
impossible for him to return to the charge, ascertain the reason
of her coldness, and dispel it by an explanation, without being
suspected of mercenary objects. Continually does it happen
that a genial willingness to bottle up affronts is set down to
interested motives by those who do not know what generous
conduct means. Had she occupied the financial position of
Miss De Stancy he would readily have persisted further and,
not improbably, have cleared up the cloud.

Having no further interest in Carlsruhe, Somerset decided
to leave by an evening train. The intervening hour he spent in
wandering into the thick of the fair, where steam roundabouts,
the proprietors of waxwork shows, and fancy-stall keepers
maintained a deafening din. The animated environment was
better than silence, for it fostered in him an artificial indifference to the events that had just happened—an indifference
which, though he too well knew it was only destined to be
temporary, afforded a passive period wherein to store up
strength that should enable him to withstand the wear and tear
of regrets which would surely set in soon. It was the case with
Somerset as with others of his temperament, that he did not
feel a blow of this sort immediately; and what often seemed

like stoicism after misfortune was only the neutral numbness of transition from palpitating hope to assured wretchedness.

He walked round and round the fair till all the exhibitors knew him by sight, and when the sun got low he turned into the Erbprinzen-Strasse, now raked from end to end by ensaffroned rays of level light. Seeking his hotel he dined there, and left by the evening train for Heidelberg.

Heidelberg with its romantic surroundings was not precisely the place calculated to heal Somerset's wounded heart. He had known the town of yore, and his recollections of that period, when, unfettered in fancy, he had transferred to his sketchbook the fine Renaissance details of the Otto-Heinrichs-Bau came back with unpleasant force. He knew of some carved cask-heads and other curious wood-work in the castle cellars, copies of which, being unobtainable by photographs, he had intended to make if all went well between Paula and himself. The zest for this was now well-nigh over. But on awaking in the morning and looking up the valley towards the castle, and at the dark green height of the Königsstuhl alongside, he felt that to become vanquished by a passion, driven to suffer, fast, and pray in the dull pains and vapours of despised love, was a contingency not to be welcomed too readily. Thereupon he set himself to learn the sad science of renunciation, which everybody has to learn in his degree—either rebelling throughout the lesson, or, like Somerset, taking to it kindly by force of judgment. A more obstinate pupil might have altogether escaped the lesson in the present case by discovering its illegality.

Resolving to persevere in the heretofore satisfactory paths of art while life and faculties were left, though every instant must proclaim that there would be no longer any collateral attraction in that pursuit, he went along under the trees of the Anlage and reached the castle vaults, in whose cool shades he spent the afternoon, working out his intentions with fair result. When he had strolled back to his hotel in the evening the time was approaching for the *table d'hôte*. Having seated himself rather early, he spent the few minutes of waiting in looking over his pocket-book, and putting a few finishing touches to the afternoon performance whilst the objects were fresh in his memory. Thus occupied he was but dimly conscious of the customary rustle of dresses and pulling up of chairs by the crowd of other diners as they gathered around him. Serving began, and he put away his book and prepared for the meal. He had hardly done this when he became conscious that the person on his left hand was not the typical cosmopolite with boundless hotel knowledge and irrelevant experiences that he was accustomed to find next him, but a face he recognised as that of a young man whom he had met and talked to at Stancy Castle garden-party, whose name he had now forgotten. This young fellow was conversing with somebody on his left hand— no other personage than Paula herself. Next to Paula he beheld De Stancy, and De Stancy's sister beyond him. It was one of those gratuitous encounters which only happen to discarded lovers who have shown commendable stoicism under disappointment, as if on purpose to re-open and aggravate their wounds.

It seemed as if the intervening traveller had met the other party by accident there and then. In a minute he turned and recognised Somerset, and by degrees the young men's cursory remarks to each other developed into a pretty regular conversation, interrupted only when he turned to speak to Paula on his left hand.

"Your architectural adviser travels in your party: how very convenient," said the young tourist to her. "Far pleasanter than having a medical attendant in one's train!"

Somerset, who had no distractions on the other side of him, could hear every word of this. He glanced at Paula. She had not known of his presence in the room till now. Their eyes met for a second, and she bowed sedately. Somerset returned her bow, and her eyes were quickly withdrawn with scarcely visible confusion.

"Mr. Somerset is not travelling with us," she said. "We have met by accident. Mr. Somerset came to me on business a little while ago."

"I must congratulate you on having put the castle in good hands," continued the enthusiastic young man.

"I believe Mr. Somerset is quite competent," said Paula stiffly.

To include Somerset in the conversation the young man turned to him and added: "You carry on your work at the castle *con amore*, no doubt?"

"There is work I should like better," said Somerset.

"Indeed?"

The frigidity of his manner seemed to set her at ease by dispersing all fear of a scene; and alternate dialogues of this sort with the gentleman in their midst were more or less continued by both Paula and Somerset till they rose from table.

In the bustle of moving out the two latter for one moment stood side by side.

"Miss Power," said Somerset in a low voice that was obscured by the rustle; "you have nothing more to say to me?"

"I think there is nothing more?" said Paula, lifting her eyes with artificial urbanity.

"Then I take leave of you; and tender my best wishes that you may have a pleasant time before you! . . . I set out for England to-night."

"With a special photographer, no doubt?"

It was the first time that she had addressed Somerset with a meaning distinctly satirical; and her remark, which had reference to the forged photograph, fell of course without its intended effect.

"No, Miss Power," said Somerset gravely. "But with a deeper sense of woman's thoughtless trifling than time will ever eradicate."

"Is not that a mistake?" she asked in a voice that distinctly trembled.

"A mistake? How?"

"I mean, do you not forget many things?" (throwing on him a troubled glance). "A woman may feel herself justified in her conduct, although it admits of no explanation."

"I don't contest the point for a moment. . . . Good-bye."

"Good-bye."

They parted amid the flowering shrubs and caged birds in the hall, and he saw her no more. De Stancy came up, and spoke a few commonplace words, his sister having gone out, either without perceiving Somerset, or with intention to avoid him.

That night, as he had said, he was on his way to England.

spoke a few commonplace words, his sister having gone out, either without perceiving Somerset, or with intention to avoid him.

That night, as he had confidence was on his way to England,

CHAPTER VII

THE De Stancys and Powers remained in Heidelberg for some days. All remarked that after Somerset's departure Paula was frequently irritable, though at other times as serene as ever. Yet even when in a blithe and saucy mood there was at bottom a tinge of melancholy. Something did not lie easy in her undemonstrative heart, and all her friends excused the inequalities of a humour whose source, though not positively known, could be fairly well guessed.

De Stancy had long since discovered that his chance lay chiefly in her recently acquired and fanciful *prédilection d'artiste* for hoary mediæval families with ancestors in alabaster and primogenitive renown. Seeing this he dwelt on those topics which brought out that aspect of himself more clearly, talking feudalism and chivalry with a zest that he had never hitherto shown. Yet it was not altogether factitious. For, discovering how much this quondam Puritan was interested in the attributes of long-chronicled houses, a reflected interest in himself arose in his own soul, and he began to wonder why he had not prized these things before. Till now disgusted by the failure of his family to hold its own in the turmoils between ancient and modern, he had grown to undervalue its past prestige; and it was with corrective ardour that he adopted while he ministered to her views.

Henceforward the wooing of De Stancy took the form of an intermittent address, the incidents of their travel furnishing pegs whereon to hang his subject; sometimes hindering it, but seldom failing to produce in her a greater tolerance of his presence. His next opportunity was the day after Somerset's departure from Heidelberg. They stood on the great terrace of the Schloss-Garten, looking across the intervening ravine to the north-east front of the castle which rose before them in all its customary warm tints and battered magnificence.

"This is a spot, if any, which should bring matters to a crisis between you and me," he asserted good-humouredly. "But you have been so silent to-day that I lose the spirit to take advantage of my privilege."

She inquired what privilege he spoke of, as if quite another subject had been in her mind than De Stancy.

"The privilege of winning your heart if I can, which you gave me at Carlsruhe."

"Oh," she said. "Well, I've been thinking of that. But I do not feel myself absolutely bound by the statement I made in that room; and I shall expect, if I withdraw it, not to be called to account by you."

De Stancy looked rather blank.

"If you recede from your promise you will doubtless have good reason. But I must solemnly beg you, after raising my hopes, to keep as near as you can to your word, so as not to throw me into utter despair."

Paula dropped her glance into the Thier Garten below them, where gay promenaders were clambering up between the bushes and flowers. At length she said, with evident embarrassment, but with much distinctness: "I deserve much more blame for what I have done that you can express to me. I will confess to you the whole truth. All that I told you in the hotel at Carlsruhe was said in a moment of pique at what had happened just before you came in. It was supposed I was much involved with another man, and circumstances made the supposition particularly objectionable. To escape it I jumped at the alternative of yourself."

"That's bad for me!" he murmured.

"If after this avowal you bind me to my words I shall say no more: I do not wish to recede from them without your full permission."

"What a caprice! But I release you unconditionally," he said. "And I beg your pardon if I seemed to show too much assurance. Please put it down to my gratified excitement. I entirely acquiesce in your wish. I will go away to whatever place you please, and not come near you but by your own permission, and till you are quite satisfied that my presence and what it may lead to is not undesirable. I entirely give way

before you, and will endeavour to make my future devoted-
ness, if ever we meet again, a new ground for expecting your
favour."

Paula seemed struck by the generous and cheerful fairness
of his remarks, and said gently, "Perhaps your departure is not
absolutely necessary for my happiness; and I do not wish from
what you call caprice——"

"I retract that word."

"Well, whatever it is, I don't wish you to do anything which
should cause you real pain, or trouble, or humiliation."

"That's very good of you."

"But I reserve to myself the right to accept or refuse your
addresses—just as if those rash words of mine had never been
spoken."

"I must bear it all as best I can, I suppose," said De Stancy,
with melancholy humorousness.

"And I shall treat you as your behaviour shall seem to
deserve," she said playfully.

"Then I may stay?"

"Yes; I am willing to give you that pleasure, if it is one, in
return for the attentions you have shown, and the trouble you
have taken to make my journey pleasant."

She walked on and discovered Mrs. Goodman near, and
presently the whole party met together. De Stancy did not find
himself again at her side till later in the afternoon, when they
had left the immediate precincts of the castle and decided on a
drive to the Königsstuhl.

The carriage, containing only Mrs. Goodman, was driven a
short way up the winding incline, Paula, her uncle, and Miss
De Stancy walking behind under the shadow of the trees.
Then Mrs. Goodman called to them and asked when they were
going to join her.

"We are going to walk up," said Mr. Power.

Paula seemed seized with a spirit of boisterousness quite
unlike her usual behaviour. "My aunt may drive up, and you
may walk up; but I shall run up," she said. "See, here's a
way." She tripped towards a path through the bushes which,
instead of winding like the regular track, made straight for the
summit.

Paula had not the remotest conception of the actual distance to the top, imagining it to be but a couple of hundred yards at the outside, whereas it was really nearer a mile, the ascent being uniformly steep all the way. When her uncle and De Stancy had seen her vanish they stood still, the former evidently reluctant to forsake the easy ascent for a difficult one, though he said, "We can't let her go alone that way, I suppose."

"No, of course not," said De Stancy.

They then followed in the direction taken by Paula, Charlotte entering the carriage. When Power and De Stancy had ascended about fifty yards the former looked back, and dropped off from the pursuit, to return to the easy route, giving his companion a parting hint concerning Paula. Thereupon De Stancy went on alone. He soon saw Paula above him in the path, which ascended skyward straight as Jacob's Ladder, but was so overhung by the brushwood as to be quite shut out from the sun. When he reached her side she was moving easily upward, apparently enjoying the seclusion which the place afforded.

"Is not my uncle with you?" she said, on turning and seeing him.

"He went back," said De Stancy.

She replied that it was of no consequence; that she should meet him at the top, she supposed.

Paula looked up amid the green light which filtered through the leafage as far as her eyes could stretch. But the top did not appear, and she allowed De Stancy to get in front. "It did not seem such a long way as this, to look at," she presently said.

He explained that the trees had deceived her as to the real height, by reason of her seeing the slope fore-shortened when she looked up from the castle. "Allow me to help you," he added.

"No, thank you," said Paula, lightly; "we must be near the top."

They went on again; but no Königsstuhl. When next De Stancy turned he found that she was sitting down; immediately going back he offered his arm. She took it in silence, declaring that it was no wonder her uncle did not come that wearisome way, if he had ever been there before.

De Stancy did not explain that Mr. Power had said to him at parting, "There's a chance for you, if you want one," but at once went on with the subject begun on the terrace. "If my behaviour is good, you will re-affirm the statement made at Carlsruhe?"

"It is not fair to begin that now!" expostulated Paula; "I can only think of getting to the top."

Her colour deepening by the exertion, he suggested that she should sit down again on one of the mossy boulders by the wayside. Nothing loth she did, De Stancy standing by, and with his cane scratching the moss from the stone.

"This is rather awkward," said Paula, in her usual circumspect way. "My relatives and your sister will be sure to suspect me of having arranged this scramble with you."

"But I know better," sighed De Stancy. "I wish to Heaven you had arranged it!"

She was not at the top, but she took advantage of the halt to answer his previous question. "There are many points on which I must be satisfied before I can re-affirm anything. Do you not see that you are mistaken in clinging to this idea?— that you are laying up mortification and disappointment for yourself?"

"A negative reply from you would be disappointment, early or late."

"And you prefer having it late to accepting it now? If I were a man, I should like to abandon a false scent as soon as possible."

"I suppose all that has but one meaning: that I am to go."

"Oh no," she magnanimously assured him, bounding up from her seat; "I adhere to my statement that you may stay; though it is true something may possibly happen to make me alter my mind."

He again offered his arm, and from sheer necessity she leant upon it as before.

"Grant me but a moment's patience," he began.

"Captain De Stancy! Is this fair? I am physically obliged to hold your arm, so that I *must* listen to what you say!"

"No, it is not fair; 'pon my soul it is not!" said De Stancy. "I won't say another word."

He did not; and they clambered on through the boughs, nothing disturbing the solitude but the rustle of their own footsteps and the singing of birds overhead. They occasionally got a peep at the sky; and whenever a twig hung out in a position to strike Paula's face the gallant captain bent it aside with his stick. But she did not thank him. Perhaps he was just as well satisfied as if she had done so.

Paula, panting, broke the silence: "Will you go on, and discover if the top is near?"

He went on. This time the top was near. When he returned she was sitting where he had left her among the leaves. "It is quite near now," he told her tenderly, and she took his arm again without a word. Soon the path changed its nature from a steep and rugged water-course to a level green promenade.

"Thank you, Captain De Stancy," she said, letting go his arm as if relieved.

Before them rose the tower, and at the base they beheld two of their friends, Mr. Power being seen above, looking over the parapet through his glass.

"You will go to the top now?" said De Stancy.

"No, I take no interest in it. My interest has turned to fatigue. I only want to go home."

He took her on to where the carriage stood at the foot of the tower, and leaving her with his sister ascended the turret to the top. The landscape had quite changed from its afternoon appearance, and had become rather marvellous than beautiful. The air was charged with a lurid exhalation that blurred the extensive view. He could see the distant Rhine at its junction with the Neckar, shining like a thread of blood through the mist, which was gradually wrapping up the declining sun. The scene had in it something that was more than melancholy, and not much less than tragic; but for De Stancy such evening effects possessed little meaning. He was engaged in an enterprise that taxed all his resources, and had no sentiments to spare for air, earth, or skies.

"Remarkable scene," said Power, mildly, at his elbow.

"Yes; I dare say it is," said De Stancy. "Time has been

when I should have held forth upon such a prospect, and
wondered if its livid colours shadowed out my own life, et
cætera, et cætera. But, begad, I have almost forgotten there's
such a thing as Nature, and I care for nothing but a comfortable life, and a certain woman who does not care for me. . . .
Now shall we go down?"

CHAPTER VIII

IT was quite true that De Stancy at the present period of his existence wished only to escape from the hurly-burly of active life, and to win the affection of Paula Power. There were, however, occasions when a recollection of his old renunciatory vows would obtrude itself upon him, and tinge his present with wayward bitterness. So much was this the case that a day or two after they had arrived at Mainz he could not refrain from making remarks almost prejudicial to his cause, saying to her, "I am unfortunate in my situation. There are, unhappily, worldly reasons why I should pretend to love you, even if I do not: they are so strong that, though really loving you, perhaps they enter into my thoughts of you."

"I don't want to know what such reasons are," said Paula, with promptness, for it required but little astuteness to discover that he alluded to her possession of his ancestral home and estates. "You lack tone," she gently added: "that's why the situation of affairs seems distasteful to you."

"Yes, I suppose I am ill. And yet I am well enough."

These remarks passed under a tree in the public gardens during an odd minute of waiting for Charlotte and Mrs. Goodman; and he said no more to her in private that day. Few as her words had been he liked them better than any he had lately received. The conversation was not resumed till they were gliding "between the banks that bear the vine," on board one of the Rhine steamboats, which, like the hotels in this early summer time, were comparatively free from other English travellers; so that everywhere Paula and her party were received with open arms and cheerful countenances, as among the first swallows of the season.

The saloon of the steamboat was quite empty, the few passengers being outside; and this paucity of voyagers afforded De Stancy a roomy opportunity.

Paula saw him approach her, and there appearing in his face

signs that he would begin again on the eternal subject, she seemed to be struck with a sense of the ludicrous.

De Stancy reddened. "Something seems to amuse you," he said.

"It is over," she replied, becoming serious.

"Was it about me, and this unhappy fever in me?"

"If I speak the truth I must say it was."

"You thought. 'Here's that absurd man again, going to begin his daily supplication.'"

"Not 'absurd,'" she said, with emphasis; "because I don't think it is absurd."

She continued looking through the windows at the Lurlei Heights under which they were now sailing, and he remained with his eyes on her.

"May I stay here with you?" he said at last. "I have not had a word with you alone for four-and-twenty hours."

"You must be cheerful, then."

"You have said such as that before. I wish you would say 'loving' instead of 'cheerful.'"

"Yes, I know, I know," she responded, with impatient perplexity. "But why must you think of me—me only? Is there no other woman in the world who has the power to make you happy? I am sure there must be."

"Perhaps there is; but I have never seen her."

"Then look for her; and believe me when I say that you will certainly find her."

He shook his head.

"Captain De Stancy, I have long felt for you," she continued, with a frank glance into his face. "You have deprived yourself too long of other women's company. Why not go away for a little time? and when you have found somebody else likely to make you happy, you can meet me again. I will see you at your father's house, and we will enjoy all the pleasure of easy friendship."

"Very correct; and very cold, O best of women!"

"You are too full of exclamations and transports, I think!"

They stood in silence, Paula apparently much interested in the manœuvring of a raft which was passing by. "Dear Miss Power," he resumed, "before I go and join your uncle above, let me just ask, Do I stand any chance at all yet? Is it possible you can never be more pliant than you have been?"

"You put me out of all patience!"

"But why did you raise my hopes? You should at least pity me after doing that."

"Yes; it's that again! I unfortunately raised your hopes because I was a fool—was not myself that moment. Now question me no more. As it is I think you presume too much upon my becoming yours as the consequence of my having dismissed another."

"Not on becoming mine, but on listening to me."

"Your argument would be reasonable enough had I led you to believe I would listen to you—and ultimately accept you; but that I have not done. I see now that a woman who gives a man an answer one shade less peremptory than a harsh negative may be carried beyond her intentions, and out of her own power before she knows it."

"Chide me if you will; I don't care."

She looked steadfastly at him with a little mischief in her eyes. "You *do* care," she said.

"Then why don't you listen to me? I would not persevere for a moment longer if it were against the wishes of your family. Your uncle says it would give him pleasure to see you accept me."

"Does he say why?" she asked, thoughtfully.

"Yes; he takes, of course, a practical view of the matter; he thinks it commends itself so to reason and common sense that the owner of Stancy Castle should become a member of the De Stancy family."

"Yes, that's the horrid plague of it," she said, with a nonchalance which seemed to contradict her words. "It is so dreadfully reasonable that we should marry. I wish it wasn't."

"Well, you are younger than I, and perhaps that's a natural wish. But to me it seems a felicitous combination not often met with. I confess that your interest in our family before you knew me lent a stability to my hopes that otherwise they would not have had."

"My interest in the De Stancys has not been a personal interest except in the case of your sister," she returned. "It has been an historical interest only; and is not at all increased by your existence."

"And perhaps it is not diminished?"

"No, I am not aware that it is diminished," she murmured, as she observed the gliding shore.

"Well, you will allow me to say this, since I say it without reference to your personality or to mine—that the Power and De Stancy families are the complements to each other; and that, abstractedly, they call earnestly to one another: 'How neat and fit a thing for us to join hands!'"

Paula, who was not prudish when a direct appeal was made to her common sense, answered with ready candour: "Yes, from the point of view of domestic politics, that undoubtedly is the case. But I hope I am not so calculating as to risk happiness in order to round off a social idea."

"I hope not; or that I am either. Still the social idea exists, and my increased years make its excellence more obvious to me than to you."

The ice once broken on this aspect of the question, the subject seemed rather to engross her, and she spoke on as if daringly inclined to venture where she had never anticipated going, deriving pleasure from the very strangeness of her temerity: "You mean that in the fitness of things I ought to become a De Stancy to strengthen my social position?"

"And that I ought to strengthen mine by alliance with the heiress of a name so dear to engineering science as Power."

"Well, we are talking with unexpected frankness."

"But you are not seriously displeased with me for saying what, after all, one can't help feeling and thinking?"

"No. Only be so good as to leave off going further for the present. Indeed, of the two, I would rather have the other sort of address. I mean," she hastily added, "that what you urge as the result of a real affection, however unsuitable, I have some remote satisfaction in listening to—not the least from any reciprocal love on my side, but from a woman's gratification at being the object of anybody's devotion; for that feeling towards her is always regarded as a merit in a woman's eye, and taken as a kindness by her, even when it is at the expense of her convenience."

She had said, voluntarily or involuntarily, better things than he expected, and perhaps too much in her own opinion, for she hardly gave him an opportunity of replying.

They passed St. Goar and Boppard, and when steering round the sharp bend of river just beyond the latter place De Stancy met her again, exclaiming, "You left me very suddenly."

"You must make allowances, please," she said; "I have always stood in need of them."

"Then you shall always have them."

"I don't doubt it," she said, quickly; but Paula was not to be caught again, and kept close to the side of her aunt while they glided past Brauback and Oberlahnstein. Approaching Coblenz her aunt said, "Paula, let me suggest that you be not so much alone with Captain De Stancy."

"And why?" said Paula, quietly.

"You'll have plenty of offers if you want them, without taking trouble," said the direct Mrs. Goodman. "Your existence is hardly known to the world yet, and Captain De Stancy is too near middle-age for a girl like you." Paula did not reply to either of these remarks, being seemingly so interested in Ehrenbreitstein heights as not to hear them.

CHAPTER IX

IT was midnight at Coblenz, and the travellers had retired to rest in their respective apartments, overlooking the river. Finding that there was a moon shining, Paula leant out of her window. The tall rock of Ehrenbreitstein on the opposite shore was flooded with light, and a belated steamer was drawing up to the landing-stage, where it presently deposited its passengers.

"We should have come by the last boat, so as to have been touched into romance by the rays of this moon, like those happy people," said a voice.

She looked towards the spot whence the voice proceeded, which was a window quite near at hand. De Stancy was smoking outside it, and she became aware that the words were addressed to her.

"You left me very abruptly," he continued.

Paula's instinct of caution impelled her to speak. "The windows are all open," she murmured. "Please be careful."

"There are no English in this hotel except ourselves. I thank you for what you said to-day."

"Please be careful," she repeated.

"My dear Miss P——"

"Don't mention names, and don't continue the subject."

"Life and death perhaps depend upon my renewing it soon."

She shut the window decisively, possibly wondering if De Stancy had drunk a glass or two of Steinberger more than was good for him, and saw no more of moonlit Ehrenbreitstein that night, and heard no more of De Stancy. But it was some time before he closed his window, and previous to doing so saw a dark form at an adjoining one on the other side.

It was Mr. Power, also taking the air.

"Well, what luck to-day?" said Power.

"A decided advance," said De Stancy.

None of the speakers knew that a little person in the room

above heard all this out-of-window talk. Charlotte, though not looking out, had left her casement open; and what reached her ears set her wondering as to the result.

It is not necessary to detail in full De Stancy's imperceptible advances with Paula during that northward journey—so slowly performed that it seemed as if she must perceive there was a special reason for delaying her return to England. At Cologne one day he conveniently overtook her when she was ascending the hotel staircase. Seeing him, she went to the window of the entresol landing, which commanded a view of the Rhine, meaning that he should pass by to his room.

"I have been very uneasy," began the captain, drawing up to her side; "and I am obliged to trouble you sooner than I meant to do."

Paula turned her eyes upon him with some curiosity as to what was coming of this respectful demeanour. "Indeed!" she said.

He then informed her that he had been overhauling himself since they last talked, and had some reason to blame himself for bluntness and general want of euphemism; which, although he had meant nothing by it, must have been very disagreeable to her. But he had always aimed at sincerity, particularly as he had to deal with a lady who despised hypocrisy and was above flattery. However, he feared he might have carried his disregard for conventionality too far. But from that time he would promise that she should find an alteration by which he hoped he might return the friendship at least of a young lady he honoured more than any other in the world.

This retrograde movement was evidently unexpected by the honoured young lady herself. After being so long accustomed to rebuke him for his persistence there was novelty in finding him do the work for her. The guess might even have been hazarded that there was also disappointment.

Still looking across the river upon the bridge of boats which stretched to the opposite suburb of Deutz: "You need not blame yourself," she said, with the mildest conceivable manner, "I can make allowances. All I wish is that you should remain under no misapprehension."

"I comprehend," he said, thoughtfully. "But since, by a

perverse fate, I have been thrown into your company, you could hardly expect me to feel and act otherwise."

"Perhaps not."

"Since I have so much reason to be dissatisfied with myself," he added, "I cannot refrain from criticising elsewhere to a slight extent, and thinking I have to do with an ungenerous person."

"Why ungenerous?" she asked.

"In this way; that since you cannot love me, you see no reason at all for trying to do so in the fact that I so deeply love you; hence I say that you are rather to be distinguished by your wisdom than by your humanity."

"It comes to this, that if your words are all seriously meant it is much to be regretted we ever met," she murmured. "Now will you go on to where you were going, and leave me here?"

Without a remonstrance he went on, saying with dejected whimsicality as he smiled back upon her, "You show a wisdom which for so young a lady is perfectly surprising."

It was resolved to prolong the journey by a circuit through Holland and Belgium; but nothing changed in the attitudes of Paula and Captain De Stancy till one afternoon during their stay at the Hague, when they had gone for a drive down to Scheveningen by the long straight avenue of chestnuts and limes, under whose boughs tufts of wild parsley waved their flowers except where the *buitenplaatsen* of retired merchants blazed forth with new paint of every hue. On mounting the dune which kept out the sea behind the village a brisk breeze greeted their faces, and a fine sand blew up into their eyes. De Stancy screened Paula with his umbrella as they stood with their backs to the wind, looking down on the red roofs of the village within the sea wall, and pulling at the long grass which by some means found nourishment in the powdery soil of the dune.

When they had discussed the scene he continued, "It always seems to me that this place reflects the average mood of human life. I mean, if we strike the balance between our best moods and our worst we shall find our average condition to stand at about the same pitch in emotional colour as these sandy dunes and this grey scene do in landscape."

Paula contended that he ought not to measure everybody by himself.

"I have no other standard," said De Stancy; "and if my own is wrong, it is you who have made it so. Have you thought any more of what I said at Cologne?"

"I don't quite remember what you did say at Cologne."

"My dearest life!" Paula's eyes rounding somewhat, he corrected the exclamation. "My dear Miss Power, I will, without reserve, tell it to you all over again."

"Pray spare yourself the effort," she said dryly. "What has that one fatal step betrayed me into! . . . Do you seriously mean to say that I am the cause of your life being coloured like this scene of grass and sand? If so, I have committed a very great fault."

"It can be nullified by a word."

"Such a word!"

"It is a very short one."

"There's a still shorter one more to the purpose. Frankly, I believe you suspect me to have some latent and unowned inclination for you—that you think speaking is the only point upon which I am backward. . . . There now, it is raining; what shall we do? I thought this wind meant rain."

"Do? Stand on here, as we are standing now."

"Your sister and my aunt are gone under the wall. I think we will walk towards them."

"You had made me hope," he continued (his thoughts apparently far away from the rain and the wind and the possibility of shelter), "that you might change your mind, and give to your original promise a liberal meaning in renewing it. In brief I mean this, that you would allow it to merge into an engagement. Don't think it presumptuous," he went on, as he held the umbrella over her; "I am sure any man would speak as I do. A distinct permission to be with you on probation— that was what you gave me at Carlsruhe: and flinging casuistry on one side, what does that mean?"

"That I am artistically interested in your family history." And she went out from the umbrella to the shelter of the hotel where she found her aunt and friend.

*

De Stancy could not but feel that his persistence had made some impression. It was hardly possible that a woman of independent nature would have tolerated his dangling at her side so long, if his presence were wholly distasteful to her. That evening when driving back to the Hague by a devious route through the dense avenues of the Bosch he conversed with her again; also the next day when standing by the Vijver looking at the swans: and in each case she seemed to have at least got over her objection to being seen talking to him, apart from the remainder of the travelling party.

Scenes very similar to those at Scheveningen and on the Rhine were enacted at later stages of their desultory journey. Mr. Power had proposed to cross from Rotterdam; but a stiff north-westerly breeze prevailing Paula herself became reluctant to hasten back to Stancy Castle. Turning abruptly they made for Brussels.

It was here, while walking homeward from the Park one morning that her uncle for the first time alluded to the situation of affairs between herself and her admirer. The captain had gone up the Rue Royale with his sister and Mrs. Goodman, either to show them the house in which the ball took place on the eve of Quatre Bras or some other site of interest, and the two Powers were thus left to themselves. To reach their hotel they passed into a little street sloping steeply down from the Rue Royale to the Place Ste. Gudule, where, at the moment of nearing the cathedral, a wedding party emerged from the porch and crossed in front of uncle and niece.

"I hope," said the former, in his passionless way, "we shall see a performance of this sort between you and Captain De Stancy, not so very long after our return to England."

"Why?" asked Paula, following the bride with her eyes.

"It is diplomatically, as I may say, such a highly correct thing—such an expedient thing—such an obvious thing to all eyes."

"Not altogether to mine, uncle," she returned.

"'Twould be a thousand pities to let slip such a neat offer of adjusting difficulties as accident makes you in this. You could marry more tin, that's true; but you don't want it, Paula. You want a name, and historic what-do-they-call-it. Now by coming to terms with the captain you'll be Lady De Stancy in a few years: and a title which is useless to him, and a fortune and castle which are in some degree useless to you, will make a splendid whole useful to you both."

"I've thought it over—quite," she answered. "And I quite see what the advantages are. But how if I don't care one atom for artistic completeness and a splendid whole; and do care very much to do what my fancy inclines me to do?"

"Then I should say that, taking a comprehensive view of human nature of all colours, your fancy is about the silliest fancy existing on this earthly ball."

Paula laughed indifferently, and her uncle felt that, persistant as was his nature, he was the wrong man to influence her by argument. Paula's blindness to the advantages of the match, if she were blind, was that of a woman who wouldn't see, and the best argument was silence.

This was in some measure proved the next morning. When Paula made her appearance Mrs. Goodman said, holding up an envelope: "Here's a letter from Mr. Somerset."

"Dear me," said she, blandly, though a quick little flush ascended her cheek. "I had nearly forgotten him!"

The letter on being read contained a request as brief as it was unexpected. Having prepared all the drawings necessary for the rebuilding, Somerset begged leave to resign the superintendence of the work into other hands.

"His letter caps your remarks very aptly," said Mrs. Goodman, with secret triumph. "You are nearly forgetting him, and he is quite forgetting you."

"Yes," said Paula, affecting carelessness. "Well, I must get somebody else, I suppose."

CHAPTER X

THEY next deviated to Amiens, intending to stay there only one night; but their schemes were deranged by the sudden illness of Charlotte. She had been looking unwell for a fortnight past, though, with her usual self-abnegation, she had made light of her ailment. Even now she declared she could go on; but this was said over-night, and in the morning it was abundantly evident that to move her was highly inadvisable. Still she was not in serious danger, and having called in a physician, who pronounced rest indispensable, they prepared to remain in the old Picard capital two or three additional days. Mr. Power thought he would take advantage of the halt to run up to Paris, leaving De Stancy in charge of the ladies.

In more ways than in the illness of Charlotte this day was the harbinger of a crisis.

It was a summer evening without a cloud. Charlotte had fallen asleep in her bed, and Paula, who had been sitting by her, looked out into the Place St. Denis, which the hotel commanded. The lawn of the square was all ablaze with red and yellow clumps of flowers, the acacia trees were brightly green, the sun was soft and low. Tempted by the prospect Paula went and put on her hat; and arousing her aunt, who was nodding in the next room, to request her to keep an ear on Charlotte's bedroom, Paula descended into the Rue de Noyon alone, and entered the green enclosure.

While she walked round, two or three little children in charge of a nurse trundled a large variegated ball along the grass, and it rolled to Paula's feet. She smiled at them, and endeavoured to return it by a slight kick. The ball rose in the air, and passing over the back of a seat which stood under one of the trees, alighted in the lap of a gentleman hitherto screened by its boughs. The back and shoulders proved to be those of De Stancy. He turned his head, jumped up, and was at her side in an instant, a nettled flush having meanwhile crossed Paula's face.

"I thought you had gone to the Hotoie Promenade," she said hastily. "I am going to the cathedral" (obviously uttered lest it should seem that she had seen him from the hotel windows, and entered the square for his company).

"Of course: there is nothing else to go to here—even for Roundheads."

"If you mean *me* by that, you are very much mistaken," said she, testily.

"The Roundheads were your ancestors, and they knocked down my ancestor's castle, and broke the stained glass and statuary of the cathedrals," said De Stancy slily; "and now you go not only to a cathedral, but to a service of the unreformed Church in it."

"In a foreign country it is different from home," said Paula in extenuation; "and you of all men should not reproach me for tergiversation—when it has been brought about by—by my sympathies with——"

"With the troubles of the De Stancys."

"Well, you know what I mean," she answered, with considerable anxiety not to be misunderstood; "my liking for the old castle, and what it contains, and what it suggests. I declare I will not explain to you further—why should I? I am not answerable to you!"

Paula's show of petulance was perhaps not wholly because she had appeared to seek him, but also from being reminded by his criticism that Mr. Woodwell's prophecy on her weakly succumbing to surroundings was slowly working out its fulfilment.

She moved forward towards the gate at the further end of the square, beyond which the cathedral lay at a very short distance. Paula did not turn her head, and De Stancy strolled slowly after her down the Rue du College. The day happened to be one of the church festivals, and people were a second time flocking into the lofty monument of Catholicism at its meridian. Paula vanished into the porch with the rest; and, almost catching the wicket as it flew back from her hand, he too entered the high-shouldered edifice—an edifice doomed to labour under the melancholy misfortune of seeming only half as vast as it really is, and whimsically described by Heine as a monument built with the strength of Titans, and decorated with the patience of dwarfs.

De Stancy walked up the nave, so close beside her as to touch her dress; but she would not recognise his presence, the darkness that evening had thrown over the interior, which was scarcely broken by the few candles dotted about, being a sufficient excuse if she required one.

"Miss Power," De Stancy said at last, "I am coming to the service with you."

She received the intelligence without surprise, and he knew she had been conscious of him all the way.

Paula went no further than the middle of the nave, where there was hardly a soul, and took a chair beside a solitary rushlight which looked amid the vague gloom of the inaccessible architecture like a lighthouse at the foot of tall cliffs.

He put his hand on the next chair, saying, "Do you object?"

"Not at all," she replied; and he sat down.

"Suppose we go into the choir," said De Stancy presently. "Nobody sits out here in the shadows."

"This is sufficiently near, and we have a candle," Paula murmured.

Before another minute had passed the candle flame began to drown in its own grease, slowly dwindled, and went out.

"I suppose that means I am to go into the choir in spite of myself. Heaven is on your side," said Paula. And rising they left their now totally dark corner, and joined the noiseless shadowy figures who in twos and threes kept passing up the nave.

Within the choir there was a blaze of light, partly from the altar, and more particularly from the image of the saint whom they had assembled to honour, which stood, surrounded by candles and a thicket of flowering plants, some way in advance of the foot-pace. A secondary radiance from the same source was reflected upward into their faces by the polished marble pavement, except when interrupted by the shady forms of the officiating priests.

When it was over and the people were moving off, De Stancy

and his companion went towards the saint, now besieged by numbers of women anxious to claim the respective flower-pots they had lent for the decoration. As each struggled for her own, seized and marched off with it, Paula remarked—"This rather spoils the solemn effect of what has gone before."

"I perceive you are a harsh Puritan."

"No, Captain De Stancy! Why will you speak so? I am far too much otherwise. I have grown to be so much of your way of thinking, that I accuse myself, and am accused by others, of being worldly, and half-and-half, and other dreadful things—though it isn't that at all."

They were now walking down the nave, preceded by the sombre figures with the pot-flowers, who were just visible in the rays that reached them through the distant choir-screen at their back; while above the grey night sky and stars looked in upon them through the high clerestory windows.

"Do be a little *more* of my way of thinking!" rejoined De Stancy passionately.

"Don't, don't speak," she said rapidly. "There are Milly and Champreau!"

Milly was one of the maids, and Champreau the courier and valet who had been engaged by Abner Power. They had been sitting behind the other pair throughout the service, and indeed knew rather more of the relations between Paula and De Stancy than Paula knew herself.

Hastening on the two latter went out, and walked together silently up the short street. The Place St. Denis was now lit up, lights shone from the hotel windows, and the world without the cathedral had so far advanced in nocturnal change that it seemed as if they had been gone from it for hours. Within the hotel they found the change even greater than without. Mrs. Goodman met them half-way on the stairs.

"Poor Charlotte is worse," she said. "Quite feverish, and almost delirious."

Paula reproached herself with "Why did I go away!"

The common interest of De Stancy and Paula in the sufferer at once reproduced an ease between them as nothing else could have done. The physician was again called in, who prescribed certain draughts, and recommended that some one should sit up with her that night. If Paula allowed demonstrations of love to escape her towards anybody it was towards Charlotte, and her instinct was at once to watch by the invalid's couch herself, at least for some hours, it being deemed unnecessary to call in a regular nurse unless she should sicken further.

"But I will sit with her," said De Stancy. "Surely you had better go to bed?" Paula would not be persuaded; and thereupon De Stancy, saying he was going into the town for a short time before retiring, left the room.

The last omnibus returned from the last train, and the inmates of the hotel retired to rest. Meanwhile a telegram had arrived for Captain De Stancy; but as he had not yet returned it was put in his bedroom, with directions to the night-porter to remind him of its arrival.

Paula sat on with the sleeping Charlotte. Presently she retired into the adjacent sitting-room with a book, and flung herself on a couch, leaving the door open between her and her charge, in case the latter should awake. While she sat a new breathing seemed to mingle with the regular sound of Charlotte's that reached her through the doorway: she turned quickly, and saw her uncle standing behind her.

"Oh—I thought you were in Paris!" said Paula.

"I have just come from there—I could not stay. Something has occurred to my mind about this affair." His strangely marked visage, now more noticeable from being worn with fatigue, had a spectral effect by the night-light.

"What affair?"

"This marriage. . . . Paula, De Stancy is a good fellow enough, but you must not accept him just yet."

Paula did not answer.

"Do you hear? You must not accept him," repeated her uncle, "till I have been to England and examined into matters. I start in an hour's time—by the ten-minutes-past-two train."

"This is something very new."

"Yes—'tis new," he murmured, relapsing into his Dutch manner. "You must not accept him till something is made clear to me. I have come from Paris to say so."

"Uncle, I don't understand this. I am my own mistress in all matters, and though I don't mind telling you I have by no means resolved to accept him, the question of her marriage is especially a woman's own affair."

Her uncle stood irresolute for a moment, as if his convictions were more than his proofs. "I say no more at present," he murmured. "Can I do anything for you about a new architect?"

"Appoint Havill."

"Very well. Good night." And then he left her. In a short time she heard him go down and out of the house, to cross to England by the morning steamboat.

With a little shrug, as if she resented his interference in so delicate a point, she settled herself down anew to her book.

One, two, three hours passed, when Charlotte awoke, but soon slumbered sweetly again. Milly had stayed up for some time lest her mistress should require anything; but the girl being sleepy Paula sent her to bed.

It was a lovely night of early summer, and drawing aside the window curtains she looked out upon the flowers and trees of the Place, now quite visible, for it was nearly three o'clock, and the morning light was growing strong. She turned her face upwards. Except in the case of one bedroom all the windows on that side of the hotel were in darkness. The room being rather close she left the casement ajar, and opening the door walked out upon the staircase landing. A number of caged canaries were kept here, and she observed in the dim light of the landing lamp how snugly their heads were all tucked in. On returning to the sitting-room again she could hear that Charlotte was still slumbering, and this encouraging circumstance disposed her to go to bed herself. Before, however, she had made a move a gentle tap came to the door.

Paula opened it. There, in the faint light by the sleeping canaries, stood Charlotte's brother.

"How is she now?" he whispered.

"Sleeping soundly," said Paula.

"That's a blessing. I have not been to bed. I came in late, and have now come down to know if I had not better take your place?"

"Nobody is required, I think. But you can judge for yourself."

Up to this point they had conversed in the doorway of the

sitting-room, which De Stancy now entered, crossing it to Charlotte's apartment. He came out from the latter at a pensive pace.

"She is doing well," he said, gently. "You have been very good to her. Was the chair I saw by her bed the one you have been sitting in all night?"

"I sometimes sat there; sometimes here."

"I wish I could have sat beside you, and held your hand—I speak frankly."

"To excess."

"And why not? I do not wish to hide from you any corner of my breast, futile as candour may be. Just Heaven! for what reason is it ordered that courtship, in which soldiers are usually so successful, should be a failure with me?"

"Your lack of foresight chiefly in indulging feelings that were not encouraged. That, and my uncle's indiscreet permission to you to travel with us, have precipitated our relations in a way that I could neither foresee nor avoid, though of late I have had apprehensions that it might come to this. You vex and disturb me by such words of regret."

"Not more than you vex and disturb me. But you cannot hate the man who loves you so devotedly?"

"I have said before I don't hate you. I repeat that I am interested in your family and its associations because of its complete contrast with my own." She might have added, "And I am additionally interested just now because my uncle has forbidden me to be."

"But you don't care enough for me personally to save my happiness?"

Paula hesitated; from the moment De Stancy confronted her she had felt that this nocturnal conversation was to be a grave business. The cathedral clock struck three. "I have thought once or twice," she said with a naïveté unusual in her, "that if I could be sure of giving peace and joy to your mind by becoming your wife, I ought to endeavour to do so and make the best of it—merely as a charity. But I believe that feeling is a mistake: your discontent is constitutional, and would go on just the same whether I accepted you or no. My refusal of you is purely an imaginary grievance."

"Not if I think otherwise."

"Oh no," she murmured, with a sense that the place was very lonely and silent. "If you think it otherwise I suppose it is otherwise."

"My darling; my Paula!" he said, seizing her hand. "Do promise me something. You must indeed!"

"Captain De Stancy!" she said, trembling and turning away. "Captain De Stancy!" She tried to withdraw her fingers, then faced him, exclaiming in a firm voice a third time, "Captain De Stancy! let go my hand; for I tell you I will not marry you!"

"Good God!" he cried, dropping her hand. "What have I driven you to say in your anger! Retract it—oh, retract it!"

"Don't urge me further as you value my good opinion!"

"To lose you now, is to lose you for ever. Come, please answer!"

"I won't be compelled!" she interrupted with vehemence. "I am resolved not to be yours—not to give you an answer to-night! Never, never will I be reasoned out of my intention; and I say I won't answer you to-night! I should never have let you be so much with me but for pity of you; and now it is come to this!"

She had sunk into a chair, and now leaned upon her hand, and buried her face in her handkerchief. He had never caused her any such agitation as this before.

"You stab me with your words," continued De Stancy. "The experience I have had with you is without parallel, Paula. It seems like a distracting dream."

"I won't be hurried by anybody!"

"That may mean anything," he said, with a perplexed, passionate air. "Well, mine is a fallen family, and we must abide caprices. Would to Heaven it was extinguished!"

"What was extinguished?" she murmured.

"The De Stancys. Here am I, a homeless wanderer, living on my pay; in the next room lies she, my sister, a poor little fragile feverish invalid with no social position—and hardly a friend. We two represent the De Stancy line; and I wish we were behind the iron door of our old vault at Sleeping-Green. It can be seen by looking at us and our circumstances that we cry for the earth and oblivion!"

"Captain De Stancy, it is not like that, I assure you," sympathised Paula with damp eyelashes. "I love Charlotte too dearly for you to talk like that, indeed. I don't want to marry you exactly; and yet I cannot bring myself to say I permanently reject you, because I remember you are Charlotte's brother, and do not wish to be the cause of any morbid feelings in you which would ruin your future prospects."

"My dear life, what is it you doubt in me? Your earnestness not to do me harm makes it all the harder for me to think of never being more than a friend."

"Well, I have not positively refused!" she exclaimed, in mixed tones of pity and distress. "Let me think it over a little while. It is not generous to urge so strongly before I can collect my thoughts, and at this midnight time!"

"Darling, forgive it!—There, I'll say no more."

He then offered to sit up in her place for the remainder of the night; but Paula declined, assuring him that she meant to stay only another half-hour, after which nobody would be necessary.

He had already crossed the landing to ascend to his room, when she stepped after him, and asked if he had received his telegram.

"No," said De Stancy. "Nor have I heard of one."

Paula explained that it was put in his room, that he might see it the moment he came in.

"It matters very little," he replied, "since I shall see it now. Good-night, dearest; good-night!" he added, tenderly.

She gravely shook her head. "It is not for you to express yourself like that," she answered. "Good-night, Captain De Stancy."

He went up the stairs to the second floor, and Paula returned to the sitting-room. Having left a light burning De Stancy proceeded to look for the telegram, and found it on the carpet, where it had been swept from the table. When he had opened the sheet a sudden solemnity overspread his face. He sat down, rested his elbow on the table, and his forehead on his hands.

Captain De Stancy did not remain thus long. Rising he went softly downstairs. The grey morning had by this time crept into the hotel, rendering a light no longer necessary. The old clock on the landing was within a few minutes of four, and the birds were hopping up and down their cages, and whetting their bills. He tapped at the sitting-room, and she came instantly.

"But I told you it was not necessary——" she began.

"Yes, but the telegram," he said hurriedly. "I wanted to let you know first that—it is very serious. Paula—my father is dead! He died suddenly yesterday, and I must go at once. . . . About Charlotte—and how to let her know——"

"She must not be told yet," said Paula. . . . "Sir William dead!"

"You think we had better not tell her just yet?" said De Stancy, anxiously. "That's what I want to consult you about, if you—don't mind my intruding."

"Certainly I don't," she said.

They continued the discussion for some time; and it was decided that Charlotte should not be informed of what had happened till the doctor had been consulted, Paula promising to account for her brother's departure.

De Stancy then prepared to leave for England by the first morning train, and roused the night-porter, which functionary, having packed off Abner Power, was discovered asleep on the sofa of the landlord's parlour. At half-past five Paula, who in the interim had been pensively sitting with her hand on her chin, quite forgetting that she had meant to go to bed, heard wheels without, and looked from the window. A fly had been brought round, and one of the hotel servants was in the act of putting up a portmanteau with De Stancy's initials upon it. A minute afterwards the captain came to her door.

"I thought you had not gone to bed, after all."

"I was anxious to see you off," said she, "since neither of the others is awake; and you wished me not to rouse them."

"Quite right, you are very good;" and lowering his voice: "Paula, it is a sad and solemn time with me.—Will you grant me one word—not on our last sad subject, but on the previous one—before I part with you to go and bury my father?"

"Certainly," she said, in gentle accents.

"Then have you thought over my position? Will you at last have pity upon my loneliness by becoming my wife?"

Paula sighed deeply; and said, "Yes."

"Your hand upon it."

She gave him her hand: he held it a few moments, then raised it to his lips, and was gone.

When Mrs. Goodman rose she was informed of Sir William's death, and of his son's departure.

"Then the captain is now Sir William De Stancy!" she exclaimed. "Really, Paula, since you would be Lady De Stancy by marrying him, I almost think——"

"Hush, aunt!"

"Well; what are you writing there?"

"Only entering in my diary that I accepted him this morning, in spite of Uncle Abner."

CHAPTER XI

ON the evening of the fourth day after the parting between Paula and De Stancy at Amiens, when it was quite dark in the Markton highway, except in so far as the shades were broken by the faint lights from the adjacent town, a young man knocked softly at the door of Myrtle Villa, and asked if Captain De Stancy had arrived from abroad. He was answered in the affirmative, and in a few moments the captain himself came from an adjoining room.

Seeing that his visitor was Dare, from whom, as will be remembered, he had parted at Carlsruhe in no very satisfied mood, De Stancy did not ask him into the house, but putting on his hat went out with the youth into the public road. Here they conversed as they walked up and down, Dare beginning by alluding to the death of Sir William, the suddenness of which he feared would delay Captain De Stancy's overtures for the hand of Miss Power.

"No," said De Stancy, moodily. "On the contrary, it has precipitated matters."

"She has accepted you, captain?"

"We are engaged to be married."

"Well done! I congratulate you." The speaker was about to proceed to further triumphant notes on the intelligence, when, casting his eye upon the upper windows of the neighbouring villa, he appeared to reflect on what was within them, and checking himself said, "When is the funeral to be?"

"To-morrow," De Stancy replied. "It would be advisable for you not to come near me during the day."

"I will not. I will be a mere spectator. The old vault of our ancestors will be opened, I presume, captain?"

"It is opened."

"I must see it—and ruminate on what we once were: it is a thing I like doing. The ghosts of our dead—— Ah, what was that?"

"I heard nothing."

"I thought I heard a footstep behind us."

They stood still; but the road appeared to be quite deserted, and likely to continue so for the remainder of the evening. They walked on again, speaking in somewhat lower tones than before.

"Will the late Sir William's death delay the wedding much?" asked the younger man curiously.

De Stancy languidly answered that he did not see why it should do so. Some little time would of course intervene, but, since there were several reasons for despatch, he should urge Miss Power and her relatives to consent to a virtually private wedding which might take place at a very early date; and he thought there would be a general consent on that point.

"There are indeed reasons for despatch. Your title, Sir William, is a new safeguard over her heart, certainly; but there is many a slip, and you must not lose her now."

"I don't mean to lose her!" said De Stancy. "She is too good to be lost. And yet——since she gave her promise I have felt more than once that I would not engage in such a struggle again. It was not a thing of my beginning, though I was easily enough inflamed to follow. But I will not lose her now.——For God's sake, keep that secret you have so foolishly pricked on your breast. It fills me with remorse to think what she with her scrupulous notions will feel, should she ever know of you and your history, and your relation to me!"

Dare made no reply till after a silence, when he said, "Of course mum's the word till the wedding is over."

"And afterwards—promise that for her sake?"

"And probably afterwards."

Sir William De Stancy drew a dejected breath at the tone of the answer. They conversed but a little while longer, the captain hinting to Dare that it was time for them to part; not, however, before he had uttered a hope that the young man would turn over a new leaf and engage in some regular pursuit. Promising to call upon him at his lodgings De Stancy went indoors, and Dare briskly retraced his steps to Markton.

When his footfall had died away, and the door of the house opposite had been closed, another man appeared upon the scene. He came gently out of the hedge opposite Myrtle Villa, which he paused to regard for a moment. But instead of going town-ward, he turned his back upon the distant sprinkle of lights, and did not check his walk till he reached the lodge of Stancy Castle.

Here he pulled the wooden acorn beside the arch, and when the porter appeared his light revealed the pedestrian's countenance to be scathed, as by lightning.

"I beg your pardon, Mr. Power," said the porter with sudden deference as he opened the wicket. "But we wasn't expecting anybody to-night, as there is nobody at home, and the servants on board-wages; and that's why I was so long a-coming."

"No matter, no matter," said Abner Power. "I have returned on sudden business, and have not come to stay longer than to-night. Your mistress is not with me. I meant to sleep in Markton, but have changed my mind."

Mr. Power had brought no luggage with him beyond a small handbag, and as soon as a room could be got ready he retired to bed.

The next morning he passed in idly walking about the grounds and observing the progress which had been made in the works—now temporarily suspended. But that inspection was less his object in remaining there than meditation, was abundantly evident. When the bell began to toll from the neighbouring church to announce the burial of Sir William De Stancy, he passed through the castle, and went on foot in the direction indicated by the sound. Reaching the margin of the churchyard he looked over the wall, his presence being masked by bushes and a group of idlers from Markton who stood in front. Soon a funeral procession of simple—almost meagre and threadbare—character arrived, but Power did not join the people who followed the deceased into the church. De Stancy was the chief mourner and only relative present, the other followers of the broken-down old man being an ancient lawyer, a couple of faithful servants, and a bowed villager who had been page to the late Sir William's father—the single living person left in the parish who remembered the De Stancys as people of wealth and influence, and who firmly believed that family would come into its rights ere long, and oust the uncircumcised Philistines who had taken possession of the old lands.

The funeral was over, and the rusty carriages had gone, together with many of the spectators; but Power lingered in the churchyard as if he were looking for some one. At length he entered the church, passing by the cavernous pitfall with descending steps which stood open outside the wall of the De Stancy aisle. Arrived within he scanned the few idlers of antiquarian tastes who had remained after the service to inspect the monuments; and beside a recumbent effigy—the effigy in alabaster whose features Paula had wiped with her handkerchief when there with Somerset—he beheld the man it had been his business to find. Abner Power went up and touched this person, who was Dare, on the shoulder.

"Mr. Power—so it is!" said the youth. "I have not seen you since we met in Carlsruhe."

"You shall see all the more of me now to make up for it. Shall we walk round the church?"

"With all my heart," said Dare.

They walked round; and Abner Power began in a sardonic recitative: "I am a traveller, and it takes a good deal to astonish me. So I neither swooned nor screamed when I learnt a few hours ago what I had suspected for a week, that you are of the house and lineage of Jacob." He flung a nod towards the canopied tombs as he spoke.—"In other words, that you are of the same breed as the De Stancys."

Dare cursorily glanced round. Nobody was near enough to hear their words, the nearest persons being two workmen just outside, who were bringing their tools up from the vault preparatively to closing it.

Having observed this Dare replied, "I, too, am a traveller; and neither do I swoon nor scream at what you say. But I assure you that if you busy yourself about me, you may truly be said to busy yourself about nothing."

"Well, that's a matter of opinion. Now, there's no scarlet left in my face to blush for men's follies; but as an alliance is afoot between my niece and the present Sir William, this must be looked into."

Dare reflectively said "Oh," as he observed through the window one of the workmen bring up a candle from the vault and extinguish it with his fingers.

"The marriage is desirable, and your relationship in itself is of no consequence," continued the elder; "but just look at this. You have forced on the marriage by unscrupulous means, your object being only too clearly to live out of the proceeds of that marriage."

"Mr. Power, you mock me, because I labour under the misfortune of having an illegitimate father to provide for. I really deserve commiseration."

"You might deserve it if that were all. But it looks bad for my niece's happiness as Lady De Stancy, that she and her husband are to be perpetually haunted by a young *chevalier d'industrie*, who can forge a telegram on occasion, and libel an innocent man by an ingenious device in photography. It looks so bad, in short, that, advantageous as a title and old family name would be to her and her children, I won't let my brother's daughter run the risk of having them at the expense of being in the grip of a man like you. There are other suitors in the world, and other titles: and she is a beautiful woman, who can well afford to be fastidious. I shall let her know at once of these things, and break off the business—unless you do *one thing*."

A workman brought up another candle from the vault, and prepared to let down the slab. "Well, Mr. Power, and what is that one thing?" said Dare.

"Go to Peru as my agent in a business I have just undertaken there."

"And settle there?"

"Of course. I am soon going over myself, and will bring you anything you require."

"How long will you give me to consider?" said Dare.

Power looked at his watch. "One, two, three, four hours," he said. "I leave Markton by the seven o'clock train this evening."

"And if I meet your proposal with a negative?"

"I shall go at once to my niece and tell her the whole circumstances—tell her that, by marrying Sir William, she allies herself with an unhappy gentleman in the power of a criminal son who makes his life a burden to him by perpetual demands upon his purse; who will increase these demands with his accession to wealth, threaten to degrade her by exposing her husband's antecedents if she opposes his extortions, and who will make her miserable by letting her know that her old lover was shamefully victimised by a youth she is bound to screen out of respect to her husband's feelings. Now a man does not care to let his own flesh and blood incur the danger of such anguish as that, and I shall do what I say to prevent it. Knowing what a lukewarm sentiment hers is for Sir William at best, I shall not have much difficulty."

"Well, I don't feel inclined to go to Peru."

"Neither do I want to break off the match, though I am ready to do it. But you care about your personal freedom, and you might be made to wear the broad arrow for your tricks on Somerset."

"Mr. Power, I see you are a hard man."

"I am a hard man. You will find me one. Well, will you go to Peru? Or I don't mind Australia or California as alternatives. As long as you choose to remain in either of those wealth-producing places, so long will Cunningham Haze go uninformed."

"Mr. Power, I am overcome. Will you allow me to sit down? Suppose we go into the vestry. It is more comfortable."

They entered the vestry, and seated themselves in two chairs, one at each end of the table.

"In the mean time," continued Dare, "to lend a little romance to stern realities, I'll tell you a singular dream I had just before you returned to England." Power looked contemptuous, but Dare went on: "I dreamt that once upon a time there were two brothers, born of a Nonconformist family, one of whom became a railway-contractor, and the other a mechanical engineer."

"A mechanical engineer—good," said Power, beginning to attend.

"When the first went abroad in his profession, and became engaged on continental railways, the second, a younger man, looking round for a start, also betook himself to the continent.

But though ingenious and scientific, he had not the business capacity of the elder, whose rebukes led to a sharp quarrel between them; and they parted in bitter estrangement—never to meet again as it turned out, owing to the dogged obstinacy and self-will of the younger man. He, after this, seemed to lose his moral ballast altogether, and after some eccentric doings he was reduced to a state of poverty, and took lodgings in a court in a back street of a town we will call Geneva, considerably in doubt as to what steps he should take to keep body and soul together."

Abner Power was shooting a narrow ray of eyesight at Dare from the corner of his nearly closed lids. "Your dream is so interesting," he said, with a hard smile, "that I could listen to it all day."

"Excellent!" said Dare, and went on: "Now it so happened that the house opposite to the one taken by the mechanician was peculiar. It was a tall narrow building, wholly unornamented, the walls covered with a layer of white plaster cracked and soiled by time. I seem to see that house now! Six stone steps led up to the door, with a rusty iron railing on each side, and under these steps were others which went down to a cellar—in my dream of course."

"Of course—in your dream," said Power, nodding comprehensively.

"Sitting lonely and apathetic without a light, at his own chamber-window at night-time, our mechanician frequently observed dark figures descending these steps, and ultimately discovered that the house was the meeting-place of a fraternity of political philosophers, whose object was the extermination of tyrants and despots, and the overthrow of established religions. The discovery was startling enough, but our hero was not easily startled. He kept their secret and lived on as before. At last the mechanician and his affairs became known to the society, as the affairs of the society had become known to the mechanician, and, instead of shooting him as one who knew too much for their safety, they were struck with his faculty for silence, and thought they might be able to make use of him."

"To be sure," said Abner Power.

"Next, like friend Bunyan, I saw in my dream that denunciation was the breath of life to this society. At an earlier date in its history, objectionable persons in power had been from time to time murdered, and curiously enough numbered; that is, upon the body of each was set a mark or seal, announcing that he was one of a series. But at this time the question before the society related to the substitution for the dagger, which was vetoed as obsolete, of some explosive machine that would be both more effectual and less difficult to manage; and in short, a large reward was offered to our needy Englishman if he would put their ideas of such a machine into shape."

Abner Power nodded again, his complexion being peculiar—which might partly have been accounted for by the reflection of window-light from the green-baize table-cloth.

"He agreed, though no politician whatever himself, to exercise his wits on their account, and brought his machine to such a pitch of perfection, that it was the identical one used in the memorable attempt—" (Dare whispered the remainder of the sentence in tones so low that not a mouse in the corner could have heard.) "Well, the inventor of that explosive has naturally been wanted ever since by all the heads of police in Europe. But the most curious—or perhaps the most natural—part of my story is, that our hero, after the catastrophe, grew disgusted with himself and his comrades, acquired, in a fit of revulsion, quite a conservative taste in politics, which was strengthened greatly by the news he indirectly received of the great wealth and respectability of his brother, who had had no communion with him for years, and supposed him dead. He abjured his employers and resolved to abandon them: but before coming to England he decided to destroy all trace of his combustible inventions by dropping them into the neighbouring lake at night from a boat. You feel the room close, Mr. Power?"

"No, I suffer from attacks of perspiration whenever I sit in a consecrated edifice—that's all. Pray go on."

"In carrying out this project, an explosion occurred, just as he was throwing the stock overboard: it blew up into his face, wounding him severely, and nearly depriving him of sight. The boat was upset, but he swam ashore in the darkness, and remained hidden till he recovered, though the scars produced by the burns had been set on him for ever. This accident, which was such a misfortune to him as a man, was an advantage to him as a conspirators' engineer retiring from practice, and afforded him a disguise both from his own brotherhood and from the police, which he has considered impenetrable, but which is getting seen through by one or two keen eyes as time goes on. Instead of coming to England just then, he went to Peru, connected himself with the guano trade, I believe, and after his brother's death revisited England, his old life obliterated as far as practicable by his new principles. He is known only as a great traveller to his surviving relatives, though he seldom says where he has travelled. Unluckily for himself, he is *wanted* by certain European governments as badly as ever."

Dare raised his eyes as he concluded his narration. As has been remarked, he was sitting at one end of the vestry-table, Power at the other, the green cloth stretching between them. On the edge of the table adjoining Mr. Power a shining nozzle of metal was quietly resting, like a dog's nose. It was directed point-blank at the young man.

Dare started. "Ah—a revolver?" he said.

Mr. Power nodded placidly, his hand still grasping the pistol behind the edge of the table. "As a traveller I always carry one of 'em," he returned; "and for the last five minutes I have been closely considering whether your numerous brains are worth blowing out or no. The vault yonder has suggested itself as convenient and snug for one of the same family; but the mental problem that stays my hand is, how am I to despatch and bury you there without the workmen seeing."

"'Tis a strange problem, certainly," replied Dare, "and one on which I fear I could not give disinterested advice. Moreover, while you, as a traveller, always carry a weapon of defence, as a traveller so do I. And for the last three-quarters of an hour I have been thinking concerning you, an intensified form of what you have been thinking of me, but without any concern as to your internment. See here for a proof of it." And a second steel nose rested on the edge of the table opposite to the first, steadied by Dare's right hand.

They remained for some time motionless, the tick of the tower clock distinctly audible in the silence of this dead-lock.

Mr. Power spoke first.

"A well-balanced position," he said. "Well, 'twould be a pity to make a mess here under such dubious circumstances. Mr. Dare, I perceive that a mean vagabond can be as sharp as a political regenerator. I cry quits, if you care to do the same."

Dare assented, and the pistols were put away.

"Then we do nothing at all, either side; but let the course of true love run on to marriage—that's the understanding, I think?" said Dare as he rose.

"It is," said Power; and turning on his heel, he left the vestry.

Dare retired to the church and thence to the outside, where he idled away a few minutes in looking at the workmen, who were now lowering into its place a large stone slab bearing the words, "DE STANCY," which covered the entrance to the vault. When the footway of the churchyard was restored to its normal condition Dare pursued his way to Markton.

Abner Power walked back to the castle at a slow and equal pace, as though he carried an over-brimming vessel on his head. He silently let himself in, entered the long gallery, and sat down. The length of time that he sat there was so remarkable as to raise that interval of inanition to the rank of a feat.

Power's eyes glanced through one of the window-casements: from a hole without he saw the head of a tom-tit protruding. He listlessly watched the bird during the successive epochs of his thought, till night came, without any perceptible change occurring in him. Such fixity would have meant nothing else than sudden death in any other man, but in Mr. Power it merely signified that he was engaged in ruminations which necessitated a more extensive survey than usual. At last, at half-past eight, after having sat for five hours with his eyes on the residence of the tom-tits, to whom night had brought cessation of thought, if not to him who had observed them, he rose amid the shades of the furniture, and rang the bell. There was only a servant or two in the castle, one of whom presently came with a light in her hand and a startled look upon her face, which was not reduced when she recognised him; for in the opinion of that household there was something ghoul-like in Mr. Power, which made him no desirable guest.

He ate a late meal, and retired to bed, where he seemed to sleep not unsoundly. The next morning he received a letter which afforded him infinite satisfaction and gave his stagnant impulses a new momentum. He entered the library, and amid objects swathed in brown holland sat down and wrote a note to his niece at Amiens. Therein he stated that, finding that the Anglo-South-American house with which he had recently connected himself required his presence in Peru, it obliged him to leave without waiting for her return. He felt the less uneasy at going, since he had learnt that Captain De Stancy would return at once to Amiens to his sick sister, and see them safely home when she improved. He afterwards left the castle, disappearing towards a railway station some miles above Markton, the road to which lay across an unfrequented down.

CHAPTER XII

IT was a fine afternoon of late summer, nearly three months
subsequent to the death of Sir William De Stancy and Paula's
engagement to marry his successor in the title. George Somerset had started on a railway journey that took him through the
wooded district which lay around Stancy Castle. Having
resigned his appointment as architect to that important structure—a resignation which had been accepted by Paula through
her solicitor—he had bidden farewell to the locality after
putting matters in such order that his successor, whoever he
might be, should have no difficulty in obtaining the particulars
necessary to the completion of the work in hand. Hardly to his
surprise this successor was Havill. Somerset had less reluctance
than before in abandoning the undertaking to Havill's
untrained judgment from the circumstance that the design was
matured, even to the working drawings, and the walls too far
advanced for any material alteration; so that mere construc-
tional superintendence was all that he had deputed—a branch
of the profession in which Havill was proficient.

Somerset's resignation had been tendered in no hasty mood.
On returning to England, and in due course to the castle,
everything bore in upon his mind the exceeding sorrowful-
ness—he would not say humiliation—of continuing to act in
his former capacity for a woman who, from seeming more than
a dear friend, had become less than an acquaintance. Though
bitterly reproaching her at every moment, he was unable to
contemn her, and could not criticise her; indeed Somerset was
still in too regretful a state to see anything in Paula but the
unattainable one who had chosen to renounce him. He blamed
himself, not her, for having been made the fool of his wishes;
and despite his resolve, half hankered for the opportunity of
being near her that the office of her architect would still afford,
whether or not she should have become the wife of another
man. But, after the diseased sentiment of moods like this, a

reasonable defiance stirred in his breast, and he saw how intolerable it would be to come in contact with her under such altered circumstances, the ghosts of sweet remembrances for ever arising before him in maddening contrast with her altered eyes.

So he resigned; but now, as the train drew on into that once beloved tract of country, the images which met his eye threw him back in point of emotion to very near where he had been before making himself a stranger here. The train entered the cutting on whose brink he had walked when the carriage containing Paula and her friends surprised him the previous summer. He looked out of the window: they were passing the well-known curve that led up to the tunnel constructed by her father, into which he had gone when the train came by and Paula had been alarmed for his life. There was the path they had both climbed afterwards, involuntarily seizing each other's hand; the bushes, the grass, the flowers, everything just the same:

"——Here was the pleasant place,
And nothing wanting was, save She, alas!"

When they came out of the tunnel at the other end he caught a glimpse of the distant castle-keep, and the well-remembered walls beneath it. The experience so far transcended the intensity of what is called mournful pleasure as to make him wonder how he could have miscalculated himself to the extent of supposing that he might return hither with controllable emotion.

On entering Markton station he withdrew into a remote corner of the carriage, and closed his eyes with a resolve not to open them till the embittering scenes should be passed by. He had not long to wait for this event. When again in motion his eye fell upon the skirt of a lady's dress opposite, the owner of which had entered and seated herself so softly as not to attract his attention.

"Ah, indeed!" he exclaimed as he looked up to her face. "I had not a notion that it was you!" He went over and shook hands with Charlotte De Stancy.

"I am not going far," she said; "only to the next station. We often run down in summer time. Are you going far?"

"I am going to Normandy by way of Cherbourg, to finish out my summer holiday."

Miss De Stancy thought that would be very nice.

"Well, I hope so. But I fear it won't."

After saying that, Somerset fell into consideration, asking himself why he should mince matters with so genuine and sympathetic a girl as Charlotte De Stancy? She could tell him particulars which, notwithstanding the anguish they would cause him, he burned to know. Moreover, he might never again have an opportunity of knowing them, since she and he would probably not meet for years to come, if at all.

"Have the castle works progressed pretty rapidly under the new architect?" he accordingly asked.

"Yes," said Charlotte in her haste—then adding that she was not quite sure if they had progressed so rapidly as before; blushingly correcting herself at this point and that in the tinkering manner of a nervous organisation aiming at nicety where it was not required.

"Well, I should have liked to carry out the undertaking to its end," said Somerset. "But I felt I could not consistently do so. Miss Power——" (here a lump came into Somerset's throat—so responsive was he yet to her image) "seemed to have lost confidence in me, and—it was best that the connection should be severed."

There was a long pause. "She was very sorry about it," said Charlotte, gently.

"What made her alter so?—I never can think!"

Before replying Charlotte waited again, as if to accumulate the necessary force for honest speaking at the expense of pleasantness. "It was the telegram that began it, of course," she answered.

"Telegram?"

She looked up at him in quite a frightened way—little as there was to be frightened at in a quiet fellow like him in this sad time of his life—and said, "Yes: some telegram—I think—when you were in trouble? Forgive my alluding to it; but you asked me the question."

Somerset began reflecting on what messages he had sent Paula, troublous or otherwise. All he had sent had been sent from the castle, and were as gentle and mellifluous as sentences well could be which had neither articles nor pronouns. "I don't understand," he said. "Will you explain a little more—as plainly as you like—without minding my feelings?"

"A telegram from Nice, I think?"

"I never sent one."

"Oh! The one I meant was about money."

Somerset shook his head. "No," he murmured, with the composure of a man who, knowing he had done nothing of the sort himself, was blinded by his own honesty to the possibility that another might have done it for him. "That must be some other affair with which I had nothing to do. Oh no, it was nothing like that; the reason for her change of manner was quite different!"

So timid was Charlotte in Somerset's presence, that her timidity at this juncture amounted to blameworthiness. The distressing scene which must have followed a clearing up there and then of any possible misunderstanding, terrified her imagination; and quite confounded by contradictions that she could not reconcile, she held her tongue, and nervously looked out of the window.

"I have heard that Miss Power is soon to be married," continued Somerset, with a boldness that astonished himself.

"Yes," Charlotte murmured. "It is sooner than it ought to be by rights, considering how recently my dear father died; but there are reasons in connection with my brother's position against putting it off and it is to be absolutely simple and private."

There was another interval. "May I ask when it is to be?" he said.

"Almost at once—this week."

Somerset started back as if some stone had hit his face. Certain as he had been that a marriage between Paula and De Stancy was impending, he had not anticipated such promptitude as this. Still there was nothing wonderful in it: engagements broken in upon by the death of a near relative of one of the parties had been often carried out in a subdued form with no longer delay.

But he could not easily say much more, and Charlotte's station was now at hand. She bade him farewell on the platform; and he resumed his seat and rattled on to Budmouth, whence he intended to cross the Channel by steamboat that night.

He hardly knew how the evening passed away. He had taken up his quarters at an old-fashioned inn on the quay, and as the night drew on he stood gazing from the coffee-room window at the steamer outside, which nearly thrust its spars through the bedroom casements, and at the goods that were being tumbled on board as only shippers can tumble them. All the goods were laden, a lamp was put on each side the gangway, the engines broke into a crackling roar, and people began to enter. They were only waiting for the last train; then they would be off. Still Somerset did not move: he was thinking of that curious half-told story of Charlotte's, about a telegram to Paula for money from Nice. Not once till within the last half-hour had it recurred to his mind that he had met Dare both at Nice and at Monte Carlo; that at the latter place he had been absolutely out of money and wished to borrow, showing considerable sinister feeling when Somerset declined to lend; that on one or two previous occasions he had reasons for doubting Dare's probity; and that in spite of the young man's impoverishment at Monte Carlo he had, a few days later, beheld him in shining raiment at Carlsruhe. Somerset, though misty in his conjectures, was seized with a growing conviction that there was something in Miss De Stancy's allusion to the telegram which ought to be explained.

Without considering how he personally would be able to explain it, he felt an insurmountable objection to cross the water that night, or till he had been able to see Charlotte again, and learn more of her meaning. He countermanded the order to put his luggage on board, watched the steamer out of the harbour, and went to bed. He might as well have gone to battle, for any rest that he got. On rising the next morning and noting how extremely vague was the course to which he had committed himself he felt rather blank, though none the less convinced that the matter required investigation. He left Budmouth by a morning train, and about eleven o'clock found himself in Markton.

The momentum of a practical inquiry took him through that ancient borough without leaving him much leisure for those reveries which had yesterday lent an unutterable sadness to every object there. It was just before noon that he started for the castle, intending to arrive at a time of the morning when, as he knew from experience, he could speak to Charlotte without difficulty. The rising ground soon revealed the old towers to him, and, jutting out behind them, the scaffoldings for the new wing.

While halting here on the knoll in some doubt about his movements he beheld a man coming along the road, and was soon confronted by his former competitor, Havill. The first instinct of each was to pass with a nod, but a second instinct for intercourse was sufficient to bring them to a halt. After a few superficial words had been spoken Somerset said, "You have succeeded me."

"I have," said Havill; "but little to my advantage. I have just heard that my commission is to extend no further than roofing in the wing that you began, and had I known that before, I would have seen the castle fall flat as Jericho before I would have accepted the superintendence. But I know who I have to thank for that—De Stancy."

Somerset still looked towards the distant battlements. On the scaffolding, among the white-jacketed workmen, he could discern one figure in a dark suit.

"You have a clerk of the works, I see," he observed.

"Nominally I have, but practically I haven't."

"Then why do you keep him?"

"I can't help myself. He is Mr Dare; and having been recommended by a higher power than me, there he must stay in spite of me."

"Who recommended him?"

"The same—De Stancy."

"It is very odd," murmured Somerset, "but that young man is the object of my visit."

"You had better leave him alone," said Havill dryly.

Somerset asked why.

"Since I call no man master over that way I will inform you." Havill then related in splenetic tones, to which Somerset did not care to listen till the story began to advance itself, how he had passed the night with Dare at the inn, and the incidents of that night, relating how he had seen some letters on the young man's breast which long had puzzled him. "They were an E, a T, an N, and a C. I thought over them long, till it eventually occurred to me that the word when filled out was 'De Stancy,' and that kinship explains the offensive and defensive alliance between them."

"But, good heavens, man!" said Somerset, more and more disturbed. "Does she know of it?"

"You may depend she does not yet; but she will soon enough. Hark—there it is!" The notes of the castle clock were heard striking noon. "Then it is all over."

"What?—not their marriage!"

"Yes. Didn't you know it was the wedding day? They were to be at the church at half-past eleven. I should have waited to see her go, but it was no sight to hinder business for, as she was only going to drive over in her brougham with Miss De Stancy."

"My errand has failed!" said Somerset, turning on his heel. "I'll walk back to the town with you."

However he did not walk far with Havill; society was too much at that moment. As soon as opportunity offered he branched from the road by a path, and avoiding the town went by railway to Budmouth, whence he resumed, by the night steamer, his journey to Normandy.

CHAPTER XIII

To return to Charlotte De Stancy. When the train had borne
Somerset from her side, and she had regained her self-
possession, she became conscious of the true proportions of
the fact he had asserted. And, further, if the telegram had not
been his, why should the photographic distortion be trusted as
a phase of his existence? But after a while it seemed so
improbable to her that God's sun should bear false witness,
that instead of doubting both evidences she was inclined to
readmit the first. Still, upon the whole, she could not question
for long the honesty of Somerset's denial; and if that message
had indeed been sent by him, it must have been done while he
was in another such an unhappy state as that exemplified by
the portrait. The supposition reconciled all differences; and
yet she could not but fight against it with all the strength of a
generous affection.

All the afternoon her poor little head was busy on this
perturbing question, till she inquired of herself whether after
all it might not be possible for photographs to represent people
as they had never been. Before rejecting the hypothesis she
determined to have the word of a professor on the point, which
would be better than all her surmises. Returning to Markton
early, she told the coachman whom Paula had sent, to drive
her to the shop of Mr. Ray, an obscure photographic artist in
that town, instead of straight home.

Ray's establishment consisted of two divisions, the respectable and the shabby. If, on entering the door, the visitor
turned to the left, he found himself in a magazine of old
clothes, old furniture, china, umbrellas, guns, fishing-rods,
dirty fiddles, and split flutes. Entering the right-hand room,
which had originally been that of an independent house, he
was in an ordinary photographer's and print-collector's depos-
itory, to which a certain artistic solidity was imparted by a few
oil paintings in the background. Charlotte made for the latter

department, and when she was inside Mr. Ray appeared in person from the lumber-shop adjoining, which, despite its manginess, contributed by far the greater share to his income.

Charlotte put her question simply enough. The man did not answer her directly, but soon found that she meant no harm to him. He told her that such misrepresentations were quite possible, and that they embodied a form of humour which was getting more and more into vogue among certain facetious classes of society.

Charlotte was coming away when she asked, as on second thoughts, if he had any specimens of such work to show her.

"None of my own preparation," said Mr. Ray, with unimpeachable probity of tone. "I consider them libellous myself. Still, I have one or two samples by me, which I keep merely as curiosities.—There's one," he said, throwing out a portrait card from a drawer. "That represents the German Emperor in a violent passion: this one shows the Prime Minister out of his mind; this the Pope of Rome the worse for liquor."

She inquired if he had any local specimens.

"Yes," he said, "but I prefer not to exhibit them unless you really ask for a particular one that you mean to buy."

"I don't want any."

"Oh, I beg pardon, miss. Well, I shouldn't myself have known such things were produced, if there had not been a young man here at one time who was very ingenious in these matters—a Mr. Dare. He was quite a gent, and only did it as an amusement, and not for the sake of getting a living."

Charlotte had no wish to hear more. On her way home she burst into tears: the entanglement was altogether too much for her to tear asunder, even had not her own instincts been urging her two ways, as they were.

To immediately right Somerset's wrong was her impetuous desire as an honest woman who loved him; but such rectification would be the jeopardising of all else that gratified her—the marriage of her brother with her dearest friend—now on the very point of accomplishment. It was a marriage which seemed to promise happiness, or at least comfort, if the old flutter that had transiently disturbed Paula's bosom could be kept from reviving, to which end it became imperative to hide from her the discovery of injustice to Somerset. It involved the advantage of leaving Somerset free; and though her own tender interest in him had been too well schooled by habitual self-denial to run ahead on vain personal hopes, there was nothing more than human in her feeling pleasure in prolonging Somerset's singleness. Paula might even be allowed to discover his wrongs when her marriage had put him out of her power. But to let her discover his ill-treatment now might upset the impending union of the families, and wring her own heart with the sight of Somerset married in her brother's place.

Why Dare, or any other person, should have set himself to advance her brother's cause by such unscrupulous blackening of Somerset's character was more than her sagacity could fathom. Her brother was, as far as she could see, the only man who could directly profit by the machination, and was therefore the natural one to suspect of having set it going. But she would not be so disloyal as to entertain the thought long; and who or what had instigated Dare, who was undoubtedly the proximate cause of the mischief, remained to her an inscrutable mystery.

The contention of interests and desires with honour in her heart shook Charlotte all that night; but good principle prevailed. The wedding was to be solemnised the very next morning, though for before-mentioned reasons this was hardly known outside the two houses interested; and there were no visible preparations either at villa or castle. De Stancy and his groomsman—a brother officer—slept at the former residence.

De Stancy was a sorry specimen of a bridegroom when he met his sister in the morning. Thick-coming fancies, for which there was more than good reason, had disturbed him only too successfully, and he was as full of apprehension as one who has a league with Mephistopheles. Charlotte told him nothing of what made her likewise so wan and anxious, but drove off to the castle, as had been planned, about nine o'clock, leaving her brother and his friend at the breakfast-table.

That clearing Somerset's reputation from the stain which had been thrown on it would cause a sufficient reaction in Paula's mind to dislocate present arrangements she did not so seriously anticipate, now that morning had a little calmed her.

Since the rupture with her former architect Paula had sedulously kept her own counsel, but Charlotte assumed from the ease with which she seemed to do it that her feelings towards him had never been inconveniently warm; and she hoped that Paula would learn of Somerset's purity with merely the generous pleasure of a friend, coupled with a friend's indignation against his traducer.

Still, the possibility existed of stronger emotions, and it was only too evident to poor Charlotte that, knowing this, she had still less excuse for delaying the intelligence till the strongest emotion would be purposeless.

On approaching the castle the first object that caught her eye was Dare, standing beside Havill on the scaffolding of the new wing. He was looking down upon the drive and court, as if in anticipation of the event. His contiguity flurried her, and instead of going straight to Paula she sought out Mrs. Goodman.

"You are come early: that's right!" said the latter. "You might as well have slept here last night. We have only Mr. Wardlaw, the London lawyer you have heard of, in the house. Your brother's solicitor was here yesterday; but he returned to Markton for the night. We miss Mr. Power so much—it is so unfortunate that he should have been obliged to go abroad, and leave us unprotected women with so much responsibility."

"Yes, I know," said Charlotte quickly, having a shy distaste for the details of what troubled her so much in the gross.

"Paula has inquired for you."

"What is she doing?"

"She is in her room: she has not begun to dress yet. Will you go to her?"

Charlotte assented. "I have to tell her something," she said, "which will make no difference, but which I should like her to know this morning—at once. I have discovered that we have been entirely mistaken about Mr. Somerset." She nerved herself to relate succinctly what had come to her knowledge the day before.

Mrs. Goodman was much impressed. She had never clearly heard before what circumstances had attended the resignation of Paula's architect. "We had better not tell her till the wedding is over," she presently said; "it would only disturb her, and do no good."

"But will it be right?" asked Miss De Stancy.

"Yes, it will be right if we tell her afterwards. Oh yes—it must be right," she repeated, in a tone which showed that her opinion was unstable enough to require a little fortification by the voice. "She loves your brother; she must, since she is going to marry him; and it can make little difference whether we rehabilitate the character of a friend now, or some few hours hence. The author of those wicked tricks on Mr. Somerset ought not to go a moment unpunished."

"That's what I think; and what right have we to hold our tongues even for a few hours?"

Charlotte found that by telling Mrs. Goodman she had simply made two irresolute people out of one, and, as Paula was now inquiring for her, she went upstairs without having come to any decision.

CHAPTER XIV

PAULA was in her boudoir, writing down some notes previous to beginning her wedding toilet, which was designed to harmonise with the simplicity that characterised the other arrangements. She owned that it was depriving the neighbourhood of a pageant which it had a right to expect of her; but the circumstances were inexorable.

Mrs. Goodman entered Paula's room immediately behind Charlotte. Perhaps the only difference between the Paula of to-day and the Paula of last year was an accession of thoughtfulness, natural to the circumstances in any case, and more particularly when, as now, the bride's isolation made self-dependence a necessity. She was sitting in a light dressing-gown, and her face, which was rather pale, flushed at the entrance of Charlotte and her aunt.

"I knew you were come," she said, when Charlotte stooped and kissed her. "I heard you. I have done nothing this morning, and feel dreadfully unsettled. Is all well?"

The question was put without thought, but its aptness seemed almost to imply an intuitive knowledge of their previous conversation. "Yes," said Charlotte, tardily.

"Well, now, Clémentine shall dress you, and I can do with Milly," continued Paula. "Come along.—Well aunt—what's the matter?—and you Charlotte? You look harassed."

"I have not slept well," said Charlotte.

"And have not you slept well either, aunt? You said nothing about it at breakfast."

"Oh, it is nothing," said Mrs. Goodman quickly. "I have been disturbed by learning of somebody's villainy. I am going to tell you all some time to-day, but it is not important enough to disturb you with now."

"No mystery!" argued Paula. "Come! it is not fair."

"I don't think it is quite fair," said Miss De Stancy, looking from one to the other in some distress. "Mrs. Goodman—I must tell her! Paula, Mr. Som——"

"He's dead!" cried Paula, sinking into a chair and turning as pale as marble. "Is he dead?—tell me," she whispered.

"No, no—he's not dead—he is very well, and gone to Normandy for a holiday!"

"Oh—I am glad to hear it," answered Paula, with a sudden cool mannerliness.

"He has been misrepresented," said Mrs. Goodman. "That's all."

"Well?" said Paula, with her eyes bent on the floor.

"I have been feeling that I ought to tell you clearly, dear Paula," declared her friend. "It is absolutely false about his telegraphing to you for money—it is absolutely false that his character is such as that dreadful picture represented it. There—that's the substance of it, and I can tell you particulars at any time."

But Paula would not be told at any time. A dreadful sorrow sat in her face: she insisted upon learning everything about the matter there and then, and there was no withstanding her.

When it was all explained she said in a low tone: "It is that pernicious, evil man Dare—yet why is it he?—what can he have meant by it? Justice before generosity, even on one's wedding-day. Before I become any man's wife this morning I'll see that wretch in jail! The affair must be sifted. . . . Oh, it was a wicked thing to serve anybody so!—I'll send for Cunningham Haze this moment—the culprit is even now on the premises, I believe—acting as clerk of the works!" The usually well-balanced Paula was excited, and scarcely knowing what she did went to the bell-pull.

"Don't act hastily, Paula," said her aunt. "Had you not better consult Sir William? He will act for you in this."

"Yes.—He is coming round in a few minutes," said Charlotte, jumping at this happy thought of Mrs. Goodman's. "He's going to run across to see how you are getting on. He will be here by ten."

"Yes—he promised last night."

She had scarcely done speaking when the prancing of a horse

was heard in the ward below, and in a few minutes a servant announced Sir William De Stancy.

De Stancy entered saying, "I have ridden across for ten minutes, as I said I would do, to know if everything is easy and straightforward for you. There will be time enough for me to get back and prepare if I start in ten minutes.—Well?"

"I am ruffled," said Paula, allowing him to take her hand.

"What is it?" said her betrothed.

As Paula did not immediately answer Mrs. Goodman beckoned to Charlotte, and they left the room together.

"A man has to be given in charge, or a boy, or a demon," she replied. "I was going to do it, but you can do it better than I. He will run away if we don't mind."

"But, my dear Paula, who is it?—what has he done?"

"It is Dare—that young man you see out there against the sky." She looked from the window sideways towards the new wing, on the roof of which Dare was walking prominently about, after having assisted two of the workmen in putting a red streamer on the tallest scaffold-pole. "You must send instantly for Mr. Cunningham Haze!"

"My dearest Paula," repeated De Stancy faintly, his complexion changing to that of a man who had died.

"Please send for Mr. Haze at once," returned Paula, with graceful firmness. "I said I would be just to a wronged man before I was generous to you—and I will. That lad Dare—to take a practical view of it—has attempted to defraud me of one hundred pounds sterling, and he shall suffer. I won't tell you what he has done besides, for though it is worse, it is less tangible. When he is handcuffed and sent off to jail I'll proceed with my dressing. Will you ring the bell?"

"Had you not better—consider?" began De Stancy.

"Consider!" said Paula, not without indignation. "I have considered. Will you kindly ring, Sir William, and get Thomas to ride at once to Mr. Haze? Or must I rise from this chair and do it myself?"

"You are very hasty and abrupt this morning, I think," he faltered.

Paula rose determinedly from the chair.

"Since you won't do it, I must," she said.

"No, dearest!—Let me beg you not to!"

"Sir William De Stancy!"

She moved towards the bell-pull; but he stepped before and intercepted her.

"You must not ring the bell for that purpose," he said, with husky deliberateness, looking into the depths of her face.

"It wants two hours to the time when you might have a right to express such a command as that," she said haughtily.

"I certainly have not the honour to be your husband yet," he sadly replied, "but surely you can listen? There exist reasons against giving this boy in charge which I could easily get you to admit by explanation; but I would rather, without explanation, have you take my word, when I say that by doing so you are striking a blow against both yourself and me."

Paula, however, had rung the bell.

"You are jealous of somebody or something perhaps!" she said in tones which showed how fatally all this was telling against the intention of the day. "I will not be a party to baseness, if it is to save all my fortune!"

The bell was answered quickly. But De Stancy, though plainly in great misery, did not give up his point. Meeting the servant at the door before he could enter the room he said, "It is nothing; you can go again."

Paula looked at the unhappy baronet in amazement; then turning to the servant, who stood with the door in his hand, said, "Tell Thomas to saddle the chestnut, and——"

"It's all a mistake," insisted De Stancy. "Leave the room, James!"

James looked at his mistress.

"Yes, James, leave the room," she calmly said, sitting down. "Now what have you to say?" she asked, when they were alone again. "Why must I not issue orders in my own house. Who is this young criminal, that you value his interests higher than my honour? I have delayed for one moment sending my messenger to the chief constable to hear your explanation—only for that."

"You will still persevere?"

"Certainly. Who is he?"

"Paula . . . he is my son."

She remained still as death while one might count ten; then turned her back upon him. "I think you had better go away," she whispered. "You need not come again."

He did not move. "Paula—do you indeed mean this?" he asked.

"I do."

De Stancy walked a few paces, then said in a low voice: "Miss Power, I knew—I guessed just now, as soon as it began—that we were going to split on this rock. Well—let it be—it cannot be helped; destiny is supreme. The boy was to be my ruin; he is my ruin, and rightly. But before I go grant me one request. Do not prosecute him! Believe me, I will do everything I can to get him out of your way. He shall annoy you no more. . . . Do you promise?"

"I do," she said. "Now please leave me."

"Once more—am I to understand that no marriage is to take place to-day between you and me?"

"You are."

Sir William De Stancy left the room. It was noticeable throughout the interview that his manner had not been the manner of a man altogether taken by surprise. During the few preceding days his mood had been that of the gambler seasoned in ill-luck, who adopts pessimist surmises as a safe background to his most sanguine hopes.

She remained alone for some time. Then she rang, and requested that Mr. Wardlaw, her father's solicitor and friend, would come up to her. A messenger was despatched, not to Mr. Cunningham Haze, but to the parson of the parish, who in his turn sent to the clerk and clerk's wife, then busy in the church. On receipt of the intelligence the two latter functionaries proceeded to roll up the carpet which had been laid from the door to the gate, put away the kneeling-cushions, locked the doors, and went off to inquire the reason of so strange a countermand. It was soon proclaimed in Markton that the marriage had been postponed for a fortnight in consequence of the bride's sudden indisposition; and less public emotion was felt than the case might have drawn forth, from the ignorance of the majority of the populace that a wedding had been going to take place at all.

Meanwhile Miss De Stancy had been closeted with Paula for more than an hour. It was a difficult meeting, and a severe test to any friendship but that of the most sterling sort. In the turmoil of her distraction, which might well have been severe, Charlotte had the consolation of knowing that if her act of justice to Somerset at such a moment were the act of a simpleton, it was the only course open to honesty. But Paula's cheerful serenity in some measure laid her own troubles to rest, till they were reawakened by a rumour—which got wind some weeks later, and quite drowned all other surprises—of the true relation between the vanished clerk of works, Mr. Dare, and the fallen family of De Stancy.

BOOK THE SIXTH

PAULA

"I HAVE decided that I cannot see Sir William again; I shall go away," said Paula on the evening of the next day, as she lay on her bed in a flushed and highly strung condition, though a person who had heard her words without seeing her face would have assumed perfect equanimity to be the mood which expressed itself with such quietness. This was the case with her aunt, who was looking out of the window at some idlers from Markton walking round the castle with their eyes bent upon its windows, and she made no haste to reply.

"Those people have come to see me, as they have a right to do when a person acts so strangely," Paula continued. "And hence I am better away."

"Where do you think to go to?"

Paula replied in the tone of one who was actuated entirely by practical considerations: "Out of England certainly. And as Normandy lies nearest, I think I shall go there. It is a very nice country to ramble in."

"Yes, it is a very nice country to ramble in," echoed her aunt, in moderate tones. "When do you intend to start?"

"I should like to cross to-night. You must go with me, aunt; will you not?"

Mrs. Goodman expostulated against such suddenness. "It will redouble the rumours that are afloat, if, after being supposed ill, you are seen going off by railway perfectly well."

"That's a contingency which I am quite willing to run the risk of. Well, it would be rather sudden, as you say, to go to-night. But we'll go tomorrow night at latest." Under the influence of the decision she bounded up like an elastic ball and went to the glass, which showed a light in her eye that had not been there before this resolution to travel in Normandy had been taken.

The evening and the next morning were passed in writing a final note of dismissal to Sir William De Stancy, in making arrangements for the journey, and in commissioning Havill to take advantage of their absence by emptying certain rooms of their furniture, and repairing their dilapidations—a work which, with that already in hand, would complete the section for which he had been engaged. Mr. Wardlaw had left the castle; so also had Charlotte, by her own wish, her residence there having been found too oppressive to herself to be continued for the present. Accompanied by Mrs. Goodman, Milly, and Clémentine, the elderly French maid, who still remained with them, Paula drove into Markton in the twilight and took the train to Budmouth.

When they got there they found that an unpleasant breeze was blowing out at sea, though inland it had been calm enough. Mrs. Goodman proposed to stay in Budmouth till the next day, in hope that there might be smooth water; but an English seaport inn being a thing that Paula disliked more than a rough passage, she would not listen to this counsel. Other impatient reasons, too, might have weighed with her. When night came their looming miseries began. Paula found that in addition to her own troubles she had those of three other people to support; but she did not audibly complain.

"Paula, Paula," said Mrs. Goodman from beneath her load of wretchedness, "why did we think of undergoing this?"

A slight gleam of humour crossed Paula's not particularly blooming face, as she answered, "Ah, why indeed?"

"What is the real reason, my dear? For God's sake tell me!"

"It begins with S."

"Well, I would do anything for that young man short of personal martyrdom; but really when it comes to that——"

"Don't criticise me, auntie, and I won't criticise you."

"Well, I am open to criticism just now, I am sure," said her aunt with a green smile; and speech was again discontinued.

The morning was bright and beautiful, and it could again be seen in Paula's looks that she was glad she had come, though, in taking their rest at Cherbourg, fate consigned them to an hotel breathing an atmosphere that seemed specially compounded for depressing the spirits of a young woman; indeed, nothing had particularly encouraged her thus far in her somewhat peculiar scheme of searching out and expressing sorrow to a gentleman for having believed those who traduced him; and this *coup d'audace* to which she had committed herself began to look somewhat formidable. When in England the plan of following him to Normandy had suggested itself as the quickest, sweetest, and most honest way of making amends; but having arrived there she seemed further off from his sphere of existence than when she had been at Stancy Castle. Virtually she was, for if he thought of her at all, he probably thought of her there; if he sought her he would seek her there. However, as he would probably never do the latter, it was necessary to go on. It had been her sudden dream, before starting, to light accidentally upon him in some romantic old town of this romantic old province, but she had become aware that the recorded fortune of lovers in that respect was not to be trusted too implicitly.

Somerset's search for her in the south was now inversely imitated. By diligent inquiry in Cherbourg during the gloom of evening, in the disguise of a hooded cloak, she learnt out the place of his stay while there, and that he had gone thence to Lisieux. What she knew of the architectural character of Lisieux half guaranteed the truth of the information. Without telling her aunt of this discovery she announced to that lady that it was her great wish to go on and see the beauties of Lisieux.

But though her aunt was simple, there were bounds to her simplicity. "Paula," she said, with an undeceivable air, "I don't think you should run after a young man like this. Suppose he shouldn't care for you by this time."

It was no occasion for further affectation. "I am *sure* he will," answered her niece flatly. "I have not the least fear about it; nor would you, if you knew how he is. He will forgive me anything."

"Well, pray don't show yourself forward. Some people are apt to fly into extremes."

Paula blushed a trifle, and reflected, and made no answer. However, her purpose seemed not to be permanently affected, for the next morning she was up betimes and preparing to depart; and they proceeded almost without stopping to the architectural curiosity-shop which had so quickly interested

her. Nevertheless, her ardent manner of yesterday underwent
a considerable change, as if she had a fear that, as her aunt
suggested, in her endeavour to make amends for cruel injustice, she was allowing herself to be carried too far.

On nearing the place she said, "Aunt, I think you had better
call upon him; and you need not tell him we have come on
purpose. Let him think, if he will, that we heard he was here,
and would not leave without seeing him. You can also tell him
that I am anxious to clear up a misunderstanding, and ask him
to call at our hotel."

But as she looked over the dreary suburban erections which
lined the road from the railway to the old quarter of the town,
it occurred to her that Somerset would at that time of day be
engaged in one or other of the mediæval buildings thereabout,
and that it would be a much neater thing to meet him as if by
chance in one of these edifices than to call upon him anywhere.
Instead of putting up at any hotel, they left the maids and
baggage at the station; and hiring a carriage, Paula told the
coachman to drive them to such likely places as she could
think of.

"He'll never forgive you," said her aunt, as they rumbled
into the town.

"Won't he," said Paula, with soft repose. "I'll see about
that."

"What are you going to do when you find him? Tell him
point-blank that you are in love with him?"

"Act in such a manner that he may tell me he is in love with
me."

They first visited a large church at the upper end of a square
that sloped its gravelled surface to the western shine, and was
pricked out with little avenues of young pollard limes. The
church within was one to make any Gothic architect take
lodgings in its vicinity for a fortnight, notwithstanding that it
was just now crowded with a forest of scaffolding by reason of
repairs in progress. Mrs. Goodman sat down outside, and
Paula, entering, took a walk in the form of a horse-shoe; that
is, up the south aisle, round the apse, and down the north
side; but no figure of a melancholy young man sketching met
her eye anywhere. The sun that blazed in at the west doorway

smote her face as she emerged from beneath it, and revealed real sadness there.

"This is not all the old architecture of the town by far," she said to her auaunt with an air of confidence. "Coachman, drive to St. Jacques'."

He was not at St. Jacques'. Looking from the west end of that building the girl observed the end of a steep narrow street of antique character, which seemed a likely haunt. Beckoning to her aunt to follow in the fly Paula walked down the street.

She was transported to the Middle Ages. It contained the shops of tinkers, braziers, bellows-menders, hollow-turners, and other quaintest trades, their fronts open to the street beneath stories of timber overhanging so far on each side that a slit of sky was left at the top for the light to descend, and no more. A blue misty obscurity pervaded the atmosphere, into which the sun thrust oblique staves of light. It was a street for a mediævalist to revel in, toss up his hat and shout hurrah in, send for his luggage, come and live in, die and be buried in. She had never supposed such a street to exist outside the imaginations of antiquarians. Smells direct from the sixteenth century hung in the air in all their original integrity and without a modern taint. The faces of the people in the doorways seemed those of individuals who habitually gazed on the great Francis, and spoke of Henry the Eighth as the king across the sea.

She inquired of a coppersmith if an English artist had been seen here lately. With a suddenness that almost discomfited her he announced that such a man had been seen, sketching a house just below—the "Vieux Manoir de Francois premier." Just turning to see that her aunt was following in the fly, Paula advanced to the house. The wood framework of the lower story was black and varnished; the upper story was brown and not varnished; carved figures of dragons, griffins, satyrs, and mermaids swarmed over the front; an ape stealing apples was the subject of this cantilever, a man undressing of that. These figures were cloaked with little cobwebs which waved in the breeze, so that each figure seemed alive.

She examined the woodwork closely; here and there she discerned pencil-marks which had no doubt been jotted thereon by Somerset as points of admeasurement, in the way she had seen him mark them at the castle. Some fragments of paper lay below; there were pencilled lines on them, and they bore a strong resemblance to a spoilt leaf of Somerset's sketch-book. Paula glanced up, and from a window above protruded an old woman's head, which, with the exception of the white handkerchief tied round it, was so nearly the colour of the carvings that she might easily have passed as a piece with them. The aged woman continued motionless, the remains of her eyes being bent upon Paula, who asked her in Englishwoman's French where the sketcher had gone. Without replying, the crone produced a hand and extended finger from her side, and pointed towards the lower end of the street.

Paula went on, the carriage following with difficulty, on account of the obstructions in the thoroughfare. At bottom, the street abutted on a wide one with customary modern life flowing through it; and as she looked, Somerset crossed her front along this street, hurrying as if for a wager.

By the time Paula had reached the bottom Somerset was a long way to the left, and she recognized to her dismay that the busy transverse street was one which led to the railway. She quickened her pace to a run; he did not see her; he even walked faster. She looked behind for the carriage. The driver in emerging from the sixteenth-century street to the nineteenth had apparently turned to the right, instead of to the left as she had done, so that her aunt had lost sight of her. However, she did not mind it, if Somerset would but look back! He partly turned, but not far enough, and it was only to hail a passing omnibus upon which she discerned his luggage. Somerset jumped in, the omnibus drove on, and diminished up the long road. Paula stood hopelessly still, and in a few minutes puffs of steam showed her that the train had gone.

She turned and waited, the two or three children who had gathered round her looking up sympathisingly in her face. Her aunt, having now discovered the direction of her flight, drove up and beckoned to her.

"What's the matter?" asked Mrs. Goodman in alarm.

"Why?"

"That you should run like that, and look so woe-begone."

"Nothing: only I have decided not to stay in this town."

"What! he is gone, I suppose?"

"Yes!" exclaimed Paula with tears of vexation in her eyes. "It isn't every man who gets a woman of my position to run after him on foot, and alone, and he ought to have looked round! Drive to the station; I want to make an inquiry."

On reaching the station she asked the booking-clerk some questions, and returned to her aunt with a cheerful countenance. "Mr. Somerset has only gone to Caen," she said. "He is the only Englishman who went by this train, so there is no mistake. There is no other train for two hours. We will go on then—shall we?"

"I am indifferent," said Mrs. Goodman. "But, Paula, do you think this quite right? Perhaps he is not so anxious for your forgiveness as you think. Perhaps he saw you, and wouldn't stay."

A momentary dismay crossed her face, but it passed, and she answered, "Aunt, that's nonsense. I know him well enough, and can assure you that if he had only known I was running after him, he would have looked round sharply enough, and would have given his little finger rather than have missed me! I don't make myself so silly as to run after a gentleman without good grounds, for I know well that it is an undignified thing to do. Indeed, I could never have thought of doing it, if I had not been so miserably in the wrong!"

CHAPTER II

THAT evening when the sun was dropping out of sight they
started for the city of Somerset's pilgrimage. Paula seated
herself with her face towards the western sky, watching from
her window the broad red horizon, across which moved
scattered trees shrouded to human shapes, like the walking
forms in Nebuchadnezzar's furnace. It was dark when the
travellers drove into Caen.

She still persisted in her wish to casually encounter Somerset
in some aisle, lady-chapel, or crypt to which he might have
betaken himself to copy and learn the secret of the great artists
who had erected those nooks. Mrs. Goodman was for discovering his inn, and calling upon him in a straightforward way;
but Paula seemed afraid of it, and they went out in the morning
on foot. First they searched the church of St. Sauveur; he was
not there; next the church of St. Jean; then the church of St.
Pierre; but he did not reveal himself, nor had any verger seen
or heard of such a man. Outside the latter church was a public
flower-garden, and she sat down to consider beside a round
pool in which water-lilies grew and gold-fish swam, near beds
of fiery geraniums, dahlias, and verbenas just past their bloom.
Her enterprise had not been justified by its results so far; but
meditation still urged her to listen to the little voice within and
push on. She accordingly rejoined her aunt, and they drove up
the hill to the Abbaye aux Dames, the day by this time having
grown hot and oppressive.

The church seemed absolutely empty, the void being
emphasized by its grateful coolness. But on going towards the
east end they perceived a bald gentleman close to the screen,
looking to the right and to the left as if much perplexed. Paula
merely glanced over him, his back being towards her, and
turning to her aunt said softly, "I wonder how we get into the
choir?"

"That's just what I am wondering," said the old gentleman,

abruptly facing round, and Paula discovered that the countenance was not unfamiliar to her eye. Since knowing Somerset she had added to her gallery of celebrities a portrait of his father, the Academician, and he it was who now confronted her.

For the moment embarrassment, due to complicated feelings, brought a slight blush to her cheek, but being well aware that he did not know her, she answered, coolly enough, "I suppose we must ask some one."

"And we certainly would if there were any one to ask," he said, still looking eastward, and not much at her. "I have been here a long time, but nobody comes. Not that I want to get in on my own account; for though it is thirty years since I last set foot in this place, I remember it as if it were but yesterday."

"Indeed. I have never been here before," said Paula.

"Naturally. But I am looking for a young man who is making sketches in some of these buildings, and it is as likely as not that he is in the crypt under this choir, for it is just such out-of-the-way nooks that he prefers. It is very provoking that he should not have told me more distinctly in his letter where to find him."

Mrs. Goodman, who had gone to make inquiries, now came back, and informed them that she had learnt that it was necessary to pass through the Hôtel-Dieu to the choir, to do which they must go outside. Thereupon they walked on together, and Mr. Somerset, quite ignoring his troubles, made remarks upon the beauty of the architecture; and in absence of mind, by reason either of the subject, or of his listener, retained his hat in his hand after emerging from the church, while they walked all the way across the Place and into the Hospital gardens.

"A very civil man," said Mrs. Goodman to Paula privately.

"Yes," said Paula, who had not told her aunt that she recognised him.

One of the Sisters now preceded them towards the choir and crypt, Mr. Somerset asking her if a young Englishman was or had been sketching there. On receiving a reply in the negative, Paula nearly betrayed herself by turning, as if her business there, too, ended with the information. However, she went on again, and made a pretence of looking round, Mr. Somerset also staying in a spirit of friendly attention to his country-women. They did not part from him till they had come out from the crypt, and again reached the west front, on their way to which he additionally explained that it was his son he was looking for, who had arranged to meet him here, but had mentioned no inn at which he might be expected.

When he had left them, Paula informed her aunt whose company they had been sharing. Her aunt began expostulating with Paula for not telling Mr. Somerset what they had seen of his son's movements. "It would have eased his mind at least," she said.

"I was not bound to ease his mind at the expense of showing what I would rather conceal. I am continually hampered in such generosity as that by the circumstance of being a woman!"

"Well, it is getting too late to search further to-night."

It was indeed almost evening twilight in the streets, though the graceful freestone spires to a depth of about twenty feet from their summits were still dyed with the orange tints of a vanishing sun. The two relatives dined privately as usual, after which Paula looked out of the window of her room, and reflected upon the events of the day. A tower rising into the sky quite near at hand showed her that some church or other stood within a few steps of the hotel archway, and saying nothing to Mrs. Goodman, she quietly cloaked herself, and went out towards it, apparently with the view of disposing of a portion of a dull dispiriting evening. The church was open, and on entering she found that it was only lighted by seven candles burning before the altar of a chapel on the south side, the mass of the building being in deep shade. Motionless outlines, which resolved themselves into the forms of kneeling women, were darkly visible among the chairs, and in the triforium above the arcades there was one hitherto unnoticed radiance, dim as that of a glowworm in the grass. It was seemingly the effect of a solitary tallow-candle behind the masonry.

A priest came in, unlocked the door of a confessional with a click which sounded loud in the silence, and entered it; a woman followed, disappeared within the curtain of the same, emerging again in about five minutes, followed by the priest, who locked up his door with another loud click, like a tradesman full of business, and came down the aisle to go out. In the lobby he spoke to another woman, who replied, "Ah, oui, Monsieur l'Abbé!"

Two woman having spoken to him, there could be no harm in a third doing likewise. "Monsieur L'Abbé," said Paula in French, "could you indicate to me the stairs of the triforium?" and she signified her reason for wishing to know by pointing to the glimmering light above.

"Ah, he is a friend of yours, the Englishman?" pleasantly said the priest, recognising her nationality; and taking her to a little door he conducted her up a stone staircase, at the top of which he showed her the long blind story over the aisle arches which led round to where the light was. Cautioning her not to stumble over the uneven floor, he left her and descended. His words had signified that Somerset was here.

It was a gloomy place enough that she found herself in, but the seven candles below on the opposite altar, and a faint sky light from the clerestory, lent enough rays to guide her. Paula walked on to the bend of the apse: here were a few chairs, and the origin of the light.

This was a candle stuck at the end of a sharpened stick, the latter entering a joint in the stones. A young man was sketching by the glimmer. But there was no need for the blush which had prepared itself beforehand; the young man was Mr. Cockton, Somerset's youngest draughtsman.

Paula could have cried aloud with disappointment. Cockton recognized Miss Power, and appearing much surprised, rose from his seat with a bow, and said hastily, "Mr. Somerset left to-day."

"I did not ask for him," said Paula.

"No, Miss Power: but I thought——"

"Yes, yes—you know, of course, that he has been my architect. Well, it happens that I should like to see him, if he can call on me. Which way did he go?"

"He's gone to Étretât."

"What for? There are no abbeys to sketch at Étretât."

Cockton looked at the point of his pencil, and with a

hesitating motion of his lip answered, "Mr. Somerset said he was tired."

"Of what?"

"He said he was sick and tired of holy places, and would go to some wicked spot or other, to get that consolation which holiness could not give. But he only said it casually to Knowles, and perhaps he did not mean it."

"Knowles is here too?"

"Yes, Miss Power, and Bowles. Mr. Somerset has been kind enough to give us a chance of enlarging our knowledge of French Early-pointed, and pays half the expenses."

Paula said a few other things to the young man, walked slowly round the triforium as if she had come to examine it, and returned down the staircase. On getting back to the hotel she told her aunt, who had just been having a nap, that next day they would go to Étretât for a change.

"Why? There are no old churches at Étretât."

"No. But I am sick and tired of holy places, and want to go to some wicked spot or other to find that consolation which holiness cannot give."

"For shame, Paula! Now I know what it is; you have heard that he's gone there! You needn't try to blind me."

"I don't care where he's gone!" cried Paula, petulantly. In a moment, however, she smiled at herself, and added, "You must take that for what it is worth. I have made up my mind to let him know from my own lips how the misunderstanding arose. That done, I shall leave him, and probably never see him again. My conscience will be clear."

The next day they took the steamboat down the Orne, intending to reach Étretât by way of Havre. Just as they were moving off an elderly gentleman under a large white sunshade, and carrying his hat in his hand, was seen leisurely walking down the wharf at some distance, but obviously making for the boat.

"A gentleman!" said the mate.

"Who is he?" said the captain.

"An English," said Clémentine.

Nobody knew more, but as leisure was the order of the day the engines were stopped, on the chance of his being a passenger, and all eyes were bent upon him in conjecture. He disappeared and reappeared from behind a pile of merchandise and approached the boat at an easy pace, whereupon the gangway was replaced, and he came on board, removing his hat to Paula, quietly thanking the captain for stopping, and saying to Mrs. Goodman, "I am nicely in time."

It was Mr. Somerset the elder, who by degrees informed our travellers, as sitting on their camp-stools they advanced between the green banks bordered by elms, that he was going to Étretât; that the young man he had spoken of yesterday had gone to that romantic watering-place instead of studying art at Caen, and that he was going to join him there.

Paula preserved an entire silence as to her own intentions, partly from natural reticence, and partly, as it appeared, from the difficulty of explaining a complication which was not very clear to herself. At Havre they parted from Mr. Somerset, and did not see him again till they were driving over the hills towards Étretât in a carriage and four, when the white umbrella became visible far ahead among the outside passengers of the coach to the same place. In a short time they had passed and cut in before this vehicle, but soon became aware that their carriage, like the coach, was one of a straggling procession of conveyances, some mile and a half in length, all bound for the village between the cliffs.

In descending the long hill shaded by lime trees which sheltered their place of destination this procession closed up, and they perceived that all the visitors and native population had turned out to welcome them, the daily arrival of new sojourners at this hour being the chief excitement of Étretât. The coach which had preceded them all the way, at more or less remoteness, was now quite close, and in passing along the village street they saw Mr. Somerset wave his hand to somebody in the crowd below. A felt hat was waved in the air in response, the coach swept into the inn-yard, followed by the idlers, and all disappeared. Paula's face was crimson as their own carriage swept round in the opposite direction to the rival inn.

Once in her room she breathed like a person who had finished a long chase. They did not go down before dinner, but when it was almost dark Paula begged her aunt to wrap herself up and come with her to the shore hard by. The beach was deserted, everybody being at the Casino; the gate stood invitingly open, and they went in. Here the brilliantly lit terrace was crowded with promenaders, and outside the yellow palings, surmounted by its row of lamps, rose the voice of the invisible sea. Groups of people were sitting under the veran- dah, the women mostly in wraps, for the air was growing chilly. Through the windows at their back an animated scene disclosed itself in the shape of a room-full of waltzers, the strains of the band striving in the ear for mastery over the sounds of the sea. The dancers came round a couple at a time, and were individually visible to those people without who chose to look that way, which was what Paula did.

"Come away, come away!" she suddenly said. "It is not right for us to be here."

Her exclamation had its origin in what she had at that moment seen within, the spectacle of Mr. George Somerset whirling round the room with a young lady of uncertain nationality but pleasing figure. Paula was not accustomed to show the white feather too clearly, but she soon had passed out through those yellow gates and retreated, till the mixed music of sea and band had resolved into that of the sea alone.

"Well!" said her aunt, half in soliloquy, "do you know who I saw dancing there, Paula? Our Mr. Somerset, if I don't make a great mistake!"

"It was likely enough that you did," sedately replied her niece. "He left Caen with the intention of seeking distractions of a lighter kind than those furnished by art, and he has merely succeeded in finding them. But he has made my duty rather a difficult one. Still, it was my duty, for I very greatly wronged him. Perhaps, however, I have done enough for honour's sake. I would have humiliated myself by an apology if I had found him in any other situation; but, of course, one can't be expected to take *much* trouble when he is seen going on like that."

The coolness with which she began her remarks had devel- oped into something like warmth as she concluded.

"He is only dancing with a lady he probably knows very well."

"He doesn't know her—I can see he doesn't know her! We will go away tomorrow. This place has been greatly over-praised."

"The place is well enough, as far as I can see."

"He is carrying out his programme to the letter. He plunges into excitement in the most reckless manner, and I tremble for the consequences. I can do no more: I have humiliated myself into following him, believing that in giving too ready credence to appearances I had been narrow and inhuman, and had caused him much misery. But he does not mind, and he has no misery; he seems just as well as ever. How much this finding him has cost me! After all, I did not deceive him. He must have acquired a natural aversion for me. I have allowed myself to be interested in a man of very common qualities, and am now bitterly alive to the shame of having sought him out. I heartily detest him! I will go back—aunt, you are right—I had no business to come. . . . His light conduct has rendered him uninteresting to me!"

CHAPTER III

WHEN she rose the next morning the bell was clanging for the second breakfast, and people were pouring in from the beach in every variety of attire. Paula, whom a restless night had left with a headache, which, however, she said nothing about, was reluctant to emerge from the seclusion of her chamber, till her aunt, discovering what was the matter with her, suggested that a few minutes in the open air would refresh her; and they went downstairs into the hotel gardens.

The clatter of the big breakfast within was audible from this spot, and the noise seemed suddenly to inspirit Paula, who proposed to enter. Her aunt assented. In the verandah under which they passed was a rustic hat-stand in the form of a tree, upon which hats and other body-gear hung like bunches of fruit. Paula's eye fell upon a felt hat to which a small block-book was attached by a string. She knew that hat and block-book well, and turning to Mrs. Goodman said, "After all, I don't want the breakfast they are having: let us order one of our own as usual. And we'll have it here."

She led on to where some little tables were placed under the tall shrubs, followed by her aunt, who was in turn followed by the proprietress of the hotel, that lady having discovered from the French maid that there was good reason for paying these ladies ample personal attention.

"Is the gentleman to whom that sketch-book belongs staying here?" Paula carelessly inquired, as she indicated the object on the hat-stand.

"Ah, no!" deplored the proprietress. "The hotel was full when Mr. Somerset came. He stays at a cottage beyond the Rue Anicet Bourgeois: he only has his meals here."

Paula had taken her seat under the fuchsia-trees in such a manner that she could observe all the exits from the *salle à manger*; but for the present none of the breakfasters emerged, the only moving objects on the scene being the waitresses who ran hither and thither across the court, the cook's assistants with baskets of long bread, and the laundresses with baskets of sun-bleached linen. Further back, towards the inn-yard, stablemen were putting in the horses for starting the flys and coaches to Les Ifs, the nearest railway-station.

"Suppose the Somersets should be going off by one of these conveyances," said Mrs. Goodman as she sipped her tea.

"Well, aunt, then they must," replied the younger lady with composure.

Nevertheless she looked with some misgiving at the nearest stableman as he led out four white horses, harnessed them, and leisurely brought a brush with which he began blacking their yellow hoofs. All the vehicles were ready at the door by the time breakfast was over, and the inmates soon turned out, some to mount the omnibuses and carriages, some to ramble on the adjacent beach, some to climb the verdant slopes, and some to make for the cliffs that shut in the vale. The fuchsia-trees which sheltered Paula's breakfast-table from the blaze of the sun, also screened it from the eyes of the outpouring company, and she sat on with her aunt in perfect comfort, till among the last of the stream came Somerset and his father. Paula reddened at being so near the former at last. It was with sensible relief that she observed them turn towards the cliffs and not to the carriages, and thus signify that they were not going off that day.

Neither of the two saw the ladies, and when the latter had finished their tea and coffee they followed to the shore, where they sat for nearly an hour, reading and watching the bathers. At length footsteps crunched among the pebbles in their vicinity, and looking out from her sunshade Paula saw the two Somersets close at hand.

The elder recognised her, and the younger, observing his father's action of courtesy, turned his head. It was a revelation to Paula, for she was shocked to see that he appeared worn and ill. The expression of his face changed at sight of her, increasing its shade of paleness; but he immediately withdrew his eyes and passed by.

Somerset was as much surprised at encountering her thus as she had been distressed to see him. As soon as they were out of hearing, he asked his father quietly, "What strange thing is this, that Lady De Stancy should be here and her husband not with her? Did she bow to me, or to you?"

"Lady De Stancy—that young lady?" asked the puzzled painter. He proceeded to explain all he knew; that she was a young lady he had met on his journey at two or three different times; moreover, that if she were his son's client—the woman who was to have become Lady De Stancy—she was Miss Power still; for he had seen in some newspaper two days before leaving England that the wedding had been postponed on account of her illness.

Somerset was so greatly moved that he could hardly speak connectedly to his father as they paced on together. "But she is not ill, as far as I can see," he said. "The wedding postponed?—You are sure the word was postponed?—Was it broken off?"

"No, it was postponed. I meant to have told you before, knowing you would be interested as the castle architect; but it slipped my memory in the bustle of arriving."

"I am not the castle architect."

"The devil you are not—what are you then?"

"Well, I am not that."

Somerset the elder, though not of penetrating nature, began to see that here lay an emotional complication of some sort, and reserved further inquiry till a more convenient occasion. They had reached the end of the level beach where the cliff began to rise, and as this impediment naturally stopped their walk they retraced their steps. On again nearing the spot where Paula and her aunt were sitting, the painter would have deviated to the hotel; but as his son persisted in going straight on, in due course they were opposite the ladies again. By this time Miss Power, who had appeared anxious during their absence, regained her self-control. Going towards her old lover she said, with a smile, "I have been looking for you!"

"Why have you been doing that?" said Somerset, in a voice which he failed to keep as steady as he could wish.

"Because—I want some architect to continue the restoration. Do you withdraw your resignation?"

Somerset appeared unable to decide for a few instants. "Yes," he then answered.

For the moment they had ignored the presence of the painter and Mrs. Goodman, but Somerset now made them known to one another, and there was friendly intercourse all round.

"When will you be able to resume operations at the castle?" she asked, as soon as she could again speak directly to Somerset.

"As soon as I can get back. Of course I only resume it at your special request."

"Of course." To one who had known all the circumstances it would have seemed a thousand pities that, after again getting face to face with him, she did not explain, without delay, the whole mischief that had separated them. But she did not do it—perhaps from the inherent awkwardness of such a topic at this idle time. She confined herself simply to the above-mentioned business-like request, and when the party had walked a few steps together they separated, with mutual promises to meet again.

"I hope you have explained your mistake to him, and how it arose, and everything?" said her aunt when they were alone.

"No, I did not."

"What, not explain after all?" said her amazed relative.

"I decided to put it off."

"Then I think you decided very wrongly. Poor young man, he looked so ill!"

"Did you, too, think he looked ill? But he danced last night. Why did he dance?" She turned and gazed regretfully at the corner round which the Somersets had disappeared.

"I don't know why he danced; but if I had known you were going to be so silent, I would have explained the mistake myself."

"I wish you had. But no; I have said I would; and I must."

Paula's avoidance of *tables d'hôte* did not extend to the present one. It was quite with alacrity that she went down; and with her entry the antecedent hotel beauty, who had reigned for the last five days at that meal, was unceremoniously deposed by the guests. Mr. Somerset the elder came in, but nobody with him. His seat was on Paula's left hand, Mrs.

Goodman being on Paula's right, so that all the conversation was between the Academician and the younger lady. When the latter had again retired upstairs with her aunt, Mrs. Goodman expressed regret that young Mr. Somerset was absent from the table. "Why has he kept away?" she asked.

"I don't know—I didn't ask," said Paula sadly. "Perhaps he doesn't care to meet us again."

"That's because you didn't explain."

"Well—why didn't the old man give me an opportunity?" exclaimed the niece with suppressed excitement. "He would scarcely say anything but yes and no, and gave me no chance at all of introducing the subject. I wanted to explain—I came all the way on purpose—I would have begged George's pardon on my knees if there had been any way of beginning; but there was not, and I could not do it!"

Though she slept badly that night, Paula promptly appeared in the public room to breakfast, and that not from motives of vanity; for, while not unconscious of her accession to the unstable throne of chief beauty in the establishment, she seemed too preoccupied to care for the honour just then, and would readily have changed places with her unhappy predecessor, who lingered on in the background like a candle after sunrise.

Mrs. Goodman was determined to trust no longer to Paula for putting an end to what made her so restless and self-reproachful. Seeing old Mr. Somerset enter to a little side-table behind for lack of room at the crowded centre tables, again without his son, she turned her head and asked point-blank where the young man was.

Mr. Somerset's face became a shade graver than before. "My son is unwell," he replied; "so unwell that he has been advised to stay indoors and take perfect rest."

"I do hope it is nothing serious?"

"I hope so too. The fact is, he has overdone himself a little. He was not well when he came here; and to make himself worse he must needs go dancing at the Casino with a young American lady who is here with her family, and whom he met in London last year. I advised him against it, but he seemed desperately determined to shake off lethargy by any rash means, and wouldn't listen to me. Luckily he is not in the hotel, but in a quiet cottage a hundred yards up the hill.

Paula, who had heard all, did not show or say what she felt at the news; but after breakfast, on meeting the landlady in a passage, alone, she asked with some anxiety if there were a really skilful medical man in Étretât; and on being told that there was, and his name, she went back to look for Mr. Somerset; but he had gone.

They heard nothing more of young Somerset all that morning, but towards evening, while Paula sat at her window, looking over the heads of fuchsias upon the promenade beyond, she saw the painter walk by. She immediately went to her aunt and begged her to go out and ask Mr. Somerset if his son had improved.

"I will send Milly or Clémentine," said Mrs. Goodman.

"I wish you would see him yourself."

"He has gone on. I shall never find him."

"He has only gone round to the front," persisted Paula. "Do walk that way, auntie, and ask him."

Thus pressed, Mrs. Goodman acquiesced, and brought back intelligence to Miss Power, who had watched them through the window, that his son did not positively improve, but that his American friends were very kind to him.

Having made use of her aunt, Paula seemed particularly anxious to get rid of her again, and when that lady sat down to write letters, Paula went to her own room, hastily dressed herself without assistance, asked privately the way to the cottage, and went off thitherward unobserved.

At the upper end of the lane she saw a little house answering to the description, whose front garden, window-sills, palings, and door-step were literally ablaze with nasturtiums in bloom. She entered this inhabited nosegay, quietly asked for the invalid, and if he were well enough to see Miss Power. The woman of the house soon returned, and she was conducted up a crooked staircase to Somerset's modest apartments. It appeared that some rooms in this dwelling had been furnished by the landlady of the inn, who hired them of the tenant during the summer season to use as an *annexe* to the hotel.

Admitted to the outer room she beheld her architect looking

as unarchitectural as possible; lying on a small couch which was drawn up to the open casement, whence he had a back view of the window flowers, and enjoyed a green transparency through the undersides of the same nasturtium leaves that presented their faces to the passers without.

When the latch had again clicked into the catch of the closed door Paula went up to the invalid, upon whose pale and interesting face a flush had arisen simultaneously with the announcement of her name. He would have sprung up to receive her, but she pressed him down, and throwing all reserve on one side for the first time in their intercourse, she crouched beside the sofa, whispering with roguish solicitude, her face not too far from his own: "How foolish you are, George, to get ill just now when I have been wanting so much to see you again!—I am so sorry to see you like this—what I said to you when we met on the shore was not what I had come to say!"

Somerset took her by the hand. "Then what did you come to say, Paula?" he asked.

"I wanted to tell you that the mere wanton wandering of a capricious mind was not the cause of my estrangement from you. There has been a great deception practised—the exact nature of it I cannot tell you plainly just at present; it is too painful—but it is all over, and I can assure you of my sorrow at having behaved as I did, and of my sincere friendship now as ever."

"There is nothing I shall value so much as that. It will make my work at the castle very pleasant to feel that I can consult you about it without fear of intruding on you against your wishes."

"Yes, perhaps it will. But—you do not comprehend me."

"You have been an enigma always."

"And you have been provoking; but never so provoking as now. I wouldn't for the world tell you the whole of my fancies as I came hither this evening; but I should think your natural intuition would suggest what they were."

"It does, Paula. But there are motives of delicacy which prevent my acting on what is suggested to me."

"Delicacy is a gift, and you should thank God for it; but in

some cases it is not so precious as we would persuade
ourselves."

"Not when the woman is rich, and the man is poor?"

"Oh, George Somerset—be cold, or angry, or anything, but
don't be like this! It is never worth a woman's while to show
regret for her injustice; for all she gets by it is an accusation of
want of delicacy."

"Indeed I don't accuse you of that—I warmly, tenderly
thank you for your kindness in coming here to see me."

"Well, perhaps you do. But I am now in I cannot tell what
mood—I will not tell what mood, for it would be confessing
more than I ought. This finding you out is a piece of weakness
that I shall not repeat; and I have only one thing more to say.
I have served you badly, George, I know that; but it is never
too late to mend; and I have come back to you. However, I
shall never run after you again, trust me for that, for it is not
the woman's part. Still, before I go, that there may be no
mistake as to my meaning, and misery entailed on us for want
of a word, I'll add this; that if you want to marry me as you
once did, you must say so; for I am here to be asked."

It would be superfluous to transcribe Somerset's reply, and
the remainder of the scene between the pair. Let it suffice that
half an hour afterwards, when the sun had almost gone down,
Paula walked briskly into the hotel, troubled herself nothing
about dinner, but went upstairs to their sitting-room, where
her aunt presently found her upon the couch looking up at the
ceiling through her fingers. They talked on different subjects
for some time till the old lady said, "Mr. Somerset's cottage is
the one covered with flowers up the lane, I hear."

"Yes," said Paula.

"How do you know?"

"I've been there. . . . We are going to be married, aunt."

"Indeed!" replied Mrs. Goodman. "Well, I thought this
might be the end of it: you were determined on the point; and
I am not much surprised at your news. Your father was very
wise after all in entailing everything so strictly upon your
offspring; for if he had not I should have been driven wild
with the responsibility!"

"Aunt, now that the murder is out," continued Paula,

passing over that view of the case, "I don't mind telling you that somehow or other I have got to like George Somerset as desperately as a woman can care for any man. I thought I should have died when I saw him dancing, and feared I had lost him! He seemed ten times nicer than ever then! So silly we women are, that I wouldn't marry a duke in preference to him. There, that's my honest feeling, and you must make what you can of it; my conscience is clear, thank Heaven."

"Have you fixed the day?"

"No," continued the young lady, still watching the sleeping flies on the ceiling. "It is left unsettled between us, while I come and ask you if there would be any harm—if it could conveniently be before we return to England?"

"Paula, this is too precipitate."

"On the contrary, aunt. In matrimony, as in some other things, you should be slow to decide, but quick to execute. Nothing on earth would make me marry another man; I know every fibre of his character; and he knows a good many fibres of mine; so as there is nothing more to be learnt, why shouldn't we marry at once? On one point I am firm: I will never return to that castle as Miss Power. A nameless dread comes over me when I think of it—a fear that some uncanny influence of the dead De Stancys would drive me again from him. Oh, if it were to do that," she murmured, burying her face in her hands, "I really think it would be more than I could bear."

"Very well," said Mrs. Goodman; "we will see what can be done. I will write to Mr. Wardlaw."

CHAPTER IV

ON a windy afternoon in November, when more than two months had closed over the incidents previously recorded, a number of farmers were sitting in a room of the King's Arms Inn, Markton, that was used for the weekly ordinary. It was a long, low apartment, formed by the union of two or three smaller rooms, with a bow-window looking upon the street, and at the present moment was pervaded by a blue fog from tobacco-pipes, and a temperature like that of a kiln. The body of farmers who still sat on there was greater than usual, owing to the cold air without, the tables having been cleared of dinner for some time and their surface stamped with liquid circles by the feet of numerous glasses.

Besides the farmers there were present several professional men of the town, who found it desirable to dine here on market-days for the opportunity it afforded them of increasing their practice among the agriculturists, many of whom were men of large balances, even luxurious livers, who drove to market in elegant phaetons drawn by horses of supreme blood, bone, and action, in a style never anticipated by their fathers when jogging thither in light carts, or afoot with a butter-basket on each arm.

The buzz of groggy conversation was suddenly impinged on by the notes of a peal of bells from the tower hard by. Almost at the same instant the door of the room opened, and there entered the landlord of the little inn at Sleeping-Green. Drawing his supply of cordials from this superior house, to which he was subject, he came here at stated times like a prebendary to the cathedral of his diocesan, afterwards retailing to his own humbler audience the sentiments which he had learnt of this. But curiosity being awakened by the church bells the usual position was for the moment reversed, and one of the farmers, saluting him by name, asked him the reason of their striking up at that time of day.

"My mis'ess out yonder," replied the rural landlord, nodding sideways, "is coming home with her fancy-man. They have been a-gaying together this turk of a while in foreign parts.—Here, maid!—what with the wind, and standing about, my blood's as low as water—bring us a thimbleful of that that isn't gin and not far from it."

"It is true, then, that she's become Mrs. Somerset?" indifferently asked a farmer in broadcloth, tenant of an estate in quite another direction than hers, as he contemplated the grain of the table immediately surrounding the foot of his glass.

"True—of course it is," said Havill, who was also present, in the tone of one who, though sitting in this rubicund company, was not of it. "I could have told you the truth of it any day these last five weeks."

Among those who had lent an ear was Dairyman Jinks, an old gnarled character who wore a white fustian coat and yellow leggings; the only man in the room who never dressed up in dark clothes for marketing. He now asked, "Married abroad, was they? And how long will a wedding abroad stand good for in this country?"

"As long as a wedding at home."

"Will it? Faith; I didn't know: how should I? I thought it might be some new plan o' folks for leasing women now they be so plentiful, so as to get rid o' 'em when the men be tired o' 'em, and hev spent all their money."

"He won't be able to spend her money," said the landlord of Sleeping-Green. "'Tis her very own person's—settled upon the hairs of her head for ever."

"O nation! Then if I were the man I shouldn't care for such a one-eyed benefit as that," said Dairyman Jinks, turning away to listen to the talk on his other hand.

"Is that true?" asked the gentleman-farmer in broadcloth.

"It is sufficiently near the truth," said Havill, in an *ex cathedrâ* tone. "There is nothing at all unusual in the arrangement; it was only settled so to prevent any schemer making a beggar of her. If Somerset and she have any children, which probably they will, it will be theirs; and what can a man want more? Besides, there is a large portion of property left to her personal use—quite as much as they can want. Oddly enough, the curiosities and pictures of the castle which belonged to the De Stancys are not restricted from sale: they are hers to do what she likes with. Old Power didn't care for articles that reminded him so much of his predecessors."

"Hey?" said Dairyman Jinks, turning back again, having decided that the conversation on his right hand was, after all, the more interesting. "Well—why can't 'em hire a travelling chap to touch up the picters into her own gaffers and gammers? Then they'd be worth sommat to her."

"Ah, here they are! I thought so," said Havill, who had been standing up at the window for the last few moments. "The ringers were told to begin as soon as the train signalled."

As he spoke a carriage drew up to the hotel-door, followed by another with the maid and luggage. The inmates crowded to the bow-window, except Dairyman Jinks, who had become absorbed in his own reflections.

"What be they stopping here for?" asked one of the previous speakers.

"They are going to stay here to-night," said Havill. "They have come quite unexpectedly, and the castle is in such a state of turmoil that there is not a single carpet down, or room for them to use. We shall get two or three in order by next week."

"Two little people like them will be lost in the chammers of that wandering place!" satirised Dairyman Jinks. "They will be obliged to have a randy every fortnight to keep the moth out of the furniture!"

By this time Somerset was handing out the wife of his bosom, and Dairyman Jinks went on: "That's no more Miss Power that was, than my niece's daughter Kezia is Miss Power—in short it is a different woman altogether!"

"There is no mistake about the woman," said the landlord; "it is her fur clothes that make her look so like a caterpillar on end. Well, she is not a bad bargain! As for Captain De Stancy, he'll fret his gizzard green."

"He's the man she ought to have married," declared the farmer in broadcloth. "As the world goes she ought to have been Lady De Stancy. She gave up her chapel-going, and you might have thought she would have given up her first young man: but she stuck to him, though by all accounts he would soon have been interested in another party."

"'Tis woman's nature to be false except to a man, and man's nature to be true except to a woman," said the landlord of Sleeping-Green. "However, all's well that ends well, and I have something else to think of than new-married couples;" saying which the speaker moved off, and the others returned to their seats, the young pair who had been their theme vanishing through the hotel into some private paradise to rest and dine.

By this time their arrival had become known, and a crowd soon gathered outside, acquiring audacity with continuance there. Raising a hurrah, the group would not leave till Somerset had showed himself on the balcony above; and then declined to go away till Paula also had appeared; when, remarking that her husband seemed a quiet young man enough, and would make a very good borough member when their present one misbehaved himself, the assemblage good-humouredly dispersed.

Among those whose ears had been reached by the hurrah of these idlers was a man in silence and solitude, far out of the town. He was leaning over a gate that divided two meads in the watery levels between Stancy Castle and Markton. He turned his head for a few seconds, then continued his contemplative gaze towards the towers of the castle, visible over the trees as far as was possible in the leaden gloom of the November eve. The military form of the solitary lounger was recognisable as that of Sir William De Stancy, notwithstanding the failing light and his attitude of so resting his elbows on the gate that his hands enclosed the greater part of his face.

The scene was inexpressibly cheerless. No other human creature was apparent, and the only sounds audible above the wind were those of the trickling streams which distributed the water over the meadow. A heron had been standing in one of these rivulets about twenty yards from the officer, and they vied with each other in stillness till the bird suddenly rose and flew off to the plantation in which it was his custom to pass the night with others of his tribe. De Stancy saw the heron rise, and seemed to imagine the creature's departure without a supper to be owing to the increasing darkness; but in another minute he became conscious that the heron had been disturbed by sounds too distant to reach his own ears at the time. They were nearer now, and there came along under the hedge a young man known to De Stancy exceedingly well.

"Ah," he said listlessly, "you have ventured back."

"Yes, captain. Why do you walk out here?"

"The bells began ringing because she and he were expected, and my thoughts naturally dragged me this way. Thank Heaven the battery leaves Markton in a few days, and then the precious place will know me no more!"

"I have heard of it." Turning to where the dim lines of the castle rose he continued: "Well, there it stands."

"And I not in it."

"They are not in it yet either."

"They soon will be."

"Well—what tune is that you were humming, captain?"

"*All is lost now*," replied the captain, grimly.

"Oh no; you have got me, and I am a treasure to any man. I have another match in my eye for you, and shall get you well settled yet, if you keep yourself respectable. So thank God, and take courage."

"Ah, Will—you are a flippant young fool—wise in your own conceit; I say it to my sorrow! 'Twas your dishonesty spoilt all. That lady would have been my wife by fair dealing—time was all I required. But base attacks on a man's character never deserve to win, and if I had once been certain that you had made them, my course would have been very different both towards you and others. But why should I talk to you about this? If I cared an atom what becomes of you I would take you in hand severely enough; not caring, I leave you alone, to go to the devil your own way."

"Thank you kindly, captain. Well, since you have spoken plainly, I will do the same. We De Stancys are a worn-out old party—that's the long and the short of it. We represent conditions of life that have had their day—especially me. Our one remaining chance was an alliance with new aristocrats; and we have failed. We are past and done for. Our line has had five hundred years of glory, and we ought to be content. *Enfin les renards se trouvent chez le pelletier.*"

"Speak for yourself, young consequence, and leave the destinies of old families to respectable philosophers. This fiasco is the direct result of evil conduct, and of nothing else at all. I have managed badly; I countenanced you too far. When I saw your impish tendencies I should have forsworn the alliance."

"Don't sting me, captain. What I have told you is true. As for my conduct, cat will after kind, you know. You should have held your tongue on the wedding morning, and have let me take my chance."

"Is that all I get for saving you from jail? Gad—I alone am the sufferer, and feel I am alone the fool! . . . Come, off with you—I never want to see you any more."

"Part we will, then—till we meet again. It will be a light night hereabouts, I think, this evening."

"A very dark one for me."

"Nevertheless, I think it will be a light night. *Au revoir!*"

Dare went his way, and after a while De Stancy went his. Both were soon lost in the shades.

two by Romney. Apparently by accident, the light being insufficient to distinguish them from portraits, the figure also brought a Raffaelle Virgin-and-Child, a magnificent Tintoretto, a Titian, and a Giorgione.

On these were laid a Raffaelle enamelled miniature portraits of the same illustrious line; afterwards tapestries and

CHAPTER V

THE castle to-night was as gloomy as the meads. As Havill had explained, the habitable rooms were just now undergoing a scour, and the main block of buildings was empty even of the few servants who had been retained, they having for comfort's sake taken up their quarters in the detached rooms adjoining the entrance archway. Hence not a single light shone from the lonely windows, at which ivy leaves tapped like woodpeckers, moved by gusts that were numerous and contrary rather than violent. Within the walls all was silence, chaos, and obscurity, till towards eleven o'clock, when the thick immovable cloud that had dulled the daytime broke into a scudding fleece, through which the moon forded her way as a nebulous spot of watery white, sending light enough, though of a rayless kind, into the castle chambers to show the confusion that reigned there.

At this time an eye might have noticed a figure flitting in and about those draughty apartments, and making no more noise in so doing than a puff of wind. Its motion hither and thither was rapid, but methodical; its bearing absorbed, yet cautious. Though it ran more or less through all the principal rooms, the chief scene of its operations was the Long Gallery overlooking the Pleasance, which was covered by an ornamental wood-and-plaster roof, and contained a whole throng of family portraits, besides heavy old cabinets and the like. The portraits which were of value as works of art were smaller than these, and hung in adjoining rooms.

The manifest occupation of the figure was that of removing these small and valuable pictures from other chambers to the gallery in which the rest were hung, and piling them in a heap in the midst. Included in the group were nine by Sir Peter Lely, five by Vandyck, four by Cornelius Jansen, one by Salvator Rosa (remarkable as being among the few English protraits ever painted by that master), many by Kneller, and two by Romney. Apparently by accident, the light being insufficient to distinguish them from portraits, the figure also brought a Raffaelle Virgin-and-Child, a magnificent Tintoretto, a Titian, and a Giorgione.

On these were laid a large collection of enamelled miniature portraits of the same illustrious line; afterwards tapestries and cushions embroidered with the initials "De S."; and next the cradle presented by Charles the First to the contemporary De Stancy mother, till at length there arose in the middle of the floor a huge heap containing most of what had been personal and peculiar to members of the De Stancy family as distinct from general furniture.

Then the figure went from door to door, and threw open each that was unfastened. It next proceeded to a room on the ground floor, at present fitted up as a carpenter's shop, and knee deep in shavings. An armful of these was added to the pile of objects in the gallery; a window at each end of the gallery was opened, causing a brisk draught along the walls; and then the activity of the figure ceased, and it was seen no more.

Five minutes afterwards a light shone upon the lawn from the windows of the Long Gallery, which glowed with more brilliancy than it had known in the meridian of its Caroline splendours. Thereupon the framed gentleman in the lace collar seemed to open his eyes more widely; he with the flowing locks and turn-up mustachios to part his lips; he in the armour, who was so much like Captain De Stancy, to shake the plates of his mail with suppressed laughter; the lady with the three-stringed pearl necklace, and vast expanse of neck, to nod with satisfaction and triumphantly signify to her adjoining husband that this was a meet and glorious end.

The light increased, and blown upon by the wind roared round the pictures, the tapestries, and the cradle, up to the plaster ceiling and through it into the forest of oak timbers above.

The best sitting-room at the King's Arms in Markton was as cosy this evening as a room can be that lacks the minuter furniture on which cosiness so largely depends. By the fire sat Paula and Somerset, the former with a shawl round her shoulders to keep off the draught which, despite the curtains, forced its way in on this gusty night through the windows opening upon the balcony. Paula held a letter in her hand, the contents of which formed the subject of their conversation. Happy as she was in her general situation, there was for the nonce a tear in her eye.

"MY EVER DEAR PAULA (ran the letter),

"Your last letter has just reached me, and I have followed your account of your travels and intentions with more interest than I can tell. You, who know me, need no assurance of this. At the present moment, however, I am in the whirl of change that has resulted from a resolution taken some time ago, but concealed from almost everybody till now. Why? Well, I will own—from cowardice—fear lest I should be reasoned out of my plan. I am going to steal from the world, Paula, from the social world, for whose gaieties and ambitions I never had much liking, and whose circles I have not the ability to grace. My home, and resting-place till the great rest comes, is with the Protestant Sisterhood at——. Whatever shortcomings may be found in such a community, I believe that I shall be happier there than in any other place.

"Whatever you may think of my judgment in taking this step, I can assure you that I have not done it without consideration. My reasons are good, and my determination is unalterable. But, my own very best friend, and more than sister, don't think that I mean to leave my love and friendship for you behind me. No, Paula; you will *always* be with me, and I believe that if an increase in what I already feel for you be possible, it will be furthered by the retirement and meditation I shall enjoy in my secluded home. My heart is very full, dear—too full to write more. God bless you, and your husband. You must come and see me there; I have not so many friends that I can afford to lose you who have been so kind. I write this with the fellow pen to yours, that you gave when we went to Budmouth together. Good-bye!

"Ever your own sister,

"CHARLOTTE."

Paula had first read this through silently, and now in reading it a second time aloud to Somerset her voice faltered, and she wept outright. "I had been expecting her to live with us always," she said through her tears, "and to think she should have decided to do this!"

"It is a pity, certainly," said Somerset gently. "She was genuine, if anybody ever was; and simple as she was true."

"I am the more sorry," Paula presently resumed, "because of a little plan I had been thinking of with regard to her. You know that the pictures and curiosities of the castle are not included in the things I cannot touch, or impeach, or whatever it is. They are our own to do what we like with. My father felt in devising the estate that, however interesting to the De Stancys those objects might be, they did not concern us—were indeed rather in the way, having been come by so strangely, through Mr. Wilkins, though too valuable to be treated lightly. Now I was going to suggest that we would not sell them—indeed I could not bear to do such a thing with what had belonged to Charlotte's forefathers—but to hand them over to her as a gift, either to keep for herself, or to pass on to her brother, as she should choose. Now I fear there is no hope of it; and yet I shall never like to see them in the house."

"It can be done still, I should think. She can accept them for her brother when he settles, without absolutely taking them into her own possession."

"It would be a kind of generosity which hardly amounts to more than justice (although they were purchased) from a recusant usurper to a dear friend—not that I am a usurper exactly; well, from a representative of the new aristocracy of internationality to a representative of the old aristocracy of exclusiveness."

"What do you call yourself, Paula, since you are not of your father's creed?"

"I suppose I am what poor Mr. Woodwell said—by the way, we must call and see him—something or other that's in Revelation, neither cold nor hot. But of course that's a sub-species—I may be a lukewarm anything. What I really am, as far as I know, is one of that body to whom lukewarmth is not an accident but a provisional necessity, till they see a little more clearly." She had crossed over to his side, and pulling his head towards her whispered a word in his ear.

"Why, Mr. Woodwell said you were that too! You carry your beliefs very comfortably. I shall be glad when enthusiasm is come again."

"I am going to revise and correct my beliefs one of these days when I have thought a little further." She suddenly breathed a sigh and added, "How transitory our best emotions are! In talking of myself I am heartlessly forgetting Charlotte, and becoming happy again. I won't be happy to-night, for her sake!"

A few minutes after this their attention was attracted by a noise of footsteps running along the street; then a heavy tramp of horses, and lumbering of wheels. Other feet were heard scampering at intervals, and soon somebody ascended the staircase and approached their door. The head waiter appeared.

"Ma'am, Stancy Castle is all afire!" said the waiter breathlessly.

Somerset jumped up, drew aside the curtains, and stepped into the bow-window. Right before him rose a blaze. The window looked down the street and along the turnpike road to the very hill on which the castle stood, the keep being visible in the daytime above the trees. Here rose the light, which appeared little further off than a stone's throw instead of nearly two miles. Every curl of smoke and every wave of the flame was distinct, and Somerset fancied he could hear the crackling.

Paula had risen from her seat and joined him in the window, where she heard some people in the street saying that the servants were all safe; after which she gave her mind more fully to the material aspects of the catastrophe.

The whole town was now rushing off to the scene of the conflagration, which, shining directly up the street, showed the burgesses' running figures individually upon the illumined road. Paula was quite ready to act upon Somerset's suggestion that they too should hasten to the spot, and a fly was got ready in a few minutes. With lapse of time Paula evinced more anxiety as to the fate of her castle, and when they had driven as near as it was prudent to do, they dismounted, and went on foot into the throng of people which was rapidly gathering from the town and surrounding villages. Among the faces they recognised Mr. Woodwell, Havill the architect, the rector of the parish, the curate, and many others known to them by sight. These, as soon as they saw the young couple, came forward with words of condolence, imagining them to have been burnt out of bed, and vied with each other in offering them a lodging. Somerset explained where they were staying and that they required no accommodation, Paula interrupting with, "Oh my poor horses, what has become of them?"

"The fire is not near the stables," said Mr. Woodwell. "It broke out in the body of the building. The horses, however, are driven into the field."

"I can assure you, you need not be alarmed, madam," said Havill. "The chief constable is here, and the two town engines, and I am doing all I can. The castle engine unfortunately is out of repair."

Somerset and Paula then went on to another point of view near the gymnasium, where they could not be seen by the crowd. Three quarters of a mile off, on their left hand, the powerful irradiation fell upon the brick chapel in which Somerset had first seen the woman who now stood beside him as his wife. It was the only object visible in that direction, the dull hills and trees behind failing to catch the light. She significantly pointed it out to Somerset, who knew her meaning, and they turned again to the more serious matter.

It had long been apparent that in the face of such a wind all the pigmy appliances that the populace could bring to act upon such a mass of combustion would be unavailing. As much as could burn that night was burnt, while some of that which would not burn crumbled and fell as a formless heap, whence new flames towered up, and inclined to the north-east so far as to singe the trees of the park. The thicker walls of Norman date remained unmoved, partly because of their thickness, and partly because in them stone vaults took the place of wood floors.

The tower clock kept manfully going till it had struck one, its face smiling out from the smoke as if nothing were the matter, after which hour something fell down inside, and it went no more.

Cunningham Haze, with his body of men, was devoted in his attention, and came up to say a word to our two spectators from time to time.

Towards four o'clock the flames diminished, and feeling thoroughly weary, Somerset and Paula remained no longer, returning to Markton as they had come.

On their journey they pondered and discussed what course it would be best to pursue in the circumstances, gradually deciding not to attempt rebuilding the castle unless they were absolutely compelled. True, the main walls were still standing as firmly as ever; but there was a feeling common to both of them that it would be well to make an opportunity of a misfortune, and leaving the edifice in ruins start their married life in a mansion of independent construction hard by the old one, unencumbered with the ghosts of an unfortunate line.

"We will build a new house from the ground, eclectic in style. We will remove the ashes, charred wood, and so on from the ruin, and plant more ivy. The winter rains will soon wash the unsightly smoke from the walls, and Stancy Castle will be beautiful in its decay. You, Paula, will be yourself again, and recover, if you have not already, from the warp given to your mind (according to Woodwell) by the mediævalism of that place."

"And be a perfect representative of 'the modern spirit'?" she inquired; "representing neither the senses and understanding, nor the heart and imagination; but what a finished writer calls 'the imaginative reason'?"

"Yes; for since it is rather in your line you may as well keep straight on."

"Very well, I'll keep straight on; and we'll build a new house beside the ruin, and show the modern spirit for evermore. . . . But, George, I wish——" And Paula repressed a sigh.

"Well?"

"I wish my castle wasn't burnt; and I wish you were a De Stancy!"

THE END

EXPLANATORY NOTES

SOURCES

Björk, Lennart (ed.), *The Literary Notebooks of Thomas Hardy*, vol. i (London: Macmillan, 1985).

Bullen, J. B., *The Expressive Eye: Fiction and Perception in the Work of Thomas Hardy* (Oxford: Clarendon Press, 1986).

Elliott, Ralph W. V., *Thomas Hardy's English* (Oxford: Basil Blackwell, 1984).

Sir Banister Fletcher's A History of Architecture, 18th edition, revised by J. C. Palmes (New York: Scribners, 1975).

Hardy, Florence Emily, *The Early Life of Thomas Hardy* (London: Macmillan, 1928).

Millgate, Michael, *Thomas Hardy: His Career as a Novelist* (London: Bodley Head, 1971).

—— *Thomas Hardy: A Biography* (Oxford: Clarendon Press, 1982).

Oxford English Dictionary (Oxford: Clarendon Press, 1989).

Pinion, F. B., *A Thomas Hardy Dictionary* (New York: New York University Press, 1989).

—— *Thomas Hardy: Art and Thought* (Totowa, NJ: Rowman and Littlefield, 1977).

7 *chevroned*: having ornamental moulding in a zigzag pattern, characteristic of eleventh- and twelfth-century Norman architecture.

gnats . . . incessantly: a reference to John Keats's "To Autumn": "Then in a wailful choir the small gnats mourn | Among the river sallows, borne aloft | Or sinking as the light wind lives or dies". The image of insignificant gnats caught up in the rays of the setting sun appears frequently in Hardy's fiction and poetry and here anticipates the narrator's comment about "human decline and death".

fillets: a fillet is a small, flat band between mouldings separating them from each other.

8 *T-square*: a ruler with a crosspiece or head at one end, used to make parallel lines.

bow-pencil: a small pair of compasses, one leg of which carries a pencil, used to measure or draw curved lines.

—dominant speculative activity . . . future human type: cf. this

description in *The Return of the Native*: "In Clym Yeobright's face could be dimly seen the typical countenance of the future" (iii. ch. 1). In that novel also Hardy argues that only young men of the past, because they were not disturbed by introspection, could be physically beautiful. Like Clym, modern men have their beauty "ruthlessly overrun" by "the parasite, thought" (ii. ch. 6). Hardy may have been influenced by Walter Pater's essay "Winckelmann".

flexuousness: one of Hardy's favourite words to describe faces and figures, suggesting flexibility and grace.

Nazarite: see Numbers 6: 5. Nazarites consecrated themselves to God by taking vows not to drink wine, shave, or cut their hair.

9 *English Gothic architecture . . . English-pointed revival*: the Gothic style that developed in northern France during the twelfth century dominated the architecture of Western Europe until the early sixteenth century. It is characterized by pointed arches and vaults, the large amount of glass in the walls, and an overall feeling of great height. The English Gothic or pointed revival refers to the renewed interest in medieval styles that began in the late eighteenth century and became one of the major influences on Victorian architecture, at its high tide in the 1860s and early 1870s.

Academician: a member of the Royal Academy.

French Gothic mania: the great interest in French medieval designs during the 1850s, perhaps stimulated by the Anglo-French alliance during the Crimean War.

Britton: John Britton (1771–1857) wrote *Architectural Antiquities of Great Britain* (9 vols. 1805–14) and *Cathedral Antiquities of England* (14 vols. 1814–35). His descriptive accounts of the ancient buildings illustrated in the volumes popularized interest in medieval architecture.

Pugin: Augustus W. N. Pugin (1812–52) was an architect, theorist, and propagandist whose work gave impetus to the Gothic revival. The title of one book, *Contrasts; or a Parallel Between the Noble Edifices of the Fourteenth and Fifteenth Centuries, and Similar Buildings of the Present Day; Showing the Present Decay of Taste* (1836), suggests his characteristic moral indignation. Pugin assisted Sir Charles Barry in designing the Houses of Parliament (1836–68), the first major public building of the Gothic revival.

Rickman: Thomas Rickman (1776–1841) was an author and

lecturer on architecture. His book *An Attempt to Discriminate the Styles of English Architecture from the Conquest to the Reformation* (1817) codified and popularized a system of classifying medieval architecture, introducing style names that became an integral part of phraseology: Norman, Early English, Decorated, and Perpendicular.

Scott: Sir George Gilbert Scott (1817–78) was an influential architect and author at the high point of the Gothic revival. His work includes the Albert Memorial at Kensington and numerous churches and secular buildings.

Palladian: influenced by Andrea Palladio (1508–80), a Venetian architect whose study of antique Roman buildings, *I quattro libri dell architettura*, was published all over Europe. The Palladian style, noted for the symmetry of its classical form, prevailed in England from about 1710 to 1750.

Jacobean, Queen-Anne: Jacobean architecture is that of the reign of James I (1603–25), Queen Anne that of the reign of Anne (1702–14). The Victorians borrowed from both styles, which had blended Classical and Renaissance details.

Revett and Stuart: Nicholas Revett (1720–1804) and James Stuart (1713–88) wrote *The Antiquities of Athens* (1762), stimulating interest in Greek architecture.

Chambers: Sir William Chambers (1723–96) was a classicist, an architect, and an author, whose most influential book was *A Treatise on Civil Architecture* (1759).

Five Orders: an order in architecture indicates the design of a column; the Greeks recognized three orders: the Doric, Ionic, and Corinthian; the Romans added the Tuscan and the Composite.

10 *empyrean*: the highest heavenly sphere in ancient and medieval descriptions of the universe.

11 *Georgian times*: during the reigns of George I (1714–27), George II (1727–60), and George III (1760–1820).

small-clothes: knee-breeches of the close-fitting type worn in the eighteenth and the early nineteenth centuries.

12 *chapels-of-ease*: chapels built for the convenience of those who live far from the parish church.

west-gallery period of church-music: Hardy refers to the period when a group of instrumentalists, sometimes accompanied by singers, provided the music for church services. Hardy's father, uncle, and grandfather were musicians in Stinsford Church; *Early Life* reproduces Hardy's drawing of its west gallery, showing the positions of the choir (13). One of their staple hymns was the "New Sabbath" (*Early Life*, 14).

the rule of Monk: William Henry Monk (1823–89) compiled and arranged the tunes for *Hymns, Ancient and Modern*, which within a decade of its first publication in 1861 had become the representative Church of England hymnal, contributing to the standardization of church music.

13 *en rapport*: (French) in sympathy or harmony.

recently-erected chapel . . . iron stove-pipe: a sharp contrast to the Gothic church Somerset has been sketching, the new chapel is made of brick and slate, cheap building materials that tended to displace local materials after the 1840s when they could be brought in by the new railways. New processes for the manufacture of sheets of glass, the repeal of the excise tax on glass in 1845, and the development of central heating, suggested by the iron stove-pipe, combined to make the use of plate glass windows feasible (*Fletcher's*, 1124).

14 *shining . . . naughty world*: an allusion to Portia's speech in Shakespeare's *The Merchant of Venice*, v. i. 90–1: "How far that little candle throws his beams! | So shines a good deed in a naughty world."

15 *Baptists*: a Protestant denomination that holds as doctrine baptism by immersion of believers only.

fugleman: a fugleman was an especially expert soldier who was placed in front of a regiment as a model during drilling; hence, a guide or exemplar.

16 *brougham*: a one-horse closed carriage, seating two or four.

white-and-black half-mourning: the black clothes worn in deep mourning could be lightened by the addition of white, grey, or lavender in the period of half-mourning.

Dissenters: a broad term for Protestant sects which did not conform to the tenets of the Church of England.

18 *ducking-stool*: a seat attached to a plank, formerly used to punish culprits (usually disorderly women or dishonest tradesmen), who were tied to it and ducked in the local pond.

recusancy: refusal to obey authority.

minims and semibreves: a minim is a half note; a semibreve is a whole note.

third chapter of Revelation: the title of the novel alludes to these verses in the Book of Revelation that reproach the Christians in the affluent trading city of Laodicea, in the Roman province of Asia Minor, for being lukewarm in their faith. "A Laodicean" came to mean someone who is half-hearted, especially about religion or politics.

19 *plain and simple man*: Mr. Woodwell is one of the "few portraits of actual persons in Hardy's novels . . . a recognizable drawing" of a Baptist minister named Perkins whose family Hardy often visted when an architectural pupil of John Hicks in Dorchester (*Early Life*, 39–40).

Raffaelesque resignation: a reference to the sweet and serene expressions characteristic of the female figures in the sacred paintings of the Italian painter Raphael (1483–1520).

20 *tergiversation*: act of desertion or abandonment of a cause.

21 *telegraph*: machines used to transmit messages by electrical impulses were patented in 1837, in the United States by Samuel Morse and in England by William Cooke and Charles Wheatstone. Generally available by around 1845, private telegraph connections were not uncommon before telephones replaced them in the 1880s. Wireless telegraphy was developed by 1896.

Sleeping-Green: Hardy borrowed the name from that of a village north of Wareham, Dorset.

dying falls: a reference to Shakespeare's *Twelfth Night*, I. i. 4: "That strain again! It had a dying fall."

Still quiring . . . cherubim: from Lorenzo's speech describing the immortal music man cannot hear, in Shakespeare's *The Merchant of Venice*, v. i. 60–2: "There's not the smallest orb which thou behold'st | But in his motion like an angel sings, | Still quiring to the young-eyed cherubins."

post-office authorities: the Post Office assumed responsibility for the telegraph service in 1871.

23 *modern mental fever and fret*: a reference to John Keats's "Ode to a Nightingale": "Fade far away, dissolve, and quite forget | What thou among the leaves has never known, | The weariness, the fever, and the fret . . ."

24 *vaulting*: arched ceilings made of stone, supported by columns.

outer ward: the open area between the outer wall and the wall surrounding the area in the centre of the castle, the inner ward.

portcullis: a heavy lattice grating of timber or iron that could be lowered to prevent passage through the gateway.

25 *Tudor*: referring to the royal house that ruled England from 1485 to 1603.

26 *coved ceiling*: one that is curved where it meets the walls.

arabesques: mural decorations composed in flowing, intertwined lines, usually in foliage or fruit designs, making an intricate pattern.

painters of this long collection: Hardy visited Kingston Lacy, the home of the Bankes family, in the summer of 1878 "to see the pictures" (*Early Life*, 160). His memories of that valuable collection, perhaps supplemented by reference to John Hutchins's description of the paintings in vol. iii of *The History and Antiquities of the County of Dorset*, may have influenced this account of the portraits in Stancy Castle. Included in Hutchins is information about a painting by Salvator Rosa "believed to be the only portrait of any Englishman by this master in existence" (237); cf. Hardy's comment about the portrait by Rosa in the final chapter of the novel. Of the painters mentioned by Hardy, only Holbein does not appear in Hutchins's description of the collection at Kingston Lacy. C. J. P. Beatty has suggested that Hardy based Stancy Castle on Corfe Castle, formerly the home of the Bankes family, giving as one of his reasons the similarity between the collections of paintings. (See "When is a Castle not a Castle?" *Proceedings of the Dorset Natural History and Archeological Society*, 90 (1969), 258–60.)

Holbein: Hans Holbein the Younger (1497?–1543) was a German painter who dominated the field of portrait painting during the first half of the sixteenth century in Germany, Switzerland, and England. His work includes portraits of the wealthy aristocrats who frequented Henry VIII's court.

Jansen: Cornelis Jansen van Ceulen (1590–1662 or '64) was a Dutch painter who painted at the court of Charles I.

Vandyck: Sir Anthony Van Dyck (1599–1641) was a Flemish portrait painter who during his nine years at the court of Charles I painted numerous portraits of the royal family and other aristocrats.

Sir Peter: Sir Peter Lely (Peter Van der Faes) (1618–80) was a

Dutch painter who after coming to England in the 1640s amassed a fortune in the country's largest portrait practice. He is known for his sumptuous portraits of the society women at Charles II's court.

Sir Geoffrey: Sir Godfrey Kneller (1646?–1723), German-born, became England's leading portrait painter after Lely's death. Hardy corrected the name when the mistake was called to his attention in 1923.

Sir Joshua: Sir Joshua Reynolds (1723–92) became the leading portrait painter in England in the 1750s, ending centuries of dominance by foreigners in that field.

Sir Thomas: Sir Thomas Lawrence (1769–1830) was the leading portrait painter in England by the early nineteenth century. With Lawrence, Hardy completes his catalogue of those likely to have painted the aristocrats of the De Stancy family since the first half of the sixteenth century.

28 *Holbein . . . blue-green*: Holbein often painted his subjects on a bright green or blue background.

29 *Correggio*: Antonio Allegri de Corregio (1498?–1534), an Italian artist whose paintings feature graceful madonnas with sweet expressions enhanced by the gentle light characteristic of his work.

30 *Built . . . stone*: from Sir Walter Scott's *Marmion*, canto 2, stanza 10.

grotesques: a style of decorative art that is characterized by a depiction of fanciful, distorted human and animal forms interwoven with foliage, etc.

capital: the top of a column.

34 *John Power*: Power has been identified with the wealthy Baptist railway-builder Samuel Morton Peto. See "John Power was Sir Samuel Morton Peto", *Dorset: The County Magazine*, issue 69 (no date).

35 *Knox or Bossuet*: John Knox (*c.*1510–72), a clergyman who led the Scottish Reformation, and Jacques Bossuet (1627–1704), a French bishop, were powerful and stern preachers.

36 *corbelled*: a corbel is a projecting block of stone built into a wall during construction.

manufacture of pottery: C. J. P. Beatty believes that Hardy had in mind Colonel William Waugh's unsuccessful Brownsea Island project, an attempt to manufacture fine porcelain in Dorset. Waugh bought the island in 1852, restored a castle, and built a chapel and cottages for the workers. See "Colonel Waugh and *A Laodicean*", *Thomas Hardy Year Book*, 1 (1970), 19–21.

fictile: capable of being moulded of earth or clay.

38 *Wardlaw*: Ralph Wardlaw (1779–1853), Scottish Congregationalist divine and prolific theological writer.

Walford's County Families: Edward Walford (1823–87) edited numerous biographical and genealogical works, including *County Families of Great Britain*, first published in 1860.

40 *antipodean*: literally, pertaining to the opposite side of the world; exactly opposite.

Deïopeia: a nymph of Juno, the goddess of marriage.

41 *pony-carriage*: a carriage with an underslung axle and lengthwise seats.

turnpike-road: a highway maintained by fees collected by a toll-keeper who turned aside a pike or bar, so that travellers could pass.

44 *How are the mighty fallen!*: from David's lament over the deaths of Saul and Jonathan (2 Sam. 1: 19, 27).

46 *myrtle*: an evergreen shrub with white, sweet-scented flowers; once regarded as sacred to Venus.

civil wars: the English Civil Wars of 1642–6 and 1647–9 split the country on religious and constitutional issues. In general, members of the nobility, who were more likely to be Anglican, supported Charles I and were called Royalists or Cavaliers. Members of the gentry divided their support, with the yeoman of a particular area usually following their lead, but the business classes of the towns, most significantly, London, sided with Parliament. Puritanism was stronger among the latter groups; the term Roundhead, a reference to the Puritans' close-cropped hair that contrasted to the long locks of the Cavaliers, became synonymous with a supporter of the Parliamentary side. Throughout the novel, the De Stancys are associated with the Royalists, and Paula and her family are identified with the Puritans and Parliament.

the old keys . . . preserved by us: Charlotte's account of the medieval door-keys may be another link to Corfe Castle (see note to p. 26). According to Hutchins, "the keys of the castle gates,

which were never yielded up by the brave lady of Sir John Bankes
. . . are still preserved as traditional trophies by her descendants"
(237). Lady Bankes defended the castle against the Parliamentary
forces in 1643, but several years later it was shelled and ruined.

Nothing can retain the spirit . . . shadow of the form?: cf. the
following passage from Matthew Arnold's essay "Heinrich Heine"
as Hardy entered it into his "Literary Notes I" in 1880: "The
modern spirit is now awake almost everywhere; the sense of want
between the forms of modern Europe & its spirit, between the
new wine of the eighteenth & nineteenth centuries, & the old
bottles of the eleventh & twelfth or even of the sixteenth &
seventeenth . . . almost everyone now perceives" (Björk, 106).

47 *Cicero*: De Stancy refers to Cicero's *Paradoxa Stoicorum*, Paradox
VI.

the philosopher's stone: an imaginary substance that medieval
philosophers believed capable of turning baser metals into gold.

48 *It is better to know . . . star lies there*: to satirize Sir William's
"wisdom", Hardy borrows from the maxims of the Spanish Jesuit
Balthasar Gracián (1601–58) which at some point his wife Emma
had copied extensively from the March 1877 issue of *Fortnightly
Review*, from an article by M. E. Grant Duff entitled "Balthasar
Gracián" (Björk, 338). Cf. this passage, as Emma entered it into
the notebook: "Know the star of your fortune. . . . Let every
man know his own luck as well as his own peculiar talent for on
this it depends whether he loses or wins" (Björk, 93).

win affection and regard . . . to the times: Hardy conflates several
of Gracián's maxims to create Sir William's final words of wisdom
to Somerset (Björk, 96).

Machiavellian theories: Niccolò Machiavelli (1469–1527) was an
Italian theorist and historian who described government that
placed expediency above morality in his 1513 treatise *The Prince*.
The name is now associated with statecraft or general conduct
characterized by duplicity and cunning.

50 *watering-place*: a seaside resort.

55 *coup d'œil*: (French) a comprehensive glance or general view.

new photographic process: a French inventor, Joseph Niepce, took
the first photograph in 1826; his technique was perfected by
Louis Daguerre, who patented the first successful process for
developing photographs in 1839. Dare's comments suggest the
technical experimentation of the decades that followed.

dog-cart: a light one-horse, two-wheeled carriage with two seats set back to back.

57 *the Establishment*: the Church of England.

Pædobaptists: Baptist sects who advocate infant baptism.

trumpery: worthless.

argument drawn from Circumcision: because the circumcision of infants was a Jewish religious rite not rejected by the early fathers of the Church, the practice was sometimes mentioned as justification for infant baptism.

58 *It happened that Somerset*: *Early Life* gives an account of how Hardy once studied books on pædobaptism and participated in arguments on that subject with Bastow, another architectural pupil in the office of John Hicks, and the sons of the Baptist minister in Dorchester, the Mr. Perkins who was the model for Woodwell (37–40).

Everything . . . long: from the description of Zimri in John Dryden's 1681 satirical poem *Absalom and Achitophel*; the Duke of Buckingham, supposedly the model for Zimri, was notorious for his impulsive enthusiasms.

59 *Aphrodite . . . Hebe*: Aphrodite was the Greek goddess of love and beauty; Hebe was a goddess associated with youthful beauty.

First Epistle to the Corinthians: I Corinthians 7: 14: "For the unbelieving husband is sanctified by the wife, and the unbelieving wife is sanctified by the husband: else were your children unclean; but now they are holy."

60 *Suffer-little-children argument*: a reference to Matthew 19: 14: "But Jesus said, Suffer little children, and forbid them not, to come unto me: for of such is the kingdom of heaven."

sixteenth chapter of the Acts: Acts 16: 33: "And he took them the same hour of the night, and washed their stripes; and was baptized, he and all his, straightway."

eighth chapter of the Acts: Acts 8: 36: "And as they went on their way, they came unto a certain water: and the eunuch said, See, here is water. What doth hinder me to be baptized?"

sixteenth of Mark: Mark 16:16: "He that believeth and is baptized shall be saved; but he that believeth not shall be damned."

second of Acts: Acts 2: 41: "Then they that gladly received his word were baptized: and the same day there were added unto them about three thousand souls."

the tenth and the forty-seventh verse: Acts 10: 47: "Can any man forbid water, that these should not be baptized, which have received the Holy Ghost as well as we?"

the eighteenth and eighth verse: Acts 18: 8: ". . . many of the Corinthians hearing believed, and were baptized."

Justin Martyr: (*c*.100–65) an Apologist, one of a group of writers whose goals were to instruct the pagans about Christian beliefs and to persuade the emperors to be tolerant of the new religion; St Justin was thrown to the lions during the reign of Marcus Aurelius.

Irenæus: St Irenaeus (*c*.135–200) was Bishop of Lyons. The Latin means: "Indeed he came to save all in his own person; all, I say, who through him are born again in God, infants and young boys and older boys and youths."

61 *renascor*: (Latin) I am reborn.

Wall: William Wall (1647–1728), theologian and author of *The History of Infant Baptism* (1705).

Tertullian's advice: Tertullian (*c*.160–230) was an Apologist who argued in *De Baptismo* the advantages of delaying baptism in the case of young children.

Cyprian, Nazianzen, Chrysostom, Jerome: St Cyprian (*c*.200–58), Bishop of Carthage; St Gregory of Nazianzum (*c*.329–90), Bishop of Constantinople; St John Chrysostom (345–407); St Jerome (*c*.340–420), the chief preparer of the Vulgate, a Latin version of the Bible.

64 *New lights*: a name given to religious groups that advocated doctrines considered advanced or extreme.

66 *open landau*: a four-wheeled carriage with a top made in two parts so that it may be closed or opened.

68 *grave end of its gamut*: at the lower-pitched end in its range of notes.

69 *traceried*: having a decorative interlacing of lines, characteristic of late Gothic style.

70 *chancel-wall*: the chancel is the part of the church containing the altar and the seats for the clergy and the choir.

Perpendicular: the last phase of the Gothic style in English architecture, from the mid-fourteenth to late fifteenth centuries.

capital . . . arcade: the upper part of one of the columns that supported the series of arches making up the arcade. See note to p. 301.

undercutting: material has been cut away so that a portion over-hangs, forming recesses and ridges that create the deep shadows most characteristic of the Early English phase of Gothic architecture.

71 *Domesday*: the Domesday book was a record of a survey made of land and property around 1086, by order of William the Conqueror.

72 *Sketching and building . . . experienced ones*: Havill's distinction between sketching and building suggests an issue much debated during Hardy's day: whether the architect who was a true artist was superior to the engineer who was more practical and suppos-edly worked mechanically. A major blow to the pride of those who held the former view was the selection of the design of Joseph Paxton, a landscape gardener, for the 1851 Great Exhibi-tion's Crystal Palace (Bullen, 133).

Institute: the Royal Institute of British Architects. See note to p. 79.

76 *Ginevra of Modena . . . Mistletoe Bough*: the Mistletoe Bough, an English ballad by Thomas Haines Bayly (1797–1839), tells the story of the bride of Lord Lovell, who played a game of hide and seek on her wedding day:

> O, sad was her fate!—in sportive jest
> She hid from her lord in the old oak chest.
> It closed with a spring!—and, dreadful doom,
> The bride lay clasped in her living toomb!

(The ballad is included in vol. 6 of *Home Book of Verse*, edited by Burton Egbert Stevenson.) Ginevra of Modena, in northern Italy, supposedly met a similar fate.

79 *Institute of British Architects*: the Institute, founded in 1837, created a code of professional conduct, but not until 1882 was admission subject to examination. As Somerset's and Havill's comments have indicated, the profession was not at the time a closed one with formal and specific requirements for membership.

83 *peristyle*: a row of columns surrounding a court.

84 *statues . . . British Museum*: Paula has no doubt seen the Elgin Marbles, a collection of ancient Greek sculptures and other antiquities removed from the Parthenon and other buildings by

Thomas Bruce, Lord Elgin, who was British ambassador to the Ottoman Empire from 1799 to 1803. Shipped to England between 1802 and 1812, supposedly to prevent destruction, the collection became public in 1822 and was quite controversial, with detractors charging that taking the treasures of another nation amounted to vandalism.

88 *Whatman's paper*: from the name of the manufacturer of a brand of drawing-paper.

90 *abacus*: a slab forming the top of a capital of a column.

95 *Cañons of Colorado*: the canyons cut by the Colorado River in the United States, including the Grand Canyon.

96 *mouse-hole*: Bullen believes that Hardy had read a note John Ruskin added to the 1880 reissue of *The Seven Lamps of Architecture* which differentiated between true architecture and "a wasp's nest, a rat hole, or a railway station" (*Works*, viii. 28). According to Bullen, Hardy "took up this animal image" but made the rat hole a little mouse-hole in a description that seems to defy Ruskin's ideas about the ugliness of railway architecture (135).

barrow: a mound of earth erected over a grave in prehistoric times.

99 *Vice-admiral Sir Armstrong Somerset*: Hardy liked to claim kinship with Admiral Sir Thomas Hardy, captain of the *Victory* at the Battle of Trafalgar during the Napoleonic wars (*Early Life*, 6).

100 *Apostolic Succession*: the unbroken line of succession beginning with the apostles and perpetuated through bishops, a belief held by Anglicans but not Dissenters, as the Baptist minister's comments suggest.

Laodicea: see note to p. 18.

101 *lord of Burleigh*: in Tennyson's poem "The Lord of Burleigh", the lord poses as a landscape painter, keeping his identity and wealth a secret until he has wed a village maiden.

102 *running dimensions*: measuring by taking the length only.

104 *Chivaler*: obsolete form of chevalier, equivalent to knight.

106 *Compuesta no hay muger fea*: a Spanish proverb: "A well-dressed woman is not ugly."

110 *cross-legged knights*: a posture indicating that the knight had fought in the Crusades.

hauberks of chain-mail: tunics of chain mail worn as armour.

wimple: a cloth covering worn over the head and around the neck and chin, especially by women in the late medieval period.

cover-chief: a cloth covering worn over the head.

Yorkist collar of suns and roses ... Edward the Fourth: two emblems associated with the House of York, who fought the Lancastrians in the civil wars known as the Wars of the Roses, were the white rose and a sun. Edward the Fourth, a Yorkist, reigned from 1461 to 1483.

112 *Archimedes*: Archimedes (287?–212 BC) was the Greek mathematician, physicist, and inventor who discovered the principles of specific gravity and of the lever.

Newcomen: Thomas Newcomen (1663–1729) was an English engineer and inventor of the atmospheric steam engine, a precursor of Watt's engine.

Watt: James Watt (1736–1819) was a Scottish inventor whose steam engine gave impetus to the Industrial Revolution.

Telford: Thomas Telford (1757–1834) was a Scottish engineer whose greatest achievements were the design and construction of suspension bridges.

Stephenson: George Stephenson (1781–1848) was an English engineer who was the principal inventor of the railroad locomotive. His son Robert (1803–59) was also an engineer and builder of railroad bridges.

113 *prédilection d'artiste*: (French) artistic preference. Hardy borrowed this phrase from Karl Hillebrand's "Familiar Conversations on Modern England", published in *Nineteenth Century*, vii (June 1880), 1014 (see Björk, 369).

Pensa molto, parla poco: (Italian) think much, speak little.

115 *phaeton*: four-wheeled open carriage usually drawn by a pair of horses.

117 *high-light portrait by Vandyck or Rembrandt*: the portraits of Van Dyck (see note to p. 26) and those of the Dutch painter Rembrandt (1606–69) are notable for the use of strong contrasts in light and shadow for dramatic effect.

119 *Miss Deverell*: in July 1878 Hardy jotted down this description of an American woman he met at a garden party given by Mrs Alexander Macmillan: "sallow, with black dancing eyes, dangling earrings, yellow costume, and gay laugh." Also drawn from

memories of that party is the thunderstorm described in this chapter (*Early Life*, 168).

120 *Jove*: the chief Roman god, also known as Jupiter; the god of light, the sky, and the weather.

123 *To everything there is a season*: a reference to Ecclesiastes 3: 1: "To every thing there is a season, and a time to every purpose under the heaven. "

Fortune . . . eye: from Pandulph's speech in Shakespeare's *King John*, III. iv. 119–20: "No, no; when Fortune means to men most good, | She looks upon them with a threatening eye."

127 *Moivre's Doctrine of Chances*: Abraham Moivre (1667–1754) was a French-born mathematician who moved to England around 1687 to escape religious persecution. He made significant contributions to statistics, trigonometry, and the development of life insurance. His *Doctrine of Chances* was first published in 1717.

128 *Vandal*: the Vandals were a Germanic tribe who invaded Western Europe during the fourth and fifth centuries and sacked Rome in AD 455. The word vandal has come to mean a "wilful or ignorant destroyer of anything beautiful, venerable, or worthy of preservation" (*OED*).

129 *Both in purse . . . the ill-used hostess of the Garter*: a reference to the Lord Chief Justice's remark to Falstaff in Shakespeare's *2 Henry IV*, II. i. 123–5: "You have, as it appears to me, practised upon the easy-yielding spirit of this woman, and made her serve your uses both in purse and person." The "ill-used hostess", Mistress Quickly, also appears in *The Merry Wives of Windsor*; the Garter Tavern is in that play rather than in *Henry IV*. Note that Havill chooses to ignore Dare's suggestion that having to compete with Somerset may damage his bank account as well as his pride.

130 *thereby hangs a tale*: from at least three of Shakespeare's plays, *As You Like It*, II. ii. 128; *The Merry Wives of Windsor*, I. iv. 159; *The Taming of the Shrew*, V. i. 60.

131 *Hörensagen ist halb gelogen!*: (German) Dare provides a translation of this adage: Hearsay is half lies.

Man Friday: Friday was Crusoe's servant and devoted companion in Daniel Defoe's 1719 novel *Robinson Crusoe*. The name has come to mean an efficient employee, or as Dare uses it here, a right-hand man, one he will rely on to carry out his plans.

Didymus: another name for Thomas, the disciple who doubted Jesus's resurrection until he saw proof. See John 20: 24–9.

137 *Inigo Jones*: Inigo Jones (1573–1652) was the first great English architect; he introduced Italian Renaissance designs, founding the English classical school.

138 *Offenbach*: Jacques Offenbach (1819–80) composed witty, cleverly orchestrated light operas.

Cupid's Entire XXX: Cupid was the god of love in Roman mythology. As Pinion explains, if Paula had partaken of Cupid's Entire XXX, she would be "passionately in love". In reference to beer, XXX indicates a strong brew, while entire indicates a blend of all the best flavours (*A Thomas Hardy Dictionary*, 169–70).

139 *en garçon*: (French) as a bachelor.

basket-carriage: a carriage made of wicker.

144 *Dionysus*: the Greek god of wine, feasting, and revelry.

Tages: a figure in Etruscan mythology, Tages was childlike in appearance but taught divine wisdom to a peasant who discovered him in a field.

chevalier d'industrie: (French) adventurer, one who lives by his wits.

147 *stout-wheeled limber*: attached to the gun-carriage, a limber is a two-wheeled vehicle that holds the ammunition chests.

148 *busby with its red bag*: a tall fur cap having a bag (usually the colour of the facings of the regiment) hanging out of the top. It was worn by hussars, engineeers, and artillerymen.

151 *amourettes*: (French) love affairs that are passing fancies.

152 *Visitation*: a bishop's tour of his district.

Doubtless . . . score: De Stancy quotes from Byron's *Don Juan*, canto 14, stanzas 17 and 18, an appropriate poem for one whose susceptibility to women has been his downfall.

154 *tædium-vitæ*: (Latin) weariness of life.

156 *Crusoe . . . sand*: Crusoe was terrified when he found a single footprint in the sand, having lived on an island for fifteen years without seeing another person; he spent many anxious moments watching and waiting. Daniel Defoe's *Robinson Crusoe* was a favourite of Hardy's.

157 *From going to and fro . . . as Satan said to his Maker*: Dare is linked to Satan several times in the novel. See Job 1: 7: "And the

Lord said unto Satan, Whence comest thou? Then Satan answered the Lord and said, From going to and fro in the earth, and from walking up and down in it."

160 *blind Samson*: see Judges 16: 18–21. The Philistines put Samson's eyes out after the temptress Delilah cut his hair, thereby destroying his unusual strength. The allusion emphasizes De Stancy's vulnerability to women.

164 *Mephistopheles*: another suggestion that Dare is the devil. Mephistopheles tempted Faust in Goethe's drama *Faust*.

165 *raison d'être*: (French) reason for existence.

168 *postern-gate*: a back gate or side entrance.

172 *Tasting . . . mirth*: Dare quotes John Keats's "Ode to a Nightingale".

173 *pink flannel costume*: as Elliott notes, Hardy often uses pink, a colour of flesh, to suggest sensual appeal (247–8). Pinion suggests that the scene is an adaptation of the scene in Goethe's *Faust* when Faust drinks the witch's potion and gazes on the image of a beautiful woman. Dare, as Mephistopheles, gives his father intoxicating liquor and shows him Paula in the gymnasium (*Art and Thought*, 62).

Lodge, Nash, or Constable: Thomas Lodge (1558–1625); Thomas Nashe (1567–1601); and Henry Constable (1562–1613).

Bona Dea: (Latin) literally, the good goddess; the Roman goddess of chastity and fertility, worshipped only by women.

174 *Olympian*: the Greek gods lived on Mount Olympus.

Ariel: Ariel is a spirit of the air in Shakespeare's *The Tempest*. Paula may be thinking of Ariel's song in Act v, scene i:

> In a cowslip's bell I lie,
> There I couch when owls do cry.
> On the bat's back I do fly
> After summer merrily.
> Merrily, merrily shall I live now
> Under the blossom that hangs in the bough.

177 *physiognomist*: one who interprets temperament and character from outward appearance, especially from facial features.

178 *gibbous*: from a Latin word meaning humpbacked; a gibbous moon appears to have more than half but not all of its apparent disk illuminated.

179 *ashlar*: hewn or squared stone.

183 *precisian*: a synonym for Puritan; one who stresses adherence to a strict standard of religious observance or morality.

first Lord Amherst's wart . . . nose-scar: Hardy refers to a painting of Lord Amherst by Thomas Gainsborough and one of Bennet, Earl of Arlington "after Sir Peter Lely".

185 *embrasures*: an embrasure is a recess in a wall for a door or window.

187 *entail was cut off*: an entail placed restrictions on the ownership of land, usually specifying that it be held for life and then passed on to a direct descendant, often to males only. The limitation perpetuated a landed aristocracy by preventing the division of large estates. A statute passed in 1834 permitted agreements to break the entail, as the De Stancy family's history reveals.

188 *court of Charles the First*: the court of Charles I, King of England (1625–49), was a relatively decorous one, following the lead of the King, a pious man who was devoted to his wife.

191 *Protean*: Proteus was a Greek sea god who had the power to assume different shapes; hence, capable of assuming different forms or playing varied roles.

Frankenstein: the monster created by Frankenstein in Mary Shelley's 1818 novel *Frankenstein* destroys him.

196 *bivouac*: a temporary encampment.

197 *troubles come in battalions*: a reference to the King's speech in Shakespeare's *Hamlet*, IV. v. 78–80: "When sorrows come, they come not single spies | But in battalions!"

200 *taking the current when it served*: a reference to Brutus's speech in Shakespeare's *Julius Caesar*, IV. iii. 223–3: "And we must take the current when it serves, | Or lose our ventures."

202 *votive building*: one offered in fulfilment of a vow.

"Wertherism of the uncultivated": borrowing once more from "Familiar Conversations on Modern England" (see note to p. 113), Hardy copied into his notebook "Methodism was only the Wertherism of the uncultivated" Björk, 134), from Hillebrand's comments about how the Evangelical movement asserted the emotional side of man's nature. *The Sorrows of Young Werther*, Goethe's 1774 novel, concerns its hero's passionate struggles against conventional society and is usually associated with a glorification of the emotions.

205 *Providence . . . shape for herself*: allusions to two lines in Shakespeare's *Hamlet*: "There's special providence in the fall of a sparrow" (V. ii. 231) and "There's a divinity that shapes our ends, | Roughhew them how we will" (V. ii. 10–11).

206 *Achates*: an ironic allusion to Achates, the faithful friend of Aeneas in Virgil's *Aeneid*.

counterscarps, and ravelins: a counterscarp is the outer wall or slope of the ditch in a work of fortification; a ravelin is a work made of two embankments constructed beyond the main ditch. As Dare's complaint makes plain, they are primarily defensive strategies, unlike the assault he recommends.

Uncle Toby: a character in Laurence Sterne's novel *Tristram Shandy* (1760–7) whose obsession is the re-enactment of military campaigns and the construction of fortifications.

weather-house: a toy house that indicates changes in atmospheric humidity by the appearance of figures (often a man who comes out in wet weather and a woman who comes out in dry weather) moved by varying tension of a string.

And, as the Jesuit said . . . two: Emma copied from the maxims of Gracián, "He spake a great word who said, Time & I against any two" (See Björk, 95 and the note to p. 48). The speaker referred to is Mazarin (1602–61), cardinal and minister of France.

207 *caryatid*: a sculptured female figure used as a column in classical architecture.

208 *stiver*: a Dutch coin of little value; a small amount of money.

212 *Phidias . . . Wykeham*: Somerset's pedigree includes designers and builders: Phidias, a fifth-century BC Greek who was the master sculptor of the Parthenon; Ictinus and Callicrates, the architects of the Parthenon; Chersiphron, a sixth-century BC designer; Vitruvius, a first-century AD Roman authority on architecture; Wilars of Cambray, a thirteenth-century French architect; William of Wykeham, the founder of Winchester School and New College, Oxford, who was also a builder.

219 *a train . . . he might save*: be in time for, manage to catch a train.

fly: a one-horse covered carriage let out for hire.

220 *escutcheons*: an escutcheon is a shield on which a coat of arms is depicted.

Lammas Day: the first of August, observed as a harvest festival in the early English Church.

quadrille: a square dance usually performed by four couples.

Hermia and Helena: the heroines of Shakespeare's *A Midsummer Night's Dream*.

221 *tournure*: (French), figure, appearance.

222 *dog might have his day*: from Shakespeare's *Hamlet*, V. i. 289–90; "Let Hercules himself do what he may, | The cat will mew, and dog will have his day." From Hamlet's comment that his chance will come to avenge his father's death.

236 *porphyry*: a hard rock, red or purple in colour, used as a building stone or for sculpture, especially by the Egyptians, Greeks, and Romans.

sang froid: (French) literally, cold blood; self-control, imperturbability, especially under strain.

237 *gallicrow*: (dialect) scarecrow.

240 *a little more than a little*: from King Henry's advice to Prince Hal about the dangers of mingling with the common people, in Shakespeare's *1 Henry IV*, III. ii. 70–3:

> That, being daily swallowed by men's eyes,
> They surfeited with honey and began
> To loathe the taste of sweetness, whereof a little
> More than a little is by much too much.

241 *Pleasance*: a pleasure-ground or recreation place, usually attached to a mansion.

chamfered: the square edges of the doorway have been bevelled off.

250 *technicist*: the *OED* defines "technicist" as "technician", giving this quotation as its earliest example of the use of the word. According to Beatty, the word is "virtually Hardy's own coinage" and implies more than what is associated with "technician", also suggesting a creative artist in charge of a building that grows organically. See C. J. P. Beatty's introduction to *The Architectural Notebook of Thomas Hardy* (Dorchester, 1966), 19.

myrmidons: in Homer's *Iliad* the Myrmidons were warriors led by Achilles to the siege of Troy; hence, hirelings.

252 *jamb-stones*: stones forming the sidepieces for the frame of an opening.

255 *refrigerator*: a refrigerator at the time the novel was written would have been one found on ships used by the meat-packing industry, a mid-century development.

263 *Paula's journey*: in the chapters that follow the characters travel to cities visited by Hardy and his wife Emma during three trips: an 1874 honeymoon in France, an 1876 tour of the Netherlands and the valley of the Rhine, and an 1880 visit to Normandy.

isothermal line: an isotherm is a line on a weather map connecting points having the same mean temperature for a given period; hence, a boundary between regions having different climates.

265 *things . . . inexpedient*: an allusion to Paul's words in 1 Corinthians 6: 12 "All things are lawful unto me, but all things are not expedient."

267 *mistral*: the cold northerly wind of the Mediterranean provinces of France and neighbouring regions.

268 *M. Aurelius*: Hardy kept a copy of *The Thoughts of the Emperor M. Aurelius Antoninus* at his bedside until he died, inscribed with the quotation in Paula's letter. The volume was an 1865 New Year's Day present from Horace Moule (Millgate, 87). As Björk notes, Paula's tone seems somewhat flippant, so it is difficult to determine Hardy's attitude toward the advice (313–14).

271 *like Cleopatra's*: Hardy may have had in mind Cleopatra's flight from the battle at Actium, where the combined forces of Antony and Cleopatra faced Octavius Caesar.

273 *romanticism . . . flying away*: cf. Hardy's note of December 1880: "Romanticism will exist in human nature as long as human nature exists" (*Early Life*, 189). Millgate suggests an analogy between Paula and the German Romantics Hardy read about in Matthew Arnold's essay "Heinrich Heine": "So the mystic and romantic school of Germany lost itself in the Middle Ages, was overpowered by their influence, came to ruin by its vain dreams of renewing them." (*Thomas Hardy: His Career as a Novelist*, 175.)

276 *the unknown God*: a reference to Acts 17: 23 which tells of Athenians who ignorantly worshipped at an altar inscribed "To the Unknown God".

279 *table d'hôte*: (French) literally, the host's table; a common dining table for guests at a hotel.

all in Lyons was quiet enough now: Hardy may refer to the brutal religious wars fought here in the sixteenth century and to the violent reprisals against those who supported the royalists during 1793's Reign of Terror.

280 *Æneas . . . St Paul*: Aeneas, the hero of Virgil's *Aeneid*, and the Apostle Paul travelled the Mediterranean.

283 *phantasmagoria*: an exhibit of optical illusions in which figures on a screen seem to dwindle into the distance or to come forward; as used here the word suggests a rapidly changing scene.

meum and tuum: (Latin) mine and yours: used to express rights of property.

Roulette: in the gambling game of roulette, players bet on which red or black numbered compartment of a revolving wheel a small ball (spun in the opposite direction) will come to rest in. They bet by placing chips on a table marked to correspond with the compartments of the wheel (Hardy's *figured diagram*).

"Messieurs . . . Passe": (French) "Gentlemen, place your bets!" "Are your bets placed?" "No more bets" "Twenty-four." "Black." "Even and high." See note to p. 284.

284 *Sept, Rouge, Impair, et Manque*: (French) the result of a spin: the winning number is seven (*sept*); the colour of its compartment is red (*rouge*) rather than black (*noir*); it is an odd (*impair*) number rather than an even (*pair*) one; it is a low (*manque*) number, literally, falling short, within the range from 1 to 18 rather than a high (*passe*) number falling within the range from 19 to 36.

Belial . . . Mesopotamia: Belial, literally, worthlessless in Hebrew, is synonymous with Satan or a power of evil. The Old Testament refers to the "sons of Belial", godless, immoral men such as those in Mesopotamia, or Babylon, in the Tigris-Euphrates river valley, who built temples to the many gods they worshipped.

purlieus: neighbourhoods.

285 *en plein . . . red or black*: to bet *en plein* (literally, fully) is to place chips on a single number, betting that the ball will fall within its compartment, with the casino paying a winner 35 to 1. To bet *à cheval* (literally, on horseback) is to split the bet between two numbers, placing the chips on the line separating them; if the ball falls on either number, the player wins, 17 to 1. Hardy corrected this passage in 1882 by deleting the words "upon two columns". To bet *the dozens*, the player places chips on one of three rectangular spaces on the tab .: the first 12, hence betting that the number will fall within the range 1 to 12, the second 12, 13 to 24, or the third 12, 25 to 36. A winner is paid 2 to 1. To bet

two numbers can only mean to bet on two numbers *en plein*, with the casino paying 35 to 1 if the ball falls into one of the numbers.

286 *napoleons*: a napoleon is a 20-franc gold piece.

297 *Strasburg*: a French city annexed by Germany at the end of the Franco-Prussian War in 1870–1 and reclaimed by France in 1918.

General Kleber: Jean Baptiste Kleber (1753–1800), a French general born in Strasburg.

Crivelli's emaciated imaginings: Carlo Crivelli (*c.*1430–93) was a Venetian artist whose sacred paintings depicted figures with slender hands, spidery fingers, and excessively pale faces with exaggerated expressions.

301 *"for his kin . . . defiled"*: from Leviticus 21: 2–3.

house in which Goethe had lived: Goethe lived in Strasburg in 1770–1 while studying law.

south transept: in the cruciform plan characteristic of medieval churches, the *nave*, or central area of the church where the congregation sits or stands, is crossed by the *transepts*, which run north and south. East of the crossing is the *choir*, then the altar and the *apse*, the circular end of the church with its central chapel, often a *lady chapel* dedicated to the Virgin Mary, and other smaller chapels that are recesses for prayer and meditation, radiating from it. Parallel to the nave are the *aisles*, separated from the main area of the church by an *arcade*, a series of arches supported by columns. Rising above the sloping roof of the aisles is the *clerestory*, the topmost part of the building with clear glass windows to let in light. Just below the clerestory, in the space between the roof over the aisles and the top of the nave arcade, is a gallery separated from the nave by a row of columns, which, because they are arranged in groups of three, led to the storey being called the *triforium*. Another name for the triforium, a dark, windowless passageway, is the *blind storey*. The nave wall is thus divided into three horizontal parts: the arcade at floor level, the triforium above, and the clerestory at topmost level.

Schwilgué: Johann Baptiste Schwilgué (1776–1856), a German clockmaker.

304 *Trink-halle*: (German) literally, a drinking hall; at a spa's Trink-halle, medicinal water is dispensed for drinking.

306 *lazy-tongs*: a system of several pairs of levers crossed like scissors which can be extended to pick up objects at a distance.

456   EXPLANATORY NOTES

308 *Falernian*: a wine mentioned by the Roman poet Horace (65–8 BC).

Charon's boat: in Greek mythology, Charon ferries the souls of the dead over the River Styx.

Horatian verses: the ironic, melancholy tone of Horace's love poems seems appropriate for De Stancy.

309 *"Charles's Rest"*: a literal translation of the German Carlsruhe.

310 *carob groves*: the carob tree is evergreen and has a beanlike fruit.

drag-chain: literally, a chain used to retard the motion of a vehicle.

317 *cream and mantle*: from Gratiano's description of people who, rather than letting their faces reveal their feelings, cover emotion like thick scum covers a motionless pond, in Shakespeare's *The Merchant of Venice*, I. i. 88–9: "There are a sort of men whose visages | Do cream and mantle like a standing pond."

320 *heliographic science*: heliography was an early photographic process that produced a photoengraving on a metal plate; in a broader sense, the term refers to photography.

sun . . . Gibeon: Joshua 10: 12–14 relates how the night miraculously did not come until the Hebrews had won a battle.

324 *faltered . . . Maid of Neidpath*: an allusion to Sir Walter Scott's 1806 poem about a girl who grieved so during her lover's absence that she wasted away and was not recognized when he returned: "Her welcome, spoke in faltering phrase, | Lost in his courser's prancing."

329 *roundabouts*: merry-go-rounds.

332 *con amore*: (Italian) with enthusiasm.

337 *Jacob's Ladder*: in a dream Jacob saw a ladder reaching to heaven. See Genesis 28: 12.

341 *"between the banks that bear the vine"*: from Byron's description of the River Rhine in *Childe Harold's Pilgrimage*, canto 3, stanza 55.

346 *Steinberger*: a German wine.

347 *entresol*: a low-ceilinged storey that projects in the form of a balcony over a main storey.

348 *buitenplaatsen*: (Dutch) country homes.

350 *Quatre Bras*: the last battle before the Battle of Waterloo that ended the Napoleonic wars in 1815.

352 *old Picard capital*: Amiens is the capital of the province of Picardy.

354 *described by Heine . . . strength of Titans*: Hardy refers to Heinrich Heine's description of Amiens Cathedral, which he probably read in a guidebook (Pinion, *Dictionary*, 128). The Titans were a family of giants who ruled the earth until overrun by the Greek gods of Olympus.

356 *Dutch manner*: like a Dutch uncle, one who admonishes sternly and bluntly.

364 *many a slip*: another of Dare's proverbs; from the adage "There's many a slip between cup and lip".

365 *servants on board-wages*: the servants are being paid only enough to buy food while the family is away.

366 *uncircumcised Philistines*: in the Old Testament, the Philistines were the enemies of the Jews; hence, those who are unenlightened or regarded as the enemy.

house and lineage of Jacob: here Power associates the aristocratic De Stancy family with the Jews, the chosen people.

368 *wear the broad arrow*: the broad arrow marked convicts' uniforms.

370 *Bunyan*: John Bunyan (1628–88) used the convention of the dream vision to form the narrative frame for his 1678 *Pilgrim's Progress*.

371 *guano trade*: guano is a natural fertilizer, composed chiefly of the excrement of sea-birds, found on the coasts of South America, particularly on the islands about Peru; before the development of chemical fertilizers, the guano trade was quite profitable.

373 *brown holland*: a linen fabric, called brown holland when unbleached, sometimes used to drape furniture.

375 *Here . . . alas!*: the last lines of "Phoebus, arise", a 1616 poem by William Drummond, appear in Francis Turner Palgrave's *A Golden Treasury of Songs and Lyrics* as "Here is the pleasant place— | And nothing wanting is, save She, alas!"

379 *flat as Jericho*: Joshua 6: 20 relates how the walls of the city of Jericho fell when the Jewish people shouted as their priests blew trumpets.

383 *Thick-coming fancies*: a reference to Shakespeare's *Macbeth*, v. iii. 37–8, from the doctor's speech about Lady Macbeth's sleepwalking: "As she is troubled with thick-coming fancies | That keep her from her rest."

397 *coup d'audace*: (French) daring action.

398 *pollard limes*: a pollard is any tree whose foliage is cut back to the trunk so that it will grow more thickly and form a rounded head or mass.

apse: see note to p. 301.

399 *braziers*: craftsmen who make articles in brass.

hollow-turners: craftsmen skilled in shaping hollow or concave vessels.

the great Francis: Francis I (1494–1547), King of France 1515–47.

Henry the Eighth: (1491–1547), king of England 1509–47.

the "Vieux Manoir de Francois premier": (French) the ancient manor of Francis I.

griffins, satyrs: in classical mythology, a griffin was a creature with the head and wings of an eagle and the body of a lion; a satyr was part human and part goat, having the latter's horns, legs, and tail.

cantilever: a bracket that may support or merely decorate a balcony.

402 *walking forms in Nebuchadnezzar's furnace*: Shadrach, Meshach, and Abednego, cast into a fiery furnace because they would not worship the golden image set up by Nebuchadnezzar, the King of Babylon, walked through the fire unharmed, accompanied by a fourth form said to be the Son of God. See Daniel 3.

lady-chapel: see note to p. 301.

404 *freestone*: any stone, such as sandstone, that can be cut easily.

triforium: see note to p. 301.

blind story . . . aisle arches: see note to p. 301.

408 *palings*: the stakes or pickets of the fence.

to show the white feather: to display cowardice; from the superstition that a white feather in a gamecock's plumage marks him as a poor fighter.

410 *block-book*: sketch-book.

salle à manger: (French) dining room.

419 *the weekly ordinary*: a public meal regularly provided at a fixed price in an inn.

prebendary: a clergyman who receives a stipend or prebend from the estate of a church.

his diocesan: his bishop; a diocese is the district under the care of a bishop.

420 *fancy-man*: a fancy-man can mean a lover or sweetheart but may also mean a man who is kept by a woman. Somerset might find the term offensive because of the discrepancy between his income and Paula's.

this turk of a while: Elliott explains that because Turks were thought to be extremely cruel, the word "turk" denoted anything formidable (229). A "turk of a while" would be a long time.

broadcloth: a fine, plain-wove, double-width black cloth used chiefly for men's garments.

fustian: a coarse cloth made of cotton and flax.

ex cathedrâ: (Latin) literally, from the chair. The expression means speaking in an official or authoritative way, as though speaking in the manner of one in the chair of a bishop.

421 *gaffers and gammers*: (dialect) grandfathers and grandmothers.

chammers: (dialect) chambers.

randy: (dialect) a noisy party.

424 *Enfin les renards se trouvent chez le pelletier*: (French) in the end foxes find themselves at the furrier's.

cat will after kind: Touchstone says these words as he mocks Orlando's verses in Shakespeare's *As You Like It*, III. ii. 109–10: "If the cat will after kind, | So be sure will Rosalind." Dare never misses an opportunity to suggest that there is a relationship between his villainy and his father's weaknesses.

425 *Salvator Rosa*: Italian painter (1615–73); see note to p. 26.

426 *Romney*: George Romney (1734–1802), English portrait painter.

Tintoretto Jacob Robusti (1518–94), Venetian painter who took the name Tintoretto from his father's occupation, a dyer of silk.

Titian: Tiziano Vecellio (*c*.1477–1576), Italian painter.

Giorgione: Giorgio Barbarelli da Castelfranco (1475–1510), Italian painter.

Caroline: pertaining to the reign of Charles I (1625–49).

431 *a finished writer*: Paula refers to Matthew Arnold. She is quoting from Arnold's essay "Pagan and Medieval Religious Sentiment": "The poetry of later paganism lived by the senses and understanding; the poetry of medieval Christianity lived by the heart and

imagination. But the main element of the modern spirit's life is neither the senses and understanding, nor the heart and imagination; it is the imaginative reason." Bullen suggests that in a "highly Arnoldian marriage" Somerset's sense and understanding will temper Paula's romantic heart and imagination (137).

461 *The changing of the old order*: a reference to King Arthur's final speech in Tennyson's "Morte d'Arthur": "The old order changeth, yielding place to new."

462 *into whose souls the iron has entered*: Psalm 105: 18 in the Book of Common Prayer describes Joseph after he had been sold into bondage by his brothers: "Whose feet they hurt in the stocks: the iron entered into his soul." With this assessment, Hardy dismisses the novel as light entertainment for those who have not suffered intensely.

whose years have less pleasure in them now than heretofore: an echo of Ecclesiastes 12: 1: ". . . in the days of thy youth, while the evil days come not, nor the years draw nigh, when thou shalt say, I have no pleasure in them."

whose lines have fallen to them in pleasant places: Psalms 16: 6: "The lines are fallen unto me in pleasant places."

the pilgrim's Eternal City: the highest ideal goal, an allusion to the Celestial City of *The Pilgrim's Progress* by John Bunyan (1628–88).

baseless fabrics of a vision: from Shakespeare's *The Tempest*, IV. i. 151, 154–6: "And, like the baseless fabric of this vision, | . . . . all shall dissolve | And like this insubstantial pageant faded, | Leave not a rack behind . . ." Although the reference to Prospero's speech about the wedding masque performed by spirits called up from his imagination suggests that the locations in *A Laodicean* are also imaginary, Hardy's primary concern as he revised the novel in 1912 apparently was to strengthen their correspondence to actual locations in the county of Somerset.

NOTES OF SIGNIFICANT REVISIONS
TO THE TEXT

Note on the Text outlines the patterns of revision illustrated by most of the notes that follow. The sigla identify the different versions of the novel from which variants are cited.

PR   Proof sheets for the serial publication in *Harper's* (in the R. R. Bowker Collection, Library of Congress).
HM   *Harper's New Monthly Magazine* (European edition; monthly December 1880–December 1881).
1881 English first edition (three volumes, Sampson Low) 1881.
TE   Tauchnitz edition (Tauchnitz) 1882.
1882 English first one-volume edition (Sampson Low) 1882.
1896 Wessex Novels collected edition (Osgood, McIlvaine) 1896.
1912 Wessex Edition (Macmillan) 1912.

Representing reprintings or resettings for which Hardy did not send separate revisions or read proof, American editions of the novel have no independent authority. In 1882 *A Laodicean* was published in Leipzig by Bernhard Tauchnitz in the Tauchnitz Collection of British and American Authors. The Tauchnitz edition is for the most part like *1881* but has some readings from *HM* and a few all its own. What Hardy provided as printer's copy is uncertain; there is no evidence that he revised separately or read proof. He may have sent first proofs for *1881*, which would not have incorporated later changes. The Mellstock Edition of the novel, published in 1920 by Macmillan, represents a resetting rather than a revision.

Hardy wrote a preface to the novel for *1896* and added a postscript for *1912*:

PREFACE

The changing of the old order in country manors and mansions may be slow or sudden, may have many issues romantic or otherwise, its romantic issues being not necessarily restricted to a change back to the original order; though this admissible instance appears to have been the only romance formerly recognized by novelists as possible in the case. Whether the following production be a picture of other possibilities or not, its incidents may be taken to be fairly well supported by evidence every day forthcoming in most counties.

The writing of this tale was rendered memorable to two persons, at least, by a tedious illness of five months that laid hold of the author soon after the story was begun in a well-known magazine; during which period the narrative had to be strenuously continued by dictation to a predetermined cheerful ending.

As some of these novels of Wessex life address themselves more especially to readers into whose souls the iron has entered, and whose years have less pleasure in them now than heretofore, so "A Laodicean" may perhaps help to while away an idle afternoon of the comfortable ones whose lines have fallen to them in pleasant places; above all, of that large and happy section of the reading public which has not yet reached ripeness of years; those to whom marriage is the pilgrim's Eternal City, and not a milestone on the way.

January 1896

P.S.—"A Laodicean" was first published in 1881, in three volumes. Looking over the novel at the present much later date, I hazard the conjecture that its sites, mileages, and architectural details can hardly seem satisfactory to the investigating topographist, so appreciable a proportion of these features being but the baseless fabrics of a vision.

However, there may remain a compensation of another sort in the character of Paula, who, on renewed acquaintance, leads me to think her individualized with some clearness, and really lovable, though she is of that reserved disposition which is the most difficult of all dispositions to depict, and tantalized the writer by eluding his grasp for some time.

T.H.

October 1912

11 *Coming to a stile*: the first indication of *1912*'s shifting geography is the addition at this point of "after two or three miles' leisurely progress".

12 *descended the hill*: ascended (*HM*). In the January 1888 issue of *Harper's New Monthly Magazine*, R. R. Bowker, Harper's agent in London at the time the story was published, recalled catching this error in proof: "Mr Hardy, having brought one of his people up to the very summit of a hill, incontinently started him up again." A postcard from Hardy to Bowker, dated 17 November 1880, survives: "for 'ascended' read 'descended'." On that date this chapter was already in print, so the error was not corrected until the first edition was published.

13 *block letter*: perhaps a typographical error carried over from *HM*,

"block letter" was changed to "black letter" (the style of heavy-faced lettering also called Gothic) in *1882*, but the inscription remained in Roman type. In *1896* "black letter" was changed to "in deep letters" and, oddly enough, "Erected 187—" was then set in black letter.

17 *brink of the pool*: Hardy deleted the next sentence in *HM*: "'Yes,' she answered, her mouth closing so firmly after the monosyllable that the red line of her lips was no more than as a scarlet thread upon the white skin around." He may have censored the description because he thought it too sensual.

she said, turning to get away: she said, in a voice which for the first time lost its calmness (*HM*); she said, trying to get away (*TE*).

18 *"Please say no more to me"* . . . *to withdraw*: "Please say no more to me: I can wait no longer," she murmured, and turned to withdraw (*HM*). The Tauchnitz version retained this reading except that Paula "hastened to withdraw" as in *1881*.

20 *upon the whole* . . . *her age*: upon the whole it was not imposs-ible—to think profanely—that her daily vocabulary might include (mentally at least) such words as flirtation, theatricals, polka-mazurka, true-lover's knot, meet-me-by-moonlight-alone (*HM*). Revisions at *1881* give Paula dignity by making her seem more mature.

two miles: a mile (*1896*).

22 *all rose the keep,*: all rose abruptly (*1912*)

towards the keep: towards a tower which might have been the keep (*1912*).

23 *civilisation* . . . *grand ideas*: editing the novel in *1896*, Hardy deleted this critique of modern architecture.

where his luggage . . . *arrived.*: added in *1912*: "He had decided to halt in that secluded spot of the reposeful name before he discovered, as he had done within the last hour, that a little town called Markton lay on the other side of the castle, not far from the foot of its slopes." Before the revisions for *1912*, the town of Markton is not as close to the castle. Hardy added such descrip-tions to strengthen the connection between Stancy Castle, near Markton, and Dunster Castle, near Dunster Village in the county of Somerset. Hardy identified Dunster Castle as the model for Stancy Castle in 1896 and authorized the equation between Markton and Dunster in Hermann Lea's 1913 guidebook *Thomas Hardy's Wessex*. When C. J. P. Beatty visited Dunster Castle to see for himself the extent to which the castle resembles the one described in the novel, he found few similarities. (See "When is a Castle not a Castle?", *Proceedings of the Dorset Natural History and Archeological Society*, 90 (1969), 258–60.)

25 *of the keep*: of the tower (*1912*).

26 *Perhaps a true account . . . present day,*: Hardy deleted this in *1896*, perhaps because in that freer atmosphere it did not seem as appropriate.

27 *north-east . . . view of the distant country*: north-west . . . view of the distant country and sea (*1912*). Hardy must not have been concerned with such details as that the terrace at Dunster faces south-east; as he imagined it, a castle in that location would have a north-west terrace with a view of the sea.

28 *the village . . . day*: the village or townlet close at hand, that he had missed seeing on the previous day (*1912*).

38 *upon the floor*: Hardy censored the description of Paula's bedroom by deleting the titillating "two or three pairs of silk stockings" that were also on the floor in *HM*.

39 *The landlord*: the landlord's speech was adjusted in *1896* to reflect the initial voicing of /f/ to /v/ and of /s/ to /z/ characteristic of the region Hardy called Wessex, a change made throughout the edition. The revisions of *1912* restored some standard forms but not all. In *1896*, the landlord says "volks", "zong", "zee", "Zundays", and "zomewhere"; in *1912* he says "folks", "zong", "see", "Zundays", and "somewhere".

41 *over to my father's*: across to my father's (*1912*).

two miles and a half: a mile and a half (*1912*).

on to the town: to Toneborough (*1912*); the geography of the novel is more complicated after the 1912 revisions. Hardy divided the Markton scenes between Markton, corresponding to Dunster, and Toneborough, his fictional equivalent of Taunton.

43 *to Markton*: to Toneborough (so the county town was called) (*1912*).

Just about one . . . she had indicated: About half past one . . . indicated, avoiding the townlet at the foot of the castle (*1912*).

After a walk . . . one of these.: in *1896* "six or eight thousand" are reduced to "a few thousand". For the whole passage, *1912* has: "After a walk of half an hour he came to another gate . . . 'W. de Stancy.' Climbing over this, he found himself on a highway which presently stretched away westward, a direction in which he had never yet been. Not far from the sea that he was approaching stood half a dozen genteel and modern houses . . . one of these."

44 *"How are the mighty fallen!"*: deleted in *1896*, probably because Hardy had since his last revision of the novel used this expression in *Tess of the D'Urbervilles* to refer to another family of fallen aristocrats, the Durbeyfields.

mushroom modernism: smallness and modernism (*HM*); an apt description of De Stancy's suburban home.

neat maidservant: trim maidservant (*1912*). Apart from the revisions relating to Wessex, Hardy made few changes for *1912*. Some appear to be insignificant matters that caught his eye as he adjusted geography.

Markton: Toneborough (*1912*).

49 *Sir William's history*: this passage was revised in *1882*, perhaps in response to charges that Hardy's description of Sir William at the race-track had been plagiarized from an 1833 article entitled "The Turf", written by Charles Apperly (who was describing a Colonel Mellish) and published in the *Quarterly Review*, 49: 381–449. An American reader of *A Laodicean* called attention to the similarities between the two passages in the issue of the New York *Nation* of 9 January 1882; the London *Academy* repeated the charge on 18 February. Although he had copied extensively from Apperly's article, Hardy said in a letter of 4 February 1882 that he had based the description on accounts of a person well known to some of his relatives and had not "drawn from other fiction, of course". Nevertheless, he revised the passage, eliminating several similar phrases. The changes in *1882* are as follows: "of fashion" became "of good company", "height of his splendour" became "height of his jinks", and the "barouche" that was "drawn" became the "ikkipage" that was "hauled". "Groom . . . another hack" became "groom, waiting with another hack—all in liveries, splendid and glorious as New Jerusalem". In *1896*, "handsome" became "jonnick" and eyes that were "black indeed" became eyes that were "black as slooes".

50 *He spent . . . silver mine*: this sentence was rewritten on PR; the original version was: "'Tis said that he would gamble to the tune of forty thousand at a sitting; yes, he once staked that sum on a throw and . . .".

to Markton: to Toneborough (*1912*).

53 *King's Arms*: inn (*1896*).

   William Dare: Egbert Dare (PR).

55 *India . . . Canada*: in *HM* Dare's background is not as obscure: he has lived only in Australia.

56 *low voice*: gentle voice (*HM, TE*). *1881* replaces references to Paula's gentle voice and manner, either with a more neutral term as in this case or with a word that emphasizes her vivacity.

61 *dignity*: stiffness (*1882*).

   looked into the question on my own account . . . remain with me.: looked into the question for a special reason. In the study of my profession I was interested in the designing of fonts and baptisteries, and by a natural process I was led to investigate the history of baptism; and some of the arguments I then learnt up still remain with me. That's the simple explanation of my erudition (*1896*). The attempt to make Somerset's knowledge more plausible is one of the few additions made in *1896*.

65 *discreet voice and soft, buoyant look*: tender voice and soft, thoughtful look (*HM, TE*).

66 *She bowed to Somerset in a way*: She bowed to Somerset, bestowing on him a smiling look of recognition (*HM*). Hardy apparently wanted to make Paula's response to Somerset more ambiguous. She is friendlier in the earlier version.

67 *Markton*: all references to Markton in this chapter become Toneborough in *1912*.

68 *inferior to both*: deleted was *HM*'s "In her presence he felt himself nothing bigger than a young student without definite standing". Revisions for *1881* tone down the serial's rather exaggerated depiction of a young man awestruck by Paula.

   I suppose I seemed: Paula is more concerned about Somerset's opinion in *HM*: "'Did I seem quite unable to defend myself?' she asked of him." Deleted is his attempt to interpret her behaviour: "Her aspect was so soft and grave that he assumed her to be quite serious in wanting to know, though, not forgetting what she had shown of lurking mischief the day before, he thought it dangerous to construe her as all gravity."

   with a remark: with a half smile, saying (*HM*).

70 *Helterton*: Toneborough (*1896*). That Havill would be driving to Toneborough makes sense in *1896* because he still lives in

Markton and has his office there. In *1912* he lives and works in Toneborough, and this reference is rather confusing.

71 *King Edred . . . long standing*: *1896* deleted this reference to Dorset's Corfe Castle and substitutes "this was used as a castle by the Romans". See the note to p. 23 for more information about the connection between the two castles. Hardy was familiar with the history of Corfe Castle, which was held in the fifteenth and sixteenth centuries by various earls and dukes of Somerset.

73 *a Canadian*: an Australian (*HM*). Hardy could not decide what characters should say about Dare's background; Australian replaced American on PR.

an East Indian: this was a change on PR; "an Australian" was the earlier reading; from the East (*1896*).

Italian: French (*HM*).

77 *something . . . refreshed him.*: a quiet power . . . refreshed him. She seemed to have been so trained and taught that art and nature were one in her (*HM*); the serial's rather vague descriptions of Paula seem borrowed from popular romances.

She signified . . . down; but finding: revision of this scene for *1881* makes Paula more dignified and reserved: "She signified with a glance which would have been called one of indifference, if her eyes had not been so tenderly constructed that one could never positively say they looked otherwise than warmly. Finding . . .".

78 *seated herself at ease*: Paula has become more graceful: in *HM*, she "flung herself" on the ottoman.

she went on: she said, smiling (*HM*).

She was reclining, and looked: She looked (*1896*). Hardy may have realized that the posture was too provocative for the scene.

79 But her sympathy . . . not great: By some nameless sympathy with his feeling she too coloured (*HM*). In the earlier version there is little doubt about Paula's attraction to Somerset. Perhaps Hardy wanted to add interest by making the love story's outcome seem uncertain.

80 *she added*: she added, laughing (*HM*).

82 *withdrew*: modestly withdrew (*HM*).

83 *coy uneasiness*: coyness (*1912*).

84 *And, blushing faintly, her eyes rested upon him*: And she allowed her clear eyes to rest upon him (*HM*). Inconsistent with changes

made in *1881* because Paula is more in control of her emotions in the earlier version.

85 *King's Arms Hotel*: to a larger one (*1896*). *1896* cancels references to the King's Arms, the name of a prominent inn in Dorchester.

   at the King's Arms: at Markton (*1896*).

86 *strolling to his rooms at Markton.*: strolling down to his new rooms in Markton, which he had taken as being more convenient for the castle than those he had first occupied at Sleeping-Green (*1912*).

87 *quietly*: shyly (*1882*).

   interest: great interest (*HM*).

   hastened to explain: blushed to a mild degree and hastened to explain (*HM*).

   so lucidly.: so lucidly he would have preferred to muse on her motive in going there as on some sweet mystery (*HM*).

89 *This community of interest . . . serious*: This flirtation—if it were not anything more serious—was growing tender (*HM*).

90 *passive*: friendly (*1882*); Hardy tried to make Paula more responsive to Somerset in *1882*, probably in reaction to a critic's comment that she showed a "strangely undemonstrative passion" for him. (In the issue of the *Saturday Review* for 14 January 1882, quoted in Helmut E. Gerber and W. Eugene Davis (eds.), *Thomas Hardy: An Annotated Bibliography of Writings about Him* (DeKalb: Northern Illinois University Press, 1973), i. 35.)

   dangerous admiration: wild and breathless adoration (*HM*).

   paused on a half-smile without speaking: paused with an affable glance without speaking (*1882*); paused without speaking (*1896*).

91 *in her eyes*: in her seductive eyes (*HM*); Hardy had added seductive on PR.

   "Thank you," . . . putting on her glove.: "Thank you," she then said softly, withdrawing her hand, brushing the dust from her fingertips, and putting on her glove, to do which she turned a little aside, her glance falling to the ground (*HM*). Note how the next paragraph makes more sense in light of this description of Paula's behaviour.

92 *the pleasure . . . suppositions*: the divine calmness of her beauty, in the young man's eye, was stained by such commonplace suppositions (*HM*).

97 *roguish*: supercilious (*HM*). Unfortunately, not the last appearance of this word in descriptions of Paula.

"*You ought not to have done it!*" *she said*: deleted in *1881* is the following: "petulantly, keeping her face turned away, and trying to calm her agitation".

98 *If we were . . . to take my hand*: Hardy added this sentence for *1881* and for *1912* tacked on "The words revealed emotion".

99 *cheerful beauty*: sweetness of manner, beauty (*HM*).

103 *King's Arms*: Lord Quantock Arms (*1896*). The new name suggests a connection to the Quantock Hills in Somerset.

104 *in very early times*: *1912* adds (enclosed by commas) "and was held in opposition to King Stephen as a centre for forays over the neighbouring country". The reference strengthens the connection to Dunster Castle, held by supporters of Matilda, the daughter of Henry I, who fought for the throne denied her in 1135 by Stephen, Henry's nephew.

107 *she asked with suave sauciness*: she murmured (*HM*); she asked with suave curiosity (*1896*).

"*Yes; off mine*": *1881* deleted a sentence here: "Her cheeks blushed more warmly than they had ever before done in his presence as she made the avowal, to the ear so softly spoken."

with ever so little reproach: with ever so little of a smile hovering on the corners of her mouth, though seriousness filled her eye (*HM*).

those nice friendly accents: those perfect eyes (*HM*).

112 *and enterprise?*: Hardy rearranged this passage on PR, replacing "nobility of talent" with "nobility of talent and enterprise." He added Paula's wish to have a well-known line of ancestors and Somerset's reply.

113 *somewhat more than usual*: like a boat on a tideway (*HM*).

114 *her natural silentness*: her natural maiden silentness (*HM*).

115 *keep*: tower (*1912*).

a blue flower: a scarlet flower (*HM*).

117 *Markton*: Toneborough (*1912*).

118 *insisted Paula*: pouted Paula (*HM*).

119 *something of a thrill*: an electric thrill (*HM*).

120 "*If you like,*" *she venturesomely answered*: "Yes," she softly

answered (*HM*). In the earlier version of this scene, Paula is skittish but submissive; in *1881* she seems more in control of her emotions and manipulative as she teases Somerset.

with roguish abruptness: abruptly (*HM*).

121   *in an undeceiving tone*: hastily (*HM*).

she teasingly demurred: she remained quite still (*HM*).

122   *"Yes," she said, "if you care to"*: "Yes," she said docilely (*HM*).

"Yes, occasionally," she murmured: "Yes," she said faintly (*HM*).

"Oh no—not yet": "I suppose so" (*HM*).

"I can give a shrewd guess," she said slily: *1882* replaces with "'Yes,' she whispered", thus essentially restoring HM's "Yes".

"Not a single word!": "I would rather not." (*HM* and *1882*).

123   *"To everything . . . away.*: on PR this prim reply replaced "'Then there,' she said, putting her finger on a particular spot of her cheek. The lover sighed and made himself content with the limitation." Hardy struck "cheek" and wrote in the margin "forehead" before cancelling the passage. He probably did not want the love affair to move at so rapid a pace and may have been anticipating the resentment Somerset feels in Book III when De Stancy kisses Paula in the play.

King's Arms: Quantock Arms (*1896*).

till the vehicle overtook him, and he got in: deleted in *1912*.

phenomenal agonies and questionable delights: entrancing agonies and painful delights (*HM*); pleasing agonies and painful delights (*1896*).

he passed . . . to Markton: he strolled down into Markton (*1912*).

131   *in the northern sky*: *1912* adds "over the sea" to reinforce the connection to Dunster.

135   *Markton*: Toneborough (*1912*).

137   *on my way to the railway-station*: in *1912* Paula must explain why she is in Toneborough: "there being no train from the nearer branch to catch the express".

139   *She looked at him*: She nodded to him (*1912*).

along the highway: *1912* must account for the stroll from Toneborough to the castle and adds: "The evening being tempting they walked further and further till they were unexpectedly near Markton and the Castle above." The distance between Taunton and Dunster is more than twenty miles. Even though their fictional equivalents, Toneborough and Markton, are apparently closer, the substitution of the former for the latter creates the need for explanations such as this.

140 *"Well, what was the use of coming here?"*: "Well, what was the use of tiring ourselves by walking these miles?" (*1912*).

146 *Markton barracks*: all references to Markton barracks become Toneborough barracks in *1912*. Added is this explanation of why the soldiers are passing through Sleeping-Green: "They have taken this route for some reason—going to camp perhaps."

Markton: Toneborough (*1912*).

148 *handsome face*: interesting face (*1912*); this modification of De Stancy's appearance is unusual because Hardy had given no attention to descriptions of characters other than Paula since *1881*.

handsome: interesting (*1912*).

149 *walked from the castle . . . detour*: Somerset walked from the castle down towards his Markton lodgings by a detour through the park (*1912*).

Cunningham Haze: PR show that Hardy tried several surnames, including Green and Woolley, before settling on Haze.

150 *Casterbridge*: Toneborough (*1896*); further on (*1912*). Casterbridge, the fictional equivalent of Dorchester, is mentioned only once in the novel. For *1912*, Hardy made adjustments so that the chief constable could have his headquarters in Toneborough, not Markton.

151 *road, having been . . . progress, bent sharply*: road, having been laid out for easy climbing, bent hither (*1912*).

but admirably made: with a tired air (*1912*).

a fine combination of strength: a due combination of training (*1912*).

somewhat striking: distinctly striking (*1912*).

155 *But he went out of town*: He passed through here (*1912*).

at his house: in the town (*1912*).

gets home: passes back (*1912*).

156 *grew sickly pale*: De Stancy's reaction in *HM* is to grow "ghastly pale". *1896* becomes even less melodramatic: his face "becomes strained" and he leans back in his chair rather than falling back gasping.

157 *Markton*: Toneborough (*1912*).

Myrtle Villa: Myrtle Villa near Markton, (*1912*).

walk past his window and down the town: walk past his window towards Markton (*1912*).

followed in the same direction: added in *1912*: "The captain went on mile after mile till Dare was almost tired."

on the other side of the town: deleted in *1912*.

in the direction of the town: in the direction of Toneborough (*1912*).

158 *Sleeping-Green Church*: Markton Church (*1912*).

159 *on my guard*: in *HM* Dare is the villain of melodrama. Deleted in *1881*: "He took from his pocket an artificial moustache and affixed it to his lip in the twinkling of an eye."

the bank here: the bank at Toneborough (*1912*).

162 *while she lives*: while, buried here in Outer Wessex, she lives (*1896*).

165 *keep*: summit (*1912*).

166 *Markton*: Toneborough (*1912*).

168 *made it his business . . . entrance*: made it his business to hire a gig and be driven back to Markton. Telling the man to wait for him at the inn he sat smoking . . . entrance (*1912*).

169 *more bewitching*: nicer and cleverer (*1896*); Hardy apparently decided to stress Paula's innocence rather than her sensuality.

170 *went on his way.*: went on his way to the inn where the man waited to drive him back to Toneborough (*1912*).

171 *walk home again*: get to the inn and drive back to Toneborough (*1912*).

173 *costume*: deleted in *1881* is *HM*'s daring description: "which showed to perfection every curve of her figure".

shocking to your weak nerves: pretty! (*HM*); the revision slightly shifts the emphasis from Paula's pride in her appearance to her boast about her athletic skill.

Bona Dea . . . fascination: Bona Dea was profanation, would have compelled him as an officer and a gentleman instantly to withdraw his eyes, had not the strange fascination (*HM*).

though so pretty: though so innocent and pretty (*1896*); a belated attempt to tone down the erotic scene.

184 *river*: brook (*1912*).

189 *"What unreasonable . . . romantic of him."*: "What romantic devotion!" murmured Paula. "And yet how foolish of him!" (*HM*).

191 *Markton*: Toneborough (*1912*).

had begun . . . moustache: still wore the heavy moustache he had fixed on (*HM*).

196 *dropping on one knee*: clasping her hand (*1896*).

199 *When he had gone . . . serenity*: When he had gone, she buried her face in her hands: she was excited, and unhappy (*PR*). The revision was needed to clarify Paula's reaction.

202 *Havill held the office*: Havill, although living some miles off, held the office of deacon, which he had taken to oblige Paula's father when the new chapel was started (*1912*). Before *1912*, Havill lived at Markton and no explanation was necessary.

203 *his own house*: his own house at Toneborough (*1912*).

204 *From the upper end of the town*: From a hill north of the town he saw in the far distance the grand . . . (*1912*).

206 *arch and serene*: inscrutable (*HM*).

reticent, independent, complicated: reticent, shy, complicated (*HM*).

211 *His father didn't know.*: 'I don't know. I have never looked at the play of late years. It is "Love's Labour's Lost." You had better read it for yourself, and do the best you can.' (*HM*). "Somerset's father did not know. He had never looked at the play of late years. 'It is "Love's Labour's Lost,"' he said. 'You had better read it for yourself, and do the best you can.'"(*TE*).

217 *Markton*: *1912* changes to "Toneborough", the new site of the Hunt Ball.

218 *. . . Hunt Ball," she replied confidentially*: Hunt Ball," she murmured (*HM*); Hunt Ball." Her low tone hinted why (*1912*).

219 *the King's Arms Hotel, Markton*: the Lord-Quantock-Arms Hotel (*1896*); Toneborough (*1912*).

221 *to take her home*: to take her to the hotel at which she and Paula had put up (*1912*).

222 *drove off with her aunt to Stancy Castle*: drove off with her aunt, to pick up Charlotte at the hotel, and thence along the miles of lonely road to Stancy Castle (*1912*).

223 *fifteen minutes' drive from Markton*: a twenty minutes' drive (*1896*); a few miles drive from Toneborough Station (*1912*).

226 *Passing through the town . . . Stancy Castle*: Passing up the townlet to the castle that dominated it (*1912*).

227 *She met his eye*: She blushed and met his eye (HM).

229 *She evasively shook her head*: She withdrew from him without replying (*HM*). Added in *1881* was "Come—yes we are!"

231 *in Markton High Street*: in the High Streets of the county (*1912*).

239 *"No," she averred . . . her head*: She flushed. "No," she said (*HM*).

    she serenely answered: she hastily answered (HM).

240 *don't expect . . . say more*: you know what that implies; and be content (*1882*).

    An elderly man: A fogy (*1896*). Captain De Stancy is 39.

245 *Markton Station*: Toneborough (*1912*).

246 *dogs*: dogs in leading strings (*HM*); spaniels (*1896*).

    King's Arms: Lord-Quantock-Arms (*1896*). In *1912* Hardy overlooked the fact that Somerset was in Toneborough, not Markton, and left the reference to his walk to the Lord-Quantock-Arms intact.

253 *saucy composure*: steady composure (*HM*).

    "Who knows? Time will tell.": "A woman may wish some things she does not care to tell!" (*1896*).

256 *"Be true to me"*: "Forget me not!" (*HM*).

259 *the last of her*: the last of his angel (*HM*).

    he went to the newspaper office: he drove to Toneborough and sought the newspaper office (*1912*).

265 *Your heart . . . disagreeable.*: although Hardy may have been trying to refocus the relationship between Somerset and Paula, revision to their exchange of letters in *1882* is for the most part stylistic, as this new reading suggests: "Your heart would weary in time, and when once that happens, good-bye to the emotions you have told me of. Imagine such a case clearly and you will perceive the probability of what I say. At the same time I admit that a woman who is *only* a creature of evasions and disguises is very disagreeable."

267 *that she . . . subject*: for my mind's eye keeps those sweet

operations more distinctly before me than my bodily sight does my own (*1882*).

268 *it is necessary not to think . . . to be*: it is best to think that, as we are the product of events, events will continue to produce that which is in harmony with us (*1882*).

270 "*I am almost angry*: this letter was most affected by the changes for *1882*. Hardy deletes Paula's lesson in the art of courtship; the much abbreviated first paragraph reads: "I am almost angry with you, George, for being vexed because I am not more effusive. Why should the verbal *I love you* be ever uttered between two beings of opposite sex who have eyes to see signs? During the seven or eight months that we have known each other, you have discovered my regard for you, and what more can you desire? Would a reiterated assertion of passion really do any good? Remember it is a natural instinct with us women to retain the power of obliging a man to hope, fear, pray, and beseech as long as we think fit, before we confess to a reciprocal affection." The letter continues with "I am going to . . .".

273 *into a chink*: amid the alien stones (*HM*).

274 *I would . . . none.*: deleted in *1882*.

I cannot help saying . . . extreme.: deleted in *1882*.

It is difficult . . . we admire.: also deleted in *1882*, softening the tone of Somerset's letter.

278 *Although his haste . . . haze of fog.*: *1896* cancels the harsh comment about Lyons' history by replacing this paragraph with: "On awakening from a fitful sleep in the grey dawn of the morning following he looked out upon Lyons, quiet enough now, the citizens unaroused to the daily round of bread-winning, and enveloped in a haze of fog."

284 *In some of the gamblers . . . and its kin*: *1896* deleted the rest of this paragraph, eliminating the unfavourable description of the casino's patrons.

290 *in intercepting . . . telegrams*: added in *1881*, probably to explain Paula's silence.

314 *aristocrats*: aristocrats, representatives of impoverished ancient families, (*HM*).

are past.: are past. We can only be saved, in the words of the apostle, as by fire—that is, by what burns the old prejudices of some of us like fire—by connecting ourselves with the new and coarse aristocracy of money, or at least the new and refined aristocracy of intellect—best of all with the two united. (*HM*) Hardy may have decided that the villain Dare should not be too conscious of his symbolic role when he later sets fire to Stancy Castle.

325 *inexpressible*: sorrowful (*1882*).

327 *brusquely.*: brusquely and with tears in her eyes for one gone (*1882*).

328 *her eyes*: her wet eyes (*1912*).

332 *with artificial urbanity*: with longing reticence (*1882*).

satirical: bitter (*1882*).

333 *to England.*: to England and did not know that when Paula got to her room she abandoned herself to long and silent tears (*1912*).

341 *his ancestral home and estates*: the alienated Wessex home and estates (*1896*).

359 *Sleeping-Green*: Markton (*1912*).

362 *in spite of Uncle Abner*: added in *1896* to explain Paula's motives: They'll say it was for the title, but knowing it was not I don't care.

365 *But instead . . . Stancy Castle*: Then he also went in the Markton direction; but instead of passing through the little town he rounded its outskirts, and so reached the lodge of Stancy Castle (*1912*).

372 *to Markton*: down the street to the inn where he had left his fly (*1912*).

373 *Markton*: Toneborough (*1912*).

374 *through the wooded district*: across the charming district (*1912*).

Though bitterly . . . altered eyes: *1896* softened the depiction of the petulant Somerset by deleting the rest of the paragraph.

375 *Markton*: Toneborough (*1912*).

379 *Markton*: Toneborough (*1912*).

along the road: along in a gig (*1912*).

380 *avoiding the town*: avoiding the Toneborough streets (*1912*).

381 *Markton*: Toneborough (*1912*).

387 *cool mannerliness*: deleted in *1881* is *HM*'s "that pride lends at such times".

a dreadful sorrow sat in her face: added in *1881*.

395 *to see me*: to quiz me (*1912*).

396 *into Markton*: to the station (*1912*).

398 *"Won't he," said Paula, with soft respose.*: Paula's response as it appears in five versions is a good example of compositorial interference with punctuation in the later texts:
"Won't he," said Paula, with dry repose. (*HM*)
"Won't he," said Paula, with soft repose. (*1881*)
"Won't he," said Paula, with soft faith. (*1882*)
'Won't he?' said Paula, with soft faith. (*1896*)
'Won't he!' said Paula, with soft faith. (*1912*)

408 *she concluded*: in a perceptibly husky note (*1912*).

409 *He doesn't know her . . . her!*: He doesn't know her! The idea of his dancing with a woman of that description! (*1896*)

416 *roguish*: playful (*HM*).

419 *King's Arms Inn . . . bow-window*: 1896 changes to Lord-Quan-tock-Arms Inn; in *1912*, "bow-window" becomes "wide window", perhaps because Hardy did not want the reference to the King's Arms Inn in Dorchester, which has a distinctive bow-window.

But curiosity being awakened by the church bells: But as he had just been helping in the castle to prepare a feast for the workpeople (*1912*).

422 *on the balcony above*: at the bay-window above (*1912*).

Stancy Castle and Markton: Stancy Castle in the direction of Toneborough (*1912*).

423 *Why do you walk out here?"*: Why do you appear out here?" "I had come in from Toneborough to Myrtle Villa, arranging for a sale of the furniture, when . . ." (*1912*).

Markton: Toneborough (*1912*).

427 *upon the balcony*: upon the street (*1912*).

429 *keep*: tower (*1912*).

two miles: three miles (*1896*); half a mile (*1912*).

hasten to the spot . . . went on foot: hasten to the spot, and with lapse of time evinced more anxiety as to the fate of her castle than she had shown at first. They went on foot (*1912*).

430 *north-east*: south and east (*1912*).

431 *On their journey*: On their way down to the little town (*1912*).

a dreadful sorrow sat in her face: added in 1881.

295 to sadden to quiz me (1912).

396 into Markton: to the station (1912)

398 "Won't he," said Paula, then soft repose.: Paula's response as it appears in five versions is a good example of compositorial interference with punctuation in the later texts:
"Won't he," said Paula, with dry repose. (HM)
"Won't he," said Paula, with soft repose. (1881)
"Won't he," said Paula, with soft faith. (1882)
"Won't he? said Paula, with soft faith. (1896)
"Won't he? said Paula, with soft faith. (1912)

408 she concluded, in a perceptibly husky note (1912).

409 He doesn't know her . . . her?: He doesn't know her! The idea of his dancing with a woman of that description! (1896)

416 roguish playful (HM).

419 King's Arms Fan . . . bore-rendezvous: 1896 changes to Lord-Quan-rock-Arms Inn; in 1912, 'bow-window' becomes 'wide window', perhaps because Hardy did not want the reference to the King's Arms Inn in Dorchester, which has a distinctive bow-window.

But earnestly being weathered by the church bells: But as he had just been helping in the castle to prepare a feast for the workpeople (1912).

422 on the balcony above: at the bay-window above (1912).

Stancy Castle and Markham: Stancy Castle in the direction of Toneborough (1912).

423 Why do you walk out here?": Why do you appear out here?: "I had come in from Toneborough to Myrtle Villa, arranging for a sale of the furniture, when . . ." (1912).

Markton Toneborough (1912).

427 upon the balcony: upon the street (1912).

429 keep: tower (1912).

two miles: three miles (1896); half a mile (1912).

hasten to the spot . . . went on foot: hasten to the spot, and with lapse of time evinced more anxiety as to the fate of her castle than she had shown at first. They went on foot (1912).

430 north-east south and east (1912).

431 On their journey: On their way down to the little town (1912).

THE WORLD'S CLASSICS

A Select List

HANS ANDERSEN: Fairy Tales
Translated by L. W. Kingsland
Introduction by Naomi Lewis
Illustrated by Vilhelm Pedersen and Lorenz Frølich

ARTHUR J. ARBERRY (Transl.): The Koran

LUDOVICO ARIOSTO: Orlando Furioso
Translated by Guido Waldman

ARISTOTLE: The Nicomachean Ethics
Translated by David Ross

JANE AUSTEN: Emma
Edited by James Kinsley and David Lodge

Northanger Abbey, Lady Susan, The Watsons,
and Sanditon
Edited by John Davie

Persuasion
Edited by John Davie

WILLIAM BECKFORD: Vathek
Edited by Roger Lonsdale

KEITH BOSLEY (Transl.): The Kalevala

CHARLOTTE BRONTË: Jane Eyre
Edited by Margaret Smith

JOHN BUNYAN: The Pilgrim's Progress
Edited by N. H. Keeble

FRANCES HODGSON BURNETT: The Secret Garden
Edited by Dennis Butts

FANNY BURNEY: Cecilia
or Memoirs of an Heiress
Edited by Peter Sabor and Margaret Anne Doody

THOMAS CARLYLE: The French Revolution
Edited by K. J. Fielding and David Sorensen

A complete list of Oxford Paperbacks, including The World's Classics, OPUS, Past Masters, Oxford Authors, Oxford Shakespeare, and Oxford Paperback Reference, is available in the UK from the Arts and Reference Publicity Department (BH), Oxford University Press, Walton Street, Oxford OX2 6DP.

In the USA, complete lists are available from the Paperbacks Marketing Manager, Oxford University Press, 200 Madison Avenue, New York, NY 10016.

Oxford Paperbacks are available from all good bookshops. In case of difficulty, customers in the UK can order direct from Oxford University Press Bookshop, Freepost, 116 High Street, Oxford, OX1 4BR, enclosing full payment. Please add 10 per cent of published price for postage and packing.